To JE
To DAVE,

" ... So, IF You HAD THE CHANCE
To LIVE YOUR LIFE AGAIN,
WOULD YOU STICK ...
... OR WOULD YOU TWIST? "

STEVENSON—

2nd SEPTEMBER 2013

CW00421693

the Water's edge

STEVENSON-OLDS

www.stevenson-olds.com

The Water's Edge

written and published by **STEVE**NSON-OLDS

www.stevenson-olds.com

This paperback edition first published 2013

1

Copyright © 2013 **STEVE**NSON-OLDS

A catalogue record for this book
is available from the British Library

ISBN 978-0-9576449-0-8

Printed and bound in Italy by **CHINCHIO UK**

For Sarah and Izzy

When I reflect on *the* light bulb moment - 2002, that adrenaline-surge of the switch concluding in my desire to write a book, the obstacle being the creation of *time* where there simply wasn't any. Outside of my role as breadwinner, my *time* would be gratefully swallowed up by the inspired creation, our wonderful six-year-old daughter Izzy, and the obligatory social whirl that goes hand in hand with the privileged position of devoted father and husband. The conundrum within all of this was simple: where do you find a spare five hours a day to write the novel that we are told 'lies within each of us?' Step forward my beautiful, patient wife Sarah, who believed in me sufficiently, to offer me the *gift of time*. She stated: sleep was overrated, that rained off days from our roofing business would see chapters realised within the blink of an eye, especially in the United Kingdom where of course 'clouds and their natural waste' are a national institution! She added smartly, that the writing of my debut novel would simply take as long as it takes - inspired logic! 2013 and the Water's Edge is complete. My exceptional daughter is now sixteen years of age, devoid of even an ounce of neglect, in fact suitably inspired and has a creative ability that I have no doubt outshines my own in spades.

So here's to you both, thank you and I love you.

I would like to make an additional dedication to inspiration:

Our home the 'Water's Edge.'

And,

to Mum with Love...

CHAPTER ONE

The Beginning Of The End

2005 – Blue Sky

My name is Ritchie Angel, and my life was absolutely perfect in every way. Apart from this one singular, isolated curve ball of a problem, I have everything a man could ever want. I am fortunate enough to say that I am madly in love … the beautiful Yasmin, the perfect wife. We have both been blessed with our dazzling, healthy and happy five-year-old daughter, Evie, and we all live at the Water's Edge, in the heart of England. The land on which our house stands was my special place as a child; an idyllic, soothing sanctuary where I would never see a soul, and I loved that. The long, lush grass, the many trees where the bluebells would shade, three acres of a spinney that would take you to the edge of the water, the unspoilt canal, just visible through the lofty reeds, and then, within a stone's throw away, bending, crossing biblically over the river via the old sandstone bridge. So for me…nirvana! I stood as a ten-year-old dreaming of how one day I would return and buy this special place, building the perfect home that would keep me and my family safe. But it's as I stand here now that my conscience is troubled. The dream *perhaps,* having been achieved at a cost – the ingredients of an obsession that endeavoured, unbending, relentless in its pursuit, a stubbornness of mind that lost sight of what was right. So here I am, 'humbled', at thirty-five years of age.

I am good at batting away the negative, and will step up and ensure that tradition is upheld. I take a deep drawn-out breath and embrace my surroundings. A wistful sigh, and a smile rises from deep within and spreads across my face – this place never fails me. I raise my eyes skyward – the primary blue and dazzling sunshine are a perfect backdrop to my dream home, built with all the love and care that this spiritual, magical place

1

deserves. I ponder all that it has taken. Only the finest reclaimed materials – every brick, tile and beam hand-picked by me and my wife. And so now stands a home that looks as though it's been here forever. The bluebell wood left alone in all its natural glory, combined with the well-manicured lawns and the long, old cobble and gravel driveway that takes you from the Water's Edge to the top of the spinney and out through our five-bar gate, easing onto the quiet country lane that takes you kicking and screaming towards civilisation and my hometown – Willow.

I lower myself down, my back resting against the arced trunk of the willow tree, its tresses caressing the water.

'Thank you, thank you, thank you...' The words leave my grateful body.

I nod my head in appreciation – the full realisation of my dream, but so aware that my life surpasses even that. The crowning glory for any alpha male is that no man – within legal means or otherwise – would or could take away his home. Peace of mind, though, is mine. I have more money than I will ever be able to spend. Since a young age, my business dealings have been shrewd and therefore highly profitable. As certain buildings in Willow were being left simply to fall apart, I spotted their potential – the dark, dank-looking canal that ran behind the forgotten properties conjured up romantic images for me ... picturesque restaurants, impressive offices, each purchased 'hook or by crook', and then renovated to the highest standards and rented out accordingly. I now have an impressive portfolio – not a single penny owing to anybody, with a five-figure monthly profit that will continue to roll in, until the end of time.

And so, as I look out across the water, desperately trying to hold onto the image of my beautiful wife reading our little angel her bedtime story, I am aware of the bails having been. Defeat admitted – my inability to maintain a clean and invincible wicket. I look up, a black and intrusive cloud having drifted onto my perfect blue sky. I so want to cut through the numbness that engulfs me, but the result from my meeting with my doctor earlier today has a stranglehold, and my head and heart drop. I swallow hard, drained by the full force of the diagnosis. An unwanted secret, begrudgingly mine, not one that I would wish to share with anyone. I have taken my time, endeavoured to digest the facts as they have been presented, reluctantly allowing them to sink into my wounded soul, but left with the need to work out a way of dealing with the problem.

My eyes drop to my reflection in the water – a conflicting healthy glow. I lift my head and stare out across the lawns to my home. I imagine myself standing with Yasmin and Evie. Without thought, I'm on my feet, taking in the girls – beautiful, faultless. But my circumstances draw my eyes to my own image, and I shake my head as what I see contradicts my supposed fate. A picture of health, alive and vibrant. Six feet tall, blonde, tanned, rugged complexion as a result of many seasons lived to the full. I stare into my steel-blue eyes and then down at the well-muscled body, but then look away.

To deflect the welling tears, I feed from my much better half, the spellbinding Yasmin. All that meet her inevitably fall in love with her – great work from the big man upstairs, a breathtakingly beautiful creation, inside and out. The deepest sparkling eyes of blue that you simply drown in. I tilt my head slightly, taking in her long blonde tousled 'come to bed' hair, and then, as though spoilt for choice as to where to look, I'm aware of an awestruck smile spreading itself from my toes to my eyes: 'Wow, Yasmin…' Making Brigitte Bardot as she appeared in *La Dolce Vita*, look rather plain by comparison. So as you can probably gather, I'm rather keen. The relationship is built on lust – a great place to start! Teamwork and loyalty, we're together because we want to be. Yasmin simply makes my heart race, faster than is healthy, I'm sure. Life without her? I swallow hard and sidestep the question.

And so to our incredible daughter, Evie. I'm sure all parents feel this way, but the love and respect that I have for this exquisite creature is incredible … nothing compares. She is an angel, with her long platinum hair, her mummy's eyes. Evie may be the smallest in her class, but she has the heart of a lion cub. Without a shadow of a doubt, she is the greatest thing that Yasmin and I ever did!

My thoughts are suddenly interrupted as a brightly painted

narrowboat creeps past me, making its way towards the fading sunset. I dwell on my hug and kiss off Evie as we exchanged our goodnights this evening. I felt that she held me even tighter than usual, almost as if she knew that I needed that extra squeeze. I sigh at the memory and my head drops. I rotate my neck and try to face the night. The chill in the air reminds me that autumn is almost upon us. I feel thankful that the summer has been so magical; so much laughter, immense good fortune, for family and friends alike. I recall the words of Sally, my best friend Jimmy's wife: 'I'm ready for the autumn; the seasons are what keep me going!' She chuckled, followed by a nod of the head. But it is only now that her words strike such a painful chord. Because I had felt so strong then – life offered no blackness, no ticking clock, no praying for extra time. My eyes start to burn. I crouch down onto the timber decking that pushes out into the reeds and sit, reliving my 10 a.m. meeting from earlier today.

As I left Yasmin and Evie this morning, I tried to act as I usually would. What I loved about our household was the fact that we were always happy. Never a cross word, no snapping, just fun, and I am *so* proud of that. It's not forced or strived for... it is purely *because* physically, mentally, spiritually we are where we want to be. We drive our friends mad... 'Oh, here we are, *at the happy house!*' And each would often say: 'Surely, when we're gone you can't keep this perfect harmony going?' But the truth is – and we love our friends dearly, 'so please keep this to yourself!' – but just the three of us, we're even happier.

I was suddenly sitting in the doctors' surgery, my eyes focusing on a pair of Georgian doors leading out into a small lawned courtyard. Two antiquated looking apple trees stood totally overpowered by the imposing grey building that surrounded them. I could see Dr Karen Malvern trying to coax a small kitten towards a large chrome bowl; the kitten seemed reluctant, happier rubbing herself up against the ancient and seemingly withering trunk, its various stages of rotten discarded fruit lying like crash victims in the sparse, sun-starved grass.

I felt increasingly cold and alone as I watched Dr Malvern

fully occupied with her little scraggy friend. For many months now my head had been filled with sharp shooting pains, my heart heavy, fluttering and tight as if it were about to splutter to a halt at any moment. And the truth is, I'm an eternal optimist, not an ounce of hypochondria in me – well, maybe a little. But I would throw a couple more painkillers into my drug-free body, the ice-cold water sending a sudden rush to my brain, and simply get on with my life. And though the pain and discomfort would dilute, they wouldn't leave me. And within an hour or two their strength would overpower me again until I felt like tearing my own head off, but barely able to lift my arms to carry out the threat due to the thunder and lightning in my chest.

'Oh, Ritchie, thank you so much for coming!'

But Karen, our family doctor, who had become such a close friend to Yasmin and I, couldn't look me in the eyes, and it was that which convinced me – today wasn't the day for good news.

A gentle knock on the door – like a click of the hypnotist's fingers – released me from my trance. I stood up instinctively, my head a little unfocused as an old, grey-haired, but distinguished-looking gentleman entered the room.

'Ahh, Dr Travis, thank you *so* much for coming. This is our Mr Angel!'

My strong handshake was met by Dr Travis's limp effort, before he hurriedly made his way round to Karen's side of the large office desk. I now had two people who couldn't look me in the eyes. I pursed my lips tightly, waiting for the damning verdict. I so wanted to say something. I was always the one with the quick, light-hearted comments, a line to ease the tension. But not today, not now … I simply couldn't speak.

Dr Travis opened his battered briefcase and took out a yellow file. I chuckled nervously, feeling the slightest optimism at the brightly coloured binder. A few whispers were exchanged, a nod of the head from Karen, and then…

'Ritchie, as I'm sure you're aware, we've had to take a little time to try to establish a prognosis here. Dr Travis has travelled all the way from America…Seattle in fact, just so that he can help me explain this rare and … umm … unfortunate illness you have.'

I tried to concentrate, but the pounding of my heart was filling my aching ears.

'So you see, Ritchie, the heart can only take so much stress, the brain can only do its best to pacify your main engine, but although we're aware of only one other example, your body is closing down … it just wants to rest! All the tests show that your brain is slowly, gradually easing to a halt. The blood flow around your body is now dangerously slow; your body, as with our other unfortunate case, thinks it can stop, and then, after a few weeks, will be able to start up again, but of course, it can't! We've considered all our options, several forms of life-support machines, but each test shows that your body will totally reject each one … it wants a complete and utter rest!'

Dr Travis's expensive flight from Seattle has simply seen him nod his head at appropriate moments, but as I finally catch Karen's eye, practical words at last leave my mouth.

'So, how long have I got? A year? A few months?'

Karen loses her nerve, her eyes now on my chest.

'I'm *so* sorry, Ritchie, but we cannot see you making it past … ummm … Wednesday evening or thereabouts … of next week…'

The cool evening breeze slaps my face and a shiver runs the full length of my spine. Suddenly, I'm aware of my feet sinking beneath the icy cold canal water. But my instincts to quickly pull my sodden boots back onto the timber decking betray me. Instead, the coldness reminds me that I'm still alive, and as I splash my legs about like a hyperactive child, I feel the burning tears squeeze out, each one rolling down my shattered face. I pull myself to my feet and take in the still, quiet night. I'm suddenly aware of a warm pair of arms wrapping themselves around me.

'Thought I'd find you here,' Yasmin whispered seductively into my ear.

I didn't turn around, but covered her arms with mine, the warmth of her body bringing some sort of normality back into my turned-on-its-head world. I couldn't talk, I just let her hold me, her chin resting on my shoulder. She leaned into my neck, kissing me softly.

'Do you want a cup of tea, gorgeous?' she asked. 'Or there's half a bottle of red left from last night...'

I let go of her arms and turn to face my wife. I lift my hands and place them against her cheeks, brushing away a soft stray curl. Yasmin beams up at me, her eyes sparkling.

'Ritchie, you seem very quiet tonight, really deep in thought.'

But she didn't need an answer, she just dropped her head onto my chest and held me, massaging my back gently. My thoughts flickered as though unsure where to engage ... clumsy and stumbling. But as we both stood beneath the moonlight, I was sure about one thing. All the medical nonsense, baked-up theories about this and that – how can all of that be real? Surely this, here and now with Yasmin, was the reality.

I pictured Evie upstairs, lying innocently without a care in the world in her little bed, waking up in the morning, and as usual, she would run across the landing and jump into bed with Yasmin and I, cuddling up, her little hands cupping my face as she kisses my nose as she did every morning. The horror struck me. Evie would wake one day very soon and realise that I wasn't there for her. She, for whatever justified reason there is, would have to carry on without me. Yasmin would have to carry on without me. They would both get on with their lives, but without *me*. Perhaps they would cope fine, but I didn't want them to, I wanted them to need me, to know that I was there and always would be there for them. It didn't seem right that these two special people should have to carry on without me, and far more importantly, that I would be cast adrift, never to return, never to see the two most incredible people in my world again.

The phone suddenly rang. Yasmin squeezed my hand.

'It will be Janey, Ritchie. Get everything locked up and I'll meet you upstairs.'

As she disappeared into the house, my heart started to race.

Was I being selfish keeping my expiry to myself? I knew she had a right to know. Good God, I would want to know if the roles were reversed. But to me, everything depended on the happiness of Yasmin and Evie – if they were happy, then so

7

was I. So the decision was made. Why on earth would I want my last few days to be spent with sad, pitying people? So I would take my secret to the very end. I kicked an imaginary stone off the decking and turned towards the house. I gave out a huge but positive sigh. A scared but determined optimism filled me, a strange sort of superhero inner voice spurring me on. *So, until the evil deed decided to deal its deadly hand, I was going to make sure that the next few days were the best ever.* I shook my head in total agreement, my inner voice adding: *Final memories for family and friends alike to be the very best possible.* So, I was going down with all guns blazing!

I hadn't been asleep long when I woke with a start, sitting bolt upright. Yasmin uttered an inexplicable array of words, her hand brushing my leg before slipping beneath the realms of consciousness – a contented sigh confirming that all was well in Yasmin's world. Carefully I pushed back the heavy quilt and slid out of bed. I pulled on my jeans, grabbed a thick jumper and made my way out onto the landing. I pulled the jumper over my head and found myself at Evie's door. The moonlight from her window danced across her beautiful face.

'My little angel,' I whispered, pride spilling out of me.

I knew that if I should die today, then I had left something wonderful. Tears welled up, stinging my eyes, my throat burning. I took a deep breath and wiped away my weakness.

None of that! I scolded myself firmly.

I backed away, desperate not to wake my little girl. I tiptoed almost silently down the stairs, wondering what the time was. As I stepped into the hallway, I stopped and took in the heady aroma of the lilies. Many shadows were being cast around me as the moonlight shone through the uncovered windows from the large swaying branches that lined the water outside. And then, as I turned my head, even the lilies were being projected several times their actual size, spreading themselves up the wall and across the ceiling. I stepped into the kitchen, my eyes focusing on the large chrome clock.

'Bloody hell, it's 3 a.m!' *Devil's hour!* Pushed to the forefront of my mind.

I took a deep breath, my head buzzing and feeling

increasingly nauseous – partly fatal illness, but no doubt added to sheer rebellion at being woken and then physically up and about at this ungodly hour. I turned on the tap, splashing the cool water onto my face before finally running a handful through my hair. I stood for a moment, just taking in the way it felt to be alive, but then couldn't deal with the alternative that was going to be mine in just a few short days as the very real horror of what lay in wait for me stung all it touched within my head. I grabbed a wet cloth and wiped our chalkboard clean – we would scribble messages, words of the day, our thoughts, daft and delightful things really. I wrote quickly: *Don't worry, girls, gone to blow some cobwebs away, will be back for breakfast! Kiss each other for me. The Husband and the Dad xxx.*

I grabbed my car keys and stepped outside. I walked past my luxurious Mercedes four-wheel drive – the vehicle that I would use for most journeys, but that wouldn't do for this morning. I patted Yasmin's pale lemon Beetle parked under the willow tree. I smiled and asked it nicely to look after my wife and daughter when they would be out together without me, but the coldness of the steel served only to reflect the stark night chill that was biting the back of my neck. As the gravel crunched beneath my feet, I pressed the remote on my key ring, and steadily the large, heavy oak garage door opened ... and there it was, my toy, the soft top already down – my silver Porsche 911. I stopped and wiped some imaginary dust off the headlight. It was the child in me that bought this car. I had simply felt the butterflies as a small boy and so, if life was to be materially kind to me, I would treat myself. But as I stood before it now I recall that when I was finally in a position to buy one, I didn't. The extravagance of it suddenly didn't sit quite so well. But Yasmin and I were in Italy, walking, blowing with the breeze, when I stood respectfully, longingly next to this very same machine, and the butterflies returned. Yasmin could see the look in my eyes.

'Promise me, Ritchie, when we get home you must buy one, even if you only use it to blow the cobwebs away once in a blue moon, then you've got it waiting for you. You could be dead tomorrow!'

And how right she was – wise words indeed. I ran my hand along the top of the door before pulling it open. I slid down into the cold creaky dark-blue leather seat. I hesitated for just a moment, but then reminded myself that once Yasmin and Evie were asleep, nothing would wake them. I pushed the key into the ignition and turned. The engine growled into life, my nerves suddenly rising and then easing as it dropped to a more acceptable spirit-tingling purr. I turned on the headlights, the strong beam illuminating the driveway, the gardens, and then I was aware of how the light was sparkling back off the water. I pushed down onto the accelerator and the car eased out onto the gravel, but the devil in the exhaust note made it clear that this machine was raring to go. I drove steadily up the long winding driveway before finally turning out through the gates and into the deserted lane. And as I thought about my two girls sleeping soundly and out of earshot, I pushed my foot down hard, the eye-watering early morning chill hitting my face with fresh pace – and it felt wonderful. It was truly a gift to be alive, and for however long I'd got, I was going to make the most of every single second.

The Porsche was breathtaking, eating up the miles effortlessly. I was heading for the coast, a small, secluded beach, a magical, memory-filled landscape that Yasmin, Evie and I love – some truly amazing times there. As I drove further away from the Water's Edge, I thought about Yasmin's warm body in our bed and how I must have been crazy to be out alone, and on such a bitterly cold night. But while Yasmin and Evie were sleeping, I simply didn't have any time to waste. I had craved a moonlit run down to the ocean for longer than I cared to remember…

So I was doing it!

Within two hours I was on the beach, all four tyres standing on the sand. Reluctantly, I turned off the engine, but I let the heater run for a minute or two before finally replacing it with the sound of the waves. Transfixed, I stared out into the early morning, the oil-black metallic glimmer of the sea gently massaging the sand. Suddenly, I was in almost total darkness, but as the clouds started to break a welcome light streamed from the twinkling of the stars. I just sat and stared, watching the movement – it was spellbinding. And as I closed my eyes for just a moment ... I must have nodded off.

The warmth of the morning sun kisses my face. I ease my eyes open and the full glare of the most wonderful sunrise hits me. I can't help but smile to myself.

Ohh, that is really something!

I climb out of the car and stretch my legs, my arms and then my back.

'Mmmm, that's good!'

I can see in the distance a fishing boat, far out to sea. I think about the guys on the boat: their lives, the time apart from their loved ones and simply getting on with each day. I hope they are happy, that they're truly aware of how priceless each and every moment is. I shake my head as I realise that I am now smiling, and then scold myself for my unheard advice. But then amusement is filtering through me, and as a consequence I start to run with an energy bursting out of me. I stop, slipping off my boots and socks – the damp sand between my toes feels wonderful. I start to run again, really running hard now, dashing into the sea as the tide rolls in and then sweeps out again. I keep running until I think my heart and lungs are going to burst, screaming at them, tormenting them to do so! But within a dozen or so more strides, I grind to a painful halt, totally and utterly exhausted. I drop my head, steadying my hands on hips, desperate to catch my breath. I turn and look towards my Porsche – it looks stunning, the sun casting its glow, and I am that kid again.

'It's only a car though, Ritchie, it's just metal!' Yasmin had said.

I feel guilty sometimes about the craving for wealth, material things, the big house, the cars. And as I have grown up, there is the constant need to remind myself that they are purely objects that don't really matter.

It's people that matter, runs through my mind – wise and true words, of course. But I will berate myself and feel it necessary to justify my methods as I progress materially.

I turned to focus on the horizon and its pure ability to level and humble you with just one look. I sighed, a calmness sifting through my concerns. I would always be there for my family and friends.

So that was enough?

But as I turned away from the sun, the draining questions returned.

The house, well, I love the setting and I feel uplifted when I am there. It's a home full of the most wonderful memories. Surely I am right to want the best for my wife and daughter – for the three of us. I start to walk back towards the car, my eyes focused as my toes push an inch or so into the sand with every new step. The questions have not finished with me yet, still spinning and buffeting my conscience.

The cars, well, they get you from 'a' to 'b', but if you're going to travel, then why not do it in something that reflects your mood? When feeling relaxed, comfort and style – but that takes money. But should you wake up and feel full of the most exuberant energy and ready to shout it from the rooftops, then it's the blood and guts of something like the Porsche – it clears the mind and certainly blows the cobwebs away. I don't think it hurts to work hard and to treat yourself a little on the way – but not at any price.

I'm looking straight ahead of me now, a vision of my funeral mixed with the breeze and metallic sunlight making me squint. I strongly believe that the friendships you forge and the gathering at your wake are the measure of a life thoughtfully walked. Show love and respect, and generally, people will love and respect you back – and no amount of money can buy you that. And though now I fully believe in being a good person, applying that extra educated effort in ensuring that you don't hurt others along the way is a crucial ingredient in how your finale unfolds. But there was a time when I didn't always act that way. But as I stand now, absorbing this incredible scenery, I try to convince myself that what was in the past would simply stay in the past. And so I had no need to worry about it ... did I?

Having grabbed my boots and socks, I run my fingers along the wing of the Porsche, and with a lift of the door handle I drop back into the safety of the car. My fingers grip the key tightly as I push it into the ignition. I take one last look at the ocean, the sunrise creating an image that is beyond words. I acknowledge the scenery, the rocks, the cliff face, all of which have been here for thousands of years; and here was I, thirty-five years young, unlikely to see this place again, and within days, unlikely to see anything or anyone again. I pushed the accelerator to the floor, the wheels biting into the sand, spinning and then catapulting me along the beach at breakneck speed before finally, erratically hitting the road that would take me home. I shake my head, twisting my neck this way and that, and then conjure up the image of my girls, sleeping, untroubled by all that lay ahead.

The roar of the engine brings a smile to my face, a perfect background symphony for my many mind-bruising thoughts. My memories are filled with love and achievement. I think about the first time I met Yasmin, her innocence so totally refreshing. I remember being so taken with her warmth, her natural inquisitiveness, making me feel so special. I was hooked, and there's been nothing in fourteen years to disappoint me about her. I know it sounds saccharin sweet to say it, but it's how I feel. I think about how I finally got the courage to talk to her, how I had a fair amount of confidence with all the other girls around, but Yasmin... I was convinced someone so wonderful wasn't going to be interested in me. But I finally got the strength to muster up the first words, and that's when it felt like the most natural thing in the world. And when we were together, nothing else mattered. And our first kiss was just so perfect. You know sometimes, how when you kiss someone it's just *so* wrong – they're either very fast kissers, devoid of warmth and connection, or maybe their mouth becomes hard, as if their lips are made of steel, unmoved by deep-rooted passion – we've all been there, right? It's rare for it to be perfect. But my first kiss with Yasmin, it was as if the rest of the world had disappeared.

The mobile phone suddenly crashed through my thoughts. I flicked the hands-free on.

'Okay, Daddy, where are you?' Evie's voice cheekily asked for my whereabouts.

'Hello, little one, how are you? Been up long?' I glanced briefly down at the car clock – 7.53 a.m. beamed back at me.

Evie tells me she's fine, but wants me home immediately,

before passing the phone to her mum.

'So go on then...' Yasmin says, chuckling.

I relay my adventure, assuring her that I would have loved for her to come with me, but she and Evie looked so peaceful sleeping at 3 a.m. that I hadn't the heart to wake them.

'3 a.m.? Wow, Ritchie, that's the devil's hour...what are you trying to tell me? You're right, I would have killed you!' Yasmin laughed, but meaning every word. 'You definitely did the right thing. I'm glad you've had fun, but we're both missing you like mad. Please hurry home, Ritchie...but be extra careful!'

I reassured Yasmin that I would be home within an hour or so.

'So get the kettle on, gorgeous!' I rang off and dropped a gear on the Porsche. I couldn't wait to get home to my girls.

The rest of the day was wonderful. Some of our closest friends had joined us and were in the very best of spirits. Perhaps with the exception of Jimmy – my closest pal – who upon his arrival had seemed a bit agitated. Twice now he had urged me to make some time for a quiet word. On each occasion I had squeezed his arm and assured him, 'No problem, Jimmy, we'll speak later, I promise!' And as the afternoon sun, red wine and scrumptious fare sedated us all, and I lay back at the Water's Edge, just taking in the beauty of all that surrounded me. I couldn't have dreamt up a more perfect afternoon: squeezing the last drop out of an exceptional summer, a day that you remember, but often failing to realise just how good it is when you are actually living it ... priceless, and then some.

The children were playing so well together, no arguments, no tantrums, just relaxed and happy. Leoni, a close friend of ours, was putting a daisy chain around my wrist as my hand lay on her lap. Janey, reliving and relaying her recent adventure in Rio with her in-laws... and I could hear Yasmin's laughter blending in reassuringly with my understandably tainted and surreal mindset. But the warm breeze gently massaging my face seemed to be overriding the twinge of panic that was every so often ready to swell as I wondered whether this could be my last day.

'You're very quiet today, Ritchie…' Sally enquired softly.
'Don't knock it…' Janey added gallantly. '…For a change, it's given me a chance to get a word in edgeways!'
I sat up, laughing at my so-called friend's comments, blowing her a kiss. Sally caught my eye, this time mouthing her own concerns.
'You alright?'
I nodded, mouthing back, 'I'm good, really good!' Now emphasising the words to all our friends, each in turn smiling, seemingly satisfied with my answer. 'I'm just very relaxed, enjoying the company of you all. Now stop your mothering, Sally, and let Janey carry on with her boring stories of Rio!'

Janey shrieked, outraged, grabbing a handful of grass and throwing it, missing me, but her sudden gleefully wide-eyed smile prepared me for the freshly mown strands now floating in my half-filled wine glass.

As had become quite a custom, we raised a glass for Scottie: our dear absent friend. It was always difficult seeing Janey and little Scottie – well, not so little any more, must be nearly nine. But seeing the pair of them, effortlessly, painfully triggered the horrific memories of the night Scottie died. I blamed myself totally for my close friend's death. But somehow, the way my wife and friends would always console me, telling me to 'simply let it go…!' seemed to get me through the awkward moments. Janey had never really settled with anyone else, apart from a brief spell with a complete bastard called Ian. But she simply lived for little Scottie, and their many, many trips around the world. And as I looked at her hugging her wonderful son, I nodded to myself, accepting that they would be fine.

Later that day, as I'm grabbing my hundredth cuddle off my beautiful daughter, Jimmy asks if we can have our little chat. We leave the others and make our way over to the garage. We climb the spiral staircase leading up to my office and push open the oak and glass door; Jimmy follows closely behind me. As I go to open a window, I turn to my friend.

'You can leave the door open, Jimmy, it's stifling in here. In fact, I'll open that other window too.'

As I turn, Jimmy is leaning against the large antique desk,

nervous and uncomfortable. I sink myself down onto the battered leather Chesterfield and take a sip of my red wine. I say nothing and wait for Jimmy to talk.

'Ritchie, how long have I known you? Have I ever been a burden to you?'

I shake my head and then tell Jimmy that we've known each other forever, that of course he's never been a burden, not to me and as far as I'm aware not to anyone.

'Get to the point, Jim!' I say, intrigued.

Jimmy takes a deep, drawn-out breath, and then there's no stopping him.

'Sally's going to leave me. I'm going to lose everything I've ever worked for, the business, *the lot!*' Jimmy throws his head back. 'Oh God, Ritchie, the twins are going to hate me.'

I shake my head, puzzled and shocked.

'Shit, Jimmy! What are you talking about … what the hell's happened?'

Jimmy steps away from the desk, now facing the door. He turns to look at me, but then his eyes drop to the floor, his voice momentarily almost a squeak but then gradually gaining in volume.

'Ritchie, 11 a.m. Monday, if I can't find two hundred grand the bank are going to foreclose. They'll get the lot, the *whole fucking shooting match!* My entire life over … *oh God!'*

Jimmy falls to his knees, tears rolling down his face, and then through the sobs his voice tries desperately to make itself heard.

'Ritchie… I'm totally fucked!'

For just a moment I am unable to move or say anything, my own predicament clouding my response. I just look at Jimmy, knowing that I should run to him and help him back to his feet, but his despair is leaving me cold.

It's only money, I'm thinking; *you'll still wake up, you'll still be breathing. Sally worships you, she'll not leave you!* It starts to sink in what he has actually asked of me. My tiring brain is running and searching in panic, but I simply cannot find any reason to get me close, my mind unperturbed, reeling off the worst-case scenario.

Okay, the material things go, and of course, initially, it kills a man's pride! But count your blessings, I'm thinking; *you'll be drawn closer together.*

And then, as the depth of Jimmy's despair seems to remind me that this poor guy needs putting out of his misery, I hear myself speak.

'Jimmy, look at me. Does Sally know how bad things are?'

My dear friend shakes his head from side to side.

'So, Jimmy, if you can pay the bank this two hundred thousand, will that clear everything? I mean, is it going into a black hole, or will you be able to guarantee a future for you and the kids? Jimmy, look at me...tell me straight!'

Jimmy finally lifts his tired flickering eyes, now totally submerged under a wall of thick tears.

'I'll be a free man if they get the money...I'll not have the crippling repayments, the *fucking* crippling repayments that have brought me to my knees. *Ritchie, they're such bastards!* They give you an umbrella when the sun's shining, and then *bam,* take it away from you just when the heavens open!'

Jimmy looks down at the floor, still on his knees, his tears exploding onto the polished floorboards, his arms motionless by his side.

'Stand up, Jimmy ... come on, man, stand up!'

I lift myself out of my comfy sofa and walk over to my best friend. I lift his head up.

'Look at you, Jim!' My face breaks into a pitying smile. 'Come on, Jimmy, stand up...stand up and then *smile* at me!'

Jimmy raises his eyes to finally meet mine. A brief show of puzzlement, but then a look that I have seen a thousand times from Evie – total trust and belief. And though I feel guilty, just for a moment, I feel empowered ... despite knowing that I will simply slip away from this mortal coil, never to be able to help anyone again. But in the here and now, while there is breath in my weakening body, I can save my best friend. His life and future have been wrapped up in one request. My ability to say yes, my conscience temporarily massaged – surely it is moments like this that validate the journey I have taken.

Jimmy glances back at the floor, but then wipes the back of his hand across his face and stiffly brings himself to his feet. He then looks at me and gradually forces a smile.

'I'm sorry, Ritchie, you must think I'm pathetic.'

I place my hands on his shoulders, trying to massage some life back into them.

'You're not pathetic, you're my friend, Jimmy, you're my *best* friend, for God's sake. The money will be transferred into your account first thing Monday morning.'

Jimmy's legs almost buckle, but then he seems to freeze as I dictate my terms.

'But, there is one serious condition attached. It's not a loan, it's a gift ... I never want to speak about it again.'

Jimmy excitedly chips in, 'Ritchie, I'll pay you back, please, I'll...!'

I stop him, my hands now on his face.

'No, Jimmy! Our friendship means *so* much more. I don't want it back, I can afford to do it, I'm happy to do it. I mean it, I don't want it back, not a penny. Our secret, *we* take this to the grave, Jim ... the girls *must* never know, just one friend helping another.'

I drop my right hand down and push it forward.

'Do we have a deal?'

Jimmy's hand is in mine and we then throw our arms around each other, an embrace worthy of the moment. As we finally come up for air, I tell Jimmy to go back to the others. I watch him as he leaves me, a spring finally in his step. As he gets to the bottom of the stairs, Jimmy runs his hands through his hair and takes a deep breath, and I feel elated for him. As I look out across the garden, I can't help but feel immense sadness at all the things I'm going to be leaving behind. And then, without warning, I can't stop the tears from falling as Evie runs across the garden and throws herself into her mother's arms. Yasmin beams, not a care or trouble in the world, and swings her daughter lovingly full circle. And as I absorb them and all their worth, I'm convinced I hear my heart break.

I ease into Sunday morning, my head pounding as if about to explode. I look down at the bedside clock; the green LCD flickers back at me – 6.31 a.m. As I finally manage to sit up, the sharp pains in my head make me feel nauseous.

'Well, it's certainly not down to alcohol,' I muttered self-righteously under my breath, counting and confirming just the two glasses of red. But the headaches and the scorching heartburn were relentless, and each day seemed to test my pain threshold just that little bit more. And as today's new high kicked in, I almost believed that maybe this was it – that today could be the day.

I threw three pills, one after the other, into my mouth, each washed down with a mouthful of lukewarm spring water. Within ten minutes or so the pain was almost bearable again. I was just about to slide out of bed when Yasmin snuggled up, her gorgeous body pushed firmly against mine, her arms wrapped around my chest and stomach, her fingers exploring me … and gratefully finding me. Yasmin's touch will see me paralysed and at her mercy. I ease submissively onto my back, her one hand making its way onto my face. I kiss each finger, her other hand leading the charge, and I'm in heaven. Yasmin's lips fall passionately onto mine, kissing me, wanting me. She suddenly pulls away, her white satin slip pulled roughly over her head and thrown to the floor. Without fumble, only perfect timing, we are one, Yasmin's body taking me totally, her long tousled hair falling over her face, her lips pouting just the way they should, her body easing itself up and down, the incredible sensation building, and the kisses and sensual touches, the birds singing in the trees, the chugging of a passing narrowboat. And as this inexplicable unique desire overrides all pain and concerns for the past, present and future, raising its game dangerously, suddenly I feel Yasmin's body tighten, in turn making my body react, my control lost as we both come together, our bodies eternally grateful for such familiarity. Yasmin slumps onto my chest, her breasts pushed firmly into me, and still nothing else in the world matters. Our hearts are pounding in unison, our breath being slowly, gradually recaptured.

As we both lie there, an intimacy built from the finest ingredients – happiness, passion and trust – the all-conquering power of the past few moments slides, the harsh reality of imminent separation fills my head, and with a burning heart and vocal mind, *Oh, how I'm going to miss this woman!* And in time, the inevitability that someone will take my place.

The bedroom door is suddenly flung open, banging against

the wall, and in runs my little angel, Evie. As this deliriously lively creature throws herself onto the bed, shouting, 'IS IT MORNING YET?' Yasmin throws her arms around our daughter, kisses her forehead, looks over at me and smiles, mouthing the words, 'That was close!'

Evie suddenly throws her arms around me, then tries to climb onto my shoulders, but my head is pounding with a renewed venom so I gently discourage her, suggesting that she opens the balcony doors and checks to see if the swans are about. Within seconds, Evie's mission is complete.

'They are! They are! I'll go and get some bread. I'll see you downstairs, Daddy … COME ON, MUM!'

After a few moments of gathering my thoughts, I take myself onto the balcony and glance down at Yasmin and Evie throwing the bread to the swans and a couple of hesitant ducks. Despite the idyllic nature of the scene, it only serves to add depth to just how serious and black my world has become, fully aware that the vultures are circling and there is not a thing that I can do about it. I swallow hard and ponder the reality: that all the optimism and money in the world cannot furnish you against looming death! And it breaks my heart. But as I turn away and simply absorb the laughter from my two most cherished people in the entire world, I once again question my deceit … and almost convince myself that I should tell Yasmin the truth. God knows, I would want to know. But I shake my head, accepting that I shouldn't tell anyone. *Stick to the original plan, Ritchie!*

As I step into the shower I search for something extreme and fabulous that we should do today. It's Sunday morning, no work, no school for Evie, just pure 'live for the day' fun. The hot water powers itself onto me.

'Oh my God, that is *so* good…this *has* to be the eighth wonder of the world!'

And yet within seconds I see the negative, my imminent demise highlighting realistically that each and every activity, good or bad, could be my last. I shake the thought away and rub my hands over my body, and engage the only antidote that I seem to be increasingly relying on to chase away the blackness. I just think of Yasmin, and picture her just as she was a few minutes ago.

Now there's a memory I'll happily take with me!

Within the hour, a drink and a quick change, breakfast for once given the thumbs down, and we're out of the house.

'Do you think it's going to rain, Dad?' Evie enquired.

'It shouldn't do, but who knows? I'll race you to the car!'

Evie charged ahead of me across the lawn and up the gravel drive, laughing hysterically, anticipating that I was about to grab her at any given second. We both ran into the garage, Evie just pipping me to the finish line. Her angelic face was so incredible, her deep blue eyes sparkling, her entire being lit up with the excitement that life has to offer.

'I'll drive, Daddy…!'

I nodded and beckoned her into the car.

'Sit on my lap, Evie, and then you can…we'll surprise Mummy.'

I jumped into the Porsche, anticipating Evie's usual trick of climbing over the top of the door. Normally I'd raise my eyes and give her a look, but I couldn't help but smile as she slammed down into the passenger seat and clumsily made her way over the gearstick, pushing the electric window button, making my side come up and then down again. She looked for my reaction; my smile cleared her of any concern.

'Come on, Dad, start the engine!'

A turn of the key and the Porsche roared into life. Evie's eyes sparkled at the sheer ferocity of the growl, but then she started turning the steering wheel from side to side.

'Right, Evie, hold the wheel straight, and when you're ready push down with your right leg … that's it, that'll make my leg push the accelerator!'

The engine roared again.

'Oohh, that sounds *very* cool, Dad!'

'Evie, push the gearstick over, that's it, where it says number one.'

The car eased forward, the gravel crunching beneath the tyres. Evie held her head up with pride. I could see her little face in the rear-view mirror and the beaming smile made my heart melt.

'Mummy, mum, look, I'm driving! Jump in mum!'

Yasmin stood laughing in front of us, taking her life in her hands. She walked nonchalantly down the side of the car and then in one impressive leap, omitting the futile exercise of actually opening the door, copied her daughter and slammed down into the passenger seat, a mischievous grin diffusing a deserved scolding from me – 'As if I would...'

The sun was rising steadily, casting a spiritual glow onto the grounds of our home, all that it kissed looking so fresh and tranquil. Though we'd been at the Water's Edge for almost six years now, the beauty of the place still takes my breath away, and I have to say I am still in awe on a daily basis. It's a wonderful place to live, and we're extremely blessed to be here.

'Come on then, Evie, you can steer until we get to the top of the driveway, but you'll have to sit in the back once we're at the top. Deal?'

I offered Evie my proposal and my hand. She pondered the details just for a moment, a smile suddenly spreading across her perfect face, her eyes widening with the excitement of it all.

'Deal, Dad!' She pushed down her right leg and off we roared, I muttered proudly beneath my breath: 'I think we're going to have a *wonderful* day today!'

'*Reach for the stars, climb every mountain higher! Reach for the stars...*' Evie sang along sweetly with her favourite band playing loudly on the car CD player, battling with and beating the challenge from the refreshing breeze that was flapping keenly around our heads.

Evie was now safely seatbelted into the back seat. Yasmin was holding and gently caressing my hand as we made our way down to Stratford-upon-Avon. I turned down the volume just a little, suddenly keen to build the tension as to where we were actually heading.

'At the end of this little journey I have a surprise for you both. Come on, your wildest, craziest ideas only, please.'

My girls look at each other, giggling, throwing out totally extreme and surreal suggestions.

'No, Evie, as lovely as it would be to visit Santa at the North Pole, it is only September, but other than that, think of something we've *never* done before.'

Some of the impressively imaginative ideas were absolutely fabulous.

'No, not the Easter Bunny … *no, not baby Jesus!'*

We were all crying with laughter. I just hoped they wouldn't be disappointed with what I actually had in store for them. Forty or so miles were quickly eaten up by the Porsche – an incredible machine. Cobwebs to blow away? Then this would be in the top three.

I turned sharply onto the gravel car park of a sixteenth-century pub, where a sign reading 'All Day Breakfasts' swung from a large oak post – the perfect antidote for my now grumbling stomach. More importantly, it would buy me the time to make a crucial phone call. I recklessly handbrake-turned the car just metres away from the main entrance, like an immature teenager, but when you realise your days are numbered, there is a temptation to live as if in a dream, or perhaps a nightmare would be a more suitable comparison. To drive too fast, to flick a policeman's hat from his head, but then making sure that you run off as quickly as possible, as of course hours locked up in an eight-foot-square holding cell is not really the best way to use up such valuable time! I smiled at the mere thought of all the things I would want to do if I wasn't going to be around to face the consequences. But then as I caught the reflection of Evie in my rear-view mirror, I realised I wouldn't be looking to embarrass my little girl, or the beautiful lady that sat beside me.

'Okay, ladies, *all out!'* I ordered, and then a little more softly, 'We'll grab a bite to eat, and then … *the big surprise!'*

The girls did their usual trick of jumping over the top of the car doors. They both went to drag me out, but I told them I'd join them in five minutes.

'Girls, just a couple of details to iron out!'

They both ran off, blowing kisses back at me until they disappeared through the black wooden doors. I grabbed my Filofax and phone, and rang my accountant.

'Hi, umm, sorry, Peter, to bother you on a Sunday…I know you don't function until you've had your first G 'n T at twelve!'

Peter laughed far too loudly into my ear.

'Don't you worry, you old sod, triple time on a Sunday! How the hell are you, sunshine? It must be important. Give me two secs, I'm just making my way into my office…'

I shook my head with concern. Peter's breathing was as heavy as his footsteps before he finally slumped down behind his desk. Peter had been my accountant since day one and was now paid a handsome retainer to manage my property portfolio, and he was an invaluable part of my financial success.

Peter's voice bellowed down the phone, 'OKAY, SUNSHINE, FIRE AWAY!'

I gave the following instructions.

'Peter, I've already put a letter together, hard copy in the post, plus emailed you, confirming all I'm about to ask you to do. There's a couple of delicate … ummm … points I've also added that I won't bother you with now, but whatever happens, it's very important that you transfer two hundred thousand pounds into Jimmy Crain's account as a *priority,* Monday morning…I've given you all his bank details, but that really is a crucial one!'

I thanked Peter for being such a good partner in crime over the years, and for all his advice and support. He did not question my slightly strange tone, but finished off our conversation with his latest joke.

'Ritchie, the psychiatrist calls in his next patient. The patient waddles in and is covered from head to toe in only cling film. The psychiatrist ponders for a moment. "Arrgh," the man in white says, *"I can see clearly your nuts!"*' Peter let out an almighty roar.

I told him what a terrible joke it was, but couldn't help but join in with his infectious, filthy laughter.

We ate and drank well, Evie declining the eggs and bacon, fluttering her eyelashes at the waitress instead and being provided with her favourite 'tuna pasta bake' – she'd eat it for breakfast, dinner and tea if we let her. Once fed and watered, we waved and thanked the friendly staff. We all ran towards the Porsche, and though I was the last to get seated, this time I didn't use the door either, and despite an imminent bruise or two I could see the attraction. The girls beamed at me proudly.

We raced off, shrouded in bright sunshine, the cool breeze blissful and making it an exceptional day to be alive. I swallowed hard, but pushed the negativity of the positive statement away.

Evie was yelling, 'LOOK AT THE PLANES! LOOK, MUM…LOOK, DAD! THERE'S ANOTHER ONE!'

I kept quiet as we eased off the country lane and onto a rough dirt track. Yasmin looked at me inquisitively.

'Umm, where are you taking us?'

'All will be revealed!' I pushed out smugly, and then pulled off the dirt track and made my way over a sparsely covered field, finally slowing down alongside a huge aircraft hangar.

The girls' wide eyes were everywhere. I said nothing, and didn't dare look at them as we clambered out of the car. I was desperate not to crack under the increased questioning. I threw Mrs and Miss Angel a couple of thick jumpers.

Evie wrinkled her nose and added, 'What on earth have we got these for, Dad? It's boiling!'

I smiled at her 'little madam' stance.

'Evie, my wonderful, *precocious,* favourite daughter…'

I suddenly raced towards her, grabbing her around her tiny waist and picking up her three-stone frame before throwing her over my shoulder, her shrieks of laughter making Yasmin and I burst into uncontrollable giggles.

'It might well be boiling down here, gorgeous, but…' I raised my eyes and pointed to the sky. 'Up there, well, it may be a *little* cooler!'

I put Evie down, suddenly grabbing both the girls' hands, dragging them and running down the side of the hangar. Yasmin pulled me back.

'Ritchie…'

I stopped. Evie ran ahead. My beautiful wife pressed her lips firmly against mine. I regretfully pulled my face away and focused on Evie.

'THROUGH THERE, EVIE. SEE THE *RED* DOOR…*THAT'S* WHERE OUR ADVENTURE BEGINS!'

Evie stopped at the red door, suddenly not so brave and now looking back at me. Yasmin pressed her body against mine.

'Ritchie, what are we doing here?'

Evie ran back to join us. The three of us, arms linked together, made our way to the red door. Just a couple of feet away, the girls filed reservedly behind me.

'Daddy?'

I turned and pressed my finger to my lips; the girls fell deadly silent. I turned the handle and then pushed the heavy bright-red door open. As we stepped through, I was like an excited child, but I just about held it together. It was huge inside the hangar, and there, right in the middle, stood my latest toy – a six-seater biplane, all gleaming white paintwork, with a beautiful platinum-haired angel painted onto the tail – a tribute to my little Evie. The girls stared in total awe. Yasmin's mouth was wide open, her eyes slowly turning to meet mine.

'Surely, well, it's not your plane ... *is* it?'

Evie ran towards the small but perfectly formed aircraft, finally getting up the courage to touch the wheels, her eyes like saucers. Yasmin grabbed my hand and dragged me excitedly towards the well-kept secret. She ran her hand along one of the wings before turning to me.

'Whose plane is it, Ritchie ... darling?'

Evie ran over to us, asking the same question.

'Daddy, the girl on the plane looks like ... me! Is this ... *our* plane?'

Yasmin placed her hand on my cheek, pulling my face towards her.

'Yes, Ritchie, is this *our* plane? And from the look in your eyes ... mmmm, oh my God! And are we going to fly in it?'

Evie jumped up, and suddenly the three of us just stared at each other.

'Well, the plane is ours. Oh, and what was the other thing? Ummm... oh yes, *we are going to fly her!*'

Yasmin pulled away from me, her hands covering her mouth. Evie was now back on the floor, jumping up and down. Yasmin stumbled towards the plane, taking a closer look.

'Have you organised a pilot then?'

I answered calmly. 'I sure have. He should be here any second ... oh, here he is!'

The girls turned full circle before I bellowed, 'ME! I'M YOUR PILOT!'

I was loving the incredible reaction I was getting; I just wish I had a camera to capture their priceless faces.

'I'm going to take you two up into the beautiful blue sky and show you what I've been doing for two afternoons a week for the last two and a half years!'

Yasmin started to shake her head, laughing nervously, then let out a scream before quickly putting her hand over her mouth as the noise boomed around the hangar, but it didn't stop her from yelling, *'You ... you!'* and then mouthing what I was sure was 'Bastard,' but then her beaming smile diffused any possible scolding that she felt was necessary.

'How the hell have you managed to keep *all this* a secret...and for two and a half years? You absolute bugger!' Yasmin shook her head and then threw her arms around me, squeezing the life out of me and uttering the words, 'I shouldn't be surprised really; Ritchie Angel, you never cease to amaze me. What other secrets are you keeping?' And as her forgiving lips left mine, her eyes widening, she purred, 'What are we waiting for?'

The thrill of climbing into the 'Angel' with Yasmin and Evie had been an ever-increasing dream of mine. I'd decided that I wanted to take up a hobby, but something a little different. Something, though, that would open up another world, and flying bit me as soon as I'd taken my first lesson – I was hooked. The freedom, and of course to now be in the position of owning my own plane ... well, it was a fabulous feeling. And to now be taking it to the next level by introducing it to Yasmin and Evie – a secret I was happy to *share...* I had hoped and confidently expected that the girls would not show any nerves, and it was proving to be the case. As we buckled in, the sparkle in Evie's eyes moved me, her look of excitement – a wonderful thing to see in any child. And Yasmin, well, her face was glowing.

I started the engine and then, after several minutes of checking all the necessary readings, we were ready to go. We eased steadily out of the hangar. I tooted to Matt, my regular flying buddy, who had carried out all the necessary safety checks to make sure everything was just as it should be. Matt raised his thumb, followed by a beaming smile and a childish wave towards the little girl behind me. I took the 'Angel' to the tip of the runway and radioed for clearance.

'Four minutes and you're free for take-off,' came the reply.

I turned and took another look at Evie, asking her if she was all set. She nodded wholeheartedly.

'Oh yes, Dad, *go, go, go!'*

Yasmin pushed her hand into mine with a slightly tighter squeeze than usual, her eyes begging a thousand questions, and then came words that were barely audible but I believed to be, *'I cannot believe we're going to do this! Oh God, Ritchie! You're really going to fly this thing?'*

I squeezed her hand reassuringly and then did nothing to calm the poor girl's nerves.

'I'll give it a go!'

Yasmin's scolding eyes told me to be serious.

'You are both going to love this, trust me! *Ten, nine…'*

Apprehensively at first, the girls joined me in the countdown.

'Eight, seven, six, five, four, three, two, one…WE'RE OFF!'

The three of us were shrieking and *'YA-HOOING'* as we made our way down the runway, the 'Angel' gathering speed at such a rate, the rattle of the concrete like that of a train track, and then the nose was up, the runway noise instantly disappearing, the strip beneath us becoming a thinner line by the second.

As we were climbing, I was suddenly aware of Evie saying and then singing, *'Oh God, reach for the stars, I can reach that rainbow… reach for the stars!'*

Yasmin and I laughed, cheering her on. I glanced down at the world below and took in the bluest cloud-free sky wrapped around us. Yasmin and Evie, their faces pressed to the glass, were pointing out this and that, my eyes excitedly joining their guide. Miniature houses dotted around the green chequered landscape, cars like scurrying ants that you felt you could blot out with the press of a thumb, but then having to remind yourself that there are real people inside those dots of metal, with their huge lives dictating their each and every move. My eyes were drawn to the winding, twisting rivers that slithered menacingly, serpent-like across our green and pleasant land,

and then our capable little bridges enabling the human race to cross from one patch of earth to the next. I pulled my eyes away. The girls were chattering ten to the dozen and I was just *so* proud of their spirit. With every excited word my smile broadens; I feel immense pleasure that they approve of my secret world.

We took in some of the most wonderful views in England, some truly amazing sights. But we could have been anywhere in the world. Everything looked so new and exciting, as if from a totally fresh perspective. Evie was so full of questions, her enthusiasm not dwindling one iota. We flew as low as legally allowed when going over some of England's more picturesque hamlets and towns, pointing out cities we'd visited and continually discovering places that we made a pact to visit. They say that time flies when you're having fun; well, today we proved that to the letter as the hours skipped by at a lightning pace.

When I reluctantly announced that we would have to be getting back soon, Evie was not happy about that, stating that she wanted to fly all night, and asked if we could nest somewhere. *A very reasonable request!* And she also wondered, 'Is America far, Dad?'

We all chuckled, explaining the reasons why we would have to give the good old *U.S.* of *A.* a miss today. Yasmin's words suddenly made my mind go blank as she offered the obvious compensatory line to Evie.

'We've got all the time in the world to explore, darling. This, I am sure, is just one of many adventures we can have, isn't that right, Daddy?'

I smiled as convincingly as I could at them both, squeaking out an, 'Of course...' and then having given a little stamina-building cough, added, 'Evie, the whole of England beckons, and then we've got Europe ... it's a whole new world opening up to us.'

Evie nodded, our hands meeting as I pushed mine towards her behind my seat. But I had to swallow hard at the untruth. To picture my little girl in weeks to come having to accept that there were to be no more flights with her daddy.

Bloody hell, Ritchie just filled my head. Wry nervous

laughter trickled through me as I pictured Evie overhearing her mummy discussing my death, and how I had known all along that I was on borrowed time. I chewed the inside of my mouth at the very thought, and then threw a little paraffin on proceedings as a full-blown picture of Evie asking Yasmin why I would blatantly lie about our wonderful fun-filled future together. But I had to console myself that I had no choice. I closed my eyes as tight as I could and pushed away all thought of it. After all, what good would any of it do?

The sunset was so incredibly bright, *spiritual*...as though we were within it rather than looking at it, and the overwhelming glow that filled our cabin convinced me that that was exactly what we were experiencing. My mouth had dropped and I was in awe, giggles spilling out of me as the girls were each bathed in sunlight, seemingly oblivious and in a transfixed state with their contented smiling faces. But as I took a long smooth turn, the sun was now falling steadily behind us and all was as it should be within the plane. The journey back was done in silence, each of us with a contented look on our faces. As we approached the airfield, I had another opportunity to impress. I talked Yasmin through my procedure in safely getting us back onto the ground, and she nodded her head a little too anxiously, her slightly animated behaviour not something I was going to take too personally. I radioed for clearance to land, and with far less delay than usual we gradually descended. Out of the corner of my eye I winced as I took in how Yasmin's knuckles were turning white as we rapidly approached the runway.

'Hold on tight, girls!'

And then *thud!* My stomach never failed to somersault, seeming to physically amalgamate with my chest as we hit the concrete. I let out a sympathetic chuckle as I took in the sheer relief on Yasmin's face, and I couldn't help but laugh as Evie yelled, *'Nooo!* I WANTED TO STAY UP THERE FOREVER!'

I shook my head and glanced again towards Yasmin.

'You looked worried, Mrs Angel.'

She just smiled and squeezed my hand tightly, and then leant over and kissed me.

'Wonderful, Ritchie, absolutely amazing. I loved every minute of it!'

The sun had now sunk, leaving only its stain and vapour trail. We locked everything up and left via the red door. Yasmin, Evie and I huddled as we walked, chatting excitedly about all we'd seen and the sheer enormity of what we'd just done together, totally unanimous in our overwhelming approval. As we approached our transport home, I shook my head.

'Damn! I should have put the roof up, it's gone really cold!'

Yasmin grabbed my hand, pulling me urgently towards the car with a reassuring, 'It doesn't matter, Ritchie, a bit of cold isn't going to kill us!'

Via the doors, we all dropped into the Porsche. I turned the key and the engine roared into life, the hood rising and slotting into place almost immediately.

As we made our way across the field, turning onto the dirt track, the heater blasting away for all it was worth, I was very happy to see the girls so relaxed and so obviously content, and amazingly, within just a few miles, they had both dropped off to sleep. I shook my head in awe as I focused on Evie, her face so peaceful and angelic; not a care in the world, safe with her mummy and daddy. I swallowed hard – I had so much unfinished business here, I did not want to be separated from my girls. I took a deep breath, seeking solace in gently resting my hand on Yasmin's delicate fingers as they lay unaware in her lap. Though I would always love to see her so at peace, there was no escaping the disappointment at not being able to simply chat with her. Normally I wouldn't give it a second thought, but now I was so aware of the seconds ticking away, each one so very precious.

Darkness fell rapidly and I was left alone with the sound of Eva Cassidy on the CD player, her rendition of 'Somewhere Over The Rainbow' a suitable backdrop for a perfect day. I drove at speed, perhaps a reflection of an uneasiness building nervously within me, possibly the stark realisation that I was another day closer… I shook my head defiantly, desperate not to mar a day that would stand as priceless. My forearms became taut, my knuckles white as they gripped for dear life around the steering wheel, the many houses skipping past me, two, maybe three a second. Just like our journey down, I had chosen to ignore the motorway, opting for the nostalgia of the old route back to Willow along the less busy B-roads. The Porsche speedometer touched one hundred miles an hour, but something seemed to slap my face and I eased off the accelerator.

'Why the rush, Ritchie boy? Where are you off to in such a hurry? You're with the girls, you have all you need right here!' The words were barely audible under my breath, but wise nonetheless.

I looked down at the clock – 8.43 p.m. I lowered my arm for just a moment and pushed 'repeat' on the CD face, giving me 'Somewhere Over The Rainbow' for the fourth time. The song was giving me *something*... almost as if it knew my secret. I watched the song title run from left to right across the display, and as I lifted my head I let my teeth bite into the inside of my cheek. I dwelt on the image of Eva Cassidy, her life taken so prematurely, and I swallowed hard at the sheer waste of a life that had offered so much. My eyes fell onto Evie's pale sleeping face – her colour always seemed to drain disconcertingly away when out for the count.

I forced my eyes back to the road ahead and was startled to see the unexpected traffic lights, and then the fact that they were turning from amber to red. I tried to brake, but it was too late. A huge dark vehicle came from my right. Any response from me would have been something, but it was all happening too quickly and my instincts stuttered and stalled, the Porsche lights dancing to whatever craziness was in control here. A mass of black steel rising up and ready to strike, seemingly inevitable that it was going to make contact with me and my girls. My head and body twisted in sheer anticipation, now all actions in slow motion, the blaring of a horn mingling with the song on my CD player. I just waited for the impact... But as the Porsche threw itself violently, I faced my own reflection in the blacked-out window of my attacker ... screaming, fearful eyes, hunched shoulders. But then, in a single blink of the eye, the van was gone and I was suddenly back in real time, the car out of control and sliding, and then a huge jolt as the Porsche whacked the kerb, throwing us onto a grass verge and sidling up to a huge oak tree. And then, as I prepared for my final breath…the whole mad scene ran out of energy and simply stopped.

Eva Cassidy was still singing in the background. Yasmin stirred for a second, wiping her eyes. She looked at me, smiled and eased back into her sleep. I turned to look at Evie – her neck craned a little, but she too was still sleeping. My entire body was shaking like a leaf and my legs had turned to jelly. My instincts slowly returning, I undid my seatbelt and stretched into the back of the car, determined to ease Evie's head into a more comfortable position, my breathing quick and heavy as I did so. I nodded in approval and slumped back into my seat. I turned and just stared at Yasmin, then shook my head, eternally grateful that everything seemed okay. All was calm.

I felt the need to get out of the car. I searched around blindly for the door handle and within a few clumsy, uncoordinated seconds the door was pushed open and I was out. The night air hit me and I just stood, my life rotating around my head. I looked at the traffic lights and then down each of the four roads – not another vehicle to be seen. I unexpectedly slumped forwards, my hands just in time resting on my knees. I was convinced I was about to be sick, but I wasn't. Gradually, my breathing became normal again. I could hear in the background 'somewhere over the rainbow…' I started to laugh. *Bloody song!* But then I looked up to the skies and thanked Eva, as I believed it was probably the volume of the song that had kept all this away from the girls. I picked myself up and then stretched my arms high into the blackness, my shaking starting to subside. I walked round to the other side of the car and checked for any damage. The traffic lights turned back to red, the strength of the glare enabling me to inspect the front wheel. It was certainly dented, but the tyre was still up. I ran the back of my hand against the aluminium wheel. I felt sick as I realised the full reality of what could have happened to us – totally horrifying! I remained stooped and worked my way along to the rear of the car. As I touched the tyre, my hand changed from amber to green as I pulled the strands of grass from between the still intact wheel and tyre.

I now stood and took in my surroundings. There were no houses, just trees and open countryside. I looked up at the huge oak tree that *so* nearly became the Angel family's final resting place. I shuddered at the very thought. I was suddenly overwhelmed by the enormity of what stood before me. Heavy, crane-like creaking branches stretching out and embracing all. And as the traffic lights repeated their monotonous routine, I couldn't help but feel embarrassed at how this magnificent creation, which had matured for hundreds of years in its natural habitat, had now been forced to share its day-to-day existence, blighted by the eternal hell of its man-made neighbour: red, amber, green, amber back to red, and so on…

I reflected on the life expectancy of us mere mortals. If we are told we are going to die, perhaps that's the best way, prepared and able to tie up the loose ends. But as I chewed over the ridiculously close shave that the three of us had just had, there would be no option of being prepared for such a brutal and untimely end, no choice as to whether I say goodbye or simply leave unannounced.

Mmm, Ritchie, and certainly not the luxury you've had to prepare for your departure!

I was guilty of carrying precious cargo without administering suitable due care and attention. I had learnt the hard way that being made aware of my imminent demise equated to a positive – the glass was certainly half full. I laughed, amused at my appreciation of my death and how it had been presented to me, but with the very serious realisation that the unexpected could still incredibly happen. My life trickling to a gradual halt, and you would think that would be the full extent of the drama, but not necessarily so. Just when you least expect it, *bang,* everything can change. I simply stared, my hands at my side, the traffic lights daubing red for probably the umpteenth thousandth time uninvited amongst the heavy swaying branches. I stood and focused on the road that would, *God willing!* lead us home. I knew Yasmin and Evie were my legacy and I was well aware that my time was limited, but I prayed that my wife and daughter would not be taken from each other for many decades to come.

I climbed back into the car and closed the door. I turned down the heater and lowered the volume of the CD, knocking off the repeat button. I pressed my foot onto the accelerator very gently, easing the Porsche off the grass verge. I waited for any obvious signs of damage, but as I screwed up my face in anticipation of the worst, the car seemed okay. As we tiptoed home, not going over fifty miles an hour, my only aim was to get the girls back to the safety of the Water's Edge alive and well.

As I dropped the indicator and turned through the open gates of the Water's Edge, I felt a huge sense of relief to be home. I let the Porsche freewheel down the driveway, the security lights around the woodland and gardens giving a welcome glow. I pushed the remote control for the garage door, the internal lights switching on automatically. The burbling purr of the car echoed loudly as I pulled in beneath my office and quickly turned off the engine. Yasmin wiped her eyes and shook her hair from her face. Evie didn't stir a muscle. I passed the keys to my dear wife, who made her way to the back door of the house. Very gently, I undid Evie's seatbelt, and as I picked her up my little girl's eyes half opened.

I reassured her. 'You're okay, baby, we're home now. Daddy's got you.'

Evie's eyes flickered, her sleepy pools of blue offering the softest sparkle, and as she slumped against my shoulder, she fell back to sleep. Yasmin and I just about managed to get Evie into her pyjamas, pleased that we hadn't woken her, before sliding her expertly beneath her soft duvet. We kissed our little angel goodnight, Yasmin and I not having to say a word, the look on each of our faces expressing how proud we were that we had created such a wonderful little creature. Yasmin cupped my face with her warm hands and pushed her lips onto mine.

'I love you, Mr Angel; thank you for how happy you make me!'

We made our way across the landing to our bedroom. I hesitated briefly.

'Ummm, Yaz, I've got a couple of things I need to do quickly before I call it a night. I'll be back *very* soon. If you fall asleep, beautiful, I'll understand.'

Yasmin kissed me sleepily on the lips.

'I won't fall asleep. There's still a drop of red in that bottle on your side of the bed, Mr Angel ... I'll share it with you!' Yasmin's eyes didn't leave mine as she walked away from me, and then blowing me a kiss she disappeared into the en-suite.

Finally, I lifted my head, my paperwork in order, all strategically placed in my office for when all of this would be someone else's responsibility. With a heavy heart I climbed down the spiral staircase at the side of the garage and made my way into the kitchen. I poured some filtered water into the kettle. The night looked particularly peaceful as I peered out of the patio doors, but then blackness and suddenly a sense of unease. The shrill from the boiling kettle broke my stare. I ran a knife over a fresh lemon, squeezing its contents into my 'Best Daddy in the World' cup. I lifted the kettle, allowing the boiling hot water to fall into the white china. I stopped for a moment, my heart seeming to gain weight by the second. I took a deep but painful breath and bit the inside of my mouth, and then suddenly, gratefully, I was able to move again. As though a respite of adrenalin had been injected into me, I opened the fridge door and removed a bottle of chilled water, but then almost instantly my arms and body were becoming slow and my throat started to burn as I tried to hold back the tears. I took another deep breath, determined to shake away the engulfing mood. My fumbling, shaking fingers wrestled with the lid before it clumsily slipped from my grasp and fell to the floor. I tried desperately to stay focused, and just about managed to pour a splash of ice-cold water into my drink *so as not to burn my lips...* Just the thought of it made me smile. I regretted adding the water. I wanted the pain, the sharpness of the melting flesh, anything to take away the focus from the heavy pounding in my weakening, dying heart.

My eyes were suddenly drawn towards the ceiling. I'd so wanted to join Yasmin upstairs, help her polish off the contents of the red wine, but something drew me outside. Cup in hand, I made my way out into the garden. I kept on walking, finally stepping up onto the two sandstone steps that led onto the timber decking. My heart jolted as I seemed to trip, spilling a bit of my drink onto the wood below, but managing to steady myself. I looked at my favourite cup, aware of the splash that was now running through the animated 'father face' that Evie would always insist looked just like me. I protectively ran my thumb across the tear of hot water. The cup shone back at me, the moonlight seeming to exaggerate the moment, and as my eyes lingered on this most prized possession, an image came to me of Evie and Yasmin out together choosing this gift, but then, through the tightness and burning of my throat, 'I love you girls *so* much…'

I lifted my head up to the sky above, a cool but comforting breeze brushing my face. The sound of the water lapping very gently against the reeds felt so familiar and safe. I lowered myself onto the oak below, placing my drink down perfectly onto a huge knot that was the exact size of my half-filled cup. I drew my legs to my chest, resting the left-hand side of my face on my knees. I started to relive my ridiculously close shave from earlier. I then slipped into a more relaxed mood, remembering the steady flight back through the dazzling sunset, the peace and tranquillity felt by all of us.

I was suddenly pulled out of my thoughts, aware of somebody in front of me. I raised my head slowly and looked into the eyes of a young girl just three or four feet away. My blood runs ice-cold as the little girl's eyes totally transfix me. She doesn't utter a word, but then something familiar about her eases me a little: her jet-black shoulder-length hair blowing gently in the slight breeze, her deep-brown eyes, her small, perfectly formed cherry lips that curl ever so slightly, her hands at her side, not moving, and then…

'Hello, Ritchie, it's been a while…'

Every single hair on my body is erect as I recognise the little girl. Her name is Rose, a very, very dear school friend of mine who died tragically on her eighth birthday. I was devastated at the loss, and her memory had lived with me ever since. We were the best of friends, and we would always sit next to each other in class. She didn't arrive at our school until she was nearly eight, and I was asked to take her under my wing. She had been someone that the other children wouldn't take to. They didn't talk to her or involve her in any of their games, but I liked her. My friends were there when I needed them, but when I was with Rose they left me to it. But then she was gone, after just one term ... Rose was no more.

I tried to stand, but was unable to move. I couldn't even close my eyes to blink the madness away. Rose simply stood and looked at me. Moments passed, and then, very slowly, she stepped forward, her tiny hands reaching out for me. I swallowed hard and then attempted to repeat the process, but was unable to. She took a final step, her fingertips now a hair's width away from my face. My skin was tingling. Her hands were suspended, my eyes focusing on the tips of her nails, slightly chewed, catching the light of the moon that now shrouded us both. Rose sighed gently, pushing away her own anxiety, very real and startling on my brow. It gave me the courage to finally breathe, the exhalation of air blowing my friend's fringe – a small Mexican wave and then gently falling back perfectly into place. Rose's lips curled and her smile that had never left me forced my eyes wide open. I am aware that I am not breathing again, her exquisite angelic face beaming at me. I feel as though I am spinning...but aware that I am totally still. My eyes then stretch to almost bursting point as her fingers brush tenderly against my lips, ice-cold, but soft and so very gentle. I'm suddenly on the verge of crying, tears building, held back by a wall of fire and then they are free. A stream of molten liquid rolling down my face. All that I was, all that I had become, flooding out of me. But as though cast in stone, I could not, dared not move. But then Rose spread her arms around me, bringing her head down onto mine, and in response my shoulders crumpled and I melted into her. All the pain and anguish that had built up, sheer toxic frustration that had wanted to scream and hurl its abuse at the unfair world, death-black resentment at being taken away from my wife and daughter, was now flowing freely. As Rose held me, my broken heart pushed out all the hurt, the anger and regret now able to boil over. I cried until there were no tears left and finally, my body became still.

Rose stepped away from me, and suddenly, instinctively, I was able to stand. As I stood, I almost expected this vision to disappear, but nothing changed. I blinked my eyes, pressing hard, and yet Rose was still standing there. She just looked back at me, almost embarrassed now that I wasn't at ease with her. I then closed my eyes, taking a few moments... and then calmly opened them again.

I heard myself say, 'I, I don't understand, you cannot be real. Surely I've gone mad, or am I dreaming? I'll wake up in a moment and you'll be gone.'

Rose smiled. She looked down at her feet and then up at me. 'I'm not sure what I am. I feel real, as real as anyone believes they are, but what I do know is that I'm here to help you, Ritchie. You see, I knew you needed a friend, and so I'm here to help you.'

Suddenly, perhaps inevitably, my temporary composure deserted me. I dropped to my knees, the shock at what I was seeing and hearing enabling me to do nothing, all human functions failing me. But then something, or someone, encouraged me to lift my head – a sudden determination to face what was before me. I raised myself up, finally standing, shaking, and tried to ignore my instincts, rationality, prejudices; and then I surprised myself as I pushed out my hands and beckoned for Rose to come to me. She stepped forward, and then, as if a little unsure herself, she looked down at her little bare feet. Then she started to move towards me and raised her eyes, just inches between us. She lifted her arms up, her fingers slipping into my hands. I encased them and then squeezed affectionately. That warm, wonderful smile returned to her face, and suddenly she laughed, sweet and infectious. I beamed, and then I was aware that I was laughing too. I pulled her towards me, hugging her tightly. We held onto each other – a twinge of calmness, but that constant battle of trying desperately to push to the back of my failing mind the idea that I may have finally gone totally and completely mad.

Rose loosened her grip and pulled away from me, letting out a relieved and wistful sigh, and then looked up at my home. My eyes followed and focused on a single soft light that lit up my bedroom window. And as if reading my mind, Rose spoke softly.

'Yasmin and Evie are sleeping peacefully, but we have a problem!' Rose's eyes were now on mine, her face uncomfortable. She ran her hands firmly down the front of her velvet dress, as if ironing out non-existent creases. 'Ritchie, there is no easy way to say this to you…' Rose took my hand, her fingers gently caressing mine, and then said, 'Tell me, Ritchie, do you feel the cool evening breeze?'

I shook my head from side to side.

'Does your head ache? Or your heart feel heavy…or in pain, the way it has done for many months now?'

I raised my hand to my chest, not looking away from Rose. I felt great. My head was light, my heart felt just fine, I felt warm not cold, the evening breeze was not affecting me; I felt extremely calm and totally well. Rose took my other hand and cupped my fingers, almost prayer-like, and lifted them to her chin. A little tear rolled from her eye, my heart sank, and was to sink a little further.

'Ritchie, when you saw me this evening, when I was finally able to show myself to you…you *had* died. You made your hot drink, and as you climbed onto the decking, here at the Water's Edge, you stumbled. It was at this point that your body closed down, your cup fell and broke. You fell…but never recovered!'

My heart was pounding. I looked at the decking. My 'Best Daddy in the World' cup was broken into two pieces, a dark stain from where the liquid had spilled out clearly visible. I turned my head, but I seemed to be operating in slow motion. I looked up at the bedroom window. I wanted to run into the house, to fearfully, desperately close and lock the door behind me, to charge two steps at a time up my stairs, kiss my daughter, hold for dear life my wife's wonderfully warm body. But, as Rose held my hands tightly I knew I could not, and would not ever again! My worst pain, my deep burning agony, was for Yasmin and Evie. *Would they find me here, dead, at the Water's Edge? Would Evie rise first? Oh my God! Or would she run into her mummy's room? Oh please, God, NO!* The full horror was too much to take.

Rose's words cut in.

'Please, Ritchie, I said that I am here to help you!'

I looked down at this person before me, and something in her deep soulful eyes told me I had to listen, but then the power of anxiousness overrode any hint of patience.

'But, Rose, how can you possibly help? How can *you*

possibly help *me?*'

Rose squeezed my hands. 'I know your concern for Yasmin and Evie is all you have left, Ritchie, but please, you must hear me out. Listen and try to understand! Ritchie, you and Yasmin are thirty-five years old, Evie is five … I take it that's correct?'

I nodded, listening intently.

Rose continued. 'I have an incredible choice for you to make. I have a way for Yasmin and Evie to never have to find you here, dead outside your home. I have a way that they will never have to shed a tear for you, a way that if you decide to take the option I have for you, their lives will be put on hold, and no harm will come to them. But you have to make, *I feel*, a simple choice.'

Rose stopped talking and then shook my arms, as though forcing some life into me. She started to talk again.

'You, Ritchie, my dear, dear friend, have had a wonderful life, a blessed and charmed life, until now. But in your blessed and charmed life you have made three fateful mistakes, three things that have let your otherwise excellent character down, unacceptably affecting the lives of others, three individually different incidents that could, if corrected, in time bring you back to here, this very evening, enabling you to walk back into your house, lock the door and to *live* your life!'

My mind was totally blown to pieces, but within this madness I trusted Rose. The vision of her, *her* words, *her* very being, it was easing over me, calming me and making me listen.

Rose continued. 'I can, if you agree, take you back in time, back to the age of fifteen, not just for a quick look, but to actually transport you back to a time of innocence. But all that you can take with you is everything that you know. You can take all your knowledge, gained from all your experiences, but you have to guarantee that you never tell a soul! Yasmin will be in your world, fifteen years of age, a time when you simply worshipped her from afar. Evie of course won't have been born yet, but there are some extremely serious conditions attached.'

I felt myself frown at the mere mention of negativity, but I was wide-eyed and listening intently. Rose was beaming as she talked, totally enthralled and full of childlike excitement for what she had to offer me.

'But, Ritchie, the conditions are non-negotiable, and I hate to sound so firm, but you must *never do the following,* or you will be transported directly back to now. But I won't be here, it will be just you, tragically lying face down at the Water's Edge, your life over, devoid of any further chances, for Yasmin and Evie to find you!'

I swallowed hard at the very thought.

'The rules are, Ritchie, that you must never tell a soul about what has happened to you. You must not, until the age of twenty-five, *talk, touch* or attempt to befriend Yasmin. Your paths will undoubtedly cross, but with genuine purpose. *Do abide by this rule.* You must move *quickly on!'*

All she was asking of me was insane, to see Yasmin and simply ignore her – I didn't know whether I had the strength. It was now Rose's turn to frown, her ability to read my mind unnerving in the extreme. But then nothing should surprise me, surely.

'*Ritchie,* your life and their future happiness relies on you being strong! Your romance blossomed at the age of twenty-one; you were Yasmin's first boyfriend?'

I nodded; a warm nostalgic glow at the memory.

'Well, Ritchie, this time you have to leave Yasmin to make her *own* way in the world…boyfriends, universities, career, all her choice! *You cannot, must not* influence her life in any way! But once you both hit twenty-five, you can make contact!'

My heart skipped at the mere thought of a reunion.

'But, Ritchie, you can never divulge any of this. She'll have no knowledge of her other life, her marriage to you, being a mother to Evie! And therefore, she'll think you're one messed-up boy should you try to enlighten her!' Rose giggled, almost in embarrassment at what she was demanding of me.

My heart was in my head, my head in my heart. I felt nauseous at all that was being said, but believing my little friend perhaps more from hope than logic.

'So, Ritchie, what do you think? Do you have the energy to go back, to do it all again? Or would you rather bow out now, like this?'

I followed Rose's eyes as she looked past me. My whole

being winced, as I saw my broken, twisted torso lying at the Water's Edge, one hand up and above my head, my fingertips brushing the reeds, the side of my face grey and sunken, my fading blue eyes open and facing skyward.

'Ritchie, please look at me. Surely the choice is a simple one?'

I turned to face Rose, her eyes now tearful, but calling me in.

'Please, Ritchie, do not doubt or fear me. It will be like old times, I'll be there for you whenever you need me, to talk, guide you as best as I can!' Rose was now smiling through her tear-sodden cheeks. 'It'll be fun, Ritchie, being able to tell you what I've been up to for the last twenty-seven years!'

Rose let go of my hands, lifting her velvet cuffs up to dab her eyes. She then walked over to the edge of the water and sat down, as though giving me a moment to gather myself, amidst the unnerving deceased body of Ritchie Angel a constant distraction just lying there, but I was simply having to deal with it. I tried desperately to churn over all that had been said, but strangely became beguiled by Rose, her red-velvet party dress looking as if it was brand new, her fresh, innocent complexion totally free from the battering that thirty-five years can acceptably ingrain. She dangled her bare feet over the edge of the decking, brushing the reeds with her toes.

'Rose...how come you don't have any shoes or socks on?'

My friend smiled softly, but didn't look up.

'Plenty of time for that, Ritchie; there will be many answers to many questions!' She turned and looked at me, a little doubting frown appearing across her face. 'If you don't go back, Ritchie, then I won't get to see you again, my chance to spend time with you will be over, *so* please...'

I stood shaking my head from side to side, amazed that Rose should doubt the outcome of her offer. Of course I would go back, without question I would love the opportunity of putting right the three big mistakes of my life, but most importantly, could any man allow his wife and young daughter to be greeted the way Yasmin and Evie would, in their discovering of me in the morning?

'Not a chance on God's given earth!'

Rose's eyes sparkled at me, but she let me finish.

'Rose, dearest Rose, if you can give me all that you have offered, then please, don't hesitate, *do it!* It should be one hell of an adventure!'

Rose jumped up and ran towards me, stopping short of jumping into my arms, but wrapped herself around me and then stepped back. Her dark brown eyes, almost black now, bore into my soul.

She then said the words, 'If you're ready, Ritchie Angel, then close your eyes!'

And so…I closed my eyes.

CHAPTER TWO

Till Death Do Us Part

After Death, 1985 – Lilac Sky

All was painfully quiet for what seemed like an eternity. My eyes were wide open, but total blackness, not a shadow … there was no breeze, not a hint of breath from my body. I couldn't move any part of me; it was how I would expect to feel if my body was taken away from me. Just left alone with my thoughts! I started to feel violently scared and instinctively wanted to scream out, but I tried desperately to contain myself. A few more seconds passed and the panic became unbearable, and then I couldn't stop myself. I was screaming, screaming for all I was worth, but there was no sound, no tightening of muscles or straining of the gut, no noise whatsoever; in fact, I couldn't even feel a mouth. And just as I thought that this was it, that maybe this is how I would be for eternity, I felt whatever I was, *whatever* shape or form I had become, starting to spin slowly, but each turn became slightly faster and faster until I was being whipped around violently. The screams of many, many voices filled my head and it just got louder and louder, *and then*, in the distance, a white pinprick of a dot appeared.

Gradually I was being pulled towards the dot and it got larger, brighter. It was a small distant light now, but I was still spinning and all I could see was the light getting larger, brighter. Suddenly the burning glow surrounded me and I was through it, into a lilac haze, but I was falling and the screams were now falling with me, like the sound of a spiralling shot-down plane. My focus was now on a world below me, the green of the land, the blue of the sea, but all tainted with the lilac dye that seemed to surround me. And as I fell faster, the earth below very quickly became the size of a fist and then so much larger so very quickly, and all I could see were the blues, browns and greens hurtling towards me and then a feeling like throwing up, excreting, ejaculating, all at once. Then I was slammed into *something* and everything stopped; my feelings of nothing were now replaced with the familiar feelings of having a body. I could feel my heart and then a tingling sensation in my fingers and toes. I started to rotate my neck, *very slowly*, but I could do it! But my eyes stayed firmly shut. I could hear voices in the distance, but no more screams, just warm, friendly voices getting louder with every passing moment. Suddenly the blackness behind my eyes became a little lighter and a warmth started to breeze itself across my forehead. I could feel a gentle hand place itself on my chest and then a body, as if lying on me.

I tried to ease my eyes open, but the brightness above me stopped me from doing so. My heart was now pounding with such venom that I felt it would burst out of me. But then familiar voices eased my building panic.

'Oh, Jimmy, you're *such* a dick! I mean, you don't see Ritchie and I moping about over girls... Play hard to get and they'll come running! Come on, Leoni, that's what you girls find attractive, being ignored, *go on*, admit it!'

Suddenly the voice of Scottie and then the laughter of Leoni forced me to sit bolt upright. As I pushed myself forward, the heavy lump lying on me shrieked and was finally gone. I forced my eyes open. The sunlight was bright, but a few blinks later and vision was finally mine. But I was immediately shocked to see the young faces before me. My eyes must have opened startlingly wide, because Jimmy burst out laughing.

'Having a nightmare, Ritchie boy?'

I couldn't help myself, I started to laugh too – either that or hyperventilate on the spot. Scottie and Jimmy joined in. Leoni was oblivious at first, her first concern being to reorganise her skirt having been so brutally rolled over by my violent wakening. But then we were all laughing uncontrollably.

Sally was making her way across Willow Park towards us all. It was perfect timing for me, because beneath my laughing was an almost hysterical man, not quite able to believe what was going on.

'So remember, Jimmy, act cool, just smile, but then make your excuses and leave. You've a girl to meet, *right?*' Scottie gave his strict instructions, and just as Jimmy was about to challenge the wise words of the master of love, Sally was literally feet away. Scottie scowled, defying Jimmy to stray from the script. 'Just do it, Jimmy!'

I stood up, looking for a place that I could run and hide. I instinctively wiped the grass from my trousers and swallowed hard. My school trousers! I looked at my white terry towelling sports socks and my black Adidas Kick trainers... So many emotions were running through my head, but as I spotted the toilet block I started to walk purposefully away from my friends.

I could hear them calling out to me, but I just yelled back, '*Won't be a minute!*'

As I walked I felt so light, a distinct spring in my step. I had my school shirt sleeves rolled up, my tanned skinny arms with their soft blonde hairs shouting back at me. I started to run – the toilet block was a good place to scream. Once inside, I had to wait a second as a couple of younger kids saw me and then skulked out. I stepped sharply towards the sinks, my hands falling quickly and gripping onto the cold white porcelain, trying to steady my shaking body. The graffiti-covered mirror confirmed everything. As I took in the long-haired would-be surfer-looking guy in front of me I was simply astounded. I couldn't believe I had ever looked this young, but then more importantly...

'You did it, Rose! Bloody hell, unless I've gone totally fucking mad, *you've done it!* You've sent me back in time!'

I couldn't take my eyes off me. My skin was perfect, not a single blemish. I leant forward, my fingers tracing my chin – a very fine, almost invisible down. But I stepped back, in total awe of the young guy in the mirror. A distant memory, an old friend but for my new life, and from now on this was me, but in the body of a mere boy! I quickly undid my shirt, my alarming reflection causing my jaw to drop. I couldn't believe how slim and toned I was, and I didn't have a single hair on my chest. I removed my shirt. I turned to the side and chuckled. Just this very morning I existed in my thickset well-muscled body, my thirty-five-year-old shell, but here, *now,* it was gone. I bit my lip, recalling my instinctive daily ritual of breathing in ever so slightly, my maturing years producing small love handles. Yasmin loved them, or so she said, but I wasn't quite so keen. But here and now there wasn't even a hint, and I missed them … I think? As I looked at the reflection before me, I didn't know whether to laugh or cry. Okay, I was alive and well, but all alone. No Yasmin, no Evie!

As somebody entered the toilets, I quickly darted into one of the cubicles. I pulled my shirt back on, but then stopped what I was doing. I tried so very hard to get my head around everything that was happening in and around me, but the more I tried, my only answer was to keep taking very deep breaths. Several minutes later, the coast seemingly clear, I left the safety of the cubicle and just stood for a moment. I was like a fox caught in the headlights of a thundering juggernaut. I was petrified, but somehow I managed to move. I eased the main door of the toilet block open and peered out. There were all my friends approaching the beginning of their grown-up lives. I felt my eyes sting, a delayed reaction in accepting that *there* stood Scottie.

'Bloody hell, Scottie, can it really be you?'

I smiled as I watched my dear friend acting the fool as he had always done; I had missed him terribly. I swallowed hard. There was so much I wanted to say to him, but of course I couldn't say a thing. I just needed to act normally around him. I looked out towards the dirty sandstone church. It was nearly 7.30pm and the sun was sinking fast. I tried to blink my eyes as everything had a lilac tinge, but no matter what I did it simply remained. Out of the corner of my eye I was aware of someone approaching me. It was Leoni, with a look of mischief in her eyes.

'Ritchie Angel, what are you standing there like that for? Aha, you're waiting for me, aren't you?' Leoni ran at me, pulling me out of the doorway, her body pressed firmly against mine, her arms slipping around my skinny waist.

It all felt so alien to me. I looked down at my friend, trying desperately to remember this scene. Had this happened originally? I genuinely couldn't recall. But as she pushed herself into me, her lips finding mine, it all felt so instinctively wrong. As if Leoni was the fifteen-year-old daughter of a good friend who'd had far too much to drink, a cry for attention, or perhaps taken leave of her senses and was making a pass at her parents' elderly friend. I was mortified and quickly lurched away, aware that I would seem to her like some scared, nerdy schoolboy. But as my head was spinning amongst the madness, the thought struck me: *but that's exactly what I am, a schoolboy!* And with mixed emotions the length and breadth of my body, as I mentally and physically endeavoured to take on the role of what I had become, I turned back towards her. Desperate not to blow my cover, I puffed up my puny chest and simply smiled. Leoni's depleted look was suddenly replaced with a bemused but wrongfully encouraged smile.

'Leoni, come on, ummm, there's plenty of time for *that*!'

The rest of the crowd were just getting themselves up and starting to make their way out of the park, the daylight seeming to dissolve around us very quickly. As Leoni and I walked, she talked, but I wasn't taking a word of it in. I was trying to remember, to recreate exactly, what my life was like. I pushed my hands deep into my trouser pockets. I could feel a bit of loose change, but as I pulled out twelve pence I recalled how I never did have any money when I was younger. In fact, the only time I started to have any kind of income was just after I turned sixteen, when I finally left school and managed to get a job.

As Leoni and I rejoined our friends at the park gates, Sally smiled, throwing my jumper at me.

'You'd have left that on the grass; come on, admit it!'

I had to smile at her forceful glare. But seeing Sally close up I was reminded of the tough, regimented, ambitious cookie she was, a million miles apart from the woman she had become – a thirty-five-year-old mother of two, and you couldn't wish to meet a more laidback, earthy, non-materialistic woman. My God, it was so great to see her, but she looked so frighteningly young!

One by one, everybody started to drift off in their different directions.

As Leoni kissed me goodbye, 'Remember what I said, Ritchie, think about it. We're not getting any younger, right?'

As she raced off towards her house, I shook my head, totally ignorant to what I was or where I stood in my revisited teenage life. Finally, Jimmy and I were left alone, steadily making our way somewhere. But as my light, nimble feet carried me forward, my head was filled with so many heavy questions. As the street lamps started to flicker into life, casting their weak glow onto the uneven pathway, it only served to remind me how real all of this could actually be. A shiver ran the length of my spine as the cool night air started to bite. I tensed my body, a rebuff to the drop in temperature, or at least that's what I told myself. My mind forced a smile, the seriousness of my situation being replaced by surreal amusement.

I kept glancing at my best friend, taking in the school blazer, his graffiti-covered Adidas sports bag. I lifted my eyes a little higher, now on Jimmy's face. I couldn't help but smile inanely at his long dark brown curly hair, his 'bum fluff' beard – his pride and joy! We were so jealous of his ability to grow such a masterpiece, but now, as I look at him, I have to bite my lip, determined not to let out the inappropriate giggles that I have building up inside me. As we walked, Jimmy talked – about a subject that I certainly hadn't forgotten. All Jimmy ever talked about was Sally, and tonight was no exception.

'It's alright for Scottie, saying to simply ignore her, you know, play hard to get, but she'll just think I'm ignorant, won't she?'

I put my arm around my friend's shoulder.

'Jimmy, don't worry. I promise you, it all works out beautifully!'

Jimmy stopped, his face looking puzzled. Firstly at my arm around the shoulder; after all, that was something we would never have done at this age. And secondly, at my reassuring outburst concerning Sally. We both stood perfectly still, our arms at our sides just looking forward.

'Ritchie, you're such a dick! Some kind of *love doctor* now, are we? Or ... or maybe someone that can see into the future?'

I winced at the mere suggestion, and not moving my head I said, 'Sorry, Jimmy.'

As Jimmy disappeared into the darkness, I suddenly felt uncomfortably alone and extremely scared. Though I knew my feet were moving steadily closer to my mum's house, I couldn't help but suddenly drop to my knees.

'Fuck!' echoed unintentionally into the night.

An eye-watering pain shot through my body as the hard concrete slabs smashed into my kneecaps. A surge of despair leapt from my body as I threw up onto the pavement before me. I heaved again, but this time nothing came out. I dragged my arm across my mouth, suddenly aware that there may be people around. But as I staggered to my feet, I was assured that I was totally on my own. I pushed my face skywards, the cool evening breeze gentle against my throat. My eyes blinked almost in unison as the stars glistened back at me. Familiar clear sky, the same sky filled with identical stars, whatever age I was. I gazed for a moment longer. I was aware that I was stalling for time, every stolen second crucial in summoning up the strength and courage that I so desperately needed, as I knew that in a few short moments I would come face-to-face with someone I hadn't seen for fourteen years.

As I stood in front of my house, a million and one memories rolled before my eyes. I forced my head up, focusing on the upstairs bedroom. For a brief moment the window was in total darkness, but as my thoughts finally seemed to catch up with my heartbeat, a warm orange glow filled the black windowpane. I was overcome with such a mixture of emotions, and the precise and descriptive term 'heart in my mouth' was exactly how I felt, and it was making me gag, nausea and blinding panic ready to spill out of me. I scrambled internally for a breath, but then realised, though being reluctant and cowardly in not making the decision to do so, that my feet were moving towards the front door. I was desperate to stop, but I also wanted, *needed* and had no choice *but* to go on. I pushed my hands into my pockets, searching for a key. My fingers clasped the cold hard metal and pulled it out into the night. The glow from the moon bounced briefly off the tip of the key as I turned it just inches from my eyes. I pushed the key into the lock, the flaking green paint revealing faint traces of old claret paintwork from years earlier. I pushed the stiff door forward and stepped into the hall. In the distance I could hear a voice on the phone. A shiver ran the length of my spine, making my hair stand on end. A breath stuttered from me. I knew I was not to imagine, to dwell or ponder, for even a second. I had to keep moving. I turned and placed my foot on the bottom stair, my eyes taking in the old house, the paintwork tatty and so dated.

'Naturally, Ritchie!' I said to myself, but smiled as I focused on my old school photographs hanging on the hallway walls.

I heard faint laughter and turned my head towards the landing. I took each step silently, my nerves unravelling. I was biting hard into the side of my mouth, but after fourteen years to now come face-to-face with someone I had so painfully grieved for, to be reunited … something that will be so very emotional, but so incredibly one-sided. I tried desperately to remember how my dear old Mum would look on this average everyday event, me coming home from school. I just kept repeating in my head, *Oh Mum, oh Mum!* I swallowed hard, accepting that she may have seen me earlier this evening after school, and if not, definitely this morning. And as all my cogs, logic and presence of mind slip and slide, the most stupid scenario unfolds in my head and makes me smile: the face of Cilla Black.

'You have not seen your mother for fourteen years, chuck, you thought she was dead. Well, love, surprise, surprise!'

The sound of my thumping heartbeat fills my ears, my ineffective breath suddenly taken by the creak of the top stair. I freeze. Mum's voice is now so clear, chatting and gossiping to someone on the phone. *Do I go in?* My thoughts are dashing between trying to act as normal as possible by choosing to simply yell goodnight and get to bed as I always would, or, the most obvious choice in these exceptional circumstances, going in there to face her, naturally scared to death of how I'm going to react and perhaps giving my mum the belief that I'm having a nervous breakdown. But my decision is suddenly made for me.

'Is that you, Ritchie?'

My mum's voice slapping my face, I try to speak, but I cannot. A higher presence takes my hands and pushes her bedroom door open, and there she is. Her smile is as I remember, reassuring and radiant, her face looking softer and younger than I was preparing myself for.

'Hang on, Sylvie, Ritchie just walked in. Are you alright, love?'

The question hammered my brain as she lay there on her big double bed, tucked up warmly in her off-white towelling dressing gown. I felt totally freaked out, but interspersed with an unexpected calm. I walked closer, bent down and kissed her cheek, hugging her firmly. I couldn't say a word; nothing would come out.

I felt her non-telephone arm go around my shoulder and I could hear her saying, 'Are you alright, Ritchie love? Has something happened? Ritchie love…'

But as I pulled away from her, my eyes facing away, I just managed to keep the tears back, and just as I thought that I would never be able to speak a word again, I managed to croak out, 'I'm fine, Mum, bit tired, umm…'

And as I fidgeted about and made a bumbling effort to leave the room, I found the strength to meet her eyes, her hand placed firmly over the mouthpiece of the phone, a look of concern on her face.

I found my voice again. 'Really good to see you, Mum!' I took a step back, hesitating briefly, but then added words that I was convinced I had never spoken. 'I love you, Mum!'

A huge smile spread across her face. 'You too, son, you too…Sleep well!'

As I closed the door, I could hear her voice.

'Sorry about that, Sylvie love, it was Ritchie. I think he's a bit tired, the stress of becoming a man, you know, what lies ahead and all that. Bless him.'

I smiled and lifted my head a little as I spotted an old familiar sight – my bedroom door. Once in my bedroom I felt totally distraught. Here I was in my childhood home, with just a few pence in my pocket. Once again, fifteen years of age, able to see my mother struggling to make ends meet. My academic skills being shown up as less than dazzling, to scrape through the most basic of exams that would merit me as extremely average to any potential employer. I was back to square one, back at the starting line. I had made a good life for myself, but it had been *bloody* hard; fifty-fifty at times whether or not I was making the right decision. And if anyone stood in my way, well, that was their mistake. Rightly or wrongly I was determined to get what I wanted out of life, and I achieved it. I was happy first and foremost: a beautiful wife and daughter, some of the best friends in the world, and to top it all off a bank balance that would give me the opportunity to do what I wanted, when I wanted. I was set up for life! But that was then. Here I was now, feeling very much alone and not totally sure of what was expected of me.

I sat on the edge of my bed, the room bathed in a lilac tinged moonlight. I could hear mum's voice faintly. I looked around as my eyes started to acclimatise to the retro, almost museum-like surroundings. My gaze fell onto my worldly belongings: my old stereo, my few albums and singles strewn across the floor. I looked at my battered oak wardrobe, the left door half open. I stood up and flicked the light switch, the low wattage bulb casting a reluctant haze on my teenage world. I was struck dumb by the poster of Debbie Harry on the wall, but then eased slightly by several photos of my mates and an old girlfriend or two, stuck almost collage-like along the bottom of the picture. I raised my eyes again to Miss Harry. I smiled, but struggled to believe that I would have put the girl with the peroxide-blonde hair and pouting lips in such a prominent position in my room. I turned to look at other strange things that may reflect my personality as a fifteen year old. There were lots of surfing pictures, but above my bedhead there was a poster of Status Quo. I giggled and raised my eyebrows, but then smiled in acceptance of the smaller poster of Olivia Newton-John.

'Mmm, looking good, Olivia, *but* Status Quo?'

I actually scratched my head, such was my surprise at that one. It was almost like looking around the bedroom walls of a stranger. But as I reflected further, droplets of déjà vu, jigsaw-like, began to reconstruct, layer by layer, my old 'young' self.

'Ha, Jimmy's bad influence!'

I excitedly recalled the reason for the 'Rockin' All Over The World' boys' posing faces that seemed to follow my every move – Jimmy's obsession. Good old Jimmy's first love, or second. I wasn't sure whom he'd lost his heart to first, Sally or Quo. But anyway, I'd been dragged to a concert and got carried away with the whole atmosphere of my 'first ever gig scenario'. And so, birthday money burning a hole, I bought the album, then the obligatory 'sticking of the free poster on the wall'. I nodded to myself, convinced. *Yeah, that would be it!* But little things started to remind me of my social standing in life as *teenage* Ritchie Angel, whom I was friends with and whom I wasn't. And as I stood there in my little room, in the middle of suburbia, I was indeed layering up a fairly reflective image of who I was, and now *was* again.

I caught my reflection in the dusty full-length mirror on the wall. My legs shaking, I stepped towards my almost childlike self and then just stood. It had been shocking enough in the boys' toilets earlier, my new self, just from the waist up, but full length… My breath seemed to freeze inside my body, my only thought being, *this is me!* I was standing face-to-face with my past. I managed to shudder out a breath, and in response the hairs stood rigid on the back of my neck. *This is you, Ritchie* echoed around my head, and of course it was so clearly me – my face, my body. The boy in the mirror smiled back at me as I recalled how I had laughed nostalgically with my friends at pictures like this when discovering old photographs. But to think that this is how I was going to be from now on, how the aging process would have another twenty years to get me back to what I know and love. But as I stood looking into the eyes of the boy, teenager, soul of a man before me, there was a burning in my heart. I bit hard into my bottom lip, suddenly overwhelmed by the fact that I would possibly never see my wife and daughter again should things go wrong or not be as they seemed. My mind was painfully filled with the image of Yasmin and Evie down on their knees, desperately trying to wake me as I lay dead at the Water's Edge, and as the tears spilt from my eyes, the vision in the mirror became blurred. And I liked it this way, blurred. I became fuzzy and fuller looking, and I could almost imagine it was an older me, but then, as if I was being told to face up to my new existence, my true and very real reasons for being here, the young fifteen-year-old Ritchie Angel returned – a now clear, twenty-twenty image of what I had become.

I took a deep breath, already tired of the crying, sad figure before me. I too wanted to see him smile, I needed him to be strong; I knew what this man before me was capable of and I had no doubt in his ability. So I puffed up my chest and ran my fingers through my hair.

'Ritchie, together, young and naive, older and wiser, it's a winning combination!'

I knew I could do this. I had to accept the cards that were now dealt to me and simply work my way forward. I thought about the confidence I had as a thirty-five year old and the advantage that would give me socially in the here and now. I reflected on the fear that I had when trying to interact with girls as a fifteen year old, all the usual, acceptable insecurities that would lurk under a falsely projected exterior. I eventually, gratefully found my feet. But as you get older, you realise that confidence is the most wonderful attribute you can have. I remember looking in awe at the mere handful of kids who didn't outwardly have a fear in the world, no inhibitions, just comfortable, cool and effortlessly popular. And as I stood, my young face and body looking back at me, I could feel a tingle running from my feet and up through my entire body, and as this surge of hope and enthusiasm filled my wise brain, I knew that I could survive. I just had to believe that Yasmin and Evie were safe and protected, and that no harm was being done. I prayed for that, more than anything else.

Rose had said that they wouldn't find me dead, and I had to believe all that she had promised me. I had to not doubt her word. I mulled over again and again my reasons for being here, the adventures that I had got *so* wrong, the conclusions that I needed to put right. I eventually lay down on my bed. The extremity of whatever I had become meant that the normality of a simple task such as undressing or getting under the covers didn't even enter my head. I just lay there flat on my back. So many thoughts running through my head, adrenalin pumping through my veins capable of putting me on the ceiling, but I just lay there and did my utmost to simply deal with it. After a while I started to feel cold, so I rolled onto my side and pulled my knees up to my chest – the foetus position. It seemed to calm me, and it wasn't long before I fell into a deep sleep.

My mind raced, twirled and soared in and out of different stages of my life. My dream settled for a while, with Jimmy, Leoni, Sally and Scottie all sitting around my large office desk, each of them puffing on a large Cuban cigar, all of us fifteen years of age. I showed them my world on a large projector screen on my office wall, the bright colours flicking from scene to scene – in every glossy shot, my large house and flashy cars prominent in the background. The sun was shining down on all of us, our fresh young images, drinking, laughing and, in our own individual way, playing the fool. I watched longingly as Yasmin walked from the house looking so beautiful. The boys were so impressed with my wife, all making sexual childish remarks about her, but I didn't mind, because I too was fifteen, and I accepted and totally expected the reaction I got. Yasmin continued to walk towards the camera. The lads were cheering as the fullness of my wife's breasts became clearly visible beneath her silk summer dress. We were all laughing and I was so proud. But then the footage seemed to falter, suddenly rewinding itself. Yasmin was walking backwards now, towards the house. The picture then steadied and cleared itself, with Yasmin striding once again towards the camera, but this time Evie was running behind, and as they both got closer tears were rolling down their faces. Evie was trying to grab hold of the hem on her mummy's dress, desperate to slow her down, but my distraught wife was now holding her hands up to her face. Suddenly their screams and sobs are cutting through the laughter of all my friends, but they are totally oblivious to the stress that is so clearly visible on the faces of my wife and daughter. Yasmin picks Evie up, and both stare lost and broken into the camera. From their dark blue eyes the tears are streaming, and then the film freezes. The screen on the office wall becomes smaller, the picture of my friends and I just stops mid-flow and then, very slowly, without a sound, the entire scene starts to fall away, and then just a white square in the middle of total darkness fills my head.

After a few moments I am awake and my face is moist with tears. As my eyes open I sit up sharply. I look around me, my eyes squinting with the strength of the morning sun streaming through my unclosed curtains, my heart still pounding with the awful images of Yasmin and Evie. I shake my head, determined to block the terrible nightmare out. As I climb off my bed my eyes become a little stronger, almost able to take the strong sunlight, but I screw up my face, a little bewildered, as I'm aware that the lilac tinge is still there. I step quickly towards my bedroom window and look out. I push out a heavy, weary breath. I have to shake my head, as the sun and its usual expected orange glow is absent, puzzlingly replaced by a purple ball with lilac entrails to the left and right of it. I open my window and take a deep breath, but there is nothing unusual about the smell or taste of the day – the cool air simply fills my lungs as it has done for thirty-five years. I'm suddenly aware of someone coming into my room. I quickly turn and see my mum's smiling face.

'Come on, Ritchie, it's nearly 8.30, love. Throw those creased clothes into the dirty linen basket will you? You look as though you've slept in them!'

And then she's gone, having left a freshly ironed school shirt on my bed. My heartbeat quickens. *School ... oh my God!* I turn and open my wardrobe door, not totally sure what I'm looking for, but then I lift a hanger on which hang a pair of black Levi's cords. I instinctively look down at the foot of my bed and see my battered dark brown leather Levi's boots. I gather my school clothes and then make my way to the bathroom. I cannot help but notice how cold the house is. As I take a general glance along the landing walls and step into the bathroom, I recall that there is no central heating. The warmth as I stepped into the hallway last night was from the old rusty gas fire that mum would use to warm up the lounge. I close the bathroom door behind me and would love to run a bath, but I relive the memory of how that's a planned military exercise in this house: the immersion heater will be put on when mum arrives home, just after 4 o'clock in the afternoon; then, if you're lucky, you'll be allowed a five-inch-deep bath and then at least there'll be just enough water for mum to wash her hair – any deeper than that and World War III would start! I had to smile as the memories came flooding back. My thoughts are cut short as mum's voice shouts up the stairs.

'SEE YOU TONIGHT, LOVE… HAVE A GOOD DAY. OH, AND MAKE SURE YOU LOCK UP. BYE!'

The slam of the door rings in my ears and then the echo of silence closes in around me. I pull off my shirt and start to douse my face in lukewarm water. I try as best I can to freshen myself up. I drift in thought back to my beautiful home and have a sudden vision of Yasmin joining me in the large shower in our en suite, twice the size of my mum's bedroom, the steaming jets of water massaging my body, Yasmin soaping my back and pushing her body onto mine. The thoughts then realistically turn to Evie running into the bathroom, all wrapped up in her large fluffy towelling dressing gown, stopping any passionate early morning play that Yasmin and I may have had in mind. Evie is suddenly naked and excitedly pushing her way into the shower, cuddling up to our legs, then washing herself in the creamy white lather that runs off our bodies and onto hers. I'm suddenly aware of my face looking sullenly into the small round shaving mirror. I take a deep sigh and manage a small smile at my own reflection.

'I miss you both *so* much…'

Bang, bang, bang! booms up from the hallway. I quickly run to the top of the landing and see the reflection of a teenager through the glass of the front door.

'COME ON, RITCHIE, SHIFT YOUR ASS! WE'RE GONNA BE LATE!'

I chuckle to myself and realise it's Jimmy. I instinctively, inquisitively run to the front window with a shoot of excitement in the sudden cold light of day as the full realisation of exactly what's happening to me seems to sink in. I see my best friend walking back down the drive and then sit on next doors front wall. I turn and quickly run back to the bathroom. An avalanche of questions and tepid answers reel through my mind, but as I clean my teeth I'm aware of the differences in my mouth. Just yesterday I had a couple of teeth that had broken over the years and then been roughly filled. But shit, now as I run my tongue over them they feel so smooth, exactly as God had given me. I open wide, my chin almost touching the mirror, and see how white my teeth look.

'Impressive, Ritchie boy; I think I'll really look after these babies this time!'

I quickly towel myself dry, throw on my school clothes and run downstairs, grabbing my leather jacket off the hallway peg. I slam the front door behind me and the lilac haze smacks me firmly between the eyes. I have to quickly stop myself, as I am aware that I am about to mention it to Jimmy, but my instincts tell me that this new sunlight 'backdrop' may only be for my benefit. I smile, shaking my head at the thought that I may indeed be the only privileged party to be seeing the world through lilac-tinted eyes.

My jaw must have dropped, but seeing my 'new, old' surroundings in the harsh lilac morning light was as strangely magical as it was breathtakingly insane. I shuddered out a feeble sigh. Everything looked so dated, naturally I suppose, but especially some of the shiny new cars on the driveways: a bright yellow Allegro stood proudly on old Mr Dimbleby's driveway, while a bold royal blue TR7 suddenly roared into life a few doors down.

'Bloody hell, it's...' I searched eagerly for his name. 'Chris...' I was now excitedly forcing the issue. 'Yesss! But Chris...' I was aware that I was screwing up my face, reflecting on the time that Jimmy and I had sneaked down to Chris's when he first bought his TR7 and waited behind the hedge next to his driveway. I shook my head at the embarrassing memory. Each night at about ten thirty, Chris would bring back Tracy Stubbs. I smiled proudly, as I realised her name hadn't escaped me. But Tracy lived just three doors away, and they'd kiss a little in the car and then each night they would get a little braver. I chuckled childishly again. Jimmy and I would be right sad gits and spy on the pair of them. I can still remember the first time Chris managed to get Tracy's bra totally off! We had such a perfect view. Well, you can imagine it was quite something for two frustrated fourteen-year-old boys.

As I stand motionless, but my face undoubtedly 'inanely' animated, I am suddenly aware of Jimmy looking at me, a wry smile on his *oh so* young face.

'WHAT THE HELL'S UP WITH YOU?' Jimmy booms.

I laugh nervously, my hands turned skyward, and my shoulders shrug meekly. He simply shakes his head as I take several large strides to join him and then we're off, pushing our hands firmly into our jacket pockets. Jimmy takes out a cigarette packet, taps two out and passes one to me. I reluctantly take the cigarette off him but feel awkward – just the feel of it between my fingers – but then I have not smoked since I was twenty-one, when I lost mum. And surprisingly, even though I'm sure I must have been a heavy smoker at the age of fifteen, I questioned the possibility of a craving now. But I didn't feel the slightest urge. I shook my head defiantly. *I don't want this cigarette!* I ponder the role of the character I have to play in my new world, keen not to blow my cover. But I question the very thought: *you're not playing a role, you prat! You just have to be yourself. If Ritchie Angel at fifteen or thirty-five doesn't want a cigarette, then that's the end of it.* I hand back the cancer stick… Jimmy looks and smiles.

'What?' he almost snarls, a look of amusement filling his brown narrowing eyes.

'I've given up, Jimmy, given up, that's it, no more!'

Jimmy guffaws, the strong breath leaving his body making my eyes blink.

'But you're always trying to give up, you're hopeless! Why embarrass yourself? Come quarter to four this afternoon you'll be gasping for one!' Jimmy holds the cigarette up, nodding for me to take it from him.

I shake my head defiantly. My dear friend laughs again.

'I'll bet you a quid you can't last a day!'

Smugness oozing out of his every pore, I shake his hand firmly.

'Okay, you're on!' I smile, realising that a pound will come in very useful to a destitute boy like me.

As we walk towards the school, the noise around me becomes loud and vibrant. I am in total and unexpected shock as I see the faces of people I have not seen for fifteen to twenty years. I feel like rushing up to each one and throwing my arms around them. I want to ask what they've been up to and find out how life's been treating them, but of course I can't do that. I'm well aware that I must restrain myself and make sure that I act as normally as possible. But I continually chuckle and gasp within, elation and awe at every turn, unspectacular characters milling around me as a fifteen year old, but as a nostalgic, sensitive thirty-five-year-old father of one, suddenly these forgotten faces from my past are as intriguing as they are remarkable.

I push my hands deep into my pockets and try to focus on the road ahead, desperate to get to school, but mixed with absolute horror at the mere thought of all it entailed. I search desperately to grasp my standing at school: cool, un-cool, was I going out with anyone? Leoni was playing on my mind, but her and I as a couple, I really didn't think so! Fifteen? My memory was serving me up as, well, a blank canvas. I hoped I was right. But amongst the butterflies was a more nagging problem, an uncomfortable memory now, but a beautiful life-changing one twenty years ago. I pulled my hands out of my pockets – they were suddenly clammy. I was aware of my neck becoming sweaty and my breath alarmingly short. I suddenly grab Jimmy's arm and hear myself ask the most ridiculous question.

'Is this our first week back? I mean, is this the second day of term?'

Jimmy's eyes narrow as they question the seriousness of what I am asking. He shakes his head and laughs, suddenly pointing out something trivial in the distance. My fingers tighten reassuringly around his arm.

'*Is this the second day of term?*'

Jimmy raises his eyebrows, but is then suddenly distracted by Leoni and Sally making their way towards us.

I'm aware that I've stopped dead, my heart pounding. I grab a young girl who looks genuinely horrified as I repeat my question but even louder and with real menace this time.

'SECOND DAY OF TERM…?' I smile apologetically, with thoughts of how I would react if someone had spoken this way to Evie. I start to back away. 'Umm, thank you, thank you, you've been *very* helpful…' I look this way and that, and as I start to run I look back at the young ashen girl. 'Sorry, thank you, *so* sorry!'

A day that no man forgets, his first love, the first time their eyes meet. And today, the second day of term, is that day.

My mind is racing. *Yasmin starts school here, today!* I am now sweating profusely, though there was the minor detail of whether it was morning break or lunch-time that my heart was taken forever. But it *was* today! And how the hell was I going to deal with seeing Yasmin? As I started to walk again, my legs felt reluctant and unsure, and before I had made any kind of decision on how to proceed here I disappeared into the side street that ran behind our school. I knew Jimmy would worry, well, all my friends would, but I needed to get away. It was crucial that I had some time to think. I pushed past the one-way traffic of school kids, paranoid and so desperately keen to keep my head down. As I put a little distance between me and the school, the pavements became reassuringly quiet. I quickly gathered my bearings and knew exactly where I wanted to go. I stepped quickly down the side of the Whippet's Fifth Leg public house, and as I looked up at the sign swinging ever so gently in the light morning breeze, I smiled, as I always did, at the mad name of our local watering hole. I climbed the wooden fence at the end of the car park and dropped down into the sports field. I needed desperately to get to the Water's Edge – it was not yet known as that, just my nickname for the place, but all in good time.

The Water's Edge had always held such special, happy memories for me. I couldn't now believe that I associated the place with my death, and though it had only just occurred to me, it made me feel very sad. My thoughts turned to Rose and how she had come to me that fateful night, and as my mind raced, a reluctant smile creased my young face as I reflected on how she had sent me off on this crazy journey. I ran quickly across the sports field and headed for the meadow in the distance, my only obstacle being the road that was the main access into Willow. As I ran, I felt very quick and nimble, as though I could run flat out and not feel remotely out of breath. As I reached the fence alongside the road, I grabbed the top rail and leapt over, stopping sharply. Though wasting valuable time, I waited patiently for the small amount of traffic to pass by. I felt so conspicuous, convinced that a teacher or parent would see me. I tried to steer my eyes away from the people in their cars, my shoulders suddenly dropping, as though keen to make myself smaller and less visible. I shake my head as I take in the view of Willow and then sigh, as it's exactly how I remember it from so many years ago. The town where I live is small, about a quarter of the size of Stratford upon Avon; very picturesque, but where everyone knows everybody else's business. But even now, I can't help but feel love for the place. From the skies above, Willow sticks out clearly – a Christian cross of willow and silver birch trees forms the nucleus, lining both sides of the river, and then, as the canal crosses over the babbling waters, a line of sixty or so willow and silver birch trees complete the perfect cruciform. Though it was mentioned from time to time by our peers, it was only when I first flew over Willow in the 'Angel' that the inspired creation fully hit me.

I'm suddenly able to cross the road, and within a few adrenalin-filled seconds I throw myself as high as possible and drop down into the poppy-filled meadow. I roll for a moment before I slam to a halt flat on my back, the lilac sunshine filling my eyes. I squint, bringing my right hand up and resting it above my eyebrows. I flinch suddenly as a poppy petal falls onto my lips. I animatedly spit it away. As my eyes focus, the drooping heads of injured poppies start to wilt in defeat at my intrusion. I sit up quickly, and the cool damp earth penetrating my cords makes me jump to my feet. I turn full circle, taking in the full beauty of what stood before me. A freak of nature, or so we're told – the incredible crop of poppies that simply thrive in this sheltered spot for up to ten months of the year. An incredible sight from the air: a cruciform of trees and water standing in a pool of red.

As a thirty-five-year-old man I want to walk carefully around the edge of the field, but as an impatient fifteen year old

I start to run, the poppies falling, cut down in their prime as I take the direct route to where I pray I'll find the answers to my many questions. I run hard, the noise of the road now barely audible. There are two ways into the Water's Edge – this beautiful access via the poppy meadow, or, for the slightly less adventurous, by turning off the main road half a mile away you would then enter a gravel driveway, a private road lined with beautiful individually designed bungalows and then make your way steadily, until the gravel became thin and sparse, potholes and overgrown hedges making access more and more difficult, until finally, just when your instincts are telling you to turn around and go back, a 'Keep Out' sign will mark the spot – bold red letters on a decaying white wooden board chained to a patched-up rotting timber five-bar gate. But today, as I search for just the smallest of openings, I become impatient and push my way through the prickly hedge. I feel a tug and a painful tear as the protective thorns pierce my flesh. But once into my special place, I simply cannot believe I'm here. *The Water's Edge*. I blink my eyes before opening them uncomfortably wide.

'My God, I'm here!' But as I look around … *bloody hell!* I knew what I would find, but I still struggled to take it in – the totally overgrown state of it, especially after all my hard work, was soul-destroying, but I knew I could not dwell, and as I held my head up, despite all that stood before me, there was an innocence and a promise that gave me peace. The memories flood back – my visits with Yasmin, the only person I ever brought here in its natural state, and the fact that Evie was conceived here. An inspiring, spiritual place for me, a home for my two girls and I, a sanctuary that would have been impossible to leave, but unfortunately for me, I had no choice. And though I was doing all I could to be strong, I was only too aware of a swirling of grief bubbling in the pit of my stomach, and though I squeezed my eyes tightly shut, hot stinging tears forced them open again and, through a haze of bereavement, all I could see were trees and the stark realisation that that was all I was going to find here. It was almost too much to bear.

I eased my feet forward, determined but awkward, almost as if forgetting how to walk. But as I made my way through the long coarse grass, it wasn't long before the sound of babbling water helped to soften my pain, and then as the trees started to thin out I could hear the gentle chugging of a narrowboat; and finally, there it was, the most beautiful spot in Willow – the view onto the water and the ancient sandstone bridge that carried the canal over the sparkling river. It was all so reassuring, so perfect, well, nearly perfect. I thought back to when I had originally discovered this wonderful place, an oasis of calm. I had never seen another soul here, so there was never a doubt in my mind. No matter who or what stood in my way, nothing would stop me – Ritchie Angel and the Water's Edge were destined to be together.

My heart and soul are on familiar and contented ground as I absorb the steady flow of the water. I've taken in the beauty of this place so many times, but today is unique. My mind is suddenly tickled by something, my eyes distracted and pulled away from the calming liquid, and then instinctively I look up at the perfect clear blue sky. I blink to make sure, but my sky is most definitely blue, not a hint of lilac. I fall back, gratefully, excitedly, onto the grass and sigh, and just take in how I love blue sky – normal, fresh, just as it should be, blue sky.

'Hello, Ritchie…'

My eyes drop and there is Rose, her exquisite face, her sparkling unassuming eyes.

'How are you coping?'

Rose's words do not get an immediate reaction. I think long and hard about what she has asked me … I don't have an answer. But my beaming smile will assure her that I am *so* very pleased to see her. I let out a huge breath. So many questions are tumbling around my head, but I simply don't know where to start. I am desperate to know exactly what she wants me to do and to explain precisely what has enabled this to happen. Rose takes my hand and sits down beside me, and without me having to say a single word she starts to talk.

'Ritchie, I have told you why you're here.' Rose's eyes look deep into mine and then she continues. 'You know what you've done wrong, and how your behaviour towards certain people has been unacceptable.' She lets her head tilt slightly forward, prompting a response from me. I nod. 'But, Ritchie, of course people do bad things all the time, and it doesn't mean that they'll die prematurely as a result of their wrongdoings! But with you, I strongly believe that it is this fact, and an admirable fact it is, being that you are a genuinely good person, that has been responsible for your death.'

Rose now takes both of my hands, her eyes focusing on my 'in awe' expression. Then her eyes widen, hopefully acknowledging my genuine inability to offer much else and that my blankness is complete and utter attention on what I hope will enlighten me.

'Ritchie, a good man will know if he has done wrong, a good man will find that the guilt stings and whittles away at the soul. The pain can be shrugged off, but the damage will only increase.'

I feel a tear slip from my eye and I look down. Rose's hands squeeze tightly around my fingers.

'Oh, Ritchie, I know, I know, but feeling sorry is not always enough. I've seen your face over the years wince, genuine embarrassment each time that you felt happy, the warmth and love you feel each time Yasmin has ever kissed and hugged you. I was always convinced that your face gave you away, as though you sneaked a little thought back to the *black* things you have done. I would study your reaction so closely, because simple things, mmm, such as each time your friends would pat you on the back, you would appear pensive, as if reflecting, an almost 'if only they knew the truth'.

I felt Rose move both my hands to rest in her lap, covered simply by her one hand, her other now rubbing gently on my upper arm.

Then almost excitedly, 'And, Ritchie, each morning, when you opened your curtains to face another wonderful day in your self-made paradise of a life, the look would be there, a shroud of guilt wrapped around you. And the final proof, should I ever have doubted it, would be the rounding of your shoulders, as if you were withering from within, in response to the priceless moments with your daughter, Evie. Mmm, the day she was born, her first smile, the first time she ever called you daddy!'

My eyes were now streaming, my vision blinded by thick resolute tears. Rose appeared to have dropped to her knees, her petite fingers tight around my shoulders.

'I could go on, Ritchie, but every time a guilt pang hit you, the stress to your heart was cranked up a painful notch, and over time we all know that stress can be a killer.' Her head is now resting on my shoulder, her words soft, gentle, almost at a whisper. 'Oh, Ritchie, your whole body has been paralysed by an overwhelming guilt... your brain no longer able to console you with justified reasons for your actions, and your heart and your brain eventually cancelled each other out.'

My tears stopped and I managed to blink my vision clear, my eyes focusing on Rose.

'Ritchie, my involvement, my reason for being here, wanting to help you, well, you were the only one that ever showed me friendship. For whatever reason the other children never wanted to talk to me, to play with me, and certainly when I was gone, suddenly disappearing from the school classroom and playground, they didn't shed a single tear for me.'

Rose paused for just a moment, and then continued.

'But you, Ritchie, showed me kindness before and after my death, and therefore, as I watched your life unfold and then became aware of how your life was going to end, I wanted *so* desperately to help you. I begged the powers that be, explained that I was convinced your wrongdoings could be put right. I knew you felt deep regret, and so I felt you worthy of the chance to do just that!' Rose's grip tightened and her soft words once again started to flow. 'You will live from day to day, but there are going to be situations that won't be totally relevant to correcting your mistakes, and therefore your life will simply fast-forward. You may fall asleep on a Monday evening and not wake up until the following Sunday, or perhaps, wake up one Tuesday morning and find yourself walking home from a night out, mmm...twelve months later, entering a more appropriate era.'

Rose lets go of my hand and stands up. I beg her not to go yet, but she smiles back at me and beckons me onto my feet.

'You see your blue sky, Ritchie?'

I nod.

'Your blue sky will only be blue when you are here. Your sky on a day-to-day basis will be tinged with lilac. Lilac is the colour of angels' tears, and you will therefore be reminded each day of their sorrow on your hands. You will only see blue sky here, because here is where you paid the ultimate price for the wrong you have done…you traded your life!'

Rose takes my hands again, her eyes judging my reaction.

'But, Ritchie, away from here you will be constantly reminded; the lilac sky will make sure of it. You'll know when you have put right your first wrongdoing, as the lilac will fade a shade or so.'

As I sat there looking at my dear friend, I felt so unworthy of her help. Rose is quiet now, pensive and desperately waiting for my reaction, but suddenly, as though impatient at my lack of fighting spirit, her face lights up and her eyes transcend a genuine spark of hope that tells me I can do this, and amongst the niggles of doubt in the pit of my stomach I feel lifted by the feasible worst-case scenario – that even if I wasn't to get my chance to go back to my old life with my wife and daughter, then maybe, just maybe, there was scant consolation knowing that I could at least rest in peace.

Rose suddenly shook her head, her arms raised.

'Defeated before we even start, Ritchie Angel! *Good God, man!* Where is your fighting spirit?'

I let out a laugh, nervous and apologetic.

'Rose, I'm sorry…If you're convinced we, *I,* can do this, then I'll give it everything I've got.'

Our eyes danced towards each other, my heart pumping at the sheer thought of all I was going to be facing. I had just one more crucial question.

'How do I deal with Yasmin? I, I am sure she's starting at my school today.'

Rose purses her lips, her eyes wide, and frown lines appear across her forehead that you could fall into.

'You know the rules, Ritchie, and on this you must be very, very clear. I accept that it's not going to be easy, as there will undoubtedly be moments when your paths will cross, but you must make sure that you do everything you can to simply keep away from her. You'll have to pacify yourself with seeing Yasmin from a distance. I've said this before, but I'll say it again so that it sinks into that *pretty head of yours…* please,

Ritchie, you *must* remember, she has to be allowed totally to live *her own life.* You must never try to influence her decisions with, say, anonymous letters, subtle hints to her friends on boyfriends, career, choice of universities, in fact *anything* at all. It is her life totally, and you, Ritchie, *have no part in it.* You will have to live with that for ten years!' Rose's face softens. 'Please, Ritchie, play by the rules and nobody will get hurt!'

And then Rose, as if someone is calling her, looks up to the skies and she's gone.

Suddenly my young bones become ice-cold. I turn and start to make my way out of the woods. I do not want to look back and am very keen to get away from here. Something is unnerving me, urging me on. I try to fight whatever force is depriving me of the usual calmness when here, and in defiance I push both my feet firmly into the rich peat beneath me. I've stopped, and the uncomfortable voices in my head have now gone quiet as if waiting for my next move. I am desperate to appear in control, but my nerves are starting to weaken. I look for inspiration. I turn my head and see the water in the distance, and I softly mutter the words 'Water's Edge.' I smile, almost baiting, but then I'm running, feeling as if I've pushed my luck a little too far with something or somebody so much stronger than I, some sort of spiritual force that seems to be stopping me from taking the route that got me here. I'm aiming in my mind to run back up the hill towards the poppy meadow, but my legs are taking me around the water through the woods towards the five-bar gate. I scramble desperately up the overgrown embankment, grabbing at the branches and brambles, anything to get away from the ever-increasing voices inside my head. Suddenly my hands are on top of the decaying gate, the moist timber crumbling between my fingers as I leap and finally land unceremoniously face down on the compacted mud. I lift my head, turning and smiling with relief as I take in the 'Keep Out' sign. I take a deep, much-needed breath and let out a small, nervous chuckle. I am aware that my hands in particular have become warm, as if the sun is shining down on them, but the intensity of the heat is as though focusing, making a point... I stretch out my fingers. The tinge of lilac is strong, and Rose's words – *You have angels' tears on your hands!* – send a shiver up my spine.

My attention is pulled in the direction of an old woman walking down the lane, her walking stick thrust skyward, I recognise her face.

Her voice bellows towards me, 'You must *not*, young man, go onto that land!' She starts to cough, her body stooped, her tone softening as her eyes meet mine. 'You can clearly see the sign! It says keep out! And I *want* you to do exactly *that*. The land belongs to a powerful man, somebody you really don't want to mess with! So I don't want you or *any* of your friends going in there. Do you hear me?'

I pull myself to my feet and nod to the lady, her outward bravado doing little to disguise the softness in her eyes. I dust myself down as best as I can. The old lady has stopped in her tracks just feet away from me. I smile, offering a sincere apology and looking for a truce in her eyes. She nods, a twisting of her grey lips as close to forgiveness as I was going to get. And as if she had pulled the trigger on a starting pistol, I then move quickly, skip around her and start to run, pushing myself faster, again feeling as though I could run forever, and increasingly tempted to do so to simply get away from this madness, but I am painfully aware that I have a very serious job to do, and so I'm heading back to school.

I question how long I've been gone. The noise of rustling trees and the gravel beneath my feet is now replaced with the sound of approaching traffic. I run quickly between the oncoming cars, a slightly over-reacting horn ringing in my ears as I reach the safety of the pavement. I can see the town hall. I try to make out the position of the hands on the old clock, but then my straining of the eyeballs is compensated by the loud chiming. Finally, as the midday signal booms out, I feel a little shocked at how much time has passed. I take myself onto the sports field and once again really push myself, still shocked at how capable this young body is. I reflect back to when I was a teenager. I was so desperate to get a motorbike or a car, keen for anything that would mean I wasn't having to pedal, walk or, on the very rarest of occasions, run. But here I was, staggeringly impressed with my fitness levels, which of course are to be totally expected at such a young age. As I sprint effortlessly towards the fence that would take me into the pub car park, I reeled off the God-given perks that you really don't appreciate when you're young. I was shaking my head, each one taken for granted, only measured as immense once they're gone and the gradual downward slope beckons, until finally left on the verge of decay, creaking and aching bones or otherwise. As I dropped down into the car park, I felt the urge to nip into the pub and have a quick pint and maybe a meal before I went back to school, but as I checked in my pockets, jingling twelve pence around, I had to sigh in defeat. I was so used to always having a roll of twenty-pound notes in my pocket that I felt genuinely and painfully deflated. It was official: *I was broke!* Being able to do what you want, when you want, was something I had undoubtedly taken for granted in my grown-up world. But then the other negative factor in my 'ice-cold beer scenario' – perhaps the school uniform wrapped around the skinny body, regardless of funds – was going to see me amusingly dismissed.

The minutes were counting down in my head, a steady rhythm synchronising with the beat of my running feet pounding on the uneven concrete slabs. I lift my head in response to the shrill of the lunchtime bell echoing from the school, and then, almost instantaneously, hordes of kids started to spill out onto the playground. But as I approached the school gates, I became nervous – classrooms, lessons, teachers, it all became such a blur. I simply had no idea as to where I should be. I stopped by the entrance to the school car park, a comfortable distance between me and the intimidating wild animals leaving the building. But suddenly I'm reeling, as an almighty thud followed by a sharp pain across my back forces me onto the hard concrete floor. I try to turn and see what on earth has happened, but then the rich-red leather of a Dr Martin boot swings full force into my face. My head is spinning and I'm instantly aware of a sticky sweet-tasting liquid running into my mouth. Then I feel a gut-wrenching blow to my kidneys. I try to crawl away, but I'm aware of people running towards me and finally being turned over onto my back. I crane my neck, pushing my nearest helper out of the way, catching a glimpse of a man running across the main road wearing a claret rugby shirt with a number seven on the back. I slump down onto the cold concrete as people are attempting to talk to me, others wiping blood from my face. I try to make sense of the attack, but my mind keeps replaying the image of the number seven. I cough and let out a deep, painful chuckle. *Number seven, Yasmin's favourite number. Not quite so lucky today, Ritchie boy!*

Gradually, I'm manhandled into the nurse's room at school. Her frustration at the crowd of helpers boils over.

'Right, out! Come on! All of you! Unless your name is Ritchie Angel, *I want this room empty!*'

As the nurse finally gets her wish and is about to close the door, Jimmy forces his way in.

'For God's sake, Ritchie, what the hell's happened?'

And in answer to his question, I really didn't know. I tried to think back to when I was this age, to try to establish whether or not I had got into a fight like this, but I certainly couldn't recall such an incident, and I was fairly convinced that I would remember such a severe beating. No, I never had any enemies, not for a good few years yet. And as the usual pangs of guilt went into overdrive, I slipped into the delves of justification, spewing out my usual drivel – that it was business, nothing personal, the end justifying the means and all that. I swallowed hard and tried desperately to focus on me being fifteen, in the here and now, and any possible provocation that could explain this, but still I couldn't.

But as I lay being prodded and poked in the narrow confines of the first aid room, there was an image that rolled over and over in my mind – the claret rugby shirt with the number seven on it. Now *that* bore some poignant significance, but exactly what, where, why or otherwise for now totally escaped me.

Despite advice to the contrary, I determinedly convince my Florence Nightingale that I'm fine and that there really isn't any need for me to go to hospital. Once outside the nurse's room, I make my way down the empty school corridor. I try to think about which class I'm supposed to be in, but then my thoughts turn to Yasmin and Evie. I take a deep breath and shake my head, but there is no escaping my craving for their love and care right now – how I long to be curled up with them both, Yasmin fussing around me, tending to my cuts and bruises, Evie lying still in my arms, just gently caressing my forehead with her beautiful petite hands. I'm instantly stopped in my tracks as I hear a familiar voice echoing further down the corridor, their footsteps getting louder and then suddenly, about five metres away, is a face that simply takes my breath away. She's looking down at the floor, her parents either side of her, the three of them being ushered into the headmistress's office. As the door closes my head is pounding, my heart feeling as if it is about to implode. I peer anxiously through the frosted glass, but all I can see are shadows. And though I knew I was wrong, and I feared the consequences could be more than I was able to cope with. I open the door. The stern headmistress suddenly looking up at me with a scowl, and then her voice booms into life. But not a single word registered.

The beautiful young lady in her office turns her head and looks right at me, and there they are, more innocent and pure than I had dared to remember, but as dazzling and blue as a sunlit ocean. Yasmin…my soul mate and wife, the mother of my precious daughter, looking directly at me, nonchalantly brushing a stray blonde strand of hair from her eye. Looking right at me, and yet *not* knowing me!

Yasmin's parents just stare at the rude schoolboy. Incredibly, but regretfully, I tear my eyes away from Yasmin and take in their serious expressions. I had never seen Yasmin's father before – in photographs, but never in the flesh. He had died a few months before Yasmin and I got together – both of us having lost a parent meant we helped each other through the difficult moments. But here and now it was surreal seeing him. Yasmin had often said, 'Ritchie, I wish you could have met my father,' but then she'd throw me one of her wicked smiles and add, 'Actually, probably better that you didn't. I think he would have definitely disapproved, you corrupting his innocent daughter!'

And as I took in his stern look now, I happen to think she was right. The headmistress steps forward, grabbing my arm, manhandling me out into the corridor, her office door being slammed behind her.

'What on earth are you doing, Angel, barging into my office? I have asked you three times to explain yourself!' Her loud, angry voice suddenly softens; I think the cuts and grazes on my face perhaps demanded another question from the bullish lady.

My mind racing, I hear an apology coming out of my mouth, explaining that I am a little dazed and had, for a short moment, not been totally sure of my whereabouts. The headmistress pauses for breath and then ushers me – a little gentler this time – back towards the nurse's room.

'Go on, Angel, keep going, I can't keep these people waiting any longer. That's it, in you go, lad!'

But once I hear her office door close I quickly turn and make my way to the reception foyer, where I hope my friends will spot me. As I stand at the centre point of the full circle entrance hall, my feet symmetrically placed onto the huge cruciform that has been etched into the marble floor, my eyes feel as though they are rotating self-sufficiently, taking in the full circumference, but then they stop, focusing on the large clock ticking down in exaggerated strides, accelerating the end of the school day. I am aware of two sets of eyes from beyond the reception desk glass staring directly at me. I nod and retreat into the shadows, and then, shuffling with purpose, busily finger through the books on the dusty foyer shelves next to the well-stocked trophy cabinet. But as I'm idly flicking through the hardbacks, I simply cannot get Yasmin out of my head. I was a lifetime away from home and yet my wife was only walking distance away from me, but I had been told that I must simply walk in the opposite direction.

I start to think about the real implications of Rose's warning and ponder the cruelty that goes hand in hand with not being able to meet, talk or even smile in Yasmin's direction. But the cost of rule breaking – such as being transported to the place where I died, where it was threatened that Yasmin and Evie would find me – well, for me it would be a pain equal to death. In light of my peek at Yasmin in the school office, I felt myself praying for forgiveness, hoping that my moment of weakness would be viewed with leniency. As I continue to flick steadily through the books, my fingers start to gain speed and I'm suddenly at the end of fifty books or so. Then I turn and see people all around me, asking questions, though I cannot hear a word, all the noises droning into one. I then move at speed out of the school, friends and surrounding people all going their separate ways. My eyes start to hurt, my body and mind out of my control, just being carried along. I'm through the front door of my house, eating my tea, going upstairs. I'm aware of the instant darkness and then the feel of heavy blankets enveloping my body. My head and stomach feel uncomfortable and nauseous, and then I seem to pass out; all I'm aware of is the subconscious feeling of night and day, dark and light, flicking in and out, gaining so much speed that I feel my head and body are going to fragment in a thousand different directions. The flashes of dark and light almost become one and then, as if slammed from space onto the side of a mountain, my madness stops. Unable to open my eyes, I start to hear sounds, very, very distant, and then I'm aware of music. I can feel my feet moving, walking steadily, my eyes still closed, but then I feel a hand on my bottom, a gentle squeeze, and my eyes finally open.

CHAPTER THREE

A Reunion With The Day That My Life Went So Very Wrong

After Death, 1988 – Lilac Sky
The full strength of the music hits my ears, and I feel a little bigger and stronger than before. My brightly coloured shirt becomes my focus as I look down at myself, and my black patent shoes shine back at me. I hear the giggles of girls and turn to see what's going on behind me. I'm then faced by three pretty faces, and one face in particular almost knocks me off my feet. Julie Andrews – I look directly into her brown mischievous eyes, her dark, shoulder-length, glossy permed hair interwoven with small satin ribbons. I recall this night vividly. I must have been seventeen or eighteen years of age,

and this girl was going to cause me all sorts of problems. And though I was now reliving the moment, this was the first time I had ever come face-to-face with Miss Andrews. Julie's friends suddenly left her side and it was just the two of us.

'Well, well, well, fancy seeing you here, Ritchie Angel!' Julie seemed to purr, putting her mouth to my ear, girlishly twirling her hair with her finger.

I try to act as though this is our first meeting, but am unsure how to handle the situation. As she talks, all that is going through my mind is that this girl will put me on the road to heartache, and ultimately make me commit my first terrible act. If I were to simply walk away from her now, would that change history and therefore stop the adventure we had together? I felt confused, but could it be as simple as that? If it was, then this whole mission of mine could be quite easy to deal with, and I would get to go back home. I hoped that somehow I could be shown what was wanted from me. I felt that I should perhaps back off from Julie, for tonight at least, allowing me time to check out the best way forward. But suddenly I was aware that my arm was around her waist. I tried desperately to loosen my grip, but it wasn't in my power to do so. And then when I attempted to make an excuse, about how I had 'some place to be', the words simply wouldn't come out. It was then that I became aware that I didn't have the control I thought I had, that there seemed to be a chain of events that I would not be able to change. It was then that Julie pulled me close and kissed me, and though my mind was filled with the full horror of how I ended up hurting this girl, my original feelings and desires seemed to take over, gaining total control of this pre-programmed body. And so the adventure with Julie proceeded. And though I was totally involved and knew exactly what was happening, it was almost as though I was looking down on us both, as I would imagine an out-of-body experience to feel. But then Julie would do and say certain things that would put me back into my body, right at the heart of the moment. All would then proceed at an every second, 'real-time' pace. Despite knowing all that I knew and being here to change specific histrionics, my actions felt spontaneous, but the reality was that I was living this moment exactly as I had over seventeen years ago.

'I'm never gonna dance again... guilty feet have got no rhythm...' filled my head as Julie and I held onto each other, our feet moving slowly, our bodies revolving full circle in the middle of the dance floor, courtesy of George Michael singing his heart out, heartfelt angst and begging for forgiveness. I knew how the poor man felt. The song and the moment had stayed with me; the combination had burned deep. Little do you realise, especially at such a young age, just how the soundtrack to your life evolves; the depth at which it sinks into your soul and just how poignant it all proves to be. Seventeen years ago, and strangely at this precise moment, a song that made me feel as though the moth was becoming a butterfly – I felt great. But in time I was only too aware how this scene would serve as a reminder of how a fateful wrong turn can affect your entire existence.

And as the lights became bright around me, Julie asked if I would be a perfect gentleman and walk her home. In my mind I was letting the girl down gently, but all I heard was, 'Yes, I would love to!' As we left the nightclub, the cold air was welcome but not sufficiently sobering.

Jimmy ran over to me, jumping onto my back, playing the fool, whispering into my ear, 'She's gorgeous, Ritchie,' before ruffling my hair and running off to join the others.

A brief moment of clarity drifted through me. All thoughts and emotions of my thirty-five-year-old self had drained out of me as the night had progressed, but then a heavily diluted case of déjà vu would flutter through me. Just as I was desperately trying to drag the intention back, it would be gone. I could feel my nerves tingling in its wake, my reason dropping away, all memory wiped totally clean. I shook my head, a *blankness,* to anything other than this moment instantly calming me. I took in my friends: thumbs up from the boys, shaking of heads from the girls. My response: smiling like a Cheshire cat.

Julie's hand slipped from mine, her friends repossessing her briefly, whispering wickedly into her ear. Though we had never spoken prior to this night, I could see exactly what I'd seen in her – she was stunning. And Julie being a year older than me could only add to her desirability. I suddenly felt cold and alone, my hands now pushed deep into my trouser pockets as I stood beneath the street lamp. Though I'd had the occasional heated moment with the opposite sex, I had never been keen to get too serious. Perhaps happier to play the field, but closer to the truth being that I had set my standards just a little too high. Once dazzled by perfection, it would appear that it blinds you for eternity, and anything less just won't do. As a result, I was a virgin. I questioned suddenly whether Julie was about to change her mind and simply leave with her friends. My heartbeat quickened at the mere thought, but I mentally prepared myself for the public humiliation should I be left standing beneath my lamp post. I shuffled from foot to foot, and was fast approaching the face-saving decision that I should simply start walking...but I couldn't. My feet were now rooted firmly to the spot, a nervous shuffle no longer an option.

'God, sorry, Angel.' Julie ran towards me. 'Sorry, I mean, Ritchie, must stop calling you by your second name, you must think me very rude.' She didn't wait for an answer, her lips pushed without warning against mine, diffusing instantly any problem I may have had with her manners.

So there I was, at two in the morning, no longer aware of how this union would end and unable to do anything to stop it.

Julie played, toyed and teased with every step. At her insistence – my resistance seemingly futile – we would, as though marking and celebrating each and every road we turned down, kiss passionately, our mouths hungry and unable to get quite enough of the other. But each time – Julie dictating the pace – I would be allowed up for air, and we would be walking ever closer to a place that held only regret for me. But as I pondered the facts, my mind would drift away to the unknown, and I would just be left with a nagging doubt and the inability to retrieve my very real concerns from just a few seconds ago. My mind was now lost totally in the moment, the glow from the full moon lighting each drunken, hazy step.

Julie stopped and turned to face me, her mouth now just a hair's width from mine. She whispered that we were now on her road. She pushed me firmly up against a huge oak tree, her tongue flicking skilfully, passionately across mine, sending an electricity that actually made my toes curl. Temporarily satisfied, Julie pulled her lips from mine, and then just stared, her face, her eyes *so* alive, simply beaming. She then grabbed my hand, my alcohol-fuelled feet reducing me to the role of a child being pulled against his will. As Julie strutted in front of me, her tight pink pencil skirt showed off her perfect figure and the moonlight bounced off the patent-clad heels of her stilettos. She walked with the confidence of a woman twice her age, and as she turned to me, her thin black jumper was short enough to show off an inch or two of her slim tanned stomach, her full breasts straining defiantly against the satin of her half-cup bra that was obviously a size or so too small. Julie had it all, and to a seventeen-year-old virgin, what chance did I have? And then, once again, just for the slightest of moments, silver strands of something – conscience, vague clarity, guilt... But for whom? And as I desperately tried to hang onto whatever had just run menacingly through my mind, I couldn't recall the slightest of notions as to why my heart would be pounding so inexplicably. I was a seventeen-year-old teenager, devoid of responsibility to another living soul, my blank canvas of a mind suddenly filled with a lust for instant gratification. Julie's hot breath was muttering something about how her parents were away for the night, and then the magical words as she pushed herself firmly up against me.

'I know we've only just *officially* met each other, Ritchie...but I've been watching you from afar, and seeing as I've got the house to myself until tomorrow afternoon...will you stay?'

My smile must have been answer enough, because I was being led – every step was fear and excitement combined, now and seventeen years ago, and as I wrestled with thoughts of rewriting even an ounce of this fateful moment, my reason for doing so evaporated.

We were now on the Oaks, a rather rough council estate; the home of the Andrews family. Julie lived alone with her mum and dad, with both her brothers living away: Kirk, the eldest, in Northern Ireland with the army, and Dirk, locked away for another ten years or so, having committed an armed robbery on one of the main banks down south somewhere – my memory fails me on the exact details. So for tonight, the baby of the family is left alone.

Julie's stilettos echoed around the alley set at the back of her house, disturbing an array of animals – dogs, cats – and falling dustbin lids. Julie amusingly placed her finger firmly on her lips.

'Sshhh, Ritchie, my aunt *must not see me!*'

Her loud whisper made me laugh. I stop her from taking another step, crouching down, and once she realised what I was attempting to do she giggled and allowed me to slip off her shoes.

But as I take in the broken glass and excrement that litters the remainder of our route home, I say, 'You hold these, Julie, and I'll carry you.'

She did as she was told, and I romantically lifted her up and attempted to carry her the last hundred metres or so, but once we reached her garden gate, I rather suddenly dropped her onto her lawn.

'There *you ... go.* You'll be alright, and ... a lot quieter on the grass!'

Julie shook her head, slipping her shoes back onto her feet, her smile matching the sparkle in her eyes. As my drunken friend fumbles around for her key, I simply stare at the vaguely familiar surroundings, and then I sense a blurred, haunting warning that this street would, in time, become quite a battlefield for me. Yet despite my instincts telling me to run and not look back, here I was shrugging away any blackness and undoubted pain that entering into this moment would bring. But as Julie closed the door behind us both, our time together seemed unavoidable, and as her soft lips pushed against mine, all concerns for a seventeen-year-old boy with only one thing on his mind simply didn't hold a candle.

Julie went around closing the curtains, smiling at me as she went from window to window. She made her way into the kitchen, telling me to take off my coat. As I did so I could hear the rattle of glasses, and within seconds my temptress had returned, a bottle of vodka being triumphantly swung above her head. I smile and nod in approval, not that I had ever drunk vodka before. Julie gave a half-hearted bow and fluttered her long eyelashes. I put my coat down on top of a brown velvet beanbag placed next to the television. Julie grabbed my coat and flung it onto the stairs, kicking her shoes off. She stood about a metre away from me, hands on hips, her face full of mischief.

'I bet you've had *loads* of those posh girls you hang around with, eh, Ritchie?'

I am rooted to the spot and don't really know what to say, but finally I decide that maybe honesty would be for the best – though it scared me that she may well laugh and send me packing. I looked her firmly in the eyes.

'Well, I'm ... well, I've had my chances, but waited ... not really met the right girl!'

Julie's eyes widened, her face stretching in sheer disbelief.

'You're a virgin?!'

Her ineffective attempt to keep a lid on her amusement lasted for about three seconds, and then my hair seemed to be forced back, such was the ferocity of her laughter that was now filling the house.

'YOU, YOU, RITCHIE ANGEL...ARE A VIRGIN?'

Julie stumbled forward, her ability to stand upright ravaged by the full emotion of my hilarious confession. She appeared to be making a valiant effort to stifle her giggles, her hands pushed firmly into the pit of her stomach. She swallowed hard and attempted to take a large deep breath. Suddenly she was looking up at me, her brown tear-filled eyes *almost* apologetic and keen for me to confirm the shocking truth.

'Ritchie, tell me seriously, surely you're not...'

In response I screwed my face up a little and heard myself say, 'I am...*really!*'

Julie turned away briefly, but then we were face-to-face. There was a moment of silence, and then she spoke, her voice soft.

'Do you think I've had loads of lads?'

Her eyes not leaving mine, as though searching for any dishonesty that may be hiding behind them, I answered quickly and truthfully, 'I don't know, but I would have thought one or two.'

Julie's smile returns.

'I've been with one, Billy Jenkins, but I had been seeing

him for over two years. I lost my virginity to him because I *did* love him.' Julie pauses, pain subduing the sparkle in her eyes, but still fixed firmly on mine. 'But I caught him shagging my *supposed* best friend... I'd bloody kill her, but sod 'em, they're welcome to each other!' Julie takes a step back, unscrewing the top off the vodka bottle before taking an impressive mouthful.

Her vulnerability was beautiful and virtuous in the absence of the tough front that I was so used to seeing. I nervously touch her arm and feel overwhelmed, but aware that the moment may have been lost. We both stand in total silence for just a few seconds, our eyes transfixed on each other, and then a look from Julie that will stay with me. Suddenly she's in my arms, her soft lips pushing firmly against mine, and then I'm aware of the tip of her tongue teasing expertly, stoking the flames. Her hands fall onto my waist, pulling my bright 'fashion victim' shirt out of my trousers, her warm fingers brushing expertly across my stomach and up over my chest. I return the gesture, my hands running up the small of her back, feeling the lace of her bra beneath her soft jumper. As Julie's grip gets more passionate, my hand follows the contour of her spine until my fingers drop down onto her skirt, lingering, taking in the shape of her tight, pert bottom. I can feel the outline of her panties, and then an urgency ups the tempo and our hands are exploring with an intensity that seems to have instinctively taken away my need to breathe, but then, like steel, tyreless wheels over a cattle grid, my entire being judders, a brutal metallic glow filling my head, and I freeze for the briefest of moments – memories, feelings, guilt... But as the light leaves me, any thoughts of my thirty-five-year-old self dissolve and I am unaware of anything other than my seventeen-year-old body and all experiences to this very point in time, and the full force of lust takes control and drives my mind and body forward. All warnings, memories, negative thoughts are gone. My trembling fingers ease the zip on Julie's skirt downwards. I'm encouraged as she assists the removal with a wiggle of her hips, and then a blur as we both drop down onto the settee, the kisses soft and teasing, then urgent and harsh. Julie takes control, slows things down, her eyes fixed firmly on mine, and her experience guides me, all flailing arms and limbs having now found their natural and rightful place ... soft, gentle, tender kisses suddenly urgent, wanting ... guidance from her demanding fingers ... and we become one, the unexpected intensity of *this* feeling, for the very first time, is one that you never, ever forget, and through the brief building of confidence a rhythm that dictates its own pace; the extremity of the sensation from head to toe builds and my control is lost.

It must have been a good four or five hours later, when a bright *spiritual* light passed through me, forcing me awake. I swallowed hard, needing to quickly take in exactly where I was – I nodded approvingly as it all came back to me. As I lay beside Julie, the sudden realisation that I am no longer a virgin hits me, bringing a great big smile to my face. I often wondered whether or not I would feel different, and now, the wonderful truth is *yes,* I feel ecstatic. With the table lamp on the sideboard shining a romantic sheen onto us both, I lift a curl of hair covering Julie's eye, the remainder of her face tucked sleepily into the settee cushion that's now lying on the floor on which we are both resting. Julie is on her side, cuddling tightly up to me. I push my fingers softly through her hair; my head, my heart, my soul, all lost in the moment. Ritchie Angel, seventeen years old, naive, lost his innocence barely hours ago. No known life beyond the here and now. I feel an inner excitement welling up, the novelty of a real-life half-naked woman beside me, and an immature and basic craving to explore. I reposition myself very slightly, my eyes taking in every detail as even more flesh is exposed as I pull my body away. My fingers instinctively brush down onto my chin several times, studious and inquisitive. I cannot take my eyes off Julie's fully pert and incredibly scene-stealing breasts, gently lifting up and down with the rise and fall of her deep and contented sleep. I shake my head in awe. Her olive skin glistens in the soft man-made light, her black satin and lace bra is around her waist and it's a sight that is stirring irresistibly from my toes upwards. I take in our clothes strewn around the room: a pair of black satin and lace panties lie closest, just inches from Julie's outstretched foot. I let the back of my hand brush feather light across her breast and let it linger there. Her nipple swells in response. She sighs. I very gently turn my hand, and with the finest of touches take the tip with my thumb and finger. This time she flinches, a smile spreading approvingly across her face, and then without opening her eyes Julie eases onto her back. I hold my breath and then a brush of her hand down my stomach encourages me. I've had my late-night fumblings, but never before have I had the naked female form so wanton and lay, so submissively before me as Julie is now. I sigh and am undoubtedly like a child in a sweet shop. Julie's breasts have my complete and utter attention, my heartbeat quickening as my hands follow the ravine and curve of each one. I bring my lips down onto her nipple. The shape and texture respond and it changes form, and though reluctant to leave this part of her body, I'm aware that I have a duty to impress and my lips move slowly and softly down her stomach, lifting my mouth when I finally reach Julie's tight, soft curls. My left hand is pushed beneath her buttocks, her back arching in response; my right hand rests, fingers spread at the top of her thighs, my splayed thumb toying at the precipice of where it longs to delve, glistening and impossible to take my eyes off. Suddenly Julie's hand grabs mine, her eyes still shut firmly, her fingers placing mine as though she had read my mind, her legs now as wide as my panoramic view, and as my shortness of breath stutters and misfires, my finger pushes gently in and then a little deeper, but finally, impatiently, and before I totally made a fool of myself, I pulled my body upwards, brushing my lips gently across her neck and then onto her pouting mouth before lowering myself into position, my eyes not leaving Julie's incredibly expressive face. And then unaided this time, entering the most precious of places, my shortness of breath and our joint symphony of sheer unadulterated pleasure a complete and uncontrollable montage of all that is primal, basic, and the epiphany of life itself, and as my head was swimming, swirling in the rapids, the cold harsh reality of being a mere inexperienced teenager was my downfall, and though my control was a little better this time I felt that lots of practice was needed ... *hallelujah!*

The screams of young children playing outside startled me

back into reality. I must have fallen into my second deep sleep of the night. Julie had pulled my shirt over her body and she too showed signs of stirring. It was now clearly morning, as the harsh daylight revealed all in its true colours. I looked around the room, taking in the teak furniture, swamped overwhelmingly with photographs. Julie's brother in his army uniform, just a school photo of the other one! Shots of relatives young and old, and then a smile spreads across my face and a pang of guilt as I spot my seducer all innocence and curls in her bridesmaid's dress. I push out a throaty chuckle in response. With forefinger and thumb I check the authenticity of the many flowers placed randomly around the room: 'impressive fakes,' mumbles from under my breath. My attention is then drawn towards the far corner of the room, where the lounge meets up with the kitchen – a drinks bar full of glasses, an impressive supply of miniature spirit bottles, toxic-looking liqueurs and cigar boxes. I imagined Julie's father pouring a drink for his mates, not having a clue about what I had just been up to with his precious daughter, but then the silver strands were back, painful and jarring, and then the full realisation, both alarming and regretful, for the entirety of the night.

I had been seventeen, blissfully unaware and experiencing everything for real, but as my head began to spin and I had a genuine belief that I was about to vomit, I was saved as a wash of calmness sieved through me. I took a deep drawn-out breath, then steadily placed into some kind of order the harsh reality that had arrived with the cold light of day. My eyes feverishly scanned the family photographs, but all I could see was the face of Evie, and then as my head spun from frame to frame, a disapproving look from Yasmin, an expression of hurt and disdain at what had happened here with Julie Andrews. But as I shook my guilty head, desperate for some form of factual clarity, I had to question: *but surely, nothing new happened here tonight?* This, and all that goes with it, was set in stone seventeen years ago. The history of this is already in the archives. My fevered and bordering on irate thoughts are suddenly interrupted by a female voice.

'Oh God, oh dear God! *Ritchie Angel!* Oh, it's all coming

back to me now!'

Julie blurts out, shaking her head, and then pulling herself up, desperate not to expose any more flesh than necessary, quickly wraps my shirt around her body, sheepishly grabbing her clothes, and then darts up the stairs before curtly yelling, 'I'M SURPRISED YOU'RE STILL HERE! THOUGHT YOU WOULD HAVE LEGGED IT HOURS AGO...'

I ummed and ahhhed for a second or two before finally vaguely reassuring her that I had simply fallen asleep too, but certainly wouldn't have just left.

I paused and then offered weakly, 'Not without saying goodbye...'

Julie finally made her way back down the stairs, having pulled on a pair of jeans and thrown back on her black jumper from last night. Suddenly her beauty looked a little less dazzling, the corduroy indentation from the settee cushion taking up the majority of her left cheek doing nothing to help. And as I caught my own reflection in the fireplace mirror, my hair sticking up outrageously ... *touché.*

Julie stops at the second from bottom stair and sits down, clumsily folding her arms. An awkward smile eases onto her face.

'You'd best go out the back. My auntie only lives next door, and she'll *bloody* kill me if she sees a lad leaving here!'

As I look at Julie, I feel as though I want to tell her that I've just experienced the most wonderful, though undoubtedly ill-advised night of my life, and to perhaps add that I know we're not ideally matched, different friends, etc., but maybe we should, could, perhaps arrange to meet up for a drink, or perhaps get to know each other. Suddenly there's a knock at the door. Julie's initial look of horror eases as the shrill of a girl's voice resonates sufficiently through the awkward moment.

'COME ON YOU LAZY COW!'

Julie runs into the hallway, letting in the excited visitor. My heart stops pounding quite so much when I hear the stifled giggles of Julie and her friend. Muffled whispers followed by shrieks of amusement. Julie and her friend finally come into the lounge, and there am I, trousers just about pulled up, with my shirt hanging over the stair banister. Julie and her notorious friend Tina Blatt just stare at me, Tina trying to contain her mass hysteria and Julie running her fingers through her hair, as if this was all a bit tiresome. Tina's voice breaks the silence.

'Virgin then, Angel? Was 'e any good then, Jules?'

Julie quickly replies, looking straight at me, her jaw almost hitting the floor.

'I swear, I never told her you were a virgin, *honest* Ritchie!'

My face must have read like an open book, because that was it. Tina turned back to look at me, full-blown jubilation spreading across her fully stretched face, ridicule and a verbal bashing not quite sure where to start.

'Bloody hell! Angel *was* a virgin! Ahh, ha, ha, ha!'

Julie looks again at me, but then, full of embarrassment, turns and runs up the stairs, with Tina *'bloody'* Blatt following in hot pursuit.

I quickly pull on my clothes, grabbing my shirt off the banister. I try to leave by the back door, but cannot find a key anywhere, and there was no way I wanted to shout upstairs to Julie and her 'wonderful' friend. So I took my chances and walked with head held high out of the front door. As I opened the gate at the end of the garden, I noticed a neighbour's curtain twitch. I shook my head, wondering whether that could have been Julie's aunt.

I was sure I smiled in her direction, but then turned away, muttering to myself, 'Sorry, Julie!' and then upped the pace and started to run, then faster, keen to get myself off the Oaks estate.

After a good fifteen minutes or so I found myself on Willow High Street, and I stopped. I glanced up at the town hall clock and raised my eyebrows in acknowledgment: 11:20. I stood still, the world appearing to rotate around me. My mind was suddenly filled with questions like what day is it, and where am I supposed to be? I tapped my fingers together and then shook my head as I reached a logically calculated assumption that it must be Saturday morning, as I always used to go to the nightclub on a Friday. I pondered for a moment, my mind now wrestling with another question. I screwed my face up, distracted by a minor detail – sudden determination in trying to name the club. I smile broadly when the penny drops: *'Don't Walk, Boogie!* That's it!' I muttered, impressed at my sudden recollection. A strange name, even now after all these years. I question again where I think I'm actually going. I don't move, and understandably receive some puzzled looks. But I've been thrust into this era, and a simple action, such as whether or not I was supposed to be at work, was leaving me increasingly anxious.

I recalled clearly my Saturday job at the local estate agents, Skirdle and Sons, which had been a huge part of my property development grounding. From a young age I had planned exactly how my career should run, and thought that being part of an estate agents would give me the perfect vantage point to learn quickly from existing developers, and to be amongst the first to know about all potential development opportunities for when I finally found myself in a position to take my first tentative steps on the road to riches. But Monday to Friday I worked for a local builder, Steve Young Construction – the best in the area. I was the lowly apprentice, but I was learning fast. Not particularly skilled on the tools, but certainly able to spot a good tradesman when I saw one. I was aware that I was unnervingly turning full circle, my eyes falling on and meeting an array of Saturday-morning shoppers, many passing me with a shake of their heads and a tut of disapproval on the narrow footpath. But then a friendly nod and a jovial 'Good morning, Ritchie' from faces that I was struggling to recognise did nothing to decrease my anxiety. The full glare of my *new real* world, and unable to remember names and the finer details of what Ritchie Angel was all about, made me want to run, but I had to stay. I needed to accept what was happening to me, and perhaps to breathe a little more! I took a much needed breath and it helped. I was desperate to hit a balance, to be calm and take things one tentative step at a time.

'Oh, Ritchie… just coming to see you about our house sale.'

I put my hand up to the elderly gentleman's face.

'Ummm, *so* sorry, you'll have to call the office,' I said, before scurrying away.

I slipped down a side alley, determined to gather my thoughts. I frantically delved down into my pockets and pulled out some money. I unfolded a five- and a ten-pound note, and a 'wow' left my lips as I also unravelled a twenty-pound note. At least I've got some money this time! I instinctively roll my shoulders, keen to shrug off suddenly feeling cold. I'm unsure what time of year it is and decide that I need to find out. I bite the inside of my mouth, my head dropping as I reflect on last night. I feel genuinely pained at not being able to walk away from Julie, and at a loss as to how to proceed if even simple actions like thought and speech are not within my control. I lift my head and take a glimmer of satisfaction from the fact that for today at least my memory and freedom of choice have been returned to me; that I am able to walk about as I choose, free to say what I want, or at least I think I can.

I reflect back to what Rose said about relevant events, and how my life would skip forward when necessary. I question the details and the relevance of now, and the outcome of Julie and I seemingly unable to sidestep history. I take another chunk out of the side of my cheek, scolding myself as I do so. But my mind is rampant. The first scene with Julie and I had been played, and the consequences... I shuddered at the mere thought.

In good old *Ritchie boy* fashion, I pushed to the back of my mind the severity of what lay ahead. I pictured my fifteen-year-old face in the mirror from earlier in my bedroom and scratched my head. As for me, as I live and breathe, that was literally hours ago, but in keeping with the mathematics of history ... two or three years ago. I smiled nervously and shrugged the thought away – I had to! I reflected once more on my young, fit body that I had to believe was capable of anything. I try to think of myself as an actor in a movie, the star of this mad adventure and how I had a part to play. I was the all-conquering hero, the lead role, and I wanted the Oscar!

I smiled to myself, uttering under my breath, 'You are such a prat, Ritchie...' But as I laughed, I felt the bulk of the fear leave me and I knew I had to be strong. Whatever this madness needed from me, I had to be ready to give. I stepped out of the alley and took a deep, courage-building breath. I raised my eyes skywards, the sun gradually warming the cool morning air, creating a pleasant breeze on my face. I clapped my hands together, as if needing a starting pistol to push my feet forward and up Willow High Street. And as my confidence grew, and I dared to take in the once so familiar surroundings of my teenage years, my eyes widened in awe at how everything had once stood. I felt my jaw drop and my head shake at every nostalgic kick. And as my spirits were bubbling and a sense of *all is possible* bounced around me, 'I love this town...' crept quietly and proudly from my lips. I reflected on the uninviting, unfashionable canal that ran behind all the shops, but how, with imagination and perceptive innovation, it became a crucial part of Willow's development. I was suddenly forced to turn around. *Mmmm* ... a welcome waft of nostalgia filled my nostrils. *My God, fresh bread! The Old Bakery!* I shook my head, a deep and sincere endorsement of approval at seeing the old place in all its glory.

My feet once again stood firm, my eyes transfixed by the painfully obvious scope that screamed out from the bakery. I swallowed hard, my mind repeating over and over, *sympathetic and traditional renovation, Ritchie.* I sighed regretfully, knowing full well how progress and greed were to be the downfall of this beautiful, priceless building. An ironic chuckle of embarrassment crept out of me, as I was only too aware that what stood before me now would become a large faceless fast-food restaurant. It was all about making a quick buck. Forget about tomorrow, it was all about the money, *my money!* I rocked momentarily on my feet, my regretful part in the demolition of the Old Bakery cutting deeper than it ever had. But as I continued to chew deep and hard into the inside of my cheek, it wasn't only the loss of such a wonderful building that had proved to be so fatal, but the ripple effect of such an action on my life. The problems that arose from my naivety and greed, and the way that I chose to solve them, cast *the Old Bakery deal* as such a daunting chapter in my short life. But despite the severity of the outcome, at the outset I believed that I could live with my route to financial security. But indeed, as I matured and walked down Willow High Street with Yasmin and Evie, I felt saddened at what I had orchestrated. I swallowed hard, feeling sincere regret at not having had the vision to try to incorporate the contemporary feel the

Americans had wanted with the true British tradition that the Old Bakery oozed. But when they said jump, the cheque was big enough for me to simply enquire, 'How high, and through how many hoops, sir?'

I drop my head and pull away, and take the dozen or so steps towards Skirdle's, with whom I may well be in serious trouble for not showing up for work this morning. I stop, so many potent memories flooding back. I am painfully aware that I need answers to the here and now, but instead my eyes are nostalgically sending me off in a different direction. Halfway up the high street is the old library, standing proudly on six impressive sandstone pillars, cars parked tightly around the centre point of the town, and suddenly I'm reeling from more painful self-pitying, life-changing regret. I try desperately to shake off my negativity and attempt to adopt a determined focus on the positives of my more mature years. I smile and approve of my most inspired decisions, spawned from a wise and contented father of my little angel. But there was no escaping the fact that as a younger man, I was indeed a different animal. Costing was the key, profit the only thing I was interested in. But with Yasmin and Evie to answer to, I undoubtedly became aware of my legacy, not only with the girls, but my business dealings too. The world presented itself to me differently, and so instead of wanting to make my fortune out of Willow and then disappear into the sunset, I rightly believed that the roots I had put down presented me as the man I had become, and blanking out the negatives of my early years, as Rose had so prudently pointed out, allowed me to focus only on what made me feel good and therefore safe. I swallowed hard. So many memories: Yasmin and I courting, making our way in the world, and of course the excitement we had when we knew Evie was on the way. This time I thought my throat muscles were about to split, and then a tear dropped in the absence of my wife and daughter.

I shook my head, the back of my hand quickly removing any sign of weakness to the passers-by. I tried desperately to focus on why I was here, and when successful, how I would be reunited with my girls. I swallowed again, a little easier this time. *Here I am*, I told myself, *but I have changed nothing yet!*

I shook my head in recognition that this was how my grown-up life began. I placed myself in the shoes of Ritchie Angel mark one – his career path was chosen and nothing was going to stand in his way. But as I stood here now, seventeen or so years young, I accepted and understood that I had made mistakes that were unacceptable and that Rose had seen me make them. I cringed at the mere thought. Shameful moments that I had never doubted to be mine and mine alone, but the reality was that they were always going to be questioned and therefore I would be answerable. And as a younger man, not being guided by religion or fearing God above, I'd simply and ignorantly presumed my life to be a private affair. To see things so differently now I found disturbing, and to be totally truthful, embarrassing. But should my sanity be intact and this all be completely and unquestionably real, then it does prove that we don't know anything at all about how the human race is governed and monitored. I smile broadly. *The world and all that sail in her, uncharted waters, Ritchie boy, so listen and learn, listen and learn!*

I am suddenly aware of someone standing before me, blocking my lilac sunlight. As I take in this familiar face, I instinctively jump back, blurting out the lanky figure's name.

'Mr... Skirdle!'

'Morning, Ritchie lad, having a good birthday? Enjoying your day off?' Mr Skirdle doesn't wait for an answer, his eyes full and dark, focusing over the top of his reading glasses. 'Ho Ho, Ritchie, looks like you've had a good night! Still in your disco gear, I see!'

And just as I was about to offer some sort of reply, Mr Skirdle was walking off at speed, as he always did, still talking.

'See you next Saturday, lad, nine on the dot! HAPPY BIRTHDAY SUNSHINE!' And then he was gone, slipping into the newsagents for his pipe tobacco, as he always did.

My birthday! I pondered, trying to calculate quickly. *Bloody hell, my eighteenth birthday! Don't Walk ... Julie ...* wow! It all came flooding back to me, and it wasn't Mr Skirdle that I was in trouble with, it was my mum. I hadn't made it home until late seventeen years ago, and I was going to be late again! I wrestled with my conscience, but then came the words *all the way home!* It will take at least fifteen to twenty minutes! And so the petulance and selfishness of my *good old* teenage years reared regretfully, presuming to reiterate words, actions and pitiful history that had only served to shame *the nicer man* that grew from within me. And though flashes of maturity struggled desperately to be heard, to rise above the youth I had been allowed to play for a second innings, they were simply batted away with a shake of the head and the line, 'I've got too much to do!' But I felt genuine slithers of what was right trying to overrule the lesser man that I found myself to be, feeling the angst and good manners of being a parent myself as I hopped from foot to foot. '...Ring her, Ritchie!' Like she always said, *Just ring me; it only takes a moment of your time to stop me worrying!* I looked around for a phone box, but then, 'What the hell is my home number?' And the truth was I didn't have a clue. I screwed my face up, as if it would suddenly come to me, but it didn't. Then smugly ... *Clever boy, Ritchie... Skirdle's!*

I ran the few steps to the estate agents, but almost froze on the spot as my hand was about to push the door open. I took a deep breath and held it in as I pushed against the glass and almost apologetically stepped inside. The breath was hot as it left my body and the memories came flooding back ... 'Ritchie, my little Angel!' And there she was, Miss Black. It was as if I had never been away.

'Good morning, Ritchie. Surprised to see you up and about!' But then, with a Cheshire cat smile, 'Mmmm, you can't keep away from me, can you?'

I quickly blurted out some weak excuse about needing a business number, my eyes looking anywhere and at anything that wasn't Miss Black. Instinctively, and not remembering that I had actually moved my feet, I slumped down into the scarlet leather office chair at my desk. I was lost in the moment for a second or two, my head perfectly still but my eyes frantically scanning all that stood on the highly polished wood that lay before me. My breathing was heavy and my heart pounding embarrassingly so, fully aware that Miss Black was watching me like a hawk eyeing up its prey. My fingers fell onto the phone book, clumsily searching for my mum's number, but I couldn't find it. My eyes now stretched painfully and fully left, my head still set at perfect centre, but I glimpsed the fat chunky phone and a white sticker with a dozen or so numbers scrawled on it. I dared to move my head, and there, in blue biro, halfway down, was *R. Angel.*

I bravely, necessarily snatched a breath as Miss Black averted her stare and took a call. I picked up the receiver, quickly pushing in the appropriate number. It wasn't long before my poor excuses were now firmly ensconced in my mum's mind. I got the tut-tutting and I felt bad.

She also announced, 'I've booked the time off work, you know.'

I now felt suitably dreadful.

She continued, 'I mean, Richard, it's not every day you're eighteen, but I won't go on, I'll see you when I see you. Oh, and Ritchie...your father's rung!'

As I put the phone down, the brief clarity of being a thirty-five-year-old father of one made me screw my face up with genuine regret. But then, as if provoked by the clicking of a hypnotist's fingers, a quick glimpse at my work colleague reinstated me devoid of thought or social graces beyond this moment. Miss Black was staring at me, teasing the top of her silver pen with her lips. I felt a twinge of a memory pushing itself forward. Miss Black and I had always had a fairly good relationship for the six months or so that I had been employed by Mr Skirdle. Miss Black – and I never did find out her first name – was in early thirties, and had seemed so much older and so sophisticated to me originally. She would play me up something rotten. She knew that she held a certain power over me and that I was a little frightened of her, and so the sexual frisson between us built up. And as I sit here now, I try to act thirty-five. I try to be cool and brush off our silly flirtation, but as much as I try to conjure up the image of Yasmin and the loyalty I have for her, I simply can't. I have only the feelings that I had as an eighteen year old. Then a shard of *something* pushes forcefully to the front of my thoughts, and though I try to make contact, determined to hear what is so desperate to be heard, decreasing flashes of light fuzzy edges gradually dissolve all thoughts and morals as a married thirty-five-year-old father.

'You're a naughty boy, Ritchie! You know Mr Skirdle's gone off for his golf!'

I smiled, wondering whether it was time for me to leave, but as Miss Black beamed, her dark, almost black eyes sparkled mischievously at me while she shuffled rhythmically in her chair. She was dressed in her usual way: black knee-length skirt, white silk blouse and black wool cardigan. She always wore very fine black seamed tights or stockings, with four-inch or so high-heel stilettos. Her shoulder-length glossy black mane was plaited and held with a black satin ribbon. But despite her prim and proper appearance, over recent months she had undoubtedly enjoyed making me blush. Not a trait that had ever troubled me with girls of my own age, but my God, Miss Black managed it with consistent aplomb!

I was aware that I was nodding my head with instinctive acceptance that she had special plans for me today. Then, as though reading my mind, Miss Black swung her legs elegantly from beneath her desk and stood up.

'Time for a cup of *tea*... Ritchie.'

As she walked, she threw a glance at me, looking down her nose and over the top of her silver-rimmed spectacles. As she entered the kitchen, I stood up, my legs a little shaky but just about allowing me to obediently follow, like a lamb to the slaughter. As I entered the kitchen, my breath juddering and evaporating before it had even left my body, despite my determined attempts to appear cool and impossibly calm, and as nonchalant as a petrified boy can be, I was finally just inches away, my buttocks pushing back against the Formica worktop. Miss Black stretched up to the top shelf, grabbing two cups and then gently placing them down on the work surface, her nylon-clad calves momentarily taut and then relaxing just a little as her feet eased back into her patent black leather stilettos. She covered up her curves well, but as she stood before me now, I knew she was ready to take our little game to the next level.

I nervously made my move, placing my hand at the small of her back, slipping my hand beneath her soft cardigan. As I did so, Miss Black arched her back a little. I placed my other hand onto her stomach, my small finger resting on the waistband of her skirt, with the rest of my fingers feeling the soft silk of her blouse. Very slowly Miss Black turns to me, removing her glasses, placing them on the work surface. Normally she would just run her hands all over me, sometimes allowing me to caress her breasts through her blouse, but today she lets her hand take the zip at the side of her skirt and pulls it down. As she does so, I take my hands away. A warm smile from her sees a nervous grimace from me, not totally sure of how far she is going to take our game today. Miss Black stares into my eyes, and without looking away she wriggles her skirt down over her thighs before elegantly stepping out of it. I am painfully aware that I have gasped loudly in appreciation. She had never looked quite so incredible as she did at this moment. She takes my hand and places it on her thigh – the sensuous feel of silk stockings, her black satin suspender belt framing a small pair of satin and lace panties. She looks and feels gorgeous. I feel as if I'm going to explode on the spot, but I try to tell myself that last night with Julie has turned this day-old eighteen year old into a man, and so I feel confident that I can handle the situation.

Miss Black, still looking me firmly in the eyes, places my hand gently between her thighs, and then encourages me to caress her. I don't need much encouragement! But as her hand starts to undo my trousers...the shop door is flung open. Though no one can see us, my first thoughts are Mr Skirdle, but I can see through the gap of the door a young couple looking at the wall displays. Miss Black is suddenly scrambling around, trying urgently to get her skirt back on, while calmly yelling through to the shop, *'Won't be a moment!'* Having organised herself, she quickly kisses me firmly on the lips.

'Oh well, another time, eh? Happy Birthday, Ritchie!'

And as Miss Black disappeared back into the shop, I remember quite clearly that there never was another time. In fact, more importantly, this incident never happened originally either, and as I tried to recall the horrific memories of what did actually happen on this day seventeen years ago, I'm left with a sick feeling in my stomach. As I tried to clear my mind, my thoughts returned to Miss Black. I tried to recall what had happened to her. But as I stood in the kitchen, taking a few moments to compose myself, I remembered that her mother had become very ill and that was that. She gave up work, and apart from one or two sightings in the high street, I never really got to see her again. But as for today, and despite being incredibly keen a couple of minutes ago, I felt that maybe it was for the best that our game had ended here – though there was no doubting a certain amount of disappointment.

As I made my way out of the shop, Miss Black winked at me. I blushed, smiled and left. Once out onto the street, I couldn't help but have a little chuckle to myself. *Wow!* I thought, the image of Miss Black standing half-dressed still very clear in my mind. As I took a steady walk further up the high street, I tried to look back to exactly what did happen seventeen years ago on my eighteenth birthday. I flicked through my memory as though sifting through a line of records. I remember eventually leaving Julie's and planning to make my way home where I knew my mum would be waiting, but whether I got there or not was still vague.

I'm suddenly snatched from my thoughts and look around in embarrassment.

'ANGEL, YOU OLD STUD! HANG ON, RITCHIE!' Scottie's and Jimmy's voices boom from across the road, and then my heart misses a beat, followed by nervous laughter, as Scottie nearly gets himself run over by an old lady driving a bright orange Mini Metro.

I give both my mates a high five, and then as they jump onto me, almost knocking an old couple through the Co-Op window, I utter, 'Sorry, very sorry,' as the flustered pair hurry on their way, Scottie totally oblivious. With a look of surprise at my politeness, he continues his interrogation.

'Come on then! Julie bloody Andrews! Come on, you lucky bastard, did you fuck her?'

I shook my head in disgust. I suddenly felt thirty-five years of age again and cringed at how basic my mates were being. I had an overwhelming desire to be totally honourable and protect the girl's reputation, and felt a glow of maturity within this teenage body. I was ready to answer my friend's impertinent question.

'Did I fuck her? Of course I did!'

More high fives and a confident, arrogant bounce of my

head.

'In fact, guys, *twice*! It was amazing! Fantastic body, and I *mean* faaannntastic body! Oh, gorgeous tits! Yeah! She's cool, I couldn't believe my luck!'

And though I was shrivelling up inside and beating myself up over the word tits and the unforgiveable indiscretion, I couldn't help myself. That's how I must have talked when I was eighteen, exactly the same as my crude mates, and of course then I wouldn't have batted an eyelid.

As Scottie, Jimmy and I make our way towards the market square, I reel off the whole night in all its gory detail, but of course swearing them to total secrecy. As we approach the square, I see Leoni and Sally sitting on the graffiti-covered bench.

The girls suddenly pick themselves up and scream, 'HAPPYYY BIRTHDAYYY' at the top of their voices and then run towards me, both squeezing the life out of me, kissing every part of my suffocated head.

The girls eventually let me go, but each stands with hands on hips and asks one question.

'Julie Andrews! What the hell is all that about?' They shake their heads in disapproval, Leoni stepping slightly forward to announce her own disappointment.

'She's just using you, Ritchie. Come on, if you were that desperate for a shag, well, Sally would have obliged!'

Sally's eyes widen, Jimmy's narrow! But our jaws drop as Sally, cringing and colouring up nicely, screams and jumps all over Leoni, desperate to cover her dear friend's mouth. The girls are grappling for dear life, and then Leoni's arm is up behind her back, with Sally demanding an apology. Scottie decides to diffuse the situation.

'Sally, Ritchie would have happily taken you home and given you a *good* shagging, but our boy is totally in love with Julie Andrews' *big tits!* Couldn't get enough of them!'

I am mortified by my friend's words, my entire soul flicking from eighteen year old to thirty-five year old and back again, all within the space of my cheeks turning crimson. Sally suddenly turns her attention from Leoni, glares at me and then dives at Scottie, who loses his footing and slips onto the hard cobbled ground, and now lies beneath his attacker. Sally impressively manages to pin his arms back with her knees, the poor defenceless, shy and demure girl demanding an immediate apology from her tormentor. I cannot help but laugh out loud at all that's going on, the sheer madness, and how it's met with such disapproving looks from the passers-by. Something then changes the light-hearted moment. Sally continues to pin Scottie to the floor, and Jimmy decides that he'll take the opportunity of getting in on the act. Plus he couldn't stand the fact that the love of his life, Sally, was so physically entwined with anyone but his good self.

Jimmy flings himself towards Sally, shouting as he makes his slick manoeuvre, *'I'll save you, Scottie! I'll get her off you!'*

My eyes watch in awe as Jimmy charges at full pelt and literally throws himself into the thick of the action, and as he does so Sally and Jimmy roll off Scottie, finally falling into the path of the passing public. Jimmy was almost getting the better of Sally, but the love of his life kicks out in a last ditch attempt to regain control, but her foot makes contact with one of the passers-by, knocking a cigar out of his hand. The freshly lit cigar spins almost in slow motion and then falls onto the road, splintering like a miniature firework. As I watch the scene unfold, I see Jimmy's look of horror, and as my gaze takes in the identity of the offended individual, my heart sinks. *Oh my God!* - Stand's ten feet tall in neon lights at the forefront of my mind. I swallow hard, and then again, but this time I am unable.

Jack De'Vil! Or, as he's fondly known, *the devil.* Jack De'Vil looks daggers at Sally, but then a wry, unexpected smile creeps onto his face and his black eyes are now clearly focused on the fair-game male that lies wide-eyed on the hard cobbles. Sally utters a sincere apology and strategically attempts to stand between Jimmy and the vengeful man, whose shoulders seem to have doubled in size within another unsuccessful attempt for me to swallow. But it's all to no avail. Jack De'Vil brushes Sally aside as if she is a rag doll. Jimmy scrambles desperately to get off the floor, but the *devil* is on him, his huge left hand grabbing Jimmy's long hair, while his right arm is pulled back and ready to strike. I blink and shake my head while screaming for Jack to stop. But the devil's fist is clenched and then, falling like a sledgehammer, his white knuckles pound the side of Jimmy's face with such venom that as Jimmy's head bounces off the cobbles, the devil is left holding a handful of Jimmy's dark brown hair.

Though I am no fighter, my instincts and love for my friend carry me full speed towards Jack De'Vil, my arm pulled right back, and while still running forward, the devil gets the full force of my fist, catching the side of his nose. My act of madness unfolds as if in slow motion. I hear a distinct tear of flesh and then a spray of blood arcs into the atmosphere, half landing like a splattering of red wine on Sally's face, with the remainder falling wastefully onto the shiny cobbles, just inches from Jimmy's feet. Everyone in the street seems to stop and stare. Jimmy is the first to move, lifting himself up, coughing out a bloodied tooth. The devil, who had fallen to his knees, shakes his head and spits out more blood onto the cobbles. He then turns, his eyes immediately focusing on my scared face. He springs to his feet, and then the once still crowd starts to stir. A concerned young lady with her small child tries to help Jimmy as a large fat guy barges through the enclosing crowd and grabs the devil, muttering something in his ear and then dragging him reluctantly away from the carnage.

Leoni throws herself forward and hugs me, her eyes looking into mine.

'Well done, Ritchie, well done. You've just belted the *devil!* I'm *so* proud…'

But as Leoni naively gave praise for my actions, I was only too aware that the stinging pain in my hand was the very least of my worries. I felt the full and daunting realisation that this was certainly not going to end here, that from this moment on I would be forever looking over my shoulder, and as sure as night follows day, the repercussions of this would be at the discretion of Jack De'Vil … the devil did not get his apt title for nothing.

Jimmy, Scottie, Leoni, Sally and I quickly leave the fuss behind, numb and just a little shocked at all that has happened.

A small ripple of laughter wells up from the pit of my

stomach and I mutter a barely audible whisper of, 'Bloody hell!' beneath my breath.

Sally keeps repeating, 'We were *so* lucky that the police didn't come!'

We're all quickly away from the high street, and one by one drop into the sports field that leads to the Whippet's Fifth Leg. We are all agreed that the pub beckons, along with the practical element of getting Jimmy cleaned up.

Scottie booms, 'Stuff beard boy, I just need a drink!'

We all laugh a little guiltily, but then Leoni kicks in with, 'Do you mean, oh where has a handful of my *hair* gone, boy?'

We are all now doubled up and almost crying with laughter, but realistically a combination of nervous energy and stoked-up adrenalin finds its release. But amidst the hysteria I am a troubled man with memories of Jack and all that did actually happen on this day originally, and though I am at pains to wipe it from my mind, in the midst of the chattering voices, the scene was rerunning line by line.

CHAPTER FOUR

Dancing With The Devil's Angel

After Death, 1988 – Lilac Sky

Firstly, let me tell you all about Jack De'Vil. The *devil* was twenty years of age, but appeared to be a good few years older. He already had a house and owned a small apartment block backing onto the town car park, at the top end of Willow. Bit by bit, as his finances allowed, the devil was doing the flats up and letting them out. To most people, Jack De'Vil was seen as a good businessman, and rightfully respected, a view that I was happy to share. But it was when I experienced his wrath first-hand that the full extent of this man's world left me physically and mentally scarred.

Originally on my eighteenth birthday, I met the devil a little earlier than today. I had stayed at Julie's – as of course I did last night – but it was just a case of timing and a different attitude this time around. I reflected back to this morning with Julie, and how before, things had ended up being so very different. Proceedings started off in an identical manner: Tina had been let in the house, and, having had a good laugh at my expense, had disappeared highly amused up the stairs with Julie – line for line, just as history had absorbed. The scene today had unfolded without incident – but originally, all unravelled quite differently. The archives would tell us that I hadn't been able to just leave as I had done so this morning. Today I was my own man as far as I could be. I was not afraid of simply walking out of Julie's front door head held high and was prepared to risk her wrath should her aunt spot me. However, originally – a little more timid, confidence that was still finding its feet – Julie had asked me to leave by the back door, and so it didn't cross my mind to defy her. Seventeen years ago, I searched and searched for that back door key, but to no avail. And so I waited, frantic and squirming, for Julie to come back downstairs, and it had seemed like a lifetime. The nerves and sweat were building; I was embarrassed, and convinced that the girls had presumed me gone ages ago. I swallowed hard as I recalled my lesser self hovering between the kitchen and the lounge, repeating my search several times over, desperate to find that *bloody* key. I shook my head as the feeling of weakness returned, the repeated attempts to will myself 'to just sod the consequences, Ritchie, just leave…!' And suddenly, I am back there…

Before Death, 1988 – Blue Sky
My feeble indecision is interrupted by an aggressive thump on the back door. All I can see is a large shadow through the frosted glass. I quickly dart back into the lounge as the visitor rattles the glass with his knuckles, hard and impatient. The girls are suddenly running down the stairs. Tina smiles sarcastically at me, whereas Julie looks concerned. She beckons for me to get down behind the settee. For a second I think she's kidding, but then I'm physically manhandled with a nervous urgency that stops me questioning the bizarre request. From my confined and demeaning space, I am aware of the back door

being opened. I rotate my neck, a douse of claustrophobia threatening to unsettle me. Tina's voice is suddenly making flirty conversation.

'Hi baby, looking good, Jack. Come on in, she's just making herself beautiful for you!'

The visitor is a little less friendly.

'Where the hell was she last night? She said she was coming round to mine. I won't be *fucked* about you know!'

My ear is becoming a little too hot against the radiator, and I just about manage to push the settee an inch or so away from me. I take a deep breath. I drop down as low as I can, and suddenly I can see Julie's legs. Tina is flitting around, in and out of the obscure picture – almost reminiscent of a video camera that's been left filming accidentally. Tina pushes the third party into view, his legs now just inches away from Julie's. Tina lingers for a second and then leaves the scene, but then without warning all breath is forced out of me. Tina, who must have leapt for maximum impact, is on the settee. My cheekbone is now at breaking point against the ribbed metal. Instinctively I want to squeal, but decide to swallow hard instead. I bite the inside of my cheek, almost convinced that this will decrease my head size. I close my eyes and start to count the seconds, praying for the moment that Julie gets her increasingly aggressive visitor to leave. In a desperate attempt to get my burning ear off the radiator, I manage to wriggle – carpet burns being the price I pay – a couple of inches closer to the edge of the settee. I swallow hard again and crane my neck, and finally I have a decent view of Julie. I am aware of the wooden leg of the settee rubbing rhythmically against my arm, a seemingly hyperactive Tina keen to impose as much discomfort on me as she possibly can. My eyes widen as Julie kisses her visitor. I still cannot see his face, but he certainly responds to her peace-making attempt. They both turn slightly, and the man seems to laugh for the first time. He slips his arms around her waist. Another kiss, and then turning into something a little more passionate. Tina quite rightly recommends that they both get a room. But then as the loving couple twist their bodies, my heart stops as the face of the visitor comes into view: Jack De'Vil.

Shit! I think. *Surely Julie's not seeing the devil.* I feel hot and extremely bothered, the full reality of my night of passion and the heavy price I would have to pay should the devil find me here becoming clear. I pray that Julie can get this man out of the house, or at least upstairs. But as I say it, my mind seems to wander and I feel strangely disappointed. I didn't exactly expect Julie and I to get it together, but I did feel very close to her after last night. I also thought it strange that she hadn't mentioned anything about Jack, but then maybe I was being naive. My thoughts are suddenly interrupted as Jack finally comes up for air.

'So, come on, gorgeous, where the hell were you last night? I thought maybe, well, you know, I'd show you what a real man is like, especially after your ex being your only shag!' Jack laughed loudly at his smooth and chivalrous line.

Tina suddenly butted in. 'She had to take me home ... er, well, you know ... bring me back here, as my dad would have killed me, eh, Jules? Pissed as a fart I was! Julie was just being a best mate. Sorry to have messed your night up, Jackie boy!'

Julie pulled away from Jack, her arms dropping to her side.

'Yeah, I should ... I meant to, but I felt really tired and crashed out. Sorry, Jack!'

But then the softening mood changed. Just when I believed that things were getting sorted out, Jack moves quickly away from Julie and I hear a scream. Suddenly, my lungs are able to breathe again as the weight of the settee is off me, and light surrounds my now vulnerable body as it is sent crashing into the fireplace. And there he is, the devil himself, standing over me, his fists clenched, with his right arm pulled back ready to attack. I look up at him, not knowing what to say, just waiting for the pain to start.

But then it's Julie's voice I hear, which seems to hold back the storm for just a second.

'Nooo, Jackkk! It's not what you think ... er ... Tina brought him back last night, or at least *he* helped me, you know, get Tina back here. They'd been together, until she fell over, isn't that right, Teen?'

Tina's voice piped up, 'Yeahhhh, I thought it was my Danny at the door, you know how possessive he can get. Nothing's gone on, but Ritchie *did* stay the night ... just crashed down on the settee.'

I hadn't moved a muscle and must have looked a right idiot crouched down in the corner of the room like a frightened spineless animal. But my breathing starts again as I see a smile cross the devil's face, and then I see his arms drop, his fists slowly unclenching. Jack's eyes turn to Tina.

'Hmmmm, nothing happened, eh? Well, it looks as though I have something on you, don't I, Teen? What's it worth to keep my gob shut, to stop Danny from killing you, and your *gay* little boyfriend here?!'

Tina glares at Julie and then smiles back at Jack.

'I told you, Jackie boy, nothing happened, so that's that! Just get him out of here!'

Jack likes what Tina is saying and grabs me by the head. I'm dragged unceremoniously, protruding limbs making painful contact with all and sundry, static and rigid in Julie's home. The nylon carpet was not flesh friendly, and the sudden drop in temperature of the vinyl kitchen floor covering was no improvement. In transit I had twisted and rotated several times, and now found myself flat on my back with all going quiet for just a moment. My eyes are fixed firmly on my aggressor, who flexes his fingers and stretches his back. But then Jack reaches down, his huge hands opening up and grabbing me around the throat, before pulling me to my feet.

I am weightless and insignificant in the hands of this animal. And then I am aware of his thumbs gouging sharply into my Adam's apple, my eyes almost out on stalks. A sudden burst of energy and, in a blur, my head catches the side of the breakfast bar as Jack seems to fling me around. He is now behind me. All air leaves my body as I hurtle towards the back door. I stumble clumsily, and instead of my arms projecting forward, protecting any imminent impact, the side of my head takes on the role, my already burnt cheek now sliding sharply down the roughly sanded, unpainted door. Everything goes quiet and something deep within me stirs, before a full red mist descends. I scramble to my feet, ready to erupt. I take a deep breath and face my attacker; he is quiet and looks at me blankly. I feel that I have nothing left to lose; my skin burning, my twisted muscles ready for revenge, I step assertively up to Jack and let him have it with both barrels.

'What's with *this* shit? You're a *fucking* wanker, De'Vil!'

My ill thought-out retaliation and the brief strength of mind behind it dampens and retreats as I take in Jack's black, hateful eyes. I feel that it's time to leave, and I can see that Jack agrees. But before I have a chance to offer an apology, or profess that I am only joking and how it's all been fairly good fun really, the devil thrusts himself forward, launching at me with such force that my back slams against the window in the door, the glass shattering on impact. There is a look of horror on his face, which seems to stop him from following up his shove with more violence. I stand for a brief moment, my eyes locked onto Jack's, and then I focus on Julie and Tina's ashen faces behind him. I turn slowly and simply open what's left of the door, praying that I don't have blood gushing from my body. I step outside and walk away, but once out in the alley, all I can hear is the girls screaming at Jack. So, just in case they get him really riled, I start to run, and I keep running until I'm well away from the Oaks estate.

After Death, 1988 – Lilac Sky

Suddenly, my thoughts are interrupted by a big hug. I blink my eyes and there is Jimmy, looking a little surprised at his own show of emotion.

'Leoni has gone in for the drinks, Ritchie. Where's Sally and Scottie?'

Jimmy always got nervous whenever Sally went anywhere without him. I wanted so much to tell him about his future, how he needn't worry about Sally, how one day he would get his wish, how he would marry the love of his life and together they would have beautiful twins! But in the here and now I couldn't help but smile. There he was, his face looking as though he'd been hit by a truck, and yet all he was concerned about was Sally. *Now that's true love*, I thought.

As Jimmy kept an eye on every window and doorway, desperate for the love of his life to return, I looked up at the sky, the lilac tinge as strong as ever. I pondered Rose's words: 'You have angels' tears on your hands...' I swallow hard, but am interrupted by Jimmy and his sudden desire to explain his actions.

'Umm, Ritchie, the hug ... ummm, well, I appreciated your help. I really thought he was going to kill me! I couldn't believe it when you attacked him, although I'm not sure it was *really* the right thing to do. He won't let this lie, you know, but anyway, thanks man!'

I nodded my head and patted Jimmy on the back. It was then that I noticed the girls and Scottie coming out of the pub door, a *knickerbocker glory* with sparklers dancing frantically, little darts of fire falling, as my best friends made their way towards me, singing 'HAPPY BIRTHDAY!' at the top of their awful but enthusiastic voices. But as they got closer, the whole scene starts to go in and out of focus, my head starts to feel sick and heavy, and then I'm gone, leaving the beer garden. I can see my friends and myself continuing the happy scene, but my spirit is being lifted. The pub grounds are now so small, but my eyes are drawn elsewhere and I can see land and the ocean. Then, as darkness surrounds me, I'm aware of a vibration that rattles my bones and I'm weightless, hovering, with major turbulence making my teeth chatter. My eyes are forced firmly shut, but flashes of black and white, day and night, and then, after a few moments of the same intrusive lights, I start to fall. A piercing droning dirge is in my head, but then total silence. My body is falling and I almost imagine that I'm being hurtled back towards earth. I feel everything, but see nothing and then I stop. No sound, and then a pin of volume, faint, a baby decibel, and then a voice, very distant but steadily getting closer. My eyes are open and slowly focus.

I'm standing in a churchyard, people walking away from me towards a line of parked cars at the side of a sleepy lane. My eyes are suddenly drawn towards a grave, the coffin sunk deep into the ground, and for me there is no mistaking exactly where I am. My feet are now standing on the edge of the deep hole, the coffin below, toasted with a few handfuls of dirt and a simple posy of daisies – my mother's favourite flowers; delicate and unassuming, she had always been drawn to their simplicity. I stepped back and looked at the mound of earth around the grave, where there were dozens and dozens of beautiful daisies. Tears filled my eyes. Though I had been given a precious chance to see my mum again, we were briefly reunited just the once and I never got to see her after that – my selfishness once again was taking over. I reflected on my eighteenth birthday and felt regret that I hadn't made my way home, where I knew she would be waiting for me. But just as I had acted originally, seventeen years previously, I had allowed history to repeat itself. I presumed that tomorrow was another day and that I would simply make amends then. But here I am, time and opportunity lost, and unfortunately in a place that brings only heartache to me.

After Death, 1991 – Lilac Sky
The voice of a young lady cuts into my thoughts.

'Hello, Ritchie. I'm so sorry to have bothered you here, and today of all days, but I felt I needed to come and pay my respects.'

I knew the voice and turned my head – it was Julie Andrews. A sense of panic was welling up inside me and I swallow hard, my mind reeling and deeply disturbed at how my life could just skip forward like this. But I strive to appear calm, and so let my eyes rest and study the concerned person stood before me – it was so surreal to see her. I was aware that I wasn't breathing and almost choked in my attempt to force the issue. I ran my fingers through my hair, stunned at the changes that had taken place in the midst of a dozen or so nauseous flashes, but the truth was that Julie and I were three years older. I hear voices from friends and family, all offering to give me a lift to mum's wake. I lift my hand and wave them off, assuring them that I'll find my own way there. As I take in Julie's face, she looks sad – and of course, I've been here before. I know exactly what's going to happen, and every word of the bombshell she's about to drop on me. But as before, I fear a lack of control, and just as I start to utter word for word my unforgivable dialogue from fourteen years ago, I manage to stop myself. The original ranting is going on in my head, but I'm starting to master a little self-control.

Julie looks up at me again, her words squeezed out between deep breaths.

'Ritchie, I had to come here. I've done a very bad thing, and I've come to pay my respects to your mother.'

As Julie talks, she starts to look at the ground, tears filling her eyes and then running steadily down her flushed cheeks. 'I'm here to apologise to your Mum...'

I butt in. 'Julie, please, you don't have to put yourself through this!'

But I am well aware that I *do* have to let her put herself through this. I turn and walk over to the large oak tree before sitting down and pulling my knees up to my chest, watching from a safe distance the poor girl who has come to confess her great secret, angst-ridden, washed-out and frightened. I had purposely moved away from Julie, stepped out of the circle from which I had ranted and responded so badly the first time around. Because originally when Julie had come to me, her news had simply horrified me. Jack was a constant thorn in my side – he hated me and took pleasure in terrorising me. So for Julie to be confessing a truth that would rile him to the point of accepting nothing less than my head on a plate, I felt that my once defensive and obnoxious reaction was the best that she could have hoped for. But this time around, I was ready for her. This moment, and this scene, had scarred me, and I had relived every breath of it a thousand times over as my life progressed. I kept quiet and shook my head, able to pre-empt her every action.

She walked towards me. I had my response ready for the words she was yet to speak, but I knew I had to let it all unfold correctly. I bit my tongue and waited.

'Ritchie, I can't keep living a lie.' She was now just a stride away, her face stretched skyward, but then a deep breath and her eyes were fixed firmly on mine. 'Ritchie, I know my timing's awful, but I needed to come and make some sort of peace, for your Mum, for you... for *me!*'

Julie's tears are making it difficult for me to simply watch and listen. I so want to take her in my arms, to just hold her, to tell her to save her breath as I already know what she's going to say. But as Julie seems to compose herself again, I let her continue.

'When you left that morning, Ritchie, I felt that you weren't interested in me other than because of the night we'd spent together, a one-off, a regretful one-night stand, and I suppose I presumed you believed me not to be good enough for your cool crowd!'

I smiled as I thought about Jimmy and Scottie, their long hair and scruffy appearances – not to mention mine – and that we should be thought of as cool! Julie leant against a huge stone tomb and continued.

'I guess, well, you would see me around Willow with Jack, and you probably believed that I had simply two-timed him that night with you, all adding up to you thinking of me as a slag.'

Julie stared at her feet as though waiting for a response, but my silence goaded her on.

'But the truth, Ritchie, and you have to believe me, is that I wasn't really seeing Jack prior to that night with you. I'd just come out of a painful break-up with my ex, and I suppose Jack and I had become close, but we certainly weren't a couple! But that night with you, well, it was sweet!'

Julie looks at me for a split second but then turns away, her face skyward again.

'Ritchie, I felt we ... sort of connected. You showed me how close and loving someone can be and I liked it. Jack, well, he's sweet to me, but, well, he's not ... well he's not you, Ritchie.'

I was transfixed, but Julie's eyes were unable to stay with me for more than the briefest of glances. The tears were now dripping off her chin, and I so desperately wanted to stand up and push her into getting to the point. But this moment needed to be orchestrated by her, so I stayed rooted, undoubtedly appearing cold and uncaring. But she turned away and stood with her back to me, and then came the words that would change my life forever.

'Ritchie, my ... my daughter, my daughter Lillie, she's not Jack's...'

I stop breathing, desperate to hear the fateful words.

'Lillie, she's yours, Ritchie...'

Suddenly I feel surprisingly numb. I knew what she was going to say, and yet it hadn't made it any easier. A tear creeps from my eye and glides down my ashen cheek. Julie turns towards me and then finally lifts her head up, her eyes searching and trying desperately to read me. We simply look at each other, not a word uttered, not a breath pushed out or taken in. The church clock chimes and a rustle of leaves lift and spiral around us, and then all is calm and silent. I want to say so much, but the most I can offer is an exaggerated and painful swallow. Then I physically shake my head and words are found.

'Julie, she's beautiful, and I can't believe that ... well, that she's mine!'

Julie, getting my response all wrong, starts to act defensively.

'I knew you wouldn't believe me, but why the hell would I lie?'

I push both my hands forward.

'Nooo, Julie, I believe you, it's just that...'

And it's as though a fear wells within me and suffocates any confidence that I thought I had just a moment ago.

'Julie, I mean, I mean, well ... *shit!* I can't offer you anything, I mean, *for God's sake!* It's you, Jack and ... Lillie! How the hell am I supposed to fit into all that?'

Julie appears suddenly vacant, as though somewhere else. She moves slightly to the left and puts her finger up at me, ready with a verbal response, but then seems to almost turn full circle, as if she's about to walk away. But then finds the strength to see this through.

'Nice words Ritchie, *really* compassionate! But Lillie, she has a right to know who her real father is...It's as if you're scared of Jack, and I don't fully understand why. But I can't deny her *her real father!* I know you'll need time to let all this sink in, but *please,* when you're ready, maybe ... maybe you'll come and see us?'

I hadn't been aware that my head had dropped, but I was focusing firmly on the thick dust on my black brogues. I lift my head up, the lilac tinge almost forcing my eyes closed. But as I am able to see a little more, I'm aware of Julie walking away from me. A sense of panic forces me to my feet and I call after her.

'*Julie!*'

She stops and turns. I lift up my hand and wave. She smiles and nods, our eyes locked for just a second or two. She then walks towards a middle-aged lady sitting and waiting patiently in a green Ford Granada. As the car pulls away, I shake my head.

Oh well, Ritchie boy... that was a little better than last time!

I wrap my arms around my body and ponder all that had just happened. I'm suddenly aware of two men walking towards me, each holding a well-used spade. The older man carries his over his shoulder, while the younger guy swings his back and forth, nonchalantly chopping off the heads of the daisies as he walks. I feel anger at his lack of respect for the flower that gave my mum so much pleasure. As he gets closer to the grave, he puts his spade down and removes his T-shirt. The older guy acknowledges me, then gently and carefully removes the posies of daisies from the mound of earth that surrounds my mum's grave. I feel humbled as I think of my mum down in the ground. As the guys finally start to drop the soil into the grave, the *thud* as it lands on the coffin lid chills me. I look down at my watch – 3:21. I know I must be on my way, but my feet don't want to move. I just watch as the men shovel more and more soil into the grave, the *thud* gradually losing volume as more earth covers the coffin. I decide that I must be going, that I must make my way to my mum's wake, but then the most incredible thing happens. A small white flower van pulls up at the side of the sleepy lane.

'Oh my God...'

A bead of sweat appears on my brow. As the driver's door opens, the most beautiful girl steps out, her long golden hair tied back with a simple satin pale-blue ribbon. The girl hasn't spotted me yet, but carries on opening up the van, pulling out a wicker basket. I know I should run and hide, but I tell myself that it's too late. The girl is walking towards me, taking in the peace and tranquillity of the surroundings, until finally her eyes meet mine – hypnotic sparkling pools of blue that I could drown in. Then the softest, sweetest voice.

'Hello...' she says, and as she goes to pass me, I smile. Though I know that I should leave it at that, I instinctively cannot help myself.

'Hello, Yasmin…'

She stops and smiles back at me.

'Umm, Ritchie Angel, isn't it … from school?'

She looks briefly into my eyes and then a small blush colours her cheeks, making her lose her nerve and look down at her feet. I want to say so much, but all I can hear are Rose's words of warning. Neither of us knows what to say, but as I stand, I am just so grateful to see her, to be able to breathe her in, absorbing her soul completely. Yasmin's eyes meet mine again. She looks a little puzzled and slightly embarrassed at our awkward silence, and so mutters a polite goodbye. She turns to continue on her way. I am aware that I have the broadest of grins spread across my face, and I hear myself call after her.

'Umm, why are you here?'

Yasmin turns, her inquisitive look followed by a warm, confident smile.

'Oh, my Mum's friend had left instructions to pick a couple of bouquets up and take them to the local hospital. I just help out now and again.'

As she stoops down, gathering up the flowers and placing them carefully into her basket, a shiver runs up my spine. My wife's delicate fingers pick up the daisies from the side of my mum's grave. I realise that because I stormed off originally, not wanting to hear Julie's words, I'd missed Yasmin by minutes! I'd no idea that she – at my mum's request – would be the one removing her flowers. Our first words would have been spoken here, at my mum's graveside. And though I'd adored Yasmin from afar at school, we'd simply never spoken.

Suddenly, she is walking towards me, her basket now brimming with fresh flowers. A thousand thoughts are running through my mind, and then as I go to say something witty and clever, Rose appears, standing directly in front of me. Though I'm standing, trying to look at Yasmin, I turn, as though instructed to do so, and see myself seventy feet or so away, making my way down the lane. Then I see a purple Ford Escort pull up and I laugh out loud as I realise it's Scottie.

Oh my God! Scottie and his first machine, his absolute pride and joy, the purple beast!

But as I watch, I see myself climbing into the passenger seat and closing the door firmly behind me. I shake my head in absolute awe at all that I am seeing. Scottie turns the car around, gravel and dust forced into the air, and drives away. But I'm *still* here, my feet stuck firmly on the sacred ground of the graveyard. I'm suddenly aware of gentle footsteps behind me. I want *so* desperately to move, to turn around, but then suddenly I feel the wind knocked out of me, as though my whole body had turned to nothing, and then the back of Yasmin's head, her blonde hair tickling my face as she simply passes through me. Instantly, as though she has taken my soul with her, I fade away. Darkness and then a warmth, building steadily with an increasing light, and then I'm in Scottie's car, looking back towards the church, Yasmin placing the flower basket into the back of the little white van.

'Sorry, Ritchie, she was a nice woman your mum. It seems very strange to think that I'll never see her again.' Scottie spoke and rested his hand on my arm, squeezing it firmly.

I did feel sad, and it did feel as though I was going through it for the first time. As we made the short journey to my mum's house, my mind was full of so many questions. I looked at Scottie, his mouth moving, words I'm sure coming out, but I couldn't hear a thing. I just turned my head and looked out of the window. The memory of Julie's tear-stained face stared back at me. But there was something in her eyes as we waved goodbye that convinced me I had left us both a lifeline, a bridge of hope – though I was in no doubt that I had much work to do. But in comparison to how vile I had been originally, simply despising all that she had told me, rejecting with full force the intrusion of an unwanted, unplanned child – I screwed up my face at the haunting memory of it. I swallowed hard as I realised my cowardly concern had been only for myself. It had culminated in utter contempt for my foolish, careless night with Julie, and the brutal fact that I had given Jack De'Vil the ammunition to make my life a living hell.

It had scared me to death, and so out of fear I took on the form of cold and uncaring – I was a despicable weak excuse of a man. But today, though taken by surprise initially – finding myself without warning at the funeral of my mum – I had managed to tread with caution, to embed subtle but hopeful steps in rectifying my relationship with Julie and our child. Today, I was only too aware how, should I have repeated the script from fourteen years ago, those words would have so fatally affected all of our lives. I shuddered at the full horror of all that had followed, my breathing suddenly a little quicker.

I sat back in my seat, my face now fixed firmly on the road ahead. I knew that I needed answers, and there was only one person who could help me. A well of panic widened my eyes; there was the very real chance that I may be in trouble. I took long, deep breaths and then pondered my state of mind. Here I was, another few years on, emotional and tired. And as my mild hysteria took a firm hold, my mind conjured up my actions with Yasmin today. How was Rose going to view that? I tried desperately to see the scene through Rose's eyes, but would I be punished? Had I overstepped the mark?

Scottie turned into my mum's road and finally I took in a word from my good friend.

'So, Ritchie, that's what you need. So if you're up to it, you know, when all the guests have gone, we'll hit the town!'

The cul-de-sac was full of cars – there had been a good turnout. Scottie being Scottie drove right onto my mum's front lawn, pulling up sharply.

'Come on, lad, let's see the old gal off in style!'

He was beaming at me, and ran round to my side of the car and opened my door while bowing his head.

'This way, sir!'

I nodded and thanked my courteous friend, as I stepped out of the car and took a deep bolstering breath. It all felt so surreal. No breeze, just a calm, anaesthetising backdrop of softness – there was no other way to describe it but as an overall numbness. I smiled as I took in the pitying faces, everyone in return shaking their heads from side to side. As I made my way around the room, quiet words would be spoken, firm handshakes and strong passionate hugs offered, whilst others, unable to speak, would just pat my back as they passed through to the kitchen, where a small spread of food and liquid refreshments were laid out.

A voice broke my conversation with mum's friend Sylvie, and as I looked, there he was. In the midst of this sombre crowd, the tanned face, the unruly hair that looked better suited to an eighteen-year-old surfer – but there he *bloody* was.

'Hello, son!'

My father's words bounced off me and seemed to lie unwanted on the lounge carpet. His steely blue eyes fixed on me, looking for a reaction, but I could offer nothing. My father stepped forward, his lips pursed tight, his hand outstretched. This time fourteen years ago I had refused to shake his hand; in fact, I was a disgrace. I had told him to go – he hadn't been in touch for years, so why had he bothered to turn up now? I stamped my feet, threw a tantrum and let off lots of steam. And of course I should have felt better for it, but I hadn't. All I'd succeeded in doing was making everyone else feel uncomfortable, and of course overshadowing what was supposed to be a dignified humane occasion.

So, having lived this scene once before, what was I going to do this time? I decided I would shake his hand, but as I tried to push my hand forward there was an awkward lack of response...As I finally, *gratefully* saw my hand stretch out in front of me, I heard a small sigh, almost in unison from us both, and I was convinced of a small ripple from the people around us. As I gripped my father's hand, there was no mistaking that this was right. I made an undecipherable gesture with my head, which was understood instinctively by my own flesh and blood. As we both stepped out into the garden, my father slid the patio door shut – polite stifling chat now replaced with the freshness of the outdoors.

'I'm so sorry, Ritchie, it must have been awful for you. I know she loved you, well, you know, *loves you* very much. She was *very* proud of you, son!'

I looked out across the garden, aware that his words had run dry. I waited for a few moments, and though I knew I should say something, it was my mind doing the talking.

So my father was proclaiming how proud my mum was of me, but the truth was that he hadn't spoken to her in years, so wasn't all this a little hollow, all a little late? I reflected on how originally I had never allowed him back into my life – the wedding, *Evie,* I simply didn't want to know. Should our paths ever cross we would chat, make the right noises about getting together in the future, but once we'd walked away from each other I'd simply want to forget him. I was suddenly aware of a hand on my shoulder and a kiss placed softly on the side of my mouth. Leoni was pensive while passing my father and me a cold beer, before leaving the otherwise deserted garden and returning into the house. I pondered how I was going to start my side of the conversation. Though I had always referred to my father as *my father* in my mind and perhaps to others, I had never done so in the flesh, verbally. It was a title that needed to be deserved, and so I found it impossible to say it. But I was ready to talk.

'Ray, why are you here? Four years ago, four *bloody* years ago you came and showed your face for a day, I hadn't seen you since I was *two* years of age. You built your bridge, satisfied your own curiosity and then *buggered* off again!'

I peeled back the ring-pull on my ice-cold beer can, the hyperactive froth shooting forward. I took a thirst-quenching gulp, tipping my head back, the burning sensation in my throat finally bringing me back up for air. I noticed my father passing his can from one hand to the other, back and forth. I ran my hand across my mouth, taking in the farmer in his rusty tractor, steady diesel chug, in the distance, barely audible as he made his way across the partly ploughed field.

'Ray...I don't know you. What do you want from me?'

My father didn't say a word, and just kept passing his can back and forth. I noticed, having now ploughed from left to right, the farmer was now at the end of his field, turning steadily by the hedgerow, ready to plough from right to left.

'You have to see things from my point of view, son. I know I should have been there for you, I *know* I've been selfish, but I now want to really get to know you, be a *proper* dad!'

I watched the tractor as the seagulls dived into the freshly churned earth, swooping and squabbling amongst themselves. The cogs jolted and clicked within my brain and I was then questioning the term *proper* dad and all that Ray stood for within my short history. I recalled having a grumpy moment whilst at infant school and the teacher saying, 'What a little *ray* of sunshine you are Ritchie Angel...' And as I sat in my class, I just repeated in my mind, *little ray of sunshine, little ray of sunshine...son of Ray!* And from that moment forward the innocent term became unfairly abhorrent to me. Full *bright* sunshine would be just fine. But little *ray* of sunshine would simply darken my mood, an image of a starved *sun*, deprived of light, a mere shadow of all that *full-on* dazzling sunshine would stand for. I let out a chuckle at my maudlin self -pity and finally heard the plea from behind me.

'Please, Ritchie, I ... I really want to be your dad!'

I stood up and stepped a metre or so forward, my toes protruding over the edge of the patio slabs. I rocked several times, finely balanced, and then stepped back and turned to face my father. Our eyes met, his chin and mouth outstretched in anticipation of what I was about to say.

'Ray, what you ask of me, *well* ... it's an impossible request.'

He let out a small breath, his head easing back now, resting into his slightly despondent shoulders.

'You are Ray, not my dad... *not* the man I have a father and son bond with. I should love and respect you... but this is where the problem starts and finishes. I *sort* of love you, but it's an unusual ... no, more of a unique feeling that I have for you. I resent incredibly your lack of interest, but the fact that you inspire any kind of emotion in me, *well,* maybe it's a form of unrequited love. As though, well... what should have been a straightforward union, though full of twists and turns, highs and lows, you and I learning off each other over the nurturing years ... well, *well* shit, Ray, we never even got off the starting block. I heard the pistol, I ... I made my way steadily down the track, but, well, where the *fuck* were you? Where for the *love of God* did you go?'

I turned back towards the field, my frustration forcing me to launch my half-empty beer can into the unploughed section of the meadow. I slumped wearily onto the edge of the patio. I could hear weak words from behind me, and yet there was nothing that seemed to change how I felt about my father. Suddenly, my shoulders lifted. This man had lost me many years ago, so this wasn't about me any more. The conclusion gave me sufficient strength to stand.

'Umm, look, Ray, take care. I'm here should you need to talk again, but you need to know I'm just, *well,* perhaps it's not really the right time, with Mum, well, you know. Once you're back in Ibiza, maybe we'll take it slow, step at a time, eh?' I wrapped my arms around him as false emotion oozed out of me. 'Take care...*Dad.'*

As I made my way back through the lounge, I shook the outstretched hands, reciprocated the hugs and kind words, and called desperately for my friends to follow me.

'Ritchie, slow down... *Ritchie,* where on earth are we going?'

Scottie's hands were now on my shoulders, his unanswered question ringing in my ears. As I finally stepped out into the cool, fresh, *now* unstifling daylight, I took a huge deep breath and finally answered my friend.

CHAPTER FIVE

Let's Rewrite History

After Death, 1991 – Lilac Sky

'Anywhere! Please get me out of here! Let's just keep walking!'

As we all made our way out of the cul-de-sac, I turned my head. Several of my relatives were standing in the window, looking surprised by my desertion. But I had suddenly felt so stifled that I simply had to get away. As we walked, I started to relax a little. With Sally threading her arm through mine, I felt loved. I smiled to myself. I could hear Scottie and Jimmy being lectured by Leoni.

'No, guys, I saw you both down at least four cans of lager back at Ritchie's Mum's. We're all better off leaving the car there.'

The boys went quiet. As we walked, my mind wandered. It was incredible just how little we really had to worry about –

the pub, partying and girls – and sometimes I feel that as youngsters we never appreciate the freedom we have. We seem to be in such a quandary about what we're supposed to be doing with our lives that we often forget to enjoy the moment. I know I did. I just had my dream, my big clever business plan, and went for it with a vengeance.

Leoni had now taken my other arm, and as the girls talked, dragging me along, I allowed myself to ponder. I reflected on the meeting with my father, and I didn't feel bad about what I'd said. Two years of age, and a total lack of interest even up to that point, but then to just walk away, with no love, no guidance, nothing. Originally at my mum's funeral I had severed all hope, totally trampled all over him, but this time I felt I had acted a little more maturely, leaving him with a belief that progress had been made. I lifted my head, taking in the early evening lilac sky, two medium-size clouds drifting into the sunset, with a small pure white cloud snapping at their heels. But all I saw were the faces of Yasmin and me, Evie in our wake. I dropped my head, searching desperately for something that would help me forget the true cost of this adventure. I literally counted through all the positives of what was happening to me and focused on the conclusion: my four best friends, manic, with each one treading excitedly forward, ready for what life had to throw at them. I knew that I had to be like them. I sighed and let out a small chuckle at the subtle differences in my friends' appearances. I recalled my full horror when I first arrived back at Willow Park. Going back twenty years in one fell swoop, the word surreal didn't even begin to cover it. And just as I was about to accept the situation, then to be catapulted three years forward. I swallowed hard, but my mind was still reeling. Time was moving on here… But God help me, was this real life, and if so, what about the day-to-day life back home for Yasmin and Evie?

I closed my eyes to the detriment of driving myself insane. I almost felt unable to walk on, broken and drained. But as I scratched around for a positive, the thought of being reunited seemed to lift me up. I also added a dose of the original antidote, diluting my negativity and focusing fully on the thickness of Jimmy's manly beard, shaking my head in patronising admiration at such a style statement. Giggles were rising helpfully from the pit of my stomach, and I knew this was where I needed to root myself. To stay within the bubble of where I would be mentally at this age and not dare to step outside of it.

As my friends chatted, I told myself that I was at ease with them now. When I had first gone back in time to fifteen years of age, I had felt alien and uncomfortable. But as the girls cuddled me, their pretty faces smiling up at me, I was starting to settle, though still in total awe at how incredibly young they looked. I thought about our wonderful summer's afternoon at the Water's Edge, each of us thirty-five years of age. Leoni still struggling to meet the right person, her plans to make a new life in America, still needing that final push of courage. And as for Sally and Jimmy, well we know how that finally ended. I thought about our last moments together, and Jimmy's desperation as his financial troubles looked set to overwhelm him. I wondered whether Sally had learnt just how close they came to losing all they had worked for. I hoped that Jimmy had put it right and was now free to carry on with his otherwise blessed life. I prayed that my gift to my best friend was sufficient – it was given with love, and when love's involved, all things are possible.

Scottie suddenly burst through the middle of us.
'Justin's place! He's got an all-day, all-night party going on! God, how could we all have forgotten that?'
The girls stared at Scottie, their eyes wide and frowning. Leoni finally added words to the black looks while nudging him painfully in the ribs.
'Ritchie's Mum, you know, her funeral? That's why we'd passed on the party!'
I interrupted. 'No, it's a great idea, I'm totally up for it!'
And so we made our way to Justin's party. I had missed it all those years ago, and the reports had been good, a night I certainly shouldn't have missed.
Oh well, I thought, *let's go and let our hair down!*

As we made our way across the main green, just on the edge of Willow, Justin's house was lit up like a beacon. The music was blaring and streams of people were heading towards the ensured madness. I could see a large guy coming out of his sandstone mansion next door to Justin's, walking hastily down his gravel driveway, and it wasn't long before an animated discussion between him and Justin resulted in a high-five, the guy being handed a bottle and then being ushered into the party with a girl on each arm. As we got closer, there were certain groups being turned away due to a selection process. I couldn't believe the number of cars crammed along the grass verge. And then suddenly, I noticed a bright yellow Porsche 944 with the registration plate JD 666.

Scottie ran a few feet ahead of us, proceeding to wipe some imaginary dust from the bonnet, before stepping back and announcing, 'De'Vil, you flash bastard!!'

My feet stopped, my heartbeat quickened and my words shot out.

'Jack De'Vil ... *what?* This is his car? *He's here?'*

Scottie looked at me and then offered mockingly, 'Yes, short memory, Ritchie boy.'

The car bore significance with my past, but my head was all over the place. Scottie continued, his total amazement at my strange reaction to the car now seemed to concern him rather more than his initial amusement.

'I would try and forget it too. If *this* had been my car and I had *sold* it to Jack De'Vil...'

My heart sank. Sally grabbed my arm and said softly, 'Take no notice, Ritchie. Think of the money you'll make having bought the Old School. The car's only metal, depreciating all the time!'

They were all looking at me now, and they did appear genuinely concerned. My eyes were suddenly wide and a false burst of laughter seemed to appease.

'HA! I'm only teasing you, I was just being ironic, you know, the fact that I would never sell a car of mine to an enemy!'

But then Jimmy butted in, a wry smile on his face.

'Enemies, you and the *devil?* More like *bum buddies* you

two!'

I didn't dare react or say another word, my eyes still undoubtedly wide, but the laughter – fake or otherwise – had long left me. And so I just nodded, grimaced, coughed and then suggested we should try to see if we could get through Justin's heavy mob manning the door. But as I floated forward, my mind was reeling: *best* friends, Jack De'Vil and I?

Scottie shrieked, 'YES!' as we were ushered forward and the full force of the music stamped all over my senses.

Justin greeted us all with open arms, passing a bottle of vodka to Sally and dropping four ice-cold cans into my arms.

'Listen, guys, plenty more where that came from. In the kitchen, you can't miss it. Have fun!!'

A blend of exhaustion and a decibel level that made your toes curl left me in no doubt that the party was going to live up to its legendary status. But I was filled with unease, and though I was going through the motions, I was desperate to get some answers to what the hell was going on. After all, the last time Jack and I had met I'd nearly ripped his nose off. And though of course three years or so had passed by, I couldn't help but look over my shoulder. I wanted desperately to ask Jimmy to bring me up to speed, fill in the blanks, but how on earth was I going to be able to do that without him thinking I was going totally insane? So, there was only one person who could help me – Rose.

Despite trying to fade into the background and slip away quietly, Leoni and Sally were particularly clingy with me, and though I would usually love the attention, and the fact that they were hanging on my every word, this wasn't the time, and it hadn't gone unnoticed by Jimmy. He wasn't being funny with me, but he did seem to be watching Sally and I like a hawk. I caught my sombre reflection in the large lounge mirror, my black suit and grey tie killing the party spirit. I looked quickly for backup, feeling a little more comfortable with the fact that my friends were all similarly dressed – Scottie's yellow tie the only exception. The girls were also looking very formal: Leoni in a short black skirt and jacket, with just the odd flash of black lace across her cleavage; and Sally in a very similar skirt and jacket, but having chosen to add a dark-blue silk blouse.

'Ritchie...You old bastard!'

And suddenly I'm confronted by the *devil,* his arms outstretched. I want to run, but feeling that it would perhaps be better to simply return the gesture, a tight bear hug ensues. And though I get through the moment without detection, my mind is blown – what on earth is going on? I shake my head harshly, as if clearing a space in my mind for a shard of clarity, for a glimmer of sense or logic, perhaps dislodging a whiff of an answer. In desperation I feel that maybe alcohol is the answer. I quickly grab the vodka bottle off Sally, who's already had a good few swigs. I then lift my head and let the bitter liquid take all the feeling out of my mouth, and within seconds my insides too. As my friends start to mingle a little, I feel the increased need for privacy. I just pray that Rose can see that I need her.

I pull my arms tightly into my sides and then ease backwards out of the lounge, almost convinced that my pose will reduce my presence. I accept that I need to be alone for Rose to come to me, so I climb the wide, elegant staircase, my heavy feet sinking into the thick carpet. I feel increasingly drained and then realise that I must have been awake for at least a couple of days. I screw my face up, as I recall my last sleep being with Julie when I was *eighteen*...I swallow hard, shaking my head at the recognition that I was now twenty-one! 'Well, that would certainly justify a modicum of weariness Ritchie boy...' sarcastically pushed out from under my breath. As I step onto the landing, I take in the junior school photograph of Justin and his sister, about eight years of age. And I think back with heady recollection to all the things that have happened since that fateful reintroduction to my old school friend Rose.

I put the vodka bottle to my lips again, letting the alcohol sink fast into my body. I come up for air, but I relish the glaze that the firewater gives my sorry state of mind, and so knock back as much as my weary body can take. Without warning I let out a painful cough, a splattering of saliva and rejected vodka clearly visible across Justin's school photograph. I clumsily run my suit sleeve across the glass, smearing from left to right. I chuckle to myself, remembering that I have somewhere I need to be, though the option of a drunken comatose sleep is increasing in appeal. I clumsily fashion my way along the landing, convinced that I need to get as far away from the mad people as possible. I notice a small door at the end of the corridor rippling, almost mirage like, and head erratically towards it. As my heavy feet and nose bump into the little doorway, I chuckle again and then finally manage to grip limply onto the brass handle. The door is reluctant to open and so I shove aggressively against it, this time granted access. I take in the small windy staircase, but suddenly, I feel a hand on my bottom, a gentle squeeze and a kiss to the back of my neck, and the tenderness brings to mind just one special lady. It would happen often, and despite my drunken haze, it could only be one person – Yasmin.

As I turned my head, soft lips quickly found mine, a gentle but increasingly urgent kiss that made my head spin even more than the powerful effects of the vodka. My eyes are closed tight as we seem to edge along the wall, my body being caressed. I return the compliment, my hands slipping the restrictive material from my lady's shoulders. I am then left with just a layer of silk covering large, firm breasts, and they feel so good. I am operating in slow motion, my head now spinning madly. But then I'm aware of being pushed into a room and then falling, but landing suitably onto a large soft bed. The kisses become increasingly passionate and I am totally consumed. I'm aware that she has my trousers undone, and then as I blindly feel her soft skin, I run my fingers up her cool thighs. My hands are pushed away from her legs, but then a brush of satin glides across the tips of my fingers. I presume a pair of panties being removed. More fumbling with my trousers, and then I feel the cool air waft across me, suddenly replaced by moist heavenly warmth, a most wonderful sensation as Yasmin pushes herself down onto me. I am now physically intoxicated and feel as though I could die happy here and now. Physical and chemical intoxication, the alcohol and the wondrous sensation building through my loins. My hands are then lifted and guided onto her cool naked breasts, but my arms soon drop down to my side as my drunken state gets the better of me. I'm totally lost in this lady's passion, and then just as her entire body tenses, her moans echoing around wherever we are, my whole body goes taut. Then, releasing all that I have, Yasmin falls onto my chest, her breasts pushed firmly against me, and then as she kisses me softly on my nose and then my lips, I manage to flicker open one eye, desperate to see my beautiful wife. But I'm mortified, as there, looking more radiant than I have ever seen her, eyes closed and a contented look on her flushed face…is Sally.

Sally's eyes eased open and sparkled at me like never before. She kissed me again, my subdued reaction doing nothing to deter my drunken friend, but suddenly I was totally sober. I started to mumble something to Sally, making excuses about why we should leave quickly, make sure that no one finds us here. Sally stumbled around, trying to pull her bra and blouse back on before falling face first onto the crumpled bed. My dear friend burst into a normally infectious bout of giggles, but my sheer horror at what had just happened here saw me urging her on with her mission, resulting in me physically pulling her to her feet, helping her to straighten her clothes. Sally stood totally still, watching intently as the flat of my hand ironed out the creases in her skirt.

'Where's my jacket, Ritchie?' she asked, and then burst into more drunken laughter. 'Oh God, I left it outside in the corridor!'

Sally stumbled clumsily out onto the landing, the music almost doubling in volume as the door was flung open and slammed into the bedroom wall. Sally grabbed her suit jacket and then looked back at me, her finger placed on her lips. I wanted to smile, but my heart was beating painfully in my ears. Sally stepped back into the room and stood before me. Then she pressed against me, her lips looking for mine. I grabbed her shoulders and shook her.

'Sally, please listen to me. I think you're wonderful, but, well, this is a mistake, *a huge mistake.* We're friends, *bloody great friends!'*

Sally smiled, her eyes dancing, and then came her mischievous reply.

'I'd say so, *bloody, bloody great friends!'*

I gripped her arms tighter, deterring her from her next embrace. I needed desperately to get the message across.

126

'Sally, you must listen to me. No one must find out about this! Promise me, because this was wrong, this, *this* was not meant to happen! I'm Jimmy's closest friend, and as you know – and if you don't then you must go around with your eyes shut – Jimmy worships you, you are all he talks about!'

Sally pulls away from me, her face suggesting that she may be sobering up suddenly, and raises her hand up to her head.

'Ummm, Ritchie, you're joking, right? I mean, he's never said anything to me. Jimmy's just the same around me as he's always been.'

I step forward, grabbing Sally's hands.

'Oh my God, exactly, Sally, because he's *always* worshipped you. I can't believe you never knew!'

Sally pulled her hands out of mine and sat down on the edge of the bed, seeming to have sobered up totally.

'What about all this then, Ritchie? With what's just happened between you and me? You didn't seem very concerned about Jimmy's feelings just now.'

Sally's words cut right through me, but I deserved them.

'I know, Sally. *Oh shit,* but you took me by surprise. I ... I've not eaten for a couple of days and the vodka just got me straight away, and I thought you were someone else, well, there are mitigating circumstances that are messing with my head, but, well ... what I mean is, you felt great! But... I'm *so* sorry, Sally, this *is* my fault, but please, just agree with me, we must *not* mention this again!'

Sally stood up, unable to look me in the eye.

'Please, Sally, let's not spoil what's just gone on between us. You're very special to me, and if it wasn't for Jimmy, well, who knows what could happen between us?'

Sally's lips creased and she gave a soft chuckle under her breath, her eyes suddenly looking right at me.

'I hate you, Ritchie Angel! Oh God, I've made such a fool of myself. I guess I knew you didn't see me as girlfriend material. *Bloody hell,* Ritchie!'

Sally just stared at me, her shoulders slumped and dejected. But then she stepped forward and hugged me, placing a small kiss on my cheek.

'Don't worry, Ritchie, I'll get over it. You weren't as good as I thought you'd be!'

My shoulders slumped and it was my turn to feel mildly dejected and deflated. But then we both started to laugh and held onto each other. As we left the room, I prayed that Jimmy would never find out what had just gone on between his future wife and me. The truth was, this would change our friendship forever, and I loved him too much for that to happen. As we were about to make our way downstairs, I made some excuse to Sally that I needed the toilet, and that I was so shattered that I might even find a quiet corner and catch half an hour's sleep.

'You lightweight, Angel,' she mocked, squeezing my arm before making her way down the grand staircase.

I made my way quickly back out onto the landing, almost breaking into a run towards the small door I'd found earlier before being so rudely sidetracked. I couldn't help but question how on earth it had happened. Though Sally was gorgeous, she was undoubtedly out of bounds. And as wonderful and as quick as the sex had been, I was convinced that nothing good could come of it. I thought about Yasmin and how I had believed, really felt as though it was her, but of course I should have known better. The door was reluctant to shift as I pushed firmly against it, but such was my keenness to gain a little privacy, I almost barged it off its hinges, but I was through and closed it quietly behind me. I made my way up the increasingly windy stairs, I prayed that Rose would come to me. I had so many questions and needed *so* many answers.

As I reached the top of the stairs, I could see a full moon clearly through large glass lantern skylights. I looked around what appeared to be some sort of attic, where box after box was piled on top of another, scribbled writing on each one: 'Christmas Decorations', 'School Reports', 'Winter Clothes', 'Summer Clothes', 'Photos' – row upon row of priceless family belongings. There was an old rocking horse with a large scruffy teddy sitting on it further down the attic, close to a large expanse of brickwork that I presumed to be one of the many chimney stacks. A shiver rippled across my shoulder blades, but then a smile crept across my face at the welcome memory. I couldn't believe the amount of stuff up here in Justin's family home – a real treasure trove. It all served to remind me of Evie and how she loved to go into our attic, looking through the old photographs, trying to talk me into taking back downstairs some of the old toys that had seen better days. I wasn't really a hoarder, but certain things, well, they held far too many precious memories to just be thrown away.

I made my way further into the attic, my eyes becoming increasingly accustomed to the darkness. I noticed a doorway that I presumed would take me out onto the roof. As I stepped before it, I slid a top bolt across and turned the handle, pushing gently, but it didn't budge. With a little more force, I pressed my shoulder fully into it, but I was thwarted once again. A glimmer of red mist descended around me as I slammed against the door with what would have been perceived as a sledgehammer to crack a walnut, but there appeared to be a reluctance for this seemingly inoffensive door to break its bond with the frame. I stood back and kicked with an almighty thump. The door squealed out and then opened. A huge smile spread across my face as I nodded and stepped through with my head held high. Suddenly, my eyes were wide and my brain turned to mush as the cold air hit me, the effects of the vodka still apparent. The music was loud, but much clearer than the throbbing bass that was booming through the house, with a backdrop of laughter, shrieking and shouting.

My mind kept drifting back to Sally and all that had just happened. I shook my head, totally bewildered and almost questioning whether I had actually dreamt that prudish Sally had just seduced me. But as I thought about Jimmy, I tried to look at the positive – at least he was going to be in very capable hands. Having now been so *wrongly* intimate with her, I was left in no doubt that he was going to be a very lucky man indeed. My mind was reeling with thoughts of Jimmy interspersed with thoughts of Jack: *friends, the devil and I?* And the Porsche that I had *supposedly* sold him. I had never had a Porsche, not until my early thirties, certainly not at the age of twenty-one, and to have purchased the Old School … how on earth had I managed that? I reflected on how I had wanted the school when seeing that it was up for sale at auction, and my big wild foolhardy plan to get it. After all, I had first-hand knowledge working at Skirdle's. But I still bore the scars of how I blew it big time first time around. So why so different now?

'I'll tell you why, Ritchie…'

I physically jumped out of my skin. I swallowed hard and turned around. There she was, my little friend Rose, sitting on the edge of the parapet wall which ran all around the roof of the house. I couldn't take my eyes off her – little bare feet swinging, her hair blowing gently in the evening breeze. I took a step forward, but my nerves were tingling as though my entire body was wrapped in stinging nettles. I turned my head slightly at an angle, focusing on her mouth and then at the stillness of her chest, questioning just how she coped with her 'disability' and so on.

'Ritchie, *disability?* You mean *dead,* right? You mustn't think of me as dead. Look at me; do I look dead? You've held my hand; do I *feel* dead?'

I smiled nervously and felt just a little embarrassed, firstly because she was so *bloody* clever and also because I was finding it just a little irritating that she was able to read my mind. But then tears were spilling down my cheeks. I was shaking my head and almost laughing through them, the palms of my hands facing skywards, questioning my inability to stop this blatant show of emotion. Rose just looked back at me as though underwhelmed at my self-pity. But then her stern face produced a warm, almost sympathetic smile.

'It's okay to cry, I guess…but you're doing okay!'

I covered my face with my hands and tried to wipe away my sudden embarrassment.

'But, Rose, am I?'

She nodded, and it helped.

'I'm sorry, Rose, I think I'm feeling a little worse for wear, tired, *very* tired in fact, tired and weak. Everything is happening sooo fast!'

Rose jumped down off the parapet and beckoned me to her. I dropped wearily to my knees and leant into her, wrapping my arms around my friend's almost non-existent waist. Her small arms were now wrapped reassuringly around me, my head gently resting on her shoulder. Her jet-black hair was so incredibly soft against my face. She just held me, her small hand rubbing the nape of my neck.

'You'll be here in this era for a few days, Ritchie. You will eat and you will sleep, you'll leave Justin's house in a couple of hours, if you've any sense. You will go back to Jimmy's, you'll get a good night's rest there; his mum will be glad to look after you, fix you a good breakfast, as she always does. She'll know you need looking after!'

The way Rose spoke made all that was happening so much easier and I was grateful, my nerves suitably sedated for the time being. And as my brain calmly rolled through my many questions, Rose read my mind beautifully and attempted to explain my circumstances in a little more detail.

'Ritchie, I know you're confused, but try to listen carefully to what I'm about to tell you. You have already changed the footsteps of your life's journey. Your meeting with Jack De'Vil at the market square, a substantial alteration to what happened originally, has seen a crucial change of opinion from him. You actually broke Jack's nose, and when something like that happens to a powerful man, it makes him question his invincibility! Every time he felt his pain, every time he looked in the mirror, he thought of you. First of all, he wanted revenge...*total* instinctive revenge. After all, his close friends goaded him, bringing his standing as number one into question.'

I found myself swallowing hard, really wishing that his friends would perhaps *stop* the goading.

'Are you listening to me, Ritchie? You've hurt him, physically and mentally, and he'll not forget it. But the general rule of thumb with bullies, after something like this, is that they tend to go for easier, far more submissive prey.'

Rose continued to explain how my worldly wise confidence was also making a difference, that people were responding to me more positively.

'You see, Ritchie, I know that you, as an eighteen, nineteen and twenty year old, were not as confident as you should have been, perhaps due to the rejection from your father... Your doubts about the big world created incisive inhibitions that of course diluted your potential power by simply reducing your confidence, just as it is with ninety-five per cent of teenagers. But you've now seen the world for what it is, and you have gone out there and made things happen. So to now find yourself at the age of twenty-one, knowing all that you do, well, it's a powerful cocktail. People are now drawn to you, in business and socially. And though it gives you an unfair advantage in life, who am I to deny you any of it?'

I nod at Rose, understanding and accepting all that she's telling me. But as I look at my serious, clever little friend, my whole being is overwhelmed by a surge of hysteria due to the sheer and extreme madness of it all, and my response is to burst out laughing. Rose looks at me, a bewildered smile crossing her beautiful young face. I try to stifle my giggles, not wanting to insult my friend. After all, I have so much love and respect for her, and perhaps a fair amount of fear embroidered around the edges. I suppose a fair response to the unknown power that I find myself involved with. But I have this incredible urge to take things down to a more playful level.

'Rose, you don't half rabbit on!'

Rose's eyes widen and then she jumps on me. Caught off-guard, I'm suddenly rolling backwards, my little friend's tiny fingers determined to tickle me into submission. But then it all stops and Rose freezes mid attack, both of us now on our knees, our hands projected forward like two attacking tiger cubs. Rose completes her retreat by dropping her hands and standing up. She appears troubled, her smile now replaced with a worrying expression. She turns away from me, ponders for just a moment and then starts to talk again.

'Ritchie, I know I'm going on, but I need to explain just a few more serious facts to you.'

I ease myself back and am now sitting cross-legged on the floor, listening intently. Rose turns side-on, pinching her nose and briefly cupping her ear, almost as though listening through an earpiece, but then her eyes are on mine.

'Ritchie, a small change of events, such as you striking Jack De'Vil, causes quite a ripple that can significantly alter your future forever. But that is not necessarily going to help you achieve the things that of course you were sent here to put right, as certain events may not present themselves as they did before. That is also why, in the early stages of you being sent back here, you were not able to change your actions. Your original thoughts and words would kick in and take control, so that you could maintain a certain crucial consistency. We really didn't expect your fight with Jack, but things happened *so* fast. And such was your fury and determination that it was too late! You were in there and *bang,* things were then altered forever. But you do realise, don't you, Ritchie, that you may have already stopped a terrible confrontation between you and him? But it can be a double-edged sword, and I and the powers that be feel that your personalities are such that your link with Julie and Lillie will, in time, no doubt create a head-to-head battle, regardless of your feelings for one another now. And should that happen, it is how you handle Jack that will help determine your destiny!'

I pondered and churned over and over each and every word, and I felt that I understood what Rose was saying. After all, I did feel differently to how I had felt as a young man the first time around. My fight with Jack at eighteen would never have happened originally, because I – as was everybody else – was in total fearsome awe of the big man. His world was alien and exciting to us, so we would never have dreamt of challenging him. And I suppose as I got older, I learnt and absorbed an awful lot about the edge that Jack's image would give him. At work I would also surround myself with mystery, which meant that I had the same ring of steel around me and therefore made my business rivals unsure as to how and if they should challenge me. Rose explained in more detail why my relationship with Jack was now so different to what it was before. And though I was moved on quickly from the age of eighteen to twenty-one after only one day, I was assured that I had continued in the same confident vein. Despite not wanting to be reminded, Rose seemed keen to impress upon me just how detrimental to my reputation my first meeting with Jack had been. Being found like a coward behind the settee, being thrown around like a rag doll, concluded fully in Jack's eyes that Ritchie Angel was *nothing,* resulting in his complete and utter contempt for me from that day forward. And though in my wiser moments I would shrug my shoulders and pretend that I didn't care what Jack De'Vil thought of me, an immaturity would overrule and my need for approval would continue.

'But, Ritchie, you must forget about all that, because now he respects and likes you, so enjoy it while it lasts!'

I sat chewing the inside of my cheek and then scolded myself for doing so. I analysed Rose's words, and on reflection realised that my fear of Jack had created the cavernous rift with Julie. Though I knew that the devil took pleasure in being such an evil bastard, I despised myself for allowing the man to make me suffer the way he did. I had been spineless and I wasn't proud of it. But time spent with my tormentor had only been a slither of my existence. On a day-to-day basis I had always felt good about myself, especially in the company of my friends, but needless to say, when the devil reared his ugly head, my confidence would dissolve. And so, when seeing Julie around Willow with little Lillie, my eyes would instinctively drop and I felt justified in denying their existence. I logically presumed that Jack would have convinced her of my frivolous and unworthy status, whereas now I accept that Julie's agenda was very different. Not caring about all the irrelevant testosterone that was flying about, she cared only about her daughter and not one jot about any futile alpha male dispute that would warrant as an excuse in me denying my link to Lillie.

Rose hugged me firmly, as though an endorsement of the fact that I might be seeing the error of my ways. But just as I felt the well of goodwill between us, I swallowed hard before attempting to ask just one more question, but she was gone. The slap of a cold chill biting where Rose had wrapped herself around me, I suddenly felt very alone.

I stood up and wearily turned almost full circle, before leaning back and sitting on the parapet wall high above the party below, my fear of heights seemingly diluted within all I was dealing with. I found it hard to believe that I was an important part of what was going on down there, more as though I was just reliving things in memory form. But of course, this was real and there were many scenes to play. And just as I was wondering whether or not I had the strength to put on a convincing performance, thoughts of Yasmin and Evie made me realise that I would do whatever was deemed necessary to be back with them.

As I made my way downstairs, as though waiting for the pulling back of the thick velvet curtains, ready for the baying crowd, I took deep stamina-building breaths. I smiled to myself as each descending step increased the volume of 'Run to You' by Bryan Adams, and gratefully my many thoughts were simply drowned out.

'RITCHIE...!'

Leoni ran over to me, her eyes large and almost scolding. Dramatically throwing her arms around me, she whispered sharply into my ear.

'Pretend we're together, pretend we're together...'

I was then aware of her pursuer hovering before us both, looking Leoni and I up and down, puzzled, and then his shoulders drooping in disappointment. He grimaced and shook his head from side to side, finally pushing his hand forward.

'Sorry, man! Sorry!' he slurred, before staggering off in search of his next victim.

'Leoni, who's the poor sod you've been leading on this time?'

I didn't get an answer, and just had my arm yanked out of its socket as I was pulled at speed through dancing and gyrating party goers.

'Oh my God, Ritchie, you're *never* going to believe this, come on!'

We were now outside, sidestepping all and sundry, but there was no stopping Leoni. The music was fading, and I gave a nostalgic sigh as Terence Trent Darby's words 'Sign Your Name Across My Heart' drifted out into the garden. But Leoni was in no mood to take in the moment. She led me away from the stone steps which were helpfully and sensibly lit, instead preferring a darkened route. In almost sheer blackness, we jumped down off the large patio wall and I'm suddenly aware that I am freefalling, before finally letting out a winded wheeze, the soft grass almost making my legs buckle as I land.

'Bloody hell, Leoni, that must have been a six-foot drop!!'

'Sssshh, Ritchie!'

I shake my head, opened-mouthed, but laugh at my friend

who is undoubtedly a little worse for vodka, the humorous result being her aggressive assertiveness. Without warning, Leoni bends from the waist and is making her way along the neatly trimmed privet hedge. I follow the example I am set and mimic my friend's animated steps as we approach the weather-beaten summerhouse. Leoni stops, quietly turns and places her finger on my lips. She darts her eyes to the movement inside the timber hideout. Under instruction, I step forward, Leoni keen and seemingly insistent on keeping her finger pressed to my lips. I slap her hand away and she frowns, but seems to get the message.

As I step off the grass, I'm suddenly aware of the noisy gravel beneath my feet. Leoni scolds me playfully, but her pursed lips and wide eyes tell me she's serious. I try desperately not to laugh and so turn away and peer through the cobwebbed windows of the summerhouse. I can see shadows, but then scan for a clear bit of glass, and there is the most comforting of sights – Jimmy and Sally, with their heads locked together. I can't help but beam, and then chuckle at the innocence of Jimmy. His hands are gentlemanly placed on her fully clothed back, whilst Sally's hands are exploring his body in the most intimate of ways. And as I discreetly pull away from the romantic scene, I take Leoni by the hand and we leave our two good friends to the privacy they deserve. I cross my fingers and tilt my head skyward – lilac clouds drifting across the full moon – and ask that nothing stops the wonderful adventure Sally and Jimmy have ahead of them.

The remainder of the night seemed to blur into one, and the last thing I really remember as my head hit the pillow at Jimmy's house was his beaming face. He hadn't spoken a decipherable word the length of our journey home. Once we'd waved Sally off, he appeared to float – a face that was basking in the glow of being struck dumb by requited love.

The next day, however, was very different. Jimmy was finally ready to spill the beans.

'I've done it, Ritchie. It must have been one of my "I love you" looks. As if by magic, she realised what I'd always tried to telepathically transmit! Oh God, Ritchie! She just walked up to me and kissed me! I thought I'd died and gone to heaven! Whatever it was that prompted her feelings, well, I'll always be eternally grateful!'

I nearly choked on my Cornflakes, but just about managed to smile and nod my head in approval. As I left Jimmy's house, I prayed that all the happiness that was finally his would not be destroyed by some pointless confession.

Though I was travelling within the realms of madness, a structure termed fondly as the rat race saw me dropping down firmly into my office chair at Skirdle's at 9 a.m. Friday. And though around me was a hive of efficiency, I was struggling to get out of first gear. Over and over again I attempted to unravel my part in the purchase of the Old School, and when I wasn't astounded by the intricacies of that, I was grappling for an order in which my projection forward had found me: *Jack De'Vil ... the yellow Porsche?* I searched back to this day in my original life, and as I ticked off the landmark details I could be sure of – Mum's funeral, not going to Justin's party – I realised that sitting behind my desk was exactly where I was at, mirroring time and date, just a different set of circumstances. And as I relived it in my mind, I turned and looked out of the window, the lilac haze now fading, and I was drifting back in time, the sky now blue. I was now firmly ensconced in my original life, with the unspoilt sun falling warmly onto my face.

Before Death, 1991 – Blue Sky

I was sitting at my desk at Skirdle's, getting ready for a meeting with my bank manager – and my bold attempt to purchase the Old School. My head, though, was drifting with my desire for Yasmin – in a time when I was perfectly free to chase her. In business, gung-ho and perilous, I would take my chances. But on the love front, I was a coward, and not having Yasmin had seemed a logical price to pay for my fear of rejection. But my business future was also in jeopardy, and all dependent on one seriously important meeting with my bank manager, whose name momentarily escapes me. I made the intrepid steps up Willow High Street, just four buildings away from my place of work, and with a handshake and offer of, 'Come in, Mr Angel,' I sat nervously in front of the man in the grey suit. I was doing my best to appear impressive. And though I'm sure the guy with the silver-rimmed glasses wasn't meaning to be patronising, he was very good at being just that.

'Well, Mr Angel, you're very young to be taking on a project of this magnitude. Mmmm, let me see, and you are also of limited funding, and of course don't really have any kind of track record as regards borrowing money or, for me far more importantly, your ability to pay borrowed money back!'

I remember feeling foolish. Why had I believed that a bank would lend money to me? But then my 'never say die' mouth would step in and seize control, offering a very one-sided view as to why the man in the grey suit and his overcautious bank should indeed lend their money to me.

'And so you see, Mr...?' I searched desperately for his name badge, or amongst the many red files on the surprisingly overfilled desk for a little plaque with his full title, clear for all to see: 'Mr ... Mr Tremble, Mr *bloody* Tremble!'

His eyes were now wide and several deep frown lines had appeared above his untrimmed eyebrows.

'I *beg* your pardon, Mr Angel?'

A shade of crimson, I coughed and apologised, and felt it wise to keep talking.

'And so you see, Mr Tremble, I believe that I can secure the school for between fifty and sixty thousand pounds. All I'm asking is for a mortgage on the property for just six months, which would enable me to get my designs accepted by the council. Which of course, with the right planning permission, would make the school a valuable asset. Perhaps we would be looking at fifty thousand pounds profit...' I grimaced and waited for a response.

Mr Tremble's lips were clenched tight, his eyes boring into me. With a deep breath, it was time to dampen the proceedings.

'Mr Angel, it's always wise to ask yourself one very good question in a situation such as this.'

I swallowed hard.

'Mr Angel, why do you not think that other, more established developers wouldn't simply outbid you, thus making their own plans to sell or develop? Subsequently making the healthy profits of which you speak, but without

138

actually having to go through you. Why do you believe these guys will see you as any kind of obstacle at auction or as a straightforward purchase?'

And of course Mr Tremble was absolutely right. But what I was not telling my grey-suited little bundle of enthusiasm was that I had a distinct advantage. Mr Skirdle had the Old School going to auction in just fourteen days. He had given me the file, asking me to make sure all the appropriate advertising was set up, and gave me the job of notifying all the potential buyers. All straightforward and above-board so far. But then the opportunity of all opportunities presented itself. Mr Skirdle was, within twenty-four hours or so, taking himself and his family away for their early summer vacation – a five-week trip to Canada. And therefore, having proved myself to be of hardworking and ethical stock, I was given full and final responsibility. Planning ahead, Mr Skirdle suggested that I took a week's holiday from my Monday to Thursday commitment with Steve Young Builders: 'Won't be a problem, will it, Ritchie lad?' Having assured Mr Skirdle that I was ready and available, I had examined the paperwork a thousand times over, and I couldn't see a negative in it. The icing on the cake for me was that in the little reserve price column was a figure of fifty thousand pounds, dutifully signed by the stern-looking local government official. And though it was usual to put a fairly low reserve price, as properties of this calibre always achieved at least thirty to forty per cent more, I was well aware that it wasn't going to this time. But of course, I couldn't share any of these impressive facts with Mr Tremble, and so I gave him a win-win scenario.

'Well, Mr Tremble, I see fully the point you're making, but maybe you should humour me, perhaps not dampen my enthusiasm, perhaps see yourself in your earlier years needing that first break. Surely you must find my hunger charming and commendable, and perhaps agree that *should* I be able to secure the Old School for the amount of fifty thousand pounds, beating, as you put it, the more established developers, and that perhaps I might warrant the backing of your bank...?'

Mr Tremble didn't look particularly impressed with my last ditch attempt. And so I decided to keep my mouth firmly shut and wait, his office clock ticking agonisingly loud and slow through the two-minute silence.

Mr Tremble looked at me and then up to the ceiling.

'I'll do it,' he said, 'but the figures have to add up. If you can get the property for fifty thousand and not a penny more – and I have to say to you now, I cannot see that happening, but should your judgment be right, and subject to a once-over from the bank's surveyor to ensure there are no structural problems – then it's a yes!'

I wanted to jump from my seat and run around his office screaming, but I chose to sit still and remain quiet.

'And, Mr Angel, looking at your bank account, you have the two and a half thousand pounds, which will be your five per cent deposit. You also have the funds for your planning application, so we will lend you the balance! Which will leave you with just enough for a bag of chips, Mr Angel! So, if you can agree to our terms, then maybe the bank will give you your first property development opportunity, young man!'

My heart skipped a beat. I stood up and offered my hand to Mr Tremble. He smiled for the first time and shook my hand, if a little limply.

As I left the bank, I was floating. There was no reason whatsoever why this couldn't work. It would be easy to keep things quiet; after all, it was only Mr Skirdle and I who had the information. So that was it – fingers firmly crossed. At the time I had a battered old pickup truck, a Toyota four-wheel drive – white with the odd chink of rust. But I loved that pickup truck, and as I crossed the market square and finally jumped into the driver's seat, I couldn't help but scream with delight. I told myself I must not waste this opportunity, I must make it happen!

As I drove out of Willow, I made my way to the next village of Holstead. Steve Young had a building job there, and though temporarily I had been taking one day off a week to work at Skirdle's, I had promised that I would make myself available after lunch today and tomorrow. Temporary roadworks forced me to stop right alongside the Porsche showroom, and it was then that I noticed a bright yellow 944 being taken off the car transporter. I tapped my fingers impatiently on the steering wheel.

'Come on lights, I'm gonna be late!'

The Porsche pulled up in front of the glass showroom doors before being reversed steadily onto a raised centre stand amongst the other suitably impressive vehicles. I shook my head from side to side as I realised that people would have to respect me if I was seen driving around in something as prestigious as that. I quickly selected first gear as the tooting of the car horn behind me alerted me to the fact that the red light had now turned to green. I pushed my foot firmly to the floor, just minutes away from getting my hands dirty. As usual I grafted hard, but my mind was overrun with the thought of buying the Old School. My adrenaline was at bursting point at the mere thought of making fifty thousand pounds sheer profit. I found myself shaking my head and chuckling about the eighty pounds a week I made for breaking my back, week in and week out, and how any profit could be the start of my empire. My thoughts turned to daydreaming about going into the showroom and throwing a banker's draft onto the counter, then simply driving the yellow Porsche away. And the more I daydreamed, the more I realised that this really could happen, that there was nothing to stop my dream from becoming reality.

Though it had only been a week or so since my mum's death, as I walked through the front door of the house I noticed a serious-looking envelope on the mat. It was from her solicitor, asking me to attend a meeting the following week. I stuck the letter up on the notice board in the kitchen. As I was getting ready to meet up with the gang later at the Whippet's Fifth Leg, I kept praying that Yasmin would be there. Yasmin had always been just a little out of my league, or at least I'd always presumed so. She was beauty *and* brains, with an aura that would draw your eyes in her direction, making it almost impossible to look away. She had her couple of girlfriends, and they just kept themselves to themselves. And though we'd smile at each other on the rare occasion I could catch her eye, I strongly believed that I didn't have a chance in hell. But then until my meeting with Mr Tremble today, I wouldn't have believed he would give me just under fifty thousand pounds. Maybe my luck was changing, maybe Yasmin wasn't so unobtainable, and so maybe, if she was in the pub tonight, I would try to talk to her.

It was just before seven as I stepped outside. It was a comfortable, fairly warm evening, the blue sky filled with gold as the sun started to slide down behind the hills. I jumped into my pickup truck and pushed the tape into the player; 'Don't Stop Believin'' by Journey blasted back at me. I wound the window down and reversed off the driveway, before speeding off towards the pub.

As I pulled into the only free parking space at the front of the Whippet's, I was surprised by how busy it was already. I stepped out of my pickup, my eyes drawn skyward as I noticed the band of thick black cloud in the distance, heading right for us. The majority of people were sitting outside – loads of familiar faces.

I stood briefly, before Scottie yelled over to me.

'Already got you one in, Ritchie!'

I stuck my arm in the air and attempted to make my way over to the table, but between me and getting to my friends was Jack De'Vil and his cronies. I could see Julie sitting obediently beside him, but she wouldn't look at me. I recalled our hostile meeting at the church and prayed she'd not said anything to Jack. It brought me out in a sweat just thinking about the repercussions such a pointless confession would bring. I took a deep breath and told myself that she was cleverer than that. But while Julie kept her eyes down, Jack looked right at me.

'Scottie got you a nice lemonade, has he? Maybe I'll get you a nice doggy bowl to drink it out of!' Jack's shoulders started to rock as he eased towards his punchline. 'Seeing as you like to crouch down on all fours...WOOF, WOOF!!' Jack barked loudly as all his friends screeched with laughter – Julie just looked uncomfortable.

I started to breathe again as I reached my friends, who had gone a little quiet having of course heard what Jack said. As I sat down, my heart sank as I noticed Yasmin with two friends just a few tables away. She looked at me, a sympathetic smile thrown my way, and then continued chatting with the girls either side of her. I listened intently to what my friends were saying, trying to nod in all the right places, keen to convince everybody that Jack hadn't got to me. But as I tried to forget about the *devil,* the black clouds were swirling above our heads and then the heavens opened. Torrential hail-like rain dropped viciously. Mass pandemonium ensued, with shrieks and screams as everybody was taken by surprise; then a mad surge for the safety of the pub, and once inside all jostling aggressively for tables. As I slumped down into my seat, I raised my eyes to see that Jack and his crowd were two tables away, but stuck between us was Yasmin and her friends. As she sat down, I struggled to take my eyes off her – I knew I had to try to talk to her tonight. But just as my confidence would build, I could hear a witty put-down from Jack, his cronies laughing louder each time.

Suddenly Jack pushed his chair back and asked out loud, 'How are your big property plans going then, Angel? I can see from your rusty old pickup truck you must be making a fortune!'

I shook my head from side to side and didn't say a word. But he was determined to push it, and with each comment, all I could do was look sideways at Yasmin – her friends were finding it all quite amusing, but Yasmin didn't look quite so sure.

'Are you listening, Angel? I've just managed to buy another small block of flats! Have you managed to actually buy *anything* yet, doggy boy? Come on, wheeler-dealer, tell me. I'm picking up my *new* BMW a week Monday!'

And as Jack really started to get on a roll, he seemed to have the attention of the whole pub.

'Yeah, Angel, probably not quite as quick or as comfortable as your rust bucket Toyota! But hey, you must love it! With all your cash … your successful business empire!'

It was then that I pushed my chair back.

'Hey, Jack! Seeing as you're *so* interested in my business affairs, maybe I'll give you a little up-to-date information! I am also, in three days' time, picking up a new car; not a BMW, though! As nice as they are, I felt I would buy myself something a *little* more in keeping with my success. Yeah, and I haven't even told my friends this yet, because I *don't* like to brag!'

It was then that my senses kicked in; it was then that I realised the depth of my stupidity should I persist with this public suicide. But I couldn't stop the madness that left my lips.

'I've just bought a new Porsche 944, bright yellow! It's been delivered to the showroom today!' Well, there it was, I'd said it.

The whole pub started clapping. Scottie and Jimmy stood up, suddenly jumping all over me, congratulating me. But then Jack stood up, not happy at all.

'Tell me, puppy boy, how the *fuck* have you financed that? There is nothing in this town that gets bought and sold without my knowledge! I take it you're not lying to me, *and all your friends?* Because you know what, Angel, I think I've just sussed you! You *have* to be lying!'

I swallowed hard, realising that I had been totally stupid – but then I became the King of Stupid!

'Well, Jack, maybe this will finally shut you up! I've had my offer for the Old School accepted, the paperwork was exchanged today! Should make at least fifty thou…!'

And that was it, just like that I had destroyed my first real chance of making a great start to my financial security. My pride, my total, flashy, show-off pride, had got in the way. But nobody else realised what a fool I was and just cheered. Inside I felt as though I was six inches tall. But to everybody else I was a giant success story. And after all the shouting and screaming, and at the expense of Jack De'Vil's stamped-on ego, he kicked his chair over, attempted to finish off with some witty final comment, which fell on deaf ears, and then left. And as I watched him running across the pub car park with Julie, getting absolutely soaked by the torrential downpour, I knew I had better make the most of the moment, because the fall was coming, and there was no doubt that it was going to really hurt.

Scottie, Jimmy, Sally and Leoni couldn't stop laughing – they had really enjoyed the show with the *devil*. And though I laughed with them, the truth was, I was a fool! Then I felt someone looking at me, and as I turned my head, there she was, pools of blue drawing me in – I just got lost in the moment. Yasmin's hand reached up in slow motion and pulled at the navy-blue satin ribbon that had tied back her glossy blonde hair, suddenly free to cascade down onto her shoulders and around her beautiful face. A few curls fell across her eyes as she continued to look at me, and then a nervous brush away with her hand – I was totally captivated. I had always found her gorgeous, but this close up, out of school, with flying colours she surpassed the fantasy.

And as the slow motion scene continued, with perfect timing, each of her friends stood up, one heading to the bar, the other making her way towards the 'Ladies'. I didn't give myself time to talk the new brave me out of my next move. My legs moved forward in time with my heavy pounding heartbeat, such a powerful thud that I was convinced she would cover her ears at any given moment to drown out the bass of it. Our eyes broke direct contact for the first time, almost killing my nerve. But as I questioned my ability to breathe, let alone talk, I toyed with the option of walking past and heading for the bar. But I stopped and slid into the chair at Yasmin's side.

'Ummm, sorry about all that, Yasmin.'

She laughed and responded that she'd found it very amusing, and that I'd handled Jack *really* well! Her first ever full sentence to me was pure poetry – I wanted to offer a line that would be memorable, impressive.

'Are you here having a drink?' I cringed; I was devastated.

Yasmin simply smiled, took a sip out of her almost full wine glass and, with a cheeky wink, said, 'I often wondered what Ritchie Angel's first ever line to me would be; brains to go with the beauty? Or perhaps a himbo?'

I went hot, her words sending me into meltdown, my mind digesting the love of my life's possible first impression of me.

Yasmin placed her hand on my arm. 'Ritchie, I'm only joking. People assume us female blondes are bound to be bimbos, so, you know, for a guy, blonde, beautiful...'

I started laughing, suddenly incredibly impressed by Yasmin's words. I would dismiss 'himbo', but she'd mentioned the word beautiful twice now, and I was going with that. A couple of drinks on, Yasmin and I were talking for England. She told me how she had been away on a modelling

145

assignment in Barbados, for a swimwear company. And though she had enjoyed the experience, she had also found it a lonely and shallow environment. She had missed her friends terribly, and had felt guilty about leaving her mum, especially after losing Yasmin's father just a few short months ago.

I screwed my face up.

'So sorry, Yasmin.'

We talked about the sadness of losing a parent so young – of course, it was something I could identify with due to my own recent bereavement. The conversation moved along effortlessly, and the moment became right for the one burning question I had.

'And a boyfriend, anyone special?'

Yasmin smiled and shook her head from side to side, before explaining that there was no 'special someone' in her life at the moment.

'I've been studying a little too hard for that, and then disappearing to do the modelling, well, you know, too much work can make you *very* dull!'

And as I watched and listened, I felt convinced that Yasmin could never, *ever* be dull. She explained that losing her father through a heart attack had made her take stock of her life. She told me how her father had been very protective of her, and insisted that she never waste her time with boys – not until she was at least twenty-five and her career well under control.

'But, Ritchie, when we buried him, I couldn't help thinking about how bothered my father was about having control, his work and family. He seemed very concerned about appearances and other people's opinions! Oh God, I'm really going on, you'll think me very rude!'

I laughed and assured her that I loved listening to her, and that I felt privileged that she felt so relaxed and able to talk to me so freely. Though I had been totally oblivious to everything around me, Yasmin's two friends, Zoe and Janey, had made their way over to my friends, and they all appeared quite happy chatting away. And as I looked through the half-open window into the pitch-black night, the evening looked perfect. The rain had passed, leaving a glistening diamond-studded sky. But then disappointment came as the barman called for last orders.

Yasmin and I were huddled together cosily, as if ours was the most natural union in the world. Her short white pleated skirt and white tennis shoes showed off her tanned legs beautifully, and the best bit was that her knees were resting against mine, and I couldn't believe how incredibly right it all felt. Our friends decided it was time for them to leave, and each one of their cheeky faces winked discreetly as they said their goodbyes.

It wasn't long before we were the last ones in the pub, and we both laughed when the barman yelled, 'Got no homes to go to?'

We took the hint and reluctantly stood up.

'Can I give you a lift home, Yasmin?'

She looked at me, a mischievous smile spreading across her perfect lips.

'What, in your rusty old pickup truck? What would my father think?'

But as she grabbed my hand, leading me out of the pub, all I heard from the back of her head was, 'I would love a lift, thank you, Ritchie.'

As I started the engine, Yasmin joked about the prospective Porsche.

'Why on earth did you feel the need to change the pickup? Bright yellow, and a Porsche, impressive! But I've got quite used to seeing you driving about in your pickup, kinda suits you!'

I smiled at her, our eyes once again just absorbing the moment, the moment I had dreamt about – Yasmin and I together. It was so powerful and strangely emotional. I couldn't think of anything to add to this perfect scene, so I said nothing and just pushed my foot down on the accelerator. As we sped off, I went to turn the volume down on the tape machine.

'Oh no, don't turn it down, I love this track!'

And as the words, 'Who's Crying Now...' were belted out by Steve Perry from Journey, I felt as though Yasmin and I were going to get along just fine.

I hadn't been sure where Yasmin lived, but as we drove down a little lane towards the back of the church, we had to pass through a fast-flowing ford.

'See? You'll never want to come and see me if you have to drive through this ford in your Porsche!'

And as she beamed at me, her blue sparkling eyes taking my breath away, my thoughts matched her words perfectly.

'No, I think this truck's ideal.'

We both laughed, and I was in heaven.

As I pulled up outside the most exquisite cottage, small but absolutely perfect – a real chocolate box setting – I turned off the engine and dropped the volume on the stereo.

An incredible silence lasted for a split second, and then we started to talk again. Yasmin asked me about my mum and what had been wrong with her. And as I explained, she just slid along the bench seat and took my hand. It was a bold and startling move, but it felt so incredibly natural. As Yasmin's fingers pushed into mine, I stopped talking, and for a few dangerous seconds I forgot how to breathe, such was the intensity of her innocent but powerful gesture. Time stood still. I could hear the music swooping in and around us, in-between my deep, exaggerated breaths. Yasmin ran her fingers along my hands and then back again, repeating the movement, but each time pushing a little further up my forearms.

She wasn't looking at me, her eyes contentedly focusing on our hands. I felt as though I just wanted to lean forward and kiss her head, longing for her to bring her lips up towards mine.

But I wasn't quite as bold and brave as the beautiful lady before me, so instead, I said, 'Tell me about your father, you must miss him terribly.'

Yasmin told me how she had loved her father very much, but repeated that he had been a very controlling and protective man. Her childhood had therefore been quite a diluted one. She had never been to the local youth club, as he and her mum would dutifully agree, 'It is a little unsavoury, dear!' Yasmin laughed out loud as she said the word 'unsavoury'. But she continued.

'I feel that in a way, they were perhaps right, because at least I haven't messed about naively with any lads, hanging around in gangs on street corners, youth clubs, discos. At least at twenty-one I feel that I'm more capable of, *well,* of making better, more informed decisions. But then, when I see who I've allowed to bring me home this evening, I wonder whether I'm capable of making such clever, informed and wise decisions after all!'

Yasmin raised her eyes, now focusing seriously on mine, and suddenly her hands are squeezing my fingers as a wicked smile stretches effortlessly across her perfect face.

'Because I can see you're a bad lot, isn't that right, Ritchie Angel?'

I screwed up my face, desperate to feign a look of hurt but failing miserably as laughter spills from my relieved body, unplanned words leaving my smiling lips.

'You cheeky cow!'

But then, instinctively, we both stop laughing, our eyes suddenly transfixed on each other. I felt an overwhelming gratitude, honour and privilege at simply being allowed to have this moment. I was captivated, compelled, destroyed and reborn a greater human being just by being here. I then felt it would be the most natural thing in the world to kiss her, and so I did, but I hadn't known what I was letting myself in for. As our lips met, I felt a charge run at breakneck speed through my entire body. A warmth that rose to white hot within nought point zero of a second, a breathtaking voluptuous spine-tingling spark that I was convinced could kill a man. As Yasmin and I pulled advisedly away from the other, our lips looking and feeling as though they were no longer part of our bodies, we both just froze and then smiled. And though I was praying for this dream not to end, the twitching of the curtains brought our evening to a reluctant close.

Yasmin sighed and pushed the passenger door open, easing herself elegantly away from me. I wanted to scream out, *'Please don't leave me!'* But I knew I had to be strong and compose myself. And as I forced a smile and uttered the words, 'Sleep well...' Yasmin beamed, before painfully turning away. As she made her way up the small path to her home, I was overwhelmed by my pounding heart, as though ready to burst out of my shirt. I was totally and utterly bereft. Yasmin pushed her key into the lock and finally turned to face me. I wanted to run to her, but something sane and advisable made me lift my hand and wave goodnight.

A horrible but familiar noise crashes into the depths of my skull. I bring my hand down heavily onto the 'off' button on my alarm clock. The house is suddenly so quiet. My thoughts are firstly of my mum and the fact that she's not here. And my sadness deepens when I think about the fact that this is how it will be from now on – waking up in a cold, quiet house all alone. I drag myself out of bed and walk to the bedroom window – the bright sunshine is starting to disappear behind dark threatening clouds. I watch intently, all the negative parts of my life being turned over in my mind, and then, as though someone, somewhere is watching over me, the sun suddenly overwhelms the cloud, shining passionately bright. It's then that my thoughts are fully focused on Yasmin, and I can't stop myself from smiling. I just think about how totally gorgeous she is – *now fancy waking up to that face everyday...* I cannot help but picture us together, and then start to get myself a little hot and bothered when I imagine her lying naked in my bed, waking me up slowly, her body pressed against mine. I laugh to myself, but then a quick look at the clock tells me I need to get a move on, as I had arranged to spend a rare Saturday working on the building site today, in an attempt to appease my boss Steve. Who was getting a little sick and tired of my dwindling enthusiasm - and whats more, I simply couldn't afford to lose the job.

'Cold water again!' I bash the tap, cursing myself for not putting the immersion heater on, even though it takes hours to heat up. But I throw the cold water onto my face and try to kickstart my day.

I slam the front door behind me, and as I look up at the sky, the black clouds are back. My heart starts to race, and there is no escaping the repeated words overwhelming all that is positive within my world: *Actions have consequences, Ritchie boy!* continues to loop repeatedly around my malfunctioning brain. My eyes roll skyward – a mass of black bruises, as if the heavens are ready to open. I jump into my pickup and swallow hard as I stare blankly at the threatening black pessimistic sky.

'Black sky, *Jack De'Vil* ... how apt!'

My mind is overrun with the stupidity of last night. Saying

about the Porsche was crazy enough, but then to have said about the school – well, that was beyond words. I knew that Jack would start asking questions – he was no fool. He would contact all the estate agents, speak to the local council, but one simple visit to Skirdle's and he'd know the lot!

I turn the engine on and the pickup roars into life. I then turn the engine off again. I rack my brains. *How the hell do I salvage this deal?* I almost feel as though I'm going to burst into tears. I keep thinking about the money and how being a success was bound to help in the romance stakes. I bang the steering wheel, my anger spilling over. *But you couldn't keep your stupid mouth shut, could you, puppy boy? You total wankerrr!!* I was fuming with myself. I wanted to go and see Jack, take the bull by the horns, but maybe that wasn't such a good idea. Perhaps the best place to be was Skirdle's, although I prayed that Mr Skirdle wouldn't drop in before his afternoon flight. I shook my head. At least I had half a chance should Jack come in asking questions. I knew one thing for certain – I couldn't just go to the building job today, as I would not be able to concentrate. So that was it, I had no choice – Skirdle's it was. I ran like a madman into the house, ripped off my scruffy work clothes and pulled on my smart suit. I took a moment in front of the mirror, desperate to build myself up. *Come on, Angel, you can do this, just keep cool!* And then I was gone – it was make or break day!

Once at the estate agents, I prepared myself for the call to my boss, Steve. He was a great bloke, but I wasn't convinced he would be happy today. I knew I was letting him down, and I couldn't just lie to him with the weak 'I'm ill' excuse. No, he deserved better than that. I needed to tell him the truth, be a man, I told myself. I dialled the number nervously.

'Hi, Steve, yeah, it's Ritchie. I've had a terrible night … yeah … at the dentist yesterday, well, it's *all* flared up again … yeah, if I can get an appointment today, a cancellation or something … Yeah, yeah I know, *sorry* mate! … Sure I will be fine for Monday … yeah, yeah, I'm *really* sorry, mate … yeah, bye!'

I wasn't proud of myself, but sometimes a simple lie can be so much easier. I shook my head in disgust, but knew he would have gone up the wall if I'd opted for the truth: 'Oh, Steve, I'm going to my other job today; that will be okay, won't it...?' I prayed that he wouldn't be passing Skirdle's today – I laughed nervously at the mere thought of it.

The ring of the shop doorbell announced one of my many unwanted visitors, but I was grateful it was my lesser concern of the three as Mr Skirdle stood with hands on hips before me.

'Surprised to see you today, Ritchie...Keen aren't you, lad?'

I laughed almost hysterically and grimaced sheepishly at my boss. Then his words seemed to hit me like a jackpot win.

'Are you planning to be here for the day, Ritchie?'

I nodded, my eyes wide, hopeful and just a little desperate.

'Then maybe...'

He walked to the shop window, his shoulder almost brushing mine as he peered up at the sky. I craned my neck too – the black clouds seemed to be passing over quickly, the sun starting to win its battle.

'Umm, I wouldn't mind getting a round of golf in, perhaps the last chance I'll get before I jet off!'

Mr Skirdle looked down at me over the top of his glasses, his long nose enabling a direct hit as he focused in on me.

'No problem at all, Mr Skirdle!' I tried to answer calmly, without falling at his feet with delirious grateful laughter. 'I've plenty to get on with here, sir...!'

And that was it – Mr Skirdle made a quick phone call and was out of the door like a shot. And as I fell into my office chair, a huge sigh of relief filled the room. At least now, if Jack did come in, I had a better chance of fobbing him off. *Oh God!* I thought. If he'd got talking to Mr Skirdle, well, it really didn't bear thinking about.

I sat and pondered for a moment, trying to tick all the appropriate boxes of places Jack was likely to scour – the car...? I wanted to create a possible smokescreen with the Porsche – maybe a surprise for Jack at this juncture would stop him in his tracks. And so I rang the dealership, and what I had to say next surprised even me.

'Yes, hello, Skirdle Estate Agents here. Your yellow 944, umm, I'm very busy at the moment, but I've just had a property left to me ... yes, and it would seem I have a keen buyer ready to roll ... yes ... indeed ... in fact, by my recently deceased mother ... yes, and well, I thought that, rather than leaving my money in bricks and mortar, maybe a fun little run-around would lift the spirits!'

The guy on the other end of the phone was the ultimate professional, though he had an over-the-top friendly tone that could become a bit too much; *almost like an over-zealous estate agent*, I thought to myself.

'Of course, sir. Should you wish to come in, we can arrange a test drive, fill her up and leave her with you for a couple of hours!'

Encouraged, I pushed a little further.

'Look, I won't get chance until later today, but would I be asking simply too much if perhaps you could bring the car to me, here at the shop?' I hesitated briefly and then started talking again, veering off the rejection. '...And then I'll give her a run out as soon as I get a moment.'

And just as I braced myself for the negative response, the man replied, 'Okay, sir, I'll send the car to you for, what, say 4 o'clock? If perhaps we can just have a copy of your driver's licence, then I'm sure you could try the car out this evening, and perhaps we would pick it back up in the morning, or maybe Monday? Skirdle's Estate Agents you say? Okay, and your name, sir?'

I almost cringed, but continued. 'Angel, Ritchie Angel.'

And that was it, the salesman signed off with a simple, 'Okay, sir, we will see you in a few short hours!'

I sat back once again in my office chair, my nerves tingling. This situation with Jack was affecting my ability to function normally. I pondered the delivery of the Porsche – *surely this is going to be embarrassing, when they come over and see that I'm a young twenty-one year old?* But I took a deep breath and thought that maybe it would be delivered by a mechanic, and that as long as I let him take my licence away with him, then why should there be a problem? And as my confidence grew, my logic finding its feet a little, I thought, *They don't know whether or not I can afford it. Sod it, enjoy it! Because after all, if my Old School deal does fall through, then it may be my only ever chance of driving a Porsche.*

The bell would ring as people walked in and browsed through the sales particulars, but as yet, there was no Jack. I tried to relax and optimistically found myself wondering whether he could have simply skulked off, wanting to be left alone to lick his wounds after last night's humiliation. I envisaged every unlikely scenario. *Perhaps, despite calling me a liar, he thinks I'm legit – that maybe he's underestimated me. And the truth is, he shouldn't underestimate me. Why should the bloody devil be the only one to have ideas and make money?*

As I sat and waited, my thoughts turned to Yasmin. I hoped that I could see her tonight. I suddenly pushed myself firmly back into my chair, frustration causing my blood to boil. I hadn't taken her phone number and couldn't believe I had been so stupid. But when I reflected on the intensity of our goodbye last night, I forgave myself, believing strongly that no man would have been thinking straight after a kiss like that. I decided that I would simply take a chance and just call round, perhaps surprise her. And as I cringed at the sheer thought of how flash I would look pulling up in the Porsche, I couldn't help but smile. It wasn't long before it was 4 o'clock ... then quarter past four came and went, and then, as I stared out of the shop window, my eyes widened. There it was – the yellow beast screeching to a halt. I rather enthusiastically punched the air, as sure enough a young guy stepped out of the car before removing a plastic sheet covering the seat. As he slammed the door shut, I was out on the street, my hand pushed forward and offering my warmest smile.

'Mr Angel?'

I shook the guy's hand firmly and tried to look as confident as possible.

'Yep, lovely!'

He offered to run through the controls with me, but I declined, simply saying that it was a similar layout to my father's model down south. And with that, the man shook my hand again, tucked my licence into his overall pocket and ran across the road to a waiting bright red van with a large Porsche logo stamped across it. The van then sped off up Willow High Street, causing many people to turn their heads and tut-tut as the mechanics tooted at the blonde crossing the road. I looked down at the bright yellow Porsche and then at the keys in my hand ... and then at the gorgeous blonde who was now within a few feet of me.

'Hi, Ritchie. I still prefer the pickup!' And as she bent down, peering through the window, 'No, Ritchie ... it's lovely. In fact, I *really* like the colour, it's fun!'

And I never gave it a thought at the time, but while in Yasmin's company, the Porsche simply didn't register with me. My breath, my eyes and my heart were totally hers, and as impossible as it would be, she was undoubtedly even more beautiful than I remembered. As the passers-by slowed down and gave the car the once-over, I was convinced that their adoration for the Porsche was eclipsed by their admiration for the blonde lady I had just had the courage to slip my arm around, my heart close to bursting with pride. As I placed a kiss on Yasmin's flushed cheek, she pushed back into me, her head now resting on my shoulder. I felt for the first time in my life complete, and the car, for tonight, was just a little bonus. Because as I looked at and held Yasmin, I couldn't believe that I would ever worry about bragging to Jack or anyone else again, because if this lady wanted me – and I really prayed she did – then I felt I had nothing to prove. With Yasmin at my side, I was simply a better man.

She turned to me. 'Look, Ritchie, I've got to meet up with my mum, but maybe you'll give me a call when you get a moment?'

I love Yasmin's words. I just purr at the content of her sentence: firstly, that she's talking to me, and secondly, that she is asking me to ring her. In any context, I am blown away. But just as I see her walking away from me, I realise I haven't replied.

'Errr, *Yasmin?*'

She turns quickly.

'Umm, tonight, yes, tonight! I was hoping to pick you up and take you out somewhere...'

Yasmin beamed, but a hint of despondency troubled me.

'Ritchie, I can't, it's just that...'

I held my breath – my life depended on her reply.

'Ritchie, it was agreed that it would be a girl-only evening, but I'll be in the Whippet's. It's Zoe's birthday, we've arranged to meet there, but maybe you could come over and talk to me, should you want to.'

I was convinced I'd just given her the most inane grin possible, and then the words spewed out without a thought for the consequences.

'You betcha, I'll come and getcha!'

I just wanted to throw myself in front of the passing bus that suddenly boomed past me, a haze of dust blowing into my face, causing me to cough and splutter, while I tried to look cool through squinting, streaming dirt-filled eyes. I was pleased that the bus had done its deed, and prayed that somehow the moment had erased my terrible *betcha getcha* thing. I'd never used a line like that – I'd never heard, or in my worst nightmares been anywhere remotely close to, a cheesy creation like that. But as Yasmin seemed to be waiting for a proper response from me to her last statement, I finally managed a more respectable combination of words.

'I'll see you in there then, looking forward to it!'

And as she smiled and turned away, I just stood and watched her walk. Now I knew exactly what was meant by the term 'poetry in motion'. I suddenly yelped and jumped as I felt a painful prod in my back. A sudden waft of cigar smoke clouded and dampened my mood, and I knew that the day had been going too well. I turned around and attempted to act as cool as possible.

'Yes, Jack!'

The devil didn't say a word, just stepped back and pushed the shop door open. Though I wanted to run, I felt it perhaps wise to simply follow him in. Once inside, Jack turned the open sign to closed – I felt my chest tighten. Jack told me to sit down and, like a scared fool, I did. I quickly undid the buttons on my shirtsleeve, then lifted the free material to try to clear some of the dirt and grit from my eyes – I wondered whether it would have been a less painful option simply to throw myself at the mercy of the bus. Jack then leant on the desk, his large arms exposed up to his elbows – his black short-sleeved shirt, his dark-blue silk tie tucked between the buttons and pushed inside. He inhaled for what seemed like an eternity on his stubby cigar, before bellowing its natural waste into my face. I tried desperately not to cough, but the now enhanced stinging in my eyes was evidence enough for his sly, wry smile.

'Your school building, Angel, it's not exactly yours, is it? Your shit and lies made me look a *total twat* last night!'

I tried to swallow but couldn't, and so I felt it wise just to listen. And as the veins on his neck started to stand out, as though ready to burst, I decided to plan the best way in which to protect myself. I looked at the stool by the filing cabinet and wondered whether a quick crack across the shins would buy me enough time to get through the front door.

'I like your Porsche out there, but oh no, excuse me, my mistake, just borrowed till the morning eh? You are so full of it, Ritchie *fucking* Angel!'

Jack stands up straight, his arms pushed out in front of him, as though strangling something invisible, but his words and anger are very real.

'I don't like you, Angel. I should have grabbed you and stamped all over your baby face last night in the pub, force you to admit your bullshit! Stamp on you until you're totally unrecognisable. Yes, that would be the only thing to make me smile today!'

As I looked at the devil, I felt totally trapped. I wondered how this little scene must look from outside, to the passers-by. Although the boards with all the house details would cover most of the goings-on in the shop, should Jack really kick off and perhaps try to kill me, then hopefully somebody would hear the commotion and call the police. But Jack seemed to calm himself down, and then his thoughts on how I could make amends to our little predicament became clear.

'Mr Angel, your school, I want it! I can only presume that you have some sort of plan. The simple fact that I didn't know about it, until your generous tip-off last night, means that no one else does either! I can only imagine that you're going to keep it quiet somehow. I'm thinking, reserve price... What is it? Forty thou, forty-five?'

I felt totally sick. As the day wore on, I had foolishly believed – hoped – that maybe Jack wouldn't waste his time looking into all this, that he would have bigger fish to fry. But as I looked at him now – this monster of a man who was plaguing me, destroying me – I felt so tempted to get rid of him. He was the one fly in my ointment. The rest of my life seemed to be falling into place. And yet, here he was, totally determined to bleed me dry. I finally managed to speak.

'Sixty thousand, the reserve!'

The devil looked at me, his eyes disclosing the fact that he wasn't convinced I was telling the truth.

'Then show me ... show me your forms!'

I tried to stand up without shaking too much. I was determined to try to act as though he hadn't totally destroyed my confidence. I had to compete, otherwise I would not make it. I would not just allow this man to crush me. Surely I had something in me to stand up to this mere flesh and blood. I took out the file on the Old School and placed it on the desk.

'Look, Jack, I really shouldn't be showing you this!'

He just laughed in my face, shaking his head from side to side before finally opening the file. He lifted up the auction papers, placing them in front of the strip lighting and squinting for a moment.

'Sixty thousand, ummmm, finally I get to the truth, Angel! Right, this is what I want you to do. I presume you feel that you can keep all this quiet, is that it, Angel ... and then buy at the reserve price?'

I nodded, hoping that my doctoring of the auction forms – having been convinced that Jack might challenge me in this way – was about to pay off in some small way.

'You cannot possibly have thought that you could get away with this, Angel, because you, as a representative of Skirdle's, cannot be seen buying auctioned properties. You're a total prat if you think you can get away with this kind of fraudulent shit!'

And as I looked at Jack, I realised that he was actually making some sense, that I hadn't thought deeply enough about the ethics – and the fact that my name would be there in black and white as the purchaser. Even up to this point, I had wondered whether I could get Jack to pay the sixty thousand in cash, I still purchase for fifty and walk away with ten thousand, but I was now struggling to breathe, let alone work out a route through all this madness. Jack scowled and continued to educate me.

'Now, if I were to buy the property, pay my sixty thousand, then there would be no questions asked. Seems quite simple, don't you think?'

I felt numb. Sure, he could go to auction and pay sixty thousand pounds and that would look less suspicious; at least we'd have ten thousand more than the original reserve. But I would have made nothing, and really there was no way of me making a penny out of this deal. So though it had cost Jack ten thousand more, there was little consolation in that. As I tried to resurrect plan B in my mind, I now baulked at my unrealistic belief that when doctoring the paperwork earlier, I had imagined that Jack might split the difference with me. Suddenly, I really felt that I didn't want any involvement with him. Jack looked at me with a pleased with himself smile that I found hard to take. He then offered his hand.

'So, we know where we stand then, Ritchie? You leave things as they are, I'll take the bidding up to sixty thou, I get my property, business concluded!'

His grimace subsided a little as I simply left his hand dangling, refusing to shake. He slowly turned and walked to the door, flipping the closed sign back to open. He then stepped out onto the pavement and I foolishly followed.

'Oh and, Angel…' Jack got his car key, looked around to make sure nobody was looking, and then dragged it deep all the way along the Porsche. Once he'd walked the full length of the car, he turned, his black eyes glistening back at me. 'Wasn't too happy when you didn't shake my hand! Makes me think that you disrespect me … makes me think that you're not committed to our little arrangement!'

He made sure I was looking him right in the eyes.

'Any shit, Angel, remember, your house, it won't take much to see that go up in flames. Would be a shame if you were, say, drunk inside of it! You know, with the recent sad death of your mother, broken heart, just drowning your sorrows, a little careless with the gas cooker. Well, I think you might get the picture. See you at the auction, Angel!'

And just when I thought my tormenter was about to finally

leave, something stopped him in his tracks. Once again, a sly smirk spread across his hard, evil face. Jack now stood right in front of me, his hand suddenly pushed forward.

'Going to offer me your hand now, Angel?'

I hated myself for doing it, but I pushed my hand forward. Jack's eyes glistened, mischievous, devious, and then his rough stubby fingers are on mine – a grip of iron. My right palm is forced skyward and then, as if in slow motion, I'm screeching out like a scolded cat. But Jack holds on vice like as the pain of a thousand white hot needles penetrate my flesh, and the smell of burning brings a sadistic triumphant sparkle to his oil-black eyes. He lets go of my hand and I yelp pathetically, passers-by looking bemused as I reel away from my enemy. As I open up my palm, I can see clearly where Jack has stubbed out his cigar full force onto the tender, now red raw, broken skin.

I look up at Jack, but he simply smiles and then purrs, 'If the car was yours, then maybe I would have settled for the damage to that! But hey, thought a little pain would remind you how serious I am, Angel!'

And with that, Jack De'Vil was content for now and nonchalantly made his way over the road to his soon-to-be upgraded BMW. As he climbed in, he looked back at me and winked. He slammed the car door shut, and with a spin of his wheels roared off up the high street.

So maybe now you can see Mr Jack De'Vil for what he was... He certainly wasn't a man to mess with. And yet I couldn't help but think that maybe, just maybe, I shouldn't take his shit any more. Surely there was something I could do. Perhaps there was a way of tripping his world up, but was it worth it? Was Jack De'Vil a man I could beat? I looked down at my hand, the deepening rouge of Jack's evil torture no longer just a mind game. I now had my first battle scar from him, and so if I wanted to take him on, I would be playing by his rules: fire with fire, kill or be killed. And this really was his game: he initiated his terms and I was a novice. Maybe the way Jack played simply wasn't a game that I was physically or mentally up to. I wrapped my fit and healthy fingers around my battle-scarred hand and walked despondently back into the shop. As the door clicked shut behind me, I stood for a brief moment simply churning over my limited options. But then I shook my head, sick and tired of all my negative thoughts. I turned everything off, and decided that closing time hadn't come a moment too soon.

I tried not to look. I just wanted to get into the car as quickly as possible and simply convince myself – at least for a short while – that the beautiful heap of metal that had been entrusted to me for just a short few hours was fine and still in showroom condition. But as I pushed the car key into the lock, my eyes fell left and then right. I couldn't believe how deep the scratch was – what the hell was I supposed to say to the garage in the morning? But as I unlocked the door and slid down into the firm leather seat, I went against the grain, took a deep, much-needed breath and then forced a smile. As I turned the key in the ignition, the spontaneous roar of the engine was incredible – like magic it seemed to put everything into perspective, and I liked this new positive feeling. I played with the controls, adjusting my mirror and seat, but no matter how I tried to keep my spirits lifted, my mind was still prepared to slide down a pessimistic path as I dwelled relentlessly on how Jack was standing in the way of all this: money in the bank, a great car and a woman who would be proud of my achievements. I selected first gear, released the handbrake and roared off up the high street, imagining the tut-tutting that I was leaving in my wake.

When I had first arranged to borrow the Porsche, I had wanted to show it off at the pub later that night. I'd wanted so much to pick Yasmin up in it, hopefully meet her mum, thinking that maybe a flash car would impress her. And of course, to whisk Yasmin off in style, anywhere she wanted to go – it had seemed fun. Then, to have seen the faces of Jimmy and Scottie – well, at twenty-one years of age it's most guys' fantasy to be racing round in a brand new super car. As I dropped a gear and floored the accelerator, my head was flung back as the turbo seemed to pick the car up and hurl it forward. *Oh, the sound of the engine!* Okay, so this car wasn't going to be as good as the top-of-the-range 911, but then you are competing with a serious status symbol. I have to say, though, that this less expensive but still suitably impressive 944 was a beast. So that was it, I was hooked. I would undoubtedly, one day, buy myself a Porsche, but for now it had to be a dream that would be put on hold. Hard work and good decisions would in time give me the option. As I pulled up onto the Porsche showroom forecourt, I just listened as the engine burbled and purred. I pressed down on the accelerator one last time and sighed lovingly, and then turned the engine off. Everything was still. My fingers were wrapped firmly around the leather steering wheel, but my head was spiralling. Out of the corner of my eye, I was aware of the salesman looking my way, suddenly grabbing his suit jacket off the back of his chair. I swallowed hard and braced myself for the commotion that was probably about five seconds away. Five – the salesman was now out through the electric glass doors. Four – I stepped out of the car. Three – he was now almost running through the line of angled Porsches that lined the forecourt. Two – he was at my side.

'You got the chance to take it for a spin then, Mr Angel? What are your thoughts?'

I turned confidently, my hand outstretched, the keys dangling in midair.

One – the salesman reluctantly took the keys off me and waited for a positive response. Lift-off. But suddenly, his eyes were drawn and his smile turned to hyperactive concern.

'Oh, Mr Angel, dearie, dearie me!'

His finger traced along the freshly ground gouge. I wanted to fall at his feet and beg for forgiveness, perhaps curl up into the foetus position and rock like a baby. After all, it had been quite a harrowing twenty-four hours. But instead, I managed to remain calm.

'That, sir, is the first thing I found as I made my way out of the shop, ready to take the Porsche out for a test drive. I can only presume that it didn't leave your showroom like that?'

The salesman stood upright, shaking his head furiously, his words forced out through gritted teeth.

'No, it certainly did not!'

I felt that the best form of defence was attack.

'Jealousy, pure unacceptable jealousy! And I regret to inform you that it is this type of reaction to such an incredible machine that means I have decided not to pursue this dream any further!'

The salesman's demeanor was suddenly jolted into a *damage limitation* tact.

'Well, yes, sir, it is of course quite sickening to see such mindless vandalism, but surely it is only paintwork at the end of the day! Umm, these ... *these* things can be sorted out, and ... *and* after all, surely best not to give in to the green-eyed thugs!'

I shook my head from side to side.

'Of course, you're right...' I took a quick look at the salesman's name badge, '...Mr Poppycock. Yes, of course, Mr Poppycock, you are absolutely right, but I feel that on this occasion I have taken the damage quite personally. The violence to this vehicle has scarred me too, and I feel that I need to reassess my values and my strong desire to own a Porsche. Perhaps I will get back to you in the not too distant future. I feel that then, I may consider going the full hog and buy my dream machine, the 911, maybe in a more sedate silver. Perhaps that will blend in a little more than the *look at me* yellow of this particular beast.'

As the salesman looked at me, his bottom lip having dropped a good inch and a half below his top lip in his keenness to digest my waffle, I thought it best to conclude while my man was on the ropes. My hand suddenly thrust into his, he returned the gesture with a fairly half-hearted handshake, which I was grateful for, as the pain of the devil's handy cigar work was reaching quite a crescendo. I eased away from Mr Poppycock, a couple of small steps and then slightly larger strides, my fingers firmly crossed behind my back, praying that this would be the simple end to the damaged Porsche saga. Mr Poppycock seemed to be stuck in an aerobics move that he simply couldn't retract from, bent double inspecting the paint, back up, arm in the air, as though keen for me to return to the crime scene. But then his inability to say anything meant that once again, he was back into the bent double position, retracing the gouge with his index finger. I was now a good forty feet or so away, and though I really didn't want to tempt fate by uttering a word, I felt that one good bash on the final nail in the coffin lid might just do it.

'I *PRESUME* YOU HAVE ADEQUATE INSURANCE COVER FOR THIS SORT OF *MISHAP?* IS THERE, *MR POPPYCOCK,* ANY PAPERWORK YOU WANT *ME* TO SIGN?'

The poor depleted salesman, now stuck in the bent double position, sort of grimaced back at me, shaking his head from side to side. That was all I needed. I turned quickly and suddenly my strides were replaced with a steady jog. And then, as I made my way across the grass verge, sidestepping the strategically placed halogen lights, I dropped my head and broke into a sprint, the relief giving me quite a spring in my step and the energy I needed for the two-mile journey back to Skirdle's. But as I ran, I screwed up my face as I realised I hadn't got my driving licence back off the distraught Mr Poppycock – *I might just write and ask for it!* - sprang to mind, suitably pacifying me, and in acceptance of taking the easy way out I ran a little faster.

CHAPTER SIX

The Wise Old Man

Before Death, 1991 – Blue Sky
It wasn't long before my impressive run towards Skirdle's became a walk. I was torn, not quite believing that I had voluntarily dropped the car back, but knowing full well that I could have kept hold of the beast until the morning. I knew that people would have sat up and noticed me should I have pulled up at the pub in it tonight. I knew all that, and yet I had still returned it. And suddenly, to add to the bitterly cold wind on my face, the rain started to fall. As I looked up at the horrendous blackness above me, blinking away soft bearable droplets, the heavens opened. Without warning I started to laugh, and as the cleansing ferocity of the storm soaked me through to the skin within seconds, my amusement was quickly

replaced with a less than enthusiastic mumble.

'Great…!'

There was an undercurrent of feeling a little hard done by, and my mutterings were continuing in the vein of, 'Great day this is turning out to be…' But though it would not have been deemed unreasonable to be revelling within the depths of despair, feeling despondent and defeated, my optimism was such, and again, without warning, my laughter was back, booming out of me, almost hysterically. My soul was drenched with hope, saturated in the irrepressible form of true love. Thus I concluded that I was far from down, and most certainly not out. The last twenty-four hours had easily been the best of my life so far: Yasmin, the Old School, and then the little ripe cherry on the top – the brief fling with the Porsche. The influence of the devil, combined powerfully with my own immaturity and my regretful brain-dead outburst, marred spectacularly all that should have been so perfect. And so it was out of respect for my mistake that I had taken the car back. Of course, I could proceed with the role of show-off and just ignore Jack. But he was definitely out for me. And the more I stuck my neck out, the keener he would be in cutting my head right off. So, I felt it wise to slip into the shadows, tiptoe through this forced arrangement with Jack and make fresh business plans. But this time having learnt that a wise and fruitful businessman keeps his cards close to his chest, that actions undoubtedly speak louder than words, and that I now had definitive proof that loose lips certainly do sink ships, left so painfully aware that there is no Kudos in bragging. And as I reflected on my own advice, I was reminded of its origin, and with a warm smile I recalled the old gardener with whom I had got chatting on many occasions.

I would often go and sit in Willow Park when I needed time to think: mum's illness, general troubles of the world. I only knew him as Mr Windell. But as he pulled up in his old but immaculate mini van, his tools placed neatly in the back, he would often wander over and chat about this and that. But one day, he'd mentioned inadvertently where he had once lived, and I looked at my old friend and remarked that the house he had mentioned was the biggest in Willow. In response, he simply smiled and appeared a little disappointed in me.

'Well, Ritchie, I am surprised to see your shock. You had seen me, seen my little old van and what I do for a living, and judged me! Isn't that right?'

I looked back at him, surprised by his reaction.

'Ritchie, this is a valuable lesson to you. You must never judge people, not by their appearance, not by the vehicle they drive, and certainly not by their vocabulary or by the company they keep, not even by the job they do! You must never feel that you have the measure of their standing in society, because that puts you at a disadvantage!'

I swallowed hard and let him continue.

'Ritchie, I feel I have got to know you over the last few months. I admit I have made a small judgment about you, but you do seem to be a bright lad, and more importantly than that, you appear to be a kind and caring human being, and I believe that you will go far in life. Having listened to your plans and strategies, you do seem to have an instinctive grasp of business. But I want to share with you a little saying that I hold in high esteem, and it's simply this: the more you know, the less you show!' Mr Windell looked at me, his studious eyes inquisitive. 'Do you understand me?'

I nodded and uttered, 'Of course!'

Mr Windell would normally stand before me, fit and lean, but now, for the first time, he took off his cap and lowered himself onto the freshly mown grass. He took a deep breath and proceeded to tell me all about his big important job: second in command at the electrical company just outside Heaton. How he used to drive a brand new Jaguar. Two exotic holidays a year. Three boys all at boarding schools spread around the country, and of course the large house on millionaires' row. But he then told me how he'd found out that his wife had been having an affair with their gardener, how it had gone on for two years and how he'd never suspected a thing. Mr Windell stopped, placed his cap back onto his head and pushed out a large breath, puffing up his ruddy cheeks as though deliberating whether he wanted to continue with his tale. He then removed his cap again and explained about his middle son – he was only fifteen, but tragically took a drugs overdose, ending his short life. Mr Windell looked away, a single tear falling onto his cheek. He took out a large white handkerchief and blew hard.

'I'm sorry, Ritchie, but losing my boy like that, well, I'll never get over it!'

But then he continued, explaining that his work was his life and how his money became his replacement at home. And only when he started to see how his world was falling apart did he finally do something about it.

'I quit my job, Ritchie. I simply walked into the MD's office and handed back the car keys. I didn't utter a word, just placed my resignation letter before him, shook my head and walked out! I made my way to the telephone box across the road from the huge factory and telephoned my wife, but she wasn't there. When I finally got home, that's when I found the note...' Mr Windell stopped, taking another large blow on his handkerchief. 'You see, Ritchie, she'd left me, simply had enough. There was the note, and it simply read: *I love Donald Windell. I married Donald Windell. The fun, loving man. But how can I still love you when you're never here. How can your sons love you, and turn to you, when you're never there for them? If you're not abroad for months on end, then you're stuck at the office. Donald, I don't love you any more ... don't even know you any more.* Simply signed: *Sue.*'

The rain was getting heavier, my shoes and socks totally saturated. Mr Windell's story had been just that up until now – a story. It had no bearing on my young life. I wasn't going to make the foolish mistakes he'd made – my life was bound to be different. At the time, I didn't really take his words in, but now, for some reason, the moral was unearthing itself. Mr Windell explained that he'd gone to get his wife back.

'Ritchie, you wouldn't have believed it, but she'd moved in with this gardener chappie. He lived in a council house on the Oaks, you should have seen it! But you know, as I knocked on the door, I could hear laughter coming from inside the house. My wife Sue laughing like I hadn't heard for many, many years. And as the door opened, there was my gardener, only one year younger than me, stripped to the waist, tanned and muscled. I looked down at my typical corporate figure, my fat belly from too many large business lunches, and as I looked back at my gardener, who didn't really have two pennies to rub together, I realised that didn't seem to matter. He was happy, and what was more, he was the one my wife loved. And my God, Ritchie, the pain was just too much!'

Mr Windell quickly blew his nose again, and then I was sure I heard a slight chuckle.

'And you know, Ritchie, as Sue joined him at the front door, she looked so beautiful. She looked at me sadly and I knew that I had lost her, because I had lost me. I didn't know who the hell I was any more. I had become a robot. How the hell was she supposed to love me?'

Mr Windell stood up, staring out across the park. I took in his now lean body, his tanned balding head, and he looked great – a picture of health. And I had felt that until his outpour, he'd seemed a very happy, contented man. He turned and looked at me, his head shaking from side to side.

'You see, Ritchie, I asked her to come outside and talk to me. She did, and then I told her, "I don't blame you, Sue, for leaving me, I would have left me, and as for your friend in there, the gardener, well, it breaks my heart, but I understand, but it's so bloody ironic that today I have walked out on my job! I've quit, Sue! I simply don't want it any more. I don't care if I have to sell the house, I mean, it's not as if you're bothered about it, otherwise you wouldn't have left it! I just want a simple job, I want to become the old Donald, I want you and I to have fun, to find each other again, and as for our poor son, Sue, I'm sooo terribly sorry." But, Ritchie, when I really felt that I didn't have a chance in the world of getting her back, she placed her hand on mine and her warm loving smile gave me hope. Just as she was about to say something to me, I placed a finger on her lips and said, "Please don't say anything, Sue! Go back into his house knowing this: I want to grab hold of life and enjoy it, and I pray that you'll see me around Willow, and perhaps fancy me again. I don't know, it sounds daft, but what I'm saying is, if you feel that I am getting my life right, then please know that it will never be too late for us. I will be waiting for you, because, Sue, I will never stop loving you. I just became blind, fat and stupid." And you know,

Ritchie, as I left there, I smiled, though my heart was smashed to pieces. I just walked away!'

But the look on Mr Windell's face told me that this little story had a happy ending.

'Within three days she came back to me, Ritchie. I was working out at my house. I had converted my office into a relaxation room and had put a jogging machine in there. As I looked out across my sprawling front garden, the 'For Sale' sign standing proud, I had to rub my eyes in sheer disbelief as I saw the gardener's van stop at the gates, and there she was, my Suzy! She was wiping tears off the gardener's face, but then she picked up her suitcase and walked up the gravel driveway. I couldn't move fast enough. I ran to the front door and I could still see her ex-lover at the gates, but as I opened the door, her face beamed at me and that was that. She walked through the door, giving me a small smile as she placed down her suitcase, and then flung her arms around me passionately, tears rolling down her beautiful face, and as she started to apologise, I shook my head, telling her that I was the one that was sorry, and that I was so happy to have her home!'

Mr Windell stopped, a tear escaping, falling slowly until it touched his smiling lips. He told me that he eventually sold the big house, or the 'ivory tower' as he called it, and bought a small cottage with a stream running in front of it, right in the heart of Willow.

'Ritchie, I now live modestly, spend a fraction of my time at work. I simply don't need the money. I've cut my cloth accordingly, and my life is rich and full of love, and extreme happiness!'

That was his message to me. And as I trudged through the relentless rain, I realised one hundred per cent what he meant: firstly, you have to be happy – the material things are purely incidental. The love and respect of a partner, family and friends, it's powerful – the material things are not an advisable substitute. I felt that although the Porsche was fun to drive around in, I didn't feel deserving and so handed it back. It needed to be in the showroom, waiting for its rightful owner. If Yasmin was the girl for me, then why was I trying to impress her with a flash car? Surely that was demeaning to her, and simply succeeded in making us both appear shallow and influenced by materialism. And as for Yasmin's mum, I strongly believed that she would be more concerned than impressed. I had been given this valuable lesson from Mr Windell, and I knew that I must try to be guided by his words and my acceptance of them. Although I seemed to get things right with my love life, my business world seemed to take a blacker, completely opposing route.

Suddenly, my thoughts were interrupted and I was back within my second life – my Rose-induced nightmare resuming its hopefully righteous and rewarding path.

After Death, 1991 – Lilac Sky

The lilac sunlight streamed through the shop windows, making me squint. And there, sitting cross-legged on my desk, was Rose. As I quickly looked around the office, Mr Ball was on the phone, totally oblivious to me or what I was doing.

'It's okay, Ritchie, he won't be able to see me, and when I'm with you, your life to others runs a scene or two behind, so he certainly won't see us together!'

I opened my eyes as wide as humanly possible, aware that my totally drenched clothing was now bone dry, the heavy raindrops no longer dripping from my saturated hair into my weather-beaten eyes. I felt as though I had just been woken from an overwhelmingly lucid dream, finding it almost impossible to comprehend and accept that I had been removed from where I so desperately wanted to be. I lifted my hands and slapped myself as hard as I was able across both cheeks. Rose suddenly stood up, a little surprised by what I was doing. I rotated my neck muscles and then the bitter sting filled my face, rising steadily up into my eyes. I winced as a small tear crept out of my left eye.

'Do you feel better for that, Ritchie?'

I didn't answer, because I wasn't sure what I was feeling. Rose was standing just a few inches away from me. I wanted to touch her. She stood totally still, not saying a word. My eyes are focused on Rose's knees, her perfect little feet. I push my hand forward, stopping just millimetres away from her left kneecap. Rose's eyes are watching me intently, but I don't look up – I can't. My fingers push forward, my breath drops a little, my nails make contact first, but then I turn my hand downwards and gently run my knuckles against her knobbly little knee – her flesh is *so* cold and disconcerting. Rose crossly kicks my arm away.

'Oh God, Ritchie, not *this* again! Yes I'm cold to the touch, but just like…A fridge, *yes* a fridge, cold inside, but warm on the outside, *whereas,* I am warm inside, *cold* on the outside…'

I cannot help but smile and I am convinced I have blushed ever so slightly.

'I'm real. We've hugged, wrestled, and I come and see you when you need me! Just believe in me, please!'

I push my office chair back, my little friend standing before me, stern and real. Our eyes meet and I swallow hard.

'Rose, I'm sorry, it's just that, well, I was *here,* and then I just, well, I started to reflect on my past and suddenly I was *there,* totally reliving …well, living it for real, not remotely aware of any of this madness!'

Rose sat down again, beckoning me to hold her hands.

'Do you think about the past, Ritchie, where and how you went wrong? We want you to reflect!'

My eyes are suddenly rolling, intense lilac lightning blurring my thoughts, and then blue dots, sharp and piercing…

Before Death, 1991 – Blue Sky
Soaked to the skin, my suit just a heavy wet rag, I finally got to Skirdle and Sons and slipped down the side of the shop to where my trusty, rusty pickup was parked. As I unlocked the door and climbed in, I couldn't believe how pleased I was to be back in it. As I turned the key, 'That's better…' blasted out and I sighed, before steadily and gratefully making my way home.

Later that night, once I'd had my *cold* bath, I felt confident that I had put all negative thoughts behind me. I simply couldn't wait any longer to see Yasmin, so I made my way to the pub. As I pulled into the car park, the butterflies in my stomach were rampant – for Yasmin or for Jack? The answer was unclear. But as I turned off the engine, I felt relieved that I hadn't made a grand entrance by arriving in the Porsche. I made my way steadily towards the door – a few hardy customers were braving the elements outside, the odd smile and wave easing my nerves a little. As I stepped into the lounge area, I could hear my heart pounding almost in unison with the throbbing of my damaged hand. I was relieved to see Scottie waiting by the one-armed bandit, and as I joined him, I was greeted with a smile and an ice-cold pint.

'Cheers, Angel my old friend. Here's to the *devil!*'

I shook my head discouragingly and Scottie seemed to get the message as I discreetly nodded towards the man himself, sat deep in thought by the inglenook fireplace. My heart was in my mouth, and though determined to look anywhere but at the devil, I finally braved a second subtle glance.

Jack, but no Julie?

I then lost my nerve and looked away. But as the evening wore on and the alcohol eased the nerves, my breathing finally seemed to resemble that of a calm and confident man. Jack threw me the odd look, but nothing more, and of course why would he? After all, his work was done. He just needed me to play my part and make him loads more money. I glanced at the pub clock for the hundredth time, but the single chime as it struck nine was a modest fanfare as in walked Yasmin. Suddenly, the butterflies were active again. Now these butterflies I loved – they were far softer, warm, feather-light, fluttering, resulting in a light-headedness – whereas I despised my reaction to Jack – steel-winged bats, bold and abrasive, razor-blade teeth and claws, with a nauseous side effect. Zoe and Janey spotted us both first and blew a kiss as they made their way to the bar. Every few seconds Yasmin would look at me, exaggerate a *looking me up and down* motion, beam her incredible smile and turn away. And though I longed to be with her, hear her voice, answer her questions, just watch her breathe, I felt contented knowing that she was here, and if I could steal just one kiss and feel the warmth of her hands on mine, then I would go home a contented and eternally patient man.

The girls were in good spirits as the barman brought over a third bottle of wine. Their decibel level suddenly leapt off the scale as they were joined by several loud and already drunken friends. Scottie's eyes seemed to light up every time Janey laughed or threw a comment our way.

'You know what, Ritchie? That Janey is absolutely gorgeous; totally out of her tree, though!'

And so that was it, Scottie moved in for the kill. Although Yasmin remained the loyal, tentative friend to the birthday girl, her subtle glances kept me going. Scottie was soon back at my side, *down but not out.*

'She definitely likes me, Ritchie, just that it's girls-only or something, some kind of ritual of theirs?'

I patted my wounded friend on the back and made my way to the bar. Within seconds Yasmin had pushed her stool back and was now at my side, her shoulder just a finger's width away from mine, but we didn't touch.

The barman boomed at me, 'Two more of the same, Ritchie?'

I shook my head and stepped back slightly, suddenly overacting...terribly.

'No, my good man, has to be ladies first!'

Yasmin laughed, giving an impressive curtsy and subtle bow of the head.

'Oh thank you, kind sir. A bottle of your best chilled champagne please, barman!'

Jeff, the pub landlord, smiled.

'Okay, gorgeous, I'll bring it over to you and your rabble!'

Yasmin put on a hurt and insulted expression before smiling and thanking him. She finally turned to face me, the noise in the room seeming to just drift away. I could feel her sweet breath on my face. My head started to spin as I took in the sensuous curve of her lips, their rich natural flush drawing me in. I am so lost in the moment that I think I will never move again. My eyes instinctively close as I feel Yasmin's hand on the back of my neck. Finally, I'm overwhelmed as her lips are now passionately on mine. I'm floating, a spiritual glow surrounding me, until Yasmin eases away, slowly and painfully, her hand dragging down the side of my face, her thumb removing any trace of lipstick that she may have left on my now abandoned lips. As I step back, breathless, weightless, I hear a rousing cheer easing me back into reality. Yasmin beams her parting smile and walks back to her friends.

I looked up to the ceiling, and for the first time in my life mouthed the words, 'There must be a God...Thank you, and I love you for this!'

As our romance blossomed, I had the beautiful moments mixed in with the downright soul-destroying ones. Jack got his Old School, and though he seemed happy with the result, it was obvious that it was only the beginning of his terrorising. And though I would keep it from Yasmin, she could see that some days I was a little distant, and it would break my heart when she took it personally.

'If you're going off me, Ritchie, then you've only got to say, I'm a big girl now!'

Each time I would simply take her in my arms. The warmth, the obvious infatuation was certainly mutual, and though words were probably not required, I would say them anyway.

'Yasmin, please, if I'm quiet sometimes it's just work, you know how it can be...'

She would give a radiant, relieved smile and then just kiss me passionately. And every time our lips met, I knew I was an addict, weak and unable to break the habit. I could never go through life, not even a single day, without her! But though she and I were incredible together, we'd not actually taken that final love-making step. With it being her first time, the moment had to be right. There was something in me that wanted her to instigate proceedings – though I would have to accept that her recent declaration of having booked a doctor's appointment to go on the pill – would have to be classed as Yasmin stepping into the *instigating proceedings* requirement! But I had never wanted her to feel even the slightest pressure – the moment, the location, I wanted it to be absolutely perfect. And even though I had my mum's house totally at our disposal, there was something a little cold about it, an aura of negativity no doubt stoked by the financial complications.

The solicitors had contacted me, promptly scolding me for not making an appointment to see them, and to further explain that my father had taken out a second mortgage – I was stunned by the news. And there was a chance that the house may be sold off against my will, something about the property never actually being in my mum's name, though I knew she had been paying the mortgage for years. When I contacted my father about the subject, he nervously explained that he hadn't meant to be deceitful, that he had got into a bit of trouble in Ibiza.

'They would have killed me, son. I had no choice but to take the money. Your mother would never have agreed, but seriously, it was a question of life or death. Ritchie, the guys were evil, I couldn't mess them about!'

There it was, another legacy of my morally corrupt father. So the house didn't seem like the secure, warm home that I craved. Yasmin would stay over, and it was painfully obvious that we were getting to the stage that she really did want us to take it further. But though I dreamt of the moment more than anything, there was no doubt in my mind that I had to come up with somewhere that we would remember forever.

I opened my eyes, easing into consciousness after the deepest sleep I'd had in weeks. I smiled to myself as I had that 'one in seven' feeling – knowing it was Sunday morning, no work, just play! I turned over and stared at the turquoise digits on my bedside clock – 10.10 a.m. beamed back. *Just as well it's Sunday!* I thought. I sat up quickly, easing my legs reluctantly out of bed, and sat there naked, gathering my thoughts. The room was cold and empty without Yasmin. I wondered how her night had gone. She had accompanied her mum to a distant relative's wedding down in Oxford somewhere, and it meant her staying the night. Although I had offered to go, we sensibly agreed that her mum would really appreciate a little quality time with her daughter. It had meant that Yasmin was away from me for one whole day and one very lonely night. But she had been staying over at mine for three, sometimes four nights a week, so it was the least we could do.

Once washed, I threw on a pair of clean jeans and struggled for something to do. I felt restless and strangely agitated. There was something a little different about today, a feeling deep down inside that was telling me certain things are meant to be. I paced round my bedroom, laughing to myself as I continued to act like a caged animal. The sun streamed in through the glass and I felt the need to open a window. I was grateful for the fresh air, and then took in the goings-on outside. I raised my hand to shade my eyes. A few doors down, Chris, was washing his TR7, and across the road Mr Hendrix was mowing his lawn, suburbia doing what suburbia does – but nothing more. I was just about to turn away when my eyes widened.

'Yes!'

I caught sight of a small pale-blue Ford Fiesta.

'My beautiful girl! Oh thank you, thank you, thankkk you!'

Yasmin's mum pulled up. She saw me looking and I quickly waved. But suddenly, my eyes were elsewhere. I watched in total awe as Yasmin stepped out of the car, looking as though she was just going to the wedding rather than returning. Her blonde hair was in ringlets and curls, a white satin ribbon twisted into a small plait at the back. Her simple, sexy, classy, floaty silk dress was clinging in all the right places, and she looked absolutely stunning. I couldn't believe that this girl was mine. Then, as she waved her mum off, she spotted me and beamed only as Yasmin can. She ran elegantly across the front lawn, and I ran down the stairs two at a time and tore the front door open. With the full force of a woman that had seriously missed me, I was pinned against the hallway wall. As I ran my hands over her beautiful body, tracing the outline of her expensive lingerie, I knew our time had come. Her soft, warm hands were caressing my back, and then easing herself away from me slightly she put her hands on my face, then lowered them slowly and massaged my chest and stomach.

Between each kiss, she murmured, 'I've missed you so much. Oh God! I've wanted you so badly, Ritchie Angel!'

I suddenly grabbed her arms, pushing her away from me, my face smiling at her. I tried to recapture my breath.

'Right, Yasmin, give me one minute to get my T-shirt. I've just the place. You'll probably think I'm mad, but trust me!'

Yasmin's initial disappointment was now taken over by eyes that oozed total unquestioning trust. We ran towards the pickup truck, both of us scrambling excitedly, unadvisedly through the driver's door. Through giggles and kisses, I finally had the engine running. The radio was playing 'Seasons in the Sun' by Terry Jacks. The words had originally drifted into my soul almost unnoticed, but this song had always been a painful reminder of Rose's death. Back then, the haunting lyrics and melody seemed to be at my every turn – on the television, the radio, in my mind. I took in the moment, sharing the intimacy though without explanation, but after thirty seconds or so I had no choice but to turn the radio off. Yasmin didn't question my solemn and glazed look, but simply slid back across the bench seat, snuggling up close, her hand gently caressing my thigh. And then, every few seconds, she planted a little kiss on my face.

I must be mad, kept repeating over and over in my mind. Taking her away from my house meant possibly killing the passionate mood I had found my beautiful girlfriend in. But I knew that this wasn't a moment of madness; the way we felt, it was here to stay. A few roads later, I pulled over to the side of the quiet lane and turned the engine off.

'Come on, gorgeous!'

As Yasmin slid out of the pickup, her dress rode up, exposing her flesh-coloured stocking tops, the white silk of her suspender belt glistening in the sunlight. She catches my eye and blushes. I quickly grab the large tartan picnic blanket from behind my seat, and then take her hand and run passed the bungalows, the gravel scrunching excitedly beneath our feet. My eyes light up as I spot the five bar gate, its decaying sign with its large red letters blazoned assertively 'KEEP OUT' I beam defiantly, *not a chance!* Nothing was going to come between us and my tranquil spot: the Water's Edge. We both stand in front of the gate, Yasmin looks at me, suddenly shaking her head from side to side, but laughing at the madness of it all. Without question, just continued trust, she takes my hand and climbs warily over the gate and drops down into the long grass on the other side. Within a moment I am at her side. Her hands are suddenly on my face again, her soft warm lips falling onto mine.

'Not yet, Yasmin, this way!'

I grab her hand and lead her off into the trees, the sound of our feet thumping softly on the dry ground as we head towards the clearing in the distance. I look up as we run, the sun glittering through the branches. And though a little cooler in the shade, once we step out into the open space beside the canal the sun hits us both, its warmth making everything so incredibly perfect. The wild flowers around us fill the air with a potent and romantic musk, the sound of the canal, with the river just a stone's throw away, masking any distant noises. I throw down the tartan blanket. We stand two or three feet apart, our arms at our sides, and turn to look around at the perfect setting. The willow trees between us and the water, a circle of silver birch to protect us, total unspoilt privacy, and as our eyes meet again I don't remember moving my feet, but our bodies are suddenly brushing up against each other, our arms still motionless at our sides.

Then, very slowly, our hands and fingers are touching, entwining – a small electric spark with each tender caress. Yasmin's face lifts towards mine and she rubs her soft flushed cheek against my cheek, her lips brushing gently against my lips, and then a little more forcefully, her tongue falling onto my tongue, totally intoxicating me. My hands are caressing her back and then falling helplessly onto her bottom, gently at first, kneading and caressing, and then more passionately, as though trying to tear her in half. I can feel her suspender belt, taut from her bottom down onto her thigh, and gradually my hand is falling lower, caressing her legs through the thin silk of her dress. She is now pushing her hands onto my stomach, kneading me with the same intense passion that I am caressing her. My T-shirt is slowly being lifted up my body and then over my head, suddenly flung and causing us both to smile and release a small chuckle as the white cotton lands like a falling parachute onto a branch of the silver birch.

I step back a little and Yasmin proceeds to undo the small row of buttons on the front of her flimsy dress. As each button is released, her breasts are heaving as though desperate to burst free, and once all the buttons are undone, she pulls the top of her dress down to her waist. Although I've seen her body many times before, it's never looked as stunning or as breathtaking as it does now, tanned and so erotic, her white silk half-cut bra barely able to restrain the rapid rise and fall of her breasts. I step forward and place my totally privileged shaking hands onto her stomach. Then, savouring the moment, I ease the unwanted dress over her thighs and she steps out of it. I have never wanted this woman more than I do now as she stands confidently in front of me, and suddenly I cannot resist any longer. My hands are on her warm back, unhooking her bra, and as her breasts are set free, exposed to the sun and now perfect blue sky, I'm entranced in the moment, my heart in my head, my mind lost and ready to die for the cause.

The gentle breeze appears through the trees to sneak a look at Yasmin, the chatter of the babbling water cheering through the branches of the weeping willow. I shake my head from side to side. I kiss her face and lips, and then as the kisses fall onto her neck I feel as though I have the strength to take on the world. Nothing could stop us now. As my mouth and gentle fingers fall lower, I give her breasts my full attention, my hands falling from time to time onto her silk-clad bottom, nestling inside her stocking tops, and then just brushing my hand gently against the silk of her panties. Yasmin decides enough is enough and pushes me back onto the grass bank, and then her perfectly manicured fingers are unbuttoning my jeans and pulling them down, until they are finally off. The concentration and wanton lust on her face is a joy to behold. Running her hands up my legs, I simply cannot believe how beautiful this woman is, better with each passing day, her spellbinding long legs, her breasts brushing against me, it was just too much. I looked to the ground and saw her expensive silk dress lying abandoned and crumpled on the grass, and then a few feet away her bra simply tossed aside.

She stood up – she had me exactly where she wanted me, naked and at her mercy. She stood back, and then with all the confidence that a girl has when she knows she's ready, her eyes not leaving mine, she pushed her thumbs inside her panties and slid them down her endless legs. Finally and elegantly she stepped out of the flimsy garment and then this *real* blonde, able to see that I was *so* incredibly ready for her, stepped forward and crouched above me, her breasts inadvertently brushing against my face. While Yasmin steadily eased herself slowly, very gently against me, her kisses became softer, flicking across my lips and cheeks. I then guided myself towards her, and she instinctively lifted her body ever so slightly until I was resting against her soft moist curls. With only the slightest of fumbles, we were one.

Her mouth is wide open, her hands gripping just a little tighter, she held onto me as if her dear life depended on it. She started to bite her bottom lip, but then moved her body, gently, easing herself tentatively, making sure, and then gradually, as her body let me in, deeper and deeper, the pleasure for me became ... oh God! Indescribably potent, electric. Her eyes were tightly closed, her short sharp breaths gaining in momentum, and then suddenly, I was unable to let her take all the time in the world. As her sighs and moans grew and grew, I couldn't help but be overwhelmed by the simple incredible fact that I was with the one woman that I fully and completely loved, the girl that I had longed for since the very first moment I had set eyes on her, that I ... I ... I... And as I shuddered to an abrupt halt, my back arched and my body gripped onto Yasmin as though *my* life depended on it!

'Oh God, I'm so sorry, darling!' My words stopped Yasmin in her tracks.

She dropped her head and then smiled, running her hands across my face and then through my hair.

'Ritchie, oh God, that was wonderful! Oh God, you beautiful man!'

She then fell against me, our bodies a perfect fit. I lifted her head and smiled, followed by another apology.

'Yasmin, that was simply amazing for me, but, well, you were just too sexy. I know it wasn't ... well, perfect for you.'

She blushed for the second time today and then grabbed hold of my head, squashing me between her gorgeous breasts. As I was smothered by this wonderful creature, I felt that I could die totally fulfilled right here and now. But then as my ability to breathe diminished, I accepted fully that I *really* could die here! With reluctance to free myself, I pushed my head up and out of her wonderful new headlock.

I looked at her again and needlessly uttered, 'No, Yasmin, please believe me, this is only the start. I will make sure that it's so much better next time.'

We both lay for at least half an hour, the sun creating a cocoon that neither one of us wanted to leave. Finally, Yasmin sprang to her feet, stretching her arms up towards the now totally clear blue sky. She turned to me and shook her head from side to side, a beaming smile just visible through the mass of ringlets and curls that had escaped the confines of the satin ribbon. She started to rearrange herself while I just lay there, taking in a sight that I felt compelled to watch. Yasmin undressing would always take the gold, but Yasmin dressing as innocently but so incredibly seductively as she was right now would be a very close silver. As she searched for this and that, she appeared to be a very happy and contented girl, and in time, I looked forward to proving that our love-making would get even better with practice. I suddenly laughed. *In time? How the hell was I supposed to resist Yasmin as she appeared to me now, strutting around in her beautiful lingerie, straightening her stockings?*

I stood and walked up behind her. She leant back into my naked body, the silk of her panties and stockings sensuous against my bare flesh. I kissed the side of her face, my hands now placed gently onto her stomach, rising slowly until they cupped her naked breasts. She placed her hands on mine, my lips falling onto the nape of her neck. I turned her towards me, her breasts pushed firmly into my chest, our lips hungry and passionate. Finally, impatient and ready, I lay Yasmin down on the crumpled blanket. I suddenly have the urge to kiss her from head to toe until some undecipherable words tell me I'm needed. We become one, and the feeling is so powerful, so incredibly sensuous, that I could so easily lose control, but I steady myself and take my time. Slow ... slow ... Yasmin is pushing into me, wanting and demanding, arching her back. I push a little deeper, touching her fire. Slow, steady, pushing deeper. Our lips kiss and tease each other, and her back arches again, writhing, total trust, demanding. And as the sun spreads itself the length and breadth of my soul, steadily, urgently, overwhelmingly, we come together. Perfect and now forever cast.

It was a wonderful moment in our brief history together as we walked away from the Water's Edge. A sanctuary that never let me down; I felt an unrivalled peace here. And though I had never brought Yasmin here before, I had a feeling it was now going to be a very special place for her too.

As we made our way out of the woods, we both turned and looked down the slight embankment, the water barely visible in the distance.

Yasmin cuddled up to me and said, 'You know, Ritchie, this is a really beautiful spot. I would love to build a house here. Could you imagine, a sweeping driveway, beautiful cottage overlooking the water, and then our kids?'

She laughed out loud, a nervous look in her eyes suggesting that she had perhaps said too much, but I loved it. I felt so close to this girl: a house together, kids ... why not? I shared the very same dream! I felt wonderfully happy when I was with her, and though I didn't add anything to her comments, I lifted her face towards me and kissed her very gently. Although it would seem impossible for us to get any closer, from that day we seemed to take it to another level. My love life was perfect. And my business world started to throw open a few options. But unfortunately, Steve, my building company boss, finally lost patience with me.

'Ritchie, you'll be getting your cards this week! We're second best for you! I know that *bloody* estate agents is your number one priority, so go for it! You're there most days anyway, so now you may as well take it on full time!'

I was shocked when Steve had his outburst, but couldn't blame him. On the final day, we chatted and I tried to explain that I did have a few plans, and should I be able to use his skills in the future – either for myself or for Skirdle's – then I wouldn't hesitate. Though Steve didn't laugh in my face, there was a hurtful smirk in response to my words as if something amused him. Perhaps he thought I was getting a little too big for my boots. But I didn't bite – I just became even more determined to succeed.

Luckily for me, Mr Skirdle was prepared to make my job full time. He stated that I had never let him down, and with a glint in his eye and a positive shake of the head, he muttered under his breath that a little more time on the golf course would suit him just fine. Miss Black had been gone for more than three years now, and though we had all muddled through, it had been very much on Mr Skirdle's mind to offer me a full-time position anyway. Mr Skirdle's right-hand man, Mr Ball, had his hands full with his residential house sales, and so would need my help with the commercial side. As the summer sun became too much for some people, Mr Ball's inability to quash his true self meant that he dropped dangerously unaware into my *favours for a rainy day* box.

CHAPTER SEVEN

A Secret To Be Kept For A Rainy Day

Before Death, 1991 – Blue Sky
It all started one hot summer's afternoon. Mr Skirdle having returned from his vacation, had telephoned me from the golf club, asking me to get myself over to his house as he'd left some important documents there relating to the sale of the Old Bakery. He had stressed in no uncertain terms that it was crucially important that I got the sales details organised for when the owner called back at 5 p.m. that very evening. I drove across Willow heading for Mr Skirdle's beautiful home – the Old Rectory – which stood a cemetery away from the church. I looked down at Mr Skirdle's house keys and recalled my boss's words: 'Mrs Skirdle is at her art class, so let yourself in. You know where my office is!'

I had felt impressed that I was so trusted and obviously seen as a long-term part of any plans he had for the company. In fact, to mark my arrival as a full-time employee, I had been given a dark-blue Ford Escort – a couple of years old, but a little more in keeping with the company image. Mr Skirdle expressed the view that driving around in my battered truck was not in keeping with the professionalism that Willow's top estate agency aspired to. When told that I would get a company car, I had envisaged a flash Alfa Romeo or perhaps an Audi. So when the car was delivered by the local Ford dealer, I had felt a little deflated.

I remember taking it home for the first time and Yasmin had tactfully said, 'The staid conservative image isn't quite you,

Ritchie...' and that she loved my pickup. And so, come the weekends, that's what we would use.

As I made my way down the cobbled lane on which the Old Rectory stood, I turned steadily and respectfully through the high stone pillars. I stopped sharply, a little shocked to see not only Mrs Skirdle's car outside the house, but also Mr Ball's blue Ford Sierra. My suspicious thoughts were quickly replaced with the fact that maybe Mr Skirdle had asked Mr Ball to pick up the papers, forgetting that he had already asked me, or visa versa. I smiled to myself at my inane ramblings, but for whatever reason, I found myself quickly turning off the car engine. I waited and then stepped anxiously out of the car. I didn't really know what to do next, dismissing the obvious course of action, to simply walk up to the front door and knock. But hesitancy about what I might discover made me act in a suspicious and candid way. I trod carefully, keen not to be heard, and suddenly felt compelled to walk around the side of the Rectory and enter the property via the back gate. It had been a stifling day in Willow and I was convinced I could hear raised voices at the rear of the house, so I walked very quietly towards the back garden. As I got closer, I could hear the splashes of water and then laughter. Mr and Mrs Skirdle had a beautiful swimming pool, and it sounded as though someone was taking full advantage of it – and who could blame them on a hot day like today?

The noise level dropped and I felt a little uneasy as I approached the back garden, almost convincing myself that I should go back and knock on the front door rather than sneaking around like this. But then, as I poked my head around the timber conservatory, I got the shock of my life. There was Mr Skirdle's son, David – about twenty-two years of age – sitting astride Mr Ball, his tongue wedged down my colleague's throat. My eyes were out on stalks and I froze on the spot. Mr Ball was running his fingers through David's hair and stroking his back. And then to my full horror, it was regrettably obvious that neither of them had a stitch of clothing on. Although I wanted to turn and run, I was well aware that it was only due to their total preoccupation with each other that I hadn't been spotted already. But I really wish they *had* seen me, because it would have saved me from having to witness the next private and wince-inducing act. Mr Ball pushed David back onto the sunlounger and proceeded to touch him, intimately, slowly. My breath was now gone and I longed for the ground to swallow me up. Mr Ball started to move his hand up and down with increasing vigour. My eyes narrowed and I swallowed hard. I blinked repeatedly and found the strength to take my first discreet step backwards, praying furiously that I could leave undetected. Two steps back ... three steps... *Oh shit!*

Mr Ball's eyes met mine. I didn't know what to do. I found myself lifting my right arm, as though waving. Mr Ball had become stuck in time. David was fidgeting and momentarily unaware as to why his lover had appeared to take on the form of a statue. I then found myself nodding my head up and down, still retreating, *willing* myself invisible. My small backward steps having become strides, I was now out of sight. My heart was beating heavily in my ears – what an overwhelming embarrassment for the three of us. I hurriedly made my way to the car, my head filled quite unnecessarily with images of all I had just seen. Just as I'm a few feet away from the safety of my car, from inside of the house I can hear raised voices. Suddenly, the front door is flung open and out runs Mr Ball, his shorts now back where they belong.

'Ritchie! Ritchie! My God, Ritchie, please, it's really not what you think!'

My body instinctively turns to face Mr Ball. I attempt to pacify and gesticulate in several useless and ineffective ways, my pleading and ghost-like colleague short of breath and his heartfelt words seeing me drop my arms and now only able to listen.

'Look, Ritchie, his parents don't know he's gay! For God's sake! I didn't really know, well ... that I was, that I am! Please, Ritchie, my wife, my daughter!'

And as I took in the grey, drained man before me, I could see the depth of desperation in his face. My eyes were drawn towards the house and I could see through the large Georgian downstairs window David hovering from foot to foot, staring out at Mr Ball and me. I looked back at Mr Ball and shook my head from side to side, swallowing hard and searching for the right thing to say.

'Mr Ball, it's nothing to do with me. You're two adults. Look, I ... I've seen nothing. I've come over here to get some paperwork!'

I became momentarily mesmerised by how his chest was pounding, every beat igniting a ripple of panic in his desperate brown eyes. But my view was clear on all I had witnessed, and I was adamant – who was I to judge? I knew that Mr Skirdle would kill the pair of them stone dead – he was always making crude and snide comments about homosexuals and lesbians, and now his worst nightmare was to perhaps come and bite him full-on. But as I looked back into the house, David trying to hide deeper in the shadows, it was him that I felt sorry for – for having such a bigoted father, making it impossible for him to tell his parents who he really was.

'Look, Mr Ball, Mr Skirdle's desk in his office ... can you just grab the bakery file? It's maybe best if I don't go in there, David looks petrified!'

Mr Ball smiled – the relief on his face said it all – and as he thrust his hand into mine, shaking vigorously, my warped mind thought back to what he'd been doing with that very hand just a few short moments ago.

As he walked back into the house, my fraught nerves pushed out a relieved laugh. I leant against the car, shaking my head. I glanced up and took in the hyperactive activity of David and Mr Ball hurriedly searching for the file. Every few seconds Mr Ball would rub David's back, and in response David would nod, a tentative, partly reassuring smile breaking out. I giggled under my breath – sympathy mixed with a modicum of empathy for how these guys had connected, two grown men falling in love. After all, it must feel so totally alien to have your sexual inclinations construed as wrong, when to those two in there, their attraction to each other is as instinctive and as normal as my feelings and desire for Yasmin.

As I let out a huge breath and focus on the barely visible wisp of a cloud across the otherwise clear blue sky, I am aware of Mr Ball now within feet of me, bakery file in hand, his small paunch hanging over the top of his shorts.

'Look, Ritchie, David and I, we're both agreed, we owe you one!'

I smiled and got into my car, the windows down and Mr Ball unsure what else to say. Once the engine was started, we waited awkwardly and then my words were out.

'Don't worry, Mr Ball, when I first pulled up I thought you were here shagging Mrs Skirdle!'

Mr Ball burst out laughing. 'Oh my God, Ritchie Angel! You've got to be kidding me – she's at least fifty, twenty years older for God's sake! You're a sick man for thinking that, Ritchie!' And as he said the words, he screwed up his face and shuddered as though someone had just walked over his grave.

As I roared off down the drive and back out onto the road, I couldn't help but laugh uncontrollably.

Back at Skirdle's, I sat and studied the bakery file. Had I found an opportunity to rival my now defunct Old School deal? I kept reading over and over again, my brain digesting and magnifying a wide range of options. With each one I would chew the inside of my mouth, but then a smile would spread as I stroked my chin and shook my head.

Mmm, this could be amazing, Ritchie boy, but do you have the balls? The butterflies that had been a constant side effect of my school deal were back. The bakery stood just across the street from Skirdle's, and I had often thought about the possibilities for the site. I got up from my desk and wedged myself between the sales particular boards to get a better view. I kept glancing down at the notes Mr Skirdle had made. It had appeared to me that the old couple who owned it were deeply set in their ways, and I had presumed that they would end their days in the rickety old building. I scanned down the notes again and then flipped quickly to a highlighted section: Repairs and running costs – far too high. And another: The property has become a liability and was keeping them up at night with the worry. I shook my head again, my greedy eyes now fixed firmly on what I had decided was an absolute goldmine.

As I sat at my desk fidgeting with excitement, I reflected on my proposed scam for the Old School. *But would it be possible with the bakery?* I knew it could be done, but once bitten and all that. I nearly jumped out of my skin as the shop doorbell rang with the entry of a stranger.

'Err, is Mr Angel here?'

I sprang up and offered my hand.

'Yes, sir, I'm Angel, Ritchie Angel. Can I help you?'

The man's steely blue eyes looked a little concerned.

'You look very young, and ummm, you're dealing with my bakery sale, are you?'

I smiled, nodding politely at the old gentleman. I accepted, without feeling insulted, that perhaps someone this old and doddery would indeed feel that I was extremely young. But I offered the straight-talking man a chair and asked if he would care for a coffee.

'Ummm, no thank you, I've just come to find out what you think the old building will fetch, whether it's best to auction, or, as Mr Skirdle had suggested, have sealed bids. I don't know; what are your thoughts, Mr Angel?'

I scanned for the old guy's name on the bakery file.

'Well, err … Mr Christian, it's, well, it's a difficult one. Auctions can be precarious things, sometimes expensive to organise and then not always a sure-fire way of getting you the best price.'

Mr Christian watched me intently, studying my every move, almost as though he was scraping back the layers of my character. I was unusually sweaty, my neck wriggling uncomfortably within my shirt collar. I laughed unexpectedly from the pit of my stomach as the word *guilt* fluttered through me. I coughed nervously, but knew that I needed to get a grip. I started to nod my head, as though studiously absorbing the figures in front of me, but in truth I was stalling for time.

'Right … mmmm, okayyyy. Are you sure, Mr Christian, I can't get you that coffee?'

He scowled at me, squinting but not uttering a word. I smiled awkwardly, biting the inside of my cheek to a depth that was going to leave a painful reminder for days to come. Then the words started to flow.

'Mr Christian, there are two problems that we have here, the first being that this building is old, very old, and secondly, perhaps not as safe as it should be! Therefore, it will scare off certain would-be purchasers, but, and this is a real concern for me, the age of the property could mean that the local council will want to step in and try to make it a listed building! There are certain features that could indeed warrant that reaction from the council!'

Mr Christian took off his glasses, rolled his eyes and leant forward a little.

'Mr Angel, are you saying I may well be lumbered with this white elephant? Are you telling me that I would have to spend money, money I have to say I simply don't have, to try to restore the bakery?'

I nodded and opened up my hands to confirm.

'For God's sake, man, I came in here wanting to sell the bloody place, make enough money to buy a small bungalow for my lady wife and I. Are you saying that I may well end up living in a ramshackle caravan somewhere?'

I dropped my hands and smiled meekly as Mr Christian clumsily slipped his glasses back on, his face suddenly turning purple. Then he caught me by surprise as he brought his fist down hammer like onto the table.

'*Well, Mr Angel...*'

My eyes widened in response, and I decided that I had thrown in enough scare tactics, and hand and facial expressions, and that calming words were now needed.

'Mr Christian, I can see you're concerned, but there *is* a way, if we tread carefully and if you put your trust in me. I can make a few discreet enquiries with a couple of also discreet developers, and see if they're prepared to make some sort of offer on the building, get some feedback and then perhaps opt for the sealed bid option. Keep it hush-hush, low profile, away from the interfering council. Try to raise enough money for that bungalow, eh, for you and your good lady wife!'

I cringed with every word, but there it was, I had set the ball rolling. I was aware that my breathing had stopped and I was now desperate to see whether Mr Christian was about to take the bait. I waited for his reaction, but he didn't move. I took a small breath and continued to wait. My eyes seem to freeze on the silent and still man before me, and then I imagined him slamming his fist down on the desk again. I swallow hard, and then some movement.

Mr Christian turned and looked over his shoulder, then back at me, shuffling forward to get as close as he could.

Then, almost in a whisper, he said, 'Okay, Angel, but all I ask is this, more for my wife than me. She loves the bakery, she was girl and woman there, and she wants it to go to good people, someone who can restore her to her original state. If you can do that for Mrs Christian and I, and get us that bungalow, then do what you've got to do. I'll look after you.'

And with that, Mr Christian was on his feet, a smile and a nod confirming that I most certainly had my green light on the deal. I swallowed hard, unable to get a word out, but stood up clumsily as Mr Christian was now heading towards the door. Within three strides I was behind him. He turned around and we shook hands. Then unprepared words were spilling out of me.

'Ummm, okay, look, Mr Christian, I … I think it best that I come and see you at the flat for any further meetings that we may need. I take it from your file that's where you're living, above the bakery?'

Mr Christian tapped the side of his nose, followed by a wink and a nod, and then he was gone, the satisfying ring of the doorbell marking his hasty exit. I stood, my arms dropped to my sides, and then the largest beam spread itself across my face. And though I don't recall my legs moving, I was suddenly sitting at my desk, mulling over the facts and the fiction of all I was about to take on. I realised and was grateful for the fact that Mr Christian wasn't quite as tough as he would like to make out, but as a consequence it did make me feel very guilty about what I was planning to do. But I convinced myself that as long as he got his retirement bungalow, then surely everyone would be happy. I prayed that I was right about the bakery and its potential. But the truth and the basis of this whole *crazy* idea had been spawned by one rogue enquiry just over a month ago, and though I wasn't able to offer anything suitable at the time, I was about to gamble my future on believing that I did now. I needed to be quick; timing would be crucial. As I closed my eyes to the pitfalls and hurdles ahead, I told myself that fortune favours the brave.

The next few days passed by smoothly, though not before

one vital ingredient had been realised. The sweat had oozed out of me as I waited for confirmation that my original enquirer had yet to secure their site. Having delved as deep as was legal, I discovered that my man was the main representative for an American fast-food chain determined to work their way into every town and city in Europe. Although they were very much in the early stages of world domination, I was left in no doubt that I was dealing with a major force. I provided every requested detail – the size, age, colour and fabric of the building, infrastructure and suitable access points – and endeavoured subtly to convince them that this was a prime sought-after spot on Willow High Street. I had them interested, but refused to reveal the exact building. I asked them for four weeks to cajole the potential seller, but pretty much put my reputation on the line with a few blatant lies.

They assured me that they would give me the time I had asked for, but stated firmly, 'No problem, Mr Angel, but of course you understand, should we secure an *alternative* site in the meantime, no hard feelings?'

I swallowed hard and turned a shade of puce that was not becoming. Each and every phone call would see me sweat and wriggle with just about the right amount of stress to keep me on my toes. Though I had failed miserably in obtaining a budget ballpark figure from our American gentleman, finally, in my last telephone conversation, he uttered the magical words that I was convinced had reduced me to purring down the phone.

'Money is not the issue for us, Mr Angel. Get us the site we need, and we'll pay the money!'

It was indeed music to my ears, and I was convinced I could hear a chant or two of gospel deep down in the pit of my stomach.

As I lay in bed that night, Yasmin's head resting on my chest, I daydreamed vividly about making a success of the bakery deal and the obscene amount of hard cash it would bring. I had quickly grasped that the company were looking to knock down any building that failed to fulfil their detailed wish list, and that of course was going to upset the Christian's. But as I pictured the scene, I knew that I would have to plead ignorance, convince them that I had no idea, and that I was equally as sorry and disappointed to lose such a beautiful old building as they were. But as I lay in the darkness, I wrestled with a more immediate problem. I could raise sufficient funds through my bank to buy the bakery, but I had to be sure that the purchase wasn't linked to me. As I felt Yasmin stir, her hand sliding from my stomach to just a little lower, all thoughts of business strangely evaporated.

Morning came round far too soon, the ugly and unnecessary banging of the alarm clock leaving me nauseous in its wake. Yasmin, as though feeling my pain, moved across me, finally turning the alarm off, before resting the majority of her body across my chest.

'Ritchie, can't you stay at home today? I've not got my interview until two.'

I said nothing, but allowed the small kisses that she was inflicting on my closed eyelids. As her lips began their downward trail, a spark of responsibility to my business needs strained to muster sufficient strength to get myself motivated and out of bed. Finally, though, and against the run of play, my eyes still closed, I was sitting side-on, my feet on the floor, my mind suddenly on Yasmin's interview for the job at a children's nursery. She wasn't yet fully qualified, but surely when you look as good as she does, who cares? *The kids will love her, and they'd be crazy not to employ her*. I laughed at my well thought-out theory, but then aware of Yasmin's naked legs wrapped around me, I was weakening, but once I had made my mind up, I was not for turning.

'Yasmin, you stay and have a lie-in. You know how busy things are at work, and though I would *love* to stay, I've simply *got* to go in!'

With a rearranging of limbs and a sudden rising off the mattress, I stood and stretched, my eyes reluctantly easing open…and there she was standing in front of me.

Be strong, Ritchie…

The words repeated determinedly in my head. But then her sun-kissed hair tumbled seductively over her exposed breasts, the thin white cotton sheet draped immodestly around the top of her thighs, and I knew that, despite my stern stance, I was going to be delayed in getting to work today.

As I roared into the estate agent's car park, forty minutes late, I knew Mr Skirdle was not going to be pleased. But as I raced through the door, my boss was being handed a cup of coffee by Mr Ball.

Mr Skirdle smiled at me, while Mr Ball simply said, 'Did you manage to check out number fifty-two Corporation Street for me, Ritchie?'

A subtle wink followed, and I simply nodded my head and uttered, 'Errrr, yes ... yes, all seems in order.'

And that was that – my back had been covered. I was barely at my desk, though, when the shop door was pushed open and in toddled a beautiful little dark-haired girl. My eyes were instinctively transfixed, and then I saw, standing sheepishly behind her, Julie Andrews. Mr Ball stepped efficiently between us, offering assistance.

'Oh, it's Ritchie I've come to see.'

She then asked if she could perhaps have a word, her eyes fixed firmly on mine. I stood up, my legs a little shaky as I made my way over to my unexpected visitor.

'Could we speak in private, Ritchie? Perhaps we could take a walk...'

Julie then looked past me and fixed her stare on Mr Skirdle.

'Would you mind if I borrowed Ritchie for a few minutes? It's just that it's quite important.'

Mr Skirdle simply nodded, taking a sip from his coffee cup. Mr Ball just smiled at Julie, and then gave me an even bigger smile. As we left the shop, Julie apologised for bothering me, but she had something important to say and it couldn't wait a moment longer.

Instead of heading up the high street, we turned left and walked off towards the park. Julie mumbled something about the weather briefly, but then opted for the straight-to-the-point approach.

'You haven't really met Lillie before, have you, Ritchie?'

I smiled down at the small child, a little unsure how much

fuss I should make.

'Ritchie, Jack's asked me to marry him. He's asked me before, the day I came to see you at the graveyard actually! But I felt I couldn't really give him an answer then.'

Julie crouched down and pointed out the swings to her daughter, which were bathed in sunlight, colourful and bright in the centre of the park. Without hesitation, Lillie ran excitedly towards them. Julie's eyes were suddenly on mine. I held her gaze for just a moment before losing my nerve and taking the easier option of watching Lillie as she made her way towards the play area. Julie was now standing, her back towards me.

'Ritchie, look, I thought ... well, although you sent me away, not wanting to acknowledge Lillie, that maybe in time you would come around, but you haven't called or anything, so I'm tempted to say yes...'

She turned to face me and I pathetically looked at the ground. Within a couple of short hesitant breaths, our feet seemed to instinctively move forward, and the remainder of the journey was carried out in silence. Finally, we reached a bench facing the pond and the ducks, which seemed to instantly multiply as we sat down.

'Ritchie, do you believe me about Lillie? She's yours, you've only got to look at her. She has my dark hair, but her face ... you must see it, she's ... *so you!*'

I watched as a drake crash-landed onto the pond, waterskiing like a novice and then clumsily gambolling up the small shale beach. Lillie was now standing before me, her eyes on mine. I eased a smile and she beamed graciously back at me. I felt an overwhelming wave of pain filter through me, cutting and jagged. I swallowed hard as I absorbed the small, sweet, adorable creature whom I was aching to hold, but I had to look away. My brain and heart seemed to fuse, my mind repeating over and over again, *she looks just like me, she looks just like me...* But a black streak of immaturity, devoid of vision for what was right and wrong, eclipsed all. My mind started to race and chastise me.

No, Ritchie! This would spoil everything, Yasmin, your career, and, oh mother of God, the devil himself! Good old

Jack De'Vil! He's going to love this, isn't he?

I closed my eyes tightly and leant forward, dropping my elbows onto my knees and resting my face onto my open hands. I took a long drawn-out breath. I was aware of Julie telling her daughter to make the most of another five minutes.

'Go on, Lillie, Mummy will come and get you when I've finished talking.'

My silence was pitiful, but the time had come for me to explain how I felt.

'Julie, Jack thinks Lillie is his; it would break his heart! You've been with him over three years now, I mean, how old is Lillie?'

Unnerved and painfully unsure, I stood up, took a few left and right contradictory steps, and then turned and attempted to look Julie in the eyes. She didn't look up. Round-shouldered and depleted, Julie focused on the twisting and turning of her hands in her lap.

'She's two and a half, Ritchie. Surely we can't all keep living with this huge lie...'

Her eyes were now on mine, a small tear ready to drop.

'Ritchie, don't you think I haven't gone over and over this at least a dozen times a day? Don't you think I haven't thought about how this could break Jack? But what right do I have to mislead Lillie? You've only got to say that you want to get to know her, get to know me! I mean, you never know, we could end up ... well, you know, for Lillie's sake, being with her real father...'

But I couldn't give Julie the answer she wanted. I sighed as I took in Lillie, now running around on the grass as though riding an imaginary horse or something, but what I did know, despite my absence in her young life, she appeared to be a perfectly happy and contented child. I swallowed hard, my throat sore.

'She's very beautiful, Julie, but...'

I was too selfish, and none of this fitted into my plans.

'You have to forget me in all this, Julie. I've told you before, your life, your child.'

And as I said it, my heart was screaming for me to stop, but I just kept going.

'Marry Jack, you're good together! Promise me, for God's sake, don't ever tell him about the three of us, because I really do think he would kill me, and then you! Just marry him, Julie.'

I wanted to drop to my knees, take her hands and beg her to see sense. I wanted Julie and Lillie to wander off into the sunset, to forget all about me and live happily ever after. My head dropped. I knew I was despicable and inhumane. I didn't know this side of me – my mother would turn in her grave.

'Julie, please look at me...'

I was now on my knees, my hands resting on hers.

'Julie, make it easier for everyone, keep the secret, marry Jack. He loves Lillie, he loves you! You'll want for nothing! Come on, how bad can that be?'

Julie's face was dripping with tears – she looked broken and empty. But how could I change all this without compromising all that I held so dear and precious? I was deeply in love with someone else. And as for Jack, I knew he would do everything in his power to break me – I was convinced that he would only feel fully compensated once he had put me six feet under. I stood up sharply, suddenly hot and uncomfortable at the mere thought of all this becoming public knowledge. I ran my fingers through my hair, my eyes briefly drawn to the sight of Lillie still running around, seemingly oblivious to all the heartache going on at the park bench.

I took a deep breath and turned to face Julie, having produced a crumpled tissue from my jacket pocket. As I stood there, limp-wristed, tissue hanging loosely, it summed me up – it was all I had to offer. And from the corner of my eye I noticed that Lillie had stopped playing. As the three of us stood, each looking at the other in the vastness of the park, I felt as though I was flatlining, my heart and soul hovering intermittently above demise. A flash of conscience flickered *neon-like* across my staring and still eyes: judgment day, when I would pay dearly for this. But I simply allowed the inevitable regret climb onto my pathetic, cowardly, slumped shoulders.

Julie, finally and reluctantly, took the tissue off me before gently dabbing her eyes. She was a beautiful girl, and Jack was a very lucky man. Lillie was suddenly comforting Julie, her petite delicate fingers stroking her mummy's hair. I smiled down at her, her large eyes taking me in, and then came the word that I imagined would haunt me forever.

'*Daddy...?*'

And whether I realised fully just how *deep* a simple word...a misguided question could cut into my iceberg heart, I felt a change pass through me that would mean I would never be quite the same person again. I blinked away any chance of a self-pitying tear and shook my head.

'No, darling, I'm not your Daddy...'

I walked away from them both.

For a while, the guilt tainted my every thought. But shameful self-preservation convinced me to forget them both and get on with my life. And as hateful and despicable as that would be, that is exactly what I did.

My mind firmly back onto business matters, I spoke to my accountant and organised a limited company. I laughed as I picked one out: Sky-Fly Ltd. I chose the name out of hundreds listed – all the titles were strange, but this one seemed to fit: sky's the limit, Angel flying high, that sort of thing. Then came the crucially important call to my bank manager. I exchanged pleasantries as far as was possible with Mr Tremble before finally getting to the only point he was remotely interested in. I explained that I was still looking to borrow an amount similar to before, the exact details of the building to follow.

'Change of building, Mr Angel? Okay, well, subject to a standard survey, that should be fine. Get your solicitor to contact us and we'll operate as originally agreed. Good day, Mr Angel.'

And as the phone went down, I couldn't resist uttering under my breath, 'Pompous git!' But the truth was, I loved him and every wonderful thing about him and his generous and trusting bank. All the relevant pieces were slowly falling into place, and this time, my mouth was firmly shut.

It was ten to seven in the evening as I climbed up the creaky wooden stairs at the back of the bakery. I tapped my knuckles rhythmically on the dishevelled door, the flaking green paint showering like confetti.

'Mr Angel, do come in, lad!'

I inched my way into the flat. Mr Christian's arms were on my shoulders and he seemed unable to get me through the door quick enough.

'Did anyone see you come here, Mr Angel?'

I shook my head in slight amusement, before adding, 'Ummm...No, no one saw me come here, oh, and call me Ritchie!'

Mrs Christian stood up – a silver-haired lady, petite and elegant. Despite the look of the bakery from the outside, the inside of the flat was immaculate, albeit crammed full of antiques, family portraits and photographs of school, graduation days and a rugby team. I stooped down.

'Surely that's not you, is it, Mr Christian?'

'Of course it is, Ritchie. I was one hell of a player. Number seven. You should have seen me go in those days, lad, I would have eaten you for breakfast!'

And as I looked at the smiling triumphant guys, the large silver cup held aloft, I didn't doubt his words for a second. Mrs Christian asked me to pass her the photo.

'Yes, Ritchie, those were good days. I remember watching Harry play his rugby; he didn't know that I had my eye on him then, but when he'd get onto that pitch, looking so dashing in his claret shirt, well, I think I knew straight away that I was going to marry him!'

And after a couple of cups of tea and a full re-enactment of many a story from their well-lived past, our meeting drew to a close. And just as I was about to leave, I assured them that the sale of their home was in good hands, and in return I received a heartfelt hug from Alice, with Harry looking uncomfortably on – but I was suitably assured that I had the blessing of them both. Although I knew I was going to be conning them out of possibly a lot of money, I conveniently convinced myself that the pair of them wished only for the retirement bungalow they had both dreamed about for so long, and I could make that happen.

As I skulked away from the Old Bakery and found myself in darkness at my desk back at Skirdle's, I chuckled as I recalled

Harry repeating several times that Alice was getting painfully breathless climbing the steep stairs up to the bakery, only for Alice to state on his final mention, 'I can still get up there quicker than you, Harry Christian. It takes you an hour and a stiff brandy to recover!'

I was burning the midnight oil, scouring the bungalows for sale that we had on our books. There was one in particular that stood out. It wasn't large, but it looked in good condition, and it overlooked the school fields.

Twenty-one thousand pounds! I stopped and stared. *Mmmm, would they go for that?* I was transfixed by the bungalow and all it meant, and suddenly my mind was racing. *If I were to give them twenty-five thousand pounds, then surely they'd be chuffed to bits.* I felt nervous, but very excited. I had originally intended to pay at least fifty thousand for the bakery, but I was now beginning to realise that I may have fallen on a better deal than I had first thought.

Five days later, I was climbing the creaky wooden staircase again. I rapped my signature knock on the increasingly fading paintwork, and then, just as before, was ushered frantically in by a little more animated than usual Harry.

'Well, Ritchie, you said that you had some fairly good news. Come on, lad, out with it!'

I nodded my head before removing my coat and opening my briefcase.

'Okay, Harry, Alice, how lucky are you feeling today?'

Alice nodded excitedly. I handed them each a set of details to the bungalow I had provisionally lined up for them.

'What do you think of that for your little retirement bungalow?'

I felt nervous as I watched them both intently. Alice peered over the top of her silver-rimmed glasses, straining, and then gave a whoop of delight that took me pleasantly by surprise. Harry kept staring at the photo on the front of the sales particulars, studious, still and giving nothing away. I swallowed hard, feeling a twinge of grating dryness as the suspense grew. Alice and I were both staring at him now. He then started to nod his head.

'Mmmm, okay then, Ritchie, do you have the envelopes with the offers in? You said we'd had a couple of offers.'

I rubbed my hands together and took a deep breath.

'Yes, Harry, of course, you're quite right. Perhaps I'm getting ahead of myself, showing you the details of the bungalow before we've even seen the offers!'

Harry was now standing behind Alice. I exaggerated the gathering of the envelopes and placed them on the coffee table. Three envelopes, each one different: two typed and one flamboyantly handwritten. Alice took hold of her husband's hands that were now resting on her shoulders.

'Do you want me to do the honours, Harry?'

They both nodded. I took Mr Skirdle's letter-opening knife and inserted it accordingly. I was surprised that my hands were shaking as I placed the knife down and pulled out the first piece of headed paper.

Without uttering a word, I scanned the information and then said, 'Okay, having inspected the above-named premises in detail, ummm, we feel that the renovation costs would perhaps be twice as much as our offer to purchase. Our offer is therefore twenty thousand pounds!'

My eyes did not leave the words on the paper, but I was aware of the synchronised sighs and the wind being knocked out of their sails. I was aware of movement from Harry, my eyes now on him as he looked at the floor and then cursed.

'God damn it! Okay, get the others open, Ritchie lad! Spare me the jargon, I just want the bottom line.'

I nodded and clenched my lips together tightly. I opened the next envelope, scanning again quickly.

'Oh, Mr and Mrs Christian, this one's a little better – twenty-five thousand pounds!'

The couple suddenly smiled and Alice excitedly squealed, 'Oh, Harry, at least we'd get our bungalow, and I know we'd hoped to be able to travel to see the kids in Australia, but we can't have everything.'

I swallowed hard, almost choking on a huge chunk of guilt.

'Hang on, Alice,' Harry offered hopefully, placing his hand firmly on her shaking hands, 'there's still one more to go!'

I went through the motions and tore calmly at the final

envelope, the knife now redundant on the coffee table. Without even glancing at the contents, I handed the letter directly to Harry. Harry pushed his finger onto the bridge of his glasses and studied what I already knew.

His head moved steadily from left to right, and then again until finally, he said, 'Well, bugger me! We might just get that trip to *Oz* after all, Alice love. *Twenty-eight thousand pounds!*'

Alice was out of her chair, and then came a burst of energy that I doubted I would ever see from these two – hugging, jumping, whooping and kissing, and then suddenly pulling me towards them, Harry struggling to get his words out.

'Ritchie lad, you're a bloody marvel! We're so grateful! I owe you one, lad. Alice, we're shot of the place!'

I was barely able to look them both in the eyes for more than a split second, but they had achieved their dream, so maybe I was berating myself unnecessarily. Alice peered over the top of her glasses with a look of concern.

'You okay, Ritchie?'

I shook my head. 'Fine, Alice, just fine!'

Harry had grabbed a bottle of sherry and was turning full circle with it above his head.

'So, Ritchie lad, what's the procedure now? How long until we get into the bungalow?'

I pondered as Harry poured the sherry into the crystal glasses.

'Mmmm, within perhaps four weeks? Hopefully less. I'll do everything in my power to speed things along!'

And once I had drunk my celebratory sherry, a shiver tracing its journey the length of my spine, I made my excuses and left. As the Christians' door closed firmly behind me, I was grateful to have got such a crucial part of my plan over and done with. I felt great, and knew that I had a smile as broad as my wallet was going to be – I cringed at the analogy. But as I disappeared into the night, any guilt was cancelled out by the fact that we were all going to get what we wanted. And I pacified myself even further as I hung on firmly to the thought that I couldn't be all that bad, as I could have got away with twenty-three or so thousand for the place, but instead I cranked it up to twenty-eight. So anything other than the positive was conveniently blocked out – I had had practice at that, and was getting quite good at it.

I was now in my pickup truck, sitting alone and content under the cover of darkness. I dwelt on the huge step forward I had taken today: *Well done, Ritchie boy, a good day's work!* And with that, my smile filtered through me and I was ready for a worthy celebration, but felt it wise to head for the safety of home. As my business head subsided and my social side eased into gear, I felt a flicker of disappointment as I remembered that Yasmin was having a quiet night in with her mum, which she tried to do at least once a week.

I stopped the pickup at the top of the high street and mulled over my options. And there it was, decision made – *one drink's not going to hurt, haven't seen the crowd in ages...* So that was that, I was going to the Whippet's. I turned the music up for Journey's 'Who's Crying Now', increasing my need for the love of my life. I questioned whether I should ask her to cut her night short and join me, but decided it would be wrong. I knew that her mum was desperate to hear all about her only daughter's new job at the nursery – Yasmin was loving working with the young children and had settled in superbly.

As I pulled into the pub car park, my heartbeat quickened as I spotted Jack De'Vil's car, and instinct stopped me from turning off the engine. I drummed my fingers nervously on the top of the steering wheel and thought about how I'd shouted my big mouth off last time, fatally wrecking my Old School plans. But then – as though a sign to get a grip – Scottie pulled up beside me, his cheesy grin and a thumbs-up meaning it was too late, I was going in.

Once inside, it appeared that the *devil* had taken over the pub. Julie was sitting surrounded by family and friends, while Jack was standing on a chair urging the barman to turn the music off. Scottie and I made our way over to Jimmy and Sally. As we sat down, Leoni suddenly joined us, placing down a tray of drinks.

'If it isn't our long-lost friend Ritchie Angel. How are you, stranger? Saw you pull up, so I got you one in!' She beamed, planting a large kiss on my cheek.

I responded by playfully ruffling her hair, which she always hated. I then felt a kick to my leg as Jack De'Vil shouted angrily towards our table.

'Excuse me, Angel, shut it!'

I just looked back at him and smiled; he shook his head and turned away.

Then, standing on his podium, he raised his glass and stated proudly, 'I would like to make an announcement. The beautiful Julie Andrews has today finally agreed to become my wife! She and my equally beautiful little daughter, Lillie, are going to become officially *Julie and Lillie De'Vil!*'

Ninety-nine per cent of the pub cheered. I finally met the gaze of Julie, who had been watching me, waiting for a reaction. But as I let out a relieved and grateful smile, she glared and looked away. I lifted my glass along with everybody else, but my heart wasn't in it. And then the sight of Julie being grabbed by her husband-to-be and their passionate embrace saw me down the contents of my drink, emptied completely into my numb and confused body.

The evening proceeded in a surreal haze. Jack ended up on the tables singing his heart out, swearing his undying love for Julie, and so for once I was not his *muse* for entertainment. And though I was waiting for the wit of the man to fly my way, instead I was able to catch up with all the latest gossip and goings-on with my good friends, but increasingly aware that I should quit while ahead. A moment of instinct told me it was time to say my goodbyes and make a wise and unscathed retreat. The cold air hit me hard as I stepped out into the car park, but a deep sigh of relief passed through me as I headed for the safety of my pickup. I smiled as I pictured the *devil* loud and proud, singing his heart out back in the pub. And then, just as I was about to duck my head to climb in, I felt the full force of a shove between the shoulder blades, propelling me sharply forward. I whacked my chin on the edge of the Toyota roof and quickly swung round, seething with anger and ready to face my attacker.

There was Jack, a big grin on his face.

'Going to congratulate me then, Angel?'

Amidst the stars and the thumping pain, I said nothing. But instead of shaking with fear, I was ready to take him on. I didn't care about any of the blows he could rain on me, as long as I landed a couple myself to inflict any possible pain he was due. Then the moment had come, but the warning bells were going off mentally and physically, and so instead I stood, not uttering a word. Jack just stared at me, amusement in his black eyes. I lifted my hand and ran it over my throbbing chin, noticing that he'd cut me badly. My contempt for him was immense, my belief, my wilting self esteem convinced: that I was powerless against him.

'Hey, Angel, any good deals that I should know about? If I find that you're keeping anything from me, you know I'll come and find you. In fact, Ritchie boy...' Jack was now right in front of me, his breath pungent and his rabid saliva finding its way onto my non-responsive face. 'Be under no illusion, *Angel fuck,* I know that you wouldn't be so stupid as to keep anything from me, as I will come and find you!'

My eyes were flickering in response to the venom as he pushed out his vitriol and unrelenting threats.

'And I will kill you, and then I'll go and *fuck* your *stuck-up* girlfriend!'

But my steel was weakening. I was anticipating a blow to the stomach or his head to drop onto the bridge of my nose at any given second, and though I stood firm before him, mentally I was retreating. As the veneer of violence wilted away from the truth, I was left with the solid and undeniable facts that were stacked so incredibly in my favour. The *devil* stepped back, his eyes dancing as he tried desperately to read my still and silent defiance. But the power was mine, and I felt the well of emotion that rippled through me, knowing that a secret opened here and now would destroy the hateful Jack De'Vil and bring his world crashing down.

But then the pub door opened and there stood the key on which Jack's world succeeded and failed – Julie. She stood suddenly motionless. The *devil* was aware of his bride-to-be watching his every move, and as a consequence his aggression seemed to melt away at her timely arrival.

'Come back inside, Jack.'

He snarled as only Jack can, our shoulders drooping in perfect unison. As he stepped another three or four paces back, he flashed his trademark smile and turned away.

'Only toying with him, babe!' he said, before grabbing her hand and heading back inside, not giving me a single backward glance.

I made my way home, back to the cold empty house. I had left at the crack of dawn, and so the serious-looking hand-delivered letter lying on the mat begged my immediate attention. I hurriedly opened it.

5th August 1991
Dear Mr Richard Angel,

REF: REPOSSESSION – Court Order – Execution No: 475329/00ANG.
Judgment Made In The Absence Of The Defendant – Mr. Ray Angel.
Please find enclosed the official 'Repossession – Court Order'.

It is with deep regret that I have to inform you of the official order made on 1st August, 1991. In reply to your recent correspondence: As acting solicitors for the Bradford & Bingley Building Society – Mortgagee: Mr. Ray Angel.
I felt obliged to write to you personally and explain the situation that we now find ourselves in. I have been informed by the building society that your mother's home is in fact in the name of your father. Despite your claims that your mother owned the house, and has paid the mortgage for the last eight years or so, your point that in view of your mother's death 'the house would be paid for and left to her estate' is in fact not so. The property fell into arrears before your mother's death. I have now received a letter from your father, having finally contacted him, notifying him of the building society's intentions. His reply to me was that he does not have the funds to clear the arrears, and therefore, due to his absence in Court on 1st August, 1991, the Court Order for repossession has been granted, and will now be executed accordingly. We are sorry to inform you, Mr

Angel, that you have seven days from the date of this letter in which to make arrangements for alternative accommodation. The building society would like to take this opportunity to point out that they have given Mr. Ray Angel over twelve months in which to bring this matter to a satisfactory conclusion.

I placed the letter on the hallway table and shook my head. *Why am I not surprised?* I sighed as I relived the assurances my father had made: 'I'll sort it all out, son, it's purely an administration problem, don't worry.' Despite my long and scathing letter to the building society in response to their threat to throw me out, they were totally within their legal rights. I slid down the wall and was now sitting on the cold floor. *Maybe I should take the mortgage on*, I thought. But I knew that it would affect my cash flow and, therefore, my business plans – and it wasn't as though I had ever really loved the place. I smiled and let out a slight chuckle from my momentarily despondent body. *Bloody hell, Ray, how on earth did you manage to remortgage the place without Mum knowing?* I thought back to when I had become of an age that I could understand, and how Mum had often said that Ray had signed everything over to her, even though she had to take on a second job to keep up with the mortgage payments. But she never once fell behind. I shook my head at just how low the man could stoop. He'd simply taken money out of the house and conned her, stolen from us both. And as I digested the morals of my father, I had to face the fact that maybe I was more like him than I cared to admit!

CHAPTER EIGHT

The Bakery Tale

Before Death, 1991 – Blue Sky
The following afternoon – Mr Ball having left for his 4 p.m.

appointment – I made the all-important phone call to my American representative. He wasn't immediately available, but within fifteen minutes or so, he called me back.

'Mr Angel? Yeah, hi, it's Nelson here, Guy Nelson...'

My heart rate quickened, each beat praying that his next words weren't going to inform me that they had secured an alternative site, but the pause suggested that it was my turn to speak, and so I embraced the opportunity positively.

'Right, Mr Nelson, umm, thanks for calling me back so quickly. Good news this end, ummm, let me just grab your file. Right, okay, I'll be ready to show you the proposed site within seven days. Could ... could you give me an indication of what this site would be worth to you?'

I was greeted by silence.

'Okayyy, it's just that I do have other interested parties, and they are, as we speak, getting their 'in-principal' offers on the table.' I closed my eyes tightly and held my breath.

'Sure, sure, I hear you, Mr Angel. We like the position as outlined on your little high street picture here; your artist's impression works well, and we like the way you've added our company logo to the outside of this 'Olde English' building. My only point is that we're not interested in the building, Mr Angel, we purely want the site.'

My worst fears were now confirmed, but I had to be cool.

'Call me Ritchie, Guy. Is it okay if we proceed on first name terms?'

'Sure, Ritchie!'

I bashed into the computer, releasing reassuring tones down the phone and across the Atlantic, then pushed a littler harder for the vital information.

'Okay, Guy, that's not a problem, I just need, then, to hear your ballpark figure. And then, with respect, we'll know whether or not we're singing from the same song sheet. Should I have faith that we are, then maybe you can fly over and see us at your earliest convenience?'

After a short pause, Guy Nelson assured me that he would be back in touch within the hour, armed with an amount that they might just be prepared to pay for this site, subject to his personal inspection. I threw my head back with relief that we were edging just that little bit closer.

'I'll, errr, wait for your call then, Guy. Bye for now.'

I spun full circle in my chair and let out a long, steady breath. I now had to wait. I had held off instructing my solicitors on the purchase of the bakery, as I had been *rightly* reluctant until I had a stronger indication of its real worth. I was disappointed to have it confirmed that the bakery had to be knocked down. One or two of Willow's historic buildings had been bulldozed and it had caused uproar, so should this deal get the go-ahead, I had better develop a skin like a rhinoceros.

It was fast approaching 6 o'clock. I was sliding within the realms of dejected and painfully convinced that my American friend had disappeared forever. Mr Ball startled me as he ran into the shop, mild amusement that I was still grafting away, parting with a word of appreciation – before disappearing quickly. I watched despondently the hands of the office clock – tick ... tick, the steady monotone of each now that of a funeral march. The minutes were passing like hours, and without fully realising how far I had fallen I was now slumped unprofessionally, defeated and broken over my desk. I was then aware of a distant ringing piercing my coma wall. My eyes thrust open in recognition of the sound and I sat bolt upright. I took a deep breath and picked up the receiver.

'Skirdle's.'

'Hi, Ritchie, it's Guy. Right, finally back to you. I've gone over the dimensions and infrastructure of your building with my superiors, and we'd be prepared to make an *in-principal* non-binding offer.'

I swallowed hard and slid forward on my seat, alert and ready.

'One hundred thousand pounds sterling. But for that, the site would need to be totally cleared, but we feel that should everything be as you've claimed, then we hope that we could be seen as favourites to purchase this land?'

I pushed the receiver away from my mouth and turned my head in the opposite direction, a much-needed exhale of air leaving my body. I knew I was smiling as I bought a little time.

'Okay, Guy, let me just make a note of that on your file...'

My business plan unrolled before my eyes, ticking off the appropriate boxes as they presented themselves. My solicitors had assured me they could complete the appropriate searches within days, once I gave them the green light. The funds were in place, the Christian's were just waiting for me, so I was ready.

'Okay then, Guy, I feel that with the figure you've mentioned, you're a realistic man, so maybe the ball's in your court. If you can get over early next week, just let me know when you're on your way.'

And so there it was – I was on the rollercoaster. I clicked my fingers and nodded my head.

'How much to clear the site?'

I was aware that I was giggling, the nerves bubbling as I envisaged Mr Tremble's reaction should he be made aware of my intention to demolish the property his bank had just lent money against. He would undoubtedly be horrified, but once I showed him the business agreement I had with Guy Nelson's company, surely it would make perfect sense to him.

As I pulled up outside Yasmin's, she was suddenly at the cottage window – a quick wave and within a breath the front door was flung open. I laughed at her enthusiasm as I stepped out of the pickup.

'Ritchie Angel, I've missed you *sooo* much!'

I was lost for words as the full force of Yasmin was upon me – soft kisses on and around my mouth were suddenly a little more forceful. I was pressed back against the side of the pickup, and though I wanted to wallow in the oblivion, I had a sudden picture of Yasmin's mum frowning with disapproval from an upstairs window.

'Mmm, steady tiger!' I uttered reluctantly.

She giggled, her head dropping onto my chest as she cuddled into me.

'Sorry, Ritchie, but I haven't been able to get you off my mind all day. Mmmm, I just want you to take me in the house, carry me up the stairs, throw me onto the bed and...'

My eye is suddenly drawn to an unamused voyeur.

'Umm, do you two want a cup of tea?'

Yasmin turned away from me instantly as if shot between the shoulder blades.

'Oh, ummm, yes, Mum, that would be lovely!'

With a frown and a look that expressed disappointment her daughter can have rarely provoked, a suitably scolded Yasmin turned to face me. I held my breath and waited, and then nodded, confirming that her mum had now made her way back inside. We both burst out laughing. I pushed my hands up beneath her hair and gently massaged her neck.

I whispered, 'I could carry you upstairs, and do all that you were just about to ask of me, or perhaps we could have *a nice cup of tea with that little old lady you live with!'*

Yasmin's lips dropped perfectly onto mine, before our fingers entwined and I was dragged submissively into the cottage, with the promise of ... *tea.*

We sat – sedate, polite – and endured. I didn't mean to be so ungracious, but there was an undoubted strain of me being seen as taking Yasmin away from her mum. But I hoped to convince her that there was room for us both in her daughter's life. Yasmin's voice cut into my thoughts.

'Ritchie, I bumped into Jimmy today. He reminded me that Justin's having another party tonight; apparently you all missed the last one, with your mum's funeral... But it sounds like it'll be fun; do you fancy it? *Oh,* and I know Janey would like to be included...as I think she's developed quite a *soft* spot for Scottie?'

I nodded slowly, feeling a little scared for Janey, but no mistaking that I was definitely up for letting my hair down.

One by one we descended on the Whippet's: Jimmy, Scottie, Sally, Leoni and finally, Yasmin, Janey and I. Within a couple of hours, the alcohol was taking an impressive hold, and I for one felt fantastic, the full weight of the bakery deal sliding from the realms of concern.

Leoni stood up, knocking her stool over.

'Party time (hic), guys. Come on!'

On my feet and mixing now with the night air, the anaesthetising effect of my several pints of strong beer had certainly worked its magic. But my legs were moving me forward and I was grateful for that. The chatter was filling my head, surreal and verging on the frantic. Scottie uncharacteristically linked his arm with mine, informing me of just how much he had been missing me, and then Jimmy followed suit and linked to my left – three guys seemingly in touch with their feminine side. I listened intently and then seemed to lose the thread as the banter leapt from subject to undecipherable subject. I focused on Yasmin and Janey, several paces ahead of us, both now chatting enthusiastically with Sally. I failed to stifle the giggles, as in their wake was Leoni, weaving half mast, the fresh air a little too heavy for her.

Gradually, the mile or so walk had allowed a much-needed clarity for me. Us boys, having overtaken the girls, were leading the way across the main green towards Justin's party, his mum and dad's grand Georgian residence alive with the sound of thumping music. There appeared to be a vetting procedure in place, as one or two unfortunate revellers were being turned away by a couple of burly guys standing guard at the front door. I was suddenly aware of Sally wriggling between Scottie and I, having deserted Yasmin. As I craned my neck to see behind me, my spectacular girlfriend and Janey were giving Leoni the stability she most definitely required. As my feet jarred sharply from the soft velvet-like grass onto the well-worn lane that circled the green, I winced, in part as I couldn't help but notice Jack De'Vil's *new* black BMW parked up against the hedgerow.

Scottie broke free and peered through the windows.

'Nice wheels! The old *devil's* certainly making some money. I bet he made a fortune out of the Old School!' Scottie glanced at me, screwing up his face and becoming suddenly quiet.

My eyes scrolled the reaction of my friends, and then a smile from me as I took in the unison daggers at our *mutual insensitive acquaintance*. But I was now laughing and a little relieved to face the subject.

'Look!! He simply put in a higher offer. I should have kept my mouth shut in the pub; it's taught me a valuable lesson and I *won't* make the same mistake twice. And you know what? I would rather you took the piss out of me than go all quiet and ignore the subject at all costs. I mean it, the school, the Porsche, history now. Don't worry, I still have a trick or two up my sleeve!'

Scottie stood with his hands now on his hips, my outburst giving him licence to take the *piss* some more, our eyes not breaking as I passed him. He then burst out laughing.

'Yeahhh, hahaha, you *stupid,* big-mouthed, *dick...hahaha!'*

The red mist descended around me and without a moment's hesitation, I leapt towards him, Jimmy and Sally pushed aside. Scottie's eyes widened as the penny belatedly dropped that he had better run. But as he turned and attempted to sprint away, I swung my foot sharply across the front of his shin. I could not have created more of an impact if I had planned it for days. He instantly catapulted full force into a neatly clipped holly bush. I let out the most almighty roar, almost immediately backed up by Scottie's dear caring friends, now almost on their knees with screams and howls of uncontrollable laughter.

I shook my head, almost choking as Scottie, firmly impaled, flailed his arms desperately to free himself, but each attempt met with a yelp and a barrage of abuse for me. After a couple of minutes of tear-inducing laughter, I almost felt guilty. And though weak with amusement, I did all I could to help free my friend. But then little shrieks of pain simply fuelled an increase in hysteria from the audience behind me until finally, and with no gratitude at all for my efforts of help...

'Ritchie! You complete and utter bastard! Ow, ow!!'

Scottie was free, though holly leaves had become affectionately attached to his nose, neck, forehead, arms, painfully, randomly – not bad coverage considering the short time he had been in there. I thought Sally was going to wet herself, she was laughing so much, and as Scottie pulled out yet another leaf, it did nothing to dampen her amusement.

Gratefully granted entry by the heavy mob at the front door, we were in, and within seconds being formally welcomed by Justin. He thrust a bottle of vodka into my hands and threw some cold cans at Scottie. Yasmin and Jimmy handed over the bottles we had brought, before being led off in the direction of the kitchen. The walls and floors were decorated with every shape and size of party animal that you would care to imagine. My eyes then jarred and locked onto Jack, his snarl even more impressive than the last one he let fly my way in the Whippet's car park. He was about to lurch towards me, but I was impressed, as one word from Julie pulled him instantly back into line. With perfect timing, Yasmin had my hand and was dragging me into an adjoining room, introducing me to a couple of her nursery work colleagues. A few swigs of vodka later and an increasing desire to flee the topic of 'Oh *little* Danny this, oh, and *little* Sophie that…' I made my excuses: 'Perhaps I'll see what the lads are up to Yaz…!'

The music was thumping and the house was heaving, the musk of allsorts thick, visible and potent. I stepped carefully between the bodies in the hallway, now in search of the bathroom, and so trod the thickly carpeted staircase. The beautifully carved banister and rails epitomised the quality of the house – I nodded my head in respectful appreciation. As I stumbled across splayed legs and finally stepped onto the landing, a smile spread wide across my face as Sally came tumbling out of the bathroom, her skirt tucked into her knickers. My friend slumped back against a large gilt-framed mirror, her legs ready to buckle. I stepped quickly towards her, shaking my head. I grabbed her arm and turned her round, keen to discover why she was displaying herself to all and sundry.

'Sally, you daft cow, you've tucked the hem into your knickers!'

My drunken friend burst out laughing. 'Oh God, Ritchie, thank God it's you (hic). I think I've drunk farrr too much! Help me un-tuck myself will you (hic)?'

I was laughing as I wrestled with Sally's skirt, almost pulling her pale blue silk French knickers down as she fell over on top of me, landing in a crumpled, hysterical heap on the floor. My sides splitting with amusement as Sally pushed her hand forward.

'Don't worry, I'm alright!' She unconvincingly confirmed.

In between more giggles, I crawled determinedly from

beneath her, and made an impressive attempt in wrestling Sally back onto her unsteady feet, only for her to fall heavily against my chest, her face almost on mine. She had a certain look in her eye that concerned me.

'Ritchie, I've something to say to you (hic)!'

Sally finally managed to stand unaided, but her wistful look remained. People started to gather outside the bathroom. She suddenly grabbed my hand and led me into one of the bedrooms.

'Ummm, what is it, Sally? *W...w...why* have you dragged me in *here?*'

As she closed the door firmly behind me and sat on the edge of the bed, her eyes were now fixed firmly on mine.

'Ritchie, I know I'm a little drunk (hic), but I need to get something straight in my head.'

She looked away briefly, took a deep breath and then her eyes were back on mine and dancing, followed by a blush to her cheeks.

'Ummm, Ritchie…I like you, I mean *really* like you! And before things get serious with Yasmin, who I really like by the way, I felt I just had to tell you how I feel (hic), or perhaps regret it forever…'

She looked so sweet, I was honoured, flattered, shocked, not to mention a little embarrassed.

'Well, Ritchie Angel, am I wasting my time? Oh my God, I suddenly feel completely sober!'

Sally was a very pretty girl, I had always thought so, but I had never seriously considered her as girlfriend material because of course Jimmy never shut up about her – he was insanely besotted. And for that reason, romantically, Sally was totally and utterly out of bounds. I pushed my hands together, almost prayer like, and took a deep breath before replying.

'Sally, bloody hell, I think you're stunning, but, well surely you know that Jimmy is absolutely mad about you?'

She looked down at the floor again and then lifted her eyes, which connected almost hypnotically with mine, and then in barely more than a whisper, 'Well, he's never said anything to me.'

I shook my head, lost for words that she hadn't known.

She sat up straight, her eyes focused on the night sky through the large Georgian window.

Then in a more confident tone, she said, 'I think a lot of Jimmy, but, well, in my band metaphor, I'd sort of seen you as the lead singer, the sexy frontman, whereas with Jimmy, he's more the bass player...'

I laughed, my eyes widening as I did so – loving the band metaphor. My ego was immensely enjoying the massage, but a sense of betrayal and despair for Jimmy was taking the edge off it.

'Ummm, Sally, if Yasmin or Jimmy were to hear this...'

Her eyes were now on mine, the room silent and absorbing the readjustment that was going to be needed here. Sally and I were destined to be firm friends – nothing more than that. Jimmy was my best friend, and God knows, I would never knowingly do anything to betray him. I sat down next to Sally on the bed and slid my arm around her shoulders.

'Sally, I'm flattered, and by the way, I *love* the silk French knickers!'

I felt a sharp elbow to the ribs, her head then falling onto my shoulder.

'But Yasmin and me, well, it's deadly serious. I know we're still a bit young, but I hope we've got a future together. As for you and Jimmy, well, I just thought it was a matter of time; I can't believe you never realised!'

Sally pushed her hand into mine.

'Ritchie, I've been a total fool. I'm thinking now that maybe the bass player is the better option, mean and moody in the background, cool but not craving the limelight the way the frontman does.'

I started to laugh, wanting to defend the qualities of the lead singer, but feeling it wise to say nothing.

'Yeahhh, Ritchie Angel, I can imagine the struggle getting the egotistical frontman away from the mirror first thing in the morning – vain, craving the eternal spotlight – whereas the bass player... Always preferred the coolness of Lennon against McCartney, John Taylor against Simon Le Bon!'

It was then that I pushed her off the bed. But though the shocked look on her face, combined with the lost-for-words

215

expression, was a pleasing alternative to what had gone before, a sudden gentlemanly twinge of guilt got the better of me, and not for the first time today I helped my dear friend to her feet. No words were spoken, our arms wrapped spontaneously around the other. We stood like that for several minutes, the background symphony of the party enough, and I had no doubt that I would remember how privileged a moment this was with my dear close friend.

Finally, we pulled away. I walked to the door, holding it open and bowing my head as she stepped out onto the landing.

'Go and get your bass player, Sally!'

As I closed the door behind us, no sooner had I turned around than there was Leoni, and just a step behind, Yasmin and Jimmy. I swallowed hard, convinced my face was ashen. The look on Jimmy's face was of hurt and disappointment. Yasmin smiled nervously, but I was convinced that I was seeing a deep-rooted trust, just edging any battle she might be having with what appeared before her. Jimmy, though, no doubt alcohol-fuelled, pushed past Leoni and pressed his face right up to mine.

'This *does* look cosy! One beautiful woman not enough for you, eh, Angel?'

Jimmy's face was angry and hurt before me; this was unknown territory, and I was numb and lost for words. But then, as if in slow motion, Sally was suddenly between us.

'Jimmy, you bloody fool! It's not what you think! Ritchie has told me, he's told me, Jimmy, you know...'

We all stood, the silence deafening amongst the riot that was going on around us. My eyes detoured over Jimmy's left shoulder, and saw Yasmin mouthing, 'Well done, I love you.' My eyes closed and opened again in disbelief at my immense good fortune at having this woman in my life. I was suddenly drawn to the subtlest of movement – Sally slipping her hand into Jimmy's.

'Ritchie just told me, you know, about you and how you feel about ... well, about *me!*'

Jimmy's puffed-out chest deflated, his eyes wide and now focused on the one woman that had captivated him from the moment his body had released its first hormone. Sally's eyes were now on mine, and then she turned and beamed at Yasmin, who in turn pushed the moment forward.

'About time, Sally; you'll be amazing together!'

Scottie suddenly raced up the stairs and onto the landing.

'What the bloody hell is going on here?!'

Sally and Jimmy waltzed past him as if he was invisible. Scottie did a double take, but suddenly lurched forward and now stood right before me, almost identical to the unfortunate stance that my accusing friend Jimmy had taken. I threw my arms around Scottie, kissing him firmly on the forehead, and then repeating his question right back to him.

'What the bloody hell is going on here? Well, Scottie, my dear, dear friend, the event of the year! And you've missed the bloody lot!'

As Scottie pulled sharply away from me – his frown lines deep enough to canoe in – I noticed Jimmy slipping his arm around Sally's waist, his chest suddenly puffed up again, and I felt great. I was sure this was the key to starting Jimmy's life – he finally had his chance. So many nights Jimmy had poured his heart out to me: Sally this, Sally that, what it would be like to hold her, kiss her… He didn't have to dream any more, he could live it, and it doesn't come much better than that.

Finally, my gorgeous girlfriend and I were left alone. Yasmin playfully pushed her face forward, a little mischievous sparkle in her eyes as her lips brushed mine.

'Yes, Ritchie Angel, one beautiful woman not enough for you, eh?'

Suddenly, my hand was grabbed for the second time this evening, and I was led urgently along the corridor. Great minds were thinking alike, so I playfully raced past her, having already spotted a small intriguing doorway. I crouched down a little, Yasmin giggling and pressed up against me. I turned the handle and pushed, but the door stood firm. I then pressed my shoulder firmly against the white gloss woodwork and barged aggressively this time, *'thank you little door!'* Left my lips as we were granted access. A small windy staircase seemed to lead up to an attic or perhaps the roof. I smiled at Yasmin, looking for her reaction – I got an immediate answer as she hurriedly pushed me through the doorway, pinching my bottom as we climbed the steep stairs. The door suddenly creaked and then slammed shut behind us, making us both jump. We gripped onto each other and continued the climb to the top. We found that we were indeed in an attic, full of family treasures, box piled on top of box, all marked with different scribbled titles: Christmas Decorations, Justin's Toys, Charlie's Toys, Magazines etc., etc. My eyes were drawn to the almost full moon through the large glass lantern sky-lights above us. Yasmin sidled past me, a mischievous sparkle lighting up her face. She took my hand again and led me to the end of the attic where there was another small door. She unlatched it and we both stepped out onto the roof. The night air was incredible, fresh and tingling on the skin. The roof was a mass of slate and glass, with a metre or so of flat walkway all around it.

The music blared out from down below, excited, inebriated voices shouting and singing. I took a step forward, ready to explore, before Yasmin tightened her grip on my hand and I instinctively turned to face her. As was becoming increasingly the case, I was unable to speak – I was just so lost in her beauty. She lifted her head and brushed her lips against mine, her body pressing against me. I turned my head towards the moon, her kisses soft and gentle on my chin and neck – a whisper of a cloud cast a brief shadow, but then we were suddenly basked in a silver light. Yasmin stepped away from me and my eyes widened with disapproval at the action, but the image before me was compensation enough: Yasmin dressed in a silk *hint of pink* ruffled skirt and a white cotton T-shirt, tousled sun-kissed hair and golden skin – I was in awe. Without warning, she roughly pushed me back onto the parapet wall. I swallowed hard as my lack of *a head for heights* made my head spin, but I was prepared to pay the price. Yasmin stepped back as far as this confined space would allow – I just watch her. She slipped her T-shirt over her head, my smiling eyes and face brighter than the moon above us – she unclipped her white satin and lace bra and let it fall on top of her T-shirt. As she posed in her silk skirt and ribbon-tied killer heels, she just stood waiting. I stepped forward and beckoned her to me; she didn't hesitate. For a brief moment, I let my eyes do the touching until I became too weak to resist. I placed my fingers beneath her right breast, my thumb easing gently across the firm satin flesh. Hungry and unable to abstain for a breath longer, I bent down and ran my tongue feather-like around her nipple. It became instantly erect and full. I then pulled away and took her left breast; same treatment, identical response.

Yasmin kept her hands at her sides, her breasts pushing into me, encouraging my every move. I take a step back, Yasmin's eyes now closed. She lifts her hands up through the fabric of her skirt and then firmly across her stomach until finally caressing her breasts; the slightest of moans, the most sensuous of touches. She suddenly arches her back, her eyes now open and on me, though barely visible through her soft sun-kissed curls. I nod towards the beautiful creature before me. She steps forward, happy with our little game. Her hands expertly undo my jeans and she slips her fingers firmly into the top of my waistband, easing the denim down my thighs. I place my hand on her chin and she steps back slightly. I kick my battered brown leather boots off, before pushing my toes into the top of my socks and successfully dismissing them too. Yasmin goes to step forward, but I shake my head from side to side. I lift my white cotton T-shirt over my head and throw it on top of my boots. I nod. Yasmin smiles and steps forward, her lips a hair's width away from mine, the tips of her breasts just teasing my naked chest. She pushes her tongue onto my bottom lip and slowly trails it down my body with light flickering movements, her erect nipples brushing my chest and then my stomach in unison, just as tenderly, totally electrifying, getting lower and lower. Her hands finally reach my ankles and I step out of my jeans. She looks up at me.

'No under crackers, Ritchie Angel!'

I nod, trying not to laugh at her underwear terminology. Yasmin stands in front of me and I pause for a moment, pondering my options. I try to stay cool and calm, but suddenly, I place my fingers on Yasmin's hips and turn her around, her hands instinctively falling onto the parapet wall. I lift up her skirt, savouring the incredible sight. Yasmin widens her stance, encouraging my next move. I gently glide two fingers against the silk of her panties, tracing all that is hidden within. Her head turns back towards me; hungry kisses become more demanding, increasingly passionate. My fingers have now slipped beneath the damp silk, pushing deeper, harder, until finally, I ease her panties to one side. I then slowly, gently enter her from behind, teasing at first, and then as she pushes herself firmly onto me I place my hands on her hips, her skirt gathered and held around her waist. I'm now experiencing the most incredible sensation, a natural high, increased rhythm, power and balance. My hands are now free to roam, to caress every erotic inch of this incredible female. I cannot resist her breasts any longer and bring my hands firmly beneath them, caressing, gently kneading, her fully erect nipples pushing through my fingers.

Suddenly, I think I'm going to lose my self-control, but then realising I might also lose my balance, I quickly place my hands on her back, my composure returning. I run my fingers roughly through her long blonde hair, pulling her head back, her back arching, her movements becoming increasingly demanding, and then, when the sensation is becoming too much, I rest my hands on her hips and thrust even deeper. Yasmin's soft whimpering moans are being drowned out by the music below, and then suddenly, totally unexpectedly, the song ends, Yasmin's oblivious pleasure increases and I quickly place my hand over her mouth, convinced that someone is going to hear us and look up. Then as romantic a song as you would want at this most crucial of moments, 'Karma karma karma karma, karma chameleon...' belts out below and a smile beams out of me. But let no man or inappropriate song divide, our bodies writhe in perfect harmony, our thrusts becoming increasingly wanting, urgent, animal, both of us totally lost in the moment. As Yasmin pushes into me with all her strength, she becomes increasingly vocal, undecipherable music to my ears, and then with an almighty shriek her body seems to buck and then stiffen within the realms of a single breath, my own body fighting and thrusting in defiance. And just as her entire being softens and retreats, I crescendo with the blasphemous, 'Ohhhhh Goddddddd!!!!!!'

The sun is warm and comforting on my face, the sound of birds singing sweetly, contentedly in the garden, and I'm instinctively aware of not being in my own bed. I sit up, and Yasmin's feminine bedroom greets my sleepy eyes. There's a soft, warm breeze blowing in through the open window. I attempt to gather my thoughts, and then gratefully remember that Yasmin's mum has gone away for a few days to stay with her sister – otherwise, there would be no way I'd be allowed to stay over, and certainly not in her perfect daughter's bed. The bedroom door is suddenly pushed open and there is a vision that is in possession of all the ingredients essential for the start to a perfect day: Yasmin, in her scandalously short white silk dressing gown, carrying a tray of fresh orange juice, some hot buttered toast and a bowl of strawberries. All topped off with a *devilishly* sexy smile that convinces me *I'm worth it!* She places the tray down carefully and then leaps onto the bed. I am then smothered with soft, sensual kisses, a single word squeezed in between each one.

'Good ... morning ... my ... *angel.* Mmmmmm ... I ... love ... you!'

Submissive and loving every breath of it, I decide to reverse roles. I bring my left hand up and around the back of Yasmin's neck and take a firm hold. Her eyes sparkle mischievously back at me. I brush a stray curl from her face with my right hand and just look at her. I shake my head from side to side.

'Yasmin, what on earth did I do to deserve you? I love you so much!'

She throws her arms around me, her lips pressed to my ear.

'Mmm, all that just because I bring you breakfast in bed? I don't usually get that kind of reaction from my other men visitors!'

She giggles cheekily into the side of my neck while I slip my hands inside her silk wrap and whisper in her ear, 'Oh yeah? Well, as long as you save plenty of energy for me!' But just as I'm getting carried away and happily lost in the moment, a sense of panic finds me scanning the room for a clock.

My eyes widen and a disappointed sigh, followed by, 'Ohhh shit, Yasmin, it's 12:20...!'

I'm just about to throw myself out of bed and take on the

animated hysteria role that I normally adopt when I'm late for work, when she says, 'Ritchie, it's alright! I've spoken to your boss, well, Mr Ball, and I've told him you're not well, been throwing up all night. I've sorted it for you, baby. He said to make sure that I take good care of you, and hopefully you'll be fighting fit for Monday.'

Before I could smile and assure Yasmin that I was fine with her plan, I scrolled through the business madness that was crucial to our future: Christian's, Guy Nelson, solicitors... I finally nodded my head. All clear; I was a free man. I smiled and Yasmin let out a relieved sigh.

'God, Ritchie, I thought I'd really messed up then!'

I felt it prudent to convince her that she had not *messed up* at all, and I felt it would exhibit a breeding of the highest order to express to my beautiful girlfriend just how grateful I was for her thoughtful and caring ways. I knew that these moments would stay with me forever.

The weekend was perfect – Yasmin and I had hardly got out of bed. And as I finally dragged myself away for work on Monday morning, I believed I was the luckiest man in the world. I drove steadily down Willow High Street, realising just how early I was – not a soul. I indicated and turned down the side of Skirdle's, and suddenly pushed my foot on the brake, surprised to see a large blue saloon car in my parking space – a bright yellow and black 'Hertz' car-hire sticker in the back window. I could just make out a large silver-haired gentleman sitting in the driver's seat. As parking was limited in our tight little alleyway, and not wanting to upset my peers by taking up the other presently vacant spots, I reversed out and parked a little further up the high street. As I ran back down the road, I was so incredibly thankful that Mr Skirdle was away on a long golfing weekend and that Mr Ball hadn't arrived yet, but one question loomed large: *surely the guy in the car isn't my American?* I unlocked the shop door and raced inside. I quickly rang my solicitors. I drummed my impatient fingers on my desk when I got the answering machine.

'Ummm, yeah, message for Mr Davenport. Ritchie Angel. Ummm, Skirdle's. Can you call me back as a matter of urgency, and give me a progress report reference the bakery? I look forward to hearing from you; as soon as you get this message would be brilliant! Ummm, thank you!'

My eyes are suddenly drawn away from the replaced receiver, and I'm aware of the silver-haired gentleman at the window, peering through the gaps in the particular's boards. I instinctively smile and wave at the unfamiliar face, my heart starting to pound a little as the door opens.

'Hello, sir. Mr Angel, is he in?'

There was no mistaking the voice; this was indeed my American.

'Ummm, yes, good morning, Mr Nelson...?'

He smiled and nodded his head. I sprang to my feet and then strode confidently towards the man who had filled pretty much my every waking thought for the last month or so.

'A good flight?'

My man nodded again, but was slightly more interested in shedding his heavy overcoat and passing me his shiny crocodile-skin briefcase.

'Well, Mr Nelson, I would say that your timing is perfect, even though I am a little surprised by your unannounced arrival.'

I placed his briefcase on my desk and stood patiently, waiting for my man to take the chair opposite and get comfortable before I took my own seat. I was aware that on the telephone we had been happy to communicate on a first name basis – but in the here and now, I was happy to follow his lead. My American suddenly took a deep breath and slumped down. Belatedly I thrust my hand forward.

'We, ummm, could have sent a car to the airport to pick you up.'

Guy Nelson looked a little surprised upon realising I was indeed Ritchie Angel – he was obviously expecting someone a little older. Nervously, and to perhaps keep the small amount of authority my heightened stance gave, I remained standing. But within a sentence or two, I gained a little inward composure, which in turn seemed to project well outwardly, and I felt confident that I was gaining the man's trust.

'Right, Mr Angel, I'm afraid I have only a whistle-stop

trip! Literally one hour to check out your proposed site, and then I'm off to inspect several other sites near to Willow!'

It is *this* that forces me to finally take my seat. My mind is churning, searching desperately for the best way forward, and I feel as though I've started to physically shake. And then just as I think I'm about to reel in the nerves to a more acceptable, workable level, in walks Mr Ball, who proceeds to panic as soon as he is in the shop.

'What have you done to your Escort, Ritchie? I hope that hire car's not being billed to us. Mr Skirdle will have a fit!'

His eyes flit from mine to the top of the head of my visitor, and almost instantly he appears to realise he may have jumped the gun. I swallow hard, and in the absence of knowing what to do next, I feel that privacy is required and so quickly stand up.

'Ummm, right, Mr Nelson, if you're in a rush, then maybe we had better get your property inspection under way!'

I keep talking, not allowing a moment for a question from my now clearly inquisitive peer, and within sixty seconds, my American and I are outside in the fresh air. Guy is wrestling once again with his coat, and then I hand him his briefcase.

'Mr Angel, do you want to take my car?'

I smile and shake my head. 'No need, Mr Nelson. As I said on the phone, it's perfect, very convenient; we're just over here.'

I place my hand across my new friend's back and guide him across the road.

'Only thing is, Mr Nelson, and I feel it wise to warn you, the demolition of the place isn't until a week today, and I have to say, though everything is in order, it's a bit of a sore subject around here, so it may be best to just let me do the talking, should anyone question our visit.'

Guy nods and just adds. 'Absolutely, Mr Angel. I know how sensitive people can be.'

As we step onto the kerb on the other side of the road, I can see Mr Christian in the bakery, but today, there is no smell of baking – just our vendor preparing for his well-earned retirement. He hurriedly opens the shop door as Mr Nelson and I draw level.

'Good morning, Ritchie, how are you today?'

I nod and shake Harry's hand, my eyes wide and attempting to provoke his cooperation.

'Good morning to you, Mr Christian. You'll have to excuse me, I've got a very important man here, so maybe you can leave me to deal with him? I'll come and see you later today.'

Harry takes a step back and throws me his trademark wink, and to my great relief he taps the side of his nose. I smile and almost have to run to catch up with Guy, who's making a beeline for the canal at the back of the bakery.

'Mmmmm, Mr Angel, interesting. I wasn't aware of the canal ... possibly a health problem, you know, with food and what have you.'

My mouth attempts to dry out within a heartbeat, but I swallow hard.

'On the contrary, Mr Nelson, it's all about settings. Like on my artist's impression to you, I feel that there is something rather *tranquil* about water. Maybe if you were to build into your design a seating area out here along the canal, I mean, I strongly believe that waterside properties are the next big thing!'

Guy walked up and down, turning his head this way and that.

'Mmm, I see your point, but a river, now that would be a more romantic setting, the babbling water, fresh, healthy, flowing. Haven't you got something by a river? Because I'm with you, I think your idea is a great one, yes, I do like the idea of the water, but let's have a river, eh?'

I swallowed repeatedly, desperate to quench my dehydrated vocal chords.

'Mr Nelson, of course, river locations are wonderful, they look fantastic, but statistics are proving that they come with a *major* downside: the risk of flooding, and it can be an expensive drawback ... loss of business ... mmmm, insurance premiums can go through the roof! With the eventual possibility of being the owner of an uninsurable property due to excessive claims! But, but canals, they're man-made, there's an overflow system about half a mile from here that runs into the river, which flows about twenty feet below, and that's why I felt this spot was so perfect for you! You've got the waterside restaurant, but without the threat of flooding!'

Guy stood still, his unflinching, unemotional face giving away nothing. But a sudden crease of the eyes and then the softest of gentle nods, which became increasingly animated, totally convincing, turned my nerves into laughter. I started to nod my head in perfect rhythm with Guy. Optimism and genuine hope filled me, and suddenly I felt it worth going for gold.

'Okayyy, so the other two companies that have shown an interest here are more interested in converting the building, incorporating some offices at the top, with a restaurant at water level. They each have plans to really use the traditional features of the bakery, you know, which would earn you some brownie points with the local community.'

But there was an increasingly steely look in his eyes that stopped me talking.

'Mr Angel, enough! I do like what I see, but *if* I'm to proceed, then I want assurance that I won't get fucked over! I sincerely hope you understand me? You using me to push your price up with your other potential purchasers, or indeed changing my plans to pacify the local do-gooders… Business is business, Mr Angel.'

I stood for a second, my eyes fixed on Guy, his eyes exaggerating his sudden need to engage with an imaginary interest in the distance – anything at all that would justify his inability to face me. I stepped before him, square on.

'Mr Nelson, if you want the building and can confirm an in-principal offer before you leave, then I will give you my word that my client's solicitors will get the contracts drawn up without delay, and we will confirm in writing that the site will be totally cleared!' I stuck out my hand. 'Do we have a deal at one hundred thousand pounds?'

Guy turned away from me and walked back out towards the road, my hand left dangling. I watched despondently as he crossed over to the other side until finally stopping. He stretched his face skyward with an exaggerated rotation of his neck muscles, and then dropped his head, his lips pursed provocatively. He seemed to ponder motionless for what seemed like an eternity, until finally, a jolt of electricity seemed to pass through me and I took a much-needed breath. My American took out a small tape recorder and started to speak into it. I swallowed hard, my throat dry and painful – I just kept reliving the act from a few moments ago of Guy nodding his head in approval, my conviction of the canal being a better bet than the river. I swallowed again, a little more able this time, a glimmer of optimism stirring my heavy breath. Though my body was numb, I pretended to take some notes myself, and then, out of the corner of my eye, I caught Harry and Alice looking down at me, wide-eyed, their thumbs up. I instinctively nodded and pushed out a reassuring smile. And then with fear and uncertainty in every step, I made my way over to Guy.

'So, Mr Nelson, what do you say?'

He turned his body and his steel-like eyes locked onto mine.

'Mr Angel, let's go back to your office, and we can discuss it over a strong cup of coffee.'

My mind raced forward a little. 'That's not a problem, Guy. Sorry, do you mind if I call you Guy?'

His eyes softened and he nodded his head. Suddenly, I was two paces behind him as he strode at speed towards Skirdle's. I was now almost running to catch up.

'Guy, ummm, GUY!'

He stopped sharply and I did all I could to stop myself from knocking him over. I swallowed hard, coughed and took a short breath.

'I need your help, Guy. There's a colleague of mine, ummm, back at the shop, well, it's one of his relatives that's very, very keen to get the bakery, so, ummm, it may well be best that if we do go back to the office, that we don't actually mention the word bakery!' I was now almost down to a whisper. 'Perhaps try to be as discreet as possible?'

Guy's eyes were boring into me – bewilderment, concern for my sanity? He tilted his head to one side, pursing his lips again, and then gave a wry, knowing half-smile.

'Okay, Ritchie. You English make me laugh, but, but no, I'll *play* it your way!'

We walked the final short distance in total silence. My heart was thumping in my ears, my footsteps surreal and worryingly forced – I didn't like the feeling. The scheming, the flying by the seat of my pants, was undoubtedly responsible for the painful twinge in every other heartbeat. But then I told myself: *if it gets you what you want, Ritchie Angel!*

As I stepped into the agency, I instantly wished I hadn't. Mr Ball stood, hands on hips, peering over the top of his glasses at my client and me. My eyes were on stalks and my shoulders were increasingly hunched and rounded as I manhandled Guy towards my desk and jostled him into a seat.

'Everything okay, Ritchie?'

I laughed and nodded, avoiding eye contact while sliding down into my own chair and hurriedly opening my briefcase, almost hiding behind it. My colleague took a step closer. I paused for a moment: *attack is the best form of defence.* So I sprang to my feet.

'Can I get you a coffee, Mr Ball? Just about to make one for my client and wondered...'

I was now bouncing from foot to foot, my temporary boss seemingly unsure of his next move, his eyes narrowing at his own indecision.

Finally, he said, 'Umm, yes okay!'

I let out a much-needed breath, but almost regretted doing so as I was sure I squealed in response to the sudden shrill of the telephone. Mr Ball answered it, and almost instantly, my coquettish friend lit up, a smile ignited as if from a thousand volts. The receiver was replaced, undecipherable words were spoken and the unwanted third party was up and out of the shop door, the bell tingling in his wake. It was music for my soul – one large patent brogue now on Willow High Street, leaving me to my misdemeanours. But my eyes suddenly widened as though someone was pushing the rewind button, and Mr Ball was back, his head popping round the partly open door.

'Oh, Ritchie, nearly forgot. The solicitors have rung, about the contracts on the bakery? They're ready to exchange. Who's bought that then?'

My legs buckled, but I managed to stay standing, now

denying the option of being able to swallow. I gesticulated with my hands, and I even imagine that my mouth was moving, but no words were forthcoming. My eyes fell unintentionally onto Mr Ball's, and I was met undoubtedly by a look of concern, but as I bore a little deeper, I was met with an expression that seemed to suggest: *I just require an answer to a simple question, boy...Nothing sinister or at all accusing...* And so I went with that.

'Yes, umm, the bakery ... a company called Fly-Sky Ltd, or something like that, have, umm, *bought it!*'

I push out my hands dramatically as if to fully emphasise how my answer is complete, almost in the same way as an energetic tap dancer would announce the completion of his final step. But there is a blankness in my colleague's eyes that suggests I have not finished, and that a little more is required from me.

'Mr Ball, I believe they've set their sights on something bigger, received confirmation late Friday, so I think we may well end up with another commission should we be able to sell it on for them.'

And though I didn't throw my hands out this time, I think I should have done, as Mr Ball nodded and smiled, and finally both of his size twelves were now on Willow High Street, his words impressively audible through the glass.

'Another commission? Excellent! Excellent!! Mr Skirdle will be very happy with that!'

Ta-daaa! filled my head, and I just about refrained from taking a bow. But I settled for the echo of the shop chime fading to nothing, a silent fanfare of relief that he was gone. I was beaming, my breathing baring something remotely healthy, instant colour flooding back into me. My eyes suddenly dropped onto Guy, immediately anticipating my next hurdle, but he seemed to be taking it all in his stride, showing no concerning emotion, until his impatient fingers rattled across the desk.

'Coffee, Ritchie? I must say, I cannot operate without a quick fix at least every couple of hours!'

I shook my head and apologised, quickly making my way into the kitchen. As I filled the kettle, I took a deep breath and as a consequence, a nervous laughter creased my face. And through the inward chuckles and shaking of my head, I could not believe what Mr Ball had just spewed out. The timing was excruciating, but I had got through. As I stretched my arms skyward and endeavoured to compose myself, I thanked my lucky stars that I had. But it crossed my mind that maybe the success of this deal was my destiny, and that I should move on with confidence and renewed belief. As I poured the steaming water into the cups, I prayed that I was right.

'Ritchie, do you mind if I use your telephone? It's a States call, though, is that okay? I have a boss who never sleeps…works around the clock, and I need to run a couple of things by him!'

I placed his coffee in front of him.

'No problem, Guy, no problem at all!'

I sat down and dropped my lips against the red-hot porcelain, the coffee black, and closed my eyes briefly as the caffeine hit the spot. My heart skipped a beat, nerves of optimism tingling carnival-like in the pit of my stomach, but as if fireworks were being released and flickering around in my chest. I took a deep breath in an attempt to quell the unhelpful activity. I was suddenly aware that I was staring a little indiscreetly as Guy conducted his seemingly in-depth telephone conversation. But despite questioning my manners for the briefest of moments, I sat firm and told myself to build on my increasing composure, and so took another sip of my coffee. My American seemed unfazed and not remotely concerned by his lack of privacy. And then the phone was replaced firmly back onto the receiver.

'Okay then, Ritchie, thank you, we want the site!'

My eyes widened and a huge smile was building behind pursed lips, but Guy wasn't done with talking.

'I'll need a contamination report on the canal, but I don't envisage a problem with it. And the price, our top bid is a straight eighty thousand sterling.'

I gulped, but didn't say a word. I took another mouthful of caffeine and swallowed hard, before placing my cup down and leaning forward.

'Guy, I cannot let you have the bakery site for that!'

My hardball American smiled. 'Ritchie, show me what your developers have paid for it.'

I didn't move a muscle – outwardly I appeared calm.

'Guy, you know I can't do that. My dealings with all clients are totally confidential! You have to understand that the company who have bought this site are simply looking to move it on, but not at a loss! They'll be extremely keen to cover their mounting expenditure with this development, and I would have to urge you to look at offering them ninety-five thousand *minimum* to even get them listening. You have to remember, we could be talking thirty thousand to take the building down. It could be *at least* that, Guy!'

He smiled back at me, his eyes narrowing and judging every breath I took. There was no doubt that he was enjoying this bit: the excitement of closing the deal, the pure sport of it. So I tried painfully hard to portray myself as cool and relaxed, but I was new to this, and it wasn't an easy game to play. I knew that I was struggling as I ran the back of my hand across my forehead and removed several beads of sweat. I wanted to say so much, but chose to leave the ball firmly on his side of the net and so said nothing. My mind kept repeating over and over again just how great an opportunity this was for me, and though I knew I needed to perhaps be a tough businessman, I was also only too aware that I didn't want to scare him off. Guy was ready to talk.

'Ritchie, I hope that we can do business, but my top offer is eighty thousand pounds!'

I shook my head from side to side, aware that my knuckles were turning white.

'Look, they will lose money at that, and I wouldn't even insult them with a phone call because I know what they'll say.'

Guy grabbed his coffee cup and quickly drank what was left.

'It's been good meeting you, Ritchie, but I have no more time. I must leave you!'

I refused to panic. I let him stand up and grab his briefcase – I had no choice but to play along, confident and unfazed. Though my legs were shaking, I stood up and pushed my hand forward. My heart was steadily rising out of my chest, the pounding now in my ears and clouding my judgment. My hands started to perspire and suddenly, I just wanted to scream, *'Okay, fine! Just sign here!!'* But I knew that Guy Nelson wanted the site, and felt sure he would go higher. In my mind I was prepared to accept ninety, but I was aware how that would look in light of what I had already said about my *imaginary client*, and so I wholeheartedly believed that he needed to come back to me with a higher offer. So I continued with the facade, but my client appeared worryingly comfortable playing it the same way.

'Ritchie, I'm sorry that we cannot do business on this occasion, but perhaps, should we be looking in Willow again, maybe our paths will cross.'

I followed Guy begrudgingly towards the door, my head and legs like lead, both ready to buckle at any second. It ran through my mind that surely I would find another buyer, should I be judged to have got negotiations so horribly wrong. But as I stood outside Skirdle's, watching Guy make his way towards his car, I increasingly believed that my dreams were leaving with him. I searched for inspiration, but I was left with a cold steel-like business streak, which was a gamble in the extreme: would it make or break me? Suddenly, I found myself in the confines of the shop, the door closed and my back firmly against it. I just stood there, waiting nervously. My heart was thumping louder and louder until almost unbearable. Surely he wouldn't just drive away; surely he'd offer just a bit more. I could hear the faint rumbling of the car, then increasing in volume as Guy reversed out of his tight parking spot and back down the side access. I suddenly couldn't help myself and stepped outside. He drew level with me and wound his window down.

'Ritchie?'

I wanted to reply, but my mouth was too dry to even squeak. My eyes and grimace assured him that I was listening, hopefully hiding my reeling mind, begging that this was it, praying that he was about to raise his stake.

'Ritchie, which is the quickest way from here to the motorway? Is it back along the outer road?'

And that was it. I just blurted out, 'Eighty-five thousand!

Come on, Guy, what do you say to eighty-five?'

But as my sad, desperate eyes pleaded for mercy, his answer was to leave me disappointed.

'I'm very sorry, Ritchie. I'm a man of my word and do not make time-wasting statements. The answer to eighty-five thousand is no. But a nice round eighty thousand English pounds is a simple and ready-to-go yes!'

Without a moment's hesitation, I thrust my hand forward.

'Okay, Mr Guy Nelson, you can't blame a guy for trying. Eighty thousand it is!'

A large and self-satisfied smile spread across my tough American's face. He turned off his engine and came back inside. Without fuss or unnecessary chat, he handed over an already drafted document, which outlined fully the company's terms and conditions, and then took out a deposit cheque for eight thousand pounds, payee as yet unwritten.

'Ten per cent okay, Ritchie? Payable to whom?' Guy scribbled quickly the solicitors' full title on the cheque and handed it to me. 'It's good doing business with you, Ritchie! We'll speak within a fortnight to see how the demolition is going, and within a week or so thereafter, our contracts should be ready for exchange.'

As Guy rearranged his documents, I noticed another cheque for nine thousand pounds, payee blank.

I couldn't help but ask, 'What's with the nine thousand pound cheque?'

My American looked at me a little sheepishly. 'Oh that ... I was prepared to go to ninety thousand!' He shrugged his shoulders and added, 'If you had told me the directions to the motorway without accepting my bid, I would have offered the ninety thousand!'

I felt the nausea rise through my body. As I looked at the amusement on Guy's face, I squeaked, 'Man of your word, eh? Don't make false time-wasting statements? *Bloody hell, Guy!!'*

I couldn't really say any more without insulting the bloke, so I just smiled and accepted the beating I had just been dealt. My client snapped his briefcase shut and, without wasting another moment, strode out of the shop. My shoulders a little slumped, I followed him to his car.

'Come on, Ritchie, you can't blame a *guy* for trying.' He raised an eyebrow and nodded, keen to provoke a reaction from me. 'You know, Ritchie, me being Guy! A *guy* for trying...? Oh never mind. I hope there's no hard feelings? After all, it's not as if it's *your* money, eh, Ritchie?' And with a wink and a wave, he was gone.

Back inside the shop, my numbness was slowly overpowered by sheer elation. Okay, I knew I'd messed up, that I could have had another ten thousand, but Guy had let me know quite clearly that he believed I had bought the bakery. It would not have gone unnoticed that I failed at each relevant point to speak to my client, which, to a seasoned professional like Guy, would have been the ultimate giveaway. But he seemed a straightforward hardball player, and perhaps had no interest in who owned the bakery. All he knew was that he had his site.

Within two minutes of Mr Ball arriving back at Skirdle's, I was out the door and on my way up Willow High Street to see my solicitors, ready to hand over the final crucial piece of the jigsaw. Sky-Fly Ltd had its wheels firmly rolling. Armed with the cheque from my shrewd American, I was *now* happy to exchange contracts for the bakery, and the Christian's could now realise their dream bungalow. I just prayed that I had enough money to flatten the site. I had agreed to borrow fifty thousand pounds off the bank, covering comfortably the twenty-eight thousand for the purchase of the bakery. My mind was full of figures, pulling them this way and that.

'Add to my twenty-eight thousand outlay, solicitors costs...' I was aware that I was now talking out loud, and continued to do so. 'And then, yeahhh, the eight thousand that I've just secured from Guy ... that leaves me with less than thirty thousand for a professional demolition job...'

I rotated my neck as it became a little hot and sticky at the sheer thought of how close I was to achieving my first business success. But then the nerves would freeze my brain, as I realised the very real threat of how victory could be snatched away from me. I reflected on the financial paper trail that I could possibly be leaving behind. I was having all the funds diverted through the Sky-Fly Ltd account, and so far, I wasn't experiencing any awkward questions when having to go into my bank. I smiled sheepishly at the mere thought. Despite keeping my head down when Mr Tremble was around, he would invariably go out of his way to come over and shake my hand, and offer his encouragement. Though on each occasion I would dread his painful probing of the finer details relating to the full renovation of my imminent acquisition. I cringed at the mere mention of it. Fair belief that any direct honesty relating to my unavoidable intention of razing to the ground the very building his bank had secured funds against, would undoubtedly bring him out in a cold and perhaps fatal sweat. I swallowed hard as I also imagined the response from the array of rabid councillors who were designed specifically to object to such sacrilege and wanton vandalism on as yet unprotected Willow landmarks, such as the potentially beautiful bakery. So anticipating such justifiable opposition, I had a devious backup plan.

Whilst such scheming and underhand dealings became the centre of my universe, I barely slept more than a couple of hours a night. Pure adrenalin, fed by the fear of failure, kept me moving, functioning on a level that just about got me through. I pushed Yasmin's love for me far more than I could imagine was wise, or remotely how a richly rested Ritchie Angel would ever venture in his wildest nightmares. But suddenly, the blackness that I assumed was only surrounding me had gone. The full glare of my favourite season, was allowed to show itself to me in all its finery, cheerful, vibrant and gratefully forgiving. For twenty-eight days I had been deaf to birdsong, laughter, optimism – fear of the path I was treading had extinguished all that – but today, I felt good.

I made my way over to the bakery – a prominent day indeed. As I walked behind the Christians' removal lorry, I smiled at the sight of all their belongings crammed up to the roof, barely an ounce of space left. I reflected on a lifetime spent at the bakery, and how today was the end of an era, and briefly pondered the fact that as the lorry closed its doors, they would be leaving a home that they would never be able to return to. But I shrugged the thought away; they would have their retirement bungalow, a new adventure stretching out into their *autumn* years.

I arrived with a large bunch of flowers and the pair of them hugged me like a long-lost son.

Harry beamed. 'Thank you, Ritchie, you've made everything so easy. We're eternally grateful!' And with that, he popped a small envelope into my top pocket. 'Told you I'd look after you, Ritchie lad!'

Alice flung her arms around my neck, hanging onto me for dear life.

'Ritchie, you truly are an *Angel!* I just wish there were more wonderful young men like you! Someone who's prepared to put himself out for others!'

And though I knew I should have dropped to my knees and begged for forgiveness, I actually felt exonerated, genuinely humbled by their kind, but of course misguided, words. But as I waved Harry and Alice off, their beaming happy faces content and grateful, I accepted a twisted sense of pride at what I had achieved for these two people. And as I stood, the bakery and I left alone, I took in the tired splendour before me, a lifetime of secrets and stories behind every pane of glass. I pondered the rights and wrongs of simply giving up on a building with this amount of presence. But then I thought about the strength of character that Guy Nelson had showed me, his cold, calculating business manner, and all sentimentality was saved for a *non-business* day. Instead, I chose to wallow in the sense of pride I felt in knowing that the bakery was mine, my first property. I patted the brickwork and whispered an apology in anticipation of what I had planned.

I made my way back over to the estate agents. As I shut the door behind me, I was aware that Mr Ball had a visitor – David, Mr Skirdle's son, and of course Mr Ball's love interest.

They looked nervous as I beamed and uttered, 'Afternoon, guys. Enjoying the new job, Dave?' I smiled inside and wondered whether it was the uniform that did it for our Mr Ball. 'So, you're Willow's new trusty postman, are you?'

They both gave me a sheepish wry smile, and the three of us chuckled politely. I felt it wise to leave them to it, and went and made a coffee. By the time I had returned, David was gone.

'Ritchie, are you still okay with, umm, you know, David and me?'

I nearly choked on my coffee.

'Mr Ball, I've told you, it's totally up to you what you do. Please don't worry about my views!'

Mr Ball shuffled on his feet nervously as I sat on the edge of my desk.

'But, Ritchie, I do worry about what you think. I mean, all this business with you buying the bakery ... I know nobody's supposed to know, but I've put two and two together. I've spoken to Mr Nelson before, but told him we had nothing suitable, and now, if I'm not very much mistaken, I presume that you've bought the bakery with a view to knocking it down. Am I right, Ritchie?'

I was totally shocked and didn't really know what to say. I put down my coffee cup and stood up, my hands placed firmly on my hips, a well of panic ready to burst out of me. There was silence for what seemed like an eternity. My eyes were looking everywhere but at Mr Ball, who was just a couple of feet away from me. Suddenly, he seemed keen to diffuse the situation.

'Ritchie, it's okay, I'm not going to drop you in it, but surely that's your plan, isn't it? But you do know, well, Willow Council are starting to get *really* tough on knocking some of the older buildings down?'

My chest was up, but I was trying desperately to keep calm. My eyes were suddenly locked onto my judge and jury, and I was feeling increasingly sick. I didn't want to hear another word, but he continued anyway.

'Ritchie, if you've done a deal with the American, then you do know they'll sue your ass if you don't deliver what you've legally committed to? Have you made an agreement?'

I nodded.

'What about a deposit, Ritchie, have you taken a deposit?'

I nodded again, but this time decided to speak out.

'Look, Mr Ball, I appreciate your concern, and you're totally right, I have done a deal, but...' I instinctively stopped, looked around the shop and then proceeded in a whisper. 'But, the bakery is coming down. Trust me, it's called progress, but please, nobody knows about this. It's imperative that you keep this to yourself, and I mean it, not a word, not even to your precious David. I'm deadly serious. One word and I'll make sure you're finished here!'

Mr Ball stepped forward, his breath warm and salty on my face.

'Look, Ritchie, I've *not* told a soul, and certainly wouldn't tell the boss's son, would I? It's just between you and me.' He stepped back, his brief anger replaced with genuine concern. 'I wish you luck; God knows you're going to need it!'

I stayed a little later than normal, needing time to think. I thought long and hard about what Mr Ball had said, and felt that maybe it was better to put my plan into action before I even called a meeting with the council. My phone rang.

'Hi, Ritchie, it's Jimmy. It's going great with Sally! I haven't really had chance to apologise for the way I doubted you the that night. I'm really sorry, mate!'

I laughed, grateful for the light relief, and then offered reassurance to my friend.

'Listen, Jimmy, you were just a little uptight, but I understand. You're a real shit, though, for thinking I would do that to you! But I mean it, you're forgiven. So anyway, everything's good? She's feeling the same and all that?'

Jimmy sighed enthusiastically down the phone. 'Ohhh God, she's *sooo* hot! I'm pretty convinced she's really into me, and it's only a matter of time until she can't resist me any more and drags me off to the bedroom! And though I am a bit scared of *that* moment, between you and me of course, I have to tell you, I really can't wait! Anyway, Ritchie, the boss will be back soon, so I'll catch you later!'

And with that, Jimmy was gone. I was really pleased for him. And with everything that was going on with me, I envied his contentment with the normal uncomplicated simple route: get the girl of your dreams, do the job you're paid to do, just steady, steady, steady. Instead, I had this bloody crazy get-rich-quick scheme, which could, if things went wrong, really blow up in my face.

I had a serious dilemma, but as I picked over the bones of the problem, I asked myself: *when is a dilemma not a dilemma,*

Ritchie boy? The answer was based on the sheer bloody-mindedness of my desperation to succeed at any cost. And so to my dilemma: *what if the council said no to my application to demolish the bakery?* And back to the answer: *what if the building was totally unsafe and there was no alternative but to knock it down?* I liked it; my backup plan was an excellent one, even if I did say so myself. But first things first: how much would it cost to knock down the bakery should the council say yes? Discretion was to be paramount. I required a guarantee that I wouldn't incriminate myself purely by requesting a quotation for the job.

Within the hour, in walked Daz – a six-foot-five muscle-bound demolition man.

'Mr Angel?' Daz shook my hand a little too enthusiastically, my fingers dissolving under the pressure. 'Sorry, Mr Angel, you know, earlier and that, not being able to give ya a rough idea over the phone. There's a lot to fink about with these kinda jobs, but I appreciate ya wanna keep this hush-hush and that, so let's avva look!'

We made our way across the road. Within seconds, Daz was poking and probing with an eagerness that was admirable, kicking the foundations and making sure it wasn't attached to next door in any way.

'Nice old building, Mr Angel!'

I tried to bat away his well-intentioned words.

'Yeah, yeah, not bad. Oh, and just call me Ritchie. I'm thinking, Daz, how much work we should be able to throw your way if you can go easy on me with the price! So maybe we should adopt a more familiar approach, first names and all that.'

My demolition man nodded knowingly, appeasing outwardly my none too clever attempt at subtle bribery. But once Daz had completed his in-depth checks, he stood back and took a deep sigh, huge arms firm on hips, and then gave a gradually increasing shake of the head.

'You're probably looking at … fifteen grand! As long as we can avva bit of time to take some of the more valuable bits down. I mean, I shouldn't really be saying this, but some of the fancy roof tiles, and some of the carved timbers, they're worth good money! So I think I would be interested, and at fifteen thousand, I wouldn't ave thought you'd getta betta deal than that.'

I shook my head enthusiastically and then raised my voice alarmingly, as I clocked a middle-aged couple pointing up at the *sold* sign – and then their eyes a little *too* keen on what Daz and I were up to.

'Yeah, yeah, sounds good money that; old tradition, skilled craftsmen are not going to be cheap on a serious renovation project like this one!'

I winked discreetly at my bemused friend, and then several times more, and then finally, gratefully, the penny seemed to drop as Daz started to laugh. I thanked him for coming and just about managed to avoid the vice-like destructive handshake by staying at his side, patting him firmly on the back and assuring him that I would be in touch once I had official word from the council.

CHAPTER NINE

More Than One Way To Skin A Cat

Before Death, 1991 – Blue Sky
At my request, ten o'clock the following morning, the council were stood kerbside looking at the Old Bakery: a gentleman in his early fifties, and one lady about thirty years of age but dressed as if several years into her retirement. Despite my attempts to use my charm, nothing – she was ice cold, and as for him, I may well have been invisible. I stood for several uncomfortable moments, and then the lady spoke.

'Mr Angel, who owns the property?'

I dutifully looked in my file.

'Ummm, a Sky-Fly Ltd.'

She jotted the name down and continued her monotone questioning.

'And why are *you* involved with the demolition of the

building?'

I shuffled a little from foot to foot.

'Just acting for my clients.'

Suddenly, the middle-aged gentleman acknowledged my existence, but was more than happy to tread me into the dirt.

'Mr Angel, I have to inform you that I rather like this building. I advise that you inform your clients that the answer is no! Of course, they can make an official application, this being a mere feasibility site meeting, but I assure you, Mr Angel, this building is here to stay, and what's more, I look forward to seeing this Sky-Fly's proposals for renovating the building back to its former glory!'

In turn, the *dream destroyers* shook my hand, and through gritted teeth I had to say, 'Goodbye, and thank you both for your valuable time.'

My sanity was kept firmly in place by my backup plan, from this moment forward to be known only as 'my one and only plan'. And though I didn't feel it wise to dwell on the negativity of the day so far, today was indeed a strange day. But nonetheless, a crucial 'sorting out all the horrible jobs' day that simply had to be dealt with, should I wish to realise my dream. I suddenly found myself on the phone to the solicitors regarding my mum's house.

'So having given you all the necessary information, if I were to send you a cheque for all the arrears, would your client consider transferring the mortgage into my name?'

'Mr Angel (laughing), it's not quite as simple as that, sir. But the building society may be open to discussion. It would usually be right to place your mum's house on the open market, but I think in the circumstances they could, *perhaps,* come up with a way that you get to purchase the family home. However, time is of the essence, so I will put your proposal to them, and push them to contact you without delay, Mr Angel. Good day and good luck!'

In an attempt to pacify my neglected girlfriend, some down time, but regardless of well meant intentions, my eyes, for the twentieth, perhaps thirtieth time, glanced at the hands on my watch – 10:15 p.m. Yasmin was sat before me, both of us trying to enjoy a romantic evening at a beautiful new Italian restaurant just off the Willow High Street. It was a really happening place: the food was wonderful, the atmosphere buoyant and the company, well, Yasmin was as stunning as was legal to be. But the whole evening was gradually spoilt – by me. Uniquely I couldn't wait to get Yasmin dropped off at home. So after much faking of a seriously painful headache, blamed on stress and overtiredness, the evening for us both was over. Yasmin kissed me softly goodbye, and expressed her deep annoyance that I wasn't taking her home with me. But she bowed to my hypochondria and waved me off, blowing lots of loving kisses as I eased away from her mum's cottage.

I arrived home and pulled onto the driveway just before eleven. I let the engine run a little longer than usual, with a few extra revs thrown in to ensure my return was duly noted. I finally, noisily, took myself into the house and went through the motions of going upstairs and turning on the bedroom light. After about ten minutes – having hurriedly changed my clothes – I turned the light off. I made my way downstairs, now dressed totally in black, with my trainers on and a thick woollen hat. I crept out of the back door, desperate not to be seen. I made my way to the bottom of the garden, my paranoia increasing with every step. I waited for a few seconds, noting every visible overlooking window. Once convinced that I was not being watched, I scrambled as inconspicuously as I could, before dropping down into the field behind. I tiptoed the first dozen or so steps, but then started to run with real purpose, but rather unsteadily, across the rough overgrown meadow. My eyes were straining against the moonless night, but gradually coming to terms with the blackness that shrouded my mile or so route towards the bakery. There was a canal lock about three hundred yards away from my destination, and I prayed that I could make my way alongside the oily black strip of water totally undetected. Once I reached the lock, the full extent of what I was about to do unnerved me, but as I carefully crossed the canal, I told myself that to succeed, sometimes you have to play rough. I nodded patronisingly at my morale-boosting line and made my way along the back of the shops, until finally reaching the rickety staircase at the back of the bakery. Just beneath the rotting timber were a couple of concrete steps which led down to a heavily padlocked cellar. I flicked on my miniature torch and reached into my pocket. I pulled out the recently acquired key, a strip of green insulation tape stuck firmly around the rusting metal: 'B.C.' roughly inscribed. I turned the key in the decaying padlock very carefully and nervously turned off the torch. I froze for a short moment, just to make sure that no one had heard me, and then, with extremely exaggerated slow-motion actions, pushed the door open.

As I made my way into the darkness, I pulled the door to.

'Shit! I can't see a fucking thing!' I scolded anxiously.

My heart was pounding. I raised my hand and brought it up to my face, and yet I couldn't see it. I fumbled for my torch, but as soon as my fingers wrapped around it, I loosened my grip – I could not risk anyone seeing the flicker of light that could possibly escape up and out through the grates at the front of the shop. So I took a deep breath and stepped blindly through the darkness. All I could hear was the scurrying of little feet, and I felt my flesh crawl. I really wasn't keen on rats, and I was convinced that one would jump on me at any given moment. As I felt my way along a damp flaking wall, I finally made my way through a small vaulted gap. I let out a positive sigh as a welcome stream of limited light filtered in through the grates courtesy of the street lamp from across the road. My eyes scoured the grey shapes, and then I beamed as I found what I came for.

'There you are, my beauty!'

And there against a central wall was the oil tank. My joy was short-lived, and an instinct to scream was replaced with a shudder that ran the length of me as I made eye contact with a rat. I wanted to blink, but instead settled for a wince, the greasy rodent now circling on top of the rusting equally greasy tank. But then losing his nerve, he dropped, lemming-like, and scurried off to join the rest of his hideous friends.

'Focus, Ritchie, focus!'

I clenched up my body in a comical defiant bulldog stance, before finally rotating my neck and telling myself: *you're an evil invincible bastard, Ritchie Angel, unstoppable!* I let out a huge breath and stepped forward, not daring to question my new words of motivation, but instead relived the moment when Harry had asked me to pass on the information to the new owners, that there was approximately a third of a tank of oil left. At the time I simply dismissed his words; it was irrelevant, until now. I crouched down and wrapped my clean fingers around the greasy nut that attached the tank to the outlet pipe, and tried desperately to turn it. I succeeded only in gouging deep crevices into my palm. I then applied both hands and squeezed until I was purple in the face. I cursed and stood up sharply, suddenly keen to rearrange my contorted back muscles. I stared at the stubborn mechanism, the large greasy nut that was being so successfully defiant, and then focused on a thin pipe just below. I ran my next move through my simple and inept brain and shook my head from side to side at the only answer I could fathom: *brute force, Ritchie boy, good old-fashioned brute force!* I rotated my neck again and stepped forward, taking a long deep breath. My foot hovered above the smaller pipe, and then I stamped downwards with all my body weight, and then again, and again, and just kept stamping until finally, the pipe was free. My triumphant proud smile beamed bright and deep from the pit of my stomach as the oil started to gloop out very slowly. I stood and let out a childlike but extremely satisfied chuckle and crouched down as low as I could, indulgently and bravely switching on my torch. The rich red shiny corrosive liquid was spreading itself surprisingly quickly now, greedily devouring the flaking concrete floor, and that made me happy. The oil would in time sink into the concrete, until soaking fatally into the foundations.

My destructive thoughts were suddenly interrupted by a large bang above my head. I stood rigid, staring up at the barely visible ceiling, waiting for the next clue as to what might be up there – but nothing. I could only presume that someone was in the bakery flat, but I didn't care: burglars, rats, I'd had enough of this place, and so I hurriedly left. My hands were shaking as I urgently wrestled with the padlock, desperate to leave the bakery just as I had found it, though of course the oil wasn't quite so well contained as when I entered the building. I shook my head at the thought, a nervous laugh pushing itself forward. I then started to run, and then a little faster, every step in painful harmony with my pounding heartbeat, but I kept running and didn't look back.

I dropped down into my garden and froze on the spot. My eyes were everywhere, desperate to make sure I hadn't been seen. As I finally closed my back door behind me, I let out a much-needed breath. I took several moments to recover my composure, before finally standing up straight and then proceeded to undress in total darkness. I threw my clothes into the washing machine and crept very quietly upstairs. I stood at the bedroom window, naked and vulnerable, questioning and trying to justify for the thousandth time what I was doing. Suddenly, the phone rang and I nearly jumped out of my goose-pimpled skin. I ran back downstairs and nervously picked it up.

'Ritchie, I'm so sorry. I hope I haven't woken you?'

I laughed with relief down the phone as my beautiful girlfriend expressed her concern.

'Ritchie, I'm *really* worried about you and want to be there to nurse you. I hate the thought of you being on your own. I'm sorry, I tried to sleep, but couldn't settle, baby. Mum's said she'll drop me over, if you want, to give you a bit of TLC.'

Just the sound of her voice and her caring words brought me back to normality. I assured Yasmin that I was okay, that all I needed was a good night's sleep, and though of course I would love her to come over, it wouldn't be fair on her mum.

'Yasmin, I love that you have called me, but it's not fair on either of you at this time of night. Get a good night's sleep, and don't give me another thought.'

Yasmin playfully sulked down the line.

'Okay, I understand.'

I suddenly had a terrible thought. 'Ummm, Yasmin, did you ring me earlier ... before this call?'

But she assured me she hadn't. Before ringing off, Yasmin instructed me to dose myself up and not to set my alarm for the morning.

'Goodnight, Ritchie Angel, I love you *so* much!'

Priceless and wonderful words to end the day with. And once I had curled up beneath my ice-cold quilt – though my mind was racing for a short while – I eventually fell into a deep sleep.

As morning arrived, I lay passed out in my bed. An insignificant repetitive noise in my ear initially did not bother me, but then the rhythm became harsh and pulled me out of my coma. I slammed my hand down on the alarm, the sudden silence almost anesthetising me again. I lay oblivious for several decadent moments, my mind totally, gratefully empty, until the strands of my life eased onto the blank canvas. The cluttered, eventful picture sobered me up and my eyes were suddenly wide open. My legs instinctively swung from beneath the thick cosseting quilt, my feet now firmly planted onto the coarse, unwelcoming bedroom carpet. I shook the sleep from my body and stood up. I pulled back the curtains and opened my window – the fresh sharp air was abrasive, but necessary. And as I stood, not backing away from the morning, the sun danced lightly across my face and chest, and I loved it. I became human again, and the urge to ring Yasmin became my number one priority.

'Good morning, beautiful woman. I really wish I had brought you back here last night, I missed you terribly!'

Yasmin playfully cursed and almost spat venomously down the phone at my change of heart. But as we kissed and cooed our goodbyes, I had already started counting the painful, empty moments until I saw her again.

After the cold wet flannel had been given the tour twice around my body, I jumped up and down and ran around in circles until I was totally dry. I pulled on my suit and stared at my reflection in the mirror, and for a minute or more I stood motionless. Then a tingle of excitement sparked my senses and suddenly, unable to resist, I was pulling inane and provocative faces at the man I had become. But within a dozen or so strides, and a concerted effort to get my day under way, I was in my company car and on my way to work.

There were seven roads and one roundabout between home and Skirdle's. As I drove, I thought about the bakery and the free-flowing oil that would be relentlessly soaking itself into the supporting structure. I smiled as I pictured the faces of the council's planning officers, and their having to admit defeat and accept that the building would have to be demolished. And if they didn't, then maybe I would have to create a plan C: 'burn the *bloody* place down!' I chuckled to myself. *Now that's not such a bad idea, and would save me fifteen grand!* But as I pondered the thought, I questioned my luck, and how I could possibly end up burning the whole of Willow High Street down, but I wouldn't be ruling it out.

As I got closer to the town, the traffic was almost at a standstill. I started to huff a bit, craning my head this way and that, and then finally stretching it out of my now open window. Then, as if appearing from nowhere, a tall starched policeman stood almost level with my front bumper.

'Excuse me, officer, *what's* the problem? It's just that I'm trying to get into work, just at the bottom of the high street.'

The young policeman took several steps forward and bent down at my window.

'Well, I'm sorry, sir, but you'll have to bear with us, as no one's allowed into the high street. There's been a gas explosion at the Old Bakery and there's not much left of the building. In fact, it's taken out half of next door too!'

I could not believe what I was hearing. I even let my fingers drop onto my forearm and pinched myself, just to make sure I was actually up and out of my bed – the sudden sharp pain convinced me that I was not dreaming. My heart was pounding so hard that I was convinced the policeman would see my body jolt with each beat. I swallowed hard, and was grateful when he moved along. My mind was running rampant, and with each desperate confused question, another bead of sweat appeared on my forehead. My breathing was erratic and hot as I tried to reverse my car back up the street, keen to escape, but then in equal measure I felt the urgency of wanting to find out exactly what had happened.

I finally abandoned the car and strode as innocently as I could towards the mayhem. My mind was juggling questions with feasible answers, negative and positive, but the one question that kept pushing itself to the front was that surely the oil couldn't have had anything to do with it? But the policeman stated gas, and yet the building ran off oil, so where the hell was there gas? As I drew level with the blue and white barrier tape, a safe distance away on the other side of the high street, my mind continued to race. I questioned reasonably that there could have been other forms of heating, and then my mind was triggered off in the direction of exactly what would have been required to bake bread and all the other wonderful things that would dispel their aroma into the Willow atmosphere. My eyes widened as I thought about the influence of the upstairs flat. It was self-sufficient from the shop, but did it run off gas? And then I was bouncing my middle finger against my lips as I pondered the possibility of the shop next door being the culprit. My face was now red hot, and it was not a self-induced sweat that I was undoubtedly guilty of, but a physical white hot fur of a heat that was wafting across my face, effortlessly scratching my eyes and throat. Several coughs reluctantly barked out of me and I looked around guiltily, my aim very much to keep any kind of attention away from me. But as I broke free from my stooped frame and stood upright, I shook my head – devastation was the only way to describe what I was seeing. There were asbestos-type sheets up against some of the surrounding shops, and the front of Skirdle's was partly covered in sheeting splattered with foam.

Without thinking, I stepped beneath the barrier tape. Steam was rising from the water-drenched pavements as I trod reluctantly towards the bakery – black confetti fluttered and swooped. But then my feet stopped. My head seemed to charge forward like a telescopic lens – the bakery was gone. Just black charcoal embers, about fifteen feet high, needle-like, out of the oily ground. And the main wall belonging to next door was being propped up by scaffolding poles and lengths of steel, foam being added every thirty seconds or so in an attempt to stop it catching fire, as there was no denying the extreme heat that surrounded us all. I moved my feet forward – nobody seemed to notice me, or tried to stop my approach. I attempted to speak to one of the firemen who had dropped back, taking a swig of water, his colleagues steadily turning over debris and giving it a quick blast with more chemicals. But as I got closer, I noticed an ambulance, and right by the side of the canal, through the wafts of rising heat, there was a small white tent, and then, as though a switch had been flicked, the unbearable heat was replaced by an ice that made every hair on my body stand on end. The side of the tent was unzipped and two medics carried out a stretcher with a body bag on it.

'Oh my God!' crept out under my scorched breath, quickly followed by, 'Fuck, fuck, fuck, who on earth is that?'

In a daze, I was escorted to safety. Several cups of coffee in the local café, and four or so hours later we were finally allowed back into the estate agents. I was incredibly numb, and despite asking who the deceased was, nobody knew. But as the hours ticked by, it was rumoured to be an old tramp who had broken into the flat, but there had not been a positive identification. By late afternoon, we had it officially confirmed that there had been a gas explosion. A shoddily fitted stop end cap had been attached to the gas pipe, and when the Christian's had moved out, whoever disconnected the cooker simply hadn't known what they were doing. Therefore, the individual was responsible for the horrific explosion, and more importantly to blame for the death of the poor person in the flat.

The fireman divulged all he knew as Mr Ball plied him with coffee. My colleague then went and offered liquid refreshment to the other uniformed men and women. I stood deflated and empty, staring out through the soot-smeared window, my demolition job complete. But it was an extreme price to pay: why did someone have to die? I closed my eyes tightly, and suddenly, I was imagining the red-hot flames melting my flesh. I turned away from the window, forcing my eyes open, and kept repeating the words of the fireman in my head: *Poor old sod, but if it's any consolation, with the strength of the explosion the old boy wouldn't have known much about it!*

Within days, the area was cleared, all evidence gone – even the cellars were dragged out of the ground. Now, instead of the grand charm of the Old Bakery there stood a sheet of pressed hardcore. Total bill – many thousands of pounds, which my insurance company duly paid for. And within a week or so, I received an offer of over forty thousand pounds to cover the costs of any rebuilding that would be deemed necessary. It seemed mercenary to talk about money at a time like this, but then I couldn't change what had happened. Suddenly, I was rolling in it. The Americans got their land and I got my profit, despite all the headaches of purchasing the site and of course the heartache with the fatality – finally confirmed as sixty-four-year-old Bill Withers. I learnt that Bill had originally drifted away from East London, preferring to take his chances on England's streets, and word had it that he had been some distant relative of our great Queen. But as the sincere thoughts of my deceased squatter left me, my business head seemed to take over. A quick push of the calculator buttons confirmed that I had made about ten years' wages at Skirdle's in six weeks flat. I'd got a taste, and I wanted more!

However, Mr Christian had taken the news of the explosion very badly. He informed the police that it had in fact been him that disconnected the cooker. And though the police weren't prepared to press charges, poor Harry's health took a serious dive. And as for me: what goes around dutifully came around! The American fast-food chain announced their plans for their monstrous new building, large and highly contemporary. It was a futuristic, forward-thinking building, and of course the kids would love it. But just when I felt convinced my detachment was complete, a local newspaper decided to do a big story on the new development, which somehow managed to unearth me as the 'shrewd property developer' behind Sky-Fly Ltd and how I had made an absolute mint from selling to the Americans. They endeavoured to portray me as an inspirational 'whiz-kid' businessman, but of course not everyone was so keen to pat me proudly on the back. It had been exaggeratedly stated that I had made over one hundred thousand pounds from the sale to the Americans, and though the headlines upset Jack De'Vil greatly and my overnight rise boosted my street credibility within the local business community, there were four individuals who weren't quite so pleased. In fact, I seriously thought Mr Skirdle's rage was going to see me strung up outside the shop.

He stated through bulging eyes, 'If it weren't for the fact, Ritchie Angel, that sacking you could very well bring a spotlight of suspicion on a so far overlooked act of dodgy dealing...' After which he went on to elaborate the murky depths of my treachery, and just how badly it would all reflect on my golf-playing boss and the up to now untarnished Skirdle reputation. I felt as if I was three feet tall and withering by the second, but I kept my job!

I can't deny that the scolding hurt. Mr Skirdle and I had never had a cross word, and so it was depressing being in his bad books. However, his final words on the subject left me with a huge dilemma.

'Ritchie lad, you will go and see Mr and Mrs Christian, and unreservedly apologise to them. And any blood money profit you have made, you give them every last penny of it, do you understand me, lad?!'

And it was this that caused the physical wince.

'Every damn penny, Ritchie!' Mr Skirdle brought his fist down on the desk with the might that would have seen the Old Bakery fall prior to any explosion.

But as I sat stone-faced and severely told, I knew without question that I wasn't ready to hand over my ill-gotten gains. But as my boss dusted himself down and my colleagues continued with their day, I knew that a visit to the Christian's was very much due. They deserved an explanation, although perhaps a colourfully embroidered, more acceptable chain of events – after all, I did have a soft spot for them both.

I turned off the engine and looked at Harry and Alice's perfect home – the garden was beautifully tended. There was an almost spiritual haze shrouding the bungalow, a glorious summer evening, not a whisper of breeze, as though holding its breath, waiting for me. I climbed out of the pickup truck and made my way up the small path leading to the front door. I knocked gently and suddenly, my nerve started to falter, but I stood firm. I could hear the shuffle of feet and then the door slowly opened. There was Alice. Her eyes once upon a time would have sparkled at me, her little frail arms clasping mine, eager to get me inside. But instead, she just looked at me, her head swaying from side to side.

'Oh, Ritchie, I really don't think you should have come

here.' The words were painful.

'Alice, it's not how you think, it's not *anything* like you may have read in the paper!'

Alice turned and appeared to look at Harry, then disappeared inside. I presumed I was expected to follow her in. I closed the door nervously behind me. There was a deadly silence as her tiny fingers turned off the radio. My eyes fell onto Harry, sitting bolt upright in his chair right next to the fireplace, a brightly coloured shawl covering his legs. He stared at me, and as I tried to look him in the eyes, determined to coax an ounce of warmth or the beginnings of forgiveness from him, all I saw was hurt and disappointment. Alice sat herself down while I just stood awkwardly by the door, my feet not leaving the floral mat.

Suddenly, I heard words break through the silence.

'Harry, Alice ... I didn't make anything like the money that was reported in the paper. I simply took the bakery off your hands because I wanted you to have the bungalow, this beautiful home. I suppose... I perhaps thought... *um,* I might make a few quid out of the sale, but I didn't expect a lot, and I didn't really get a lot.' But as I spoke, my own words sickened me.

Harry beckoned me to him. I left the safety of the doormat and stood before him; our eyes lingered for a brief moment. Harry's pupils started to dance and increase in size, a sparkle that offered me a glimmer of hope that I may just be forgiven. My heartbeat quickened and I felt a half smile puff out my embarrassed cheeks. But then suddenly, like a man possessed, Harry lurched forward, his fists clenched tight.

'*YOU FILTHY, CHEATING LIAR!!*'

My eyes were now as wide as my attacker's and I instinctively sprang back, almost yelping as Harry's outstretched fingernails scraped the side of my nose. But as Harry floundered and missed his target, he dropped like a rock and struck his head on the brick hearth with a sickening thud. All I could hear from behind me as I quickly dropped to my knees, grabbing Harry's head, were Alice's screams.

Harry's eyes seemed to roll into the back of his skull as my fingers disappeared under the life-draining amount of blood that was escaping from the tear in his temple. I heard the crack of Alice's knees behind me as she collapsed to the floor. I simply couldn't catch my breath at what was happening. My shaking hands placed Harry's head back down onto the blood-sodden carpet – his eyes were wide open, flickering, as if wires were fusing, but he was fading fast. In a panic, I threw my arms around Alice, desperate to comfort her, but she just screamed and lashed out, her fingers outstretched, but feeble and ineffective. The tears were rolling down my face as I turned my attention back to Harry, Alice's hands thumping increasingly weakening blows across my shoulders. But all I could do was shake my head – I knew it was too late. In one last ditch attempt I fumbled clumsily for a pulse, but there was nothing, and suddenly, the room was quiet and still.

I stood up, unable to feel my legs as I did so. My eyes drifted around the room and took in each lifetime possession that these two people held so dear, and then finally, I found the strength to look at Alice. She was no longer crying and just stared up at me. I hesitated, but instinctively lowered my arms in an attempt to help her up. As my hands dropped towards her frail shoulders, her eyes widened and she went to scream out, but this time nothing came out. Her arms and hands were stretched and shaking in front of her, her face contorted and wretched. She continued to scream, but the volume was set at zero. I just stood, my shoulders rounded and my arms dropped helplessly. I screwed my eyes up as Alice fell onto her side, lying there still and broken. After several lost moments, bewildered and indecisive, I finally rang 999, and then, as per their instruction, dialled the number clearly marked by the phone, for their doctor. As I sat and waited for help, I had never felt so painfully disorientated. I knew I was scum – I had no other description for the part I had played in this tragedy. Ironically, I winced and reflected on how I had felt vindicated by getting them their little bungalow, but once they knew the truth, they had nothing but contempt for me. And as I sat and continued to wait – Alice lying motionless on the floor and her dead husband just feet away from her – unworthy, self-sorrow tears rolled helplessly down my ashen face.

The ambulance soon arrived, closely followed by the

doctor. When asked what had happened, I said that Harry had fallen out of his chair, hitting his head on the hearth. And as for Alice...

'Well, Doctor, I think the shock has seriously affected her, and now she doesn't seem to be able to speak!'

As Alice was strapped into a carry chair and taken out of the bungalow, she didn't utter a word – she couldn't, wouldn't even look at me.

The weeks that followed simply passed by with me in a haze. The only time I seemed to relax and act remotely normal was around Yasmin – she seemed to bring peace to me. And when she expressed effortlessly her love for me, I didn't feel quite so worthless.

One rainy afternoon I had an overwhelming desire to go and see Alice at her nursing home. I'd heard through the grapevine that she had not spoken since the accident, and that finally, they had had to commit her into care.

'I'm Ritchie Angel. Yes, I've come to visit Alice Christian.'

The nurse smiled and offered much-needed encouragement.

'Oh lovely. Alice doesn't get any visitors, this will make her day!'

I sighed pitifully as the nurse said it, but still my thoughts were of concern. I hoped that she would be okay when she saw me, and as I pictured the scene I so nearly turned and ran for the door. But I genuinely felt a hand of strength or guidance rest on my shoulder, convincing me that I had to see this through. And so with a deep breath, I did what I had to do. As I was shown into her room, Alice was sitting quietly in an oversized chair. She resembled a fragile baby bird, with grey and transparent skin, just waiting for a thick flourish of feathers. Alice craned her neck towards me, her bloodshot eyes growing in size, and then a huge smile spread across her face. She stretched out her arms towards me. I remembered how Harry had lurched at me, but as I stepped hopefully towards my welcoming little friend, I didn't hesitate in simply wrapping my arms around her, and she hugged me for all she was worth.

The nurse loitered by the door, and then Alice spoke.

'Lovely to see you, Davey! Oh, I'm so glad you could come!'

The nurse looked at me with a beaming smile and a shake of the head.

'I really didn't think I would ever hear our Alice speak!' And then she uttered, almost in a whisper, 'Please don't try and correct her, that's if you don't mind?'

I nodded reassuringly as the nurse slipped back outside. Alice was at sixes and sevens, such was her childlike pleasure at seeing me, or whoever she thought I was. But then she passed me a small letter, urging me to look at it.

Dear Mum,

Trust that this letter finds you as well as can be expected? We would so love to come and see you, but you know how it is – three young sons, time and money! Will write often and send you more photos as we get them developed. Hope you like the one of baby Harry in the pool.

Your loving son, Davey

X X X

I noticed the Australian postmark, and as I passed the letter back to Alice she hugged me again.

'Davey, I knew you would come and see me! Oh thank you, dearest, dearest Davey!'

And so that became the routine – every Friday, for a couple of hours, I would visit Alice, and how she loved my visits. The nurses told me that the only time she ever spoke was when I was with her. And strangely, perhaps conveniently, I believed that this was the start of scratching the surface of making things up to her. And if Harry was looking down, I hoped that he felt a little less angry towards me...

CHAPTER TEN

The Calm Before The Storm

Before Death, 1991 – Blue Sky

Whilst I had many things on my mind, I at least felt that life was back on a fairly even keel. I had got away with the bakery deal – *just!* Mr Skirdle never mentioned the incident again and simply resorted back to his old cheerful self – and for that I was eternally grateful. And word had it that Mr Ball had stepped in, expressing a positive opinion on my dedication to the job, saying that I was young, and it would appear that I had acted out of character, and that of course everyone deserved a second chance.

And due to the healthy nature of my bank balance, I had official confirmation that the building society were prepared to let me purchase the family home. But prior to signing my life away, out of courtesy I telephoned my father. After five minutes or so of insipid pleasantries, Ray concluded that his own financial situation was poor to bankrupt – which I felt was a fair description of his morals – so it would be impossible for him to clear the arrears. And so, I was left with a decision to make. Much deliberation later, the heart said no! But the business brain said yes! Despite the rather hefty mortgage that remained, having now received all the appropriate figures from the building society, I realised that there was an equity figure that could surpass five figures should I choose to purchase the property, with a view to then sell. So, who better to reach the conclusion that I would have been a fool not to have taken advantage of the situation. Once the house was legally mine, Yasmin expressed an interest in us making it our home, that perhaps we should consider her moving in with me. I pondered her suggestion for a millionth of a second. I loved the idea of living together, but I had also dreamed of our first home being a place that we had both chosen, fallen in love with and ached for the moment we were handed the keys. And so our search started, each piece of the jigsaw arranged and prepared.

'Yasmin, I've had an offer on Mum's house today, and I'm tempted to accept it.'

Yasmin looked at me as though keen to say something, but she remained quiet, just offering an agreeing nod, so I continued.

'I think I've found the perfect place for us!'

Yasmin's eyes grew, and then in synchronised harmony we both blurted out, '*Sky Cottage!*'

We just stared, suddenly racing to get out our words.

'On the edge of the main green?'

'Bloody hell, Yasmin, yeah! I think it will be absolutely perfect for us!'

It would seem that we had both been monitoring the same *perfect* home for weeks, and as we uncorked a bottle of red, we excitedly discussed our plans and dreams for the rather rundown place – but to apply the estate agents' speak, a chocolate box cottage, main green setting, totally original features, in need of love and renovation. We give you: Sky Cottage. And so within weeks, our cold unwanted house was gone and we were on the *verge* of purchasing our dream, albeit, tied up with red tape and lethargy, compliments of our incompetent solicitors. Therefore, I was homeless.

Yasmin's mum was initially reluctant, but with a serious lecture and sincere swearing on the *Holy Bible*, I was eventually allowed to move into the small spare room, which just happened to be tucked downstairs, accessible via the kitchen only – therefore keeping our vow of chastity while under Yasmin's mum's roof totally in the realms of my new landlady's wishes. On the whole, we respected her house rules, and though sometimes a little frustrating, at least we were under the same roof, and that was all that mattered to us both.

Financially, I was chasing my dream. Though I was in boundary and Grade II listed disputes over Sky Cottage – I was up for the battle! And amidst the madness I had managed to negotiate the purchase of the now closed-down record shop, just five doors up from the Old Bakery site. I had plans to turn it into offices, as it was a Tardis of a building at four storeys high. I felt that the street-level section would make a wonderful upmarket restaurant, enhanced by the plans I had to develop the rear of the property, which led down to the canal and open countryside. It was a wonderful opportunity. At least this time,

I had gone through the correct channels and, most importantly, I had discovered a niche that was as yet only obvious to me. Jack De'Vil was shrewd and had good vision, and we seemed to be the only young blood amongst the local property developers. But Jack was keen to purchase and restore the old buildings, making them into flats and offices, and hadn't grasped the potential of the canal. And for that, I was eternally grateful, because it was really starting to fall into place for me.

Before Death, 1992 – Blue Sky

Jack would leave me alone for a while, and then he'd be back – his venomous black eyes would bore into me, his usual threats gathering fresh momentum each time he felt I was getting too big for my boots. It had been many months now since the newspaper had printed the story about my involvement with the bakery, but Jack, true to form, paid me a visit.

I was the last to leave Skirdle's late one Tuesday evening. I walked happily, totally unsuspecting, down the side alley towards my car when out stepped Jack.

'Good evening, Mr Big Shot Wanker!'

I stopped suddenly, my keenness to get home to my beautiful girlfriend now pushed firmly to the back of my mind. He stepped up to me, the stench of whisky and cigar smoke sour and warm on my face. I waited for his next threat, but instead, his knee was forced sharply into my groin, and there was no amount of pride or inner strength that could keep me standing. I dropped to my knees, breathless and nauseous. I then felt the full force of the *devil's* spit hit the back of my head. Through the pain and humiliation, you question your resolve, your lack of backbone, but should you challenge your demons? Will you win or lose? Jack's shadow seemed to step back away from me and I felt the air around me lighten. I rolled over onto my back, the pain almost bearable in this position. The *devil* stepped forward with a grin and pouting lips.

'Good doggy, now that's the Ritchie Angel I know and *love!*'

In defiance and with the fact that I felt just about able to, I staggered painfully to my feet, relying heavily on the bonnet of my company Escort.

'Jack, *okay!* This time I've managed to buy something for myself.' I coughed and spluttered. 'And make a few quid!' I turned my head to face him. 'For God's sake, if I hadn't, and you were to cripple my every move, then I would have left Willow by now! So how would you have had your pound of flesh then, eh? *For fucks sake, Jack!*' I cradled my groin in my hands and endeavoured to stand up straight while pleading my case. 'You... you must be making a fortune out of the Old School development, plus all your other bits. There'll be stuff for you! But don't push me too hard, Jack. I need to take the odd one for myself, otherwise there'll be nothing to keep me here!' I leant forward, buckled and pained, my hands on my knees and felt the need to take a moment.

Jack's black eyes started to dance – I think the message was hitting home. He grunted and snarled.

'Okay, Angel, but don't go getting *too* greedy! I'll be watching you!'

The *devil* started to walk backwards out of the alley, his eyes teasing me with every step until finally, he turned around and was gone. I ran my hand across the back of my head and screwed my face up with disgust as the *devil's* cold spit spread like slug-slime between my fingers. I ground the saliva into the brickwork and despairingly got in my car. I instinctively locked the doors and slumped back angrily into the car seat. I thought about what I'd said, but I totally despised myself for even explaining my actions to him. I mean, here I was, twenty-two years old, trying to make my way in the world, and yet I had this evil thug hanging over me. It was ruining my life, and the more I thought about it, the more I felt determined to sort it out for good.

Yasmin and I *finally* got Sky Cottage. As we stood, the sun setting around us, we were simply in awe of how beautiful our stone and render dream home was.

'Oh God, Ritchie, it's just *so* perfect... Look, we've even got the roses around the door.'

I didn't feel the need for words – anything that I could say would simply detract from this special moment. I took in the chocolate box cottage – my estate agent's head accepted that although a bit small and the garden not the biggest, it was nirvana for Yasmin and me. Without doubt the place needed to be totally renovated, but it was our home, and we loved it. During the summer months we would spend nights there, our large sleeping bag laid out on the old bare creaky floorboards, a couple of bottles of wine, the open fire lit should we need it, and so it was a wonderful time that would stay with us forever. The honeysuckle that almost covered the front of the cottage filled the air with a perfume that was intoxicating.

Amongst the renovations and heavy drinking sessions, I felt that it was only a matter of time before Scottie accepted that Janey was the girl for him. And the romance between Jimmy and Sally, well, they became totally inseparable. So what more could I ask for? An inspiring, passionately addictive girlfriend. A warm and snug character home very close to completion. And to cap it all off, some of the most wonderful friends you could ever ask for. Nothing was ever too much trouble for them, and they also knew when not to outstay their welcome – what a wonderful combination!

Before Death, 1993 – Blue Sky
Time gathered pace and Sky Cottage finally resembled the initial dream. Yasmin and I were fortunate that our ideas and taste were as compatible as our attraction for each other. We rarely, if at all, disagreed on anything, and so, together, we created a beautiful home.

Summer slipped away, the rusty autumn easing us into an icy-cold winter, and just as our fingers were starting to thaw, spring gave us all renewed hope, and then with grateful arms, summer was back. The long drawn-out days, many late evenings sitting outside on the patio, drinking smooth full-bodied red wine, lapping up the deep and sometimes totally inane conversations with our valued friends. And then as the nights started to draw in, and thoughts of hibernation crossed our minds, autumn would hoot its final warning, and winter would rear its ugly head once again. Though one might argue that winter cannot be described fairly if offered as ugly, for me, it has only a handful of ugly moments: the dark and bleak icy-cold Monday mornings, the slaps of sadistic hail and the biting wind numbing your face. But then, when the blue skies frame the coldness, the glorious top coat of freshly fallen snow covering our scene, perhaps ugly is most definitely ill chosen.

Before Death, 1995 – Blue Sky
And so, our young lives were ticking away with increased prosperity, and the seconds that came and went would leave us unnoticed, gone and never to be recaptured. On this particular evening, maudlin and questioning, we once again found ourselves inside Sky Cottage. The logs in the original inglenook fireplace blazing away, a perfect backdrop for us to continue our wallowing, unaware that in years to come it would be now, times like these, that we would look back and yearn nostalgically. I raised my glass, the rich red wine close to spilling.

'To each of you, my very dear friends!'

We all cheered totally out of unison, clumsily but sincerely. My sombre thoughtful mood was interrupted by the gorgeous, still single, Leoni, who beckoned to me and looked inquisitively, and then repeated something her dad had said to her.

'Ritchie, my dad's started working at Mercedes, and he said (hic) that he was surprised you were still driving around in the *old* pickup truck (hic).'

I laughed and thought a little about my answer. Though I liked nice things, I suppose I never really forgot the words of the wise old man, who had his large house and flash car, all the trappings of success, but the recipe didn't work for him. And the little saying that he would quote to me: 'Ritchie, the more you know, the less you show!' And so when Scottie and Jimmy would get onto me, just like Leoni was now – 'When are you going to scrap that old pickup truck of yours?' – I would simply smile, and then say, 'It's doing its job, almost a lucky charm, and at least the company rep-mobile is still there when I need it!'

Yasmin raised her glass, her words endearingly slurred.

'Hey, I love that pickup truck! It always reminds me of when I would *lust* after Ritchie (hic) from afar!'

Everyone laughed, Scottie pretending to throw up. I kissed

Yasmin and got lost in the moment, eternally grateful for such a beautiful creature. As I slumped back into the soft cushions of the settee, the conversation amongst the others vibrant and animated, I reflected on what I had achieved in such a short space of time. Sky Cottage was ninety per cent done and wonderful. My purchase of the old record shop was now fully developed – I had hired Steve, my old boss and his building company, and they had done me proud. I had beautifully converted the record shop into seven luxury self-contained offices, with a large street-level restaurant as planned, but had also grasped with both hands other opportunities that had presented themselves. I was in no doubt that I had stretched myself painfully and dangerously thin, but I felt vindicated – the light at the end of the tunnel was dazzling. Steve had drafted in backup contractors and worked tirelessly in creating an impressive portfolio for me. The Old Bakery deal had turned out to be overwhelmingly fortunate, and had given me a tremendous amount of hard cash to invest wisely in several gift-horse opportunities. The secret was to reinvest any profits back into what had been kind to you, and so, I had no hesitation when the historic but beautifully built library block right in the centre of the market square became available and couldn't believe my luck when I was confirmed as the successful purchaser. The overall size of it meant that four large shops could easily be achieved, retaining the grandeur of the building. So I was doing okay. My unbending commitment, my *ball and chain,* was having to pay out seventy per cent of my rental income per month for the next ten years at least, but the property values were escalating better than my business plan forecasts. After that time, should I ever feel the time was right to sell, I believed strongly that I was set up for life. But every single penny made, was at the expense of an intimidating visit from the *devil* himself. Snarling aggressively, devoid of an ounce of respect for my ability to thrive in his acidic, toxic attempts to shut out any sunshine, good fortune or otherwise that would see me successfully forge forward. The visits were dwindling, perhaps three or four a year, but just when I let myself believe that Jack was losing interest in me, he would be back. And each time, I swore: that next time I would be strong, take him on – but guess what? I wouldn't, couldn't, didn't! Instead, to pacify him, I would throw Jack a few crumbs, a business opportunity for him to temporarily quench his unwavering hatred, and I would chastise myself for it. But the result was that I was still alive, but each time he would leave me, I was left with no doubt that he would be working on that! I nervously shook the thought away, concentrating on the positive. I swallowed hard, bewilderment risen from the sheer fact that I had kept my problem with the *devil* away from Yasmin – but so very grateful for that! And though of course Yasmin was totally behind me in whatever venture I wanted to undertake, I didn't bring my work home with me. As far as she was concerned, the buildings, the money in the high-interest accounts, that was all mine – not my choice, but hers. She would argue that she had her job, her money, and wasn't interested in taking anything from me. But in time, I knew that she would accept that whatever I achieved in business, I was working for us, for our security, for our future!

CHAPTER ELEVEN

Sheer Bloody-Mindedness

Before Death, 1996 – Blue Sky
'Fluffers! Yasmin, can you see her?'

Yasmin shook her head. 'Come on, Ritchie, we'll have to run! I think she's gone into the Major's garden again! Oh, Ritchie, she has… That dog's got the devil in her!'

I ran after Yasmin, pulling her back just as we approached the Major's cottage just on the other side of the green to us. The snow was thick on the ground, but the sky was a perfect blue.

'Hey, Yasmin, just walk normally, then maybe the Major won't notice us. Let's just call Fluffers *very* quietly.'

Yasmin tried to stifle her giggles. Fluffers, our very fluffy golden Labrador, had once again gone into the Major's prize-winning garden – she had a total fascination with it. As we got to the boundary of his garden, where he joined up with Mrs Jeffers – his next-door neighbour and bridge partner – I tried to call Fluffers again.

'Oh God, Yasmin, she's bloody rolling around on top of his Buxus thingummy! The snows meant it's just the right height! Fluffers! Fluffers! Come on, Fluffers! The Major's not going to be *too* keen on that. Fluffers!'

But then it was all too late.

'*What the hell!* Bloody Angel's dog again! Shooo! *Get off there, you BASTARD dog!!!*'

Fluffers barked and playfully lolloped about, quickly chasing her tail for a couple of spins, and then ran towards an embarrassed Yasmin and me. The Major gave chase, red-faced and seething, his cane raised high. But then he spotted us.

'Oh! Mr and Mrs Angel...oh *how* embarrassing!'

In a slow motion movement, the Major looked up at his raised cane – his eye flicking from the cane to us, and then back again – and then brought it down to his side in a swift regimental fashion.

'Arrgh! Wouldn't have hurt her. Dreadfully sorry, Mrs Angel my dear...Mr Angel!'

Yasmin smiled at our embarrassed neighbour, and then tried to lighten the moment.

'Not at all, Major. Come here, Fluffers! You're a very bad dog, you really are the very worst!'

I coughed and uttered, 'Sometimes she can be so good, Major, but then she just goes deaf on us and starts acting like a daft puppy! Even though she's over a year old now! But of course any damage, you'll have to let me know. But more importantly, we'll try and keep her on a lead...until she understands!'

We quickly got Fluffers back on her lead and waved at the Major, who responded politely. So we continued our walk. It was just after 2 o'clock Tuesday afternoon – just a week to go until Christmas.

'Ritchie, have you noticed how the Major always calls us Mr and Mrs Angel?'

I smiled and pulled her close to me.

'Yes, I think everybody around here presumes we're married.'

Yasmin took my hand and pulled my arm roughly, seemingly keen to discuss the matter further, but not totally sure how to go about it. Fluffers finally seemed to calm herself down, now walking steadily as though interested in the outcome of our conversation.

'Ritchie... I want us to get married!'

I coughed and spluttered, shocked at the directness of her proposal. And in response to not knowing what to say, I started to respond rather negatively.

'Yasmin, but we had always said that we would only get married should we run out of things to talk about. And we'd agreed that should we run out of things to talk about, then it was time to part! So what's changed?'

The love of my life squeezed my hand tightly in hers.

'Ritchie, we're never going to run out of things to say to each other! I want to be Mrs Yasmin Angel, and in time, I want us to have a child. I want to be with you, and so I just feel that I'm *really* ready. I mean for God's sake, we're both twenty-six now!' Yasmin stopped talking and pulled me to her.

As our bodies stood still and silent, thick snow around our feet, there was something magical about this lady: a courage that never seemed to waver, an inner beauty that seemed to burn brighter with each passing day, and a warmth that simply overwhelmed me; her hands, her eyes, her voice. I let my head fall back, simply taking in all the positives. I had on occasion thought seriously about asking Yasmin to marry me, but there was an inbuilt fear about marriage and how it seemed to be the *beginning of the end* of any promising relationship. My mum and dad's marriage had been a disaster! So that hadn't exactly inspired confidence in the institution of 'I do'. And I often watched married couples, and listened to their constant bickering and moaning at each other behind the other's back *or to their face*...and I wasn't quite sure which was worse. And it would never cease to amaze me how the guy would stop off at the pub on his way home from work, leaning against the bar, a vision of disinterest and undoubted fear as the last dregs of his pint would disappear down his neck: 'Oh well, best go and face the wife and kids...' And you would often hear the wives talking with their friends: 'God, he's *so* useless, should have listened to my mother!' And so I wondered whether or not staying together forever, happy, in love and wanting to be with the other *till death do us part...forsaking all others,* was all that feasible, if it was possible to still love and cherish your partner until your dying breath. But as I reflected on Yasmin walking away from me, not looking back, never to kiss her again, never to feel her perspiration on my chest, to push the stray curl out of her sparkling mischievous eyes, to have her whisper how much she loved me, to have her shout at the top of her lungs in our local *crowded* supermarket that she longed for me 'to take her now!', to just know that she often watches me as I sleep, and for me to be able to just watch her sleep, breathe, twist and turn amongst the bed sheets the way only Yasmin can. If I could live without all these traits, if I could walk away and still function, totally convinced that someone else out there could make me feel *this* complete, then I should turn down her proposal.

I stepped away from this person before me, this flesh and blood human being. Surely she was just the same as a thousand other girls capable of taking my heart? I stood just two feet away and Yasmin didn't move. She just stared at me, a small flushed pout of the lips and the slightest closing of her blue eyes. I took a huge deep breath. Could I walk away? It would be cruel, but she would undeniably get over it, although perhaps hate me for a few weeks. But then the sheer force of what Yasmin stood for in my life hit me, as it did every day, but suddenly, questioning her power, I dropped to my knees.

'Yasmin, please would you do me the *honour*...of being my wife?'

And as Yasmin stood pondering my proposal for what seemed like a lifetime, my thoughts continued to process. As I looked at her little cold nose and dazzling blue eyes, I knew I could never deny myself the opportunity of waking up with her every day, for the rest of my life. To be blessed and honoured having her pregnant with our baby, and to experience first-hand what a wonderful mother she would make. Yasmin suddenly threw herself fully onto me and I staggered back, laughing uncontrollably, her hot tender kisses in between, 'I do, I do, I do…I DO!'

Finally, we were home – twenty paces in thirty life-changing minutes – wet, icy cold, but delirious with excitement. We let Fluffers off her lead and could hear the telephone ringing inside the cottage. Yasmin ran towards the front door, pushing it open, just managing to grab Fluffers before she carried all the wet snow into the hallway. We were falling over each other, but I finally got my boots off and made a dash for the phone. It stopped just as my hand touched the receiver. Yasmin laughed, pinching my bum as she walked past me.

'Do you want a Drambuie coffee, Ritchie? Thought it might warm us both up!'

I enthusiastically accepted my future bride's inspired offer, and the phone then rang again – this time I was ready.

'Ritchie, where have you been?' Jimmy's excited voice said on the other end of the line. 'Listen, Ritchie, you're going to kill me, but I've something to tell you! It's Sally and I…we've run away to Gretna Green! We're getting married at 9 o'clock in the morning!'

I couldn't believe what my best friend was saying to me.

'*Fuck, Jimmy!* Why Gretna Green? And how come *now*? And you *can't* get married without *us* there!'

Jimmy yelled down the phone at me.

'*I was hoping you'd say that! Shit!* The pips are going to go any minute, but this is why I'm ringing you. I want you and Yasmin to get here, bring Scottie, the girls, *but please*, make sure you get here!!'

And with that, the pips kicked in and the phone went dead. I walked ever so slightly numb into the kitchen and put my arms coolly around Yasmin's waist.

'Ummm, Yasmin my darling, what's the chance of you breaking up a couple of days early from work?'

She carried on pouring the boiling hot water into the cups, but inquisitively uttered, 'Why?'

'Because, Jimmy and Sally, well, like all the best couples, they're getting married!'

Yasmin quickly put the kettle down and turned to face me.

'Oh that's absolutely brilliant! Oh God, Jimmy will be *sooo* happy! But why a couple of days off?'

I shook my head, still mystified and shocked.

'Because, my love, the pair of prats have run off to Gretna Green! Don't ask me why, but that's where they are, and that's where they want their friends! Oh, and by 9 o'clock in the morning!'

Yasmin laughed out loud, as did I. We couldn't get hold of Janey and Leoni, they had gone down south to see Leoni's dad – who had suddenly become very ill, but we all had our fingers crossed that he would respond to treatment. And so it left Scottie, Yasmin and I. I felt bad that I couldn't get everybody together. I knew that Jimmy and Sally would be disappointed. But then, they had taken a chance by shooting off up to Scotland just like that, so they only had themselves to blame.

Scottie soon arrived at Sky Cottage. He was really excited about our mad dash to the Scottish border. As we loaded up the car, I could hear Yasmin apologising on the phone to her employer. As I walked back through the hall, I could see her face, worryingly depleted.

As she replaced the handset, she said, 'God, she can be an annoying cow!'

I took a step forward and wrapped my arms around her.

'God, Ritchie, I've never *once* had a day off! And yet, I know it's short notice, but she's moaning because we've got health and safety in tomorrow, and she insists I be there!'

I lifted Yasmin's chin towards me.

'Look, gorgeous, I know you're probably not going to like this, but seeing as Janey and Leoni aren't coming, well, maybe just Scottie and I should go. I'm sure Jimmy and Sally will understand, and the way the snow is, maybe it would be wise if we took the pickup – at least it's a four-wheel drive.'

Yasmin took a deep breath and sulked petulantly for a moment, before stamping her feet and bursting out, 'Oh God! But these are our *best* friends. I wouldn't have minded if she'd asked me nicely, but instead, she just goes all huffy and starts questioning my loyalty, and then demands me there *or* face the consequences, Yasmin!'

I hugged her tightly.

'Yasmin, let Scottie and me go, and I think that when I get back we should really talk, you know, about you opening your own nursery. You'd be a major success!'

As Scottie and I ventured off, easing the pickup truck through the icy thick snow, Yasmin waved frantically, blowing kisses and warning me, 'Please, Ritchie, take extra care! I've just heard on the radio how we're in for more heavy snow!'

I blew a kiss back, Scottie mimicking every soppy gesture. Within twenty miles or so, darkness started to fall, along with light gentle snowflakes batted away by the intermittent wiper blades. I drummed my fingers on top of the dashboard.

'See, Scottie? My rusty four-wheel drive heap has its uses; should be perfect with all this snow about!'

Scottie looked at me unconvinced. 'It's a piece of corroding shit, Ritchie, and you're a madman and a tight bastard for keeping it!' He laughed excessively; I laughed a little.

Though there was a thick freezing fog developing, I felt convinced that all we needed to do was take it easy. Scottie turned the music up, and then started yelling to make himself heard over the noise of it.

'Ritchie! Janey is one hell of a woman!'

I turned the radio back down, enough to stop my teeth from hurting. Scottie shook his head and tutted his disapproval, but then continued in a more sedate tone.

'Seriously though, Ritchie, she's *so* into me. She has great taste! But joking apart, I *am* without doubt a very lucky man!'

I nodded approvingly, and felt quite impressed that Scottie had tiptoed into the realms of being 'almost humble' for a moment there. But as the dire weather conditions demanded my full concentration, I felt relieved to finally hit the motorway, and we started to really eat up the miles. Though I had always been closer to Jimmy, you couldn't help but love Scottie. Though to most people he came across as cocky and arrogant, deep down and to his close friends, we knew he was extremely cocky and breathtakingly arrogant! But Scottie didn't suffer fools, and he was very fussy about who he had as friends. If you crossed him, that was that – no forgiveness, no second chance. But we'd known each other since junior school.

We'd sat next to each other for the first two terms or so, that was until Scottie broke his leg badly when he was about seven years of age. We didn't see him at school for nearly a year. And as I reflected, I thought about the summer term that Scottie was away, and my mind was then filled with thoughts of Rose.

Rose started school just after the Easter holidays. I remember her standing there, with our teacher Miss Shaw. Rose was a very quiet girl. She always wore her straight jet-black hair down, beautifully combed, not a strand out of place. I remember as I sat leaning on my desk, chewing the end of my pencil, thinking that she reminded me of how Snow White would have looked as a seven year old.

'So is that okay, Ritchie? *Ritchie Angel?'*

I quickly answered Miss Shaw. 'Sorry, miss! Oh yes, miss!'

And then Rose pulled out the chair next to me and sat herself down. The other children in the class giggled. But as I stole a look at Rose, the faintest of smiles crept across her lips. I then beamed back, an impressive, more accommodating grin, but Rose shrivelled away with embarrassment, looking down at her lap. The rest of the class never did take to her, and the truth was, she never made any effort to make friends with them. But I, for some reason, would spurn the offers of joining my friends to play at break-time, because I knew full well that Rose would not join in and I didn't want her to be left on her own. And so, Rose and I became inseparable – at school at least. When my mum collected me at the end of each day, Rose would be picked up by her father – a very sullen, grey-looking man, always dressed in his grey sombre suit, though he made the effort with a claret-coloured tie. As Rose's father opened the back door to their grey *sit up and beg* Ford Popular car, Rose would give me a sneaky wave, keen for her father not to see this show of friendship. And then Rose and her father would drive off down the road. I can still see clearly how she would turn and look at me through the back window, her face a little drained, before finally sliding back down into her seat. I would always watch as the bright orange indicator flicked out at the side of the car, before turning right at the end of the long avenue.

'Ritchie?'

My thoughts were suddenly interrupted by Scottie.

'Ritchie, I've something serious to tell you, but you mustn't say a word! Not a *bloody* word to anyone, you wanker, or I'll kick the shit out of you!'

I smiled, struggling to keep my laughter in, but then glanced at my friend.

'Why so serious, Scottie? What's your big secret?'

Scottie shuffled about in his seat, his head bobbing up and down as the pickup continued its journey up the snow-covered motorway.

'Say you promise then, Ritchie…'

I smiled again, this time telling him not to be such a prat and that of course I wouldn't repeat anything that was so obviously important that I *had* to make a promise. Now I was laughing, but Scottie was in a world of his own and a little agitated.

Then he blurted it out. 'I'm gonna be a *Dad!* Janey's pregnant!'

My eyes were suddenly uncomfortably wide with the shock of my friend's news. I looked across at Scottie and took in his proud face. I shook my head from side to side and then laughed out loud.

'You bloody star! Oh my God, and of course, it's what you both want … you're both chuffed to bits?'

Scottie looked at me, his grin subsiding a little.

'Yeah, we're chuffed! But I know Janey's mum and dad are gonna go mad! *Bloody ballistic* in fact! They're very protective towards her, and they're not that impressed with me really, think I'm a bit of a wanker! Suppose because I'm a bit quiet with them, but hey, that's just me with old people – they're well into their forties.'

I looked at Scottie, suddenly his face full of excitement again, and I felt very happy for him. He was doing well at work – he had recently been made gym manager at the local sports centre – and he deserved it. He was brilliant at his job and a talented athlete. And had he not broken his leg so badly as a child, who knows what he could have achieved.

After a couple of hours or so, Scottie started to drift off, and so, as the quietness consumed me, my mind turned back to Rose. She would often enter my thoughts, and I would always feel a great sadness at losing her. It had been at the end of term, when we were all breaking up for the summer holidays. It was about 2 o'clock in the afternoon, and we were finishing shortly after. Rose had been very excited about her eighth birthday party the following day, and though I had asked her to invite a couple of the girls from our class to help her try to build a friendship or two, she simply wouldn't hear of it, not for a second.

'Ritchie, no! None of the children in this school like me, they never even look at me. I think that they feel I've stolen you from them. You must notice it?'

I nodded my head. Rose was right.

'But, Ritchie, I don't care. Just promise me you'll come to my party tomorrow, 3 o'clock!' Rose beamed at me, placing her hand on mine.

I suddenly looked around at my classmates, embarrassed that they may have seen Rose's show of affection, but I breathed a sigh of relief as I realised no one had noticed a thing.

As we left school that day, the sun was very warm – I could feel the strength of the heat tingling my arms and face. Rose's father was there as usual, his grey Ford Popular looking old and out of place amongst the other cars parked close by. I was surprised to see Rose in her smart but long thick coat as she walked obediently towards the open passenger door. She always wore her coat, but with the intense heat this afternoon I found it strange. With an out-of-character act amusing me even further, her father had, for the first time, removed his suit jacket, his tie loosened slightly and his shirtsleeves rolled up to his elbows very neatly. And as Rose stepped into the car, I noticed her father smile; though very slight, it was, nonetheless, the first smile I had ever seen him produce. As the car pulled out of the school gates, passing me as it always would, through the open window I could hear the song *Seasons in the Sun* by Terry Jacks. The words seemed to drift hypnotically out of the car: 'Goodbye, my friend, it's hard to die…when all the birds are singing in the sky!' And then the music faded as the car pulled further away. Rose didn't turn around this time, but simply lifted her arm up and gave a very slight wave, before quickly pulling her arm back down.

On the day of Rose's party, I woke very late and jumped quickly out of bed. As I flung open my bedroom curtains, I felt a little disappointed. There were a few drops of rain on the window pane and the sky looked pessimistically grey. I remember running down the stairs, anxious and uncomfortable. I became sullen and cross as I noticed that it was nearly 2 o'clock in the afternoon. My Uncle Dan, though not my real uncle, for a change wasn't around, but my mum was sitting quietly at the dining table, reading her *Cosmopolitan*.

'*Mum!* How come you didn't wake me? It's just, well, it's Rose's party at *three!* '

My mum lifted her slightly bemused eyes towards me and smiled.

'Sorry, love, you looked so peaceful up there, I thought that maybe you needed the rest. And your Uncle Dan, well, you know when he's in one of his moods. Surprised *we* didn't wake you.'

My heart sank a little as it always did when they rowed. My mum got up and headed into the kitchen.

'Some toast, Ritchie? Oh, and what party? You never mentioned your little friend was having a party!'

I stormed into the kitchen.

'Of *course* I told you! 3 o'clock, her house! *Soon!* '

My mum totally ignored my outburst and simply continued to place some bread under the grill. And with a wry smile she glanced half-heartedly at me, and lethargically uttered, 'Sorry, dear, my mistake.'

I finally managed to get mum out of the house, and we headed off to Rose's party.

'Ritchie, love, are you sure you know where we're going?'

I huffed and pulled mum's hand to try to quicken her up. I had never been to Rose's house before, but I knew where she lived – or at least I thought I did. I presumed she lived in a grand but hidden away house at the edge of the village, which had converted the gatehouse into a little sweet shop. And to the side of the shop there was a narrow driveway – a private road with large gates further down the drive that always appeared to be locked. Eventually, we reached the shop. I stopped and looked up at my mum.

'Rose is not going to be very happy. I've not *even* got her a card, and I really wanted to get her a present. I thought you would have got one earlier in the week...'

My mum shook her head, a forced smile on her face.

'Mum, can I just get her some chocolates or something from the shop? Please, Mum!'

It wasn't long before I was making my way down the narrow driveway, clutching my last-minute gift from the shop. The nice shopkeeper had allowed us to use his pen to write Rose's card. And the flowery paper bag he gave us didn't look too bad for my dear friend's chocolates: *Cadbury's Roses*. I felt inspired, totally convinced that Rose would be tickled pink by my clever and original idea. But suddenly, my smugness was being tinged with confusion and uncertainty. We seemed to be walking forever down the twisting driveway, my mum repeating her concerns.

'Are you sure it's down here, Ritchie love? I've never seen a house down here!'

But then my heart leapt with relief as I finally spotted the gates, fully open, just a dozen or so steps away. I felt excited and quickened my pace, dragging my mum along.

'Ritchie! Slow down, love, it's only *just* gone three!'

But then the gates started to close and a tall old man in a black suit clanged them together. My mum lurched forward.

'Excuse me! There's a party here; 3 o'clock?'

The man looked sad, a vacant look on his tired face.

'Very sorry, but there's no party here today.'

I suddenly pushed past my mum.

'But I'm invited. It's Rose's eighth birthday party... she's expecting me!'

The man looked at my mum and then down at me. I seemed to focus on his pencil thin lips, and then just with the slightest of glances took in his white ashen face. I was then drawn back to his lips, which started to move and then horrible words came out.

'I'm sorry, son, but Rose won't be having a party.'

Totally focused on the man's lips, I heard my own words spill out.

'Please, sir, why? Rose is my best friend!'

The man's mouth turned to my mum as if looking for some inspiration, and then his lips seemed to face me again.

'Son, I'm very sorry... but Rose died this morning. She's not been well for some time, but it's still been a shock. I'm very sorry... but you've had a wasted journey.'

My head had become separated from my body. I was knotted, numb and nauseous, totally devastated, but not able to express any outward emotion. I remember being dragged home, my mum between the deafening silences trying to offer words of consolation, trying to explain how sometimes these things can happen. But I couldn't speak – I could hardly breathe. I remember staring at my feet as I made my way home, the memory of Rose and her last wave goodbye from the back seat of her father's car repeating itself relentlessly. As I walked beneath the trees that lined my route, the deafening rustle of blowing leaves battled with the haunting words of: 'Goodbye, my friend, it's hard to die ... when all the birds are singing in the sky', intermingled with the intermittent disfigured shadows being cast around my best shoes as the sun appeared and then disappeared again behind the clouds. I lifted my eyes as I arrived home and noticed my *uncle's* car. And as I entered the house – my flesh tender and in pain – I felt his rough, strong hand ruffle my hair. I remember him saying something about me being mardy, and then my mum whispering something to him. I stepped away quickly, desperate for the solitude of my bedroom. As I climbed the stairs, I couldn't believe my uncle's sudden burst of laughter – not out of malice, I was sure, perhaps a nervous reaction. But as I closed my bedroom door and slumped onto my bed, I had to try to deal with the loss of Rose.

Scottie suddenly cut into my thoughts, sleepily, clumsily turning off the tape, before finally flicking onto the radio.

'Ritchie, seriously, how can you see, mate? The snow's *really* coming down. Are you sure this is a good idea?'

I glanced quickly at my concerned friend and gave him a

reassuring nod of the head, before my squinting eyes firmly fixed on the torrent of white before me.

'We'll be alright, Scottie baby, we're making progress.' I swallowed hard, my temples burning with the relentless concentration. 'I can't let them down, we've got to get up there! Men or mice, Scottie, men or mice?'

Scottie punched me sharply in the arm, fear and concern bubbling over.

'Yeahhh, I know! But it's *really* getting bad, you twat. Remember, I'm going to be a Dad, I have responsibilities, I don't want you and your Kamikaze attitude killing us both ... well, more importantly, *me!*'

I shot my eyes sharply left, taking in Scottie's unusually furrowed brow.

'Come on, Scottie, have a little faith. Have I ever come close to killing either of us?'

Scottie tutted and leant forward, shaking his head and fiddling with the radio, muttering about a news and weather update. A distorted voice screeched in and then drifted away.

'That's the one, Scottie!'

'Yesss, Ritchie, I gathered that! It's just that it's really shit reception!'

I opened my eyes wide, desperate to regain focus on the road ahead, my knuckles white. My ears pricked up as we started to receive the information we desperately needed: 'Serious weather conditions are making it almost impossible for drivers the further north you travel. We seriously advise that unless your journey is of an urgent nature, then stay at home!'

Scottie flicked the radio back over to the tape, his head now nodding vigorously at the radio warning.

'See, Ritchie? She's just said it: unless you are a really thick, stupid, mad-headed *wanker,* do not attempt to use the roads!'

I chewed the inside of my mouth, a faint ripple of amusement passing through me. But it *was* getting bad, and I knew that Scottie had a point. But I felt *so* determined to make it to Jimmy and Sally's wedding, I wasn't about to let a bit of snow and Scottie's nerves get in the way of that. And so I remained focused, although more than aware of my agitated red-faced friend snarling at me, shaking his head, before finally leaning forward, flipping the tape over and turning the music up.

Eventually, Scottie dozed off again – not surprising really since we had been on the road for nearly six painful hours and were now literally crawling along. Either side of his sleep, Scottie had talked non-stop about Janey and the plans he had for her, and their joint excitement at the prospect of having a son.

'A little lad, Ritchie, I would love that, a little Scottie, a cracking little lad!'

I was thrilled for them both. My thoughts drifted to Yasmin. I felt overwhelmed by the fact that we had finally decided to get married. And then I started to daydream about us both having a child. As I created the perfect family in my head, I thought that I would like a daughter – I don't know why, I just felt that Yasmin with a little girl seemed to fit better somehow – and the whole blessed picture filled me with an overwhelming desire to realise the dream.

We were now well over seven hours into our journey, and for the last hour or so, it had become increasingly difficult. And just to bolster proceedings, Scottie was snoring like a foghorn. From what I could gather, we were just a few miles short of the Scottish border. My head was pounding and I was squinting constantly, desperate to remain focused, almost second-guessing what actually lay before the heavy snowflakes that were hitting the windscreen with such ferocity that for each one beaten away by the wiper blades, there were at least a dozen or more ready to overpower us. Suddenly, I caught the slightest glimpse of a sign.

'God, was that for a hotel?'

I craned my neck back, thinking that a good night's sleep would perhaps be wise, convinced that daylight, however hazardous the weather, had to be easier than this madness. I tried to look for somewhere to turn around, muttering to myself, 'Mmmm, a bite to eat and a nightcap, ohhh, and a comfy bed. As long as we get a nice early start, yep, that would be cool, get there for nine easy!'

I became a little complacent, desperate to turn round before I got much further along the road that was already framed by four-foot-high snowdrifts. The wheels were increasingly twitchy, the temperature having dropped to around minus ten, the crunch of compacted ice startlingly loud. As we had proceeded under the cover of darkness, we experienced several hairy skids and swerves, but my nerve had held this far. My lights suddenly beamed onto a sign again.

'Shit! Was *that* for the hotel?'

I craned my neck like a contortionist as I cursed myself for once again missing what it said ... then another sign!

'Oh for fucks sake! Come on!'

I felt it best to stop, but before I'd even had chance to take my foot off the accelerator, the steering became incredibly light and then came the almightiest *bang.* I was thrown towards the dashboard, and Scottie, as if weightless, was flung like a rag doll in his sleep-induced state against the windscreen – the whole scene as if in slow motion. My head was jerked back, and suddenly the whole windscreen shattered, but instead of Scottie being dragged back into his seat, another jolt and his head and then his shoulders pushed through the disintegrating glass, blood replacing his pale flesh. I then feel the pickup fall, weightless, sickness filling my body, crashing and tearing into my heart, lungs and brain. I'm trying to stretch forward, trying to pull Scottie back into the truck. But then as we hit *something*, we rotate, and Scottie is dragged through the glass and into the darkness. As the vehicle continues to fall, my heart pounding as if about to ignite, I am screaming Scottie's name, and then suddenly, as the truck slams to a halt, I feel as though I've broken every bone in my body ... and then silence.

It was three days later that I woke up in Cumberland Infirmary, Carlisle. My eyes were closed, but I could hear voices around me, and then a warm familiar voice cut in.

'Oh God, Ritchie*! Nurse?* I think he's waking! Ritchie! Darling, please, it's Yasmin!'

I can feel tears in my eyes, and my heart is desperate to wake. I try to will my eyes open and then I am aware of light cutting into my darkness. I see a white line, a stronger dazzling light – it's a fluorescent tube above me. And then as I try to move my head, I see Yasmin's face come into view and then the most wonderful, welcome smile. Suddenly, tears are rolling down her cheeks, falling onto my face; then one of them drops painfully into my left eye, and a stinging sensation forces me to close them again. Yasmin quickly wipes away the salt, her apology echoing through my head. I squint my eyes open again, and see her being pushed aside by a nurse, and then a doctor hovering over me. He's beaming sharp piercing light into my pupils. She's attaching more cables onto my chest, and then as the stinging leaves my eyes, I hear my own voice.

'Scottie? Yasmin, please... where's Scottie?'

I gradually manage to focus, but then I don't like the pained look that greets me on Yasmin's distraught face. The nurse pushes her aside again, and a soft unfamiliar voice breathes over me.

'Scottie's fine, Ritchie. Just concentrate now, forget about Scottie, just look up! That's it! Everything is fine!'

I feel a sudden sharp sting in my right arm, and then a swab of cotton wool or something pressed firmly against the pain.

One by one, the nurses and the doctor leave my bedside. And then I see the face that always calms me.

'Yasmin, oh God, Yasmin... What on earth has happened?'

Yasmin drops her head, her face now against mine. And then, very softly, her lips brush my cheek, then a gentle measured kiss.

'Ritchie, you've been *so* lucky. They couldn't get to you. Your truck... *your* truck hung dangerously on a cliff edge!'

Yasmin's voice falters and she wanders over to a nurse. I cannot understand why they're both whispering, but then as I try clumsily to sit up, Yasmin is back at my side, her fingers wrapped painfully tight around mine.

'Ritchie, about Scottie...'

She didn't have to say another word. I felt a venomous lava rise up from the pit of my stomach, flood through my chest and spill painfully through my eyes – I already knew. But as her words squeaked out through her sobs: 'Ritchie... Scottie had no chance. When they found him, he was already dead. There was nothing they could do!' I just kept reliving, over and over again, what Scottie had said to me, how he had wanted us to stop, but I hadn't listened. I had been too stubborn. Convinced I could get us there, that nothing could stand in my way. And now, as my head raced and my heart ached, my throat burning, I knew I was guilty of killing him. As the tears rolled uncontrollably down my cheeks, all I could think about was Janey and their unborn child.

Before Death, 1997 – Blue Sky
Amongst the blur of hours, days and long painful nights, Jimmy and Sally came to see me, as did Janey, as did all our friends – not one of them blamed me. But they knew the truth, the truth that rolled around my broken mind relentlessly. I couldn't accept that I had risked our lives like that. I survived, but poor Scottie, so young, everything to live for, and yet through no fault of his own...gone.

I left hospital two months after the accident. I had broken my leg and a few ribs, but a couple of complications had meant that I was constantly being denied my one wish – to simply go home.

I didn't feel right for a long time – the power of guilt was totally overwhelming. Jimmy and I would go off and get ourselves tiresomely drunk, and I know for the length and breadth of my self-pity I caused Yasmin immeasurable heartache. For the brief moment sobriety enabled me to judge, I saw the disappointment and frustration in Sally's eyes. But one Wednesday morning, after a particularly heavy night, my head pounding, I looked at Yasmin, her beautiful, innocent face asleep and therefore momentarily oblivious to the crap I was giving her day in, day out. But I considered that soon her eyes would be open, and her first thoughts would be: will he be in a bad mood today, or a terrible mood? It made me shake my head with shame, and that was it! I knew I had to take responsibility for my precious life. I scribbled a loving, optimistic note for Yasmin and placed it on her bedside cabinet. I threw on a pair of shorts and a T-shirt. I then scratched my head as I searched as quietly as I could for my trainers. Finally, I opened the front door. The sheer strength of the magnificent morning grazed my eyes. But the large defiant breath I took carried me off, running and skipping like a hyperactive child. And though I took the chance of the neighbours believing I had finally flipped – why would I care about that? I was alive, and I needed to live! - I was soon on my own, in acres of unspoilt countryside. Though my one leg was a little thinner than the other and the muscles were hurting like hell, I simply didn't care. I just wanted to run and keep running, desperate to get the chemicals and lethargy out of my under-used body. And from that morning on, I made sure that as a tribute to Scottie, I would live every day as if it were my last. And so the self-pity stopped. And seven weeks later, Janey gave birth to a beautiful baby boy.

Yasmin had been Janey's birthing partner. And as my bride-to-be came running out of the delivery room yelling, *'It's a boy!* He's a beautiful, perfect *baby boy!'* before rushing back to the proud mother, my knees buckled and I sobbed uncontrollably and looked up to the ceiling. 'You got your son!' I said. Two guys sitting close by came over to me. They didn't utter a word, just patted my back in an attempt to console the madman. And then before me, coffee cups in hand, stood Scottie's parents, concern and fear in their eyes.

'Ritchie, is everything alright? Janey, any news?'

I scrambled to my feet, nodding and thanking the two gents for their kindness, a glimpse of how I must have looked with my excessive outpour of emotion, down on the waiting room floor, passing through my mind. But as Scottie's mum and dad stood before me, their eyes wide and their mouths open in anticipation, I told them what they wanted to hear. They grabbed hold of each other and then Scottie's dad turned to me.

'Ritchie, what's she called the little mite?'

And then the delivery room door opened and out walked the nurse holding the newborn baby.

'Janey heard that you were both here. She wanted you to see your *perfect* grandchild while we clean the clever mum up!'

And as the proud grandparents peered and cooed, the nurse made an announcement that stunned us all.

'Yes, Scottie...these people are your dear Grandma and Grandad!'

And the looks on the faces of my dear friend's parents said it all – tears of deep joy and sadness combined. But something told me that they approved of Janey's choice of name.

CHAPTER TWELVE

You Have To Have A Dream

Before Death, 1997 – Blue Sky
Yasmin and I decided that we needed to fix a date for our forthcoming marriage. We had considered waiting, but in the end, we both felt it was the right time. And as we started the whole thing rolling, I had a visit from my old friend Jack. He'd left me alone for nearly a year, and I had dared to think that maybe he had grown up. After all, he was a wealthy, happily married father. But for some perverse reason, Jack decided it wasn't quite enough.

I had decided that I wanted to give Yasmin a wonderful wedding present, a gift that would mean the world to us both. Though Sky Cottage was beautiful, it was undoubtedly small and without scope for further development. And of course, I had my childhood fantasy to create the perfect 'Angel' family home – a place for Yasmin and I to lay roots that would run deep. The practical details within the dream included a desire for an impressive office, separately encasing my business life, ideally many healthy steps away from the house. I'd thought about a grand four-car garage, with an impressive business space above, but I wanted an outlook that would inspire me. In the perfect world, a view over the ocean, but seeing as we stood within the heart of England, and that my business dealings and the people I love most in the entire world were all here in Willow, I was more than happy to settle for the next best thing. I had never wavered from wanting to buy the Water's Edge, with the views over the canal and the river, surrounded by beautiful unspoilt countryside – an incredible spot that had never once failed to raise my spirits. *Peace and spiritual calm.* Then when I met Yasmin, it became a special place for us both. And though the spinney would appear as though it had been simply abandoned, after much searching, the man with the legal rights to it was finally unearthed. I believed strongly that everything had its price, and I had no doubts that I could convince this elusive owner to sell. But unfortunately for me, Jack had similar ideas. So, as Yasmin made all the arrangements for our special day, I was busy working out my strategy against the devil himself. He made it fiercely clear that he was going to make the land his, and should I even think about challenging him for it, then I should be left in no doubt that I would not live to see my wedding day. But this time, however convincing Jack was, I was ready to fight.

I went to turn into the high street and get myself into work early at Skirdle's. But then I had an overwhelming desire. I quickly spun the car around and headed off towards the Water's Edge. I smiled, just knowing that I was going there. I would be overwhelmed by shoots of immortality running through my veins when standing in the long green grass looking out across the water. I wanted to own the land *so* much that it hurt, and the mere thought of failure lifted my thumping heart up and between my ears. I swallowed hard and pushed all negativity away. I wound down my window and assessed frantically my purchase strategy.

As yet I had not spoken to the owner of my dream, but I knew that the Water's Edge belonged to a Mr Heart. I had read, studied and digested several times the man's business history, in an attempt to unearth his Achilles heel, discover the chink in his armour, but I found an impenetrable force. Our man appeared to be a shrewd and weathered businessman. The Land Registry records revealed that Mr Heart owned many buildings and thousands of acres of land in Willow and the surrounding villages – a millionaire many times over. So there was a possibility that this acquisition was going to take more than cold hard cash.

As I approached the Water's Edge, I felt a calmness brush refreshingly over me. It was 8 a.m. and the 21st of June – the longest day of the year. The warmth in the air was wonderful. We had been having a glorious spell; the lead up to summer was just how I remembered as a child – endless hot days. I pulled up at the side of the road, easing the car tightly against the hedgerow. The hedges and trees were so high and overgrown around the Water's Edge that the beauty behind was lost to the passer-by.

Despite my intention to stand up to Jack, I found myself looking for him at every turn. I stepped out of the car and made my way tentatively along the gravel driveway. I tried to ignore the row of bungalows sat proudly along the private drive. The crunch of gravel beneath my feet provoked barking from a couple of dogs, but I just looked ahead and kept walking. A smile spread across my face as I was about to step reassuringly onto the sparse woodland earth, just a hundred metres or so away from the rotting five bar gate...but then forced to turn my head towards a loud aggressive knock on one of the bungalow windows. My heart sank like a scolded child as my eyes met with those of a small white-haired old woman mouthing angrily towards me and throwing her arms about, wanting to make it quite clear that I was not welcome. My gut reaction was to ignore my voyeur and run, to throw myself over the gate and move on, but my instincts stopped me from doing so.

I took a deep breath and smiled. Then, making my own animated arm and mouth movements, my smile firmly fixed, I was now a little surprised to find myself stepping purposely across the gravel and down the lady's driveway. She looked a little concerned now – the bold, angry lady I'd witnessed just a few moments ago was now looking timid and defensive. I slowed down a little and softened my smile, concerned that I may very well have entered into the realms of a grimace. The lady had now disappeared. I stopped by the front door and waited. I started to bite the inside of my mouth and then scolded myself for doing so – I hated the sore, annoying lump that would appear within half an hour or so. I started to feel a little foolish, almost expecting a police car to come screeching along the gravel driveway at any moment. But then I heard the reassuring sound of a bolt being pulled, and then another. It went quiet for several seconds, and then a third bolt was slid back and the door opened, though just a few mean inches.

'What do you want?' the old lady demanded. 'That's private property. I've seen you going in there before! What do you want?'

I apologised for alarming her and also added, 'Haven't you got a safety chain for that door? You never know who's knocking!'

The little old lady pulled the door back slowly, but sufficiently for me to now see the whole of her sweet pink face. I pushed my hand gently forward and spoke softly.

'I'm Ritchie Angel, I work at Skirdle's Estate Agents, not that this has anything to do with, ummm, *well,* Skirdle's...'

Two fingers and a thumb wrapped weakly around the tips of my fingers.

'How do you do, Mr Angel.'

I explained that it had never been my intention to upset her. That the spinney was my place of solitude – the perfect spot for mulling over the problems of the world. A sigh and the faintest trace of a smile crept across her faded lips. Slightly encouraged, I continued to explain, and mentioned that I'd even gone as far as to name the beauty spot the Water's Edge. I now had a full smile, and then slowly the door was pulled fully open. My little friend peered up at me as though weighing me up, and then uttered words of encouragement.

'Well, you seem a decent young man.' A smile now reached her eyes, warming her wrinkly face. 'But you do realise that Mr Heart owns that land, and he's not one to mess with, you know. In fact, he's been known to blast a shotgun at any intruders in the past! Just thought you'd best know.'

I smiled again, taking the opportunity of enquiring about Mr Heart and what she knew about him. She looked at me, squinting, her face now just inches away from my chin.

'Why are you asking questions about him?'

I thought for a moment. Should I tell this lovely lady that I wanted to try to buy the land? I hesitated, but then felt that I had nothing to hide.

'Well, I wanted to speak to Mr Heart actually, as I want to discuss the possibility of purchasing this delightful spot. It's, umm, it's just that it's totally overgrown and certainly doesn't seem to be doing anything. Nothing would change as far as your outlook is concerned, one single home, tucked away amongst the trees.'

Suddenly, every wrinkle seemed to stretch, horror and disdain greeting what I had thought was an acceptable and reasonable description.

So I quickly added, 'It's just that I would love to see a single family home, in fact my home, on there, you know? Better than some developer trying to get it, and sticking twenty, perhaps even thirty boxes on it!'

Gratefully, the old lady offered an understanding nod of the head, but remained tight-lipped. I waited in silence for a few painful moments, but then her words started to flow and so I listened intently.

'Mr Heart wouldn't be interested in selling the land. He's sixty-five, you know?' And as she went to say something else, she stopped, a wistful look taking over her entire face.

I touched the old lady's arm. 'Are you alright?'

Suddenly, I had about three stone of skin and bones in my arms, and my heart seemed to somersault uncomfortably as I genuinely believed my little unnamed friend had gone and died on me. I patted very gently on her frail cheeks, desperate for a sign of life. Her eyes suddenly rolled back into her sallow sockets.

'Good God, you gave me a scare!'

She pulled herself away as I tried to utter some words of comfort.

'Umm, look, it's not a problem, you just seemed to faint. You were talking to me, remember? I'm Ritchie, Ritchie Angel, from Skirdle's.'

A smile led to a flush of welcome colour.

'I'm Ivy, Ivy Heart. I'm so sorry, Ritchie, I sometimes do that. It's him, the bugger! If I think about him, mention his name … you must think me an old fool.'

I was firstly relieved that her time was not up, but then

startled at the possible link.

'Ivy Heart? So tell me, Ivy, are you related to Mr Heart? Perhaps his younger sister?'

Ivy's eyes sparkled back at me, and though she did look ten or so years older than Mr Heart's sixty-five, I didn't think it wise to dwell on the fact, and it appeared that my corny line was appreciated.

'Oh, Ritchie, you are very kind! But no, I'm not William's younger sister or otherwise, but I was his first wife, many, many years ago you understand, but he's always been a bit of a rogue! And once I'd had enough of his womanising, I left him. It was thirty-five years ago; I had just celebrated my fortieth when I packed my bags. William was always one for the ladies, and though he was ten years younger than me – when he first chased me he was only twenty – he couldn't resist the older woman. I finally gave in and married him, and he was a good provider, but he was also a selfish bugger! Oh, Ritchie, listen to me going on!'

I squeezed Ivy's hand and smiled. 'He must have been a fool, Ivy. I'm sure he's regretted it ever since!'

Ivy looked out across her front garden and spoke softly.

'No, Ritchie, I wasn't young and glamorous enough for him. We had ten fairly good years, and I think, well, I think he expected me to let him have his meaningless flings, but I couldn't. I loved him far too much for that! And so, in the end, I walked away. He was already a wealthy man at thirty, and I could have sued him for a fortune, but I just wanted a small, peaceful bungalow, and so he built me this!'

Ivy's eyes moistened and she sighed.

'But, typical bloody William Heart, he built me my little bungalow on its own. I had a beautiful large garden, and then within two years he went and built the rest of the bungalows, squashed up against mine!'

I didn't know what to say to her. But then suddenly she looked at me and burst out laughing, grabbing onto my arms, making sure she didn't topple over. Once Ivy had regained her composure and her balance, I enquired as to whether her and William ever spoke.

'Ritchie, you'll be surprised to hear that yes, we do! Every now and again, once a month, he'll come and have a pot of tea and a good chat. He's still a handsome boy, but oh God, when I look at us both together now... I have not worn well, whereas William, he still looks good. Trouble is, Ritchie, he *bloody* knows it!'

I felt that I had bothered Ivy enough and that I really should be getting to work. But as I made my way down the driveway, Ivy offered a few heartfelt words.

'I'll tell him! I'll tell him he should sell to you, that you're a nice young man and that you love the land, that a young happy family deserve to unlock the spinney. Tell him, Ritchie, if you get to him first, tell him you want it, tell him Ivy approves! I'll try for you, Ritchie, I promise!'

And as I walked back down the drive, my heart full, I waved back at Ivy, her old, tired face suddenly taking on a glow, the many years seeming to just fall away. As she blows a kiss, I send one back; a youthful, beautiful woman waving and encouraging me on. *Mr Heart, you were the love and passion of her life, and like a fool you let her go!*

But suddenly, as a cloud passes over the strong morning sunlight, Ivy's tired and aged frame returns, her thin colourless lips pursed and sad, before she shuffles off into the shadows of her bungalow.

As I step lightly, the gravel crunching beneath my feet, I notice the air is thin and lifeless, the branches still and despondent above me. As I step off the loose stones and out onto the lane, an instant breeze pushes against my face. I stop and close my eyes, simply letting the wind whip around me, waking me, dragging me back into the harsh reality of the day. I ease my eyes open wide, but feel cheated by what stands before me: a black BMW parked right up close behind my car, JD 666 on the number plate.

Shit! How the hell did he see me here, and what on earth does the bastard want now? I walk hesitantly towards the vehicles. I can see Jack's large frame through his rear window, and then I am aware that he can see me. He is quickly out of his car.

'Mr Angel, how the *fuck* are you?'

I nod and smile at the warmth of his opening line.

'Good, Jack, very good!'

I feel tempted to just walk and get into my car, but I can't, physically or mentally. I stop, just six feet away from him.

'Ritchie, my dear, dear friend, there is disappointment in my generous heart to find you here when I have already told you that you are *not* getting this land. So I am left puzzled by your need to be here. I know how desperately you want this scruffy marsh, and it is for that reason I have felt the need to check up on you!'

Jack's eyes widen, his pupils spreading like an oil slick and ready to burst. He steps forward, his breath dancing across my face, circling its venom that very nearly brings tears to my eyes. He goes to turn away, his fingers now stroking his chin, but then he changes his mind and steps even closer to me.

'I shouldn't have to check the perimeter of this site on a daily basis, Angel, my mischievous, not-to-be-trusted *piece of shit*, but hey ho, here I am…'

The devil's eyes start to twinkle before me, as though diamonds have risen to the surface of his pools of black. A menacing smile spreads across his face, and I instinctively do the same.

'Mmmm, funny isn't it, Angel, verrrry funny? But what's *far, far* more amusing to me is the fact that I only want this land because you want it soooo badly, so I am going to have it!'

His words sicken me, his hatred for me only matched by my contempt for him. The devil takes a step back and then rotates his neck, his eyes not leaving mine.

'Arrrgh, *Angel, Angel, Angel,* it would seem that I simply cannot help myself. As I've said, I've checked on this land every day since I gave you my warning, so when I see your crappy little vehicle parked up and it would appear to me you are making plans that go against my own, I'm not pleased with *that* at all!'

Jack rotates his neck again and steps forward, at such speed that it makes my eyes blink furiously as I brace myself for an attack. But instead we are now face-to-face, and then Jack is gradually growing in stature as he pushes himself up from the balls of his feet, his chest and shoulders increasing in size. He swallows hard, his lips almost on my forehead.

'I can't help it, Ritchie Angel, there's just something inside that makes me despise you, and I have to say, for a man of my gentle nature I am shocked by how I strongly believe that nothing would give me greater pleasure than killing you...'

My eyes widen and I have an overwhelming feeling of being trapped, and then as easy as that I drop my head and step around him. My head is craned slightly forward, waiting for the onslaught from the beast behind me as my feet scurry towards the safety of my car. *Will I make it?* is repeating over and over again in my head. I had foolishly but genuinely started to believe that the threat from Jack was not so bad, that he had left me to get on with my life. But once again, he was back, twice as ugly and more evil than ever. My hands are shaking as I clumsily try to push my key into the lock. I am aware of Jack having turned and his eyes boring into me. Against my better judgment and willing myself not to, I glance towards him and I am greeted by a face of mild amusement at my petulance.

'Going somewhere, Angel? I wasn't aware that we had finished our conversation!'

The devil steps forward and then stops, no more than a foot away from me. He is dressed in his trademark black suit and black open-neck shirt. His jet-black hair, though slightly tousled, is always combed neatly back, the obvious smattering of Brylcreem giving it a greasy shine. But his whole calculated appearance reflects the hard, cool businessman that he is. But as he stands in front of me, he places his hands on his hips and I almost giggle nervously, feeling that the stance is bordering on the effeminate. But his black eyes dispel all doubts as they bore into my soul. Jack pushes the left-hand side of his jacket back a little, exposing the rich red lining. And there it is, encased in a leather holster – a cold and serious-looking black and chrome pistol. I look at the gun...then back at Jack.

'Angel, I wanted you to be the first person I use this on, but unfortunately, I've had a couple of business problems just lately, and therefore I've had to test its capabilities elsewhere!'

I swallow hard.

'I'm pleased to report, Angel, that I'm getting rather handy with it now. I suppose what I'm trying to say is that if I hear a single whisper from anyone that you've made a solitary effort whatsoever to get this land, then I will happily pump a couple of bullets into you! It's no idle threat, Angel, it will be the excuse I need! Mmmmm, and with you out the way, with the smell of your blood still on my hands, my next port of call would be consoling that fiancée of yours! Yeahhh! I can imagine she'd appreciate a good fucking from a real man!'

Jack winks and then turns away from me, and with ice in my veins I watch him stroll back to his car. He opens the door and then looks at me again.

'Take care now, Ritchie. Enjoyed our little chat, and I *really* hope that you've listened to what I've had to say, but it might well be worth looking over your shoulder anyway, because I'm really getting a taste for the harm this little pistol can do! Mmmm, really must try to control the urge to use it. Good day, Ritchie!'

I hadn't planned to stand there like a petrified, crushed schoolboy, but as Jack pushes his foot hard onto the accelerator, dust and gravel hitting my face, through to my soul I feel so completely ineffective, not remotely worthy of the air I was breathing, and I despised myself for my lack of a backbone. It was all I could do to get myself back into my car. As I slump into the seat, I wrap my fingers around the steering wheel in an attempt to stop my hands from shaking. I just sit and stare out through the windscreen, fear gradually being replaced by a fury that was building up inside me. I finally start to breathe deep and meaningful breaths. I have everything going for me: Yasmin, money, a wonderful future, but it is all tinged with an immense black cloud in the form of *Jack De'Vil*. I must have sat for an hour or more, pondering with increased ingenuity my options, my imagination running riot on how to solve my problem.

Over the next few weeks, the threats from Jack slid down my list of priorities. And as a total act of defiance, I ensured that I was in the right place at the right time to finally meet up with William Heart. He was reluctant to talk business as regards the Water's Edge with me at first, but once we got onto the subject of Ivy, we undoubtedly found common ground. But despite the clinking of our glasses and the mutual toast of good fortune, Mr Heart dismissed out of hand all thoughts of selling me the Water's Edge.

'Ritchie, why should I sell? I don't need the money! I certainly don't need the aggro from the people who live in the bungalows there. And though I'm not calling you a liar, I do have to say the chances of you *actually* doing what you say, and building just the *one* house, well, please excuse me, but there's over three acres there! You'd be a bloody fool not to want to build a couple of dozen, eh, Ritchie? Surely you take my point?'

But of course, that wasn't my plan. I didn't need to develop the land. I had my money, I had my properties; I purely wanted the Water's Edge because I loved it.

'Mr Heart, I will put in writing, with any solicitor of your choosing, that I just want to build a family home! Name your price.'

But he wasn't for budging. In fact, he couldn't have looked less interested if he had tried. But then suddenly, Mr Heart half closed one eye and turned to look at me, a small smile creeping across his lips.

'Did you say that your company is Sky-Fly? The company that owns the newly developed old library in the centre of Willow?'

I nodded suspiciously back at Mr Heart.

'Then you may just have your land, Ritchie!'

My heart started to race – it was music to my ears. After all, the land was everything to Yasmin and I. But then I couldn't help wincing as Mr Heart's logically impossible terms were laid on the table.

'Straight swap, Ritchie! Your library in exchange for what you call the Water's Edge!'

I swallowed hard, my throat suddenly a little dry.

'Ummm, but William, ummm, *Mr Heart*, the library's fully developed! Has to be worth over a million!'

But as his eyes narrowed and he stared deep within me, he knew that if I really wanted the Water's Edge, I would pay anything. I turned away, taking a much-needed breath. The library was a prime building, and as wonderful as the Water's

Edge was, it was only worth a fraction, maybe a tenth, of the library's value, especially with its lack of planning permission. Mr Heart was watching me intently; then he leant in close.

'Ritchie, I'm not sure that you'll understand what I'm about to share with you, but then I have a strong feeling that you might... When I was just a young lad, maybe seventeen, eighteen years of age, I used to love going into the old library. I can see it now, the many shelves, stacked with all the literature you were ever likely to need. But my heart wasn't with the shelves and the books, Ritchie, but with the girl behind the counter, ten years older and undoubtedly out of my league – Ivy! Every day for two years I went in there – oh my God, the lure of the older woman – until finally she agreed to go on a date with me.'

I knew I was smiling, wishing that Ivy could hear what the love of her life was sharing with me.

William continued. 'The old girl thinks I'm a cold-hearted bastard, but the truth is, I have never loved another the way I love dear old Ivy! But I was guilty of having a wandering eye, Ritchie; simply couldn't, and even now cannot, resist a pretty female! I want the library because my heart is there, Ritchie. I feel that I would like to put the deeds in Ivy's name, as a gesture of what she means to me! Not for us to rekindle our romance – we have both moved on physically – but here, Ritchie, deep down in my selfish heart, it's Ivy who got to me the most, by a long, long distance, and it will be my way of showing her!'

So, for Yasmin and me, Ivy and William, I wanted to push my hand forward and cement the deal, but good business sense was stopping me. The old boy beamed at me, urging me to agree. After all, I was convinced I'd seen real emotion, and even the hint of a tear in William's eye.

'Ritchie! Do we have a deal?'

I stood up and paced the room. The library accounted for about a third of my wealth, and the power in this deal had balanced itself out; this was about more than money for us both. But then, just as I was about to revise the terms, my eyes fixed on Mr Heart's and he threw in his ace card.

'One of your rivals, a Mr De'Vil, he's prepared to trade,

should I feel tempted by anything in his portfolio!'

And without a second thought, I smiled.

'Okay, William, you old rogue, as much as you're totally ripping me off, you've got a deal!'

We shook hands, raised a glass to the loves of our lives, and exchanged solicitors' details.

With the wedding only three weeks away, it was imperative that all parties concerned were on top of their game. Despite my accountant's advice, and he being convinced I was losing my touch, contracts were finally exchanged. I felt very sad letting the library go – there were seven separate businesses installed, seven separate incomes per month! But I shrugged it all off. I knew I was letting my heart rule my head, but as I finally held the title deeds to the Water's Edge, I felt a warmth pass through me – a sense of how certain things in life are *just* meant to be. And then a smile broke out, totally unexpectedly, across my face. All I could see in my mind was the long green grass being blown gently in the breeze, the sparkle of the water, the sunlight dancing around the ripples created by the breeze. Financially I knew I was being a fool. But when I pictured Yasmin's face, I knew it was the right thing to do. It was the perfect wedding present. And she never need know just how much it had cost me!

It must have turned midnight, and though I was restless, Yasmin had fallen into a deep sleep. I eased carefully from under the single cotton sheet, the moon shining brightly through the undrawn curtains. I stood almost hypnotised by my bride-to-be. She was undoubtedly the most beautiful woman I had ever set eyes on. I wriggled my bare feet into the sheepskin rug, preparing them for the stark contrast of the cold oak floorboards. As I tiptoed gently down the stairs of Sky Cottage, I felt the need for the fresh midnight air. I stepped out onto the patio, not totally sure what temperature my naked body was going to be hit with. *Mmmm, that's beautiful!* I needn't have worried, as the embers of the scorching hot day had left a comfortable night. I took a slow, deep breath, the sleepy aroma from the surrounding shrubs and flowers enough to make me want to set my alarm and experience this unexpected pleasure night after night. I nodded my head with self-satisfaction as I took in the splendour of all that Yasmin and I had achieved out here: the garden full of shrubs, lovingly planted by us both, now running rampant in the small plot that we had. My thoughts turned back to the sleeping Yasmin – safe, contented, happy, hopefully not a worry in the world.

I thanked my lucky stars for everything that I had achieved. And when faced with all the blessed and positive aspects of my life, I pondered the not so good, concerning fragments that perhaps I could improve on. The biggest hurdle by far being Jack De'Vil. But negativity in my personality? Well, I reflected on how dangerously ambitious I was! And the fact that I was often far too focused on making money to stop and enjoy every precious moment that each day offered. I tried to sum up the sort of guy I was, and to picture how others perceived me. It wasn't an issue I would normally give a second thought to – if people liked me, fine, but if they didn't, also fine! But I actually wondered whether that philosophy was realistic. People who spout that they don't care what people think – can we believe them? Is it not more a case of: 'No, I'm going to be *me* regardless!' But then deep down they resolve to accept and learn from the criticism.

I smiled at my late-night ramblings, but still pondered my progress as a good human being. I felt, though a little reluctantly at first, that I should do a bit more for the community – perhaps be a little more giving with my time. Though I felt a genuine warmth when reflecting on my weekly visits to see Alice. But that kind of effort needed to start here, at home. Yasmin's mum, for example – she could be very demanding! And therefore, I would switch off, leaving Yasmin to deal with her, but hoping that it wouldn't eat into our time together. Although Yasmin would sometimes joke about my selfishness, she would often, for a quiet life, try to see her mum when I was perhaps working, keen to keep the harmony. My soul-searching was interrupted by the gentle distant chime of the church clock and I playfully scolded myself under my breath for being out at this time. I closed the patio doors, a sudden shiver reminding me that I was naked and covered in goose pimples. I crept back up the stairs and slid beneath the welcoming sheet. I felt the strongest urge to cuddle up to Yasmin's warm body for instant heat, but realised that my progress as a kind, less selfish human being would face its first major setback at such a cruel manoeuvre; but then the new reformed Ritchie Angel could start when I rose for the new day...

'Oh *my* God! Ritchie, you're *bloody* freezing!!'

Yasmin yelled up the stairs, *'Ritchie! My lift's here, darling, I've several things to finalise before going into work. I can't believe we've only got two days until our big day! Love you, sleepyhead!'*

A smile crept across my barely conscious mouth, my eyes still welded together, *love you, sleepyhead,* still resounding around my grateful brain. I wanted to jump up out of bed and wave Yasmin off, but instead I succumbed to the easier option. My slumbering body suddenly jumped, startled at the volume of our house phone. I grappled around on top of my bedside table, finally picking up the receiver and putting an end to the horrendous ringing.

'Ritchie, I had to *call* you... I know that Jack De'Vil is not your closest friend, but my mum has just come back from her night shift at the hospital and she told me that Jack and Julie's little girl *died* in the early hours of this morning!'

My heart stopped. It was Leoni, and her voice started to falter, each word tripped by the welling-up of emotion.

'Oh God, Ritchie, (sob) she's only eight; the poor little thing...her whole life in front of her, but she's gone...' Leoni suddenly apologised and hung up.

I lifted myself up and out of bed, but then stopped, cold and unable to move. After what seemed like an eternity, I raised my hand to my mouth and rubbed around my lips. I staggered back onto the bed and sat down. My heart seemed to have stopped beating, but then, as though keen to contradict me, it was pounding with such force that I couldn't hear myself think. I tried to lift my head as high as possible, convincing myself that that would enable me to rise above the volume, and suddenly, the previously fragmented words sank in: *little Lillie had died.* I pictured Julie's face and how she would express so much passion for her daughter in utter abundance, in her eyes, her words, every pore. And though I would conveniently choose to disbelieve that I was Lillie's father, the compassionate man in me would say, *There wasn't a valid reason on earth for her to lie!* But I would take the coward's way out and simply deny the truth – and so the problem and the emotions that went with it would conveniently disappear. I just erased it from my mind and got on with my life. But this didn't feel right at all – depths that were until now undiscovered were pushing themselves painfully forward. I picked myself up and ran across to the bathroom, urgent and grateful as I dropped onto my knees before the toilet.

I feel as though my entire intestines are being wrenched from me as I am violently sick. I have no control; the tears are rolling down my face, dropping like small explosions onto the *contemporary art,* now splayed at random on the white porcelain, in and around my mouth, pungent, chunky remnants in my nose. I feel blindly for the damp flannel, finally placing it across my face as I slump down against the hard, cold radiator.

I tried to gather my thoughts, desperate to regain my sanity. I resorted to *type,* convinced myself that the only way to sidestep this tragic news was to deny my role. And once I let the questions come – surely Julie would have pestered me more than she did; Jack *had* to be Lillie's father, he was no fool, he would know if he wasn't – and though the full force of my sadness for Julie and Lillie remained, I found it far easier believing that Lillie wasn't my child.

As I took a deep breath and stood up, trying to get myself ready for work, my mind wandered onto Rose. I couldn't believe that Lillie should die in her eighth year, just as Rose had done. I physically shook as a shiver ran the full length of my spine and out through the bottom of my feet. But then, in typical Ritchie Angel style, I took a deep breath and pulled myself together.

Despite my attempts to pull a veil over the tragedy, I found as I drove to work my thoughts inevitably wandering back to the De'Vil family. Though I was of course devastated for Julie and Jack, with the loss of *their* child, my mind was filled with the devil's threats concerning any efforts I might make in attempting to purchase the Water's Edge. I had been convinced that now the contracts were exchanged – even though I had asked all concerned to keep quiet until after the wedding – Jack would somehow, perhaps inevitably, find out, resulting in one of his visits. But it callously dawned on me that with the death of his daughter, surely even *he* would feel that my land purchase had simply paled into insignificance. And though I tried to wipe such a practical thought out of my mind, I couldn't. As incredible and unforgivable as it was, I thought that this might soften Jack up a little, at least relieving me of a major problem – a sort of silver lining.

Word travelled quickly around Willow; the news of little Lillie was all anybody could talk about. Nobody seemed to know for sure how and why she'd died, even though many different views were expressed. Therefore, an exact cause of death was never confirmed, and nobody liked to ask.

CHAPTER THIRTEEN

Mr And Mrs Angel

Before Death, 1997 – Blue Sky

My stag-do was set up in the traditional sense – the night before the wedding. I really wasn't up to it, but Jimmy and a few work associates got together to give me a good send-off. We started off at the Whippet's. Jimmy pushed me through the door first, and then I couldn't help but smile, as there was Yasmin, surrounded by her old college and work friends, many empty bottles of champagne on the table. Yasmin and her hen party had achieved a good two-hour start on us boys - compared we were miserably slow out of the blocks. My bride-to-be stumbled towards me, her long blonde hair having been set in ringlets by the girls, now wild and free across her face. She kissed me passionately, slurring her rescue plea.

'Ritchie! (hic) My Angel, take me home! Please save me

from these *supposed* friends of mine … I think they're trying to kill me! Death by (hic) champagne!'

But as the girls dragged her off into the night, my head shaking from side to side, I couldn't help but smile nervously, wondering seriously whether I would ever see her again. My thoughts were interrupted as I was spun around.

'Oh shit! Where the hell did he dig you lot up from?'

As old school friends thrust their hands forward, some not so concerned with polite etiquette were suddenly jumping all over me. I was genuinely shocked as over the space of half an hour, more faces from my past crawled out of the woodwork. As my reunited friends exchanged stories and brought each other up to speed with what they'd been up to for the last decade, Jimmy wrapped his arms around me, his eyes beaming disconcertingly. He then pushed his face right up to mine, his eyes boring deep into my soul, his voice barely audible above the noise.

'Tonight's a celebration! Tonight's in memory of Scottie! Right, Ritchie? RIGHT?!'

And though I raised my bottle with the rest of the lads, the words totally mortified me. Though outwardly I'd successfully moved on, inwardly the pain was as sharp as ever. I still blamed myself for Scottie's death, as I absolutely and rightly should. But I had allowed that to damage me before. I knew that I had to be strong, as anything less was a slippery slope that I simply couldn't afford to go near.

From that moment on, the entire night was a blur. So many faces, heartfelt handshakes, emotional kisses from girls that I vaguely recognised. I know that there was a stripper in there somewhere, who expertly humiliated me in front of a room full of people. But it was as though I was looking down on the whole scene – a total out-of-body experience. And as I watched from above, peering through finger-covered eyes, I was totally naked, sitting on what looked like an old school chair, with a buxom blonde bouncing half-naked on top of me. I winced and prayed that it wasn't quite as bad as it all appeared, and felt heartened and convinced that my intimacy with the lady was pure theatre – I certainly wasn't capable of anything else! Far too much champagne and several *Bloody Marys* later, I must have passed out.

I could hear the gentle tweeting of birds and the noise of a milk float not too far away. Every now and again, a toot of a horn could be heard, but I couldn't open my eyes, and I was aware of a sharp pain in my arms. I was unable to move, as though being restricted. In an attempt to open my eyes, a painful thumping increased alarmingly in my head. The more I tried to focus, the more intense the throbbing became. I closed my eyes again, and the beating eased a little. The discomfort now seemed predominantly in my wrists. As I tried to move them, I screwed my face up in reaction to a sharp shooting pain. I then became aware of feeling particularly liberated as a cool breeze wafted across me, particularly noticeable around my lower regions. A cog seemed to drop into place, my brain suddenly aware that all was not well.

My eyes instinctively opened wide as I yelled out, *'Shit! Where the fuck...?!'*

And there I was, on the small traffic island just outside Willow, tied to the maypole, naked apart from a pink satin bra strapped strategically between my legs – although the bra had slipped down a bit, exposing sufficient to get me arrested. My heart started racing as I tried every trick in the book to try to untie my hands. As I wriggled, regretfully devoid of an ounce of progress, I focused on a milk float heading towards me.

'Oh shit, it's a *woman!*'

The milk lady so far seemed oblivious to me and my predicament. But then suddenly, the bra was intent on sliding an inch or two lower, at which point my potential saviour's eyes widen and she has undoubtedly spotted me. She lifts the peak of her cap, her eyes suddenly wider than is perhaps healthy, with a hyena-smile spreading across her entire face. Within a moment or two the milk float is pulled to a hasty stop, abandoned in the middle of the road. As the red-cheeked buxom lady gets closer, I realise that I know her and she quickly recognises me.

'Mr Angel! Well, well, well, fancy seeing you here! I take it you haven't tied yourself to the maypole, illegal to do so you know, been the law since 1912. Only kidding! Cruel sods; what have they done to you?'

The milk lady's name is Rita. I had recently sold her house with Skirdle's – she had been vivacious and tactile from day one. And now, as she looked me up and down, her tongue darting in and out of her mouth, I made my plea.

'Ummm, please, Rita, perhaps you could untie me? I'm due to be married at twelve!'

Rita raised her eyebrows, her smile devouring every inch of my predicament.

'There, there, Mr Angel, you've plenty of time, it's only just gone six! Mmmmm, I can't let this opportunity pass. Just give me one second, I've got my camera on the float!'

And as I watched Rita run back into the middle of the soon-to-be-busy road, her arms and legs flailing as she rummaged excitedly in her milk float, I cursed Jimmy and all my so-called friends. Rita was soon back and snapping away.

'Mr Angel!' Rita's hand slid down to the pink bra, now leaving nothing to the imagination. 'Mr Angel, from the size of those satin cups she was a big girl, naughty you! Oh, I'm sure the intended Mrs Angel will forgive you; after all, it was your last night of freedom!'

I try to encourage Rita to untie me, but she seems more interested in pulling the bra back up.

'Must protect your modesty, Mr Angel!'

But as she wrestles with the bra, trying to put my bits back into it, she blatantly handles me!

'Oh, Mr Angel, there you go. Hang on one second, let me see if I can push Mr Sausage back in there with his two little *double-barrelled* friends, Mr and Master Plum-Tomato! That's a little better; after all, you could get arrested for such indecent exposure!'

I simply lifted my head up to the skies above, uttering under my breath, 'Mr Sausage, Mr and Master *bloody* Plum-Tomato! God give me strength!'

Several photographs later, Rita finds it in her generous heart to untie me. I thank her several times and ask politely if I might borrow her apron, but she won't have any of it. And as she wanders off back to her milk float, she utters something about the rules and regulations of the milk marketing board, and how it would be frowned upon for anyone other than an employee to be impersonating a milk person.

'And, Mr Angel, I'm not sure my husband would take *too* kindly to me being seen with you in *such* a state of undress!'

I follow two steps behind, shaking my head in total disbelief. Here I am, cold and naked – apart from a bra wrapped around my privates – more than a mile away from home. And despite wanting to be a million miles away from my sexually molesting saviour, I decide that Rita is probably my best option. After all, she's seen and touched me now – suitably bonded, you might say.

'Rita, please! Ummm, hang on, Rita, please! I'm in serious need of your help here. Please can you drop me home, *please?'*

Rita stops and looks at me with a wry smile, even becoming a little coy, but finally realising that she can't just leave me here. She beckons for me to get in the milk float. As we make our way home, she just keeps looking over at me, her hand every few minutes sliding over and patting me tenderly between the legs, the only thing protecting me this time from actual contact being the warmth and security of the pink satin bra.

As the milk float made its way around the main green, I thanked my lucky stars that most people were still in bed. I was relieved that it was a quiet Saturday morning, rather than the madness that normally showed itself this time on a weekday. As Rita pulled her float up outside my cottage, I slid carefully off the cold plastic seat and dropped down onto the harsh road.

'Thank you *so* much, Rita, you have really saved my life!'

And as I made my way to the safety beyond my front door, I realised that Rita hadn't pulled away yet. I quickly turned around to see her with her camera clicking away.

'Got some great posterior shots there, Mr Angel; yep, they'll come out *very* well!'

I was past caring and simply lifted my hand.

'Ummm, thanks then, Rita, thanks again, I won't forget this!'

Rita laughed out loud, suddenly surging forward in her blue and white milk float.

'No, I won't forget it either! Should have the photos back in a day or two. *Congratulations, Mr Angel! Enjoy your wedding!'*

The sheer relief as I closed my front door firmly behind me – the cottage had never looked so welcoming or beautiful. The sun was already streaming through all the south-facing windows – I basked longingly, the natural warmth gradually thawing out my cold feet and body. I tried not to make any noise and was just about to creep up the stairs. As the second tread creaked loudly, I held my breath. I looked around me – there were no drawn curtains.

Ritchie, you prat! She's not even here! I had totally forgotten that Yasmin was staying with her maid of honour, Janey, until being dragged kicking and screaming to the church at midday to of course become Mrs Angel. It stopped me in my track's, I turned back and made my way into the lounge, staring out into the garden, the full glare of the early morning sun magnificent. *Mrs Yasmin Angel!* It was beautiful, and I loved the very thought and sound of it. I would often just stop what I was doing and simply take in what Yasmin was up to – to see her going about her day-to-day existence, her wheels rolling within mine. I would just watch her, this other person in my world, going about *her* life but so totally connected to me. I would reflect on life before Yasmin, when it was just me feeling my way, my plans, my dreams. Then once you leave school, life seems to plod a little, and then once you start work and find your feet – for me at least – life gathered momentum, and then like a giant roller-coaster, whoosh! We were off. Work, money, meeting Yasmin, spending money as though it was going out of fashion, but then making more money, more plans, more schemes! And this was my life, the *two* of us!

I had questioned myself relentlessly prior to asking Yasmin to marry me, and from that day until this it had been perfect and then some. But here, on the day that I was about to take things to the next level, I reflected on some of my less proud moments. But right or wrong, I realised that these incidents didn't touch Yasmin, and I was eternally grateful that I was able to keep this unfortunate side of my life away from her: Mr and Mrs Christian, Jack, Julie and Lillie – I kept these things locked up inside of me. And so for Yasmin, these negatives simply didn't exist. It had to be this way, because I was convinced that the truth would undoubtedly tarnish whatever love and respect she had for me. Though the reality would probably be that she could and would accept the real me, it was safer this way – my *ivory tower* intact and unblemished. Then, at least, as I lay in Yasmin's arms at night, I could leave all that was bad outside in the cold. I didn't have to look in her eyes, her knowing my dark side – I had taken control in the only way I believed I could. Why should Yasmin be handed the burden of carrying around my wrongdoings? And could I take the chance of her leaving me should she know the real Ritchie Angel?

Suddenly, as my thoughts start to drift and my focus across the garden fades, I catch my reflection in the patio doors.

'Oh my God!' I laugh out loud, my hand clutching the satin bra to my groin.

All my deepest angst being raked over, and yet here I am, standing almost naked, looking totally ridiculous...*Bang, bang, bang!* I turn around quickly as the loud knocking on the front door kills the surreal moment. I quickly run upstairs and pull on a pair of jeans. The door is thumped loudly again.

'ALRIGHT, ALRIGHT, I'M COMING!'

When I finally open the door, there is Jimmy, with a smile that would put the Cheshire cat in therapy.

'Ritchie boy!' Jimmy didn't bounce forward and into my home as he normally did and was a little hesitant, my un-smiling face leaving room for doubt as regards how I had taken my wonderful friends' little prank.

I frowned at my best man for just a second longer, and then said, 'Jimmy, *you* are a *total* bastard! I really cannot believe you *left* me there!'

But then as the image-provoked smile crept across my face, Jimmy's suppressed amusement suddenly came flooding out.

'Oh God, Ritchie! All I've done since we left you there...' Jimmy is now leaning against my hallway wall, clutching his stomach as his laughter starts to gain control of his balance. 'Oh God, Ritchie! I mean it, every few minutes, the lads and me, we would just burst out laughing! You looked such a complete dick strapped up to the pole. Oh God, you were snoring your head off; it didn't matter what we did to you, you were totally out of it!'

Jimmy's laughter became reluctantly infectious. And as I wiped the tears away from my eyes, I couldn't help but be impressed – the lads had done me proud. Something to tell the grandchildren: a stripper, got me totally smashed until I finally passed out, and then the icing on the cake, tied me naked to the town maypole! Who said that tradition was a dying art? The lads, led by Jimmy, had succeeded in making my stag night a memory that would live with us all forever.

The next few hours rolled by chaotically and at times uncomfortably, crouched over the toilet, the full force of last night determined to leave its mark. Finally, though, the guests all seated, my head beating and a rumbling of nausea in the real depths of my gut, I was standing next to Jimmy, the church bells ringing. I was swallowing hard and gasping for any air that I could find in the mustiness of the vaulted ceilings.

Suddenly, there were voices yelling down from the back of the church, 'She's here! No going back now, Angel! She's here!!'

I swallowed hard again, the nerves fluttering and my fingers going numb at the sheer enormity of what I was about to do. The organist finally coaxed a tune from his hesitant, faltering machine, and the church was suddenly alive and filled to the rafters with 'The Arrival of the Queen of Sheba'. The decibel level battled with my alcohol-sodden brain, and just as I felt it was about to admit defeat and go into meltdown, I turned my head. Suddenly, there was no music, no people, just Yasmin and me. Our eyes locked onto each other as she made her way, step by perfect step, towards me – a spiritual, powerful silence around us. Having floated away, lost in the moment, I slid motionless and acceptingly back to Jimmy's side, the music and our guests now very real. Yasmin coolly and elegantly made her way between our family and friends, her mother dutifully ready to give her away. I swallowed hard, and within seconds I stretched out my hand. Her delicate warm fingers slipped into mine, and her sudden coolness escaped her as she tried to stop the tears from falling. I smiled, shook my head from side to side and mouthed, 'You look so beautiful!' I squeezed her hand and together we regained our composure.

The words spoken by the vicar came and went, a blur of tradition, questions popping in and out of my head about sins and forgiveness, an exchange of bands of platinum. But as I proudly announced the words, 'I do,' and the love that bore through me as Yasmin made her commitment to me, and then the softest of kisses, her warm cheek against mine, I knew that with this lady I was a far better man.

The ring of applause rang out. Yasmin and I stepped instinctively apart. She looked me up and down, with a smile of approval and the faintest whisper.

'You look wonderful, Ritchie!'

I took in the simple floor-length silk gown, accentuating every mind-blowing curve of my wife's beautiful body. And the appropriate understated posy of fresh daisies twirled coyly in the blushing bride's hands, complemented by more delicate flowers in her hair. I literally gasp at just how ridiculously perfect she is, and swallow hard as the full force of what I have been given threatens to totally overwhelm me. But I stand up straight and take a huge breath. The power of the church, the unity of our family and friends, the unlimited expectation of our future together; but Yasmin's eyes, there was nothing quite so potent or so totally immeasurable. I knew beyond all doubt that my decision to marry her was inspired!

They say that for a woman, her wedding day is the best day of her life, and perhaps that is true. But for me, in the blink of an eye, a black cloud had drifted into my perfect sky. In the build-up to the wedding, I had almost managed to lull myself into a sense of calm and security, believing that in the wake of Lillie's tragic death, just maybe, Jack De'Vil wouldn't bother me again. But as I stepped out from the church, the camera flashlights going off like small fireworks, I saw him. I tried to blink his image away, but he was still there, standing outside the church grounds, looking awful: his black hair uncharacteristically unkempt, a thick razor-edged stubble seeming to cover most of his gaunt face. Though the sun was shining and the air was warm, he had a thick black leather coat on, his hands pushed deep into the pockets as though desperate for warmth. My mind raced. Surely there was nothing he could do, certainly not with all these people around? But for the first time I feared for a different reason. I thought of Julie and Lillie. Perhaps Julie's heartbreak at losing her daughter had caused her to tell Jack that Lillie was mine. I felt sick to the stomach. After all, no man deserves that. To find out that your child, the little bundle that you build your whole world around, isn't yours. The trust and love that had been the sheer backbone of the De'Vil family. If Jack was now armed with the truth, then I had a right to be afraid, very afraid!

The softness of Yasmin's lips breaks through my thoughts – and another pose for the photographer. The throng of happy smiling faces before me hide Jack, but I keep looking. I try to keep cool and calm, but the perspiration around my starched collar causes me to fidget uncomfortably. Forty minutes later, my eyes having searched every blade of grass, every cobble and distant tree, I take a breath and let myself believe he's gone.

Eventually, we leave the church and all make our way to the reception. I had kept the location a secret, and so everyone was following the pale lemon Rolls Royce that Yasmin and I had hired as our wedding car. Yasmin was begging me to tell her where we were going, but I just kept smiling and telling her to have a little patience. Within a mile or so, I beckoned to the driver to pull over. I pushed the heavy door open, the tired burgundy leather seat creaking as I got out of the car. I walked over to Jimmy, who was already running towards me, a slightly vacant expression under his unruly mop of curls.

'Plan A, Jimmy! Plan A, as we discussed. Take this map, mate, but remember to make sure everyone parks their cars down on the bottom field!' I peered anxiously over the top of the map and pointed my finger. 'Marked X, see? There, look!'

Jimmy nodded his head and beamed at me. Then my best man turned and ran back towards his car.

He hovered briefly, and I stated nervously. 'Yasmin and I should *just* about get down to the marquee in the Rolls, Jim! Keep your fingers crossed!!'

Jimmy's curls dropped forward as he turned his map this way and that.

'It's marked 'M', Jimmy...got it?'

Jimmy stuck his thumb up and dived eagerly back into his car. As I slid back into the Rolls Royce, Yasmin hugged me, tender kisses interspersed with, 'Oh, Ritchie! Where are we going?'

But as everyone drove past us, tooting their horns as they went, I pulled a white silk scarf out of my jacket pocket. Yasmin didn't utter a word and just turned away, allowing me very gently to cover her eyes. After a few moments, the Rolls purred back into life and we were on our way. Within five minutes Yasmin's grip suddenly tightened as the once smooth ride became a little shaky, the crunch of gravel and the odd pothole testing the coil suspension. The sunshine was now streaming in through the car windows and it felt good on my face. I wound down the window, waving back at an animated, beaming Ivy Heart. I take in the fresh air, nerves of anticipation fluttering through me. I pushed my hands together, prayer like, and started to gently clap them together. We were now driving at a snail's pace. I placed my hands back onto Yasmin's and a small nervous giggle came from behind the silk scarf. A broad smile spread across my face as a guy in a Queen's Guardsman uniform stood to attention at the side of a *new* five-bar gate. As we turned through the narrow entrance, the driver eased to a halt at our pre-planned spot. I kissed Yasmin lightly on the cheek and gently undid the scarf. I couldn't believe the view myself, and yet I had already seen it. But as Yasmin opened her eyes, she blinked and blinked again. There before us, in all its natural glory, was the Water's Edge!

My eyes followed the temporary cinder driveway down the slight hill, a mixture of trees and wild rhododendrons lining its route. Yasmin's hands gripped my fingers, as if needing reassurance that she wasn't simply dreaming.

'Oh Ritchie! ... Wow!'

I took in the marquee surrounded by silver birch trees, and then just beyond, the line of willow trees, their heads hung elegantly, their fine delicate tresses stroking the water. There was a six-piece orchestra playing Handel's 'Water Music', and to top it all, Yasmins mum and our closest friends, waiting to usher us in. Yasmin looked at me with tears in her eyes.

'Ritchie, it's beautiful, but I don't quite understand...'

I gently wiped a small tear off my wife's flushed cheek.

'Well, Mrs Angel, I felt it appropriate that we should have our wedding where we plan to build our family home, and in time have our children, and *so*, as we'd always dreamt that the Water's Edge would be the perfect spot, I thought maybe I should try very hard to buy it for us!'

Yasmin's eyes widened, and then a curious questioning frown crossed her face, as though she was unsure what I was saying.

'But, Ritchie! Surely you haven't...'

I had never experienced quite the depth of Yasmin's eyes as they bore deep into my soul, but gradually a smile, starting in her eyes and then rippling from her head down through her body, convinced me that she knew exactly what I was saying. Her arms are suddenly flung tightly around my neck with screams of sheer disbelief.

'Oh God, Ritchie! I can't believe it! The Water's Edge? Oh my God! You mean we've actually, *really* bought it? We own all this wonderful, amazing, beautiful land?'

And as special moments go, just when I thought I couldn't be any happier, any luckier, I realised that this really was going to be the most wonderful marriage, that was getting better with every twist and turn.

Thirty-six hours later, as Yasmin and I landed nervously in the seaplane, delivering us into the instant tranquillity of the Maldives, our feet stepped dream-like onto hot silky sands. We were instantly surrounded by half a dozen smiling faces and within minutes escorted into our private honeymoon suite, standing majestically in the shallow turquoise sea. Cocaine-coloured sands and lush green palms seemed to put the icing on the very special cake that was my life – *our* life. And for three wonderful weeks, spiritually and physically we wanted for nothing in paradise. Though now and again my thoughts would reluctantly produce the regretful image of Jack *bloody* De'Vil, I was quick to usher him away, opting instead to make the very best of this exotic island, and to make sure that I built up my strength. Should I really have a battle on my hands once I returned home, then I would be ready. To feel mentally and physically able to handle whatever Jack had to throw at me. The funny thing is, looking back I really believed it. But if I had had any sense at all…I would have stayed on that island!

CHAPTER FOURTEEN

No Place Like Home

Before Death, 1997 – Blue Sky
As we touched down on British soil, I felt a buzz of adrenalin shoot through me; an anticipation and impatient desire to slip back into the real world as Mr and Mrs Angel. The excitement of designing and building our dream home, and so keen to see all our family and friends.

'Ritchie! Yasmin! I'm over here!'

There he was – my best man. We excitedly made our way over to Jimmy, Yasmin and I both hugging the life out of him. Yasmin enquired after Sally.

'Oh, a little bit of a development there!' Jimmy couldn't help but look very pleased with himself.

And then, as though we'd both been married for a hundred years, Yasmin and I screeched together, *'She's pregnant?!!'*

Jimmy couldn't contain himself. 'Yep! Oh my God! I'm gonna be a Dad!!'

We couldn't shut Jimmy up on the way home. But when we stopped at the motorway services and Yasmin had gone off to the ladies, he told me the bad news.

'I'm sorry, Ritchie, but I can't take you and Yaz back home. I've booked you into the Grange. It's Sky Cottage… I'm *so* sorry, mate, it's been broken into and, well, it's disgusting. Graffiti everywhere; it's been totally trashed.'

My heart dropped about a mile and a half through the orange tiles of the service station floor; all the goodness and well-earned optimism of the last three weeks drained instantly out of me. Jimmy placed his arm on mine.

'I just thought, Ritchie, that maybe you could tell Yasmin

you were having it painted while you were both away? And that, well, they've been a bit held up? I just thought... Well, the state of it – I think that she'd be devastated, I don't think she'd want to go back there *ever* again. I tell you what, Ritchie, whoever's done it, well, they're a real *sick* bastard! The stuff that's been written all over the walls, it seems all a bit personal... I only went round last night to put some supplies in the fridge and that, you know, check that everything was okay. My first instinct was to get the police straight in, or maybe just the decorators... Oh shit, Ritchie, I didn't really know what the hell to do for the best, but I thought you would want to have a look first. It's just that, whoever's done it, they've daubed messages: 'Tell the police and Yasmin's dead'... For God's sake, Ritchie, who the hell have you upset?'

I did what Jimmy suggested and took Yasmin to the Grange. It was a lovely country club hotel, but Yasmin just wanted to go home, as did I, back to our little cottage. But there was no other way.

As Yasmin soaked in a hot bath, Jimmy drove me over to Sky Cottage to collect a car. It was getting quite dusky now, and as I pushed the key into the door lock I was almost overcome with nerves – and I had good reason to be, as once inside I thought I must have walked into *hell*. Jimmy hadn't scratched the surface with his description of the mess. Everything was smashed up; every picture, every vase, everything electrical, just littered around the place. But the worst thing was the stench! It totally turned my stomach. There was blood and shit everywhere. And the writing on the walls and carpets: 'DIE', 'YOU'RE DEAD', 'RAPE MRS ANGEL', 'DESTROY YOUR WORLD, BASTARD' – it just went on. I had no doubts as to who it was. I was convinced that the truth was out, that Julie had told Jack about Lillie – it was the only thing that made any kind of sense of this madness. I needed to speak to Julie somehow. Then it crossed my mind that maybe he had done something to her – there was so much blood! My mind was running riot. I thought that perhaps I should tell the police, but an inner voice was stopping me. And the more I thought, the more convinced I was that I needed to get this mess cleaned up – not just the blood and the shit, but the *devil* himself! Though my anger was rising, I knew I had to tread with severe caution. I prayed that Julie was okay, and that she held all the answers I needed.

As I stood outside our hotel room, I took several large breaths, because once inside with Yasmin I was going to have to act just as before. But I hadn't wasted any time – I had called in a huge favour from a local company I had used on several occasions for Skirdle's and for my own developments. I relayed the nightmare situation to Dave Complete – his company specialised in preparing show homes. Though the full horror of this request would perhaps be a first, he assured me that he would get his best team into my home at the crack of dawn and erase the devastation I had described. Dave was also instructed to organise the best security system available; I never wanted a repeat of this, not ever.

I pulled up outside Yasmin's work and my reluctant wife pushed the car door open just a few inches.

'Ritchie, I love you! I can't believe after all these weeks together we've got to part today. Can't we just forget work?' She smiled, not waiting for an answer, but pushing her lips onto mine.

As she opened the car door fully, her gorgeous body now leaving me for the day, my mind momentarily wandered away from the important mission that lay ahead. We exchanged the obligatory waves and blowing of kisses, until Yasmin disappears behind the brightly coloured wooden doors. I catch my reflection in the rear-view mirror and try desperately for a few seconds more to keep up the pretence, squeezing the last smile from my seething body as the image of Jack once again fills my head. My breathing becomes heavy and strained, my mind racing with a determination to face this battle head-on. Sudden adrenalin shoots through me, my foot instinctively pushes to the floor and there is a squeal of burning rubber as I head for the Old Church – the home of Jack and Julie De'Vil.

I ease the car up alongside the high hedgerow that surrounds the beautiful gothic church. I lean forward, taking in the splendour of Jack's inspired home. But as I envisage the tragedy that lies within the thick stone walls, I bite my tongue.

I think about Lillie, but then proceed to beat myself up as I struggle to create her face in my mind. I turn off the engine and get out of the car, the subdued morning air creating a feeling of vulnerability. I look up into the thick swaying branches of the centuries-old oak tree, grateful for the symphony of watching birds, their song almost drowning out the distant drone of traffic two fields away. A shiver runs down my spine as the full force of what I am about to do hits home, the unwavering determination from earlier now waning dramatically.

My footsteps seem noisy on the threadbare tarmac, but within three paces or more I am stood in front of black glossy iron gates – twice the size of me – with bars the thickness of Blackpool rock. I peered through the unwelcoming iron and took in the gravel driveway. I couldn't see Jack's car – there was just a white BMW, with the registration number JD 21. My heartbeat eased a little, as I knew Jack's number was JD 666, so I presumed the white car to be Julie's. As I studied the church, I looked for signs of life. I could see under a covering arm of an oak tree branch, almost brushing the rear of the church, a huge double garage, and I questioned whether Jack's car could be in there. I surprised myself as I turned the iron hoop that lifted the latch to the gates. As I stepped through onto Jack's drive, I kept questioning what I was doing, but I knew I had no choice. My first couple of steps were intimidating and the temptation to turn back was immense. But as I got used to the gravel crunching beneath my feet, the fact that I was still alone gave me a little encouragement. As I got closer to the church, I could hear the faint ripple of music escaping from the small leaded windows. I stopped briefly, tempted to just knock on the large oak front door, but instead crept towards the garage. I could see a small arched window, the sun reflecting off a barely visible section of the leaded glass, almost entirely covered in ivy. I stepped forward, brushed away some thick cobwebs and peered in – there was no car inside. But I could see a small pink bike, a paddling pool and a child's climbing frame that appeared to have been thrown into the corner. I pulled away from the glass, aware that the music had suddenly got louder, as though a door or a window had been opened. My nerves were running rampant.

'Only Jack De'Vil can do this to me…' I muttered.

I shook my head in disgust and scolded myself for being so weak. I felt less conspicuous as I walked down the side of the church and into the back garden. I could see a gothic arch and then realised that it was a patio door – it was open. And so I stepped carefully towards it across the daisy-filled lawn. The music was now hauntingly loud, and with every step the song became clearer until there was no mistaking the ballad, the sudden break in the music, and then 'I …will always love you!' filtered out into the garden – Dolly Parton pouring her heart out. I was now just feet away from the doors, but the song ended and I froze on the spot, waiting for another song, or perhaps a disc jockey to start speaking. But the silence seemed to last an eternity. Then the familiar voice of Dolly Parton started again – the same song simply being repeated.

I waited for the song to build a little, hoping it would cover any noise I was making. I pushed my foot onto the mossy stone patio and stepped forward. I was now able to peer into the lounge. I could see a dark cherry-red leather Chesterfield settee with loose photographs strewn all over it; cushions had been discarded onto the floor, the thick cream carpet was covered with scrunched-up tissues and open photograph albums, and a red wine stain lay next to an empty glass. I pushed my head into the room. I could see that many photographs were ripped up, leaving empty spaces in the open albums. I hesitated for a moment and then stepped into the church, the thick carpet beneath my feet. Dolly's voice was now deafening. I turned and looked at the stereo. I felt a sudden urge to turn the music down, believing that it would at least bring Julie, if she was here, into the room. And so I did. As I watched my hand connect with the chrome dial, I turned the sound down a little – not too much to start with, but then a little more. Nobody came. Finally, I pushed my finger onto the off switch and the music stopped. Dolly's voice echoed around the large church, gradually fading and then silence. An unsettling, deafening nothing. I couldn't move – I just seemed to freeze into the moment.

But then suddenly, I half turned my body as I heard light footsteps from upstairs. I was taken over by extreme panic and sorely tempted to run, but I couldn't. The footsteps stopped and then very slowly…one more, then another.

'Is that you, Jack?'

I couldn't speak. I was then aware that someone was coming down the stairs. And then I was confronted by Julie, standing on the bottom stair. She was beguiling, dressed only in a black silk slip, her long curly hair tumbling off her shoulders, her tanned body glistening – but her once brown sparkling eyes offered only sadness, framed by red rings, evidence of her recent tragedy. She just looked at me – no show of emotion, not a word from her lips. I pulled my hand away from the off switch on the stereo and let my arms fall to my side. I couldn't think of a word to say. But then the one question prominent in my mind spewed out.

'Is Jack here?'

She shook her head from side to side, and then in a tired weary voice said, 'Typical of you, Ritchie. This has always been about Jack, hasn't it?'

I lifted my hands, desperate to offer words of comfort, but I gestured clumsily and the words wouldn't come. Julie stepped off the richly polished stair and then sat herself down on a small footstool. As she did so – though totally inappropriate – I couldn't help but notice how high the lace hem of her slip rode, exposing herself to me. As she leant forward, her ample breasts pressed firmly against the silk, her nipples suddenly hardening beneath the thin material. But as Julie's eyes looked at me, a tear starting to roll onto her cheek, she instinctively pulled the hem of her slip down, covering herself fully. I felt helpless as another tear dropped from her eye and disappeared into the thick cream carpet. My throat became dry and my eyes started to sting, suddenly overwhelmed by the full emotion of what was going on here. And then as Julie said the words – 'You never wanted to believe me, did you, Ritchie?' – my remorse released hot beads of guilt. They just fell, rolling like loose pearls down my face.

'Ritchie, Lillie was everything to me, but it always appeared that she meant nothing to you…'

The words were harsh but fair. Julie shook her head slowly from side to side, her regret pushed out from her tear-drenched lips.

'I owed it to her, to allow her to meet her real father, but you, Ritchie, denied me that!'

Despite shutting out the obvious truth to firstly myself and of course to Julie and Lillie, the broken soul that now sat before me was my Judgment Day. And as I questioned my reasons for denying the truth, I could only presume that it was out of fear: Jack, losing Yasmin ... both. But what I did know for sure was that the pain in my heart was for not having known my little girl, and for the heartache that I had caused this poor broken woman before me. As I stood within the walls of this sacred place, I was full of longing that was threatening to overpower me. Though I was fully aware of how contemptible my feelings were, as I stood in front of this woman at this moment, I was lost. My mind was reeling with the belief that I had missed out on the full journey, the completion of an adventure with something, someone wonderful. I swallowed hard, feeling guilt and embarrassment at how Julie would react if she knew what I was thinking – and in God's house, too. I knew I should console myself as an undoubtedly privileged man to have had such an important bond with her and leave it at that. I also had to accept that she must hate me for my unforgivable behaviour from start to finish.

I took a long deeply drawn breath in an attempt to distract myself and looked around at Jack's wonderful home: the many, many photos of his beautiful family, the sheer financial success he'd made of his life. I realise that my fear and respect for these two people is paramount. I feel totally unworthy as I stand in Jack's home, in front of his heartbroken wife, finally accepting that I have been a major part of all that Jack and Julie are. My face is drenched with tears and I know that Julie is talking to me, but my thoughts are working overtime. I'm suddenly looking at her, almost as though I'm having an out-of-body experience, and I start to picture all that I have missed: the winter nights, Julie putting Lillie to bed, reading her bedtime stories – Jack, having the privilege of it all – the outings to the park, the bedtime cuddles with Lillie. Priceless. And regardless of who Lillie's biological father is, to Lillie, it was Jack. She undoubtedly would have loved him unreservedly, and as for me, I was nothing to her; I simply didn't exist. So, as I look at Julie, I realise what a fool I have been. Her words start to cut in.

'Jack's a good man, Ritchie. He might be hard to the outside world, and I am sure there are things in his business life that I don't know about, but God, Ritchie, you have been such a coward. I didn't want to disrupt my world, cause heartbreak for Jack, rejection for Lillie, eternal damnation for myself! But you, Ritchie, chose to live a lie! You have totally discarded Lillie and me, shunned the truth!'

Every word this bereaved and broken woman spoke could not be argued with. And then Julie really summed up my existence.

'Ritchie, Yasmin is a lovely girl from what I hear and I envy her your love, but whatever you and your wife have, it's built on lies and denials! She doesn't know the real you – a flawed Ritchie Angel with a *huge* secret. Tell me if I'm wrong. She doesn't know about Lillie and me, does she, Ritchie?'

I raise my face to the church rafters, and then, as the breath leaves my body and my head sinks, my eyes fall on line after line of stained glass, dozens of biblical figures waiting for an answer. I swallow hard, wanting desperately to be able to tell her, '*Of course she knows, my wife knows everything and still chooses to love me unreservedly,*' but of course I couldn't tell her that because it would only be more lies.

I walked wearily and defensively over to her and just stood for several moments before her. I hadn't planned to, but suddenly my fingers were brushing gently across her cheeks, wiping away the remnants of her tears. Julie looked up at me and then placed her hand on mine. Time seemed to stand still.

And then she offered her first smile, quickly followed by an exasperated, 'Oh, Ritchie, you are *such* a shit!'

As our fingers entwined, I chose to say nothing at all. The strength of the moment resulted in an overwhelming closeness and I felt increasingly strange, frighteningly so. In fact, in Julie's company, I felt as though I was two different people. There was the *kind,* successful, loving husband that was married to Yasmin, but here, in Jack De'Vil's home, with Jack

317

De'Vil's wife, I felt like someone else. My thoughts were neither rational nor appropriate, but the simple gesture of Julie's hand on mine was taking me over. I ached for her, her forgiveness, her warmth. I tried to think rationally. I could see the words creeping out from the depths of my twisted logic: maybe the pain that we were both feeling, our joint grief for Lillie, maybe we were both craving anything, as long as it masked the hurt. Maybe this would justify such a welling passion, a desire that was frighteningly overwhelming. Yasmin didn't seem to play a part in this. The man that I was, here with Julie, was a different man. The performers in this scene felt the irresistible bond that had been made bigger than ever in the light of Lillie's death. But what happened next, despite it being what I wanted, shook me to the core.

As I knelt down at Julie's side, my hand on hers, her tears starting to ease, I was totally taken over, her smell intoxicating me. As her naked leg brushed against the hairs on my arm, the electricity that passed through me, well, I had never felt a power quite like it. And every time she sighed, her breasts straining once again against the bodice of her slip, I felt such an overwhelming desire to kiss her. Julie may have easily looked past me, or let her eyes fall to the floor, and then the moment may have passed. But she looked right into my eyes, and suddenly there seemed to be a fire, a burning intensity that I was convinced had been long extinguished. I felt my head falling, my lips brushing against hers. Julie pulled back slightly, and then her lips were back on mine, gently at first, and then as I lifted my hands, pulling her face forward, the passion took control and it felt so totally right. Any thoughts of Yasmin trying to ease into my mind were pushed out – this wasn't me, it was something much stronger than that. And, as Julie pushes me away, I feel as though I'm going to die, but as she stands up, she takes my hand and leads me upstairs, every step more potent than the last.

As we reach the most sumptuous bedroom, I look around. Julie's exquisite clothes hanging in the open wardrobe, her silk dressing gown strewn across the large bed. But the whole scene makes me feel as though I'm being allowed into Julie and Lillie's special world. Julie's lips are suddenly on mine again, and as I find I cannot resist another moment I run my hands over every twist and curve of her body, finally releasing her breasts from the confines of her silk slip. My hands and then lips are on them, kissing, taking in the wonderful smell, kneading passionately, textures and colours rising and enriching with every passing second. Then, as my hand falls down between her cool thighs, my fingers slip hesitantly into the most privileged of places – a volcanic heat welcomes me. Just as I feel my desire is going to take the roof of the church off, we become one! As our ill-advised passion seems set to destroy both of our lives, the tears are streaming down our faces. The feeling is as though *spiritual* – earthy, basic and animal, but *so* incredibly necessary. There is nothing that could stop us doing what we were doing.

Finally, we lay still, drained and burnt out, our legs entwined, Julie's head on my chest, and none of it felt wrong. I couldn't love Yasmin any more than I did – she was everything to me. And from the little things that Julie was saying to me, here and now, it was abundantly clear that she loved Jack totally. But somehow, the emotions had been running high – the nine years of hurt had perhaps required closure. A deep-rooted love and respect that I had for Julie had shown itself and totally overwhelmed me. So here we were, our actions set in stone for eternity.

The sun streamed through the large stained-glass window. I was transfixed on the image of the Virgin Mary cradling baby Jesus. Shades of green, purple, blue and red as the midday sun fell across my chest, the outline of Mary and her baby boy clearly visible on Julie's face. I almost mentioned it to her, but felt that maybe there were words on certain occasions better left unsaid. And I didn't want anything to spoil *this* moment.

'Ritchie, you do realise that this must *never* happen again?'

I sadly agreed.

'Ritchie, since that night with you there's only been Jack. I did the honourable thing and kept him waiting for a good month, but then when I realised I was pregnant I panicked, didn't sleep for days. I became scared, figured that you wouldn't be interested in me, especially with a baby on the way, and I suppose, well, I didn't mean to, but perhaps I took the evil but undoubtedly easy option and seduced Jack.'

Julie and I just stared into each other's eyes with blank, numb expressions, both lost in all that had happened between us from the very first night together. I brushed a stray curl from her forehead. She smiled and took a deep breath.

'Ritchie, Jack has always treated me like a princess, you know? I've never asked him for anything, yet he gives me everything!'

Like a spoilt child, I started to feel a bit agitated. *Okay, Julie, so Jack's a great guy!* But I sensibly stopped myself. I had no right to shatter any illusions that she had of her husband. And though my feelings for her were strong – after all, she took my virginity – I knew that she belonged with Jack. But then the obvious hit me, and I had to ask *the* question.

'Have you told Jack the truth about Lillie? You know, in light of, well, you know?'

Julie sat up sharply.

'God *no*. I should have done, but years ago; how can I do that now?'

Julie drew her knees up to her chest, guilt sinking sombrely through her.

'Ritchie, I may be wrong, *so* totally, totally wrong, but perhaps the truth has died with Lillie…' A single tear dropped from her eye and it took several moments for her to compose herself, she then let out in almost a whisper. 'Maybe I have to accept this incredibly high price for what I have done.'

My heart broke for her.

As I kissed Julie goodbye, I told her how I loved her and that I would always be there for her, should she ever need me. We held on to each other for several minutes, and it was painful to step away. We had been brought together today – closure, new beginnings, I wasn't quite sure which – but if I was supposed to feel guilt and regret, well, at this precise moment, I didn't. And as I walked away, with every step I felt a tremendous loss. I scratched my head as I clunked the gates shut. But despite the thousand or more questions repeating the same meaning within my tired, broken mind, I knew that we were never meant to be together. What had gone on between us today, what we had all those years ago, we weren't supposed to have anything more than that. Any thoughts of whether or not Julie and I could have made a go of being together would have meant that Yasmin and I would have missed our chance, and that was something I simply couldn't comprehend.

The midday air seemed to sober me up, and suddenly I was riddled with guilt. As I climbed back into the car, my mind was rampant with the image of Yasmin. I slammed the door shut. Never, not once, had I had any inclination or desire to cheat on her – my life with her was perfect. But maybe I had to accept and try to understand that Julie and I needed the moment we had shared, but now we should both move on.

I went to start the engine, but then my car door is pulled open with such a force, and then the largest fist hurtles towards my face and all I feel is my head being slammed back. As I lay open to blow after blow...I must have blacked out.

Eventually, my head spinning, the taste of wool in my mouth combined with the sweet stickiness trickling steadily down the back of my throat, my mind tries to recognise who I am and what the hell has happened. There's a whooshing in my brain and I can hear a voice, a familiar voice.

'See, Julie? He's coming round now; no harm done, eh!'

I manage to roll over onto my back, my ribs hot and resentful at the simple movement. I try desperately to open my eyes and gradually they succumb, but my vision is blurred, with a red-tinged frame. I painfully blink away the distortion and then recognise the vaulted church ceiling, finally aware that I am back in the devil's home. Pure fear enables me to sit up, and there is Julie, sat on the leather settee in her black dressing gown, her lip split open. Standing beside her is Jack, a familiar shiny black and chrome gun in his hand.

'Good afternoon, Angel! Nice to see you, sunshine!'

I pull myself to my feet. I start to cough and splutter, blood and mucus falling on and around the scattered photographs. Jack laughs and quickly points the gun at me.

'Stop there, Angel! Nothing, and I mean nothing, would give me more pleasure than sinking a bullet into your forehead and then watching you die, fading away and out of my life forever, but first I have something I want you to do for me.'

I look at Julie, her eyes petrified and totally shocked at all that is going on. I lower my head a little and focus in on Jack's delirious inane smirk. But as our eyes meet, his are dead and empty, as though destroyed and running on dregs. Nervous, desperate words suddenly spew out of my mouth.

'For God's sake, Jack! What the hell is all this about?'

Jack walks towards me and spits full force into my face.

'Shut the *fuck up*, Angel! None of your *shit*, I mean it. You'll get to know what *all* this is about soon enough!' The power and venom of Jack's words and the sheer force of his breath behind them make my eyeballs ache, and forces his earlier gift of saliva to spread across my ashen face.

My shoulders ease with relief and I feel genuine pleasure seeing the back of Jack's head as he walks over to his wife. He drops down onto one knee, taking Julie's hand in his, and looks her straight in the eyes.

'I loved you so much, Julie, and yet you have totally betrayed me. I have tried to make you love me, be a good husband, a good father. I have tried to give you everything!'

Julie attempts to place her hand on Jack's face, but he brushes it aside. The tears once again start to roll down her cheeks, the words barely audible from her swollen lips.

'Please, Jack, I love you. I...'

But Jack stops her. 'Julie, you have allowed *him* into our home, you have allowed him into our bedroom ... and opened your legs!'

Jack turns his head towards me, his words pushed out through gritted teeth and his face taking on the caricature of a rabid Doberman.

'So that he, *that* scum, can fuck you! You have allowed that piece of shit to *come* inside you! You...'

Jack turns back and faces Julie, his words suddenly faltering and momentarily placid.

'The woman I loved, the woman I felt deserved everything I could muster...'

Julie cut in, her hands now allowed to press onto his face.

'Please, Jack... I really don't know why it happened. I think the emotion of Lillie... God knows, Jack, but...' Julie stopped, knowing that she couldn't say any more.

I let out an almost paralysed squeak of relief, but then my

last thread of hope of actually managing to walk away from this situation snapped as Jack sprang to his feet and snarled, 'Julie, I know all about your *big* secret! I am well aware that Ritchie *fucking* Angel is Lillie's father! *I know* ... I've always known!! What do you think I am, some kind of docile thicko? Your stupid little slag of a friend years ago told me you'd spent the night with Angel, but I had only just started seeing you. It totally ate me up! I either killed him, or you both, or just got on with it! And you know what, Julie? Your love, what we had, made up for it. I waited for you to say when you were pregnant that it wasn't mine, and I dreaded the day because I believed you *would* tell me and then leave me. And so, when the words never came, I, like a bloody fool, believed it must have been out of love for me, that deep down you wanted the baby to be mine! And I *loved* that, and I could happily live with *that* belief. So, when Lillie was born, I couldn't have loved her more, and because I believed that you *really* loved me, I could cope. My love for you both just got stronger, but now...'

Jack slumps down into a chair and I try to say something.

'Jack, all Julie's said today is how much she loves you!'

Jack turns and looks at me, suddenly rising to his feet, his evil smile making me step back.

'Get Yasmin on the phone and get her to come here!'

My mouth goes dry and I shake my head.

'No, Jack! I don't want her having anything to do with this.'

Jack turns to Julie and then back to me.

'Okay, Ritchie Angel, here's the deal. Either you get Yasmin on the phone and get your precious bitch over here, or I'll kill Julie! I mean it, Ritchie. I've nothing left, you've made sure of that by coming here today. Trashing your house, sure, I wanted to scare you, frighten your wife and make her question what you are, but that was all! But now, coming here, you and my wife, *fucking*... Well now, any reason I had for being with her has gone. So get Yasmin here, Angel, so that I can tell her everything that's been going on, and then we'll *all* have lost everything! You see, Ritchie boy, then we can all walk away on level terms.'

I look at Jack and then down at Julie. I feel totally wretched. I have destroyed her life. Jack paces up and down a little, then points his gun at Julie's face, just twelve small inches away.

'Go on, Angel, call Mrs Angel. And make sure she gets here soon.'

I thought about Yasmin and how all this would destroy her, and there was no way that I could do it. I knew that Jack wouldn't kill Julie; he may well take it out on me, give me a good kicking, a few cuts and bruises, but it was a small price to pay. So I look at him, a liberating assuredness showing itself just when it was needed.

'I'm not ringing her, Jack.'

My judge and jury hung his head with an exaggerated chewing of the inside of his mouth.

'Is that your *final* word, Angel?'

Jack's eyes stare at me. I nod, resilient and sure. Jack's eyes crease, his tanned stubby fingers squeeze the trigger and my eyes widen in sheer disbelief at the most horrendous scene that I will ever witness as Julie's head distorts and explodes, blood cannoning back and splattering the church wall and window.

Jack just looks at me, the gun still pointing at Julie, tears rolling down his face, his body shaking.

'You see, Ritchie? Look what you've made me do! I asked one simple thing of you, but you couldn't do it, could you? Ritchie, *you've* killed my wife!'

I suddenly start to shake uncontrollably and then fall to the floor. I feel that my stomach is going to leave my body as I wretch. My head becomes blurred and I believe that I am going to pass out. Finally, I am rid of the last bit of vomit. I glance at the photographs on the floor, all the pictures of Lillie cut out.

'Why have you done this to the photos, Jack?'

He speaks softly. 'She wasn't mine, and when she died, I just felt that maybe the best way to cope with the pain was to cut her out of my life, try to forget about her. Julie went mad when she saw the pictures, but I couldn't help it, and I didn't tell her I knew her secret.'

I am suddenly aware of the gun pointing directly at me.

'Ring your wife, Angel. I mean it, or I'll shoot you too!'

I stagger to my feet and stare down the end of the gun, the stench of death all around me. Jack's words just tumble out – same theme.

'I have nothing more to lose, Angel. I think I might as well kill you! The police will believe that you broke in, trying to harm me and my wife, and I will tell them I had to shoot you because you had raped my wife. No one will doubt me. And then here's the best part, Angel, I will get together with Yasmin, we will comfort each other until finally we become lovers, and we can have a child of *our* own!'

Jack's eyes cut into me, his smile broadening. I don't doubt he means it. My heart seems to be competing with my brain for air.

'Okay, Jack...Give me the phone.'

As the devil bends down, a self-satisfied smugness stretches across his triumphant face. As he grabs hold of the telephone I take my one chance. I kick with all my might, the full force of my boot connecting with the devil's wrist, and the gun instantly spins into the air. I suddenly scream out as I barge at him with all the strength I can muster, and the devil falls back crashing through the glass coffee table. I race for the gun, and as I grab it I pray that it's loaded. I simply turn and point it at the devil, but he doesn't bat an eyelid. As he climbs out of the remnants of the coffee table, clusters of glass falling from his body, my clear indecision gives him the one chance he needs. As he lurches towards me, I squeeze the trigger. The blast into the devil's stomach pushes his legs and head forwards, whilst his midriff is propelled backwards. He slumps off the edge of the thick cream carpet, his back cracking against the highly polished stone floor. He looks at me, his hands clutching his stomach, unable to stop the surge of blood seeping between his drenched fingers. Then he utters his last words, his black eyes flickering in and out of consciousness.

'I'll haunt you forever, Angel! Mark my words, I'll...'

His eyes seem to seize half open, and suddenly I am surrounded by silence.

When I had been lying next to Yasmin last night, unprepared but determined to face Jack head-on, the full horror of what lies before me now had not been one of the many pre-empted scenarios. The gun is still pointed at Jack. I start to shake venomously, totally unable to loosen my grip, until the shaking becomes so violent that the gun leaps and lands amongst the now bloodstained photographs. I stagger back, waiting for my senses to return. My legs instinctively give way and I drop down onto the thick carpet; the shaking continues. It may have been two minutes, it could have been ten or more, but I finally raise my head from between my legs and advisedly some urgency returns. I stretch my arm towards the gun, my fingers taut and tense. I ease my still shaking hand around the murder weapon and turn it full circle. I walk quickly into the kitchen, grabbing a warm tea towel from off the Aga and rub furiously, desperate to remove the blood and my fingerprints. With the gun wrapped in the tea towel, I walk back into the lounge, tiptoeing around the devastation, my entire being squirming as I push the gun between Jack's blood-engulfed fingers, and just lay the tea towel in the centre of his pool of blood. I heave violently, but nothing comes out. I look at my earlier effort – mustard yellow and all too visible. I know I need to clean it up. I start to perspire, and within seconds heavy beads are running down my forehead. My hands starting to shake again, but then I look at Julie and tears start to merge with the stream of sweat trying to drown me. I feel an overwhelming urge to kiss her goodbye, but as I take in her shattered face, I close my eyes quickly, desperate to shut out this madness.

I start to edge backwards away from the carnage, deciding that I have to leave my vomit untouched – the link unsettling me terribly, but I know I have to go. As I turn, I take a last look at Jack – I am completely numb. I step outside; the fresh clean air potent and so very necessary. I walk with purpose to the window of the garage, wiping frantically with my sleeve any marks I may have made earlier. As I try to walk calmly down the driveway, an almost dream-like determination to float across the uncompromising gravel denies me my desire for a quiet getaway. I finally reach the point of departure to this nightmare – the imposing iron gates. I physically shake as taunting words fill my head: *You needed bigger and stronger gates than this to protect you, Jack...* I wipe the handle clean and head towards my car, which mockingly seems to be drifting further down the lane with each step. I look around me, shaking this surreal feeling away, rotating my neck and trying to sober up my hindering thoughts. All was clear – not a soul about. And as I take my last few steps to relative safety, I pray that I am leaving the scene of the crime undetected.

As the car door clunks shut, the sudden quietness feels like a prison cell. But the increasing decibel level of my pounding heart highlights the urgency in getting away from here as quickly as possible. I look around again and nervously start the engine. I ease the car back down the lane and reverse into a shallow opening; the bumper nudging the farmer's gate a little, the slightest tremor from the knock seeming to ricochet through every nerve end in my body. I push my shaking foot onto the accelerator and kangaroo away.

It takes several roads until I even dare look at another vehicle. I turn into the top of Willow High Street, the sudden welling of nausea ready to overwhelm me, but a line of optimism climbs through me, unexpected, but I cling on to it. I question the chances of getting away with what I've done, the line of hope thickening and inspiring me to believe that I just might. But then my mind is instantly filled with the tragic image of Julie, and the pessimism surges back loud and nagging. Incriminating pictures in my mind of how just a few hours ago we had made love ... forensics, my sperm, my vomit, all powerful and capable of seeing me locked up for life. But I have to believe, I need to be strong. I keep telling myself: if they don't put me in the picture, then how can they possibly link me? I need an alibi, every detail consistent with having lived a normal day, doing everyday *acceptable* things. I look and squint at the clock in the car. It was twenty past three – where had the time gone? But when I reflect on just what has been achieved in just a few short hours, I felt it wise to ignore the question. I bang the steering wheel hard as I turn down the side of Skirdle's. *Come on, Ritchie boy, you can do this. Deep breaths, and keep focused.*

My legs start to buckle just as I am about to step out into the spotlight of the high street. I face the crumbling brickwork and ease my forehead onto the cold, unforgiving Skirdle wall. I rub my repentant numb flesh against the bricks and mortar, trying desperately to erase the horror story running rampant through my conscience. I start to whisper nonsensical words, unsettling and unhelpful, but then, just as I am beginning to doubt my ability to cope, I hear myself utter, 'Be strong, Ritchie, for Yasmin. You can do this.' I attempt to rotate all that is negative and raise a positive, and then settle on a crazy strategy: *If Julie's poor tragic face appears, then think of Yasmin, instantly.* I shudder as I am confronted with Jack's dead contorted body: *Think of the Water's Edge, Ritchie! Come on son, think of the Water's Edge! Your dreams and plans for the place, peaceful and calm.*

I shake my arms and rest my fingers against the bricks, slowly easing my forehead off the wall. I run the back of my hand across my face, a fine terracotta powder brushed exaggeratedly away. I finally manage to stand up straight, and as an inner belief lifts me, I push out an absurd smile. With my chest pumped up, I barge characteristically through the shop door, and then, right on cue, bravado and radiance beamed directly at Mr Ball, who was listening intently on the telephone. He tripped over his words, returned a concerned smile and stuck his thumb up. I sat down and tried to look busy. Mr Ball replaced the receiver, suddenly jumping to his feet.

'Ummm, *shit*, Ritchie! Welcome home and all that, but wow, she's either a very passionate woman or you have just gone ten rounds with Mike Tyson!'

I didn't look up and simply gave a dismissive wave of the hand.

'*Umm,* Ritchie? You need cleaning up...'

As though triggering an acknowledgement to the possible state of my beaten face, the pain seemed to ignite with immediate effect. But all I heard was a feeble excuse leave my swollen lips.

'Oh, *bloody kids*, ummm...their bikes left lying outside of the paper shop, wasn't looking, went flying. Looks far worse than it is, don't fuss!'

Mr Ball took a step back, grimacing at my dismissal but prepared to play it my way.

'Well, bruises and co aside...you look *really* tanned! How's the stunning Mrs Angel?'

I felt normality creeping back into my world as Mr Ball

stepped forward, his hand placed firmly in mine, his dancing eyes expressing genuine warmth.

'Yasmin and I are both feeling fantastic. I mean it. You and young Skirdle would love it there, very romantic, just amazing!'

Mr Ball suddenly looked quite overcome with emotion, his hand once again thrust firmly into mine.

'Good to have you back, Ritchie. You're a good man, Ritchie Angel! Yasmin's a very lucky woman.'

I smiled and cheekily replied, 'Hey, I hope you're not flirting with me!'

Mr Ball laughed more openly than I had ever seen him do before. Suddenly looking at his watch, he grabbed his briefcase and made for the door.

'Ritchie, are you okay to hold the fort for a couple of hours? I've got three visits to do. I had planned to do them before now, but Skirdle senior hasn't got back from his weekend away yet!'

I seized with both hands the opportunity.

'Umm, sure, Mr Ball. Umm, would you mind saying that I've been here all day? You know, should Mr Skirdle or anyone ask. It's just that I had planned to get in earlier, but you can perhaps imagine how difficult it was to get my head off the pillow this morning – jet lag, and of course the passionate honeymoon!'

Mr Ball winked at me as though not a care in the world.

'You can count on me, Ritchie lad. If *anyone* asks, you've been slaving away at your desk all day!' Mr Ball did have one condition, though. 'Ritchie, so that you don't scare all the customers off, I'll just leave you this foundation, just your colour. Will work wonders in disguising the face damage. Umm, okay, *sorry,* I'm going now!'

And as Mr Ball patted the side of his nose with his beautifully manicured finger, he left. Within seconds of the door closing, I unexpectedly found myself running towards the bathroom where I instantly threw up again. As I wiped my mouth, I just shook. All I could think about was the devastation that someone would find at the Old Church. Though it was the last thing I wanted to do, I relived how Julie and I had made love only this morning – but now, her and Jack were dead! As my nightmare was interrupted by the opening of the front door, I made my way back into the shop, my acting ability to be tested to the limits.

CHAPTER FIFTEEN

The Murderer And Adulterer Is Back In The Arms Of His Loving Wife

Before Death, 1997 – Blue Sky

That night, back at the Grange Country Club, I don't know how I managed to contain myself. I felt as though everyone was looking at me, as though they all knew what I was guilty of. Naturally, Yasmin was her normal wonderful self, but I simply despised myself for what I had done. Married for just over three weeks and yet I had already committed adultery. And of course, if you're looking to trump that horrendous act, then how about a cold-blooded murder? I shook my head furiously.

'Are you alright, darling? I'm serious, first thing in the morning I'm going to have a word in that shop. What if it had been someone pregnant, or an old age pensioner sent flying?' Yasmin was not impressed.

But as I smiled and told her that I thought it was quite funny actually, and that she would too if she had seen me drop like a sack of potatoes across the bikes, she joined me in a wry smile, begrudgingly seeing the funny side.

I quickly changed the subject.

'Not impressed that the decorators haven't completed Sky Cottage, *tiger,* but never mind, we'll be back home soon!'

And as I continued the ruse of a crushing headache, we gratefully found ourselves back in our room and within record time I slid between the cool cotton sheets. Yasmin kissed the back of my head, and under the cover of darkness I took on the foetus position. Finally, I fell into a deep but disturbed sleep, my head pounding, every pore producing a hot, clammy sweat. I tossed and turned, each and every hostile step of my real-life nightmare simply repeating over and over again.

The next morning I showered away the aftermath of my restless night. Yasmin and I exchanged words, touches, kisses, but I felt and heard nothing. I made my way to work on automatic pilot, keeping my head down, just trying to fade and hopefully disappear for good into the background. I hadn't wanted to visit the Water's Edge; I didn't want to take the guilt there. I dreaded the morning papers and imagined far too vividly the boys in blue handcuffing me and dragging me out of Skirdle's. I couldn't even look up from my desk as different people came into the shop, and with each new and familiar voice I just waited, expecting the dreaded announcement about the tragedy that had been thrust upon our community – but there was nothing. I simply lived and tiptoed through the next three days, almost questioning my sanity – surely Jack and Julie must have been discovered? And then, just as I had mustered the strength to lift my head above my desk, I came face-to-face with the paperboy.

'Here you go, Mr Angel!'

I smiled and thanked the young lad. I read the bold black lettering above the leading story, but perversely didn't digest a word. I focused instead on a small column at the bottom right-hand side of the paper: *Local Estate Agents up for National Award!* I shook my head positively and proudly as I scanned the nominated company – Skirdle's– and my very own name linked with the success we had achieved here. I raised my eyes back to the headlines: *Heartbroken Couple in Suicide Tragedy*. I read every word, and then again…yet unable to take it in. Mr Ball and Mr Skirdle walked in from the kitchen, the latter placing a steaming cup of coffee in front of me. I folded the paper quickly and handed it to my boss. I was several feet above my body at this point, aware that I was downing the contents of the red-hot liquid.

'Steady on, Ritchie lad, you'll take the roof off your mouth!' warned Mr Skirdle.

I watched as I placed down the cup and walked calmly towards the bathroom. Once inside, I locked the door and fell back against the wall, slumped and slowly slid down the stark white bathroom tiles. Within moments I was back in my body, my mouth dry and burnt. My mind was running rampant, the report's poignant points racing through my head, one after the other: the death of their little girl, the unbearable grief, suspected joint suicide. There had been a mention of the photographs and how the gun was registered to Jack – and how he'd used it on them both. As the icy-cold bathroom floor forced me to stand up, I felt an incredible optimism. I prayed that this was the end of it. I assumed that the police would have to make further enquiries, but I hoped they were *truly* satisfied with it being a suicide.

Over the next few days, it was all anybody could talk about, and of course, who could blame them? Drama like this simply didn't happen in Willow. This was a major event. It even made the headlines on the national news. The power of it all filled every ounce of me. I dreaded closing my eyes at night, because once asleep, the nightmare would be relived again and again. I was shocked by the way I felt – I had always presumed that I could cope with anything. But I was unable to eat and I was incapable of sleep, and that was a combination that in time would send me insane – or kill me. But gradually I managed to operate through the numbness until I assumed that I was starting to get on with my life, making minor plans and moving tentatively forward. And that expanse of nauseating darkness that would welcome me when I woke each morning was now replaced with a glimmer of optimism. But I would cringe as I felt that unforgivable silver lining feeling that I despised in myself – the gratitude that at least Jack De'Vil was finally out of my life. And though I would try to balance the *silver lining* school of thought with the belief that the broken-hearted Julie would be reunited with Lillie, for the first time in my life I questioned my religious beliefs, my hopes and aspirations – heaven and hell, life after death…

Two weeks on, and Julie and Jack had their funeral. I pondered furiously over whether I should go. But to the outside world I had no links with the De'Vil family, so I stayed away. I felt it wise to concentrate on my responsibility: Yasmin and our future. As I carried my bride over the threshold of Sky Cottage, I felt an incredible relief at the freshness and welcome that our home had to offer. The guys had done a wonderful job, and the huge bonus that I handed over to the individuals involved in eradicating the devastation caused by my late foe was given with immense gratitude. All I asked for in return was total discretion. I stated, *rightly* so, it was 'for the sake of Yasmin', but as I woke suddenly in the small hours of the night, I appreciated that the police may have been prepared to ask a question or two, should they have been enlightened. Combined with the chain of events that regretfully followed at the Old Church, their conclusion could have been devastating!

Married life and all that went with it held no disappointment for me – I loved Yasmin being my wife. And though we had made lengthy strides with the design and detail of the Water's Edge build, we were yet to lay a single brick. Though we had both found immense satisfaction in clearing an area of ground for our new home that best suited our requirement of maximum light and unrivalled views. Yasmin and I would stand in awe on the chosen spot, our imagination for what we should and could do running riot and knowing no boundaries. But the *cold light of day* reality, and the *real world* restraints of the tortoise-pace planners and their attempts to suffocate us with the obligatory red tape, concluded the fact that we were ready for battle. And so there wasn't really any time for negative reflection.

As autumn took on the guise of winter, we all stood around yet another Water's Edge bonfire. Jimmy seemed to have something on his mind; he was buoyant and ready to combust unless he spilt the beans.

'Right, everybody! You have all commented on the fact that Sally has the largest bump ever … well, we're having twins!'

We all danced around like idiots, thrilled at the news. I pulled Yasmin tightly to me, and we both commented on how deliriously easy Sally made pregnancy look. She just glowed – a perfect advert for a beautiful mum-to-be. And so life really did seem to find its feet again for us all, even though every time a police car drove past the shop window I would climb out of my chair to see whether it was parking up or not. So for now at least, paranoia was the price I paid.

Before Death, 1999 – Blue Sky

Two severe winters and two summers later, the dream home was finally a blood-sweating reality. But as I stood back and took in the fruits of our labour, the manic goings-on around me were not able to penetrate my peace of mind. After the death of the De'Vil family, I had expected from then on in – with thoughts of karma and 'what goes around comes around' – that my life would never be the same again. That surely I could not expect to be blessed with good fortune and the strength of happiness that I presently found myself with. Despite a scarred conscience, my life was perfect. Everything possible in my wildest dreams was all around me. Yasmin now stood at my side, all our close friends gathered for our other special day – the official opening of the Water's Edge. The whole project had taken an excessive amount of time to complete, but the planning alone had taken over ten months to be approved. We knew exactly what we wanted, and we made sure that the three men in their grey suits from the local council were not going to sabotage and dilute our labour of love. Every reclaimed brick, sections of weathered sandstone, mortar colour, warped clay roofing tiles and hundred-year-old oak timbers, it all had to fit the life-long dream. But as Yasmin's hand slipped into mine I had no doubt that we had created an inspirational home, with a backdrop that seemed to purr in approval.

'Ritchie! Come on, mate! We've saved this one for you!'

Steve, our faithful builder, climbed down off the scaffolding and made his way towards me, before finally holding up the sculptured ridge tile. My heart lurched.

'Ummm! Steve mate, you *really* want me to do this?'

His steely-blue eyes gave me my answer, and everyone started cheering.

'Shit!' I uttered under my breath, bowing and grimacing at my sadistic audience. 'Alright, alright! You had all better catch me when I fall!'

My legs shook as I made my way towards the waiting ladder

of death.

'Hey! And, Ritchie, once that ridge tile's on, we want a speech!'

I laughed nervously as Jimmy and Sally's banter swooped in and around my pounding heartbeat, painfully risen and now making my skull shake. But then a warm smile would leave my blood-drained lips as I was drawn to my best friend's twin toddlers, Danny and Daisy, fully focused on their mad Uncle Ritchie, each with their arms wrapped around the leg of their chosen parent. Yasmin called out and ran up to me, kissing me gently, the look in her eyes aware of my unfortunate fear of heights. I gripped her hand, not wanting to let go. But like a limpet child on his first day at school, I finally broke the bond and made my way, brave face forward, each step lead-filled. I rose above the cheering crowd, a moronic grin etched firmly from cheek to cheek.

My respect for Steve and his gang of fearless roofers tripled as I finally got to the top of the scaffolding. Steve nodded towards the awaiting cat-ladder that was to take me even higher. Once climbed, a symphony of encouragement boomed from below, with whistles and cheers as I swung my leg over the ridge line like I was mounting a terracotta horse. Uncomfortable and petrified, I inched myself towards the edge of the gable end. I had seriously never felt so scared in all my life – perhaps a statement that wouldn't quite hold water if I were to allow myself a moment to reflect. But regardless, my previously shaken skull was now whooshing, as though slamming across the choppy seas in an out-of-control speedboat. Steve passed me the antique ornate dragon-shaped ridge tile – a suitable finial looking down and taking care of us all in and around the Water's Edge. With arms that I no longer had control over, I lowered the ridge tile onto the mortar that Steve had trowelled out ready for me and pushed it firmly into place.

'IT'S NOT STRAIGHT!' Yasmin yelled up at me, everyone laughing and adding their own little unsympathetic verbal abuse.

And then as I announced our family home complete and our door always open for our wonderful family and friends – '*and please God, can I get down now?'* – everybody cheered. With a little help from Steve and the guys, I shakily made my way back down to solid ground, and though I tried to put on a brave face, my legs felt as though they were going to buckle at any moment.

The rest of the afternoon was a worthy celebration. Everyone was there: the builders, the landscapers, the architect, anybody who had been involved with the creation of our new home. The roof was only just finished, but we had been watertight for many months, allowing us to complete the inside. I had to raise a glass to them all, as at no time had there been the remotest of problems, and I have to say that in all the years I had taken charge with different building projects, this was the first time all those involved had seemed to take that extra little bit of care – as if they had felt the magic that was here at the Water's Edge. Once we had our plans approved, the journey from then on had been an absolute pleasure: 'Amen!'

As Yasmin and I waved off all our well-wishers, I doubted that greater happiness could exist – but I would be wrong thinking that.

'Ritchie darling, I've got something to tell you!'

And as I looked into Yasmin's sparkling excited eyes, she didn't need to say another word.

'Oh my God! You're pregnant?'

As I lifted my beautiful wife up and off her feet, giving her the most passionate, heartfelt hug, I quickly, safely placed her back on the ground.

'Oh God, Yasmin! I'm *so* sorry! Are you alright? I haven't hurt you, have I?'

But my clever wife just laughed and threw her arms around my neck.

I ran Yasmin her first bath in our new family home, and as she sank her fabulously fertile *baby house* of a body into the deep bubbled water, I looked out through the bathroom window. The crystal-clear diamond stars twinkled back at me, but a twinge of negativity made me question their motive. I was now a man with the sweetest cherry dropped firmly onto the thick snow-white icing on my large blessed cake of a life, but still something was unsettling me. I brushed Yasmin's stray curl from out of her eye and blew a kiss as I made my way downstairs – I needed a moment alone.

As I stepped outside, I prayed that our baby was going to be a beautiful, healthy specimen. I knew I was due a fall, but I hoped that despite any punishment I may be due, my child wasn't going to be the beating stick. And as I walked across the moonlit lawn and stepped up onto the large timber decking area that faced the canal, it was there that the tears welled up. I looked up to the skies above and offered my words of forgiveness: for Scottie, for Harry and Alice, for Lillie and Julie, and even for Jack.

'Please! If you wish to punish me…then I beg you! *Not* my baby, *not* my innocent wife!'

A single tear rolled down my cheek as the words left my vulnerable and desperately sorry body. I took a deep breath and lowered myself down, my arms resting on the tops of my raised knees. Many pictures passed through my mind, and as a consequence I tore into the inside of my cheek before scolding myself. I let out a long drawn sigh, lowering my head onto my forearms. My eyes scanned the surface of the water and then dwelled on the activity that was causing the many ripples amongst the canal reeds – silver moonlit circles, the only outward sign that there was life stirring within the depths. Several moments later I lifted my head up, a shroud almost extinguishing the scene, the stars now lost behind a passing cloud.

Gradually, I was aware of a smile increasing across my face – one solitary but dazzling and proud star, and then several, and then in the blink of an eye dozens, and then a sky-full. You simply couldn't help but feel a world of optimism with a show as extravagant as that! And as I beamed back with the powerful image of Yasmin and, God willing, our little baby-to-be, my thoughts turned to Julie and Lillie. I made a promise into the night that I would dedicate this new baby to them both. I prayed that they were together and okay, and that maybe in time they would find it possible to forgive me. As I wiped away a determined tear, I questioned whether or not they could hear me. But I believed that they might, and my love went out to them both.

Before Death, 2000 – Blue Sky

As a New Year clocked in, the winter fierce and vocal around us, it was baby-soft fleeces and roaring fires that protected our unborn child. I counted down the days, Yasmin's bowling-ball bump growing ever larger. But within a skip and a jump, as the buds of spring uncurled their yawning limbs, our anticipation and nervous excitement crossed boundaries that we never knew existed. Then, with withering patience, we were out the other side and into in my favourite season – though collectively we could not help but doubt the weatherman's word that summer was finally ours.

But alas, today, with the full strength of an untainted blue sky and the exuberance of a capable sun finally unleashing a sample of its potential, we raised our glasses high. As the quenching cool offerings of the Chardonnay valleys slid effortlessly down my parched throat, I looked on in awe as I watched Jimmy and Sally running around after Daisy and Danny. Though my best friends had safely predicted that their lives were never going to be the same again, I couldn't help but smile. Since the arrival of their perfect, fit and healthy bundles, the change to their lives was overwhelming and then some. But the unfortunate, totally un-ignorable fly in the ointment for us all was that the pair of them looked the spitting image of their father – minus of course, and welcomingly so, the scruffy hippy beard that still featured as our Jimmy's proud and reluctant-to-lose feature. But give Danny another twelve years and I was convinced he would be able to sprout facial hair that would put his father's offering to shame.

Then the amusement would subside a little as young Scottie ran around the garden, and my heart would feel so very heavy over the fact that his father would never see or hold the wonderful little lad he'd helped to create. Janey had brought her new boyfriend Ian with her, and on first appearances he seemed a nice guy. We all hoped that maybe this was the one – she had certainly built him up. I had prayed perhaps more than anyone for Janey to find love again, a partner to enhance her life and to share in the joy of little Scottie.

Yasmin attempted climbing unaided onto her swollen feet,

but once we had all gallantly tried to ignore her clumsy futile efforts, the laughter spilt into the air. Jimmy was the first to the rescue, his hand outstretched, his words doing nothing to soften Yasmin's receding sense of humour.

'Come on. Wow! Feels like my mate Angel has impregnated you with a baby elephant, Yazzy!'

A flush of pink, blossomed instantly within my beautiful wife's cheeks, followed by a reluctant squeal of amusement, resulting in them falling into each other's arms – though Jimmy looked slightly strange, as he was sticking out his bottom due to the extent of Yasmin's protruding *baby house*. I chuckled child-like at the goings-on, a deep contented sigh rising up from within. Apart from Yasmin and Jimmy's contortionists' cuddle, everything else just seemed to fit. The here and now? I wouldn't change a single ingredient. The future? An excitement and expectation that just filled me up – I knew I was a lucky man. And just as I was about to address murmurs from my past, I'm drawn quickly to the smiling safety of my friends. I feel the touch of cast iron nestle against my lower back, Yasmin's caress, and then planting a kiss between my shoulder blades. Our hands entwine for several priceless moments before gently slipping free. I turn and watch her now lowering herself onto the blanket next to Sally. Though I'm deep in conversation with our guests, my eyes notice how the twins hover adoringly around my wife and I admire their impeccable judgment.

My head tilts towards the largest willow tree and I see Ian and little Scottie out of sync with the rest of the happy, relaxed guests. A frown crosses my brow as I notice an unexpected sternness towards the child. Ian catches my eye and an instant smile extinguishes the thunder in his previously tight jaw. I almost feel pacified as Ian ruffles the hair of the bemused little lad, but only temporarily as the nagging doubts build.

The sun was now at eye-level, intrusive visually and a little cooler, but my hand screening sufficiently above my eyes while chatting with my dear friend Leoni. As the red wine flowed, I became a little maudlin. I slipped away to the side of the house and slumped down onto the cool gravel, my back against the spiral staircase leading up to my office. I looked out across the woodlands – natural and unspoilt. I felt bad that I had left my friends, but it was occasions such as this that my heavy heart would hang like a boulder. The deep regret that I had for the loss of my friend Scottie meant a day could not pass without me thinking about him. Once I was on the trail of deep, wretched remorse, the questioning faces of Julie and Lillie would sit before me, and then as I worked through the negatives in my short life, the hate-filled sallow eyes of Harry would force my head back, and then at his shoulder an entire frail figure of disappointment – Alice. And a heavy drenching sweat would cover me.

I jumped out of my torment as Janey suddenly sat down beside me, placing her hand on mine. We both just sat. She knew me; we'd been here before. Her fingers twirled gently the thick blonde hairs on my forearm, her head now resting on my shoulder.

'You okay, Ritchie?'

And as she gave me an extra squeeze, she told me how she'd been watching me, and scolded me for my inability to look her in the eyes today. I felt a tear escape unexpectedly, and I wasn't proud of my self-pity – but there are depths to a soul when it's impossible to rationalise.

As Janey searched and forced my eyes to meet hers, she playfully frowned and uttered, 'Hey you...' followed by the softest of smiles.

No need for words – we had spoken them all so many, many times, and so we settled for watching the sun lower itself through the trees ... catharsis and then some. And as the evening light gradually drained away, suddenly, as though we had both set our watches to do so, we jumped up, each with a flurry of goose pimples bringing an unexpected laughter and a shudder from us both.

'Brrrr, suddenly gone cold, Ritchie. Give me a hug!'

As we held on to each other, the backdrop of our friends became more prominent in the distance.

'What do you think of Ian, Ritchie? Do you approve?'

I loosened my hold, my arms now resting around her waist. I nodded my head with determined optimism.

'Seems a really nice guy. I've only had the briefest of

words, but I'll grab a drink and have a good chat...' I then pulled away completely. 'Yeahhh, need to ask him what his intentions are. Realistically the kind of lifestyle that he can offer little Scottie and my beautiful, mate!'

Janey punched me firmly in the arm. 'You bloody dare, and I'll beat you severely, Angel!'

But Ian and I did chat, and he did seem like a nice guy. Though it was early days, he certainly shone protectively around Janey and Scottie. And so, as Janey kissed Yasmin and me goodbye – nightfall shrouding us all – I gave her an optimistic thumbs up.

I was in the deepest of sleeps when all of a sudden I felt a sharp nudge in my side.

'Ohhh God, Ritchie! You need to get me to hospital, I think the *baby house* is about to have its front door kicked open!'

My head was spinning, but I didn't need telling twice. I tripped and stumbled around the bedroom, trying to get mother and bump out and into the car. I couldn't believe the speed at which I drove. Normally a good half an hour haul to the hospital was completed in just over sixteen minutes. But as I rushed into the reception area, my uncoordinated frantic gestures just received a blank look from the two nurses stood bemused on the other side of the counter. I turned to my left and then to my right, and it appeared that my inability to keep calm had meant that I had taken several strides forward but concluding in twenty, perhaps thirty gigantic steps backwards as I realised I'd left Yasmin in the car. I raced back to my poor deserted wife, spewing out a jumble of words – had they been pushed out correctly, they would have been deciphered as, 'I'm *so* sorry, darling!' But in between short bursts of breath, her look of amusement at my hyperactive insanity said it all. As I finally handed over all responsibility to the calm, almost worryingly blasé maternity staff, I stood, the sweat dripping from my pounding forehead.

Though of course I had been convinced that every second saved would be of life-creating significance, it was several hours later, when the sharp pains seemed to become far more frequent and Yasmin would draw blood each time she dug her nails into my hands and forearms, that I realised true arrival time was worthy of such a fuss. Up to now the nurses had been steady and unfazed, but then, as Yasmin produced a scream a little sharper, her eyes the size of a full moon, I saw a nod from the midwife and suddenly: camera, lights, ACTION! Within seconds, like a well-rehearsed Formula 1 pit stop, Yasmin was eased back, legs stretched out towards the bright lighting. My pounding forehead stepped up for its encore, my original frenzied foolishness now replaced with a numb, awestruck waste of flesh, but within twenty minutes or so I could see the top of a head, the appearance of a coconut inside a coconut. I shook my head at the thought, my face contorting and twisting out of sympathy. Just as I was beginning to think that there was no way it could be legal for Yasmin to have one of the most beautiful, private parts of her body stretched in that way, I soon realised that this was only the beginning. And as the excitement and fear grew, the anticipation at meeting the little creature that Yasmin and I had created was just getting unbearable. But then my breath went, seeing the unmistakable sight of a whole head. I started to pant intermittently, totally out of sync with Yasmin's slower, far more productive efforts. But my concerns were huge. How was my baby going to get out? I was at a loss – surely a creature so delicate was never going to manage to push itself out into the cruel, cold world. But then, as though reading my mind, a demure little midwife stepped forward. I couldn't help but frown at her as she roughly eased her fingers around my child's head and seemed intent on decapitating my firstborn. But then, like a bullet from a gun, the baby was out, covered in blood and slime, with almost a metre of purple cord attached to the poor little miracle's stomach.

'Yasmin, Ritchie, you have a beautiful baby girl!'

And as the little Angel was placed onto Yasmin's chest, the tears that had already been threatening to spill were suddenly rolling down both my cheeks. I beamed at the pair of them, taking in the proud, radiant look on my clever wife's face as she was introduced to our new extra special friend. Time seemed to simply stand still, as though all that had passed before had simply been building up to this moment. Then as our baby made eye contact with her mum, I felt as though I was being lifted onto a higher plane, that the power of all that I was experiencing would change me forever.

'So, what are you going to call her?' The midwife's words cut into my thoughts.

Yasmin looked at me and I nodded back at her.

We both announced, 'Evie ... Evie Angel.'

And as the name resounded around the room, her arrival was now official, she was really here: to look at, to touch, safe and sound, and perfect.

Once the midwife had congratulated us both and given us the all-clear, Yasmin's mum and our closest friends were allowed into the room to make their acquaintance with Evie. And as the chilled champagne and the ice-cold beers were handed out, we gave Evie the welcome she undoubtedly deserved. Within a surreal hour or so, Yasmin, Evie and I were left alone. Not a word was spoken – just looks of pride and bewildered eyes expressed how blessed we knew we were. Though I was reluctant to leave, tiredness all round forced the issue. I kissed my girls goodbye, leaving them both in the capable hands of the nurses. I felt very strange as I stepped out into the cool evening. The words, *'I'm a Dad, I have a beautiful daughter...!'* just kept rotating round my frazzled brain. I pushed my hands deep into my pockets, a small self-satisfied chuckle gurgling within as I made my way back to the car. I raised my eyes up to the skies, offering thanks – I was good at recognising a greater being when I was getting my own way, and I promised that I would try a little harder to give thanks on a more regular basis. I kept reliving Evie's birth. I pictured how Yasmin and I had started that way too, how we all came into the world this way, and just how incredible nature is!

And then my thoughts turned to when they would both arrive home within a couple of days. When Evie would see her home for the first time – the home where she would cut her first teeth, learn to crawl, and eventually start walking and running around, the wonderful garden where she would experience many an adventure with all the little friends she was yet to meet. But I started to laugh as I slid into the driver's seat of my car, the full adventure slapping me firmly on both cheeks, as from this moment on it was going to be the three of us, our little family unit – for Evie to get to know her parents and for us to get to know her – and it was as scary as it was unrivalled and beautiful.

CHAPTER SIXTEEN

Playing God And The Kangaroo Court…!

Before Death, 2000 – Blue Sky

With everything in life to celebrate, we had many wonderful parties at the Water's Edge, days that will stay etched in my mind forever, though there were certainly one or two nights that bordered on the raucous and wild, compliments of our amazing friends, who of course were a constant feature. But with one painfully noticeable exception – Janey. Her having finally got together with Ian had resulted in us being totally excluded from their lives. Frustrated and thwarted by the telephone, Yasmin and Sally would attempt to visit every chance they got, but with only marginal success. As our concerns grew, and on the one occasion they got to see Janey, she was a shadow of her former self – lost and withdrawn. But it all came to a head the day I bumped into Janey and Scottie on Willow High Street. And this time Janey couldn't look me in the eyes. As for Scottie junior, he had lost all his sparkle, a hesitant nervousness replacing his usual confident, cheeky character. But within minutes of trying to make conversation with my two close friends, Ian suddenly joined us, his chirpy manner and firm handshake more than making up for the lack of life in the meeting of Janey and little Scottie. Within a moment more, Ian was ushering his newfound family away from me.

'Sorry, Ritchie, Janey and I are already late for something…nice seeing you!'

And as Ian nodded and waved back at me, I felt

resoundingly uneasy.

Later that evening, I discussed the meeting with Yasmin,
Jimmy and Sally – we all nodded instinctively, well aware that
something needed to be done. If Janey wanted to pull away
from us as friends, then we would graciously accept her
wishes, but as long as it was Janey's decision. For the sake of
her and little Scottie's happiness, we would do anything she
asked, but the girl I had witnessed today didn't seem happy,
just lost and scared. Yasmin in particular had been friends with
Janey since they were at infant school together, and so we all
agreed that we could not just stand by and do nothing; we
needed to know that all was well.

The very next day Sally and I had parked the car several
houses away from Janey's. We waited patiently for Ian to leave
for work. Within half an hour or so, we were suddenly giggling
nervously as we kept our heads down, giving Ian time to turn
out of the road. Within seconds we were pressing the doorbell.
Janey finally opened the door – she didn't look pleased to see
us. A moment of silence and awkwardness resulted in my
grabbing of Sally's arm and barging our way into the house.

'Janey, I am *so* sorry, but please look at me.'

But she couldn't. The red rings around her eyes said so
much. And despite trying to coax softly the reason for Janey's
sadness, Sally and I took it upon ourselves to take drastic
action.

'Janey, Sally and I are *seriously* worried, and so we're
taking you home with us, where Yasmin and Jimmy are
waiting, and if you don't come willingly, well, I'm afraid we're
prepared to kidnap you and Scottie!'

I hoped that our firmness would force a smile, coax a
plausible explanation, but we got nothing.

'Get your things, Janey, you're coming back with us, back
to the Water's Edge.'

Janey didn't say a word, but her eyes were frightened. I
hadn't noticed Scottie sitting on the stairs. And though Janey
started to mutter about how this was her home and why would
she want to leave, I couldn't help but notice a sudden spring in
Scottie's step. He was soon racing up to his bedroom, and from

the sound of it gathering its entire contents and throwing them into a huge trunk. And though Janey was a little more reluctant than her son, who now had the front door open and was excitedly yelling at us all to hurry, finally, Sally and I had them both safely in the car.

For the first day or two, Janey wouldn't say much. Although we were convinced that we had seen Ian at the gates of the Water's Edge, he didn't come on to the property, seemingly reluctant to confront any of us. But it was on the third day that finally our actions were deemed justified. Yasmin had accidentally walked into the bathroom and caught Janey naked. And as she looked at her closest friend, Janey burst out crying as Yasmin's eyes widened at the number of bruises all over her stomach and upper arms. Having then checked Scottie for similar marks, the results left us feeling physically sick. Once given the news, Sally and Jimmy came rushing round.

'Ritchie, I want to kill him for this!'

But Janey heard Jimmy as he ranted at me in the hallway, and a sudden burst of emotion stopped us all in our tracks.

'No! No more violence! I'm sick of it! Pleassse, two wrongs won't undo any of this!'

And she was right – it wasn't the answer. But as the full extent of the story unfolded, I couldn't believe the extreme jealousy and how controlling Ian was.

'Look...' Janey would start, 'he doesn't mean to do it. He says that he loves us both so much and that it's for our own good. He's demanded that I cut all my friends out of my life! He's even stopped me taking Scottie to playschool!'

But as Janey's words spill the truth and the tears continue to roll down her face, Scottie tries to console his mum. I look at Yasmin and Sally, and then without another word an almighty force envelops me. All I can see is my dear departed friend Scottie's face, the look in his eyes confirming what I had to do. Without further hesitation, Jimmy and I are out the door and heading quickly towards Janey's house. As we pull onto the driveway, I spot Ian in the lounge walking towards the window and then quickly disappearing back into the shadows. I cannot get out of the car quick enough, Jimmy matching me stride for stride, our fists finally falling heavily onto the front door.

Silence, baited breath, our heads spinning, but Ian doesn't answer.

'Stay here, Jimmy. I'll try round the back.'

But as I run down the side of the house, Ian is making a hasty retreat across the back lawn.

'Ian, *stop!* We're not here to hurt you!!'

Ian stops and turns to look at me, and I put my hands in the air.

'I mean it. Though you *seriously* deserve the beating of your life, we know it's not the right way.'

Ian just stares, his eyes suddenly focusing on Jimmy as he joins the stand-off.

'Think you're *sooo* great, don't you? Big *fucking* tough guys! I bet she shagged the pair of you! Is that the deal? You've got her at your *bloody* palace! I bet that's it! I know she doesn't mean to be a slut, but she can't help herself, and that's why I have to punish her.'

I felt like grabbing him and kicking the *proverbial* out of him, but I was determined not to. But Jimmy wasn't so restrained and was suddenly on Ian, slamming him up against the garden wall, ready to let his fists do the talking.

'Jimmy *no!* Remember what Janey said?'

Jimmy stepped back, the veins on his neck prominent with rage.

'You're going soft, Ritchie! *Oh God!* How can you keep your hands off him?'

I was desperate to keep calm and deal with this as fairly as possible. I took a deep breath and swallowed hard.

'Ian, whatever screwed-up vision you have of Janey, it is just *so* totally wrong! She is a great girl, she's no slut and you know that. If you cannot see what a beautiful, *loyal* girl you've got, then you're a bloody fool! But regardless of what you think of her, it's over, sunshine. I mean it! Jimmy and I have a simple choice for you, one hour to get your things out of Janey's house and to get yourself out of Willow – the train station beckons Ian...and we're deadly serious! One solitary, single second after that hour, if we see you, even smell your hatred within a mile of Willow, then Jimmy will get his wish! Let you have some of what you've been dishing out!'

Ian edged past Jimmy and me, his eyes narrowing in an attempt to weigh up just how serious we were. We followed the control freak into the house and helped him pack, all in total silence. Finally, we were done and I pulled Janey's front door shut behind us. The three of us just stood, Ian with his head bowed, suitcase in hand. I broke the silence.

'The clock's ticking, big man…'

He didn't move. Jimmy nudged me, his eyes darting from left to right, fuming silently at *our* man's reluctance to do the right thing. I placed my finger on my lips, and then proceeded to warn Ian that it was his last chance to leave unharmed. He suddenly burst into life, ranting and yelling that he needed money, that he had nowhere to go, that if Janey wanted out of the relationship, then she and Scottie should leave. Without a word or a look between my friend and I, within several anger-filled strides Jimmy and I were bundling Ian into the car.

All I could see was Jimmy's back, his words booming, *'The car, the house, it's all Janey's!!'*

As I opened the driver's door, I watched as Jimmy's fingers suddenly grabbed the red thunderous, snarling face of Janey's ex.

'You came with *nothing!* You're leaving with *nothing!!'* Before slamming the car door shut, Jimmy asked: 'Do tell me that bloody child lock's on, Ritchie?'

I nodded and smiled nervously. We drove for several miles in silence – at mile eight, the vile ranting started in earnest. Ian spewed venomously that all women were programmed to cheat, not one single female could be trusted, that Janey had told him many stories about how Yasmin and Sally had betrayed us both, and his disgust at our inability to control our women. Jimmy and I both laughed, our amusement doing nothing to dampen the spirit of our guest. Jimmy's laughter turned to a perturbed smile, and then from a smile to instant anger, Ian's words igniting my friend's fuse, his sense of humour failing miserably this time.

'Yeah, that barbecue at the Water's Edge, remember it, Jimmy? I had two fingers wedged up your Mrs…she pulled me into the bathroom and wanted me to take her there and then. You didn't know that, did you, you gullible prick?!'

Jimmy's eyes widened, and within a split second he's leant into the back and unleashed hell.

I yelled at him, 'NO, JIMMY, COME ON MAN, YOU KNOW HE'S JUST WINDING YOU UP!'

And then jamming the brakes on, my partner in crime was thrown painfully and unceremoniously back into his seat, his head slamming sharply against the glovebox.

'*So* sorry, Jimmy! I'm *really* sorry, mate, but we need to stick to the plan!'

Jimmy scowled at me like I've only seen once before, and this time I couldn't blame him. I pushed my foot to the floor and we roared off. But despite a brief respite from Ian, it had simply served for his stories and threats to sink to a new and unfounded low. And as he spewed his evil, something inside me snapped. This man was no good to anyone, and the more I questioned his mere existence, Scottie's face was right in front of me, as though egging me on. Up to that point the boundaries of my intentions had become increasingly blurred, but suddenly, I knew what I had to do. I recalled a bridge which I had visited as a child with my school, spanning the Avon Gorge, and so I kept driving. Ian became increasingly agitated as he realised we weren't station bound. He tried frantically to get out of the car, his fists pounding relentlessly against the windows, followed by a flurry of blows to the back of mine and Jimmy's heads. I just pushed my foot hard to the floor and turned the radio up as loud as I could. I became fully focused on the road ahead, though vaguely aware of Jimmy getting his way, having now joined Ian on the back seat, the extent of my sidekick's rage convincing our guest he'd be wise to keep his fists to himself. Whilst almost having to sit on Ian, Jimmy had a question.

'Where the *hell* are we going, mate?'

I assured him it wouldn't be much further. But the truth was, we seemed to be travelling forever, and the inevitable, intermittent rantings of Ian flaring up and the tussles with Jimmy almost forced us off the road on a couple of occasions, tethered fraught nerves almost at breaking point. Suddenly, my eyes widened as I dropped – just as I had imagined – onto the mountain pass that I had prayed hadn't been a distorted childhood memory. We twisted and turned, with the backdrop of a distraught and venomous Ian, until we could climb no more.

We pulled up along the strangely quiet road that led onto the bridge and I turned the engine off. Jimmy was swallowing hard, but chose not to share his thoughts with me. Trance-like and numb, we manhandled Ian out of the car, his leg's kicking and his fingers gouging. With sheer brute force and whatever means available, we dragged him over to the edge of the metal railings, my fear of heights starting to make me shake. But somehow my anger was overpowering my phobia. The wind was getting up, and we were having to shout to make ourselves heard. After a desperate wild struggle, we finally had Ian pinned to the floor, his head over the edge of the bridge, his eyes able to see just how high up he was.

'You pair of fucking bastards! You can't frighten me! You'll never get away with this!'

The tirade of abuse continued, blood and strands of torn-out hair all over the three of us. But as I gulped for air, desperate for any possible way back from what we were about to carry out, I attempted to ask calmly a couple of questions. Jimmy gripped Ian's jaw to shut him up.

'Ian, *for fuck's sake, PLEASE stop struggling.* Prove to me that you're not the *evil bastard* we so strongly believe you are, save yourself and get to see another day!'

Jimmy let go of Ian's jaw, and the three of us just took a moment and looked at each other. The wind blew harder, and still we waited for something positive to grasp hold of, for Ian to convince us that what we were doing was so very wrong, unjustified. Then, as though the result of a successful exorcism, Ian's body became limp, his head now dropped backwards. I looked at Jimmy, but he didn't take his eyes off Ian. Suddenly, with the cry of a banshee, Ian's body pulled taut, releasing warm phlegm across my face. I dropped my sodden cheek onto Ian's. I was shaking with rage as I returned and smeared his excess body fluid back onto the face from which it came.

'*Right*, my *scummy* little friend, Jimmy and I, and certainly for the good health of Janey and little Scottie, want *you* gone! Not necessarily the way that you may presently be thinking, slamming onto the nice hard road down there, or perhaps the twisting river that runs beside it! No, I still favour our first offer, the simple exit, dropping you off at the train station! But I am increasingly overwhelmed with negative foresight here, a putrid image of Jimmy and I watching you leave on that train, but only too aware that you could come back and bother Janey and her son whenever the mood takes you. And *that* seriously worries me! But should we get our wish and you are actually never seen again in Willow, aren't we being a little naive, aren't we just passing you onto some other poor, unsuspecting woman and child, who you can bully and control, you know, *punish?* Because they need to be taught a lesson! What do you think, Jimmy? Quite a dilemma!'

Jimmy's eyes were boring into me, and he was swallowing hard. I was almost hallucinating now, and I heard my words grate against the strong winds.

'I say we throw him over!'

But as Jimmy tried to judge my mood, I could see him showing a justified concern, his eyes telling me that he wasn't sure how far I would go to teach this evil bastard a lesson. Ian looked up at us both and did nothing to help his cause.

'You're a pair of pussies! You don't have the balls! You're just pathetic, the pair of you. Just stop this shit!! Get back to your slag wives, and enjoy screwing Janey, the little tart!!'

My eyes were pulled skywards. Scottie's presence was all around me, and there were tears in his eyes – a frustrated inability to take care of the two people he loved most in the world. The right thing to do was pull Ian back to his feet and get him safely back in the car. But my mind was racing, and my ability to make the right decision was slipping away from me. The inescapable fact that this excuse for a human being was not worthy of compassion kept flashing before me, combined with the plea from Scottie...the heart-wincing point that was tipping the balance to the extent of no return. And just as I thought I was about to grab reason and go with it, I knew that unless we made a statement of relentless intent to this guy – a man that was seriously disillusioned in his judgment of Janey and Scottie – could Ian *ever* believe he was wrong? Would he, could he ever change? My arms started to shake as I held on to the son of some poor mother somewhere, but then trumped with a vision of bullied little Scottie cowering in the corner of his bedroom, courtesy of the *piece of shit* I was holding onto here! How could anyone harm a child? I lived daily with the guilt of hurting little Scottie the most, for it was me that had condemned him to a life without his father – a poor, innocent little lad being deprived of such a crucial relationship because of my mistake. I swallowed hard at the mere thought – nothing would, or could top that pain. So maybe it was for this reason that I would do whatever it took to make sure that little Scottie should not have to suffer further because of this bastard's evil. As I looked down at Ian, he was still spewing his nonsense. He had the mad idea in his mind that Janey was sleeping around, but what on earth could he have against Scottie?

I spat the words at him. 'WHAT ABOUT SCOTTIE, IAN? YOUR REASONS THERE?'

Jimmy suddenly lost patience with me and what I was doing, and so attempted to pull Ian back up. But as we tussled, I seemed to have the strength of two men and kicked Jimmy away while begging him to trust me.

'I'M ONLY GOING TO SCARE HIM JIMMY!' I dragged Ian further along the bridge edge, directly above the river.

But then this charming man spurted his best line. *'Scottie, bloody bastard child Scottie! He's just a constant reminder. The little bastard is the proof that she's been a fucking slag and opened her legs to some randy bloke! Yep, precious Scottie is the proof that she's just some worthless tart that needs putting on the straight and narrow!'*

Jimmy was suddenly on my back.

'NO, RITCHIE!' But the red mist was choking all my senses; my ears were filled with Scottie yelling all around me, *'What if it was Evie? What if it was Evie that he had scarred for life?'* But despite the full horror of what he was saying, a sober moment of borderline clarity almost made me pull him back to safety, but as my arms were full stretch with the entire weight of this writhing rabid animal, Scottie's words were slapping around my head and starting to stick black snowflake on top of black snowflake, a full gory *negative photo shoot memory* of Scottie's death being replayed over and over again!

'Ritchie, you are my spirit, my reason, my only source of revenge!'

The veins on my forearms were ready to burst. I aimed for reason, my *reason* for not doing what Scottie wanted me to, but then, just as another rant spewed venomously out of Ian's filthy mouth, I pushed him with full force, my head now filled with his screams. Jimmy was at my side, his fingers gripping my jaw, forcing me to look at the sheer horror on his ashen face, but I shook my head free and focused on Ian as he fell the few hundred feet or so, hurtling towards the swirling river.

It seemed an eternity before he finally slammed against the metallic glass of the water and disappeared beneath the surface. My arms were shaking uncontrollably. I couldn't take my eyes off what I'd just done. The tear into the water seemed to repair itself almost instantly; he was gone. I scoured the line of gunmetal grey, but still nothing. I almost fell backwards as I suddenly saw his black spot of a body resurface. It bobbed along for a second or two, but then was drawn under again. My eyes wide and straining, I searched desperately for him, but then came fear, raw emotion and an inability to focus mentally, visually. All clarity or perspective of what I had just done left me frozen and unconscious in the moment.

And then, as though two fingers had clicked me out of a trance, Jimmy and I slumped onto our backs, not saying a word. My thumping heart was in my ears. We just lay on the cold asphalt, the strong winds buffeting accusingly around our sorry heads. But as our faces fell to look at each other, I think the full force of what I had done kick-started a real nerve-fuelled bout of the giggles. And then the more we thought and mimicked Ian's flailing arms as he fell, our laughter was suddenly uncontrollable.

Once again, for the next few days, every second, every minute, every hour I waited for the heavy forceful knock on the door. And at night, as I closed my eyes, desperate for sleep, I imagined the house being surrounded by police. For Yasmin to see me taken away, my hand's handcuffed behind my back. But as the days passed by, Jimmy and I would just look at each other, not daring to utter a word that might tempt my justified fate, and as the weekend came and went our eyebrows would raise a little higher, still no words uttered, but a single blade of belief that I might have just got away with it.

Janey and little Scottie accepted without question that Ian was gone. They both nodded in unison when Jimmy and I passed on Ian's *sincerest apologies* for his unacceptable behaviour, his *wretched guilt* forcing him to move on. And as we both continued to lie and overact, Janey's arm sliding protectively around her son's frail shoulders, we contrived their abuser's request for forgiveness. Janey shed a tear at speed down her cheek, but the relief in her eyes, well, it was only the beginning. But as we continued to nurture them both back to physical and mental health, we started to see the old Janey again. And as for Scottie? On the surface we had our happy, excitable little boy back. The bruises had gone, but would there be any long-term effect? We could only pray for the very best.

Jimmy and I would continue to look sheepishly at each other, no words spoken about *that* fateful day, but my guilty eyes begged for forgiveness from my unfortunate accomplice. I knew I was wrong to have thrown Ian off the bridge like that, and as I said the words I had to look away else my nervous laughter might return. It was only many weeks later, miles away from home, that Jimmy and I dared to utter a word on the subject. We concluded that there was a good chance that Ian had been killed on impact, but of course we couldn't be sure of anything. And as the weeks turned into months, Janey shared with us a vital piece of information – the fact that she had never met any of Ian's family, and that she had felt it strange that he had never mentioned friends of any kind. Welcome words that encouraged Jimmy and I to hold our nerve. And as each day drifted to a close and I turned out the lights, I prayed that there would not be a price to pay for my moment of madness.

Before Death, 2005 – Blue Sky
So as the dark and fearful months turned gradually into lighter and increasingly optimistic years, there was still the inability to escape that split second of fear that would greet me as my mind woke to each new morning. That painful opening of the eyes as

I religiously wondered whether this would be the day, the day that I would get the heavy, life-ending knock on the door – penance for Jack, for Ian. For now my prayers continued to be answered, but the black smothering guilt lived with me. I ached for a chance to wipe the slate clean. Faith? Confession? I knew I was a lucky man. I knew that everything else in my life was perfect. But when my days of required optimism were overpowered by the sheer determination of pessimism, the pain in my head, the ache in my heart, the blatant brute force of it made me feel as though I was going to die... But as the black clouds were ushered away, I would shrug my strong shoulders and accept that physically I was a perfectly fit and healthy specimen, and surely guilt had never killed anyone. The mental scars would heal, and so my blessed life continued.

Evie was now five years of age – the time had gone so quickly. And for a man that believed all things were possible, Evie was indeed a creation of sheer genius. Her beautiful face would take my troubles and breath away every time. Her words, her laughter, her fingers, her perfect feet... I would even fawn over the sheer intricacy of her shoulder blades, her knees, her shin bones, *her cry* – all features that would see me rightly humbled. And though our little girl wasn't a crier, it was how she dealt with even this that I admired. If she fell and hurt herself, I would be in awe at her determination to fight the tears; she would be brave and strong, pick herself up and dust herself down. Though Yasmin and I would always be there to give her that special hug and kiss, at least a reserved thousand times a day. Her slender arms sliding around our necks, the tear-inducing pursed lips – it is obvious that we both love her unreservedly. And though I pronounce that Evie is the most wonderful thing in our lives, that is of course also how I feel about Yasmin. Our love undoubtedly gets stronger every day. Though I stand amazed on occasion how mathematically, physically or otherwise that's possible.

And so, what about Janey and little Scottie? Well, finally, a good man came along – Peter! They both started out as friends, giving each other the support they needed. But during one Sunday afternoon get together, we were dealt an almighty announcement. The three of them stood proudly as they relayed the fact that they loved being together so much, and that the worst part of their day was when Peter returned to his home just three miles away – that the answer to their problem was a simple one. They were all in excited agreement that they never wanted to be parted again, not even for a single night. And so it became the most natural thing in the world to live together, and because it worked so beautifully, they felt the need to express their commitment to the rest of the world. And so, on Evie's birthday – a perfect summer day – they married. And little Scottie's beaming smile was priceless, enabling I was sure, the beginning of a much needed healing process – certainly for him, and in some part, for me.

But it wasn't long after Janey and Peter's wedding day that I actually blacked out, such was the intense pain of my headache. I was alone, and perhaps only out cold for five minutes or so. But as I stumbled to my feet, I realised that I needed to see my doctor. Several tests were carried out, and the daunting day to see Dr Malvern arrived far too soon. Of course, if you've read my story thus far, then you'll know exactly the result of our meeting. And so it would seem that my life was medically over.

But sometimes, something out of the ordinary comes at you and you're left questioning your sanity. But the fact that my expiry date was ticked off on the calendar of life, before Rose appeared before me, seemingly having the power to avert my demise in exchange for my efforts to redeem myself. So a new, crazy adventure begins.

CHAPTER SEVENTEEN

You Only Get One Life

After Death, 1991 – Lilac Sky
So there I was, aged twenty-one, desperate to see Rose – but she was a little more elusive than I would have liked. I had sat for two hours at the Water's Edge, and yet she didn't come to

me. Back on Willow High Street, my thoughts are disturbed by a car horn, and there is Scottie his window wound down. '*Get in Ritchie boy!* Justin's a glutton for punishment, mum and dad away again, the States I think? *So party time!*'

And so within one hour, I was sitting at the top of Justin's parents' house, with Rose, finally prepared to show her face and attempting to explain away the continuing madness.

'So, Ritchie, do you see? The pieces of the jigsaw have changed. Your past, your battles with Jack, all may work out very differently now, but only you can do it! Already the one simple difference is that Jack *likes* you!'

Rose jumped up onto the parapet wall, high above the partygoers down below. She pushed her little bare feet right to the edge of the coping stones.

'And the Porsche, Ritchie, it's a subtle consequence. Your friends know that you bought it, impressed that you had the means to do so, but then respected your decision to sell it! You simply showed a maturity that you didn't need the status symbol. Now wasn't the right time, you had far better things to invest your money in! After all, you're simply at the beginning of your property development, and you've a mountain to climb to get that fortune growing, and the small profit from the Porsche, not to be sniffed at!'

Rose giggled as she pushed her arms out to her sides, increasing her balance. But then as she started to turn on the spot, her eyes looking up to the stars, I was becoming increasingly nervous, as she looked decidedly unsteady on the narrow ledge. But the smile on her little face convinced me that she didn't have a care in the world.

'And another thing, Ritchie, Yasmin let you into a little female psychology first time around, that to any self-respecting lady, the Porsche was purely a statement to the world – *look at me, see how well I'm doing!* Well, as I said before, you're a mature man now, and you know that it's far better to play things down. Remember the words of Mr Windell, the wise old man … the more you know, the less you show!'

I shook my head from side to side. I understood the sentiment of what Rose was saying, but how would these changes ultimately affect what I was here to do? Rose peered down at me, her eyes as though looking over the top of reading glasses, peeling the questions directly from my mind.

'The long-term effect? Not really sure yet! Oh, Ritchie, I know that you're skipping through time a little awkwardly, but you will get used to it, I'm sure. This is about trust, Ritchie. You have to trust and have faith in your closest friends, and *me* of course!'

I looked at Rose, my nodding head and determination to accept this madness simply creating a whooziness around my frazzled brain – as had happened on a few occasions since my return to my younger years. I was suddenly struggling to focus, as though sliding down a maturity ladder. I seemed to have moments of clarity – the wisdom of a thirty-five year old – but then for whatever justified reason, and with a painful crunching of cogs in my grey matter, I pulled my clenched fists up to my head, my eyes started to flicker and with an electrical fusing of dates, young faces, I forced my eyes closed, determined to escape the searing pain. But then an uncomfortable crick of tendons seemed to bring a balance, my eyes gave a gentle butterfly flicker and then I simply opened my eyes.

'Ritchie, you're okay! Just breathe normally.' Rose ran her fingers across my forehead.

I felt fine, but certainly wasn't looking for a repeat of what had just happened.

'What *did* just happen?' Rose paused for a moment. 'Mmmm, well, mentally we can accept changes, but *this* extreme? Your brain can absorb a malfunction, but there is a cost!'

My eyes were raised and my breath baited as Rose appeared to be choosing her words carefully.

'In laymen's terms, Ritchie, it can push you to insanity … it was our one gamble!'

I briefly nodded my head while absorbing her words, and then…

'*Insane!* You certainly didn't warn me that I could end up a *basket case* with all this second chance malarkey!'

Rose stepped back, her hands now firmly placed on her hips, a look of disdain simmering in her black eyes.

'Well, excuse me! A fifty–fifty insanity gamble may be

worth a chance, don't you think? When I came to your rescue, Ritchie Angel, unless you've forgotten already, you were dead!'

We looked at each other, and suddenly we both burst out laughing, uncontrollably. Finally, we are both sitting with our backs safely against the parapet wall, Rose's hands on mine. I tried to gain some perspective, small steps, settling for knowing where I actually stood socially, enabling me to continue my journey.

'Sooo, I did buy the Porsche? But then sold it to Jack? And for a profit you say? Ummm, I hope that I got to thrash it around a bit first.'

Rose frowned at me and then smiled.

'So okay, Rose, I've sort of got it over the car, but how come Jack doesn't hate me over the Lillie situation?' I didn't wait for an answer. 'Or has Julie's *lovely* friend Tina not told him yet?'

'Correct, Ritchie! We have no control over Tina, but it seems that you're not such a joke in her eyes as of course you were before!'

I laughed at Rose's matter-of-fact condemnation of my original standing in society. She continued, ignoring my outburst.

'And therefore, Ritchie, she's extremely wary of crossing you, and her risk of ruining your friendship with Jack, which in turn could destroy her friendship with Julie! Your social standing, well, you're higher up the league table now, meaning that she'll probably keep her mouth shut. But, and despite all the social grading, if I were you, I would make sure you keep yourself in Tina's good books; it could well save incredible heartache!'

I pushed my back firmly against the sandstone wall, trying to quash the nerves creeping steadily up my spine. I let out a deep breath while churning Rose's words over and over, trying to convince myself that these subtle differences *could* really save my life. As I tried to work through the cast in my rewritten play, I became nervous about some of the supporting roles.

'But, Rose, what about the way I treated Julie at the

churchyard the other day? Surely my negative response could tip the balance. If the mother of my little girl decides that Jack should finally know the truth, are we not back to square one?'

Rose shook her head. 'I cannot answer that, Ritchie, because I don't know. We have no control over the things other people do, we don't have total control over you. Sometimes things just happen too quickly! But we will try our best to guide you, to steer you wisely where possible, if we think you're making the wrong decisions.'

I must have sat calmly and in silence for at least five minutes, but suddenly, I started to pat my lips with my fingers. Something deep within was unsettling me, rising up, alarm bells sounding!

'Oh God, Rose! What about Sally and me? You know, ummm...'

Rose stopped me, her little cheeks blushing; I was sure she was reliving the dreadful image in her young mind.

'I don't know, Ritchie. I was totally shocked by you ... God, *you* men! You simply let it happen!'

I interrupted Rose sharply. 'It *was* Sally! I mean, *she* surprised me.'

I felt unconvincing sitting down, so I jumped defensively to my feet, parading up and down as I gave my version of events.

'I know it sounds a weak excuse, Rose, but there was a familiar warmth about her, *that* and the alcohol! And on an empty stomach! And then the lack of sleep...it was such a surreal moment, you know, dream like.'

Rose stopped me. 'Look, don't worry too much about it. I pray for your sake that Sally can keep it quiet, because you know full well that it would destroy Jimmy!'

And as Rose's words imitated exactly what I was thinking, I prayed that Jimmy would never, *ever* get to know.

I was now perched bravely on the parapet wall, with the belief that I finally had a grasp of what I was dealing with. My eyes dropped to the floor. I was just about to ask Rose one more question, but this time nothing at all to do with me – her bare feet.

'Why, Rose, do you, you know, never wear any shoes or socks?'

But it was too late. Whether Rose was avoiding the answer or my timing was dreadful, my little friend was suddenly gone.

As I sat all alone, my mind drifted back to the distant memory all those years ago, right here, with Yasmin, and our passionate love-making. But I couldn't bear it and tried to extinguish the image from my mind. And just as I stood up, ready to make my way back downstairs, Rose appeared before me once more.

'Oh, and, Ritchie, your attempt to talk with Yasmin at the churchyard? If you try that again – I hate saying this to you – but all this would be over. You have to trust me, you have to keep away from her. Another attempt to speak, touch or otherwise, and it really would mean the end of our arrangement!'

My shoulders suddenly rounded and, forlorn, my eyes widened in an attempt to coax a little sympathy, but then, once again, she was gone.

I stood silent, wanting to move forward, make my way back to my friends, but my head was spinning and my body numb. My mind was filled with the long, hard journey ahead of me, and I could feel the sheer panic welling up from deep within. But I needed to face this, I had to be strong. Maybe after a good night's sleep, it would look so much better in the cold light of day.

As I made my way downstairs, different people were coming up to me, patting me on the back, talking about everyday things, subjects that each person presumed I would understand. And though I recognised one or two of the faces from my distant past, many of them didn't register at all. I just accepted that I must have met them at stages of my new life that I had simply skipped through. But I wondered whether or not that was possible. Then I thought about the fact that I had bought a car and then sold it; I certainly had no recollection of that. So I was beginning to believe that anything in my new world was possible. But the next situation that was to unfold was up there in *the hardest to handle yet* column.

I was standing about three stairs up from the hallway as my eyes fell on a scene that turned my soul to ice. There, standing in the lounge, were three girls: Janey, a mystery girl and

Yasmin, talking to two lads. My breathing could hardly muster an out. There she was, *all I longed for*, just twenty feet away. And should I be allowed to hold her, never letting her go, then I would feel normal again. But as my heart thumped painfully, I knew I couldn't. I had to heed Rose's words. I tried to look away, but she was compelling viewing...but with the beauty came the inevitable pain.

As one of the guys slid his arm around Yasmin's waist, it was just unbearable. I couldn't take my eyes off his hand rested on the waistband of her flimsy skirt, while his thumb brushed against her tanned naked midriff. I felt like running over and screaming at the guy to get his hands off my wife, to then catch that magic that I knew existed. Something that was so natural for us both, someone that craved my touch and had eyes for only me. But now I was just another face in a crowd of many.

I sat down on the stairs, hiding behind the banister. But as my fingers dug into the stark white paintwork, I couldn't bear it any more, I had to get out. I was sure that no one would miss me if I simply slipped away. But though I wanted to get up and leave, where would I go? I sure as hell didn't want to go *home* – the place only succeeded in spooking me with all its memories. So maybe the best place to be was here with my friends. Perhaps I just needed to act normally, try not to look at Yasmin. But as I mulled the option over in my mind, I had to ask myself how I was supposed to do that. Suddenly, Scottie was in my face, his arms around me, pulling me to my feet.

'*Shit, Ritchie!* Where have you been? There's a couple of *right* sexy birds here, that *real* snooty babe from our old school days, and the other one...*well,* she'll do for you! *Come on!* We'll have to be quick, they've already got a couple of *slimy* geezers all over them!'

I walked reluctantly behind Scottie, ready to run should his intended target be my wife. Every step I took seemed to sanction a stroll through hell – though brief, my eyes widened, a temporary reprieve, as the guy that had been all over Yasmin was suddenly walking towards the kitchen with Janey. I wanted to punch the air. But then as the torture level was about to be cranked up, I could do nothing but crave the other guy back as Scottie stopped. I was suddenly rocking on my feet, the room spinning around me, a mass of blonde curls turning instinctively to face my dear, uncouth, unworthy, arrogant friend. Suddenly, nobody else in the room existed. Yasmin, face-to-face with Scottie, appeared to be hanging on his every word. I started to spin in the opposite direction to the room, my hands now covering my eyes, my legs like lead, but somehow I was drifting away, escaping, until finally managing to step off the merry-go-round...the nausea and madness leaving me instantly. Without warning I clumsily fell to my knees on the damp evening grass. I looked around. The dizziness easing and I was now in the temporary safety of the garden. And as the night air hit me, I could offer no explanation other than being in hell. I was *convinced* that I was in *hell;* that *must* be it! Surely this was indeed *hell!* As I stood with my back to the house, my mind raced, tormenting me with images that had only ever appeared in my sweat-induced nightmares. Though I knew I was getting a little ahead of myself, it did nothing to ward off the image of Scottie and Yasmin. *God, what if they hit it off?* And though I told myself that I was being ridiculous, they were young, attractive people, so why shouldn't they? They were both single and after all, why shouldn't my torment increase?

For the sake of my sanity, I needed to escape. I looked for a side gate – any kind of exit would have done as long as I didn't have to go back through the house. But after a frantic futile search, going back through the nightmare I had just stepped away from was my only option. So as I proceeded with my walk through the potential minefield, I tried to focus firmly in front of me, ignoring all that was· left and right. As the music boomed out and several accomplished steps forward, I just kept hoping, but then there they were, Scottie and Yasmin, slumped comfortably, knees touching, on Justin's settee. I just stood and stared, the exact opposite of everything my arms, legs and eyes were telling me to do, but she was stunning, beautiful, everything I wanted, everything I *had*, but now with my *mate*. *What if they became close?* Like Yasmin and I had all those years ago. Gorgeous, sweet and innocent Yasmin, just waiting for Mr Right. Originally it was me and then the rest was history. But tonight? And for the future? Maybe that person was going to be Scottie. And in my mind I was struggling to see Evie's face. All I could create in my battered weary head was someone who looked a little like Evie, but it wasn't her! I had to do something to stop this pain, so I headed for the kitchen and grabbed a bottle of tequila tucked behind the mountain of beer cans. I couldn't get the top off quick enough. Finally, gratefully I tipped my head back and let the bitter liquid scar its way down my throat. Instantly I coughed, almost spraying Leoni as she stepped in front of me.

'Steady, Ritchie! Wow! Someone's in need of a drink!' She grabbed the bottle off me, taking a small swig herself, creasing her face up and handing it back with a look of distain. '*Yuk!* How can you drink that stuff? *Shit,* I need some wine! *Anything* to take that *taste* away. Any white, anyone?'

As Leoni opened up the fridge, she had a look of triumph as she grabbed hold of an open bottle of *Black Tower*, nodding her head and giving me the Leoni trademark double blink of the eyes, never failing to create a warm feeling in the pit of my stomach. She grabbed my hand, and I obediently followed my guardian angel back through the lounge and down towards the river at the bottom of Justin's garden. My eyes had been helplessly drawn to Yasmin and lecherous Scottie – his hand had been on hers! And though I tried to console myself with the fact that it was his hand on top of hers and that she could hardly be rude and just shrug his hand away, I had to dilute this torturous pain by whatever means possible. I recalled Rose's words: 'You must not try to influence Yasmin's life in any way...' I simply couldn't go near her. Her life had to progress totally without me. How the hell was I supposed to do that? How on earth was I going to be able to stand by watching the mother of our daughter build herself a life that didn't include me? Simply watch as she moved further and further away from me? But I knew I couldn't do anything about it, and so, for tonight, the bottle of tequila and the company of Leoni, well, it might just get me through.

Leoni and I slumped down onto the grass embankment. I smiled as she leant against me, flicking an intrusive strand of hair out of her eyes. Leoni was a good friend, a pretty turquoise-eyed blonde. Loads of guys fancied her, but she didn't seem that interested in having a boyfriend. She was very sporty and clever. And though I wasn't entirely convinced, the rumour was that she *may* be a lesbian. But that was really only a culmination of jest and perhaps wishful thinking between the other guys and me. And should our playful, uneducated presumptions be correct, I for one would be shocked – and it would undoubtedly break the hearts of at least half the guys in Willow. So, as Leoni leant on me, trying to console a friend – her obvious conclusion being that my sombre mood was due to the recent death of my mother – I had to just play along. Despite having laid my poor mum to rest, I had of course had fourteen years to come to terms with the fact. Instead, my severe bereaved state, though unbeknownst to the girl beside me, was due to the *oh so* very recent loss of my wife and daughter. And as we both drank away our sorrows, it wasn't long before the pain of this night became a welcome blur.

'Come on, you *lazy* bastards! It's time to get yourselves up and out! My parents will be back within hours, so come *on,* I need you *up and gone!'*

Justin's voice smashed violently into my sodden brain. I could hardly feel a thing from the waist down. And then, as I managed to get my eyes slightly ajar, I was aware of Leoni lying comatose on top of me. My crotch was her pillow. I screwed my face up as I realised that I was stripped to the waist … and so was Leoni, apart from a skimpy bra that was so twisted and incapable of doing the job it was designed for, she might as well have not been wearing one. I peered over the side of the bed. There were my jeans and T-shirt lying on the floor, and Leoni's excuse for a dress tangled up with a discarded blanket. I tried gently shaking Leoni, seeing if she was going to wake. She uttered a few words.

'Not morning yet…! Pleasssse let me sleepppp…!'

I looked around the large bedroom, the high ceilings and traditional decor blending beautifully with the many expensive antiques. I couldn't believe how Justin kept getting away with having these parties. As a responsible thirty-five year old, I certainly wouldn't want my house being trashed like this. But then I couldn't stop a smile spreading across my face. *Loosen up, Ritchie, you're supposed to be twenty-one for God's sake!*

Leoni stirred a little. And as she pulled herself further up my body, resting her face on my naked stomach, her breasts now pushed firmly into my groin, I couldn't help but respond in the way that any red-blooded male would at 9 o'clock in the morning. And then, just as I thought that things didn't seem quite so terrible in the cold light of day, the heavy bedroom door was pushed open, and there was Scottie, bleary-eyed, looking straight at me.

'Ritchie boy, thought you'd left ... until Justin said he thought it was you in here!'

And then, peering over Scottie's shoulder there was no mistaking those blue eyes. Yasmin, her hair scraped back, her tanned, beautiful face taking in the scene of me, stretched out on the bed, complete with entangled girl face down on top of me in only her underwear. My heart stopped instinctively. After all, Yasmin *is* my wife. How on earth would she act stumbling across this scene? But of course, as she looked at me, sadly there was an unconcerned smile. Scottie, being the polite guy he was, decided to introduce us all.

'Ritchie, you old stud! This is Yasmin, the girl we have *all* lusted after from afar! True, yeah, come on, admit it to her, she thinks *I'm* bullshitting... But, umm! Seeing as you have your lap full of blonde, I think we'll leave you to it! Perhaps catch you later? Once freshened up? Midday? The pub? Bye!'

My wife and her boyfriend closed the door firmly behind them. There was nothing in my mind, I simply couldn't allow it. How could I begin to work out the words to cajole myself forward? So I switched off all thoughts of Yasmin, but as Leoni wriggled about a bit more, my mind just steamrollered over my new rule. *Yasmin and Scottie! Please God! Tell me nothing's happened between them ... PLEASE!*

As Leoni finally woke, her eyes taking in the seemingly unexpected surroundings, she gave me her double wink special, and a definite blush as she straightened her bra. Up to that moment, it was all I could do to think straight let alone talk, but now Leoni had got me laughing. Though I knew I was being basic, perhaps that was the answer. Presumably I needed to look at Leoni as the antidote to my pain. And as she stood there, looking totally gorgeous, stooping down for her dress, disappointingly covering up her impressive body, it wasn't such a bitter pill. Leoni passed me my jeans. I turned and looked out of the window, my eyes following Scottie and Yasmin as they made their way across the green. Though they weren't actually holding hands, they were giving each other gentle playful shoulder barges, and I *hated* it.

'Ritchie, we didn't … well, surely we *didn't,* did we?'

I turned and smiled teasingly as Leoni wriggled into her dress.

'Oh, Ritchie, just tell me!' Leoni pushed her feet into her high-heeled shoes. 'Ritchie Angel! Tell me, pleasssssse!'

I started to really giggle as she placed her hands firmly on her hips, reminding me of when Rose was losing her cool with me.

'Leoni, I don't remember us, well, you know, penetration, *part* or otherwise!'

We both laughed nervously.

'Yeah, but, Ritchie, I don't remember you undressing me either, and I *was* undressed!'

I shrugged my shoulders, shaking my head from side to side. I walked over to her and placed my hands on her face.

'Let's just agree that nothing happened.'

We both smiled and then hugged warmly. The moment suddenly shattered as Justin's now slightly agitated voice boomed through the bedroom door, we decided perhaps we should leave.

As we made our way out of Justin's house, our 'GOODBYE, AND THANKS!' echoing around the huge hallway, we ran down the drive and onto the green. I stopped, turning to Leoni and pulling her to me, kissing her gently on the lips. She blushed for the second time in less than twenty minutes, squeezing me tightly in response to my instinctive gesture.

'Thanks, Leoni, you're a good mate. It was a difficult night for crazy…*crazy,* reasons, wasn't so sure I could have made it through on my own, *so* thanks!'

I got the double wink and I couldn't help but shake my head. Leoni's eyes opened wide in response.

'What? Why are you shaking your head like that, Ritchie

Angel?'

'I don't know, *you,* you make me smile, and that double wink of yours is, well, it's a beautiful thing!'

Leoni looked at me as though I was completely insane. But then she pushed her arms around my waist and we continued on our way. A dozen or more steps forward, both almost centre of the main green, and I had a question. As though reading my mind Leoni turned to face me, her head inquisitive and tilted slightly to one side.

'What is it, Ritchie?'

I almost lost my nerve, my eyes breaking away from hers, but then I said, 'It's the dumbest question I am ever going to ask you, and, I mean it, if you want to just slap me and not honour the question with an answer, I will take it as a no...'

Leoni stepped away from me, her eyes inquisitive as she waited patiently for what I had to say.

'Umm, no easy way to ask this, so *fuck it!* Are you gay? I'm *so* sorry, a man with a small mind asks small-minded questions. I'll shut up now!'

Leoni's eyes sparkled at me, her nose wrinkling as she appeared to mull over my impertinence. She stepped forward and took my hands in hers, but then stepped back and pulled away from me, just a foot or so, her eyes now looking down at the floor.

'Ritchie, I don't know! I'm not sure! Maybe, but then maybe not... Shit, I don't know!'

I pulled her back to me, kissing her on the top of her head. And then finally, we turn and walk, my arm around her shoulders, not saying a word to each other. As we quietly make our way, not really sure where we're heading, I cannot help feeling far more in control than I ever did originally as a twenty-one year old. I felt an inner confidence that enabled me to be, well, me! Gone was the posing, the pretending to be something I wasn't. Realising that girls are just as confused and lacking in confidence as I was, and knowing that suddenly makes it all so much easier. I felt as though I was a thousand years old in this environment, and though it would be naive to believe I had all the answers, I did genuinely feel that I had a few. And for now, I felt a little more capable of perhaps living my new life with an advantage.

Finally, Leoni and I parted company. I didn't go to the Whippet's Fifth Leg pub – I mean, how could I? How could I possibly meet up with Yasmin and Scottie, and act remotely normal? Besides, it was against the rules, and I simply didn't trust myself when Yasmin was around. I seemed incapable of following my head – with Yasmin I was overruled every time by my heart.

Leoni and I did, however, promise to meet up later that night. She felt amazed that I had asked her outright about her sexuality. But she wasn't indignant, defensive or insulted! There was a confused, wistful look in her eyes when she explained that she felt closer to me because of the question. But now, as I stood alone, staring up at the lilac sky hanging heavy over the Oaks estate, I needed to visit Julie and had an ever-increasing urge to see Lillie. Don't get me wrong, the thought of upsetting Jack De'Vil didn't really bear thinking about. Though apparent to the rest of society, but morning fresh to me, Jack was my friend. Our bonding moments I could only imagine had been enhanced while I was surging forward suddenly in time. Because for my side of the friendship, one hug and several words shared at Justin's *funeral* day party, well, that was it! I shook my head, an unnerved smile crossing my lips. I still viewed Jack as a very shrewd tough businessman – you crossed him at your peril! And of course, I knew that only too well. As I stood looking up at the sky, I noticed how rich and ruddy the lilac was, but changing quickly – a calmness etching out the anger. Within a few hypnotic minutes it was a beautiful day, the clouds having been broken down and, well, gone, leaving a very clear, albeit lilac sky.

I turned and made my way towards Julie's parents' house. But as I got closer, I wasn't sure whether Julie and Jack had moved in together. I hadn't really given it much thought. And not knowing for sure gave me the excuse to be weak and stop. I was already on the right road, but now, leaning against a waist-high brick wall covered in graffiti, and a recently trimmed privet hedge towering protectively behind it, despite my dithering I knew that I must not leave this visit any longer. I took a deep breath and started to walk again. My eyes were suddenly focused on Julie's house, several doors down.

Come on, Ritchie boy! Keep moving, sunshine! You can do this! I kept repeating again and again. What would I say, faced with Julie, or perhaps her mum, or even her dad? I wondered how much they knew. Her mum had driven Julie to the graveyard that day, so I presumed that she would know the secret. I suddenly turned, alarmed by the roar of a powerful engine and then the screech of car brakes.

'Ritchie boy! What are you doing in this neck of the woods?'

And there he was, with the largest, warmest smile, which somehow just didn't compute for me when looking at the *devil*. As Jack stepped out of the car, slapping me firmly on the back, I was already trying to create an answer in anticipation of his second time of asking, 'So, Ritchie, what *are* you doing here?'

I smiled, and then laughed a little nervously.

'Oh God, Jack! You've got me! There's *a* girl, a little blonde that lives around the corner, next street *I* think.'

Jack smiled, punching me sharply in the arm.

'Good lad, Angel! That's my boy!'

'So anyway, Jack, how's tricks? Are you and Julie living together?'

Jack couldn't keep the smile off his face as he rabbit punched me again on the top of my arm.

'You're a fucking tease, Angel. I *know* we should have moved into the Old Church last month, but you know how it is. Fucking idle builders! I even had to give the one carpenter a right good slap, taking fucking liberties! Ah well, give some people an inch and they take a *bastard* mile!'

And as I simply listened, I established that Jack had bought the church a little over twelve months ago, and that they were now just days from moving in together. My mouth was now desperately dry, every other sentence littered with glowing anecdotes about Lillie this, and Lillie that.

'Look, Ritchie, if you've given up looking for this little blonde tart, then why not come back and see what we're up to with the church?' Jack looked eagerly at me, willing me to accept his invitation. 'Wouldn't mind your opinion! *Go on!* Two secs, just got to grab something from Julie's mum and dad's, and we'll shoot back!'

So that was it, my first official invite to the De'Vil residence.

As we roared off, the Porsche claiming attention from everyone we passed, I felt understandably uneasy. After all, how was Julie going to react as I strolled into her home? Would she be able to act normally, not causing Jack the slightest concern? It wasn't long before Jack swung the car through the large imposing iron gates and onto the church driveway. As he pulled the car to a halt, he pushed his foot to the floor, revving the engine before letting the car idle, and then quiet as he switched the engine off. He turned to me, grinning from ear to ear. I smiled back and massaged his ego.

'Wow, Jack! You've got it all, stunning home, and what a great car, mmmm, just as I remember *of course,* and your beautiful girls, Julie and Lillie! Yep, Jack, you've got it all, got *it* all!'

I then looked towards the church. It did look fantastic, very impressive. And as we both stepped out of the yellow beast, Julie appeared at the front door, her face suddenly white as a sheet. I stared at her, breaking into a sympathetic smile. I tried to act as normally as I could. Julie forced a smile my way, then at Jack.

'Julie love, picked Ritchie up just outside your mum and dad's! He was chasing a bit of skirt, but managed to drag his tail away. Thought I'd let him see what we're up to!'

Julie half turned her face to look at me, flecks of paint and plaster dust randomly settled in her tied-back hair, before forcing another unconvincing smile, making her excuses and hurrying back inside.

I walked hesitantly towards the church, Jack talking at a rate of knots. But all I could feel was my heartbeat getting louder and louder. Such was my anticipation at seeing Lillie, especially after the incredible bond I had with Evie and being torn away from each other so ruthlessly. Being a father, and finally understanding the simple power of what that bond meant, my years of regret over my denial of Lillie, well, to be given this opportunity! And though I had acted like a total prat at the churchyard with Julie, I simply hadn't had the control to say what I wanted. But now, as I walked each intrepid step towards the De'Vil home, my mind was racing. After all, being here, at the home of Jack and Julie, when you consider what happened last time – a scene that I would never be able to forget – just made all this feel so totally crazy. As Jack talked, explaining how they had changed this and moved that, all I could think about was Lillie's tragic death. After all, I never did find out what had been the cause. Surely, knowing that there was going to be a problem I could perhaps change things. But suddenly my thoughts were sent scurrying away as we turned down the side of the church and into the back garden. There was Julie, holding Lillie in her arms. The words only just squeaked out.

'Wow, you two, you both look *so* beautiful!'

Jack stepped forward, an unsure frown crossing his forehead, but he took Lillie off Julie, kissing *my* daughter's face, and then lifted her into the air, blowing a raspberry on her bare stomach.

'Say hello, Lillie! Yes, yes, yes! This is Ritchie, Daddy's friend!'

A horrified look appeared on Julie's face as Jack surprisingly passed Lillie to me, but I didn't bat an eyelid. I just took the beautiful little girl in my arms and the world suddenly stood still. I pulled Lillie instinctively to me – I didn't dare look for a reaction from Jack and Julie. I raised my grateful eyes to the sky. The sun seemed to shine brighter than ever and the lilac tinge was gone – just beautiful *pure* blue sky. I was astounded. The strength of the natural sunlight was almost blinding me, and the lilac shroud, something I had become so used to, something that seemed to dilute the strength of the sun, was now wonderfully normal again. But as I felt Lillie's soft cheek rest against mine, I think I held the moment too long, as Julie stepped forward, seeming quite keen to take her daughter away from me. I simply stretched out my arms, placing Lillie into the safe hands of her beautiful mother. The lilac reminder was back instantly!

Julie looked at me intently; her eyes appeared cold and questioning. Totally oblivious to all the high emotions going on around him, Jack continued talking about the roof, and then pointed over to where certain trees had been before they were ruthlessly felled.

'But, Ritchie, we needed those two out of the way! After all, we needed a garage, didn't we, Jule?'

Julie simply nodded, before turning and walking away from me, but as she made her way indoors, the smile that Lillie gave me brought a lump to my throat.

Jack strode forward enthusiastically, beckoning me to follow him inside.

'That's a good idea, Jule! Cuppa, Ritchie?'

As I stepped into the lounge, my heart was leaping somersaults. A thousand images made my eyes widen with each dreadful moment that built up to the horrific tragedy that had gone on here. But amidst the black was an undercurrent of warmth. The staircase that led up to Jack and Julie's bedroom gave me a sense of belonging – her and me together in the De'Vil matrimonial bed. But I could feel my palms going sweaty as I tried desperately to shake off the vivid memories of what followed. All I could see was the hatred in Jack's face as he told us both that he knew what we had been up to. But here, right now, as I looked at him, I was with the man that Julie and Lillie knew – excitable, warm and friendly.

'Ritchie! Come and see this, *you'll* love it!'

Jack sprung gazelle-like up the stripped wooden staircase. As I made my way onto the first step, my eyes met Julie's as she stood in the doorway of the kitchen. I stopped for a second, our gaze fixed. I creased the smallest of smiles, desperate to encourage something similar from her, but her face didn't flinch, and she just turned and disappeared out of view. I physically sighed, swallowing hard, before climbing the rest of the stairs, where Jack was conducting his tour, totally unaware that I had momentarily been absent.

'Look at the light, Ritchie! Can you believe the architect wanted me to rip out these stained-glass windows? The dick! He said that they were unsafe and not environmentally friendly, too cold! Bollocks, I told him, they're bleedin' beautiful!'

I watched as the sun slipped from behind the small cloud and then became transfixed as the scene of the Virgin Mary cradling baby Jesus shone clearly onto the bare wooden floor.

My mind swept back to Julie and I, lying together on the bed, and the same reflection across her face. But then Julie had just lost Lillie, and though we weren't aware of it at the time, our actions meant that we had signed Julie's death warrant.

My thoughts were suddenly interrupted by the loud shrill of the phone ringing downstairs. The noise stopped, but then Julie yelled upstairs. Jack apologised and left to take his call. There was an eerie silence as I stood alone in the bedroom. I stepped towards a small Gothic arched window and looked out across the garden. Lillie was playing with her pink doll's pram. I hadn't been aware that anybody else was in the house, but an older woman wandered out into the garden – it was Julie's mum. Footsteps were suddenly behind me, and as I turned, there was Julie, three or four feet away.

'Why are you here, Ritchie?'

I looked at her; her face was still stern.

'It was Jack, he, well, he insisted really! Very persuasive... It just seemed easier to come over rather than make up some poor excuse.'

Julie turned away in response to Jack's voice echoing through the church, saying that he would be back in ten minutes; something about documents and photocopies. I felt relieved that he was leaving, giving me a chance to talk to Julie. She turned back towards me, looking a little more relaxed.

'I'm *so* sorry, Julie. I needed to see you. That's what I was doing when Jack pulled up outside your mum and dad's. I just, well, I needed to apologise for the way I behaved, you know, at the graveyard!'

Julie pulled her lips together tightly, dropping her gaze at the memory. She then spoke softly, almost whispering.

'You're a shit, Ritchie Angel. It took all my courage to tell you about Lillie, and you, well, well, I don't know, maybe I should have expected the reaction I got, but none of this has been easy. Jack's a great guy, and it's been hell lying to him! But I should have known you wouldn't be interested, and yet I risked upsetting everyone, just by trying to do the right thing.'

I swallowed hard, my lips tight and imitating Julie's deflated spirit. A small tear trickled down onto her tanned cheek. I stepped forward, placing a finger to catch it. Julie's hand was suddenly on mine. I was confused by the gesture, but then instinctively pulled her towards me. I couldn't believe how wonderful it felt to hold her. I had been haunted by her horrendous death, and here she was, fit and well, Lillie playing outside in the afternoon sun. We just stood still and *this* felt right, as though a healing process had begun. I hated not being with Yasmin and Evie – it was the most unimaginable savage feeling. But losing Julie and Lillie without the chance to make amends had just left me with a backdrop of regret, perhaps the biggest guilt-ridden regret of them all.

Julie tactfully pulled away from me, and I sensed that the intensity of my hug had confused her. But I smiled, and at a loss as to what to say, I simply apologised again for my bad reaction at the graveyard. We both shuffled about a little awkwardly, and there was no mistaking the chemistry between us. But I was under no illusions; maturity was enabling me to look past the beauty and intensity that was so fatally attractive to me. Without question, I needed to make sure that she and Jack stayed happily together. That this secret we had *stayed* just that. But as Julie turned and greeted her mum and our daughter at the top of the stairs, I think we both knew that there would be another chapter in our already potent relationship.

But for now I needed to get away and gather my thoughts. I made my excuse to leave. Lillie was now in Julie's arms. I shook hands with Julie's mum, even though I was well aware of her angry eyes and the biting of her lip, but we both stayed calm for the sake of her daughter. I unintentionally brushed my hand against Lillie's leg, her smile instant and dazzling. As I took in Lillie's beautiful face, the curl of her lips, the shape of her eyes, there were incredible similarities with Evie. Without warning my legs almost buckled, an overwhelming wave of grief at the loss and panic, the sheer enormity of how I was missing my little Evie. But I knew I had to wipe it all from my mind. The pain of thought and wonder at how and where Yasmin and Evie fitted into all this madness defied me and threatened to undermine my ability to carry on, but carry on I must.

Julie put Lillie down, who then ran obediently towards her

grandma's open arms. Julie walked with me down to the end of the driveway and out through the open gates. As she peered down the lane she looked up at me, and a beautiful smile filled her face.

'I don't regret it you know, you and I, our one night together.'

I took Julie's hands in mine, but she sharply pulled them away.

'Ritchie, because of Lillie... She's the most wonderful little thing, and until you've experienced the full-blown pleasure of being a parent, then you'll never understand the power of it!'

I nodded my head, desperate to explain that I understood fully what she meant, but instead just uttered, 'Julie, *she's* perfect, beautiful, just like her clever mum!'

We both cringed as I said it, but she knew that I meant it.

As I started to walk away, she said, 'Ritchie! What am I going to do? We still need to meet and talk.'

I nodded and waved back at her.

'I will be in touch, Julie, just need a bit of time to digest it all.'

I finally turned around and made my way down the narrow lane. As I walked, I felt a flicker of cloud envelop me, a shiver of negativity and doubt shoot the length of my spine. I looked up at the lilac sky – there wasn't a cloud in sight, and the sun was beating as strong as ever. But as I looked down and to my left, there was Rose, walking with me, her little bare feet making me smile. My dear friend looked up at me, her own smile turning her cherry-red lips up at the sides.

'See, Ritchie? That wasn't so bad, was it?'

I beamed in agreement. But then panic set in as Jack's yellow Porsche turned into the lane and roared towards me.

'Oh great, *bloody* Jack! He'll see me and think it strange that I've simply left.'

Rose gripped my hand. 'He'll not see you, Ritchie, look around you!'

My feet, my body, I was slightly elevated from the security of the ground, belied and out of synchronicity with the trees and hedges that lined the lane. Rose squeezed my hand.

'You're already sliding further into the future. These few

steps and words spoken have seen a couple of hours pass by already. Jack won't be remotely surprised that you're gone, and will simply feel bad that he's left you for so long. In fact, Ritchie, every step we take together, one hour on, two hours on, but gradually multiplying at a tremendous rate! So, I reckon by the end of the walk home…' Rose started counting on her fingers, screwing up her lips and eyes as she worked out her sum, '…we'll be nearly a month on!'

Rose couldn't contain her childish laughter, and as the light turned to dark, and then back to light, I felt wonderful, happier that time was moving forward, perhaps getting nearer to my journey's end, even though I knew I still had *much* to do.

And as the days and nights passed by with every few steps, 'Tell me, Rose, how come I'm able to say what I want now, able to express how I'm feeling to these important people in my life, whereas before I simply slipped into the tracks I had cut before, my original persona?'

Rose squeezed my hand again. 'It's *your* doing, Ritchie, the simple fact that you're starting to grasp what all this is about. We feel a little more confident in what you're thinking and saying, and so, we're taking more chances with you, having a little more faith shall we say. Well, up to a point anyway!'

As we walked together, getting closer to Willow High Street, I asked Rose about Yasmin, and if things would develop with her and Scottie. Rose laughed a little nervously.

'Ritchie, I shouldn't be telling you this, but I, and the powers that be, well, we've had a little bit of a brainwave, so yes, things do move on a little, and of course you're not allowed to influence Yasmin's judgment, so on and so forth! So, to make things a little easier for you *not* to break the rules, in your absence, you, Scottie, Yasmin and the rest of your friends have got together on a couple of occasions, and luckily for you, well, you've made a total idiot of yourself! So far as to say, Yasmin believes you're not a very nice guy, and therefore she now wouldn't make the mistake of being interested in you!'

I let go of Rose's hand, and it was my turn to place my hands firmly on my hips.

'In what sense, *an idiot?*'

Rose tried not to smirk. 'Well, Ritchie, let's just say that you're pretty good at being an idiot when it's forced upon you!'

'Oh, *bloody* great! So my carefully atoned character over the years has in one foul swoop simply seen me branded as the new village idiot? God, Rose! How come you can't run these little gems of strategy by me first? Couldn't you have just kept us apart until we reach twenty-five? At least then I can start with a clean slate. Instead, now, I've got to totally eradicate any opinions she has of me.'

Rose seemed amused by my outburst.

'Ritchie, come on, it doesn't matter! We had said to you that your paths must not cross, but we've now realised that that's not always going to be possible, so if she sees you as a fool, and has absolutely no respect for...*or* interest in you, then you cannot be of any influence over her choices in life. Quite brilliant really, and it takes the responsibility off you. After all, you do show a bit of a weakness in this area! I think I remember my father calling it, ummm, cruel to be kind?'

Rose started to walk on, leaving me with my hands raised high above my head. I simply didn't know whether to laugh or cry. But I *was* close to tears, feeling emotional and exasperated. It suddenly dawned on me that Rose was disappearing far too quickly into the distance, so I quickly ran to catch up with my antagonistic friend. I was beginning to feel quite nauseous as the light and dark, day and night were now flashing past me at an ever-increasing speed.

I was barely able to keep up with Rose, her steps almost stretching into a run.

'Rose! Please answer me this...' I knew that I couldn't argue with the powers that be, but all the same, I had one simple question. 'So, Rose – *please stop* – are you saying that I will have *no* control whatsoever when Yasmin is around?'

Rose finally stood still and turned to face me, a warm smile beaming towards me.

'You'll have control when you're physically with her, but when your life is skipping forward, you'll still exist and play an active part, you just won't be aware of it, that's all. We sort of work you in your absence; quite clever really!'

Rose looked at me, well aware that I wasn't comfortable with what she was saying. And though I pleaded in vain that perhaps they could present me in a slightly better light, it seemed to fall on deaf ears and I realised that I was wasting my time in challenging them. After all, I didn't know how I was being showcased, but maybe it really wasn't as bad as Rose was painting. And perhaps I should remain focused and grateful for what they were doing for me.

I pushed out beneath my breath, 'Mmm, maybe I needed to be a bit more trusting and gracious.'

Rose smirked and walked on again. I scratched my head while watching my little friend continue her journey. *Where on earth is she going?* I shook my head as I asked the question, my head pulling back slightly as she began to go a little fuzzy around the edges to then disappear completely. I looked up to the dark skies, taking in the thick lilac swirls forming around the full moon, whilst determinedly trying to convince myself that *trust* was certainly the way forward.

Suddenly, I could hear Rose saying in a child-like, patronising tone, 'My God, Ritchie Angel, I do believe you've got it! Yes, I do believe that we're starting to hear words of gratitude!'

But as Rose's voice seemed to echo and fade into the night sky, I was hoping that she would answer me just one more question.

'Rose! *Please* put me out of my misery on *one* thing; why the bare feet?' But though I waited…nothing!

Several lonely minutes passed by, and so I had to accept that Rose was gone. I continued my walk, every step seeming to bring on the night, quickly followed by day. I raised my head skyward, feeling nauseous and increasingly exhausted. Calmly and politely I asked for Rose to come back, and then an exasperated plea, one last vain attempt as I turned a full three hundred and sixty degrees…but nothing.

I witnessed the sun drop like a stone out of the sky, my face drawn to the cloud. A large relieved smile creased my lips. I had stepped off the surging merry-go-round and my life was now back at a normal pace. It was early evening and I could see all my friends gathered around one of the outside tables at the Whippet's Fifth Leg pub.

Scottie spotted me, and yelled, 'ANGEL! OH COME ON, ANGEL, YOU CAN'T *RUN* FOREVER. COME AND HAVE A DRINK WITH *US!*'

As I crossed the road, I could see Yasmin trying to get up from the table, but Scottie was pulling her back down onto the bench seat. But though everyone else was looking at me and laughing, Yasmin was plainly not amused. It broke my heart to see that look in her eyes, a distaste that had only been reserved for perhaps one or two people in all the years we'd been together.

'Oh God!' I uttered under my breath. How I longed for those simple, straightforward days.

'Hey, Ritchie, come and sit next to me!' Jimmy spoke sympathetically, and beckoned again.

As I sat down, Yasmin stood up, this time without restraint or a glance, and made her way into the pub.

'Something I said?'

Everybody except for Jimmy laughed out loud.

Scottie bellowed back at me. '*Something you did!* I forgive ya though, because I love ya, and it actually *was* very funny! But I think you need to go and catch up with her, and *really* apologise!'

I was totally baffled of course, but I stood up and stared at Jimmy. He got the message and followed me towards the gents.

Once inside, 'Look, Jimmy, I know you're going to think I've gone completely mad, but, well, I've no idea what I could have said *or* done to Yasmin to upset her.'

Jimmy looked extremely puzzled. 'Ritchie, come on, how can you *not* remember? I'm sure as hell *never* going to be able to forget it!'

But as Jimmy looked at me, his eyes seemed to offer a sympathy that suggested he knew I wasn't kidding. He tactfully started to fill in the blanks.

'Well! Yasmin's cousin, do you remember, Dean, Sunday night? You know, just turned eighteen, got his girlfriend with him, little Abbie?'

I shook my head from side to side and Jimmy continued.

'Remember how you pulled Abbie's boob tube down, and

grabbed her breasts? Are you seriously telling me you cannot remember *that?*'

I shook my head again.

'*Shit, Ritchie!* You didn't seem all that out of it! So, there you were, Abbie's breasts in your hands, Dean going mad and throwing a punch at you! And then *you,* well, kicking the *shit* out of him! Then, once everyone had dragged you off, the first chance you got, well, you *bloody* well legged it, *with* Abbie!'

I fell back against the cold white tiles of the toilet wall. I was totally devastated. No wonder Yasmin couldn't bear to be anywhere near me. All the time she had known me I had never once been remotely lecherous, and she had certainly never seen me throw a punch at someone, never mind beat some poor young lad up! I was totally mortified. I simply had to talk to her. But it was no good. I tried to move my legs, but I couldn't.

'Ritchie, I think you need to get yourself home, mate! Do you want me to drive you?'

I declined Jimmy's offer, and just about squeaked out a no thanks. I took a deep breath and did everything in my power to go and talk to Yasmin, who was now sitting well out of my way with some other friends of hers. I was so confused, perspiring and unable to move forward. Suddenly, I was turning around, brushing harshly against Jimmy and walking straight out of the back door of the pub. Once out of sight, I finally came to a stop at the back of the car park, falling onto my knees amongst some empty beer barrels. All I could think about was Yasmin's state of mind, how she would now perceive me. A nasty thug! Something that I had always managed to keep away from her, for our entire time together! I had never, ever wanted her to see my dark side, but now, in one mad moment, she had seen me in a different light. Had she, in my absence to control, seen my alter ego and worse? My thoughts then turned to the rest of my friends. At least they would know that it was totally out of character for me to do such a thing. But how on earth could Rose and *whoever* controlled this journey – if they really were on my side – allow me to be seen in this way? I felt scared and vulnerable. Just when I was beginning to believe that I was making some kind of progress, I suddenly felt as though my whole world had once again come crashing down around me.

I eventually made my way home. The house looked uninviting as usual. But as I turned my key, I knew I desperately needed some sleep. As I walked into the dining room, there was a note on the table.

Dear Ritchie,

Hung around for a few days, hoped to be able to catch up and maybe sort a few things out. Trust that you're okay.

Love Dad x

I was shocked as I read the words. But then I suppose I had gone a little easier on him this time. It was well documented that originally I had humiliated him and really, apart from upsetting him, the only other thing achieved was that I had caused hurt and regret for myself. So this time, being a little kinder, well, it felt far better. I thought that I would write to him, and should I actually put pen to paper then maybe we could keep the bridge built.

As soon as my head hit the pillow, I fell into a deep sleep, my dream painfully real. I trudged on foot and stood at the top of the long driveway that led down to the Water's Edge. My eyes were drawn up to the sky, searching for proof that perhaps my nightmare was over and that this was my final homecoming. A sharp stab of bitter disappointment passed through me as my eyes squinted through the strong sunlight, only to see that the lilac tinge was as strong as ever. I pushed my tired feet forward and walked slowly down the driveway, a small grey suitcase gripped tightly in my right hand. As I got closer to the house, my mood lifted, as I could see Evie, her platinum-blonde hair lifted by the breeze. But as if in slow motion, as she trotted around on an imaginary horse, a small baby boy was crawling in circles, central to Evie's fantasy showground. I stopped, my feet still on the gravel drive, my toes just tickling the neatly trimmed grass verge. I placed my suitcase on the ground and tried to call out to Evie, a surge of excitement filling me, ready to boil over in anticipation of our eyes meeting. But all I could do was whisper. The frustration and panic building up inside me made me stop. Suddenly I didn't want Evie to see me – I simply didn't want to upset her, and I felt unsteady and fazed.

I turned and looked at the garage, the heavy door open and my silver Porsche convertible clearly visible inside. My eyes followed the large swaying branches of the oak tree, almost brushing against the open office windows above the garage. I took a couple of steps towards the house and a warm sea-breeze type air wafted gently around me, in part soothing my anxiety. Yasmin's Beetle stood – dirtier and a little less cared for than she would normally allow – on gunmetal cobbles set beneath the dining room patio doors. I walked towards the back entrance of the house, and though this was my home, I felt as though an outsider, an unwanted intruder skulking suspiciously. I placed my hand firmly on the doorknob, but I was unable to muster the strength to turn it. I tried again and again...until in defeat I rested my head against the unopened glass and timber. My sombre defeatist mood was suddenly lifted by the gentle sound of a narrowboat making its steady journey past the house. I stood up straight and moved my heavy lead-like legs towards the front door, that lay parallel with the canal. As I trudged, seemingly invisible to my surroundings, I couldn't take my eyes off Evie, but I was aware that my face was crinkling as my much loved daughter appeared a little younger than before. I blinked furiously, and then frowned as the little boy running around in circles suddenly appeared to have aged a handful of years within minutes, his jet-black curls glistening in the evening sunshine. I lifted my feet wearily up the three large slate steps, double oak and glass doors before me. As the chug of the passing narrowboat filled my ears, I instinctively turned around, and a familiar face smiled and waved back at me. My eyes strained again and locked onto the lady's eyes – it was Julie De'Vil. I could do nothing, and just watched as the boat eased slowly past me. Julie appeared to be alone, but I was totally transfixed. Then my eyes are drawn to a curtain covering the small porthole window. The white floral material is curled back at the edge, but then pulled across sharply. I smile and wave as the face of Lillie beams at me, but looking almost of teenage years. We all just wave, and I watch as they chug away slowly. I finally turn and face the doorway to my home. I place my shaking hands on the doorknob, praying that this time I am able to turn the handle. I heave a huge sigh of relief as the door glides open.

As I step into my spacious hallway, white long-stemmed lilies stand elegant in a tall glass vase in the centre of an antique maple table. I feel a calmness sink through me, totally comforted by the fact that I am home. I can see through to the kitchen, a pan simmering gently on the Aga. But I am aware of footsteps upstairs, and then silence. I make my way to the stairs and begin my climb, every step seeming to take an absolute age. I finally reach the landing. Three large windows line the curved wall overlooking the front and side lawns. I can see Evie, her little face seeming to get younger with every new glance. The boy is now standing, taking over the role as leader, Evie now toddling clumsily in the inner circle. A well of panic bubbles painfully in the pit of my stomach. But I'm again aware of noises coming from the bedroom. I try to call out, but cannot. I attempt to walk, but once again my feet are defiant and unwilling to do as I ask. I ease at a snail's pace towards the voices behind the door. My hair is being blown by the breeze that I experienced outside, but a little more harshly now. I place both hands on the doorknob, ready for it to resist me, but I suddenly let go, as I can hear the distressed cries of a baby. I make my way across the landing, my feet a little quicker this time, as if I am flowing with the current rather than against it. I push the nursery door open. I swallow hard as I see Evie's cot standing in the middle of the room, lots of cream muslin hanging from the ceiling, blowing harshly in the breeze coming from the open window. I tread fearfully, each step quickening the beat of my heart, and I am aware that I am physically shaking. I look down into the cot and there is Evie, five years of age, a look of heavy distress on her face, her head and feet touching the top and bottom of the cot. I want to whisk her up into my arms, hold her and never let her go, but I can't. And as I stand there, powerless and rooted to the spot, Evie is lying totally still, breathing, but *so* very weak, and her eyes are straining, as though willing me to read her mind, to save her from her misery. Suddenly, I'm drawn to the window, praying for a happier image, Evie happily running around, making a mockery of what is happening here in the nursery. But as I stand looking out across the once happy garden, the little girl looking back at me isn't my daughter. Her eyes are locked onto mine, black and piercing, an indignant index finger twirling strands of oil-black hair, and the little boy has his arms wrapped around his sister. They both stare at me, taunting me. I quickly turn to Evie in the cot again and still she cannot move, her eyes showing signs of tremendous stress. I can feel the stench of desperation filling my veins, a pain that would rather see me gouge my own eyes out than watch my little girl suffer in this way. With tears rolling down my cheeks, I feel as though I'm drifting out of the room, pulled along by an aggressive reversal of current that's making it clear that my time here is up, the painful images of Evie being challenged by the anticipation of what I might find in the main bedroom, my bedroom, in my house.

Without having taken a step away from the nursery, I am suddenly stood face-to-face with the main bedroom double doors. I push them open and there is Yasmin, on our bed, on her back, totally unaware of my presence, her cream silk slip nightie pulled down around her waist, her full breasts pushed into the chest of her black-haired lover. And as he thrusts enthusiastically into her, I can see all that I don't want to see so painfully clear, my eyes as though held in a vice continuing to witness my wife's blatant infidelity. I want to run forward and force this travesty apart, but I cannot even blink, so as the impostor pushes in and out of my beautiful Yasmin, I have to witness first-hand how her nails are digging into his back. Though I am willing my body to react and take control of this horror show, I do nothing, and I am left witnessing the sheer look of ecstasy on her face, a look I have seen a thousand times before. A shard of what is happening to me sees me willing myself to wake up, but I can't, and so I wrestle with the belief that this may be real. Then, unable to turn away, I manage to look up, and I can see swirls of lilac smoke blowing across the ceiling. My head is suddenly thrust, as though by hands of steel, to witness further the nightmare unfolding on my matrimonial bed, and there she is, the woman that had only ever slept with me, the woman that was – and I pray still is – my soul mate. As I witness the finale, the man's black eyes lock onto mine. I struggle to focus, nausea and lack of breath threatening to overwhelm me, but then clarity punishes me with the almost hypnotic, sickening slow motion image of this man, this alien-type creature, his hands explorative and creating pleasure all over her body, sufficiently to finally make me physically sick. As the floodgates open and I feel as though I have been whacked with a huge sledgehammer, I wake up in my cold empty house, the warm, thick substance covering my pillow and sheets. Instinctively I jump out of my bed and try to run quickly towards the bathroom, my hands over my mouth. I believe that I might be okay, but then as the painful images of Yasmin and Evie fill my mind I fall to my knees, and this time, though my body is heaving continuously, there is nothing left to give.

CHAPTER EIGHTEEN

Christian Angel!

After Death, 1991 – Lilac Sky
As the morning arrived, I felt dreadful, my head and heart pounding. I slid my legs out of bed and sat up, the nightmare still painfully clear in my mind. I chewed the inside of my mouth, heart-kicking memories churning over and over. And though I labelled it a nightmare, with all that's happening to me it just seemed to blend in with the rest of the so-called reality of my present existence, therefore making it difficult to simply dismiss it as a *mere* nightmare. But I had to see it as nothing more than that otherwise I was convinced I would lose my strength to continue. But suddenly, as though I'd clicked an on switch, I started to move with a little urgency, as though governed by a preordained schedule, and the only way to survive was to get this ordeal over and done with as quickly as possible. I was ready for work and jumping into my company car, heading for Skirdle's. A nagging shard at the back of my mind, mulled over and over, finally revealed itself – I had a

meeting with *Harry Christian* today, and as I said the name, the hairs pulled tight on the back of my neck.

I was dutifully sat at my desk when Mr Skirdle strode, high spirited, into the office. Kelly, our new part-timer, Mr Ball and I all waited for his usual 10 o'clock announcement.

I glanced down at my watch and muttered softly under my breath, 'Three ... two ... one...'

'Well, team, I can see that you don't need me getting in the way, slowing you all down! I have an important meeting at the golf club, so if there are no objections...'

Mr Skirdle scoured the room, his eyes coaxing an approval from each of us – the outcome never being in doubt. He stood up straight, and a beaming smile and jolly farewell larger than life filled the room. And then came the words that had left their scar.

'Oh, Ritchie lad! The Old Bakery ... a Mr Christian said he would call in later this afternoon, about 5pm. He collared me at the golf club last week, assured him that I had just the man to look after him. All yours then, sunshine!'

He tipped his new bowler hat, his eyes lingering on mine for confirmation that I had it all under control. I nodded my head reassuringly. I quickly skipped through the diary. There was nothing about Mr Christian, and I wasn't sure whether to be impressed or a little spooked by my anticipation of our meeting today. I started to smile and ponder another incident that had happened on this very day in my original life. I didn't look at the watch and do the countdown, but within ten minutes there it was. Mr Ball looked at me and announced that he needed to get out of the office and see a few people, so he too would be gone for most of the day. Though accepting without question his intentions originally, in the here and now I was suitably enlightened, shall we say ... hot weather, swimming pool. But as I peered back, eyebrows raised, I was almost tempted to share my knowledge – 'Look, I know about you and Skirdle junior!' But of course, it would be unwise and straying from the original script. As I chewed the inside of my mouth, I knew that I was pulling a face, uncomfortable at the memory of having caught the two of them in the act. After all, Mr Ball and I became pretty good mates in the end. But was it because he knew I had something life-changing on him? Or was it because he genuinely liked me? I would never really know, unless I was prepared to wait and see how things developed naturally. And as I pondered, I felt that I should just let things progress at their own steady pace.

However, the choice was suddenly taken away from me when the phone call came from Skirdle senior.

'Sorry, Ritchie, but there's a file on the Old Bakery, *meant* to bring it in, old forgetful fool that I am! But if you could fetch it before your meeting today, it's in my office at home. Thank you, lad!'

And as voyeuristic and questionably indulgent it may seem, touch for touch, note for note, word for word I endured the full uncompromising love fest between Mr Ball and Skirdle junior unfold in all its wondrous and scarring detail.

As I slumped back down into my office chair, Kelly enquired as to whether I was okay. I shook all thoughts of what I had just witnessed firmly out of my mind, and assured our sweet assistant that I would be fine. I accepted gratefully her offer of a cup of coffee to bring my colour back.

Mr Christian soon showed his face, and as though pushing the play button on the video recorder, everything went as it did at our first meeting together. But despite the perfect re-enactment, the *devil* was lurking in the detail – there was undoubtedly a problem. But as I chewed the inside of my mouth again, I considered exactly what my options were, here and now. After all, this time around I had got the school. As far as I could establish, I obtained it by illegal means, but because Jack was my friend I can only presume that no one was standing in my way. But Rose hadn't mentioned anything about the Old School; she hadn't questioned or condemned my methods. And so now, with Harry Christian, I didn't really need the money quite so desperately! So would I be doing the right thing in playing this one straight? I pondered the situation, and in truth, it seemed that all I needed to do *was* my job. Then, hopefully, I wouldn't create a situation where I ended up with Harry's blood on my hands!

My mind was racing as I recalled my meeting with Harry

Christian. It had gone well, but then at the end of talks, just as he stood up and thrust his hand forward, I shook it limply, as though guilt had left me weak. My eyes suddenly struggled to connect with his, and the briefest of glances offered little comfort. There was a confidence about him, a knowing smile that unnerved me. I swallowed hard as I focused beneath his silver floppy fringe – a raw wound, roughly stitched and ugly to look at. Instantly I was shaken by flashes of light, and then the image of Harry being turned over by the doctor after his fatal fall. I felt the breath draining out of me. I could hear my voice apologising to Mr Christian for my funny turn, but unable to stop myself, I slumped back into my office chair.

'Can I get you a drink of water, Mr Angel?'

Though my eyes were still closed, I nodded, his voice bashing around my short-circuiting brain.

'I bet you've skipped your lunch, eh, lad?' was all I could hear over the clatter of cups and closing of cupboard doors.

I forced myself forward, resting my head in my hands, before cold, clammy fingers lifted my head up and pushed the glass to my mouth. I took a few sips and brushed the offering away.

'Thank you, thank you, Mr Christian, umm, *thank you*. I'm fine now. I'll see you out.' Kelly was on the telephone, seemingly oblivious to *all* that was going on.

As I stood up, my eyes now able to focus, Harry was *un-scarred* and appeared to be his usual self and my heartbeat steadied. I smiled warmly at the tired and timid, eager-to-please man that stood before me. He then whispered an invitation to perhaps conduct our business at his flat above the bakery, should I feel that it would be more convenient and *discreet* to do so. But just as I scolded myself for my inappropriate reaction to such an unthreatening soul, it was his final line that had me reeling again.

'Alice is looking forward to seeing you, Ritchie!'

And as the shop door shut firmly behind him, I watched Harry make his way back to the bakery, and my blood ran cold. Never before had I met Alice Christian – not in this lifetime anyway! And Harry's sudden use of Ritchie rather than Mr Angel seemed instantly familiar and out of context with how professional the meeting had been. And as for meeting at the flat...Originally I had instigated the secrecy of their home so as not to raise unnecessary suspicion in the shop. As for this occasion, at no time had I suggested that we would need privacy to conduct our business.

I sat for what seemed like hours at my desk. Kelly had long left and I had turned the lights off and flipped over the 'closed' sign. But I simply couldn't raise the energy to leave. I just needed to think. The darkness within the shop contradicted the bright summer evening that was there for those that wanted it, outside in the real world. I was aware of the faces peering through the glass, looking for more available houses than the shop window had to offer, but they couldn't see me. I was safely tucked away in the shadows, and that was just how I liked it.

I didn't make it home that night. After all, there was no one waiting there for me – there was certainly no Yasmin. And as I sat and pondered my existence, I wondered whether or not suicide would result in me being found dead back at the Water's Edge, aged thirty-five, or whether I would be found here, in the office, aged twenty-one.

As I fell into a light, gentle sleep, my head slumped onto the cold hard table. I could feel the tears rolling down my cheeks and into the small opening of my mouth. But as I fell deeper, I felt the reassuring hand of Evie gently brushing my forehead with her small, warm fingers. So I held on to the belief, and I made it through the night.

The next few days seemed to pass in a daze. I kept my head down, just nipping out for a takeaway sandwich at lunchtime. But then the most difficult of situations made me realise that I had to get a grip. I had just managed to get the last hot beef baguette, and as I stepped out of the café and onto Willow High Street, I bumped full force into Yasmin. As she bounced off me, falling back sharply onto her bottom, the cold hard slabs making her scream out was quickly followed by my clumsy panic.

'Oh shit! Yasmin, I am *so* sorry!'

As Yasmin lay unceremoniously on the ground, her short

floaty skirt revealing far too much tanned thigh and a glimpse of pale pink lace panties, I knew I should look away – my chance to perhaps prove that I wasn't the letch that she presumed me to be. But true to type, my eyes seemed to linger just below the level of her skirt, which was now resting around her mid-riff. She simply glared at me, pushing her skirt back down.

'Let me help you up, Yasmin. I simply didn't see you!'

As I pulled her to her feet, she uttered.

'On the contrary Ritchie, I think you've seen *plenty* of me…' She shook her head, her eyes staring back at me with scolding contempt, and it was totally destroying to see someone you love view you in that way. Especially when even our worst rows would never show even the slightest glimmer of what I was seeing now. But they say that the eyes are the windows to your soul, and so, as I looked at her, desperate for a connection, she held my stare. Three, four seconds, and then she broke away, a little flustered and a little natural rouge to her beautiful face.

Yasmin made her excuses and strode off up the high street. I watched her walk, praying that she would turn around. Just as I was about to give up hope, she turned. She didn't smile, but she *looked* at me, her eyes unable to break away. Four, five seconds, before finally ending the moment and continuing her journey. Suddenly, I was jolted back into reality. I felt hot burning against my chest, looked down and pulled the hot baguette away from my grease-stained shirt. I shook my head from side to side, but this time a small chuckle gurgled through me.

'Hi, gorgeous!'

I turned around, startled to hear any words of affection from anyone, such was my present self-loathing. It was Sally. She smiled sweetly, but then grinned, highly amused as she took in the totally un-cool stain on my work shirt.

'Need a bib, Ritchie?' But then her amusement seemed to subside. 'Ritchie, I need to talk to you.'

As we made our way back towards the estate agents, and having now lost my appetite, I slung my baguette into the overflowing bin, having to push it down amongst the chip wrappers so that it didn't simply drop back onto the pavement. While my fist was a foot deep in waste, I pictured myself from above, and it was then that I knew I needed a change of scene. Seeing Yasmin, and now with Sally at my side, I realised that I had a desperate need to escape, an incredible desire to get out of Willow.

As I pulled my tomato sauce and beef grease-stained arm out of the bin, I shook my head and uttered as calmly as I could, 'Sally, once I've cleaned this disgusting mess off my arm, how about you and I taking a drive out into the country?'

She nodded. I gave her the keys to my car and said I would join her once I had made my excuses to my boss.

Though the words were exactly what I wanted to hear, Mr Ball was unable to look above the modern art-like stain on my chest.

'Sure, Ritchie, Kelly and I will manage. I think you're right, you've perhaps been overdoing it a bit lately. No offence, but you *look* like shit!'

I couldn't argue, and simply grabbed my jacket, leaving quickly before they had the chance to change their minds.

As I stepped out of the agents, my mood lifted, but then I heard, 'Ritchie! Can we have *that* talk?'

There was no mistaking the voice.

'Julie, umm, arrhh, umm, sure, umm, *you* need to give me a minute!'

I looked down the alley, where my closest friend's girlfriend sat waiting in the passenger seat. Julie looked at me, and then at Sally.

'I thought she was going steady with Jimmy…'

I unintentionally hesitated.

'Oh God, Ritchie! You're not…'

I shook my head vigorously, suddenly aware of how things might appear.

'Julie! For God's sake, *no!!* We're just mates! But it might seem odd to her that I'm with *you.*'

But Julie seemed to be past caring. And so it was that I made my way towards the car. Sally had spotted Julie and stepped out onto the car park.

'You'll have to pass, eh, Ritchie? You have a better offer?'

I took Sally's hand.

'No, this is just a bit delicate. I promise you I'll come to yours after! Perhaps that would look better than us being seen driving out of Willow together!'

Sally nodded, and as she walked back out of the alley, passing Julie, both girls simply nodded their heads to each other.

Julie climbed into the passenger seat. It felt strange being with her like this; it also reeked of stupidity and danger. Jack and I were friends now. But he wasn't the sort of guy, well, me being seen out with his fiancée – I'm sure you take my point. As we drove off up Willow High Street, I waved to Sally and she gave a wistful wave and half smile. I tried to work out why she had come to see me. It wasn't unusual for us to spend time together, we were close friends after all, but for the few months she had been with Jimmy, the word was that they were inseparable.

So Julie and I headed out of Willow. A thousand thoughts ran through my mind, but I couldn't think of a single thing to say. I needed Julie to start, I needed confirmation of where we were at. Finally, when the fields couldn't get any greener and we hadn't passed a house or building for over ten miles, I pulled the car over onto a gravel track and stopped.

'Who's got Lillie?'

Julie looked at me, our eyes finally meeting.

'My mum. I would never feel happy leaving her with anyone else.'

I wasn't having a go at her, but her defensive tone suggested she might have thought so. I found the courage to take hold of her hand.

'Julie, you must *never* tell him. You have to take this secret to your grave. But tell him, well, mmmmm...' And then of course I recalled Jack's words to Julie just before he killed her. 'That's it, Julie! Perhaps you *do* tell him, but explain that I was a huge drunken mistake, that you would never, *ever* want me to know because you simply don't want me to be the father. You wish *so* strongly that Lillie was his!'

Julie scowled at me, pulling her hand away from mine. As I looked at her, I could see that she was chewing the inside of her mouth, furiously mulling over the words she had just heard.

'So, Ritchie, you suggest I tell him the truth, but taint the intention with carefully chosen lies to make him *feel* better? Don't you think I've done enough of that? Don't you think it's time that I cut out the bullshit and tell him the complete truth?' Julie didn't wait for an answer. 'But no! Ritchie *bloody* Angel simply wants to keep the lies alive. Wouldn't it be a lot simpler if I just accepted that you want *nothing* to do with Lillie and I ... and that I continue to just *bloody* lie to him? Wouldn't that make things easier for you?'

Julie had every right to be angry, I knew that, and momentarily I couldn't meet her tears. But surely the main thing here was keeping Julie alive. History had already revealed that it wouldn't be long before Tina found it necessary to divulge the painful truth to Jack, therefore giving him the ammunition to destroy my life. But this way, maybe coming clean early on would make a difference. Jack now being my friend and having the privilege of bringing up my beautiful daughter, with his stunning fiancée and perfect life – surely he wouldn't want anything ruining that. It even crossed my mind that he could possibly feel sorry for me. I couldn't be sure of anything. But maybe, if Julie and I were to make a pact here and now to agree to never meet up again, ensuring that we never, ever give Jack the chance to suspect that Julie was lying, or worse cheating on him, mentally or physically, then just maybe, Jack and Julie De'Vil had the chance to grow old together. That would then leave only one problem – saving Lillie.

We both just sat motionless in our seats, no words, just questions and answers stacking up in different orders in each of our minds. But I was confident, armed with surreal facts that gave tried and tested rhyme *and* reason to mine, but how could I convince Julie? After all, I couldn't explain how history had already reacted to this predicament.

I wound down my window, the warm afternoon air soothing me a little. I looked up to the lilac sky, praying for some divine intervention. I took a few minutes, and then finally turned towards Julie and took her hand again.

'Look, you're due to be married soon. You may well feel

that I'm being totally heartless, but I'm not!'

Suddenly, a burst of desperation and frustration crept over me and the tears started to roll down my face. All that kept rushing in and out of my mind were the facts that I had lived with for all these years – little Lillie, how I never took the chance to know her, and then for her to die at the age of eight... Well, it was madness. And then the horrific death of Julie, and to simply be with her now, it just suddenly became too much and I thought the tears would never stop.

Julie eased forward a little awkwardly, patting my back gently, but then finally pulled me towards her, holding me tightly, squeezing some kind of reassurance into me. I think for a few moments she thought I was putting on a show, but these tears were not false – each one stung like hell. My heart felt as though it was about to burst, something it was getting used to just lately.

'Ritchie, I know you haven't asked for *any* of this grief, and maybe this is all too soon after your mum's death, but you're confusing me.'

I finally managed to lift my head up and look her in the eyes. I laughed, a little embarrassed by my outburst. Julie smiled and chuckled with me, wiping my eyes, compassion filling her concerned face. I felt an incredible bond; a spiritually unrequited love perhaps? I think having lost my virginity to her, well, that lasts forever, however bad, good or otherwise. But knowing that she's the mother of my daughter, well that's an honoured level in itself. The tears today? For the daughter I simply dismissed and for the inhumane way that I had treated Julie, and once we did finally commit to some kind of closure, within a couple of hours any positive memories were splattered with her own innocent blood.

We both sat in silence, simply looking at our entwined hands. I reflected vividly on us lying in bed together on her final day. As we lay there, there was undoubtedly something incredibly natural between us. But we both knew it could never be allowed to happen again. Had Julie been allowed to live, I believe wholeheartedly that we would have gone our separate ways. After all, I never doubted she loved Jack. And my love for Yasmin, well, it made our decision an easy one. So, the love we felt? The bond that we had? It was set in the stars! But the conclusion was that it was a mixed-up destructive union. And had it gone undetected, well, fine. But of course, there was one man that couldn't live with any of it, and so his way of handling the hurt was to torture me. Once Julie and I took our story to the next level, he couldn't be satisfied with simply torturing me; he would undoubtedly want to destroy me! And of course, who could blame him? But to kill Julie, to wipe her out, *just like that*, surely he wouldn't have been able to live on knowing what he had done. And as for me killing Jack? Well, I will always believe it was him or me.

And so, as Julie looks for answers from me, I can almost see it in her eyes – she sees me as a weak, spineless guy, blubbing like a spoilt child, just trying to get his own way. But there's a change in her tone and she seems to gain new strength from my weakness.

'Ritchie, take me home. I agree with you, I'll have to pick my moment, but maybe I should tell him, and the way you've advised.'

But as she says the words, my heart starts to race. I feel as though the floodgates are going to be opened and that the power of the torrent will sweep me away. My mind is trying desperately to cover every possible scenario: Is it the right decision? Maybe Julie needs to just make sure that Tina keeps her mouth shut! But the more I question and try to anticipate the future, how can I possibly? Circumstances will change, it's inevitable. Tina is bound one day to spill the beans. Though she thinks the world of Julie, I can't help but believe that her jealousy is an accident waiting to happen. I think Tina's sad life, in her squalid flat with her drunkard boyfriend, brings her down, and that's when she's at her most dangerous. So *maybe,* Jack hearing it from Julie, perhaps making it clear that they go into their marriage without any secrets, perhaps a logical and ethical approach, will appeal to Jack's better nature. And as I start the engine and we make our way back to Willow, the words *better nature* keep rotating in my mind... Better nature – does Jack have one?

I dropped Julie off as soon as possible, and as I watched her head off towards her mum and dad's house, I realised that I would have to look over my shoulder for the next few days. I nearly jumped out of my young skin as I felt a small hand on my leg.

'Good God, Rose! I *wish* you wouldn't do that!'

Rose laughed mischievously, but then flicked her hair back, trying to stretch up and check her reflection in the car vanity mirror.

'Well done, Ritchie, I think you've done the right thing there. I know it won't be easy keeping away, but I agree with you. Julie coming clean? He's no reason to doubt that you're being kept in the dark. Just make sure you *do* keep away. I know you'll be tempted to see Lillie, but that would simply confirm to Jack that he's being misled, and as we both know, that would be suicide! Anyway, you managed it before.'

I frowned, a little hurt by Rose's flippant comment. Lillie was a sensitive subject.

'I'm sorry, Ritchie, but it's true!'

Rose tweaked her fringe, but as I looked in her mirror there was nothing! I felt an unnerving reality check travel the length of my spine and I shook my head, determined not to start questioning my sanity levels again. Rose slumped back into her seat, continuing to offer her opinion.

'But the trouble last time, Ritchie, was that Jack started to fester, like a time bomb! He just ticked away, his resentment building, until ... *BOOM!*'

I jumped again.

'For God's sake, Rose! *Please,* not today, my nerves can't take it!'

Rose spluttered through her fit of giggles, but, staunchly determined to force her words out, 'But, Ritchie, I really think you might just manage it this way. I'll keep my fingers crossed!'

I laughed at Rose. 'Fingers crossed? This is serious stuff!! If it is only a matter of keeping our fingers crossed to achieve what we're after, then this should all be easier than I thought!'

Rose pulled an indignant face. I laughed and shook my head.

'Sorry, Rose, no, you're right. I really hope that he does end up feeling sorry for me, a bit of pity in my direction, bring it on! If it means we don't end up arch enemies, then that's exactly what I'm after, my *over-dressed* little friend!'

Rose leapt up, now standing on the car seat, her fingers suddenly ruffling my hair and then, totally unexpectedly, blowing full force into my ear.

'*Rose!* You *little* bugger!'

We both looked at each other, and between bouts of playful giggles, I managed to sum up what I was desperate to achieve.

'So, Rose, you would agree with me, right? All that matters is that Lillie and Julie get to make old bones.'

I drove away from the Oaks estate, not convinced that being seen talking to myself in my car would be a positive step in eliminating my new 'village idiot' title.

Rose continued to talk. 'When are you seeing Harry Christian, Ritchie?'

I looked at my suddenly serious friend, a little surprised at the slightly concerned look on her face.

'Tomorrow at 3 p.m., but I'm playing it straight.'

'I know, Ritchie, but, well, there's something we're a little concerned about.'

I nod, keen to hear what Rose has to say about good *old* Harry.

'Now, Ritchie, it may genuinely be nothing, but this is all quite new to me ... us! And we, as your guardians, feel it necessary to warn you, well, to take extra care with Harry. In fact, though we all felt it sensible to rewrite history here, on wise reflection we now mathematically know you have to play it exactly the way you did before.'

I pulled the car sharply onto the grass verge, stopping quickly.

'But why, Rose? How the hell is that going to help anything?'

Rose took my hand, her vague expression searching for the words.

'Ritchie, we all felt the same concern, but none of what you're out to do can be fully achieved if the change of events don't present themselves in the order and depth that's required. In a nutshell, your life needs to tread the same path as before, and we're now so totally convinced that you need to go through the motions in the same way, even down to tampering with the oil tank, your dealings with Guy Nelson, Harry Christian, William Heart, Mr Ball! When we've tried to predict a chain of events that would steer you successfully through this journey that will eventually save your life, *all* strategies fail. The only proven path is a tried and tested one, the very same path you walked previously; simplistic, embarrassingly obvious, but painfully necessary! So, *carry on as before.* It's how you deal with things once you receive your ill-gotten gains that you will be judged for.'

Suddenly, a loud toot of a car horn made me turn around, and there, headlights flashing, was the bright yellow Porsche of Jack De'Vil. My heart stopped. I quickly turned to Rose, but she was gone. I stepped out of the car, my legs shaking in unknown anticipation, but I smiled as I usually would as Jack strode calmly towards me.

'Ritchie, you old *fucker!* What are you doing parked at the roadside? Car trouble? The bland rep-mobile fallen asleep on you?'

I laughed, almost inanely, with the sheer relief that it wasn't a confrontation, which I didn't have the energy for.

'Oh thanks, Jack. No, everything's fine, just a little splutter, but I think it's cleared itself now!'

Before Jack jumped back into his car, he yelled, 'RITCHIE! FANCY A DRINK? WHIPPET'S? TWENTY MINUTES?'

I was taken aback, keen to keep my distance, but without the time to think up a believable excuse I nodded, and that was it, he roared off. I knew it wasn't a good idea going for a drink with Jack. After all, it would seem strange to Julie. But it was too late, I'd said yes, and perhaps if I was to make it a one-off, then maybe there would be no harm done.

I pulled into the car park and nearly drove straight off again as I saw Yasmin getting out of Scottie's car. She looked *so* painfully beautiful, and it felt like yesterday when I was the proud man that would walk into the pub with her. I cannot fully explain the agony and frustration that I felt, but it was as though a knife had been pushed into the pit of my stomach and being given permission to pull the weapon out, but having insufficient strength to do so – so the life would drain out of me, a slow drawn-out death. And for me to be seen drinking with Jack De'Vil, well, I know she wouldn't approve. Yasmin had never been keen on him, simply felt that he came across unnervingly cocky and aggressive. Her opinion being, that when he stood before her, he would be undressing her with his eyes. And the truth: absolutely yes, that's Jack's way. Totally confirmed as I've got to know him more. But to his credit, he would be the first to admit that some girls didn't feel comfortable around him, but then to others, his arrogance and self-assuredness would undoubtedly appeal.

I waited in the car park for Jack, as I wasn't keen to enter the pub alone. As I sat reluctantly, wanting to be anywhere but here, I could see Yasmin and Scottie ordering their drinks at the bar. Their little kisses and touches, simply another twist of the knife! I shook my head with relief, momentarily grateful as they finally disappeared into a cosy corner and out of sight. But then imagination can be *far* more creative than reality. I drummed my fingers impatiently on top of the steering wheel, shaking my head vigorously, questioning how I could be so weak. Because of my fear of upsetting Jack, I was physically unable to walk away from this dreadful scene. Despite suffering inexplicable pain at the mere mention of Yasmin and Scottie's names, here I was having to watch their obvious intimacy unfold in front of me, simply because of the hold the *devil* had over me. I was astounded by his power. You feel that being older and wiser, you would consistently handle things better. But when you're thrown back into the context of the situation that unnerves you the most, it would appear that nothing changes. My mind resorted back to my wife and her boyfriend – were they now sleeping together? Just thinking the words nearly choked me. I was now slumped onto my steering wheel, such was my inability to hold my head up.

I know that Yasmin and I waited for quite a while, but that was *us*. I had wanted everything to be *so* perfect, the taking of her virginity to be something that we would both remember forever. And though Scottie was a close friend, I felt so unhealthily envious. Severe moments like this almost touching on inexplicable hate. I recalled an incident with Scottie and a wonderful girl when we were all just fifteen years of age. He had confessed his undying love for the poor deluded creature. His unquestionable sincerity in her eyes having procured her virginity within the space of a fortnight. Having achieved his goal, her use now at an end, I painfully recall the moment he ended it, me having been dragged in as an unwitting witness to what proved to be such a hateful moment in my life and hers. He started off so promisingly. 'Look, it's not you, it's me...' I winced as I vividly remembered the hurt in the poor broken girl's eyes, though a pain that was about to get cranked up a notch or two further as Scottie added, 'It's just that I think, well, that I can do *so* much better than you...' He of course thought it was incredibly funny, but I was sure I heard the poor girl's heart break. My loathing for Scottie on the romance front wasn't something I was proud of, but nonetheless justified. I knew that Scottie wouldn't think twice if Yasmin came on to him. Taking her virginity would be just another notch on his bedhead.

'OH SHIT!' I yelled. 'I really cannot bear this!'

I tried to think of something else, but I had become increasingly agitated and hot. I opened the car door and stepped out, desperate for some fresh air. Just as I did so, the roar of an engine made everybody turn and stare, a crescendo of rubber on dusty tarmac bringing the devil's Porsche to a halt. Just nudging my shin bones, all I could do was fall forward onto his bonnet, my hands slamming hard against the bright yellow paintwork. I lifted my eyes just in time to see the full spectrum – from amused to not so amused, just visible through the heavily tinted windscreen. Jack was out of his car in a flash.

'Oi! You silly bastard! *Get the fuck off it!*'

As I finally managed to get myself upright, and as my breath returned,

'Jack, you cheeky git! *You ran into me!*'

Jack slapped my face hard and my head rocked. For a few ear-ringing seconds, there were three Jack De'Vils standing before me. I was suddenly aware of Jack's middle face stepping right up to me, his cigar breath intrusive around my mouth and nostrils. There was now just the one Jack and I waited, not saying a word, the sheer anticipation of what was about to happen striking me dumb. I lurched back, startled as Jack threw his arm around me, my recoiling manner suddenly reassured as I was led obediently towards the pub.

As we stepped into the lounge, Jack leant right into me, his lips almost brushing against my ears as he spoke.

'Mmm, Ritchie! That player mate of yours is in here with that *well* fuckable Yasmin bird!'

We started to move forward again, Jack's arm finally leaving my shoulder as we stood elbow on bar, mirroring each other, Jack now aiming his words teasingly towards Romeo and Juliet in the corner.

'Shit, Ritchie! What *does* she see in him? When she could have me!'

Scottie didn't respond and Yasmin gave a withering look of tiresome amusement. I dropped both elbows onto the bar, the sheer frustration of just not wanting to be here almost bringing on an uncontrollable fit of the giggles, or as I pondered the thought an unstoppable outbreak of tears, finally resulting in me curling up into the foetus position, right here at the bar, to be finally taken away and sectioned. But instead, I heard a *hanging on in there* line of questioning leave my lips.

'What about Julie? I thought it was real love with you two! Getting married and all that...'

Jack turned to me, a look of disrespectful amusement on his face.

'Angel, you *soft* shit! Of course I love Julie, and so what if I make her Mrs *bloody* De'Vil? Doesn't mean I can't look! I'm a *hard,* desirable bastard, and that's what women want, not some puppy dog! I treat Julie like a queen, but she knows, scratch the surface of Jacky boy and I'm as crude and slick as the oil that runs through my veins!'

As I downed my fourth pint of ice-cold lager, my mind started to seek alternative ways of survival. I simply couldn't look at Yasmin, and so I questioned my ability to move on and perhaps forget about her. As I stood there, I was a single man. Not really answerable to anyone. The only reason I was putting myself through all this pain was simply to get back to being thirty-five, fit and well, and able to be a family again with my wife and daughter. But what if I didn't want to play ball? What if I decided that the chances of making amends were painfully slim? And that perhaps I should just build a new life, try to meet someone else? Maybe in time have a child or two of our own? And as I contemplated this perhaps *easier* option, I felt uncomfortable and a well of panic rose within me.

I looked around, keen to ignore my heart, my soul, and so in trying to see if there was anyone who remotely tempted me, my eyes just fell towards Yasmin. I was totally hooked, and the more I knew she was slipping away from me, the more I knew I had to fight to get her back. But being positive, totally determined, wasn't going to be easy. I was going to need help. As Jack's irrelevant ranting bounced in and out of my floating mind, I closed my eyes and prayed for strength. But though cocooned and feeling happier behind closed eyes, I knew I had to be strong and open them. As I did just that, suddenly brave enough to face my demons, the torture simply increased. Scottie and Yasmin, their kisses intense and searching, Scottie's hands caressing intimately. Then, as though my tormentor knew I couldn't take any more, as though my prayer was being answered, my eyes were unexpectedly covered, two soft hands blacking out the hateful scenes.

'Guess who, gorgeous?'

A heartfelt gratitude rose up from the pit of my stomach as I placed my hands over petite warm fingers. I knew instantly that it was Leoni. I turned and leapt a little gung-ho into her sparkling, life-saving eyes – turquoise, several shades lighter than Yasmin's, but she was *just* what I needed. I could see her lips moving, though synchronicity wasn't totally mine just yet, so whatever she was saying was blurring into the vision of Jimmy and Sally hesitantly making their way into the pub, and then to Jack's eyes absorbing every inch of Leoni, his usual smarmy banter convincing me that the flurry of words and visionary madness were simply the result of my imminent insanity. But then came a hard slap on the back.

'Ritchie, my bestest buddy! How the hell are you?'

Jimmy thrust his hand into mine, almost breaking my fingers with his new clumsy handshake, and suddenly my head was back in the room. Sally gave me a gentle peck on the cheek. Her pensive look concerned me and of course reminded me that we still needed our chat. But the much needed friendly gathering had one serious side effect – Scottie and Yasmin joining us. And so, as I took a couple of excessive deep breaths, I felt that the only way to get through tonight was to get positively steaming drunk. It wasn't really my way, but due to my newfound circumstances, it was beginning to become a bad habit. For tonight at least, any thoughts of reform would have to be put on hold.

The subject of my disgraceful behaviour was raised by Scottie, but nicely buried when Jimmy and Sally made it quite clear that it was totally out of character for me to do such a thing, and that in all their years of knowing me – and, in their words, 'loving me' – they had never seen me do anything quite like it. And therefore, everyone should simply forgive and forget. I raised my glass hesitantly, waiting for the support from the rest of my now fairly inebriated friends. Jack unfortunately was the first to add his views.

'Fucking hilarious if you ask me, Angel! I'll drink to your forgiveness!'

Everyone seemed to wince at Jack's insensitive response, and I couldn't help but shake my head as I noticed Yasmin turn to me, the obvious biting of her tongue keeping a lid on her keenness to respond. Scottie thrust his glass forward, amusement and embarrassment in his shaky voice.

'*Hear, hear!* We'll let you off with a warning, just this once, eh, Yaz?'

Yasmin didn't need to say a word, her eyes spoke for her. I had to look away and bury myself in the search for the bottom of the glass.

In my steadily increasing blur of an evening, I prayed that I wouldn't do anything to undo their forgiveness. Yasmin of course being the exception, in her bow of defiance to the majority. And though I craved a smile, a new beginning, a chance, I had to settle for the support from my friends, and be grateful for that.

As I left the safety of half a dozen pints of lager, my logic was slowly drowning in the wake of three or four glasses of *Jack Daniel's*. I questioned whether or not I could possibly be thrown forward in time. The inescapable joy of finding out three or four weeks down the road that I had indeed managed to disgrace myself further! Once and for all losing the respect of those that mattered to me. I escaped to the toilets, suddenly desperate for water. As I finally pulled away from the magical sobering effect of the warm putrid *council pop*, it dawned on me that Rose and her cronies would leave me be, especially as I had my important meeting with Harry Christian tomorrow. And so I decided to relax, safe in the knowledge that whatever I achieved tonight, it would be down to me. I stepped back into the pub lounge and hovered for a second before finally squeezing in between Jimmy and Leoni. Despite intentions to the contrary, my eyes were drawn to Yasmin, and though her gaze crossed from left to right, she simply would not engage in a moment that would possibly let me off the hook. And so – perhaps fickle, but more realistically simple for survival – I decide to focus on the antidote, and as Leoni rested her head on my shoulder, coaxing a smile, we created a haven in which I felt cocooned from reality.

As the evening wore on, Leoni finally developed a taste for the *Jack Daniel's* too – despite glass one making her face contort and her shoulders tremble, she seemed to like the after-effect. And so it would seem that not only was Leoni being converted on alcohol preference, but as the little touches and the small intimate kisses increased it would appear that I was managing to convince her that the male of the species may be a little more appealing than she had first thought. And within seconds of my deep, meaningful wishful thinking, Leoni whispered the question I had thrown at her about her sexuality, her giggles covering any embarrassment. So, our little private in-joke almost became my personal crusade – to find out for definite whether she was gay or not, for her own good of course. As a friend, I felt that maybe she could test herself, me being the self-sacrificing guinea pig. Our discretion was obviously a little off, as Jack pushed his evil grin between our scheming heads.

'If you want a *real* man, Leoni, forget Angel. Bit of a *faggot* I've heard! Jacky boy will happily oblige!'

I winced for the second time this evening at Jack's subtlety and waited for Leoni's response, but I needn't have worried, as she just laughed and shoulder-barged Jack out of the equation. He looked a little hurt, but then simply shrugged his shoulders and seemed to feel that this was as good a time as any to bid his farewell.

'Lovely evening, guys! *Fucking* marvelous company! Must now go home to the wonderful Julie!'

And with his drunken slur, he made his way pinball-like out through the pub door. Our chat stopped dead and our heads craned as we witnessed Jack clumsily dropping into his Porsche, and within minutes speeding off into the night. So there we all were. My beautiful wife, but with my mate Scottie, sitting happily and unchallenged on his lap, brushing the side of his face with her soft, delicate hand – how on earth do you deal with that? On the other side of the table was Jimmy, totally on cloud nine with the love of his life, Sally. Even though affectionate with her man, she appeared to have something on her mind. And here, right beside me, was my painkiller! Though not having ventured down the romantic road with Leoni originally, as of course I only had eyes for Yasmin, with that union totally out of bounds Leoni was a wonderful sight for battle-sore and bereaved eyes. And her warmth and interest? Well, it was becoming quite intoxicating.

And though foolishly believing that I was immune while enveloped in my haven, my eyes were drawn to Scottie, who seemed to be suggesting to Yasmin that it was time for them to leave. But as my heart seemed to stall, to my sheer delight Yasmin slid off Scottie's lap, and perhaps having also seen the distance in Sally's eyes this evening, felt it necessary to be a true friend. But within five minutes or so, Sally having suitably reassured Yasmin that she was just tired, Scottie got his way, and I simply couldn't look as they disappeared into the privacy of the night.

Sally finally stood up, beckoning to Jimmy.

'Home, James!'

Having left Leoni and me to simply gaze into each other's eyes, I asked *the* question, 'So, Leoni, where do we go from here?'

And there was something about the innocent face before me,

the touch of her warm hands, the depth of her teasing smile, that stirred a basic carnal response from deep within, that increased the potency of my aim for this evening.

'Leoni, you are without any doubt *ridiculously* gorgeous!'

As my hand pushed firmly onto the small of her back, I stroked gently and just let her eyes devour me. Twenty, thirty seconds later I felt it time for words.

'Well, Leoni, have you decided whether or not you want me to walk you home? Or were you hankering after the charms of Yasmin, or perhaps Sally?'

Leoni laughed out loud, and then rested her fingers very gently on mine. She didn't have to say a thing. I wasn't imagining what was happening here. As we left the pub, I waited for the chemical reaction of alcohol and fresh night air. I laughed, surprised as a degree or two of sobriety seemed to frame the moment. Leoni pulled away from me, turning around, arms stretched out at her sides, spinning, her face turned up towards the stars. I watched intently. Were Yasmin here, wanting me, then I would without hesitation walk away from this girl now. But, as I stand and watch Leoni, I am painfully aware of my absolute inability to have Yasmin, that she is in the arms of another man, and so I'm a completely different person. Not wanted by Yasmin makes me somebody else! And as Leoni stands powerful and challenging before me, there is a charm that appeals to the new me. My cards are dealt! Leoni stops dancing and walks towards me, her turquoise eyes hypnotising me with every step, and I simply pull her to me. Her body is so warm, and her warmth is exactly what I cannot let go of.

Suddenly, the lights of the pub are switched off and our eyes adapt slowly to the darkness that has encased our haven. Just a small outside light is shining close to the entrance. My bland hatchback is the only vehicle in the car park. Leoni's hands caress my back and I don't want her to stop. She pushes against me; her breasts beneath the cool cotton of her white gypsy blouse have my undivided attention. My hands wander slowly and gently beneath the soft cotton, my fingers following the contours of her spine. Our eyes smile with a hesitancy, a fear of where this is leading. I take in the fullness of Leoni's lips. I test my resolve, try and hold myself back, but then I weaken, desperate to brush my lips teasingly against hers. She tries to provoke some urgency, soft, urgent kisses, and then the slightest touch from her teasing tongue. I pull away, feeling the need for a secluded spot. I notice the five- or six-foot-high entrance sign propped up firmly on the grass verge, the light beaming against the front of it, but a discreet shadow cast behind it. I take Leoni's hand and lead her to the soft grass. She pushes her lips onto my face, her hands now firm on my stomach. I open my eyes, taking in the moment, and I notice how small beads of light are filtering through brail-like holes in the sign, creating a subtle haze around us. I slip onto my knees, my lips and hands taking in every curve of Leoni's body. I pull her to me, her short floaty skirt covering my face. My hands caress her firm bottom and I can feel the outline of her panties. I bring my hands slowly around to the front of her skirt, no curve or contour untouched. I raise my eyes to meet Leoni's – her urgent sparkle gives me confidence. I lift the hem of her skirt, and as the light catches the white silk of her panties, she takes the hem in her hands, lifting it higher. Her slender thighs shimmer in the man-made light and I shake my head in total admiration. As though reading my mind she steps out a little, widening her stance, and suddenly I cannot resist the invitation. I run my fingers onto the soft silk and, in response, Leoni opens her legs a little further. I gently caress her, and then press my lips onto the moist white silk. Leoni pushes herself against my mouth. I bring my fingers up and gently slip the panties down. The blonde curls glisten like gold in the light. I run a firm, hungry finger between her legs, her wetness *so* incredibly welcoming. I quickly ease Leoni's panties to the floor, and she steps out of them. My fingers stiffen in sheer anticipation as I run them around her ankles and then firmly up her calves, before the final straight of her shaking thighs. I push my face into her hot moist curls and eventually let my tongue taste her. My hands are now clenched onto her bottom as my tongue is pushing and teasing, her body writhing rhythmically.

Eventually I rise to my feet, her flinching body demanding more. I lower my eyes, Leoni looking up at me, her wide-eyed appreciation urging me on. I wait teasingly for just a few seconds, Leoni still holding up her skirt. I raise her blouse above her head, her white satin bra heaving beneath the moonlight. I sigh as once again I take in yet another incredible sight – her breasts threatening to break free. A sudden urgency pushes through me, so I roughly unclip her bra, her breasts spilling forward – huge, pert and heavy – and as I stare in awe I feel like a child in a sweet shop. My honoured hands gently caress and knead her breasts, my lips, suddenly unable to resist, fall softly onto her nipples, which swell, erect and wanting in my mouth. As Leoni's moans become more and more demanding, my hand falls once again between her legs. My lips are drawn up to her hungry, urgent mouth. And then, as Leoni lets her skirt hem fall back into place, she caresses me through my suit trousers, finally undoing my belt and unzipping me. I feel huge as she releases me into the cool night air. As her soft warm fingers devour every inch of me, small currents of electricity paralyse me in their wake. And though I could allow myself to be caressed in this way forever, suddenly my hunger for her becomes overwhelming. I cannot get enough as my hands are everywhere, loving each private place on her wonderful body. But as Leoni's kisses start to border on biting and I feel her stretch up onto her tiptoes, I lift her one leg and guide myself quickly and expertly. And as I finally hit the warm heavenly spot, I push very gently into her, and though tight and resisting, I gently tease and coax. Leoni puts her arms around me, pushing her breasts hard into me, and then, just as the moment seems to step up a level, I push my hands beneath her bottom and push a little deeper, each thrust becoming just a little more powerful than before. Leoni's hands are holding on for dear life, up onto my head, back down onto my shoulders. My deep searching thrusts have taken over all that I am and our moans become harmonious, but steadily climbing off the scale. As all my experience as a thirty-five-year-old man finally serves me well as a twenty-one-year-old, it isn't long before Leoni reaches the climatic moment, and through the sheer strength and power that makes me feel as though I could simply take my arms from beneath her and carry on forever, suddenly, unexpectedly, I feel the whole wonderful experience overwhelm me, and as my entire body becomes taut, the world

409

seems to stop *here* and *now*. My eyes roll wide open, taking in the sheer brilliance of my unique lilac moon, but suddenly, as my mortality returns and Leoni slowly slides down my body, we both slump onto the ground until the heavy beating of our hearts steadily, gradually subsides, and we lie totally drained on the fateful, and now *historic* grass.

Neither of us utters a word – we simply bask in the afterglow. But within ten minutes or so, a cool breeze blows cruelly across us. We both shudder and suddenly seem to sober up to the enormity of what we have just done. We quickly gather up our clothes, a smile etched firmly on both of our faces. I watch transfixed as Leoni struggles erotically back into her bra and blouse. She appears a little flustered as she picks up her panties before letting out a small blush and pushing them into her skirt pocket. But the intimacy and warmth that is thick and potent around us will stay with me forever. Determined to erase all thoughts of my past, I feel it best to accept where my life has taken me. And so, based on that, I cannot believe my luck. Leoni is without doubt one of the prettiest girls in Willow. In nearly every conversation you have with a guy on the subject of girls, she will strongly figure, along with the obligatory question concerning her sexuality. So as Leoni takes my hand and leads me away from the pub, I happily follow. I sidle up to her and slide my arm around her waist. She turns towards me, flicking her hair back in that special way that confident gorgeous girls can.

'Ritchie…'

My eyes drop onto her stubble-rash lips, courtesy of yours truly, and *God* it suits her! Leoni looks down at her feet, but then continues.

'Ritchie, I think I know the answer!'

I squeeze her hand tightly, knowing exactly what she's talking about.

'Leoni, there's no need to say a word; I think we *both* know the answer! You were absolutely amazing! I think I'm *still* in shock!'

But Leoni stops and takes both my hands in hers, her eyes now fixed firmly on mine.

'No, Ritchie! I mean, I now know for sure…That I'm gay!'

My breathing stops; the look on my face must have been comical.

'But, Leoni ... *how?*'

'Ritchie, I've only ever had sex once before, with an older guy. Total pervy friend of my dad's, a real shithead! And it really shouldn't have happened. But what I'm trying to say is...it was crap with him, and so, well, I wondered whether it was *that* which made me question my sexuality. But here, tonight with you, I just got caught up in the moment, really enjoyed the closeness with you, and perhaps more importantly trusted you. And, oh shit, it *was* amazing! But, well, when your hands were on my breasts, your tongue inside of me, your, well, you know...' Leoni contorts her face and peers briefly down at my crotch area. 'You know ... *him* inside of me! And as wonderful as it all was, I was fantasising that it was Dana doing all those things to me! Oh God! I know you'll probably hate me, but shit, Ritchie! Please say I haven't hurt your feelings.'

I stepped back, determined not to let the hurt show, but I was devastated. The stuffing had been totally knocked out of me. And as I looked at Leoni, I knew I wasn't in love with her or anything, but given a little time... And yes, I think I could be very serious about this girl! But as I look at her, her confession changing her character suddenly, I know it will never be. After all, this stunning creature that stands before me is crazy about her best mate, spiky-haired Dana! Willow's judge and jury had already summed up and accepted the sexual preference of Dana, but wow, Dana was an extremely lucky girl if she was to end up with Leoni.

As we walked home in the heavy lilac moonlight, Leoni talked and talked, trying to explain how she and Dana had only ever cuddled, never anything more, but now her one big question had been answered.

'Ritchie, for a guy, I wanted you *so* much and I can't imagine it ever being as wonderful as us tonight! I couldn't believe that I would ever be like that, but, although it was physically amazing there was something more spiritual missing, almost as though ... I can't explain it. As though I wasn't being true to myself. In fact, the only way I could really let go, well, was to imagine it was *Dana!*'

'I know, Leoni! You already *said* that!'

Leoni scowled at me and then flung her arms around my neck, suddenly attempting to squeeze the life out of me.

'Ritchie, I love you! I'll never be able to forget tonight, and it will be *you* that made me realise that I was one hundred per cent gay! It will be *you* that I am eternally grateful to!'

I shuffled uncomfortably, almost reading the newspaper headlines now prominent in my head.

'Oh God, Leoni! Perhaps we had better keep that little fact to ourselves.'

Leoni laughed out loud, suddenly feeling the urge to ruffle my hair and run off. But as I watched her run, turning, trying to goad me into playing, I couldn't. It had been a long, long day. My brain was totally done in, my morale down on the floor, my heart full of black painful bruises. And so I think now, all I wanted was to walk Leoni home and then get myself into the safety of my bed.

As I put on my best happy, unhurt and accepting face, I waved Leoni off, her front door closing safely behind her. Alone, walking back home, the effects of the alcohol starting to wear off, my mind inevitably wandered to Yasmin. Was she sleeping with Scottie? Tucked up and happy in *her* new world? And convinced that it was pointless and futile to imagine anything different, accepting logically that it was only natural...*But bloody hell! Would she end up with him long term?* As I walked with heavy painful steps, I couldn't believe how far away from my world I was. How incredible it would be to walk to the Water's Edge, to open up my front door and make my way upstairs to bed, checking first on Evie, just watching her breathe as she slept. I don't think there can be much to match that. And then to finally slip into my bed, the cool cotton sheets, and then Yasmin instinctively cuddling up to me, and when morning finally came around, the three of us planning the simple day ahead. It all seems so incredibly far away. But then to think that Yasmin is only a couple of streets away – or at least I pray she is. In her mum's house, safely out of the clutches of Scottie, dare I believe? I so wanted to see her, to knock on her door, to just look at her. And as I stop in the middle of the road, the vindictive lilac moon shining down on me, I can't help it – my mind is made up.

I ache to see her, and so I start to run, my heart pounding. I look up at the moon and the lilac stars, the backdrop of my running feet echoing in the dead of night. As I turn into Yasmin's quiet little lane, I almost expect Rose to appear, standing before me, making me stop. But then it crosses my mind, and I start to mutter to myself: 'Surely, Rose and the *powers that be* have to sleep…surely they cannot watch me *all* the time!' But as I try and look for weaknesses within their surveillance system, I doubt strongly that there would be any! I laugh as I splutter out: 'they've got their famous archives remember, Ritchie boy!' But my alcohol fuelled stubbornness drives me forward. I walk carefully along the narrow foot bridge at the side of the babbling ford, and as I finally reach the small white picket gate, I look up at the thatched cottage, simply shaking my head at the sheer anticipation of what I'm doing. I know I should turn and walk away. I know that I am risking everything. But as I push the gate open, I feel that just knowing she was here, out of the clutches of Scottie, would at least enable me to sleep tonight. I go to thump on the door with my fist, but stop suddenly. I try to think rationally, but my mind is racing all over the place, and in the absence of waiting for a sensible conclusion I take a few steps back. I bend down and grab a handful of small pebbles. I throw one up at Yasmin's bedroom window, and as the stone clatters across the glass, my heart is in my mouth. I wait, but nothing happens. I throw another, and this time there is a sharper, louder noise. I wait a few seconds, and then the curtain is pulled back and the window is quietly opened.

'Who's there? *Oh God, Ritchie!* What on *earth* are you doing here? It's nearly one!'

I am almost unable to speak, such is the emotion of relief. Tears streaming down my face, I just about manage to squeak out, 'I'm *so* sorry, sorry for everything. I need to speak to you urgently.'

Yasmin looks flustered.

'Ritchie, *please* go home!'

I just stare at her, the beautiful girl that has never refused me anything. But as a few wordless seconds tick away I'm thrown a look that suggests she's had a change of heart. Her window closes, and then I notice the downstairs light go on. The front door opens, a little noisier and quicker than I had expected, and then I step back startled as Yasmin's mother appears.

'What on *earth* do you think you're doing, *young* man? If you don't go now, I will call the *police!*'

I try to reason with her, but she steps forward, her face urging obedience. As I turn, feeling it wise to leave, I glance back quickly.

'Please! Just tell Yasmin that I apologise for *everything*. I mean it! Please tell her that *one day* she'll understand.'

I hear the slamming of the cottage door ringing in my ears, but I'm suddenly moving at an incredible pace. My first fear is that it's all over, that I'm being hurled forward to the dreaded death scene on the decking at the Water's Edge. But then I'm off my feet, being twisted around and hurtling backwards, and then I'm slammed into a hard cold wall. The screeching of a howling wind in my ears finally stops. I look around and I'm back in my room at my mum's house. And then I see the face I expected, sitting, arms folded, on the end of the bed – my *friend* Rose.

'Oh dear me, Ritchie! I really thought I could trust you. You are a *total* fool. Well, that's it, it's *all* over!'

I suddenly feel nauseous.

'God, please, Rose! I couldn't help it!'

The tears start to roll down my cheeks, the full horror of Yasmin and Evie waking up and finding me dead by the side of the water just too much. I knew I had been a fool.

'But it doesn't stop you, does it, Ritchie? I told you! I warned you!'

But I knew I had pushed them too far this time.

'Please, Rose! I'll do anything! Please give me one more chance. I mean it, I'll do anything!'

Rose rocks from side to side and then climbs down off the bed.

'Ritchie, I can't promise anything, but I'll try for you. But we're not happy at all, and I doubt they'll go for it.'

Rose rests her hand on my arm, her thumb rubbing gently, a

look of pity filling her young face.

'Ritchie, each time you do this, they simply feel that I have been misguided in wanting to help you, but I will try, and I'll let you know their decision in the morning. For tonight at least, you'll sleep here and not the Water's Edge.'

Rose was gone, and as the full horror of my actions sank in, I pushed all the air out of my lungs. Then my heavy eyelids closed and I drifted into a much-needed deep sleep.

As the morning arrived I waited, simply expecting every moment to be my last. My heart felt genuinely sorry, and in the cold light of day I knew that I had to finish what I had started here. But Rose didn't come, and my day proceeded as planned.

'So, Mr Christian, that's everything. I feel that in the circumstances, the bakery should fetch sufficient funds for the retirement bungalow you have mentioned. But of course, the bakery is not in the best of health, which will reflect in any offers we get.'

Harry Christian looked at me, his eyes sparkling more than I ever remember, but I felt that I was just being paranoid. There was no way that he could have any knowledge of what I was proposing to do. I finally managed to convince myself that it was my guilt, nothing else. *Just the sheer power of guilt.* I should understand above all others that guilt could be the instigator of weird and incredulous happenings, so it was this that gave me an unsettled feeling when faced with my past. As I shook Harry's hand, I referred to *his* suggestion that we perhaps should meet at the flat instead. Harry tapped the side of his nose and gave a friendly wink before scurrying off towards the bakery.

The rest of the day passed uninterrupted. I felt that if I kept my head down and concentrated on the job in hand, perhaps my actions would speak louder than any self-pitying apology. I had spoken to Guy Nelson, the American fast-food representative, a couple of times now, and I have to recommend to all you business entrepreneurs out there that knowing exactly how the script is set gives you an incredible business advantage. That, and an inner confidence, not only raised my stature in his eyes, but also enabled me to override the weeks of limited sleep that played havoc on my exhausted complexion first time around. And as I punched the buttons on my calculator, planning my property empire, it all seemed rather like taking candy from a baby. But more importantly, it got me a step closer to purchasing the Water's Edge. As I rolled through my business plan, I recalled Rose's words, and exactly how crucial each piece of the jigsaw was going to be. I accepted that I needed to make sure that I set myself up well in the here and now. I knew that my aim was to get back to my old life, and I prayed that this could be achieved. But it was only just starting to dawn on me, what if this was it? What if I was never allowed to go back? What if all my seed sowing now was to be all that I reaped? I knew that once I had turned twenty-five I would then be allowed to pursue Yasmin, but what if she was to create a world that I couldn't penetrate? Scottie? Three screaming kids around her ankles? If they were my children, then fine, but somebody else's? I couldn't be sure I could handle that, not after all we'd had together. But whatever went on in Yasmin's world, I undoubtedly needed to make a success of myself, and along the way ensure that I made amends for the three bad things I had done. But maybe – and of course I was purely speculating – just maybe, regardless of how I make amends, perhaps as a booby prize I will at least be able to stay with the new life I create for myself? But as I considered this I felt uncomfortable deep within – a life without Yasmin? Without Evie? It burnt and singed my soul! And yet, there was a *very* real possibility that I may not have *any* life at all, as Rose hadn't come back to me with her punishment for yesterday's rule-breaking yet!

My working day was drawing to a close. I had telephoned Scottie asking whether or not he would mind picking me up after work, as of course I had left my car at the pub. He readily agreed, stating that he was more than happy to do so, and that it would give us chance to have a pint and a chat. He excitedly informed me that Yasmin and he were getting on brilliantly, and that he would fill me in on the details. As I replaced the receiver, I couldn't help but say to myself under my breath, 'Great, can't wait for that, Scottie boy!'

Scottie was a good twenty minutes late, but as I eventually

jumped into his car we sped off towards the Whippet's. As my dear friend drove, it was painfully how I had envisaged: Yasmin this! Yasmin that! Really, there was only one thing that I wanted to know, but I simply didn't have the courage to ask him, not yet at least. I deliberated the word courage; it wasn't the question that troubled me, but of course the pain of the answer.

The pub started to get quite busy, but Scottie and I kept ourselves to ourselves. Yasmin had decided to stay in and spend some time with her mum. Though I wanted to believe it was a good sign, that maybe her interest in Scottie was waning, I knew full well that every few nights Yasmin had done that with me. So I didn't build my hopes up too much. Scottie left me on my own for a few moments while he disappeared to the gents. Suddenly, as I'm looking around the pub, my eyes start to lose clarity, the lilac tinge that I was so used to now a couple of shades darker. I looked at my hand holding my glass, and the colour of my lager is almost the colour of blackcurrant. I can't help but feel that this does *not* bode well. And then, from nowhere, on Scottie's stool *is* Rose. The rest of the pub, though still active, seemed now to be running on a continual loop over a two-second cycle; it was incredible to witness.

'Ritchie, I didn't like to leave my news a second longer, but I have to tell you, you really have upset the powers that be! I mean it, Ritchie. I know you see me as only eight, and I don't like to swear, but they're really pissed off with you! They weren't having it at first; that was it, they were sending you back. They don't believe you are capable of achieving our aim, and I don't really believe that they trust you now to complete your task.'

I was extremely nervous and started to interrupt.

'Rose! Please, if I don't make amends here, am I allowed to continue in *this* life, thirty-five years of age and beyond?'

Rose frowned at me. 'Not now, Ritchie! I don't know the answer to what you're asking me. Twelve hours ago you had *no* life, it was over. I have had to beg, even *cry* to help you. You have to listen to me. Thanks to my feminine and childlike charms combined, you do have another chance, *but* – and you're not going to like this – you cannot, as a punishment, make any attempts to see Yasmin until you're twenty-seven! They have put another two years on!'

My mouth drops open.

'Two years, Rose? Oh shit! *Why?* I know I was a prat, but I was drunk, pissed off! And it's not easy all this you know. It was just a momentary lapse…'

'Ritchie, it's not the first time you've broken the rules. But we know this is hard, and it's in understanding that, that made them see you were perhaps worth another chance. But I have to say, this morning you were going back! Water's Edge … *dead!* They simply felt that you weren't up to the challenge.'

Rose's words chilled me. I think the trouble was that four years was such a long way off, but each day survived seemed to just keep me hanging on. But then, just like that, two more years. Well, I was totally devastated…

Rose slipped down off her stool, and came and hugged me.

'Ritchie, you've got to stay strong. I really don't think that a third chance would be an option. In fact, you must be warned, this really *is* your last chance.'

As Rose let go of me, she let out a pitying smile and then disappeared. The toilet door swung open and Scottie strode across the room, the lilac haze fading fast.

I felt so very numb, but I knew I only had myself to blame. Scottie was really downing his drinks – a man who perhaps had his own problems. I pushed a twenty-pound note across the table.

'Keep them coming, Scottie!'

The next hour was a blur. Although Scottie was chatting, my mind was drowning in many questions and half-hearted answers. Had my visit to Yasmin changed her opinion of me? If so, then maybe I had to believe that the extra two years was a small price to pay. And as I straightened my back, a strength of spirit seemed to pick up my mood. Had I won a battle with the powers that be, after they had tried to destroy Yasmin's image of me? I knew it unwise to provoke my helpers, but should I continue to skip forward in time whenever necessary, then perhaps I should take encouragement in the genuine belief that this journey would be shorter than I first thought. Two, even three years could be swallowed in the flicker of a dozen sunsets

– an era that could be brushed aside in a walk the length of Willow High Street. I pondered the thought. *Was I being foolish, flippant?* If Yasmin had spent just a moment or two thinking about me today – my mad, compulsive visit – she may just feel that it was quite a romantic thing to do. If my actions had really changed her opinion of me for the better, then I was utterly justified in accepting my punishment with a smile. But Yasmin at twenty-five, perhaps just in time to sweep her off her feet. But twenty-seven…What if someone else, at twenty-five, perhaps twenty-six, was to step in and make her his? Perhaps I was wrong to dismiss too easily just how significant two years could be, but how could my worrying help me now? I simply needed to learn the lesson, to swallow hard and keep focused. I scratched my head roughly with my nails, the sudden rebellious sting lifting me out of my surreal comatose state of mind.

Scottie was mouthing off to somebody at the bar, but I didn't bother to even look around. I just kept replaying it in my head – sunrise, the Water's Edge, reunited with Yasmin and Evie. If successful, that would be my reward. I sat there on my pub stool, my optimism rising with my brainwashing chant of: *make amends, be allowed to grow old with my wife and daughter, simple business transaction!*

'Oops, sorry, Ritchie!' Scottie said as he splashed an ice-cold dollop of lager down the back of my shirt.

How could I *not* smile? Scottie clanked his already frothing pint clumsily against mine, a wave of alcohol crashing over the top of the glass now soaking my shirtsleeve. How could I *not* laugh? My mood was now acceptingly buoyant. And as Scottie started to become a little maudlin, the steady flow of alcohol inspiring a show of honesty, my ears pricked up and my mood was to be lifted even higher. Scottie divulged Yasmin's lack of interest in giving herself body and soul.

'Come on, Ritchie, tell me! How can she resist the sheer charm of yours truly? But resist me she does! Sure, we'll kiss and mess around a little, but as for what's really important, I mean, come on, I know she's a virgin and all that, but, well, a man can only have *so* much patience!'

How I contained myself from firstly jumping up onto the

table and giving a little *'Yasmin's still a virgin'* dance and then buying a celebratory drink for everyone in the pub, well, I never knew I had such willpower! Instead, I kept my elation deep inside and rewarded myself with giving Scottie a gentle persuasive punch on the arm.

'Oh well, mate, I'm *sorry* to hear that! But maybe you need to start stamping your feet a bit, explain that you may consider looking elsewhere, that there are at least a couple of girls in Willow that would jump at the chance! And, well, that she should be grateful that you have chosen her!'

Scottie was now leaning into me, his head nodding in appreciation at my seemingly *sincere* advice. I felt as though I was walking on eggshells as I continued, but still I offered my support.

'There's always that *Janey!* You know, Yasmin's mate? I have it on excellent authority that she's *really* keen on you!'

Scottie looked at me, mulling over my words. 'Naa, couldn't do that! I mean, Janey's gorgeous, but Yasmin, well, she takes first prize every time!'

I pushed the positives of Janey and called upon *libels* version of poetic licence to reveal the negatives of Yasmin. But as I tried to influence the downfall of this nightmare relationship, would the *powers that be* punish me? Was I blatantly breaking the rules? Scottie staggered to his feet, tottered unsure for a second, but then stretched his arms up to the ceiling. His crotch thrust forward and I seemed to almost leer at my friend's loins, a self-satisfied smugness at *its* lack of success with my beautiful wife. I had to smile, and I was very proud of her. But as Scottie made his way unsteadily to the bar, I reflected on my own weak-willed liaisons, a sudden gust of guilt causing my face to screw up: *one rule for you, one rule for me,* filled my head. Scottie was suddenly slumped back onto his stool.

'Anyway, Ritchie, you sly old dog! What's the score with Leoni? Now, she might well be worth cheating on Yasmin for! Mmm, good tits! *Very fit!'*

I shook my head from side to side, praying that Yasmin was standing behind us, Scottie unwittingly digging his own grave. I felt bad feeling this way towards one of my best friends, and

God knows being responsible for his death originally I sort of owed him one. But Yasmin? That was *far* too high a price to pay.

'Ritchie, you gormless git! Leoni! Spill the beans!'

'Scottie, keep your voice down! I'm sure there's people outside that didn't quite hear you!'

But as it all went over Scottie's alcohol-sozzled head, he goaded some more, and so I decided to let him down gently.

'Okay, Scottie! Well, we're close, but just friends, a bit like you and Yasmin!'

Scottie spat his drink all over the front of my shirt.

I just shook my head and uttered under my breath, 'I suppose I deserved that.'

Scottie sprayed what was left over my face as he challenged my denial.

'Yeah right, Angel, I believe you! Oh, and don't worry about Yasmin and me, I'll soon have my evil way there!'

And then, though seconds too late, there was Yasmin, standing directly behind Scottie. She smiled at me, putting a finger to her perfect lips. She then slid her hands over Scottie's eyes.

'Guess who?'

Scottie turned around as quick as his drunken coordination would let him, placing his hands on Yasmin's thighs, making her short skirt ride up a little. Yasmin lowered her head, placing a small kiss on Scottie's forehead. I took all this in and hated every painful second.

'Mum was tired, wanted an early night, so thought I might pop down here and catch a last drink with you. Oh, and Janey said she might make it down too!'

Yasmin pulled a chair up next to Scottie, his hands all over her. She looked at me, I chose to believe a little embarrassed by Scottie's octopus ways.

'Hi, Ritchie!'

I seemed to slip into her eyes and couldn't help my response to her question.

'High? No, Yasmin, but I *really* wish I was!'

I pushed my chair back and stood up. Scottie gave me a none too subtle wink. Yasmin's eyes didn't leave mine.

'Drugs eh, Ritchie? That would probably explain a lot!'

I shook my head and felt it wise to offer a hasty denial.

'You *do* realise I was joking…?'

Yasmin just smiled, and I felt it wise to simply let it go.

'Can I get you a drink, Yasmin? Same again, Scottie?'

As I stood at the bar, I felt as though I was drowning. How the hell was I going to keep Scottie and Yasmin apart, without facing the wrath of the Gods?

'Yeah, umm, a medium white wine, and the same again for Scottie and me!'

When I'm on my own, away from Yasmin, I feel that I can cope, get on with the task in hand. But then, when I have to see her, well, it's just impossible.

'Oh, and a bottle of Jack Daniel's as well please, Pete, and a glass!'

Pete, the landlord, frowned and then explained why.

'Getting into the booze a bit just lately, aren't you, Ritchie lad? Oh, and while I've got you on your own, your little session didn't go unnoticed with the pretty blonde in the car park last night either! I don't want a repeat of that, well, not unless you warn me next time and I can sell a few tickets first!'

I felt myself blush, a full rerun of our little show causing me to think, *oh nice one, Ritchie* as I paid Pete and made my way back to the table. Janey had now arrived and sat herself down. And as I took my place at the table of torture, she joined me in a glass of Jack Daniel's. The more I drank, the less capable I became of taking my eyes off Yasmin. Her lips, every word she spoke, every time she brushed a stray hair out of her eyes, her simply breathing in and out, the way her breasts would rise and fall… And though I tried to look away I would be pulled back in, it was official: unsurpassed adoration!

Scottie was all over her, but despite the steady loss of his faculties, he seemed to have taken notice of Janey's interest. Yasmin made her excuses and headed off towards the toilets. I waited a moment and then followed her. As I reached the door of the gents, I froze. My breath started to burn and ache, but I didn't move. Why was I being so totally suicidal? But I still didn't move, and then someone stumbled out of the gents, bumping into me, and we made our mutual apologies. But as the slightly worse for wear guy disappeared through the exit, I was left standing face to face with Yasmin, who was now staring straight at me. And there was the look that I had been praying for, had doubted wholeheartedly whether I would *ever* see again, but it was here as we stood, both of us unable to step away from the other. We both seemed to be content with just standing, absorbing each other's breath, but finally it needed one of us to break the moment.

'Yasmin...do you fancy some fresh air? Not being funny, but I don't think those two will miss us for five minutes!'

Yasmin didn't say a word and just nodded. As we stepped outside together, sharing this simple intimacy made me feel almost human again. I just wanted to grab her hand and run, and run, never stopping.

CHAPTER NINETEEN

Suicide Blonde

After Death, 1991 – Lilac Sky

It was dark now, the pub garden empty ... except for me and my wife. We both sat down at one of the garden tables, straddling the bench, our knees touching. I didn't say a word and just looked at her. Yasmin appeared to be quite content, saying nothing and looking at me. She was so young, *so* beautiful, and as we both sat in silence together, it seemed the most natural thing in the world. I glanced towards the pub, the rich tapestry of bodies framed by the glass windows. I could hear a dull roar of laughing, yelling, cheering, and I was glad to be away from it, especially sat here with Yasmin. But after a few moments, she looked down at her knees and spoke softly.

'What was last night about, Ritchie?'

I paused for a moment, waiting for our eyes to lock onto each other again. I almost sighed loudly, as there they were.

'I'm *so* sorry, Yasmin, but you're all I think about! And so...last night, I felt this overwhelming urge to come and tell you…'

But Yasmin didn't seem to mind, and then chose the best seven words that filled my empty, drained heart.

'What do you think Scottie will say?'

And then as to ensure beyond all confusion, that I understood fully her response to my startling confession, her fingers grazed mine. I placed my hand on top of hers and felt the warmth, the sheer electricity that flowed through us both. Yasmin gave me a look that I was beginning to think I would never see again. I raised my right hand and placed it on her cheek, and she pushed her face into my hand. I don't even remember moving my head, but my lips were suddenly on hers, and the softness was incredible, the passion overwhelming. But then the pub door was flung open and we both turned around quickly. It was Janey. Yasmin stood up, and reacting on guilt and sudden nerves, ran over to her friend. Words were quickly exchanged, then they both turned and looked at me before going back inside. It was then that I felt the stinging sensation in the side of my face and the warmth of a rising sun across my back. I couldn't move, not a finger, not a toe. My heart was thumping very slowly. I couldn't open my eyes, but in my mind I could see an entire scene unfolding. The sound of running water seemed to pass by very close to my head. And of course I knew only too well where I was.

Yasmin was throwing cold water on her face, and Evie was running around on the polished wooden floors, her platinum-blonde hair cascading down her bare back. Evie was tanned, and only wearing a pair of white brushed-cotton pyjama bottoms. Yasmin pulled on her silk dressing gown, now covering her naked body. Evie ran down the stairs, excitedly shouting for me.

'DADDY! DADDY! How *come* you *didn't* wake me *up?*'

And as she made her way through the house, I couldn't move; my heart just thumped harder, quicker. Yasmin was now close behind Evie, their happy smiling faces all that I seemed to be focusing on, but gradually, as the scene became slower and the girls had given up looking for me inside the house, Evie ran first to the patio doors. A glance across the stone slabs and the short run of lawn and they would see me on the decking, stretched out, lifeless...I screamed out, but it was only inside. I screamed and screamed, begging for forgiveness, desperate for Rose to help me. And as the small hand turned the door handle, the scene froze. The running water, the late summer breeze, it all simply stopped. Deadly stone-cold silence filled every pore.

But then, as though I am looking down from above, Rose is standing over me. And suddenly, as though the vision is turned off, I'm back in my body and slowly getting to my feet, dusting myself down. There are tears in my eyes and I'm unable to look at Rose.

'Ritchie, the time has come! Look at your house, look at Evie and Yasmin. Within seconds they will walk through that door; it is then that all this is over! I won't be here, and I won't be able to return. Your life will have run its natural course. It happens, people die every day! But they don't get the chance that you have had, and to be blunt and honest with you, I have misjudged you and wasted everybody's time!'

The tears that are rolling down my face are for the fact that I'm here at the Water's Edge, and everything that I want and need is there in my house. Yasmin and Evie are looking for me, and I so want them to find me. I turn my eyes back to Rose.

'Yes, Ritchie, you do want them to find you, and if you could have been a little less selfish, maintained the strength for what was required of you, then *in-time* you would be waiting excitedly for Evie's little hand to turn that handle, perfectly able to wish them good morning.'

I push out my hands to Rose, but she shakes her head and breaks my heart.

'No, Ritchie, *you've* failed.'

I'm aware that I'm being forced back onto the decking, the next hateful scene being prepared. As I buckle and fall onto my knees, large powerful hands seem intent on snapping my spine. I start to pray, and as I beg for forgiveness, an invisible force all around me, my mind is filled with distorted images of Yasmin and Evie, but as I push out my prayers, my neck is suddenly relaxed, all force removed – though I am painfully aware that I am unable to move from the position I have been *so* determinedly placed. Running through my mind is self-pity and tears of despair, but then the images of Yasmin and Evie become clear and detailed. Evie is now, hands raised, on the lawn looking up to the skies. My words, *begging for forgiveness*, are falling like newspaper cuttings around her feet. Evie drops to her knees and is now frantically shuffling the letters around, but as *though* breaking up my last desperate plea! My eyes are now drawn to a distraught Yasmin, holding my painkillers and heart tablets that I had hidden away. I hadn't wanted her to *ever* see them. But then my eyes are back on Evie, and I cannot understand why she is trying to destroy my cry for one last chance. Suddenly, having gathered up all the letters, she disappears. I wait. I'm suddenly looking at a clearing. It's not quite at the edge of the water, but amongst a flourish of lilac crocuses, and Evie is talking to someone. I squint my eyes as the letters are laid on the ground, and I can just make out...

TAKEAWAYTHEKISS!

I'm suddenly walking out of the Whippet's Fifth Leg public house, and Yasmin and I are heading for the outside table. I'm painfully aware that I've lived this moment before, but I dare not question it. If this scene delays Yasmin and Evie finding me dead on the decking, then I'll take it and relive it a thousand times. Yasmin and I straddle the bench, our knees touching. I don't say a word and just look at her. Her eyes are bubbling brighter than I can ever recall. No words are spoken, both of us just happy to let the moment steal us away. She is so young, *so* beautiful, and as we both sit in silence together, it is unquestionably the most natural thing in the world. I glance towards the pub, the rich tapestry of bodies framed by the glass windows. I can hear a dull roar of laughing, yelling, cheering, and I am glad to be away from it, especially sat here with Yasmin. But after a few moments, she looks down at her knees and then speaks softly.

'What was last night about, Ritchie?'

I pause for a moment, waiting for her eyes to look up, to engage fully with mine. Suddenly, I am aware of sighing loudly as her eyes are on mine, and she waits for my answer.

But Yasmin's face is suddenly replaced by Evie's, and all I can see deep within her eyes is 'take away the kiss!' I blink furiously, as I am now face-to-face with Yasmin, a look of undoubted concern in her fading eyes at my mere inability to offer her anything at all. My heart is aching to do and *say* so much, yet I am empty, unable, just a shell. The furrow of her brow questions my lethargy to whatever it is she thought we may have, and of course I know that I have to simply walk away.

As I walk, total blackness surrounds me for twelve, maybe fifteen seconds. I question whether I've made a terrible mistake and misread the signs. But then I'm back at my mum's cold empty house the morning after the *horrific* night before. I think about the kiss with Yasmin, a special life-changing moment, but not in the way I had hoped. I now fully accepted the terms. I knew that my crazy short-sighted moments of weakness were just that; not helpful and not welcome.

There was no other reason for being here – I had to make amends. My old life? My new life? They both led to the same place – the Water's Edge, on the decking. It was up to me whether they found me *dead* or *alive*.

'So, we have a deal then? Thank you, Guy!'

The bakery was sold. As Guy Nelson handed me the prewritten deposit cheque for nine thousand pounds, I felt elated – ten grand more than before! This time I let him ask me the quickest way to the motorway and, as cool as a psychic cucumber, I told him. I even threw in, 'Have a safe journey!' And that was that. He got out of the car and finally agreed to ninety thousand pounds.

I enjoyed banking the money, adding it to what I had already made from the Old School. I was now well on my way to financial freedom and security, rather than just praying that I was, as I had done originally. And I was pleased that I was now getting into the spirit of all that was expected of me. I had resisted the tendency to feel tired and uninspired by simply re-treading my original steps. If I was to be convincing, I needed to put on the performance of my life – second life! And after my horrendously close call on having blown my chance of retribution, my mind was now well and truly focused. As I strolled down Willow High Street, wrestling with the exact path that I needed to tread, there was one thing that I had no doubts about. Should I at any time have my tunnelled vision creep even briefly over the safety line, drawing me within a hundred feet of Yasmin, then I knew exactly what to do. To simply, painfully, activate the next scene in Rose's little play: *Evie turning that door handle!* And so, until I'd made amends, I believed that this would be enough.

I was literally twenty paces away from Skirdle's doorway when suddenly, I came face-to-face with Sally.

'Ritchie Angel! Are you trying to avoid me?'

I screwed my face up and uttered my apologies.

'Sally, Sally, Sally! I've, well, I've just been *so* busy, but what is it that's so important?'

She slumped her shoulders and a look of bewilderment convinced me that our talk should not be delayed a minute longer. I popped my head around Skirdle's door.

'I need a couple of hours. If I'm not back tonight, then I'll see you in the morning.'

Mr Ball smiled, eyes large and nodding like a lovesick puppy, then continuing his telephone conversation. As I closed the door, I laughed. Our Mr Ball only ever had that expression when talking to the love of his life, Skirdle junior!

Sally followed me quietly to the car. I turned to egg her on a bit.

'Come on! You look as though you're off to the gallows!'

Sally threw me a forced, un-amused smile, which only added to my increasing-by-the-second concern. My first thought, which of course horrified me, was that I had got her pregnant – a wisp of hysteria fluttered through me at the mere thought. I dwelled on the image of Sally and Jimmy playing with their twins on the Water's Edge lawn. Anything less than that for their future would be tragic; *surely our ill-advised liaison couldn't avert that!* I shuddered and dismissed the pain of such news. I took a deep, much-needed breath and convinced myself that surely with all that was going on in my death, my life, just lately I deserved a break, a brick of optimism to build on. Certainly not a sledgehammer to proceedings just as I was starting to get some kind of grip.

As we headed west out of Willow, the mood was steadily lifted as Sally started to chat about this and that, but nothing so far that would be deemed life-threatening. I felt a wry smile crease my face as I recalled the drive out into the country with Julie – once again, when the fields became greener and we hadn't seen a house or building for miles, I finally pulled over onto the same gravel open space that I had with Mrs De'Vil. I switched the engine off and turned to Sally.

'Come on then, gorgeous! Out with it, what's *he* done?'

Sally turned and looked at my chest, seemingly unable to raise her eyes any higher.

'Ritchie, I'm pregnant!' And then finally, her eyes were on mine. 'I know you're going to ask me how I know, but I just do! Ritchie, it's *your* baby!'

I blinked hard, desperate to sit up with a start, throw off my quilt and realise it was all a horrendous nightmare. But instead I became mentally and physically numb, my breathing having stopped. I failed to simply force myself awake, and I was unable to say anything. My eyes were wide and scanning the inside of my car, the world through the windscreen still and momentarily unreal. A shard of regret for how this must be for Sally, eventually, finally provoked a verbal response.

'But, how do you know it's mine? I mean, well, surely *Jimmy* is the more likely?'

Sally took my hand and let out a deep breath.

'Jimmy and I ... we have only just started sleeping together! We waited and waited. I think Jimmy's been the nervous one, quite a gentleman in fact, but, ummm, once we, well, *did* the evil deed, it was then that I found out he was a virgin! I'd only ever slept with one other guy, before you that is, and that was several months ago! So when Jimmy and I got together, because it was special it felt natural to take our time. I've already been to the doctors, and the dates, *well,* they prove it's yours, Ritchie. I'm *so* sorry.'

My breathing started to quicken and a sense of panic welled up within me. I was suddenly aware of rubbing the sides of my head furiously – it was as though I was overheating. I pushed the door open and jumped out, desperate for air. I walked this

429

way and then that, until returning to the open door, placing my hands on the car roof and leaning in looking for answers.

'So, are you saying, Sally…that you and Jimmy only started sleeping together recently, and so it's a *total* impossibility?'

Sally nodded. I just hung in the doorway, my head resting against my raised arm. Just as I was starting to view my new world a little more positively, simply knuckle down and do the time, I'm suddenly faced with one hell of a dilemma. I couldn't help but wonder what good could possibly come from this.

I slipped back into the driver's seat, trying desperately to keep calm. I twiddled my thumbs for a few silent moments, thoughts and concerns for Sally temporarily dissolving my shock. Of course she was looking for support and answers from me, and the 'out of her depth' look in her eyes seemed to displace my self-pity and pass it over to my partner in crime. But at the same time, I couldn't believe she could be *so* stupid. I was convinced that she would have been on the pill. But of course the truth was, I should have asked. But then, if we're reviewing our actions fairly, then it was just a mad irresponsible moment of passion. As we both sat there in total silence, though, it was undoubtedly an immense price to pay.

I knew that I had to treat Sally right here. I was a man well versed with how emotional a pregnancy can be. As Sally talked, I listened, but my mind was blown to bits. After all, the shock originally when Julie came to me with the news that I was the father of Lillie, it was a lot to take in. And being immature then, perhaps not knowing any better, I had dismissed the pair of them. But now, given a second chance to do the right thing by Julie and Lillie, it was dawning on me that I was going to have to do exactly the same thing for Sally and *our* baby.

'So you see, Ritchie, you know that I think the world of you, but you made your feelings perfectly clear that night that we had … well, I'm sure you remember, but now, well, I've *totally* fallen for Jimmy, and there's no doubt in my mind that *he's* the man for me. So I take it that you agree, that perhaps I need to tell him the truth, gamble that he'll be happy to take me and the baby on even if it's yours?'

My eyes widened, realising that I must have missed part of

what Sally had been saying, but as the words slotted home like three cherries on the one-armed bandit, the truth was that I thought it a terrible idea. Jimmy would without doubt hate me forever. I believed strongly that there was only one answer.

'Sally, I know you'll despise me for saying this, but you have to look at the bigger picture here. I believe more than you can ever imagine that you and Jimmy are meant to be. I know he worships the ground you walk on, but for you to tell him that you're carrying *my* baby... No matter how much he loves you, it will break his heart! How far gone are you? It's just that you could consider...'

Sally's eyes narrowed.

'You *total* bastard, Ritchie Angel! The answer to that *is no!!*'

Sally was furious, her arms raised skywards. I quickly grabbed hold of her hands, trying to calm her down.

'That was despicable, I know, but please try to understand, Sally. You and Jimmy, you have to make it, you can't risk your future because of *our* mistake.'

But as I bore into Sally's hurt and accusing eyes, I was overwhelmed with images of Evie and Lillie, and how they meant the world to me. And though there was no doubting the problems the birth of this baby could cause us all, I also knew that aborting the poor, innocent child was out of the question.

'Sally! Please forgive me. I mean it, I'm not thinking straight. Come here!'

I wrapped my arms around my dear friend, giving her all the warmth and love I could muster.

We drove home very slowly that afternoon, our deep life-changing conversation seeming to have brought about a familiar plan. Mentally my head was reeling; physically, I had the same gut-wrenching feeling when I knew Julie was going to tell Jack that Lillie was mine. I couldn't quite get over the curveball that life was throwing with this fresh and totally unexpected problem. My thoughts were interrupted.

'So, Ritchie, we're agreed? I tell him that it was a terrible drunken mistake, my night with you, and that I don't want him ever telling anyone that the child's yours, that he should never, ever talk to you about it, because I haven't told you. How I don't want it to be Ritchie Angel's baby, but how I wish with all my heart that it was his child. God, Ritchie, I think it might just work. Wow, I have to pray that he really loves me enough to actually go along with it.'

As we drove, idling along well below the speed limit, I repeatedly churned over the ideals of living this lie, Sally's words were drowning in my déjà vu regrets.

'But, Ritchie, should he totally flip out about it, then I'll tell him that you raped me…'

My trance-like gaze suddenly smashed, my panic-stricken eyes now on Sally's. Her serious face suddenly burst out laughing.

'I'm sorry, couldn't help it! It was just your face had gone so expressionless that I wanted to provoke a reaction!'

I shook my head at Sally, uttering, '*Well,* mission accomplished!'

A wry, beaten-into-submission, fearful smile crossed my face as Sally continued with how she was going to break this important news to Jimmy. I had to wonder how all this madness had been allowed to happen. The lilac sky was rolling along quickly in the increasing wind while Sally expressed the depth of her love for Jimmy. I stopped the car just a road away from her house.

'The thing is, Ritchie, as much as I could never terminate a child's life, if I was faced with the dilemma of losing Jimmy…then I suppose I would have to consider it an option.'

Sally seemed to lose her way, hers eyes suddenly moist.

'I love Jimmy that much! And though it goes against all my principles, and though it would haunt me forever…'

Her tears were then falling uncontrollably down her now defeated face. I grabbed and squeezed her hands, and within a few silent moments she seemed to gain some strength from somewhere.

'Ritchie, the only problem I think we might have is that he'll believe he's letting *you* down, you know, with not telling you such an important thing. He's a straightforward guy, and I'm not sure how he'll cope with the lies and the deceit of it.'

Sally had a point, but she also needed to realise just how much her man loved her. I was prepared to bet that Jimmy would rather live with this dreadful secret than live without the love of his life – I believed it to be that simple, and I prayed I was right. As Sally finally climbed out of the car, she looked pensive. I scolded her for chewing the inside of her mouth. We gave each other a good luck hug, and then waved our goodbyes.

As I drove away slowly, I wondered what Rose would make of this mess. But then I imagined what it was going to be like having to stand back and watch Sally and Jimmy bring up my child. My heart felt increasingly heavy and troubled at the mere thought.

As I pulled onto my driveway, I turned the engine off. I didn't want to go into the cold empty house, but the reality was that I had nowhere else to go. I couldn't go to the pub, just in case Yasmin was there. I suddenly caught my reflection in the rear-view mirror and my mind steered away from my nightmare for a moment. I could still be shocked by my appearance – my face looked so young. There were a couple of moles that had appeared on my cheek and forehead over the age of about twenty-five, and a scar that I had picked up when falling out of a canoe and hitting a jagged rock in my early thirties. But as I looked at my face now, there was not a single mole, nor a blemish or scar to be seen. I ran my hand across my chin, the skin still reasonably smooth. I hadn't shaved for a couple of days, and still didn't really need to.

I slumped back into my seat, reflecting once again on the situation with Sally and Jimmy. I prayed that my best friend wouldn't hate me. He was a kind and decent human being, and I loved him. To be responsible for causing him such heartache, well, I was devastated by it. Any change to the dynamics of our friendship would be a huge loss to my life. We had known each other since infant school. But I just had to believe that life has a way of absorbing such a crisis, that people adapt and move on – I hoped wholeheartedly for that. A nervous giggle lifted itself from the pit of my stomach as I digested Sally's confession to Jimmy of just how drunk we both were, and how she will play on the fact that she couldn't believe his infatuation with her, and to attack him for keeping such a secret to himself. Had she known, she would never have given me a second look. I took in the increasing strength of the angry lilac sky and begged to the heavens above that their love would get them through.

I finally made my way into the house. I stood aimlessly for several lost moments before being drawn to the lounge window, suddenly aware of a car pulling up outside.

'Oh no, not now!'

It was Julie. She looked stressed and anxious as she ran down my drive. Before she had chance to ring the bell, I opened the door and she stepped inside.

'Ritchie, have you seen Jack?'

Those words never failed to unnerve me. I shook my head and begged the question that I really didn't want to know the answer to.

'No, why? Have you told him?'

Julie nodded. The look in her eyes did nothing to calm me.

'Shit! What did he say?'

'Please, Ritchie, have you any brandy? I'm not joking, *I need a drink!!*'

Finally, Julie sat down in the lounge and I handed her a half glass of brandy.

'Bloody hell, Ritchie, you trying to get me drunk?'

We both smiled nervously, but I pressed her to tell me what Jack had said.

'Not much really! He just looked totally shattered by it, just stared out of the window for a bit. I tried to talk to him, repeatedly begged him to forgive me, explained that I was petrified of losing him, and when I said that, he turned and took me in his arms. He held onto me as though his life depended on it! But then Lillie ran into the room and that was it. He looked at her, then back at me, and he walked out of the church! That was late last night and I haven't heard a thing from him since. I'm at my wits' end!'

Sheer fear seemed to mute us both; not knowing Jack's thoughts or next move did that to you. Julie made her excuses and left, and I was glad to see her go. But as I had hugged her goodbye, I felt an incredible sense of betrayal towards Jack. If we were to be spotted together and he should react as before... I watched as Julie's car drove off out of the cul-de-sac. I half expected Jack's yellow Porsche to come screaming into the road, but it didn't. In fact, the road had never seemed so quiet. For the entire night I just waited, sitting in silence. No television, no lights; I hardly drew breath. As I sat slumped on the lounge floor, my back against the wall, my mind would jump from what could be happening with Sally and Jimmy. Would she have the nerve to come out with it tonight? And then back to Jack. What on earth was he thinking? Would he want revenge? Or would he accept and continue the secret by simply sauntering back to Julie, licking his wounds, and then concentrate on rebuilding his world? I squirmed uncomfortably in realising that I had to deal with all that I had created. And then a small, wry, ironically optimistic smile crossed my face as I thought that things couldn't get any worse. But then the smile was gone as I pictured Leoni at the door with tear-stained eyes, announcing, 'Ritchie! I'm afraid I'm pregnant!'

I must have drifted off, because suddenly I woke with a start. I reeled forward, having bashed the back of my head against the wall.

'Fuck! That hurt!'

I clambered to my feet, looking for the light switch, desperate to find out the time.

'Shit! Midnight?'

I quickly ran upstairs to change into my darkest gear. I needed to get to the bakery to release the oil. I hadn't felt it necessary at first because of the gas explosion and all that. But I recalled the fire report, stating that had it not been for the oil tank leaking so severely, the gas explosion would have probably only blown a few windows out. But the intensity of the flames once the oil caught fire meant that the building didn't stand a chance. And of course that's exactly what I needed to satisfy Guy Nelson – his money! Generous insurance payout! All crucial pieces of my ongoing business plan.

As I finally made my way across the canal and along the back of the shops, until finally reaching the rickety staircase at the back of the bakery, I knew I had an extra job tonight. The bump upstairs in the flat, the tramp, I wanted him out. I would sleep easier for many years to come knowing that I had saved his life.

I crept carefully down the concrete steps that led into the cellar, and it wasn't long before I had the padlock off. I pushed the door open, and instantly I went from dark to pitch-black. I could hear the scurry of tiny feet and it made my skin crawl. I took a deep breath and stepped into the blackness. I dreaded every step, my fingers being greeted by damp flaking brickwork as I sidled past a steel and brick supporting wall. I crouched down and pushed through a small vaulted gap – and was welcomed by a stream of faint lilac streetlight, that had filtered through the grates that led up onto Willow High Street. I shook my head excitedly as I located the oil tank, but suddenly gave out a slight, *'Urrgh!'* as I spotted a rat that was now looking right at me, standing proud on top of the corroding metal. I stamped my foot in an attempt to scare the rat away. It looked unimpressed, but suddenly seemed to politely oblige, jumped down and scurried off to join the rest of his busy gang. I tried to recall how I'd managed to disconnect the pipe originally as I continued to puff and pant, succeeding only in removing layer after layer of my knuckle flesh. Eventually, virtually defeated and on the verge of screaming, I kicked all my frustration venomously onto the neck of the stubborn pipe and it was off. The oil started to glug out reassuringly. I moved quickly, desperate to get out of the cellar – tiptoeing blindly through the minefield of rats was not a great way to end any day.

Once back outside, and though the moon had temporarily disappeared behind a cloud, in comparison to the cellar it was as though I'd stepped out into broad daylight. I snapped the padlock shut. I turned and looked upstairs towards my next port of call. There had been no loud crash this time, but I presumed the tramp would still be up there. I felt nervous as I climbed the wooden stairs, finally reaching the top and then peering blindly through the frosted glass in the door. I pushed the key into the lock and turned it. As I entered the bakery flat, I was anticipating someone suddenly rushing at me, eager to get away. But instead, there was nothing. I left the door open and made my way inside. I tried to cajole myself into thinking positively. The street lamps lit the flat in lilac and shades of black to grey. The place smelt suitably scrubbed.

'Good old Alice, you've left the place spotless!' I muttered softly under my breath.

It was rather sad as I recalled all the antiques and the dozens of framed photographs that had stood here for so many years. There was now nothing but bare walls and empty floors. I stood in the doorway of the lounge, a cold clammy welcome replacing the warmth and hospitality of less than a week ago when Alice and Harry were still very much in residence. But as I stood, and despite the bakery's best efforts to simply erase their memory, there was a distant spirit that seemed to ooze out of the sheer heart of the building. My eyes were suddenly drawn to the floor, the strong lilac moonlight shining into the centre of the room. I found myself looking at a single framed black and white photograph in the middle of the bare floorboards. I stepped nearer and sunk to my knees to get a closer look. I felt my stomach muscles tighten and a shiver run the length of my spine. There was Harry Christian standing proudly holding a silver trophy, inscribed with *National Champions. Captain: Harry Christian*. I stood up quickly, feeling agitated and threatened. I looked around the lilac-drenched room, but then suddenly enveloped in darkness. I backed out of the lounge and into the hallway. I stood totally silent for just a handful of seconds, waiting for footsteps, proof of life, but there was nothing. The walls were suddenly lit up with the shadows of the outside trees, framed in bold lilac flashes. My eyes fell on a tempting chance of an early exit. I was spooked enough to simply quit and run, but I knew my work here wasn't complete. I needed to check every inch of the place to make sure that the tramp was gone. Room by room, my heart in my mouth, I threw open each door, but a quick glance inside brings a sigh of relief. Finally, I'm done. I wait again. Total silence, nothing. I'm now at the farthest point from the front door and it looks *so* far away. I wait, my patience ticking down. *Three, two, one...* And then I run, desperate to get out.

When I finally get back outside into the reassurance of the night, I slam the door firmly shut behind me, my hands shaking furiously, pathetically. I gratefully turn the key and lock the place up, a building I will never enter again. I step back and look at the door – it feels as though I am sealing a coffin lid, and I pray any visitor is long gone. I take a deep breath and then glance up at the huge gable end.

I mutter under my breath an apology. 'Sorry it has to be this way, bakery my dear friend, nothing personal.'

My eyes suddenly widen and a well of panic rises.

'Meant to check the gas pipe...*damn!* Did I smell gas?'

I retraced my steps in my mind. Maybe I did, but was too busy with the *bloody mad* picture on the floor. I crouched down and pushed the letterbox open. I took a deep breath in. Is that gas? I couldn't be sure. I took another deep breath, but my head and heart were pounding and jarring with every blink of my eyes and twitch of my nose, and all I knew was that I was sure of nothing. I had to leave circumstances to chance now – I could do no more. But my resignation to what may or may not happen here made me recoil. The picture of Harry Christian spooked me and I knew I needed to leave, and quickly.

I lay on the bed desperate for sleep, but my overtired mind denying me that. After an hour, maybe two, just churning all that was affecting my life over and over again, I got up and walked to the bedroom window. The street lamp offered a subdued, but comforting haze. As I pondered the scene and my role in it, I felt so strange, placed back in time, at an age that I had happily passed through and onwards. But here I was again, reliving each day and the drama that that brings. The positives: a pleasure. The negatives: painful. Certain decisions and appropriate consequences that I had simply wanted to forget, but this time trying to make things right. It was an awkward and difficult task. There was no simple black and white scenario here, just subtle changes here and there, and it concerned me. As I made my way through my new world, I wasn't convinced that I was making a good job of my second chance. But as I returned to my bed, I lay down, pulling my knees up to my chest, and closed my eyes.

Brrrrrrrrrrrr! I slammed my hand down onto the off switch of my alarm. I felt nauseous, and my brain seemed to rock from side to side.

'Shit!' The word just rolled off my tongue as the thought of what lay ahead rightly made me nervous.

I quickly pulled on my clothes and rushed to the bathroom to throw some cold water over my face. I hurriedly brushed my teeth and couldn't get myself out of the house fast enough, such was the anticipation of what I was going to find this morning. I ignored the company car and stepped towards my own vehicle today. The pickup truck roared into life, as reassuring as an old friend, dependable, and in a strange way it helped calm me a little. I drove slowly to work, my original keenness suddenly replaced by a not-wanting-to-know. I was almost at a snail's pace as I approached Willow High Street. But this time around there was no police blockade, and as I turned into the high street itself I felt my face wince with disbelief. Everything was perfectly normal, not a police car, fire engine or ambulance in sight. As I pulled up outside of Skirdle's, I could see that the bakery was still standing. I banged the steering wheel with immense frustration.

'WHYYYY...?' As my breathing became deeper, I tried to be logical. *Maybe, by me going into the bakery to try to find the tramp, I had simply got there first. Perhaps he had been planning to go in, but I had simply scared him off?* Whatever the reason, I was beginning to realise what a total fool I was being. After all, it was quite clear that it *was* the tramp, perhaps smoking, that had caused the gas explosion. And though I had been desperate to make sure that there were no casualties this time, to avoid the nightmares of the faceless down-and-out, perhaps I was being unrealistic in looking to alter the fate of it.

I parked the pickup at the back of Skirdle's and made my way into work. As I turned the key in the lock, I felt a strong unnerving slap on my back. I turned around quickly, fearing the worst: Jack? Jimmy? It was Mr Ball.

'Good morning, Ritchie lad! Nice and early!'

I smiled, flicking on the light and making my way to my desk. The day passed slowly. I was unable to do anything constructive, my mind racing, totally convinced that the bakery was going to explode at any moment. Lunchtime came and went, and as I looked up from my desk, the ticking of the large clock on the office wall seemed to get louder and louder. And then, just as my feelings were about to overwhelm me, the shop door opened. Mr Ball quickly stood up.

'Can I help you, sir?'

But as I pushed my chair away with the backs of my legs, I stood quickly too.

'Umm! No, *it's* okay, Mr Ball, this, *umm,* gentleman is here to see me. Hello, Jack!'

Jack De'Vil stood, his eyes sunken, the sparkle extinguished. He didn't move. And though this time around Jack and I had been friends, there was something in his face that seemed to resemble the hatred that I had so reluctantly endured the first time around.

'Angel, we need to talk.'

Jack turned and stepped out of the shop. I nervously, obediently followed him. He went to walk up the high street, but then stopped. He looked lost, undoubtedly making it all up as he went along. Suddenly, he turned around and made his way down the side of Skirdle's towards the car park.

'Look, Angel!'

Jack stopped and pulled out a small cigar from his coat pocket, lighting it quickly, then taking a deep draw. I shuffled nervously on the spot, rubbing my fingers against the once burnt palm, all courtesy of the man before me, but all I felt was smooth unblemished flesh, as of course Jack had caused me *no* harm in this life.

'Angel, I know you and I have been friends…but you've fucked things up for me!'

'Jack!!'

'No, Angel, please shut the fuck up! I mean it!!'

My mind was turning somersaults. I needed time.

'Please, Jack, I, I really don't know what I'm supposed to have done. But we need to talk later. I've got an appointment, umm, a client due in the shop any moment!'

Jack lifted his eyes away from the floor and was now staring at me through a cloud of cigar smoke. He had an almost sorry look on his face, disappointment etched into his body language, but I doubted that it was enough to save me. There was no mistaking the intent in his eyes.

'Jack, it's *no* problem, I'm happy to meet up with you later, upstairs flat, the Old Bakery. What shall we say, seven…see you there *at* seven?'

I quickly dug into my trouser pocket, pulling out the bakery keys, separating the flat key. My hand started to shake as I passed it to Jack.

'See, Jack, to show I'm serious about meeting you!'

He didn't say a word, just took the key and walked away.

I needed a few moments. I couldn't go straight back into Skirdle's. I looked skyward – a calm combination of white fluffy clouds on a lilac canvas, totally at odds with the evil that was brewing down here. I fell back against the brickwork. My nerves had got the better of me, and I started to laugh, brought on by the surreal proportion of my plan. I wondered whether or not I could really let Jack walk into the bakery. All it needed was him to be smoking his cigar. Again, the nervous laughter squeezed out of me. I knew it was unforgivable, but I had seen that look before. I thought about Julie, and how last time Jack had taken no prisoners, he felt wronged, he felt totally betrayed, and so surely this time he would be thinking along the same lines. My gut instinct convinced me that history *just might* repeat itself. Rightly or wrongly, I believed that it was kill or be killed.

As I sat and watched the final person leave Skirdle's, I became indecisive. Part of me wanted to sit and wait, make sure that Jack made it to the bakery. But then part of me felt that I shouldn't let this happen; surely, me allowing Jack to walk into the gas-fumed bakery, well, I may as well just put a gun to his head. Would the powers that be feel that my actions were unforgivably calculated? Or would they perhaps overlook it? After all, they were well aware of what Jack De'Vil was capable of.

I quickly stood up. *Of course, Rose!* I needed to talk to my friend, and quickly. Before I knew it, I was out of the shop; I had total tunnel vision, and a real panic, a desperate urgency took over my mind and body. I didn't even bother to grab the pickup truck, I just ran, faster and faster, my legs pushing harder and harder into the concrete pavement. I flashed a smile and nod of the head to several people that I passed. But as I made my way to the edge of Willow, the sun was dropping quicker than I wanted. The heavy background noise of evening traffic started to fade, the peace and quiet of the countryside soothing me a little. Finally, I made it to the five-bar gate and leapt over it. As I landed, I stopped still. I could hear the distant sound of a narrowboat, the soft slapping of the wake against the water's edge. I whispered to myself, 'How I love it here!' I stood up, breathing deeply, replenishing my empty lungs. I started to make my way down the embankment, through the trees, and finally into the overgrowth. I let my hands brush across the fruits of the grass before turning a full three hundred and sixty degrees.

'Rose! Please, Rose, I *really* need you!'

I turned a further half circle, still unable to see my little friend. I moved quickly towards the willow trees, turning urgently this way and that, calling her name, each time more urgent than the last. I suddenly stopped altogether and looked through the light green leaves of the most prominent willow... the flicker of sparkling water, barely visible between the long branches... And there she was, the rich claret of her velvet dress, her little bare feet, her jet-black hair. Rose stepped forward, her reassurance immediate.

'It's alright, Ritchie. *Really,* it's alright.'

Rose pushed her hand into mine and I gratefully covered it firmly with my other hand.

'Rose! I'm *so* relieved to see you. I'm convinced I'm making a terrible mistake.'

'Ritchie, I've already told you, *it's* alright! We've been watching you, and we've been watching Jack. We've, *well,* we've decided we need to turn a blind eye. We're aware that there is a certain inevitability about how you and Jack proceed. Stay with your plan, but don't go back to Skirdle's! You need to go somewhere visual, public. Maybe a drink at the Whippet's?'

Rose brought her other hand and pressed it against mine. Her eyes sparkled at me, and I felt that everything was *okay* when I was with her. But the virtues of the day had worn me down, and I just wished she would take me home, back to Yasmin and Evie. But as the thought filled my head, a smile spread across her young lips.

'Ritchie, take care now, I'll see you soon.'

And then she was gone, my hands still cupped together. I looked up at the now dark sky, the lilac tinge strongly visible across the full moon. I felt concerned. Normally here at the Water's Edge I had my clear sky, day or night. But then, as the moon disappeared behind a dark cloud, I knew it was time to leave. I made my way back up to the road, keen to get myself back into the glare of society.

I ran for most of the journey, but once, just a few hundred metres away from where I needed to be, I eased into a walk, keen to remove the flush of colour that had taken me over. I stepped into the bar, quickly glancing up at the clock, and within seconds it chimed seven times. My heart seemed to seize with a paranoia that everyone would know what I had done. I ordered myself a drink, almost expecting with each passing second to hear a boom. The barmaid smiled sweetly as she served my ice-cold pint of lager, but just as I handed over my money, the door swung open and in walked Yasmin, Janey two steps behind her.

Yasmin looked at me, her cheeks matching my sweaty glow. I nodded, barely forcing a smile. In fact, I was almost convinced I'd frowned at her. But as my eyes dropped to the safety of the floor, I knew I had to get out of there. I turned and made my way to the toilets. But once in the corridor, instead of stepping into the gents, I kept on walking, outside and into the night, craving the safety of home. My brain and body were tired and aching, and I was desperate to curl up into a ball, away from all this madness.

Brrrrrrrrrrrrrrrrrrrr! I once again slammed my hand down onto the off switch of my alarm clock, the shrill echoing around the room before escaping through the open window. As I eased into consciousness, I really didn't want to open my eyes, but if I didn't, then the dreaded day couldn't begin for me. I knew I had no choice, and my first question was, what would today bring?

I jumped into the *Escort* and drove into Willow, it wasn't long before I was turning into the high street. And this time there were police and firemen everywhere.

'Sorry, sir, you'll have to turn around. We've had to close the whole street off, there's been an explosion! The Old Bakery has burnt to the ground!'

I reversed quickly, parking the car up and onto the pavement. The policeman stepped towards me.

'You work at Skirdle's, don't you, sir? You're Mr Angel? You sold our house for us!'

I nodded, vaguely placing the face.

'Well, sir, Skirdle's is in a bad way. The explosion has ripped out your front door and windows...'

I was floating as he spoke. I couldn't feel my legs and doubted whether I was able to speak, but then said, 'Ummm, bloody hell, *really?* You're joking, as bad as that?'

The keen policeman took my arm.

'Well, sir, it's worse than *that.* There's been a casualty, though there's nothing much left of the poor sod!'

My head starts to pound, my numbness returning, but I can hear myself prompting the policeman.

'Oh, how awful. Any ideas *who* it might be?'

'Well, sir, the blast happened just after seven last night, and the only bit of evidence we have as regards an identity is a wallet found outside the back door of the shop. A bit scorched, but the detective was telling me, and you must keep this under your hat, sir...it was a Jack De'Vil!'

I stood open-mouthed for a few moments.

'Are you alright, sir?'

I nodded as reassuringly as I could, desperate to regain my composure. So Jack was gone. He'd died six years earlier than he had originally, and I wondered how significant a detail that would be. But as the policeman chatted aimlessly on, my mind was racing and I was struggling to keep up with any of what he was saying. But as I strained my eyes on his intermittently mute but moving lips, I just about hung on. I finally nodded at about the right time in an effort to seem only acceptably fazed by the news.

'But, sir, as is often the case in an explosion like this, the bodies can be *so* badly burnt that it can take ages to identify the corpse. But we have his car, though virtually damage free, tucked away close by, but as for our Mr De'Vil, there wasn't much left of this one!'

And as I wandered off, not sure where I was heading, my mind continued to race at the immensity of all that this meant. As I tried to let it all sink in, the one prominent line that kept floating back to the top was that my actions had resulted in Julie being allowed to live on, and with Jack gone, there was now no reason for me to keep away! And as I accepted the enormity of that, it gave fresh hope for Lillie.

The next few days and nights passed intensely. Hours of questioning by the local constabulary was not something I wished to repeat. And once finally left alone to regain some sort of normality, my concern was for Julie, who of course would be heartbroken at the loss of Jack. But mixed with the desire to offer my condolences and to comfort her, I was increasingly aware that she may be questioning my part in Jack's death. There was no escaping the fact that should the police deem it necessary to divulge that the bakery belonged to me, well, Julie was no fool.

After I had made a few enquiries, it was confirmed that Jack, Julie and Lillie had finally moved into the Old Church, though Jack had only had the pleasure of spending a week or so there. And so the moment had arrived as I stood before the huge iron gates of the De'Vil family home. The clunk of the latch dropped behind me. I turned and took in the power of the old place, stinging memories screaming out at me. As I stood on the sacred site, for the first time I reflected on how totally inappropriate this choice of home was for Jack. And even though he had been pleasant company this time around, I couldn't get the old Jack De'Vil, capable of causing me so much pain, out of my mind. It was his cold callousness that always crept up, justifying my every negative thought and painful image of my now departed foe.

A cool breeze passed over me, as though sent as a reminder as to why I was here. Our history meant that I couldn't and didn't want to escape the bond that I had with Julie and Lillie. And despite all the negativity that I related to the Old Church, I had this *questionable* affinity with the place. All that had happened had never left me. The day that Julie and I had made love, despite the unforgivable deceit to Yasmin, it had felt spiritually right at the time. I could never fully explain the strong emotion that it had fired up in me. I think that just being in her home, Lillie's home, Jack's home, the time that they had spent creating their family dream, well, it all screamed at me from every brick, every door, every window, and it was a powerful cocktail. And as I stood now, free of the fear of Jack, I felt as though I was *home?* Well, a home while forced apart from Yasmin and Evie. As I knocked on the large oak door, I turned towards the double garage. Jack's yellow Porsche was standing under an old creaking tree, the subtle shades of the autumn leaves clashing against the primary colour. I quickly turned back towards the front door as suddenly, I stood face-to-face with Julie. I swallowed hard. She looked tired and drawn. But her heavy eyes seemed to lift a little, as though I had been expected, and so she beckoned me in. At a loss as to what to say, I enquired after my little girl, Julie's back towards me.

'Umm, Lillie's at nursery. She's been keen to go. For the best, keeping a bit of a routine up, I suppose.'

We were now face-to-face, my composure ebbing away. I felt unquestionably strange, and as a consequence sought solace in stepping away from the moment, taking bold strides towards the lounge, aware that Julie was following closely behind. But then something rose up from deep within me, an acute and face slapping reminder that Jack was gone and that I had nothing to fear now. I stood for just a moment, taking in the almost revelation of a boost that resulted in a newfound confidence that had simply never existed for me here. And though there was no escaping the full horror of all this room had meant to me, I was able to face it, embrace it and accept it, for all it stood and just how it had shaped my life. My mind was filled with the need to hold Julie, but I waited, trying desperately to imagine her reaction in doing so. I closed my eyes briefly, counting down from three to one, and turned. We just stood, her face tilted up towards mine, my face dropped and taking in all she was trying to tell me, and then the moment presented itself. With immense bravery I eased my arms around her. She froze for a breath or two, but then her stiff and momentarily unyielding guard relented and she eased into me, and then she melted. I could hear the faintest of cries, a gentle sobbing that I hadn't expected. But then as she held onto me, her tears stopped and we just stood. I was increasingly sure that being here with Julie gave her the same comfort that I was craving. And though consciously I was unsure of what I was striving for here, I did increasingly see that if I couldn't have Yasmin and Evie, then at least I had more than I deserved to keep me occupied within the Old Church. It may sound hard and callous, but Julie and Lillie were definitely the antidote that I needed to get me through. And though it was undoubtedly convenient for me, it was also a perfect opportunity for getting to know the wonderful Lillie. Something about our union felt right. And for the first time, apart from my one wonderful, but *expensive* kiss with Yasmin, this did feel right, as right as it was going to in this mad adventure. From that day, I barely left Julie's side. And though we were as discreet as possible, Julie, Lillie and I became a family.

Finally, the funds from Guy Nelson and his American fast-food company were in my account. And the fateful day came for me to go and see Harry and Alice Christian. I was determined not to let the story hit the papers as before without making things right with the Christian's first. I desperately needed most of my profit, as I knew that the Old Library was crucial to my future, and the money for that, in part, had come from the success of the bakery deal. However, I felt that I could give more than originally, and perhaps I needed to explain things a little better this time, to diffuse all chances of a misunderstanding.

The Christians' bungalow looked beautiful, but my legs felt a little unsteady as I rapped my knuckles on the front door. Alice opened it quickly, her sparkling eyes thrilled to see me.

'Oh, Ritchie! How lovely. Do come in, dear. Look, Harry, look, it's Ritchie!'

Harry was sat in his chair. And though nothing should have given him cause to be upset with me, there seemed to be something very strange indeed. I quickly got the conversation started.

'Can you believe the terrible explosion? It must have come

as a terrible shock to you both. After all, how many years had you both lived there?'

Alice looked a little upset as she seemed to reflect on her many years at the bakery. Harry didn't flinch, his smug smile now a permanent fixture on his wrinkled face, and it unnerved me. Just as Alice ushered me to sit down, Harry suddenly burst into speech.

'Oh look, Alice, *our* knight in shining armour is here! Come to give us *all* the profit from the sale of the bakery!'

Alice scolded Harry for his unnecessary tone. She seemed understandably upset and embarrassed by her husband's reaction towards me.

'Shut up, Harry, you *stupid* old fool! *Please* don't start. Ritchie has been wonderful to us both, and *that's* how you treat him!'

I took Alice's hand and Harry eased back in his chair.

'I need to explain a couple of things to you both.' I waited nervously for Harry's reaction, but felt slightly encouraged when he remained silent. 'Harry?'

He just stared back at me.

'Look, I need to explain the intricacies of how I managed to sell the bakery. In an effort to help you achieve a sale *I've* taken a huge gamble, which has fortunately worked out well, but it could have gone *terribly* wrong.'

Harry started to rock slightly in his chair. I wasn't keen on him doing it, as he appeared more menacing by the minute.

I continued. 'I knew I could make more by selling it to a developer, but I didn't know when, and I certainly didn't know for how much. *So,* in an effort to keep the worry away from you both – after all, I knew you just wanted *rid* of the bakery – I bought it! I did then get a buyer quickly, but the plans they had for it, well, that is of course irrelevant now it's burnt down! Oh God! I know I'm making a terrible mess of this, but, well, if you remember what our concern was, firstly to get you your retirement bungalow, which I think is just perfect for you both, and though I did warn you that the likelihood of there being enough money to get you over to Australia, to see your son, well, in truth, was very slim, well, after taking out my expenses I have a cheque here for fifteen thousand pounds!'

Alice squealed with delight and then jumped around with a spring that belied her age. I found that I had to raise my voice over the singing animated figure before me.

'But I must warn you both that there is likely to be a newspaper article highlighting my sale to the Americans. And though it's very flattering to be hailed as a successful businessman, I have to prepare you that they'll probably quote some figures, you know? How much I *supposedly* sold the bakery for... But *please* believe me, they're *grossly* inflated! I will be happy to show you *any* documentation that I have.'

Alice stepped towards me and gave me a huge hug, but then Harry called me to him. I cannot explain how eerie his words sounded, but there was a depth and strength of menace that seemed to grow before my eyes. Harry curled his finger, beckoning me to come closer. As I stepped tentatively forward, my eyes dropped onto his and he stared deep into my soul for ten seconds or so.

Then he lurched forward, yelling out, 'HE'S JUST TRYING TO *SAVE* HIMSELF! THE CONNIVING *EVIL* BASTARD IS JUST TRYING TO *SAVE* HIMSELF!'

And though having missed me originally, this time Harry caught me perfectly, his clammy hands held tightly around my throat, as the full force of the man pushed me onto my back. Harry's fingers dug tighter and tighter, until I could feel his thumbs gouging into my Adam's apple. And though I felt that I should be able to restrain him, such was his determination that he seemed to have the strength of a lion. Suddenly, amidst screams from Alice and my borderline passing out, I heard the cracking of bone. Harry suddenly winced and fell on top of me, his hard skull smashing into my nose and cheekbone with such force that I felt convinced I was about to black out. I floundered for a few seconds, catching my breath and waiting for Harry to fall away from me, but he didn't move. I suddenly, urgently wanted him off me and I pushed up with all I had, but Harry's dead weight of a body was moulding into mine. With one last desperate heave, I finally managed to crawl from beneath Harry, his body falling onto the fire hearth. I sat up quickly as Alice was walking backwards towards the kitchen door, a look of total horror on her ashen face, a large brass poker gripped tightly in her little hands. Her eyes darting from Harry's to mine, and then back to her lifeless husband. Her mouth then opened, the poker dropping to the floor, her hands being drawn up to her raging face and the full recreation of *Edvard Munch's* 'The Scream' was alive and well in the Christians' lounge. But as Alice continued to tense and strain every conceivable muscle, nothing was coming out, and she finally fell onto her knees, her arms now dropped to her side. No movement … paralysed and silent.

The police and medics soon arrived. All I could see was Alice as she was when Harry killed himself the first time round. The look of total disbelief filling her frail face as the medic pronounced Harry dead.

First Alice and then finally Harry were taken away from the bungalow. I felt total horror at what had happened. How could Harry have known of my deceit? Even in our previous meetings he'd seemed to be biding his time, as though well aware of my less than honourable intentions. And here, tonight, it all seemed *so* premeditated. He was totally determined to seek revenge for something that he simply couldn't have been aware of. As I pressed the ice pack to my battered face, I looked out of the lounge window. The police were talking to the neighbours. I let the cream floral curtain, starched and new, fall back into place, just inches away from the vase of silk flowers. I let out a sad despondent sigh, still numb and amazed that I had failed so miserably in trying to do right by the Christian's. I turned and looked around the room. My eyes are suddenly drawn to a familiar picture on the sideboard. I bound forward, picking up the antique silver frame – there is a young man in a black and white photograph, in a rugby shirt, his face slightly distorted. I could almost taste the sweet sticky blood in my mouth as I recalled the second day after I was sent back in time. The appalling unexplained assault from behind, my attacker, wearing the claret number seven rugby shirt, running off into the distance. I raised my arm, scratching my head, recalling the black and white photograph sitting perfect centre on the floor at the bakery flat. I turned the picture over, looking for clues as to the identity of the rugby player. I almost took a double take at the surreal image of seeing the *back* of the young man displayed in the photograph. My eyes widened as I focused in on the number seven. I quickly turned the picture back around…And there was Harry's smiling face! I rocked on my feet momentarily, my breath escaping me. *My attacker was Harry Christian! But how, and why?* I slumped back onto the Christian's settee, my brain searching for answers, I instinctively threw the picture onto the floor. But though I tried to ignore it, Harry's face was staring back at me happy to goad me. It's as though he had slipped back in time with me, knowing all that he did, desperate for revenge.

I finally managed to slip away from the Christians' bungalow. I climbed inside my pickup truck and sat in silence for a while. So, first Jack, and now poor old Harry, both dead, both gone. I was supposed to be putting things right!

No matter how bad things would get for me in my original life, the simple thought of home, Yasmin and Evie, and the tranquillity that each would give me got me through. No matter how bad things *were,* however destructive and painful the day had been, my gorgeous girls were always at home, waiting for me. But here and now my reality was Julie and Lillie, and the Old Church. And somehow, as much as I loved them both dearly, it wasn't the same. No matter how hard I tried, it was *never* going to be.

CHAPTER TWENTY

My New Family

After Death, 1994 – Lilac Sky
The years started to pass steadily, rewarding, though not quite as quickly as I would have liked, but I knew better than to take for granted my time with Julie and Lillie. The fast-forwarding of my younger years had now stopped. I felt frustrated on the tough days, desperate and longing for Yasmin and Evie, and it would be this that would sap my patience the most. But Rose would simply pacify me and beg for trust.

'The *devil* is in the detail, Ritchie. Each precious moment, the level of love you're building here is crucial. Please don't wish your life away!'

It would be the morning times that I was at my most vulnerable. I would wake up, holding onto the warm body beside me and the comforting reassurance that it would bring. But every sunrise, without fail, I would wake and it would take only the opening of my eyes to remind me of my changed circumstances. As loving and as pretty as Julie was, she simply wasn't Yasmin. Lillie – it was the greatest privilege to spend so much precious time with this wonderful little girl, but each and every second spent with her reminded me without let-up just how much I longed for Evie. But pushing pain and regret aside, I relished and accepted the price that I was paying in receiving my second chance with my precious daughter, an innocent child that had succeeded in making me a far better man by having got to know her.

But despite the everyday pace, I kept my head down. I found it hard, but submerged myself in the necessary empire-building that was required to enable my progress. And my meetings with Rose helped guide me through. She had constantly reminded me as things were progressing, that I needed to try to achieve what I had materially acquired first time around. Because of course my purchase of the Water's Edge was going to be a critical piece of the jigsaw. Although Sky Cottage was no longer a necessary purchase, I couldn't help it and bought it anyway. After work, I would often just go and sit in the unrenovated cottage with a bottle of red wine, simply reliving memories of Yasmin and me. Julie would often be a bit quiet when I finally arrived home, but she never nagged me, never moaned, and after half an hour or so she would come and hold me. But I could see a depth of puzzlement in her eyes, in her face the simple frustration that she wasn't getting all of me.

Business wise, my portfolio grew impressively. I had to cheer, as without doubt the most crucial piece of the jigsaw, the Old Library, was purchased. But the day I handed my money over for the Water's Edge *bait* was a day that I reflected on a small business matter that hadn't received acceptable closure.

My reason for my last visit to see Alice and Harry Christian was with the full intention of handing them a cheque for fifteen thousand pounds. But of course the circumstances that developed, changed all that. And so I had kept the money, placing it in a separate high-interest account, not wanting to touch it. Though I was fortunate, as when I did go to see Alice at the nursing home – just as before - she was always delighted to see me, as she simply believed me to be her son Davey. The question of money of course never arose, but it didn't stop me wanting to make amends.

On one of my Friday visits to see poor, frail Alice, I wrote out a cheque for fifteen thousand pounds and placed it in my suit jacket pocket. I wanted one of the nurses to pay it into Alice's account, with the suggestion that perhaps some of the funds could be sent to her son Davey, so that he could then bring all his family over to see my little friend. But as I sat having my second cup of tea and my fourth *Digestive* biscuit, I had a change of heart. The confusion for Alice would be too much. She just seemed so bubbly and excited when I was with her that I simply didn't want to risk spoiling the relationship I had with her. So for now, the money was put on one side. I was going to have to find another way of making amends with the ill-gotten gains.

As I stopped off for my daily visit to Sky Cottage, I would often question my reasons for buying it, because without Yasmin, I was never going to live there. But I did eventually get the place renovated, along with some sparse furniture and basic home comforts. Not with the time and love that Yasmin and I had administered, though, as that was simply our history, our place together. Sky Cottage would never be the same without Yasmin, but I was still grateful to own the wonderful place, and to be able to wallow in all the memories that it held. As far as Julie was concerned, it was purchased for investment reasons only. And though my new *common-law* wife would take a little more interest in my day-to-day business activities than Yasmin, Julie would never question or challenge my purchases. As for us all living there, well, as nice as Sky Cottage was, the Old Church was Julie and Lillie's home, and I didn't want to change that.

The day that I heard Scottie and Yasmin had moved in together brought me to my knees emotionally. There had been rumours flying around that Scottie was seeing Janey as well, but there was nothing concrete. Anyway, I felt it best not to even think about it.

My situation with Jimmy and Sally was incredibly problem-free. Jimmy, to his total credit, never said a word. His friendship still seemed totally committed to me, and for that I was eternally grateful. Sally would sometimes struggle in certain circumstances, but we muddled through. But the thing that had always amazed me was the fact that Sally gave birth to beautiful twins, just as before, and they were adorable, even though I do say so myself. Because, whereas the twins originally looked the spitting image of their father, the painful truth was that they did this time too – my eyes, my nose, my colouring! I simply couldn't get over the fact that Sally had had twins again, and chosen to name them as before, but hey, who was I to question the path of fate? Danny and Daisy were now in their second year, and we all loved them to bits. And though I always thought of the children as Sally and Jimmy's, there were of course many moments when I would see my own characteristics, and it would act as a painful reminder.

Leoni finally ended up travelling the world, though I would tease her in any letters I wrote that she was simply running away from herself, that she should stay and face her sexuality. But she was adamant that there was something prehistoric about Willow that made her feel uneasy about coming out. After a long telephone conversation, she finally admitted that she had met a famous young film star, and that they would both be in England within the week – I couldn't wait to see my friend. It was only a day or two later when I realised that Leoni had never said on the phone whether or not the star was a girl or a guy, and so I just sort of presumed that perhaps it was best not to *presume*.

A couple of days before they were due to arrive, Leoni asked if she could rent something off me – a house would be perfect, a flat would suffice, but it would be for at least six months. Oh! And could I pick them up from the airport. So I happily obliged.

It was almost midnight when I arrived at the private airfield, only to be informed that there had been a delay. I sat and waited patiently for well over an hour, finally rewarded with the sight of Leoni running towards me, her arms outstretched, her new friend trailing in her wake. I loved the intensity of her hug, but we were close, and *only time* would show exactly how close. Leoni introduced her special lady friend, Tia, her headscarf and sunglasses making her barely recognisable. But as the twinkle of dark Italian eyes peered over the top of her sunglasses, I couldn't believe who I was confronted with. It was someone I had had a major crush on, and I was seriously shocked that she was *that* way. Finally, after much chat and excited storytelling, I got the two girls back to Willow, turning down the stereo and easing off the accelerator as we pulled onto the driveway of Sky Cottage. I hadn't rented the cottage out before – I hadn't bought it for that. But for Leoni? Well, for her, anything!

It was nearly 3 o'clock in the morning, and after sharing a couple of bottles of wine together, we all finally crashed out. Having first thrown the large settee cushions onto the floor and having grabbed several duvets from upstairs, and as the early hours chat became a heady inebriated affair, there was no mistaking the sexual tension. Though nothing other than platonic hugs and kisses were exceeded, there was just an undercurrent, a feeling that both girls were toying with me. Not in a bad way, but certainly in an intriguing and *yet* to be explored way. Perhaps keen to conduct a moral and righteous life – Julie having steadied my hedonistic streak – I did feel old before my time, comfortably submerged in the respectable depths of normality. So I was painfully aware that a little encouragement from the wrong quarters could see Ritchie Angel's *halo* slipping.

The morning arrived far too soon, and it was sunglasses on as I made my way to Skirdle's in a hung-over haze. Once at my desk, I picked up the phone and called Julie, who unsurprisingly was a little cool with me, but seemed to loosen up a bit once I told her that I would definitely be home tonight and that it was just business getting a little out of control! I hated the way that I treated her sometimes, it certainly wasn't intentional, but I wasn't as eager to please her as she undoubtedly deserved. As I considered things overall, when I was with her I was loving and considerate, and so I suppose it was the good times that we shared together that made her tolerate my indifferent, less than attentive days. But as per usual, my mind was being taken over by other matters, pushing Julie a little further down my list of priorities, and as though to prove the point, once my business day was done I instinctively made my way to Sky Cottage.

As I pulled up, the interior lights reminded me of my mistake, but it was too late to slip away unnoticed. Leoni had seen me, and ran outside and proceeded to drag me inside. As I made my way through the front door she was very excitable; there was a real whiff of something illegal in the air. Leoni ushered me into the lounge, before disappearing into the kitchen. She soon joined me, pouring a large *Jack Daniel's*. I couldn't help but smile as she handed me the almost full glass.

'Wow, Leoni! I've got to drive home!'

My incorrigible friend looked stunning in a cream satin wrap barely covering her bottom, the sheen of the fabric showing off the fullness and pertness of her breasts, which resulted in me whispering under my breath, 'Wipe it from your mind Ritchie boy!'

I could hear high heels on oak floorboards upstairs and then a voice calling. Leoni answered her friend from the bottom of the stairs, before rejoining me.

'Tia has really taken to you, Ritchie. In fact…'

We were suddenly interrupted by the phone ringing. Leoni looked at me, and I shrugged my shoulders.

'You answer it, Leoni! I've never given the number out here!'

But as Leoni answered, her voice suddenly shrieked, *'Oh, Jimmy baby!'*

She exchanged a quick few words, but the phone was soon passed to me.

'Ritchie! I'm in Gretna Green. Sally and I, well, we're *finally* getting married!'

The words Gretna Green filled me with horror and I almost freaked at how Jimmy had got through to me on this phone. No one knew the Sky Cottage number; this place was my private retreat. But as I had damagingly learned from my second life, it wasn't wise to question certain happenings. After all, this whole thing was so much bigger than me.

'Ritchie? *Please,* my mum's got the twins. Try to get everyone together! Look, it's a bad line, *just* get here! We came up thinking we'd just get married and then return and surprise everyone, but now we're here I think it would mean the world to Sally, well, to us both, if our best friends were here with us! Oh and, Ritchie, you need to be here for nine in the morning!'

The phone then went dead, just as it had done before. Leoni looked at me, a little concerned by my ashen face. I explained Jimmy's lunacy, but she winced apologetically, stating that she had arranged to meet up with her mum and dad tomorrow, to finally tell them the truth.

'Leoni, it's not a problem, but I've got to go. Need to get a few of us together!'

And as I made my apologies to her, yelling a goodbye up the stairs to Tia, I couldn't help but swoon as my house guest stood at the top of the landing, stunning in some little silky number. I shook my head, scolding her with a wagging finger at her sheer inability to cover any of her famous curves. All I received in reply was a smile that almost succeeded in stopping me from walking out of that front door. But as I gritted my teeth and left, the door slammed firmly behind me and my heart almost stopped. If the shock of Leoni and Tia's plans for me weren't enough, then the sudden heavy snowflakes falling thick and fast around me were like an arrow through my forehead.

I turned the key of the truck and the engine roared into life. My first thoughts were to do as Jimmy asked, but then it seemed totally obvious: if nobody went, then nobody would die! So I sincerely tried to make my way steadily home. As I hit the final T-junction, I stopped, hesitancy filling my head. If I turned left, I went home to the safety of Julie. If I turned the steering wheel right, then within a couple of minutes I would be in the Whippet's car park in pursuit of Scottie. *Left it is...please take me home!* I turned the steering wheel *right,* and within minutes I was in the pub car park. My palms were clammy, my brow perspiring – this was wrong. But then maybe *this* was a new test? Maybe this was meant to be? Perhaps my inability to turn left and retreat to the safety of my new family was to test me, to prove that the journey could be tackled safely? Or perhaps... I *simply* didn't know! I hung my head for a few moments, pondering my next move, but all I could settle on was that I needed a drink. I took a deep breath and made up my mind to go home. I knew that was the right thing to do – I certainly didn't want to risk meeting up with anybody. But I was finding it difficult. I was being pushed, pulled, gradually being worn down until I felt convinced that my control was gone. I turned off the engine, opened the pickup door and made my way into the pub.

'Ritchie, old chap! How the hell are you?'

I looked in the direction of the loud drunken voice and there was Scottie, his dishevelled appearance taking me a little by surprise. As I sat down next to the loud drunk, he let it all pour out.

'Ritchie, I've really *fucked* things up. Janey (hic), well, you probably know I've been giving her one?'

Well, I hadn't known for certain, and I couldn't believe he'd want to cheat on Yasmin, but Scottie continued.

'Well, Janey, the *silly* bitch, has got herself pregnant! (hic) And Yasmin, bless her, she's *not* best pleased. In fact (hic), I got home this evening having done the decent thing, you know (hic), telling her the truth, and she's *gone,* cleared off! Left a note and buggered off! Her mum won't tell me (hic) where she is, says she's better off without a two-timing *rat* like me!'

I felt like thumping Scottie and then telling him a few home truths. But just as I was trying to contain my self-righteousness, I heard my voice above the noise of the pub.

'Scottie! Janey's pregnant? Your baby? Baby Scottie?'

I winced as I realised what I'd said, but then the fact that Janey was pregnant just as I was about to drag Scottie off up to Scotland made me begin to sweat. Suddenly I knew that I had to take control and walk away from Scottie now. I went to jump up, with a sudden desperate yearning to race round to Yasmin's mum's to try to coax an address out of her. But I had no intention of signing my own death warrant. I knew I should have simply walked out of the pub, but I turned to Scottie and told him about the phone call from Jimmy. Scottie nodded his head, but as his intentions became clear, his reply was tantamount to entrapment.

'No, Ritchie (hic). I know I should go with you, but I *need* to find Yasmin (hic), tell her that I'm sorry, maybe propose to her (hic). I'm sure that will swing it! *Shit!* I dunno! I'll do whatever it takes to get her back, though...'

Suddenly, I grabbed Scottie's arm and dragged him out towards the pickup.

'No, Scottie! You need to leave Yasmin to sort herself out, and we need to be there for Sally and Jimmy! Come on, mate, you can sleep the booze off while we drive!'

As the wheels of the truck crunched over the ever-thickening fresh snow, I just listened as Scottie went on and on about his love for Yasmin, and how she was a stupid cow for not understanding that a man is allowed at least one minor discrepancy. My dear friend was also adamant that it wasn't really his fault, that Janey made him feel special. I tried to delve a little deeper, asking him to explain. Scottie started to giggle, revealing how he had always insisted to Janey that it was her he really wanted. But then, when back in the arms of Yasmin, he would tell her the same thing!

'Ritchie, it's not my fault! It's just, well (hic), with Yasmin I don't feel that I've got her full attention, it's (hic) as though her mind is elsewhere, as though I don't have all off her...'

I was beaming inanely as Scottie shared the intricacies of his crumbling relationship. My mind was racing. I knew that this drunken wreck beside me was my friend, perhaps even like a brother to me, but in these circumstances my loyalty and love for Yasmin meant that Scottie would always come second.

The wiper blades were just holding their own as they battled bravely against the increasing snowfall. I started to think about when Yasmin and I first got together, how easy and wonderful our relationship was. It's like any successes in life, especially relationships, it's all about luck. If you fall for Mr or Mrs Right and it all works out, then great, you're *given* for having good judgment. But the honest truth is, if you fall for someone, then you fall. Whether they're right for you and whether you can make each other happy, only time will tell. So the walk of love by design is blind. Physically we may be attracted, but the sexual chemistry, day-to-day compatibility, is that not down to luck?

My fear and jealousy of all that Scottie and Yasmin could mean to each other kept me on that treacherous road to Scotland. The snow was coming down thick and fast. And like a lamb to the slaughter, Scottie started to snore. I recalled how he had shown his concerns on our original, fateful journey. But in his drunken state now, I had only my conscience to wrestle with. I tried to convince myself that this wasn't about Scottie, that this was about Jimmy and Sally, making sure they knew I loved them, that I wouldn't allow anything to stop me being at their wedding, a small consolation for the negative I had introduced to their lives. I didn't want to believe that I was signing Scottie's death warrant – perhaps even my own. I was now convinced that any control I thought I had was gone. But as Scottie's snoring started to resemble that of an injured boar, I was aware of a small hand on my leg.

'Ritchie! Keep your eyes on the road!'

Rose's words hit me hard and seemed to wake me from my trance. My eyes concentrated on the snow-covered road ahead.

'I'm confused, Ritchie. You *know* you shouldn't be doing this, this journey will only lead to tragedy!'

My heart was beating uncomfortably fast with guilt and having been caught out doing something I shouldn't.

'But Rose, this isn't my choice. I didn't go looking for Scottie. Surely this is all *you,* the powers that be, *fate?'*

Rose told me to stop the pickup truck. I pulled over to the side of the road, almost steering us into a snowdrift. Every hair on my body stood on end, guilt and embarrassment taking over me.

'Ritchie, you know that your reasons for this are wrong. You just want to punish Scottie for his lack of respect for Yasmin. This lack of power over your own destiny that you talk about is pure *fallacy.* You, Ritchie, have total control, just as you have over most of your choices now.'

And as I watched the wiper blades make everything a little

clearer, I turned to Rose to say something, but she was gone.

I drove at a snail's pace, apologising again and again to the blissfully unaware, unconscious Scottie. I finally got my friend home, struggling terribly but eventually managing to get him onto his settee. I threw his boots into the corner of the room and stepped back. I felt my eyes sting and my heart hang heavy. But as I stepped forward, I broke into a smile, feeling sheer elation that I had been forced to turn around as it dawned on me that Scottie would get to see his child. I prayed that his son or daughter would get the love and protection they would need for many, many happy years. I bent down over Scottie, placing a soft kiss on his forehead. As I made my way to the front door, I looked back at him and thanked the heavens above for Rose's intervention.

I was just about to leave when Janey turned up. She could tell from just looking at me that I knew her secret.

'Ritchie, please don't think badly of me! Yasmin is my *best* friend, but it's been torture watching her together with the man that I love! She could have anyone. I don't believe that she loved him with *all* her heart. In fact...' Janey stopped as though wanting to tell me something, but averted her gaze and continued. 'I haven't meant to be a bad person, Ritchie, but love can make you do unforgivable things!'

Her words sank deep into my soul and of course I knew exactly what she meant. I stepped out of the house, but then turned, taking her hands in mine.

'Janey, I know he loves you *very* much, and you're quite right, it was never meant to be, with Yasmin. Just make sure that you keep him to yourself this time, *never* let him forget how amazing you are!'

Janey threw her arms around me, kissing my cold face.

'Thank you, Ritchie, *my* angel! Don't worry, I'll not let him out of my sight!'

I jumped back into the pickup truck and sped off, a sudden surge of jubilation shooting through my body. As I turned into Vine Street, two roads away from the Old Church, I simply didn't have a chance. A thunderous thump and sickening slam of metal against flesh filled the cabin of the pickup truck. As I jammed the brakes on hard, I slid out of control and hit the kerb. My heart was in my mouth as I flung open the door and quickly jumped out. I couldn't see anything or anyone for several seconds, but then I stopped a couple of feet away from the body of a man. As I crouched down, I turned my head, as I was aware of a woman watching me from a well-lit open doorway, her little boy crying at her side. My hands started to shake as I focused on the damage I had done. As I watched the blood pour from the injured man's head, I turned him over and felt myself go very light-headed, almost to the point of blacking out. I felt that I aged ten years instantly as I recognised the face. It was Ian...Janey and little Scottie's abuser, the man I had originally thrown to his death. As I looked at him, his eyes stared straight at me, but he was already gone. The lady and the young boy walked towards us both, but as I stood up, ready to apologise, I noticed the bruises on her bare arms, the tear stains on her cheeks, as though she'd been crying all day. I looked at the poor woman and her young child; she would never know that I totally understood the relief clearly visible in her eyes.

I clung onto Julie that night for all I was worth. But as the sweat of guilt and questioning insanity poured off me, I simply tossed and turned within my broken hallucinating sleep, Julie's haunting quizzical eyes just staring at me, offering pity, questioning concern at what I had relayed to her. But how could she understand? Just another twist and blow that I was having to digest and make sense of. I had explained about the man, how I hit and killed him. Julie just held onto me, not letting go. But after hours of sympathetic words, she uttered the inevitable.

'Ritchie, that poor woman and child!'

I tried to explain her bruises, and the fact that she seemed relieved, but I could see Julie didn't understand. As I pulled her towards me, I simply had to ask her to trust me. What had happened to this man tonight was actually okay.

A few days passed by, and I had kept away from Leoni and her friend. I think I'd had enough excitement for a lifetime or two. It was Sunday morning and the snow was still on the ground. I was standing in the middle of our gravel driveway, hot cup of coffee in my grateful hands, my faced stretched up to the ineffective lilac sun. The temperature had risen a little and so the snow was starting to thaw, slipping slowly and sliding off the weary branches of the ancient trees that framed our home. Lillie was putting the finishing touches to the snowman we had both built on the front lawn. Julie stepped out of the front door, her red fur hat and gloves giving her that festive look. She lovingly snuggled up to me, my now cold bones gratefully absorbing her yet untapped heat. We stood silent and thoughtful for five minutes or so, until Julie broke the moment.

'Ritchie, look how the rust is marking the snow as it drips onto the drive, look! From your rusty pickup!'

As I took in her large brown eyes sparkling mischievously, I felt honoured to know her, but totally unworthy of her love. She compensated enormously for my passive attitude towards our relationship. And though I had my positive days, undoubtedly the negative regretful moments would see her eyes sadden, but it was as though she dare not ask me why. Lillie, however, was a happy young girl. And though they would have each received total devotion from Jack, I prayed that deep down they both knew that I loved them very much.

My eyes wandered through the sugar-dusted skeletal trees in the orchard as the wrought iron gate to next door was forced forward. Lillie's school friend was pushing her Wellington-clad legs through the untouched snow until greeted by Lillie, and excitedly joined in her snowman dressing. Julie and I beamed simultaneously at the excited girls. We linked arms and walked a few steps.

'Ritchie, seriously though, you have your company car, so you really should consider selling the old truck. Or perhaps scrapping it is more realistic!'

I pushed her playfully away from me, uttering, 'Ha, ha, funny girl!'

Julie ran back at me, a playful hurt expression on her face, before pushing her arms around my waist.

'Ritchie, *we're* alright, aren't we?'

I hugged her tight, desperate for her to feel reassured. We stood silent and peaceful, and then I broke the moment.

'Julie, what do you want to do for Lillie's fifth birthday?'

It had played increasingly on my mind to make the most of my beautiful daughter's birthdays. For the ones I had missed, and far more importantly, in recognition of the countdown to her eighth: the mere thought of it brought me out in an overwhelming sweat! I had become understandably paranoid; any sniffs and sneezes, then straight off to the doctor. Though I had tried to be as subtle as possible, I could see my numerous requests and excuses to get Lillie in for this test and that had unnerved Julie. And so I had tried to ease off and accept the doctor's repeated claims.

'Mr Angel, she's a perfectly *healthy* little girl.'

Julie's words cut through suddenly.

'Mmmm, I don't know, Ritchie, so you plan to stick around then?'

Julie laughed, a playful nudge of her shoulder into my ribs, before stepping away from me, her hand now pulling the timber garage door open. 'Ritchie, it really is a waste you know! If you're not going to use the Porsche you *really* should consider selling it. We must have lost fifteen grand on it since Jack, *well,* since he died.'

She was right of course, but I felt strange letting it go. I'd not changed anything in or outside of the house, and I felt guilty about my reasons. I just felt that perhaps changing things would erase Jack from his home, and that my time here was simply as a *passer through.* I know that sounds disrespectful to Julie and Lillie, but I didn't want to be here forever for obvious reasons – I just didn't want to leave an indelible mark. That said, I knew that I should make a decision, that perhaps the pickup should go. And the Porsche? Well, that had to be down to Julie. But as I considered a suitable replacement for the pickup truck, I knew it was an impossible request. The memories of my former life were in every scratch, in every rusty section – I knew it would break my heart to let it go. *No!* I definitely didn't want it gone.

Later that day, I received a phone call from Leoni.

'Ritchie, we've got a leak! There's quite a bad damp patch on the ceiling in the main bedroom. Maybe you could send someone out to fix it, *or* perhaps have a look yourself? Roof, plumbing, Tia and I are not sure which.'

I didn't think anything of it, just promised to get out before four later that day.

Suddenly, there was a loud knock on the front door of the Old Church. As I turned the heavy latch I shook my head in total surprise, before throwing my arms around our unexpected visitors.

'*Jimmy! Sally!* Get yourselves in! I'm *so* sorry we couldn't get up to you, but the weather was dreadful.'

As I stepped back, taking in their proud beaming faces, Julie ran through from the kitchen, giving them both a congratulatory hug. Lillie came bounding down the stairs, all snug and warm having had a nice hot bath after her many hours of fun in the snow – she too made sure they knew we were extremely glad to have them home safely. We cracked open a bottle of champagne and toasted the newly married couple. And as the bubbles hit the back of my throat, I smiled to myself, eternally grateful that Scottie was alive and well, being given the chance to start his own adventure with Janey and her bump. After catching up with all the details of their special day, I felt disappointed that none of us could have been there with them. And though I was keen to be sociable, I felt a small rumble of butterflies, causing me to glance at my watch several times in anticipation of my 4 o'clock appointment.

Finally, just after five, I made my excuses to Sally and Jimmy, explaining that I was needed at Sky Cottage. At the front door, Lillie was reluctant for me to go, but I assured both my special girls that I would be back before they knew it, and that I would be able to help with Lillie's kitten project for school. The temperature was now below zero again, the thaw halted and encased with a shimmering glaze.

As I crunched my way across the driveway, I yelled back to them both, 'LILLIE, PARTY! YOU NEED TO START THINKING *REALLY* BIG! BYE...!'

Suddenly, Lillie broke free from her mum, her bare feet now carrying her at the speed of light towards me, Julie's screams of laughter ordering her to come back. Lillie jumped into my open arms, the intensity of her stature-defying hug almost breaking my neck, her sudden gasps of, 'Daddy, that snow *is* freezing! My toes are tingling!' And then my heart flipped.

'Please hurry back, Daddy, I hate it when you're not here with me and Mummy!'

Leoni opened the front door.

'Ritchie, come on in, you're late, you bad boy!'

She looked gorgeous – whatever she was getting up to with Tia, well, it certainly gave her an incredible glow.

As I slipped off my heavy winter jacket I sighed and commented, 'Wow! It's really hot in here!'

Leoni just smiled and grabbed a bottle of red wine from the kitchen, the cork already pulled. My friend kept putting her arms around me, her small white vest top hardly containing her tanned breasts. She handed me a large full glass of red and ushered me into the lounge. As I turned ready to sit, she playfully pushed me back into the big chair by the open fire.

'Steady, tiger! Bloody hell, Leoni, it nearly went everywhere!'

As the wine slipped over the rim and oozed around my fingers, Leoni smiled and walked away from me, her navy blue and white polka-dot shorts leaving nothing to the imagination. She had certainly picked up a good all-over tan while abroad. And as I tried to steer my eyes away from the forbidden, Leoni pulled the curtains across, shutting out the pitch-black night.

'Oh, Leoni, the leak, in the bedroom?'

Leoni looked at me, and then the penny seemed to drop.

'Oh, *the* leak, silly me! Seems to have sorted itself. Maybe it was just a bit of snow blown in or something…'

I stood up. 'Well, if you don't mind, probably best I check it out; maybe the drop in temperature has stopped it temporarily.'

Leoni looked at me cheekily and then smiled. 'Okay, you know where it is!'

I made my way upstairs and stepped into the main bedroom. I stopped suddenly, as there was Tia, sitting at the dressing table, in her pale-pink expensive-looking satin and lace underwear.

'Oh, Tia! I'm *so* sorry! Leoni didn't say that you were up here!'

Tia looked at me via the mirror, a huge smile spread across her face. She didn't turn around but simply stood up, checking her reflection and then straightening the seams on her flesh-coloured stockings.

'Oh, don't worry about me, Ritchie, just do what you've got to do!'

I walked around the bedroom, trying to find the stain on the ceiling, while Tia continued to preen herself. I simply couldn't believe how stunning she was! And then just as I was about to leave the room, Tia bent down. I seemed to freeze, unable to peel my eyes away from her small satin panties, pulled extremely taut across her pert cheeks. At that point Leoni walked in.

'Ignore her, Ritchie! She's just seeing how you react!'

I had to smile at them both, suspecting that I was showing myself up as the small town boy that I was. Tia stood up straight and then stepped towards Leoni. The well brought up gentleman in me felt it polite to step out of the room and leave these girls to their privacy, but I didn't feel ready to leave just yet. Tia placed a very soft gentle kiss on Leoni's lips and I questioned again in my mind whether perhaps *now* I should slip away. But whether I was to stay or go, both the girls seemed quite unperturbed about their audience of one. Totally without warning, Tia pulled Leoni's vest top up and then over her head, and my eyes couldn't help but widen in response. Both girls' eyes were on mine, Leoni looking away first, the back of her hand dropping down between Tia's legs, a gentle caressing, Tia's eyes not leaving mine. I was simply rooted to the spot. Leoni started to probe a little more, seemingly oblivious to my existence. Though after several moments Leoni's eyes were on mine, judging my reaction. I didn't move. Leoni smiled.

'It's okay, Ritchie!' She then beckoned me to join them. 'Tia has never, ever been with a man. On screen, *yes,* intimately*, no.* I'm serious. I told her about us, you know, I mean, it *was* amazing!'

The girls suddenly looked away from me as Tia started to peel off Leoni's shorts, and then as Leoni pushed Tia onto the edge of the bed I had to gasp in amazement as Leoni returned the favour and slid Tia's panties down her long, slender legs, at which Tia lifted her feet and the wisp of satin was gone. The girls were now both looking at me as though having raised the stakes. Leoni's eyes lingered on mine, an inspired invitation, desperate for an RSVP.

'Please, Ritchie! You're the only man I trust. *Pleasssse?*'

I couldn't help but ponder the fact that this was a totally surreal situation. I physically blinked, convinced that I'd wake up. But as my eyes met Tia's, there was an endearing innocence about the pair of them that made my inability to walk away as a twenty-three year old, unmarried red-blooded male caught in the moment, forgivable. Two beautiful, adventurous girls waiting for me, just feet away. Leoni let her hand fall between Tia's thighs, her middle finger exploring successfully, Tia arching her back in response. The girls *again* looked for my reaction; Tia's face as though I would be doing her the biggest favour in the world. I looked skyward, and then within seconds ... *to hell with it! Where's the harm?* I lifted my thick wool jumper over my head, Leoni sprang excitedly towards me, almost gazelle-like, helping me undo my jeans.

'Wooooh, not so fast, girls! I need to take things a *little* slower. Call me old fashioned, but maybe start with a kiss first?'

Leoni pushed her lips onto mine, gently, sensuously, slowly, her tongue just touching the tip of mine. Bit by bit I started to acclimatise, adapt to the situation. I then moved towards Tia, her eyes sparkling in anticipation. I simply couldn't resist lowering my lips onto hers. Her kisses were a little harsher, wanting; her hand suddenly on the back of my neck, our kisses starting to devour each other, our tongues entwined. I pulled away for breath. I looked at Leoni, her breast pushed into my arm, and I let the back of my hand gently brush her nipple; instantly it became erect and I dropped my mouth onto the protruding flesh. But then Tia pulled me towards her and I was as though a child in a sweet shop! I turned away from Leoni briefly, but then her lips were on mine. I could suddenly feel two sets of hands across my back, my buttocks, pleasuring me unreservedly. As Leoni's mouth started to retrace the steps of her hands I lifted my head skyward, thanking my lucky stars, every muscle stretched and taut, maximising the incredible sensation in every fibre of my body.

I dropped down amongst the warm available flesh and ran my hand down the full length of Tia's body, admiring, kissing, touching, before finally unclipping her bra as she arched her back. I welcomed her breasts as they lifted up towards me, my fingers pushing beneath her satin and lace suspender belt, and as my body writhed against hers I left the remaining lingerie in place, adding that extra sensual *something* to the proceedings. I was now stretched out above Tia, Leoni's mouth and breasts soft and tingling down my spine. I continued to tease Tia, not allowing my body to touch hers, but then as she kept moving towards me, lifting her body up to meet me, I felt Leoni's soft warm hands placed onto my thighs. I then placed a gentle kiss onto Tia's lips. She tasted *so* good! But then Leoni took control of proceedings, her fingers guiding me into her beautiful friend. The wetness of Tia sent a surge of electricity through my entire body, and as I pushed very gently, slight tender touches, for a split second I thought I would lose my composure and embarrass myself, but then as I relaxed and pushed a little deeper I started to find my rhythm, slowly, gently…But as I pushed a little harder Tia would lift her body, her aroused nipples brushing my chest with every teasing stroke, and each time I felt as though I was going to explode. I managed to hold on, temporarily saved from ridicule, and then as Tia seemed to get lost in the moment Leoni started to kiss her friend passionately. After a dozen or so harder, more forceful strokes, Tia pushed her lips onto mine and Leoni slumped onto the bed, pushing her fingers deep into herself, arching her back, her pleasurable moans adding to the potency of proceedings. Tia pushed her body towards me, each time harder than the last, until for both of us the moment was too much. Tia clung onto my body for dear life just as I pushed myself all the way.

Tia looked so relaxed and breathtaking as her body slumped beneath me. She was more beautiful than I had ever seen her in any of her films, and here I was, well, I was overwhelmed! The girls both looked after me very well that night. Once they had bathed me, refreshed me, sharing with me a bottle or two of chilled champagne, Leoni decided it was her turn.

'Please, Ritchie! Tia was my way of saying thank you for

your wonderful friendship, and I will never forget the hurt in your eyes when I explained that I was definitely gay. But I thought that this way you'd know that you weren't to blame!'

And as Leoni climbed on top of me, her eyes sparkling, wriggling herself into position, she cooed, 'Mmmm, Tia! You forget how good the *real* thing can feel!'

And as strange as it may sound, though I had never fantasised about making love to two beautiful women before, believing that one on one was best, quality not quantity, I have to say that tonight was a night I would never have wanted to miss.

As I crept away the next morning, leaving the two girls huddled together, I didn't feel quite so proud of myself. The cold light of day and betrayal to Julie produced a heavy heart and a sick feeling to the stomach. The crunch of icy snow beneath my feet expressed exactly how I felt – uneasy, as though I was ready for a fall. As I walked towards the pickup, the lilac morning sun bounced off the shoddy paintwork. I stopped, just feet away from the truck. I looked up at the sky, and turned very slowly three hundred and sixty degrees. I then looked out in front of me, taking in the individual homes. As my eyes scoured, each house produced a memory: Old Fluffers, and how she'd run off, driving everybody mad as she bounded through the beautifully kept gardens, throwing herself around without a care in the world. I recalled how I would be laughing so much inside, watching as Yasmin ran one way and then another, finally having to dive at Fluffers, as she'd taken the game to a higher level. I could feel the tears welling up inside of me as I thought about my beautiful wife, how she would run towards me with her flushed face: 'Oh God, Ritchie! Please stop laughing! Come on, you *must* help me, the Major will go crazy, she's wrecking his garden!' And her simply taking my hand, her pale-blue gloves encasing my cold fingers – the warmth, the electricity that would pass through me, that simple touch. Oh, how I longed for *that* touch, her face to press up against mine! But here I am, cheating on my girlfriend, the mother of my daughter, just because I had got carried away. Julie would be waiting with a heavy heart, Lillie worrying because I wasn't home, seeing full well that once again her daddy was making her mummy unhappy. I hated hurting them both, and yet it was all I seemed to do. I mean sure, I was there for them, most of the time. But increasingly I would catch them both looking at me, as though they knew my heart wasn't totally in it, as though my passion, mind and soul were elsewhere – and of course they were right.

I turned and looked back at Sky Cottage. I reflected on my wonderful memories – and now? I'd tarnished without thought such a precious legacy to what had gone before. As accepting as I was that last night had just been a bit of fun, it wasn't quite as simple as that. The price that I paid, the guilt that hangs so heavy the morning after the night before, for Julie, for Lillie, was also for Yasmin and Evie, but most of all I just felt, well, as though I was a bit pathetic really!

CHAPTER TWENTY-ONE

Heaven To Hell

After Death, 1994 – Lilac Sky
I couldn't face Julie and so went straight to work. It was 7.20 a.m. by the time I stepped into Skirdle's. I sat before the telephone, and finally lifted the receiver. It rang out for a while, but then a sleepy voice answered.

'Julie, it's Ritchie. I'm *so* sorry darling, I, I, well, having been and seen the leak, I remembered something I needed to do at work. And well, time passed quickly and, well, I've just woken up.'

Julie didn't say anything for a few painful seconds and then her words smacked my face hard.

'Don't worry, Ritchie, Lillie came in and slept with me. In fact, she's looking at me now, wondering what lies her daddy's telling her mummy!'

The phone was then put down, and though I knew she had hung up,

'Julie, Julie, please!'

I tried to concentrate for a few hours, but the urge to go home and make things right became too strong. Just as I was about to get up and leave, a policeman came into the shop.

'Mr Angel?'

Mr Ball pointed to me, and a huge sigh of relief left my colleague's pursed lips.

'Ahhh, Mr Angel. Can I have a word, in private?'

Mr Ball stood up, grabbed his coffee cup and headed off into the kitchen. The policeman sat down, taking off his helmet and placing it on my desk.

'Right, Mr Angel. I thought I had best call in and see you, stop any unnecessary anxiety you may be experiencing. Mr Hunt, Mr Ian Hunt, we've gathered all the evidence concerning his death and your unfortunate part in it, and suffice to say, well, there won't be any charges brought against you. Though you will be called upon to attend a hearing, we will be purely concluding that you had absolutely no chance, and as his wife has been keen to stress that it was Mr Hunt, her husband – though only for six months or so – that was to blame and that you had no chance whatsoever of avoiding him.'

The policeman finished his speech, got back to his feet and bid me good day. Once out of the shop, he placed his helmet back on his head, checked his reflection in the shop window, positioned both his hands behind his back and proceeded up Willow High Street in the traditional guise of a real 1950's British bobby – I liked it.

My amusement quickly turned to relief, but I would have felt very hard done by had things turned out any differently. But my guilt was calling me elsewhere. I couldn't believe it was just after 11 a.m. and here I was trying to work when I had serious issues to address back at the Old Church. So I stood up, made my excuses and headed home, finally realising that I couldn't rest until I knew Julie had forgiven me.

The large iron gates were open, which was unusual. I turned off the engine and stepped out onto the driveway. I pushed my key into the front door and stepped inside. I had heard the thud of bass from outside, but now in the church the music was painfully loud. As I walked into the lounge, my head was filled with horrific memories – the loud music, and all the heartache that I had witnessed here. I repeated my actions, walking slowly up to the stereo, but turning the volume right down this time. I almost expected footsteps, or perhaps a yell from upstairs, but nothing. I finally pushed the off button, the echoes of the song ringing around the church. As the deafening silence eased, I was aware of distant sobbing – my guilt was filling me up. Determined to make amends, I ran towards the stairs and then, striding two at a time, finally reached the landing.

'Julie! Julie, please! Darling, I am *so* sorry.'

But as I ran into our bedroom, expecting to see Julie on her own – Lillie having been dropped off at school at least a couple of hours ago – that was not what I found. Instead, a scene that can simply kill you on the spot. The sun was shining through the stained-glass window onto Julie's ashen face. Her brown sparkly eyes extinguished. And though I knew she was holding something, I was afraid to look. Then, as my eyes found the courage, there, on Julie's lap, was Lillie – her limp body, her blue lips. Something inside seemed to kick-start my instincts. I threw myself towards them both, trying to grab Lillie away from Julie, but she quickly dropped her body over our daughter.

As I tried once again to touch Lillie, to hold her, Julie screamed at me, 'IT'S NO USE! *IT'S NO USE!!'*

Finally, Julie fell to the side, letting the precious bundle slump forward. My heart was trying to break out through my mouth as I grabbed Lillie, scooping her up in my arms. My tears spat out like venom. She was gone, her once soft, warm body now cold, the life drained out of her. As I held onto her small frame, my heart seemed to convulse and I started to splutter. The red-hot molten tears fell unrelenting down my face. I tried to hug her, push my life into her. I wanted so much, like she'd done a thousand times before, for her body to mould lovingly into mine. But this wasn't *my* little girl, this was just a lifeless, empty shell. The only thing that was the same was her beautiful silky hair. The shivers started to run up and down my spine as I placed Lillie onto the bed. She simply didn't look real.

Julie crawled towards us both, trying to pull herself up, but she didn't have the strength. She just looked up at me; hate, pity, her eyes asking a million questions. But as I stood, my eyes on Julie's, she somehow managed to speak.

'She just died, Ritchie. I, I, I think she had some sort of heart attack. She got herself upset.' Julie, suddenly unable to look at me, dropped her head, her voice barely audible. 'Ritchie…she got *very* upset and she just started shaking…couldn't get her breath, started a weird sort of screaming, holding her heart. I tried to calm her down but she just kept screaming, until… Oh God, Ritchie, until she couldn't scream any more. She couldn't even cry…her eyes just looked at me. Her eyes, Ritchie, just begging me to help her! Calling for you…*wanting* her *daddy* to help her!'

My tears were dropping onto Julie, mixing with her own, her face drenched.

'Please believe me, Ritchie! I couldn't save her, I couldn't save my *little* baby!'

I fell to my knees, trying desperately to hold Julie, but she wouldn't let me in, just kept pushing me away.

Between her gut-wrenching cries came, *'Ritchie, I couldn't save my beautiful little girl!'*

And as her sobs became uncontrollable, my tears falling like raindrops, we both cried inconsolably.

The three of us died that night; the pain was like nothing I had ever experienced. I thought I had had it bad, thought I had been through every conceivable emotion, but this was so painfully final, guilt-ridden and murderous. Yasmin and Evie – I lived with the hope that I would see them again. But losing Lillie in these pitiful circumstances, it was a pain that could so easily kill you, and the way that I felt now I wished it would.

Once I had finally closed the front door, I leant with my back against it. In the distance I could hear the iron gates clang shut – finally everybody was gone. And the one little person that should be here with her mother and father, well, she was gone too. While Julie and her mum and dad were falling apart around me, I just kept asking myself, *why now, why three years or so early?* I recalled the black plastic body bag that they put Lillie in. I saw Julie's reaction, but all I could do was shake. I couldn't talk, and as I watched Julie's body crumple up with the pain, we just looked at each other. Julie's mother wrapping her arms around her daughter, Julie's father not quite sure what to do, just staring down at his feet, but the tears that fell from his eyes simply summed everything up. *Why?* And as the night plodded on, surreal and desperate, I raised my eyes to the high ceiling and thought about Julie in our bed, heavily sedated by the doctor. I hoped that she'd fallen asleep. I knew that I couldn't cope with the hurt in her eyes.

I thought back to how I had originally felt about Lillie's death. And of course, despite my outward denial, there was still that feeling of hopelessness, but it was nothing like this. I didn't know Lillie then, but I loved her completely now. I think it was the image that kept pushing itself into my mind of her little fingers, unable to push and curl into mine, that hung lifelessly when she was placed into the cold man-made body bag. I recalled earlier the many questions from police, from the doctor, all answered through a veil of tears. Originally, my first life, I knew that I had to come and see Julie, and we were reunited through our grief. My eyes suddenly widened, as it painfully hit home: being in Lillie's life meant that she had died three and a half years earlier than before. Jack had taken better care of *my* little girl than I had. My blood ran cold and my breathing stopped. But as the tears of guilt rolled relentlessly down my cheeks, I repeated the words of the doctor: 'It's very rare for a young child to have a heart attack. But if there is a mechanical fault, then often, too much emotion or excitement, the heart cannot cope! But we'll know more once the coroner has had a chance to carry out an autopsy.' I thought about how upset Lillie would have been about me not coming home last night and I cursed myself. I knew that I could be selfish, I knew that I looked after number one far too much and would get lost in the moment, telling myself *to hell with the consequences! I'll deal with that when the time comes!* Well, as I sat with my back against the bare stone wall, I couldn't help but believe that I had killed Lillie, and that had I been a better, kinder person, she would be here with us now.

I looked at the hall clock. It was nearly 3 a.m. – it only seemed like a couple of hours since I returned home. But as I thought about how the last twenty-four hours had totally destroyed what was dearest to me in my new world, I couldn't help but cry out, but all I produced was pain and noise, as all my tears had run dry.

I must have drifted off, and a shiver and coldness surrounded me as I forced my heavy, crusted eyes open. The sun was starting to show itself, flickers of light beaming through the small stained-glass window from the landing down into the hallway where I lay broken. I didn't move for a further hour, until I found the strength from somewhere and made my way upstairs. I crept into the bedroom, sliding in next to Julie. She was snoring very gently, as she would if sleeping really deeply. As I nestled down into the bed, I slid my hand over hers. I breathed a sigh of relief as her fingertips instinctively acknowledged mine. And there we lay. It wasn't long until I fell into a deep but troubled sleep.

The days passed by. Our friends didn't find it easy; they appeared to struggle terribly, not really knowing what to say. But they were there for us, whenever we were ready, and that was all we really needed from them.

The day of Lillie's funeral was dreadful. I just felt so totally useless. Julie was barely managing to breathe all day; she just about kept going. And though she would come and have a hold every now and again, I would really hang onto her, *too* much really, and so she would finally push me away, uttering apologetically, 'Sorry, Ritchie, but you're suffocating me.' But I understood. I knew I wasn't getting the balance right, but when you're *this* numb it's not easy to judge.

Julie's mum moved into the Old Church. I wasn't asked, and I wasn't happy about it. Her dad would come and bring bits and pieces, giving me little snippets of advice, how I needed to be at Julie's and her mum's beck and call. 'After all, Ritchie, this sort of thing always hits the girls worse.' As I stepped away from him I knew he meant well, and perhaps he was right, but I wasn't convinced. Julie and I had both lost our daughter – surely we needed some time alone to grieve and repair our broken hearts together. But I think the deep-set guilt within me was making me resentful and angry, and I was beginning to feel that walking on eggshells in my own home couldn't be healthy. Having put up with Julie's mum for just over two months now, I knew it wouldn't be long before I found an excuse to lash out.

Another grey, painful day came and went. Julie's mum had brought Julie some hot milk.

'Drink it up now, dear. Go on, Ritchie, go and turn the electric blanket on, get the bed ready for Julie.'

I looked at Julie's mum and then noticed Julie staring at me.

'Ritchie, don't look at my mum like that.'

I turned and smiled, sharply adding, 'And how would that be, dear? Perhaps a look as though I'm just about ready to throw her through the stained-glass window if she doesn't start giving me just the smallest amount of respect in my own home!'

Julie's eyes narrowed, and her mum then decided to throw some petrol onto the smouldering coals.

'*Your* home eh, Ritchie Angel? This is *my* daughter's home!'

Julie stood up.

'Mum, please!'

'No, dear, I won't have it! This *is* your home, yours *and* Jack's! He moves in here, thinks he can take over, leads you a *right* song and dance! You need to tell him how you feel. Your father's already told you he'd be happy to beat some manners into him!'

I stepped back, not quite believing what this delightful woman was saying to me. I was just about to defend myself when I was drawn to Julie's face – I thought she would be ashamed of her mother's rantings, but instead she seemed to be agreeing with every word. And so I stood and looked at the pair of them – Julie saying nothing, but her mother letting me have it with both barrels.

Finally, I felt it was my turn to speak. But then, just as I was about to explain a thing or two, in flew Julie's dad, his words adding a firecracker to the proceedings.

'Right, young man! *Now* what trouble are you causing?'

I looked at Julie's mum, her words suddenly drying up, and then back to Julie's dad, his chest all puffed up, his fists clenched. Then I turned to Julie and started shaking my head from side to side. Julie's dad stepped closer to me.

I pushed my hand up to his face and he suddenly spurted some macho nonsense, so I felt it wise to warn him, 'Step any nearer and I promise you, I will embarrass you in front of your wife and daughter!'

I didn't look at him, but he wisely stepped back. I was seething, but determined not to lose my cool. Such was my anger that I could barely talk, but I managed to get a sentence or two out.

'Julie, I know I'm not perfect, but I'm part of something special here with you and Lillie! We didn't have the best of starts, that was my fault, but you were with Jack. As for the last few years, well, I felt that we were good. I've never tried to take over here, I've certainly not made any changes or tried to make my mark, never, not once! So *why* the continued hostility from your parents? I know they feel as though they owe their loyalty to Jack, but what about their loyalty to *you,* to your choices…*your* decision to be with me?'

I looked at Julie's mum, and she stared straight back at me before finally losing her nerve, her gaze falling to her feet. I waited anxiously for Julie to reassure me that things would be okay – a hug, a smile, taking my hand. I waited, and when I felt that I would have to wait forever, I stepped forward, wrapping my arms around her. I sighed, relieved, as she seemed to melt into me, burying her head into my chest. We held onto each other for dear life, but then, unexpectedly, she pulled away.

'Ritchie, I love you with all my heart, but you keep breaking it. I so much want to give you everything, but I can't reach you! I think you're incapable of love, *total love!* I could see it, not just with me, but with poor Lillie too! You would be going through the motions, but there was always something stopping you from giving us one hundred per cent.'

The tears rolled down her face, and though I hadn't been aware, they were rolling down mine too.

'Ritchie, I love you *so* much that it hurts. *You're killing me!* I know where you were the nights you weren't here, and I should hate you for it, but the truth is, *I don't,* I just *pity* you. But you *are* killing me! I've got to let you go. I've got to carry on without you, because you're no good for me...'

Julie's sobs start to build between her words.

'Ritchie, when Lillie died, she'd been in my arms for over an hour, but all I kept imagining was you not wanting us, just being with your tarts, doing whatever!'

And how could I argue with one single bar of what Julie was saying? It was all true. I did love her and Lillie, but just being there wasn't enough. She'd already experienced total commitment from Jack; she knew what it was like to be cherished. But of course, she would never understand why I couldn't give her my all. I hated having made her feel like this and I prayed to God that Lillie hadn't felt unloved. *With all my heart I prayed for that.*

I left the Old Church that night having thrown all my clothes into one small suitcase. Julie's mum and dad stood behind her as I left. As I hugged Julie goodbye, I thought I would never be able to let go, but she finally pushed me away again, lifting her hand to wipe away my tears. Julie's mum and dad just stood and watched the break-up of our relationship. I looked at them both, and though the words that left my mouth surprised me, I realised the words were right.

'Mr and Mrs Andrews, I am *so* sorry not to have taken better care of your daughter, and of course Lillie...' I swallowed hard, trying to keep it together, '...and you are absolutely right to protect Julie the way that you do.'

Their expressions didn't change, but I'd said exactly what I had finally realised. As I turned and took the first few steps, the heavy oak door clunked shut behind me. And as darkness surrounded me, I couldn't escape the sudden pained cry that came from inside the Old Church.

And so, having rented out my mum's house since moving in with Julie and Lillie, I found myself homeless. Though it would have perhaps been the most comfortable option, and had I not linked Tia and Leoni so blatantly with the night of Lillie's death, then maybe Sky Cottage would have been an obvious choice to put my head down for a few days. But there was no doubt that I would have hated it if Julie had found out I was living there. I tried Scottie's, but they didn't really have the room. And so I tried Jimmy and Sally's. I was nervous, but I needn't have been; they welcomed me with open arms.

But the world of Ritchie Angel had become such a sham. I loved Jimmy; he and I had always had a natural bond. We had total trust and respect for each other. So how could I have been so *bloody* stupid, when I was so aware of what my friendship with him meant? To have ended up creating a secret between us, a horrible festering time bomb that made me question all that we had together. But actually, living for a few days with Jimmy, Sally and the twins Danny and Daisy, had been extraordinarily magical. Though I would see them at social gatherings, I'd not really allowed myself to get too close. And though I felt positive about this stolen time I was aware of a slightly cool breeze from one person in particular. Questionable paranoia? No, there was no escaping the concern in Sally's eyes every time I played with the twins. But here I was, in Sally and Jimmy's home, and despite the contradictory see-saw I felt as relaxed as I was ever likely to be, especially in such unforgivable circumstances. But you cannot argue with the protective instincts of a mother, and so I proceeded with caution.

I'd taken a few days off work, totally necessary to make sure I didn't lose my sanity. I'd tried to telephone Julie on a couple of occasions, but each call resulted in her mum answering, stressing that I was *not* to talk to her, but promising that she would pass on the fact that I had rung. As I put down the receiver, Sally would offer words of encouragement: 'Give her time, Ritchie, the girl has been through hell!' I nodded and smiled, then focused on the twins as they asked me to watch this and that. Sally poured some red wine, and handed me a glass.

'Go on, Ritchie, it will do you good! It certainly does me good! I need at least a glass a day with these two!'

We both smiled, raising our glasses.

'To friendship!' I spurted.

Sally nodded enthusiastically and then shouted, 'TO FRIENDSHIP! AND MAKING SURE THAT WE DON'T *TOTALLY* FUCK IT UP!'

I laughed out loud. Daisy flicked her head in the direction of us both, looking shocked but bemused by her mum's outburst.

As the giggles left my friend, I knew we were about to step into more serious territory.

'Ritchie, you know Jimmy and I are happy to have you here, but, it's *not* ideal, is it?'

I smiled, reassuring her that I would be gone in the morning. Sally didn't say another word and just clinked her glass against mine, followed by a deep sigh of relief.

CHAPTER TWENTY-TWO

Half Man, Half Fish

After Death, 1994 – Lilac Sky
Spring morn, cold and fresh, but despite swimming against the tide, I was surprisingly buoyant. I waved goodbye to Jimmy and his family, approval I was sure from Sally as I climbed into my trusty rusty pickup and headed out into the country. I had been so very tempted to seek sanctuary at the Water's Edge, but was determined not to take my grief there. To have my death so devastatingly clear in my mind, lying there for all to see if I didn't make amends, well, it was sufficient incentive to salvage success with the challenge thrown down by Rose. I drove out towards Shrewsbury and pushed on towards the Long Mynd, a place I'd loved as a child. Eventually, as I made my way steadily up the thin mountain road, deserted and barren, I finally pulled up onto a slate and gravel clearing, one of the highest points of the county. I climbed out of the truck and took in the rawness of the fresh sobering wind. It felt so good as I drank it in, my lungs bristling, startled by the intrusion. I turned slowly, taking in every detail of this inspiring landscape.

My spirits stirred. I kicked the truck door shut and made my way over to the dark slate rock that stood proud, offering the best standpoint. I raised my eyes skyward, longing for clear blue sky. But as the wind wrapped itself around me, my flesh almost vibrating in its midst, it was as though the swirls that rolled across the face of the clouds and bustled with the struggling sunlight were being ravaged by lilac, edged in sombre greys and veins of black. My neck was thrust back as though the wind was intent on damaging me, each blow managing to disorientate, almost pushing me to the ground. I stood firm, determined to withstand its brute force.

Just as I believed I had the measure of my attacker, I saw the brightest lilac swirl yet twist and turn and then slam itself into my stomach, the wind leaving my lungs, forcing me to stoop forward. Then, without the speed or instinct to react sharply enough, from the rear a ridge of wind slammed hard between thigh and calf. I felt the air leave my body and heard the crack of bone as I landed on my back, sharp damp slate breaking my fall. Without warning I started to laugh, rolling slowly to my side and bringing myself up onto my knees, my fingers gouging deep into the moss-filled crevices. I suddenly felt a little more rooted, holding onto the side of the mountain. The decibel level of the wind seemed to soften, almost as though ticking over, waiting for inspiration. I dug my nails deeper, questioning whether I had upset the powers that be. *Was I making such an awful mess of my second go at life?* I feared wholeheartedly that the answer was *yes* to both. Over halfway through my journey – twenty-three years of age – knowing all that I did, and yet where had it got me?

But as my destructive doubts started to sink deep into my mind, the wind eased further as though offering a reassuring nudge. I lifted my weary eyes to face the sun, which was trying to break behind the deep-claret clouds. I begged for some kind of sign – not a request that I had ever needed or asked before. Hesitantly, I gradually stood up, but I waited. Several minutes passed and increasingly the depths of being alone sank to a new level. I wanted to turn and despondently walk away, but the urge was insufficient to move my legs, causing an increasing belief that I was taking root deep into the mountainside. I continued to wait. I swayed gently as a flicker of lilac danced around my eyes, the heat and glow instinctively making me want to blink, but there was a fresh resilience that kept my eyes wide and focused. An energy passed through me, my fingers started to tingle, a warmth from the unhindered sun soothed my face, and then set amongst the sunburst were Yasmin and Evie, with happy smiling faces, hugging and kissing each other. The power of the image filled me with fresh optimism. I stretched out my body, once again taking in the cold air and loving the sting in my lungs, the burn in my heart. And as the image in the clouds started to drift, I thought about my twenty-fourth birthday in just under a week's time. Though I was praying for a fast-forward, *desperate for that!* I had to reflect on the positive. I had completed nearly nine years, I was still alive, and so I begged shamelessly that I was still in with a chance of achieving my dream. The image of Yasmin and Evie was back and a little clearer...But then fading, leaving me...

I instinctively screamed out, 'YASMIN!...*EVIE!!'*

...And there they were, clear as day, smiling, then blowing me a kiss before their image shot away as you would imagine a UFO to take off.

I clapped my hands together, yelling into their wake, *'I LOVE YOU GIRLS!'*

It rang out into the busy sky, ricocheting repeatedly down into the valley. And with the buoyant echoes as my soundtrack, like an excited child and now able to escape the hold of the earth, I ran in circles, my arms outstretched. Suddenly, I was spinning around and around, until finally falling to the ground. I laughed as I felt the cold damp breaking through my jeans, making my body feel uncomfortable, but I didn't care. The numbness that I had felt since Lillie's death was very slowly starting to ease. So any feeling, however uncomfortable, was really very welcome. And as my eyes became increasingly drawn to an initially uninviting lake, right down at the bottom of the valley, I was suddenly running like a man possessed towards it, with total disregard for common sense. I threw my coat to the ground, and as I ran a little further my legs were suddenly no longer in control of my downward descent. I flung my T-shirt into the bracken, falling and gambolling, little nicks and scuffs, from flesh challenging jagged rock and sheer slate. As I flipped over for the sixth or seventh time, I pushed my feet firmly into the earth, gradually easing to a jolted stop just inches from the glass top of the lake.

As I sat, breathless and vaguely disorientated, the urge to

break the sleeping water became vital. I undid my heavy boots and kicked them away. I stood up, desperate to get my jeans off, taking my socks off at the same time, and hurling everything into the distance. I looked around, the cold air touching every part of me. And then, with the most powerful surge of energy I had ever experienced, I threw myself into the cold black lake. As my naked body sank into the deep, dank icy water, I felt my breath leave my body as I resurfaced.

I splashed around, but my body simply wanted more. As I pushed myself into the depths of the now inviting waters, I found that I could swim freely, moving about swiftly. Though I had always been a competent, but average swimmer, for some reason I was now moving like a fish. My eyes, normally uncomfortable as the water stung and my vision became blurred, were able to see unhindered. And as I swam around underwater, darting this way and that, I could hold my breath for minutes at a time. Eventually, I rose to the surface, the piercing lilac light causing me to squint. As I blinked away the discomfort, I began to focus on my breathtaking surroundings. The stark imposing mountains looking down on me, I suddenly felt a little uncomfortable, an increasing vulnerability replacing my confidence and vigour.

The silence of the valley was eerie. As the cool water rippled around my shoulders, the more I trod water, the little splashes would slap against my face. I was ready to get out and away from here. But then, against my wishes, as though pulled, I sank back down beneath the water, and any nerves or fear were replaced by a confidence and longing to use this powerful body. I swam faster, deeper, pushing closer to the bottom of the lake. The shiny slate looked so smooth, the flags of green fluffy weed blowing in my slipstream and the suddenly noticeable current. The water had seemed so still from the mountainside, but now, beneath the black surface, I could feel the energy, the movement all around me.

I turned quickly, pulling my arms down to my sides. I was whipping my feet up and down like a mermaid using her tail to push herself quickly through the sea. I moved *so* sharply through the water, and though I was aware that the lake wasn't that big, suddenly I seemed to be swimming in acres of icy-cold mountain water.

I rose once more to the surface, shaking the water from my hair, and blinked the intrusion from my eyes. I found myself at the top of a severe waterfall, an access to the many pools below. I took in the dangerous journey that would eventually lead me to the final lake in the distance and tried to weigh up whether or not the stream down to the next level would be able to take me without cutting me to shreds with its jagged rocks sticking out like the spikes on the back of a dinosaur. I suddenly lost my nerve and decided not to risk it, not today at least.

I raised my eyes towards the powers that be, grateful for proof that I wasn't *quite* so alone. And as I nodded in appreciation, the lilac sunrays seemed to brighten, tainting the falling droplets as I vigorously shook my head. But as I took in my sheer insignificance – my humble speck on this daunting landscape – I was unnerved. I dragged myself slowly to the side, grabbing onto clumps of bracken. I slipped and slid my way up and onto the embankment, until finally slumping unceremoniously onto the greasy, muddy mountainside.

I lay there for a few thoughtful minutes, mulling over the significance of today and all that it had delivered to me, a cool breeze slapping over my naked vulnerable body.

Suddenly, I was startled by laughter and turned quickly. There on a rock was Rose, her arms hugging her knees close to her chest. I was inquisitive as to her embarrassed amusement. But then, as a fresh northerly wind blew bracingly across me, I was reminded of my nakedness. I started scrambling around, searching in vain for something to cover me. I finally admitted defeat and stood awkwardly, my fingers outstretched protectively. Rose pulled her hands to her mouth, stifling a snigger, typical of any eight year old and how they would react in this embarrassing situation.

'I'm sorry, Ritchie, it's not you being naked, it's just your face! You get yourself *so* flustered sometimes; you need to relax. You forget, I get to see you at *many* points during your day-to-day life; nothing shocks me any more! But then again, Leoni and Tia, well, maybe we'd better not get into that!'

I felt my cheeks blush with sheer horror at how I had

unintentionally corrupted this innocent child.

Rose climbed off her rock, suddenly holding a pile of neatly folded clothes, my boots balanced on the top. She looked right into my eyes and took a step back. I started to shiver, a frown crumpling my brow.

'Umm, can I have my clothes please?'

Rose appeared to chew the inside of her mouth and suddenly turned her head towards the lower lake.

'Ritchie, I will hold onto these clothes, but you need to be brave, you need to trust me.'

Her words made me extremely uncomfortable. There was barely a breeze now, but the air had a distinct chill and the sky appeared to be waiting for something. I wrapped my arms around my increasingly cold body, now desperate for Rose to share what she wanted from me. She placed my clothes down on a rock and stepped to the tip of a steep drop on the mountainside, her eyes focusing on the lake in the distance.

'Rose, what's with the water? How come I can swim so well? I felt amazing, almost invincible in there.'

'Ritchie, you need to get down into the bigger lake. You could have today, if you hadn't lost your nerve! Via the stream you may have gained a cut or two, but it wouldn't be life-threatening!'

I inspected the deep swollen cuts and bruising that I had acquired already – a little sore, but as Rose had so sympathetically stated, *I would live.* Finally, she turned to face me and I pushed my hands out.

'Clothes, Rose, just until you tell me what it is you want me to do. I'm going blue here!'

Rose didn't move, a wry, almost patronising smile creasing her perfect lips.

'Ritchie, you haven't asked me about Yasmin. I need to tell you how happy she is.'

My face must have said it all.

'Hell, Rose, go easy on the feelings, why don't you!'

'I'm serious, Ritchie. When the time comes for you to find her, you are going to have to test *just* how powerful this love story of yours is.'

My face must have reflected how I was feeling inside.

'I'm sorry, Ritchie; sometimes it's best not to ask the question if you're not strong enough to handle the answer!'

My eyes widened.

'I didn't *ask* the question!'

Rose wasn't listening, but I think she was ready to tell me what she wanted.

'The lake, Ritchie, get back in the water and keep going until you reach *that* lake!'

Her petite finger was pointing out towards the horizon. I was breathing deeply. Though I had been drawn to and loved the water today, there was something that I didn't want to face within that huge black lake. Rose wouldn't look at me, and then suddenly and without question I lowered myself into the green slime-edged water, in my mind repeating over and over again, *what the hell are you doing, Angel, what the hell are you doing?* I moved slowly until my shoulders sank beneath the water. My breath escaped me, but the more vibrant my strokes became, the sooner I was acclimatising and able to finally turn and face Rose. Her lips were pursed and my eyes transfixed. I pushed my body backwards, further into the lake, which now seemed vast. I felt a warmth spread through me as my little friend lifted her arm, and then a wave; though weak and dispirited, I found it reassuring. Lilac splashes dropped onto my face, my eyes still firmly focused on Rose's diminishing image on the mountainside. I blinked and waved back. Rose appeared to be smiling, both arms now above her head, small kisses blown towards me. I turned and dropped beneath the surface of the water. There was a power and an energy around me. Strands of algae were caught on slabs of slate, taut and upright with the sudden increase of the current. I pushed my head up through the surface of the water, shaking the droplets from my hair and eyes. I turned my head, drawn towards the waterfall that was about to drop me into the pool below, one of three or four that would finally take me to the lake it would appear was my destiny to enter.

But then a fear, a sense of panic enveloped me and I attempted to swim back the way I had come, but it was no use. I slammed into the mouth of the waterfall, my body suddenly becoming weightless and my arms flailing in response. Water was trying to enter me through every orifice; no matter how far left or right I twisted my neck, I was at the mercy of nature. Then a quietness as I dropped deep beneath the water, and then compliance as I pushed myself towards the light. I gasped for breath as I broke through the surface of the next lake and yelled out excitedly, the echoes resonating around the mountains that had me surrounded. Without a moment's hesitation I was surging forward, drawn towards the powerful thrash of the waterfall twenty or so feet away from me now. My breathing quickened, my adrenalin pumping. I dropped below the water and pushed towards the next drop.

My eyes were open wide beneath the surface of the lake, and I could make out the draw of the water several hundred feet ahead of me, the mouth of the next waterfall drawing me mercilessly towards it. My arms were pulled tight in at my sides, my feet pointed back, but barely an effort from me as I was reeled along, my nerves and concerns barely able to keep up. Within seconds I was flipped over, the air leaving my body, my mouth inadvisably wide open. I could feel the brush of rock and slate, convinced that I was leaving souvenirs of my flesh for the fishes, but for now I felt no pain. I was tossed above the froth and terror of the water, the ice-cold air brushing my body, and then bouncing and dropping within the nurturing steel armour of the torrents heading towards the lake below. Once again my neck was twisting and contorting left and right in a desperate attempt to retrieve the air that had been relentlessly knocked out of my insignificant frame. I finally felt my muscles relax as I dropped beneath the calm waters, a dense and distorted volume as I pushed my battered body towards the light.

I gasped for breath amongst my own laughter and tears, hysteria and insanity relentless amongst the splashes of ice-cold lilac. *I wasn't ready for the next waterfall.* I continued to tread water, determined not to be drawn beneath the surface. All I wanted was to swim over towards the steep slate sides of the lake, but my eyes widened as I took in the tomb-like circle in which I found myself. I turned a full three hundred and sixty degrees, and felt as insignificant as it was possible to feel. My life flashed before me – happy smiling, loving faces, each wishing only care and kindness for me. But as I splashed around, fuelled by painfully strained nerves, I felt as though I was offered only harm and heartache at all I had left behind. *Where are you, Rose? My God, Rose, why am I here?* I felt the answer pass through me – I wasn't where I was supposed to be yet. Perhaps once there, I would find the meaning to all of this.

I started to swim hesitantly, my head firmly above the surface, the final waterfall offering nothing but fear in the distance. I reflected on when I was a child, standing alone and petrified on the top board at our local swimming baths. Having been full of bravado prior to climbing the concrete steps, my friends and family watching intently, I couldn't back down, admit defeat, take the route that had got me there – so I jumped. It hurt like hell and I nearly broke my body in two, but I did it. I swallowed hard at the memory, the waterfall taunting me, calling me forward, I had to accept that I had no audience, and there was no route back. I closed my eyes and psyched myself up with the image of Yasmin and Evie holding their arms out to me. I dropped beneath the surface and pushed my body as hard as I could. The noise of the final waterfall was ear-shattering, the mouth frothing and shards of black rotating and pulling me forward. I am suddenly twisted and slammed as though forced through a blender, my head losing sense. Rolls of black filled my nostrils, dropping down through every organ in my defenceless body as though toxic and life-taking. I suddenly flipped and fell, cold, biting air around me, my hands grasping for the security of the falling water just inches away, but I just kept dropping, arms and legs flailing. I felt an arrow through my heart as I sunk beneath the icy cold water below and I was unable to move my arms or legs. I just drifted and sank further into the depths of whatever it was that had got me.

I am physically and mentally at peace, my body gone, all pain spirited away, cosseted by something or someone.

A proportion of what I am, physically and mentally, starts to grow. A shudder of faint light draws me in from deep behind my eyes, and what is left of me is welcomed back. I have the weight of the world pressing against me, my eyes squinting and desperate to focus. I am pushed firmly against the bottom of the lake, every crag and knot pressed into my back. I cannot move, and yet I'm strangely calm. My face screws up as I ponder the words: *the water's edge.* I picture my home, my beautiful, happy home at the Water's Edge. How I would love to wake up to the sound of the narrowboats idling by, to stand with Yasmin and Evie as we throw bread to the ducks. But then I picture myself as I am now, at the opposite end of the spectrum, trapped between the earth and the *water's edge* – my *so* loved life lost, out there somewhere but taken away from me.

I suddenly swallow a mouthful of water and start to convulse in response, my arms and legs flailing and thrashing. Then the hold on me is gratefully removed and I start to lift, rising slowly. My head gradually clears and a surge of urgency pushes me to swim. I push harder and harder. The surface of the lake seems so far away, but I am using all my strength; increasingly my lungs are burning as though ready to burst. I focus on the brightening of the light above me, almost in touching distance now, so desperately close. Finally, I burst through the surface, my eyes squinting as the freshness of a sun-drenched day welcomes me. I start to laugh out loud, hysterically; the lilac sun kisses my face, and I love it. I can feel the emotion and relief welling up in me, the fresh air filling my lungs back up, the trees and greenery around me at the top of their game. But then I drop unintentionally back beneath the surface. I scramble furiously, my legs gripped and unable to fight the force, the water making me cough and splutter. But *then,* totally unrestricted, I drift back to the day above. I keep looking down into the water, desperate to see what has been attacking me, but I can see that I am quite alone. As my breath returns, I concentrate on taking more air, but I frown as I notice the day is now grey, and the leaves are falling off the trees. I spin round, my face puzzled, and I am increasingly desperate to get out of the water. But I slip deep beneath the surface again, my legs kicking out in defiance. Nervous laughter ripples through me, I am dropping further, my paranoia keeps me kicking out, as though grasping limbs are desperate to keep me here. My eyes are scanning furiously, determined to avoid another attack. Finally, I look up, desperate to leave this hellhole, but there is a darkness all around me, a thick sheet of black above, and I can't push through it. I start to panic. I dart this way and that, desperate to escape my tomb. I can feel the tears leaving my eyes beneath the water, my hands sliding across the smooth bottom of the sheet of ice that encases me. I don't want to die like this! But as I flounder, desperate for an answer, my eyes are drawn to my right. There is a brightness, holding a perfect line, working its way across the surface towards me. I dive to my right, pressing my hands against the ice, praying, and then I'm laughing as the ice is dissolving, my hands pushing through it with ease. As my head lifts above the surface I scream out to the powers that be, offering a mixture of emotions, but *so* grateful to be free. The water appears to be rising in temperature as I swim for the safety of the shore. Tired and exhausted I drag myself out of the lake, the thick rich grass breaking my fall. The intensity of the lilac sun is comforting; I am desperate to get warm.

As my body starts to dry, I feel sharp stabbing pains all over my arms, legs and back. I brush my hands against the worst areas and notice how badly cut I am, but then I turn to face the sun as it passes from behind a cloud, and slowly the blood recedes and the wounds heal. Humbled and full of emotion, I blink back at the sun in recognition, questioning the power of what goes on up there, and then…

'Hello, Ritchie. You took your time, didn't you? I've been holding these for ages!'

I don't know how to respond and just keep looking at my little friend, but then I push out my hands and take my clothes from her. I swallow hard and shake my head, at a loss as to what to say.

'Bloody hell, Rose! You wouldn't believe what I've been through for the last couple of hours!'

Rose started to laugh. I wanted to share the joke, but for some strange reason I wasn't feeling it.

'Sorry, Ritchie, but I told you to trust me. You're still alive, right?'

I nodded my head while hurriedly pulling my clothes on, Rose adding:

'It's just funny, that's all!'

I pulled my T-shirt over my head and scowled at my amused little friend.

'Funny, *that's* all? Those idyllic-looking lakes and their *bastard* death-drop waterfalls have tried to kill me in many weird and wonderful ways, *SO PLEASE*...excuse me...if I don't *quite* feel the amusement that is *so* obviously tickling you.'

Rose tilted her head to one side. 'No, Ritchie, I'm aware of all that, but the last couple of hours bit? What I mean is, you'll be twenty-seven in ten days!'

She now had my full and undivided attention, though the words wouldn't come out.

'Twenty-seven, Ritchie! I asked you to trust me, and my God you've earned the reward. I'm not lying to you, from the moment you dropped into the top pool, until you slumped down here on the fresh spring grass, three years on! Thirty-six little baby months! Ten days and Yasmin is yours to find, you've just got to *find* her, but I have faith in you!'

After Death, 1997 – Lilac Sky

I was undoubtedly elated – a little broken, twisted and torn, but the physical scars of proof were gone. But I knew I would never, ever forget what I had just been through. I scratched my head as I pondered the thought: *as though I had been baptised to the highest degree.* Rose and I looked at each other, a giggle here and there. Finally, I had my boots on and stood up. I absorbed the cold air, breathing deeply. There was something about its sharpness, its freshness that seemed to wake me. The full heat of three lost summers appeared to have left this May sun drained of power, but I was happy to take what little was left. But I had another question, determined to steer all thoughts away from Yasmin and her present happiness. It may have been three years since Rose had said it, but the words were as real and painful today as they were then.

I thrust my head into my hands and started to rub furiously, screaming out, 'WHAT THE *FUCK* IS GOING ON, ROSE?'

Rose stepped towards me, her arms wrapped around my head, her fingers forcing my hands to my side.

'Stop it, Ritchie. You're now ready, be grateful for that.

Now you've got to get on with what lies ahead. Move yourself! Just trust, and you cannot go wrong.'

My breathing was deep and hurried, my arms compliant and seemingly happy to forget my desperate mood from just moments ago, and slowly I lifted my head up.

'That's my boy, Ritchie, *go!*'

My young friend looked at me, her smile increasing gradually.

'What are you waiting for, Ritchie? I thought you would be racing back up that mountain, nothing able to stand between *you* and *your* family!'

I started to shake my head, a huge excited smile taking over my entire face, but as I raised my eyes to beam at Rose, she was gone.

'Bloody typical! You could have at least climbed back up the mountain with me, it's miles back to the truck!'

But as I took my first step of many, I was feeling good.

Within an hour I was back to where my water adventure had started. I was turning full circle, the cold air stinging my lungs, my pickup nowhere to be seen. My breathing was quick and heavy, but now tinged with a rising panic. Suddenly, something forced me to turn sharply, almost cricking my neck in the process.

'Lost something?'

Rose jumped off a large rock, her smile mischievous, bordering on smug. I didn't say a word and just followed my little friend, even though I was beginning to question the term. Rose turned briefly.

'Huh, I find that quite hurtful, Ritchie Angel!' she said, before concentrating on the path ahead.

Within a minute more, we were both stood at the top of a narrow driveway, sparse wind-battered hedgerow lining the entrance to a whitewashed stone cottage, smoke rising from the chimney.

'Come on, Ritchie, but we need to be *very* quiet!'

She pressed her finger to her lips as we tiptoed animatedly down the lime-dusted driveway. Rose pulled at a heavy-looking rusting corrugated sheet of steel that was posing as a garage door, and then disappeared behind it. I stood for a moment, looking nervously through the small filthy windows into the cottage. My attention was soon back with Rose as two large pieces of corrugated steel scraped noisily across the ground; and there was my pickup. I shook my head, a smile beaming from ear to ear.

'Quick Ritchie, we *need* to be quick!' she berated in a breathy whisper.

As I entered the garage, pheasants hung above my head, their lifeless bodies tied together by the neck.

'The key is behind the sun-visor, Ritchie…'

I patted Rose on the arm as I slid into the driver's seat, quickly discovering the key. Rose was prompting me to get a move on, her eyes wide at my supposed lack of urgency to the job in hand, but I was moving as quickly as I could, well aware that we needed to be on our way. Rose closed the pickup door, a warm proud smile released from her perfect lips. I pushed the key into the ignition and prayed for an instant response. The sudden roar of the engine was alarming, and I searched frantically for reverse, my heart pounding furiously. Rose screamed out as I became aware of a huge hairy man grabbing my arm through the open truck window, his breath pungent – a mix of stale whisky and sheep. I pushed my foot firmly onto the accelerator and the pickup bucked and screeched its way aggressively through the corrugated doors, their sharp jagged edges engraving impressively into the already challenged paintwork of my beloved vehicle. But as my heart raced, there was nothing that was going to stop me as I reversed erratically up the narrow driveway, before spinning the pickup around once out onto the mountainside. I was searching frantically for Rose, but she was nowhere to be seen. Instead, my eyes were filled with the huge monster of a man, battered leathery skin, snarling nostrils, hands like shovels, charging towards me, and suddenly, all thoughts of my little friend were revoked as I rammed the gearstick into first and roared off across the epic scenery that had been my backdrop for the last *three years!* As the man became a fading shadow in my rear-view mirror, I started to chuckle, laughter pushing out through heavy lungs. I screamed out, bellowing thanks to Rose, fuelled from the excitement for all that lay ahead.

Within a few miles or so, a very obvious thought threw me completely. Depleted, I eased my foot off the accelerator pedal. *'My God,'* pushed out on the wave of a heavy exasperated breath. The unavoidable fact bounced around my head that of course Willow and all those that sailed in her were very likely to have moved on since I jumped into my truck this very morning and felt a need for fresh country air. Who would be doing *what* and *where* three years on, *Ritchie boy?* What on earth could have changed? The sheer horror of how I could have been construed in my physical and mental absence left me shaking my head. I had now brought the pickup to a standstill at the side of the quiet lane, my fingers dropping nervously and tapping furiously on top of the steering wheel. I remembered only too well how I had been presented previously, unable to effect a jot of my character as my life had surged on within my second life, Yasmin's opinion of me being my prime concern. So what was I going to find this time? Curious, frustrated and deeply concerned, I pushed my foot firmly to the floor and sped off to find out.

Darkness was setting in and the roads were incredibly quiet, with a mist descending, eerily thick and almost immediate around me. I flicked my full beam on, but quickly dropped back down to main beam in an attempt to see anything at all. Steadily my eyes became a little more accustomed and I managed to pick up the pace to an almost death-defying twenty miles an hour. My head was just inches away from the windscreen in an attempt to make sure I kept myself safe. After all, my mind was still keen to bubble over with excitement about the fact that in just five days' time, I would be free and able to go and find Yasmin. I flinched back suddenly as my lights lit up an old tramp-like character, his thumb held up firmly and a look that spoke volumes as to his need for a *Samaritan* on this dreadful night. Despite wrestling with my conscience, I carried on forward, my instincts as usual advising me against pulling over and picking the poor guy up. But though my mind was ready to dismiss the twinge of guilt I was feeling and concentrate on the road ahead, I stopped the truck.

My passenger door opened, and the old guy stooped down and beamed humbly at me.

'Thank you *so* much, very, very grateful to you! Once again, thank you so, so much, you won't regret this, young man!'

I swallowed hard as my new travelling companion climbed in beside me. He carried a stench of stale alcohol and cigarettes, his crumpled face only surpassed by the ground-in dirt on the time-ravaged rags that clothed the poor soul. But there was a warmth in the man's eyes that forced a genuine smile from me, and my hand suddenly pushed into his as though I was greeting a long-lost friend. The man pulled his bulging bags from off the grass verge and dropped them into the foot-well of the pickup, finally pulling the door firmly shut. We smiled again at each other in perfect unison, and then with pinpoint timing faced our heads forward, ready for the journey ahead.

Strangely, we travelled for several minutes without uttering a word. Then I heard myself speak.

'My name's Ritchie. What's your name, sir?'

The man smiled again, the teeth he had left, brown and yellow, matching the nicotine-stained fingertips visible through his threadbare gloves.

'Nice to meet you, Ritchie!'

Before turning away and concentrating on the limited view through the windscreen, I repeated, 'Do you have a name, sir?'

The man turned to look at me again, his smile subsiding and a momentary distinguished glaze dampening the previously excited sparkle of his hazel eyes.

'Ummm, I don't have a name, Ritchie, don't have a need for one!'

I laughed nervously, his answer taking me by surprise, but then as I mulled over his words and the thought behind them, I nodded my head, as I felt that he must have good reason. Moments of complete silence followed, the noise of the pickup truck was all that was bothering my ears, and then instinctively I could hear myself asking my friend why he had chosen the life he had. He didn't answer for several minutes, pushing himself firmly back into the seat, his head dropping and staring at his lifeless fingers spread evenly on each leg. I was aware that I was chewing the inside of my mouth, before scolding myself at the mere thought of the swollen lump I knew I would

496

have as a consequence in the morning.

'Do you have any children, Ritchie?'

The question bit me hard, and small short breaths crept out from my suddenly heavy heart. I could feel my friend's eyes boring into me.

'I do...*two* girls.'

I couldn't look at the man beside me, and I was grateful as I instinctively knew he had turned away. After several moments I stretched my eyes to my left without moving my head and glanced his way for a split second. His eyes were now focused on his hands, no longer still, fingertips wrestling, anxious and wrought.

'I had a daughter, Ritchie, perfect, beautiful. My little flower girl, I liked to call her.'

I dropped the indicator down to the left, edging slowly at the junction, and then turned onto the deserted main road that would gradually take me back to Willow.

'Life was full for me, Ritchie, good job, happy home, beautiful wife, and my *perfect* little flower girl.'

I smiled nervously.

'But it's the incidental things in life that can kill you. My childhood sweetheart was the world to me; I was the happiest, proudest man when I was with her. Funny, really. We got married and we had our plans, *big plans, Ritchie*. Ambitious man, you see! Great job, *loved my job*. And then my wife became pregnant, planned, wanted! But I was striving forward, ambitious, driven! The flower girl arrived...'

The fog was now thicker than ever and I was struggling to drive faster than ten miles an hour – my eyes fixed firmly on the road ahead, my heart and soul transfixed by my friend's story.

'I tell you, Ritchie, sometimes you just don't see things clearly, like tonight. The fog, the unclear road, we know we need to be somewhere, would do anything to get there.'

I started to think about my life, new and old.

'But my spirit was broken, Ritchie. I didn't see it coming; busy, busy, busy. The order of wealth was simple – marry a good woman, for love, for love, Ritchie. Needs to have the right attributes to be a great wife and a fabulous mother to your offspring, eh, Ritchie? But the job, the house were what people would judge me on, and of course my good lady, the family unit. But my pack of cards came tumbling down, Ritchie. I underestimated my love for the little flower girl. She would grow, flourish, marry, inevitably have children of her own, make me a proud grandad one day. But she didn't make it, Ritchie…'

His fingers became still again, his breathing heavy, and his head dropped onto his chest. I wanted to pull the truck onto the side of the road, but I daren't, as the fog was thicker than I could ever recall, my eyes almost on the windscreen now, and I was struggling to get above five miles an hour. I swallowed hard, my left hand dropping onto the clammy mixture of harsh wool and wrinkled fingers.

'You know what, Ritchie? When my little flower girl died, I carried on for a while. That's what you do, isn't it? Stiff upper lip, can't stop, keep going. But one day, I just faded away, never made it back home. Just loved that little flower girl more than life itself.'

My head was shaking with the sadness of my friend's broken and lost world, and our hands gripped together. I let out a sigh of relief as the 'Welcome to Willow' sign meant that home would soon be in sight. I asked my friend where he wanted to be dropped off, and then heard myself offer him a bed for the night. He declined and said that as long as he was in Willow he was going to be okay with that, and so I pulled the pickup to the side of the road. My friend stood, his bags at his feet, the thick fog surrounding him. I grabbed some money out of my pocket and handed it to him. He smiled warmly.

'Ha, I don't need your money, Ritchie. Where I'm going, everything is taken care of!'

I screwed my face up, concerned by what he was saying, but my friend's eyes shone brightly at me.

'Know this, Ritchie Angel, you weren't helping me when you stopped and gave me a lift tonight, but helping yourself. The threads of your life are hanging just as you left them.'

He then handed me a crumpled up piece of paper. I looked around me instinctively, feeling as though someone had walked over my grave, and then as I turned back to shake the hand of my new friend, he was gone.

I just sat, every hair on my body standing on end, my eyes focused on the open pickup door, watching as the fog lifted, physically and mentally unable to loosen my grip and read whatever might be written on my scruffy bit of paper.

I must have sat numb and lifeless for almost half an hour, until finally pulling the pickup door shut. I then sat for a further half an hour or so reliving every line of what my hitch-hiker had shared with me. He had called me Ritchie Angel, yet I certainly hadn't mentioned my second name. I was at a loss, having deciphered nothing.

I uncurled my fingers, the crumpled paper seemingly insignificant, but my reaction and my undoubted concern for it finally forced me to open it up. I swallowed hard as I read the crimson-coloured letters: *PUT YOUR TRUST IN TIME.*

My breathing steadily returned, and from somewhere I finally found the strength to carry on with my journey, to take the final handful of roads and search for a bed for the night.

Back within Willow, I shook away all that had been brought to me on this crazy day. Choosing only to settle unquestioningly on the conclusion of *put your trust in time,* I shouted out above the noise of my engine, *'AS IF I HAVE A CHOICE!'* borderline insanity spewing out of me in the form of inane laughter. But I hoped that I understood exactly what the old tramp meant.

Unable to suppress my impatience for what was so close, I knew I was beaming from ear to ear, knowing that in just ten days' time I would be free to find Yasmin. The image of our reunion kept repeating over and over in my head, and I was ready to burst with the incredible excitement of it. I was like a seven-year-old on Christmas Eve, and wondered exactly what I should do to keep myself sane for ten days. I frowned as my concern focused on the very real chance of not being able to get through the long nights. I was aware that I only really had one place that I could go, and that was Sky Cottage. I wondered whether Leoni and Tia had moved on. But regardless of how that would look to Julie and her family, my intentions were purely platonic. After all, Yasmin was within touching distance from being brought back into the legalities of my arrangement with the powers that be, and I now had no need to simply pass the time or reach out for extremes to numb my pain. But a nagging concern for Julie returned, a questioning of where her life may have taken her.

I turned off the engine, the warm glow of Sky Cottage suggesting that someone was home. I was surprisingly nervous as I took the dozen or so footsteps towards the front door. I knocked. There was no response. I hesitantly put my key into the lock and pushed the door open. Though I had been here only a couple of months ago, *plus three years,* it felt hazy and a little surreal around the edges. As I stepped from room to room I could see that the girls were still living here, and so I waited for their return. As the clock ticked, I felt an increasing urge to write a letter that I felt was very much overdue, and though it would be deemed as perhaps timely in the context of how my life *should* be ticking down, I was also aware that communication from me after the *supposed* three years that had now passed would perhaps only serve to confuse the recipient, but I still felt the need to do so.

Dear Julie...

As I scribbled away, I underlined *purely a friendship, a place to put my head down* and *short term,* and then signed off, *should you need me for anything, anything at all, then please call.*

I ran across the main green, my eyes taking in the lilac, though clear night sky, more stars twinkling back at me than I could ever recall. I placed my hand against the red post box and took a moment, before finally loosening my grip and letting the envelope drop, ready for early morning collection. As I stepped away, screwing my face up with almost instant regret, I realised my handful of days with Leoni and Tia were perhaps of no concern to anyone, as I had to accept that Julie and I were no longer a couple. Her life? My life? Our decisions and actions were now down to us as individuals. And as I questioned my ability to actually comply with my promise, my sheer elation at being able to run and find my beautiful wife convinced me that I would be immune to all temptation, however powerful.

As the next few days unfurled, there was no doubt in my

mind that I had stepped into the most rigorous of tests. Leoni and Tia had a magic that could hypnotise, but as for me being their plaything, a few well-chosen words seemed to establish new ground rules. And each night, as I headed off to my bedroom, I would proceed unchallenged, or maybe it was just that I wasn't that irresistible after all. That said, Sky Cottage was straining at the rafters with an erotic presence. Jimmy and Scottie were forever popping round with one excuse or another to justify their visit. But though the girls would smile and tease, they would always walk away, giggling to themselves.

As another midnight stepped forward, I lay alone in my bed, the haemorrhaging black cherry moon reminding me of the bigger picture. In the midst of my dreams and schemes, I could hear across the landing the odd burst of laughter, the moans and groans that could only mean one thing. I couldn't deny the fact that the girls were incredibly attractive, and despite my insistence to them that we shouldn't make a repeat of our fateful night, it seemed to bring a sigh of relief from Leoni, but a challenging 'we'll see' from Tia. But Yasmin stood effortlessly in my every thought. So, despite Tia ticking all the boxes in the fantasy category, I was okay.

My thoughts were once again interrupted as I heard my name being called and I dared not utter a word. I would be woken by the creaking of the landing floorboards, my name whispered through the door, as though *Sirens* calling the fishermen onto the fatal rocks, but undaunted I turned over and pushed my head into the pillow. I heard a giggle as they both scurried away. I shook my head, proud of myself. I reflected on the buzz around Willow, the pride of having an Italian-American film star in our midst, but nobody was quite sure how to handle the situation, so the girls were gratefully left alone. And though I had been keen not to unearth any answers to questions that I was too preoccupied to handle, the girls did relay a story or two about this and that, things I had supposedly got up to in my physical absence over the last three years, but I resisted a reaction. After all, whatever response or otherwise I could give would surely raise questions about my sanity, so undoubtedly it was best served with a shake of the head and a change of subject. But as for Tia and Leoni, they had been back and forth, jet-setting around the world in between films, but were spending a month or two at fairly regular intervals at Sky Cottage as it suited them.

Though my eyes were closed, I was aware that it was morning. I pushed out a satisfied *'Yes!'* as another day on the calendar was ticked off. I pulled on my jeans and crept along the landing, then hesitated outside their door, my hand falling towards the handle, but I stopped just inches away. I pulled my arm back, exaggerating the motion, and then tiptoed, continuing the animated style down the stairs until safely outside. I slumped down onto the sandstone step of Sky Cottage. Though the day appeared warm and inviting from inside, the truth made me stand back up very quickly as I felt the bite of ice, reminiscent of winter, rather than the spring morning I found myself facing. I knew I was just trying to kill time until my birthday, the loss of direction until then the cause of my wandering around like a lost soul. I looked for inspiration up above, the impressive lilac sky offering controversy. Did today's strength of lilac bode well, or not? The sun was also lacking in answers – dazzling, but ineffective and empty.

I made my way towards the familiarity of my pickup truck, climbed inside and quickly pulled the door shut. I smiled as I caught my half-dressed reflection in the rear-view mirror. I turned the key and the engine roared into life. I waited a few moments before sliding the heating up full. I ran my hands around the steering wheel, then along the door. The memories of Yasmin – our first date, how we had come and gone from Sky Cottage before finally moving into the Water's Edge. I hadn't sold the pickup until two months before Evie was born. I recalled the day that finally made my mind up to let the old 'ever faithful' go. I hadn't wanted the pickup back after the death of Scottie, but for some mad reason, the damage hadn't been as bad as the fatality would have suggested, and so the insurance company had it patched up and sent back to me. But the day I relented, finally making the decision to sell, was just a build-up of the strangest of incidents. It had been an indifferent day. I remembered driving towards my gates at the entrance to the Water's Edge and suddenly waved at somebody I thought I knew, but then without warning I hit something – a loud thud and the wailing of an injured animal. I pushed on the brake hard and skidded to a halt. I jumped out of the truck and kept looking back at the person I had waved at, but there was no one there. I turned a full three hundred and sixty degrees, my hand now scratching my head furiously. There was nowhere that they could have gone, a gap in the hedgerow, a pathway, nothing. They had simply vanished, unless I had imagined it. My head dropped and I looked down at the road. I screwed up my face as I took in a black cat, bloodied and twisted. 'Oh fuck,' left my lips as I realised it was too late, the cat was dead. I was hesitant and unsure what to do, whether to gather the cat up and take it home to bury it, though the coward's way out did strongly cross my mind – to simply jump into the truck and drive away. But I decided to settle for a compromise. I felt jumpy as I looked at the cat. I became strangely agitated, almost freaked out at the thought of how this recently fatally injured pet would feel to the touch. But I knew that if I just left it there, there was a very good chance that Yasmin would be next along the lane, and if she were to find the cat, she would undoubtedly have the strength of character to bring it home and give the poor thing the burial it deserved. Despite being pregnant it would upset her greatly, but she wouldn't think twice about doing *just* that.

So faced with what my cowardice could bring, I quickly ran to the back of the pickup and grabbed an old shovel. Within the last hour I had mixed a small amount of mortar with it, and there were traces of wet cement on the well-worn tip. I almost closed my eyes as I tried clumsily to ease the shovel beneath the cat's body. As I wrestled the glossy saturated fur and bones onto the cold steel, the cat's blood ran onto the cement splatters, the two curdling together. I walked awkwardly towards the hedgerow, a full grimace on my face. I pushed the shovel into the undergrowth, steadily trying to shake the poor creature off. I winced with relief as the shovel became light and a reassuring thud filled my ears. I gratefully pulled the shovel back, a shiver mingling with my rotating shoulder blades. I tried to wipe the blood and cement onto the thick grass while looking around, thinking that somebody was watching me. I inspected the shovel again, but could still see a painful reminder of what had gone on here. I grabbed a handful of dock leaves and rubbed them furiously over the evidence. I felt a bead of sweat run down my forehead, and then an itching sensation on my hand. My thumb was ingrained with cement and blood. I rubbed it furiously on the thick grass until a green stain appeared right up to the nail. I stopped, taking a moment to question my madness, and then took a deep breath and stood up straight. I carried my shovel back to the truck, the engine still ticking over. As I climbed back into the cab, I forced a smile, craning to catch a glimpse of my insane self in the rear-view mirror. I shook my head and looked back towards the hedgerow, expecting to see nothing, but then, as the bright sun caught the cat's bloodied eye, I was dazzled by a beam of lilac.

I was spooked enough to put my foot down hard and head for the safety of home. And though I tried to simply forget the incident, I couldn't shake the compelling urge to finally sell the pickup truck. I was physically unable to wash away the blood that I had found on the front wheel and so, for no logical rhyme or reason, my ever faithful friend and I were ready to part company. And like some suspicious thief, I sold the truck for two hundred pounds to a backstreet dealer in the big city. I remembered walking away from the garage feeling a calmness that had eluded me since the accident with the cat. I headed back to the centre of the city in search of a cab. As I walked, the two hundred pounds in my right pocket that I had kept separate from the cash in my left pocket simply played on my mind. I took another dozen steps or so, but finally stopped. I pushed my hand down deep into my pocket, pulling the contents out. I was aware of somebody or something watching me. I was almost relieved that my paranoia wasn't getting the better of my fragile state of mind as my eyes dropped onto the tired, desperate figure of a tramp huddled behind a rusting shopping trolley, sheltering inside the doorway of an old closed-down TV repair shop. From across the street he simply stared at me, and then dropped his eyes, seeming to lose his nerve. I stepped off the kerb, making my way towards him. He looked up again, finally lifting his hand, his voice cutting open this surreal moment.

'Enough for a cuppa, guv?'

The man seemed to cower as I bent down towards him. I forced a smile, keen to assure the man that I meant him no harm.

'Don't be alarmed, old son!'

Taking the man's arm, our eyes met, his growing larger by the second. I then pushed the two hundred pounds into his dirty hand, closing his yellowing fingers tightly around it.

I shook my head at the distant memory as I sat in my truck outside Sky Cottage, the heater finally blasting a much-needed warmth. I simply couldn't understand why I had been so spooked by the death of the cat. I chuckled nervously to myself as I recalled my actions. But the whole scenario seemed to sum up my personality somehow. All bad things... Regardless of whether or not it was my fault, I simply wanted it gone. I didn't want it bloodying my doorstep, affecting my life or wife in any way. God forbid that anything remotely unsavoury or controversial should be allowed to penetrate the barrier I had installed around her. It wasn't healthy, and what's more, it undermined and patronised her existence. Julie, Lillie, the Christian's, Jack De'Vil, even the killing of Ian. If I didn't like it, then it wasn't allowed to enter my perfect world with Yasmin.

As the heater worked its magic, I wondered whether or not I had changed at all. Surely a second go at life would see all original mistakes erased? I almost laughed as I said it, scratching my head nervously. After all, I'd sent Jack to his death at the Old Bakery. The motive? The result? I simply felt confused and nervous as to how the powers that be would be summing up my new existence. Rose simply evaded the question! Would not? Could not? Hint at how the Judge and Jury will view my actions. And of course, my role in Ian's death this time around, that one was certainly puzzling me. How the hell did that happen? If you were ever going to believe in fate, then that was surely it. But as I screwed up my face, confusion and uncertainty leaving me short of breath, maybe I had to accept that it was purely coincidental. But my gut feeling told me it was more than that.

They say that when you're walking through hell you should simply keep walking, and so I did. The days, the nights, took forever to pass, but pass they did. And as another day revealed itself to me, I smiled, as within two days I would finally be free. Yasmin, wherever she was, could finally be approached. I prayed that I could find her, and wherever her new life had taken her, I hoped beyond all reasonable hope that she would give me a sign of encouragement. But what if she was married? And to someone that she loved very much! And what if there were children? How was I going to feel, trying to break up a happy home? And should we be destined to be together, how was I going to feel taking on another man's offspring? After all, my life had been *perfect,* Yasmin, Evie and me. Yasmin had no history with anyone else, no baggage; it was just us and I loved that! We knew and trusted each other implicitly – I let out a sigh as I accepted that my wife only knew what I *chose* for her to know about me! But I brushed the thought aside and concentrated on where Yasmin's life may have taken her now. Would her change in circumstances have changed her personality too? And though Rose had said very little to me about how things could end, she had made it increasingly clear that I needed to recreate my old life to perfection, thus making the changeover – should I be successful – as easy and as straightforward as possible. I took a huge deep breath. It was moments like this that made me question my sanity, and more importantly my actions in my new world. I reflected glumly on my weakness with the female form. When I saw the hypnotic glint in the eyes of Tia I saw an escape route out of this madness, and wondered if I should simply change direction totally and take a chance with her. But though it felt fun and exciting under the cover of darkness, as a new day arrived a sense of clarity would ensure that the novelty left me, and the bereavement would undoubtedly set in. There was something so deeply rooted about my feelings for Yasmin and the longing to just hold her, to kiss her, that I felt as though the pain in my heart was taking over my body, my mind, and suddenly, I was so intensely agitated and suffocating with the heat of it all.

I sat up straight and turned the heater off. My pickup had

become my comfort blanket, and inbetween the day-to-day goings on, I was at my calmest when cocooned within it. Once again, my first thought as I woke this morning, was the need for my early morning contemplation, and as though someone had set fire to my bed, I was out of Sky Cottage and nestled cosily in my faithful battered truck. I wound the window down and let the cool air in. My heart was leaping. What the hell was stopping me from going to find Yasmin now? After all, as long as I didn't approach her... But at least if I could find her I would be saving valuable time later.

I excitedly released the handbrake and selected first gear. But just as I was about to pull away, there was Rose standing in front of the truck. She didn't smile, just pushed her hand against the bonnet. I could only just about see her, her four-foot-nothing petite frame almost crushed beneath my enthusiasm to get on with the task in hand. I shook my head, quickly turned off the engine and jumped out of the truck.

'ROSE! FOR *GOD'S* SAKE, I COULD HAVE *KILLED* YOU!'

Rose gave a wry smile. '*Very* funny, Ritchie. Look, I need you to go and see Julie...But I suggest you put a top on first.'

I wanted to say that Julie wouldn't want to see me; after all, she had her *guard dog* parents there. But there was something in Rose's eyes that told me not to question her request.

I pulled up outside the Old Church and turned off the engine. I felt it would be more polite if I simply left the truck at the bottom of the drive; after all, this wasn't my home any more. As I climbed out of the pickup, I recalled my last moments here. I clanked open the heavy gates, and memories of Lillie came flooding back...Suddenly, I had to take a very deep breath to physically stop the tears from falling. *That's the last thing Julie needs, Ritchie boy.*

I knocked on the door gently, but there was no reply. I waited a little while longer. Julie's car was parked up, very close to the garage door. I knocked again, a little louder this time. I waited, but still no response. I rummaged for my keys, before tutting to myself, as of course I had handed them back when I was asked to leave. I walked to the front windows, but couldn't see anyone. I thought that there was a possibility that

Julie may well be at the back of the church, and it was sometimes difficult to hear the door if you had the TV or stereo on. I made my way into the back garden and sheepishly stepped up to the patio doors. As I peered through the thick glass, I could hear very faintly the sound of Dolly Parton's 'I will always love you', and my throat instantly struggled to swallow. I turned the patio door handle and stepped into the lounge. I called out softly, not wanting to startle anyone.

'Julie, Julie, it's Ritchie...'

I waited, but nothing. I suddenly felt foolish. Perhaps she was out with her mum and dad, in their car. *But then...why the music?* And why was Rose asking me to come here? I started to feel nauseous – there was something not quite right. Every foot forward was a step already taken, but a lifetime ago. And just as before, I made my way over to the stereo and switched it off. The silence seemed to boom back at me until all I was left with was a painful memory – *déjà vu* at its most poignant.

After a few moments of nothing, I screamed out, 'JULIE!...ARE YOU *OKAY?*'

I climbed the stairs, my legs feeling like lead. Everything about this felt *so* wrong – and of course I had good reason to feel like this. First with Jack, then coming here and finding Julie with Lillie. When I finally reached the bedroom door, my heart was ready to burst out of my shirt. I wanted to turn and walk away, but instead I opened up my palms and pushed the door open, and there she was, lying on top of the bed. In a white silk dressing gown; her hair as if it had just been washed and styled. I felt a calmness descend over me. I don't know why, because my eyes told me something *very* different, but then compared to the scenes that this place had offered me in the past, maybe I could understand the optimism so far. But as I walked towards Julie, I noticed the empty vodka bottle lying by her side. The cogs in my brain seemed to take an age, but then I threw myself at her as the large brown pill bottle seemed to glare back at me from the floor.

'Julie! God *no, Julie!* PLEASE GOD! *NO! JULIE!*'

I lifted her at the nape of her neck, her body rolling into mine. I shook her clumsily, screaming, begging, pleading with her to wake up, my eyes wet and wide. I pushed her back onto the bed, taking her by the tops of her arms, shaking her far more effectively now, and I kept on shaking her, desperate and coaxing, then softer, my voice less menacing now, but nothing changed. Her head was slumped back, her hair hanging glossy and vibrant, but the body beneath it... I shook her again. How could I accept this? I rolled Julie onto her side. Pushing my fingers into her mouth, I could feel partly dissolved tablets in her throat, but as I pushed my fingers deeper there was simply no reaction. My brain seemed to freeze and a surreal haze formed around me. I finally slumped down on top of her, my tears soaking her face. I noticed how warm she was, but as the minutes ticked by in the deathly quiet of the church, the heat was leaving her, just as my desperate hope was deserting me. All life seemed to have drained from my dear friend. I kept stroking her hair, my heart broken, tears dropping like bombs. More excruciating pain, cutting into the barely knitting wounds of all that had gone before. All I could hear as I rocked backwards and forwards with her was my own echoing voice ringing around the high ceilings – *'Why, oh God why?'* – until eventually the cries faded and I sat still, simply holding the dead mother of my dead daughter.

I had no idea how much time had passed, but as I begrudgingly pulled my face away from Julie I shuddered at just how cold her body had become. I rearranged her arms and legs, keen to see her regain a pose of dignity in the spot where she had chosen to end her short life. As I stepped back, my eyes were drawn to the stained-glass window. Dusk had now replaced the late afternoon sun. The figure of the Virgin Mary cradling baby Jesus; a mother's eyes proud and protective. I turned away, reflecting on the happier times that Julie, Lillie and I had shared here. Through thick misting tears, my eyes stopped and focused on two envelopes on the dressing table. Though I wasn't aware of moving my legs the few short steps, the tear stained envelope addressed to me was in my hands and I reluctantly opened it. I physically shook as I unfolded the pale blue paper and sat down on the edge of the bed.

Dear Ritchie,
I am sorry, but life can be so hard. My existence without

Lillie became unbearable, even a slither of pleasure on a day to day basis became almost impossible to recognise.

I tried so desparately hard to keep going. On the handful of occasions that our paths would cross Ritchie, for the brief moment our eyes would meet my heart would lift with genuine joy at seeing you. But then your inability to continue looking me in the eyes would disappoint me so much, that I would always walk away from you feeling less of a person than when I had woken that very morning. My love for you Ritchie Angel was fuelled without question from the birth of Lillie, and our brief time together as a family was a time that I felt almost complete, almost centred, almost happier than I had ever dared imagine possible. But almost isn't quite enough is it Ritchie.

For three New Year's Eves I prayed that each new breath drawn would realise peace – but it never came Ritchie. I blindly trudged forward, searching for a life raft, a purpose for carrying on. But instead the empty vessel that I had become craved the ability to simply disappear, happy to sink to the bottom of the ocean.

Please forgive me Ritchie, but the blankness in your avoiding eyes taught me that you could not bring me what I was longing for. But then I began to believe that the emptiness I saw in you was simply my own reflection, and that as a consequence it was time for me to go, to finally be with my baby. I pray that I am with her now.

I wish you peace and I will always love you.
Julie xxxxx

I couldn't move; I could hardly breathe. I took Julie's hand. As I looked at her, I knew that I loved her *very* much and I felt deep remorse at not being able to be 'so much more' than I was for her. I pondered my meetings with Julie, my inability to look her in the eyes – but the truth was, I hadn't seen Julie since the day she asked me to leave.

I knew from that moment that you *could* love more than one

person, and that love can take on many forms. I knew that the overwhelming depths that love could administer itself were without boundaries, parameters, structure or code of conduct. It was a living, breathing, out-of-control monster that could stretch and knew no confinement to etiquette, formality or simply how it would be perceived by polite society. My heart was wrenching with a pain that burnt against the hot breath in my increasingly cold body. I placed a final kiss on Julie's brow. I stepped back and took in the shell that had carried around her beautiful soul and swallowed hard. I admired her commitment to Lillie, and the fact that no sacrifice is too high for the love of your child. And so I prayed that she was now with our daughter – she undeniably deserved that. They both had to be together. *Please let it be so.*

I was suddenly aware of movement all around me and was immediately caught up in a frenzy of activity. Julie's mum and dad running around, both screaming. My eyes widened as Julie's dad grabbed me by the throat and slammed me up against the wall, venomous nonsensical words and saliva bounced on and around my face. He then threw himself at the bed, frantically trying to revive his daughter. Julie's mum was tearing open her letter, within moments, deep unrelenting sobs and more words that simply failed to ignite a meaning. She was then clawing at her husband, pulling and grabbing, both of them jostling blindly for prime position. For reasons out of my control I dropped my letter to the floor and left.

I couldn't get my head off the pillow the following morning; there was something stopping me from opening my eyes. It was grief – pure, raw grief. I didn't have the energy or inclination to go and look for Yasmin, and I despised myself for even thinking about her. There was no question about it, out of sheer respect for Julie and Lillie, all thoughts of any search, well, it simply didn't feel right. I believed that should I have been opened up and my heart taken out, it would undoubtedly be bruised and bloodied, with lumps torn off it, twisted and unable to function. I felt scared and empty, and whatever time could heal, for now, in the safety of my bed, my brain was unable to offer an opinion. *Putting my trust in time?* I wasn't so sure.

I asked Leoni and Tia to thank any callers, but I was unable to see anyone. As I traipsed back up the stairs, I felt that my words were self-absorbed and melodramatic, but losing Lillie and then finding Julie, the way she had ended it, and her final words… Perhaps I was right to feel sorry for myself. But then I also knew that I had to question my contribution in all this. I had to look closely at how I hadn't been there for her. Sure, I felt hurt when Julie threw me out, perhaps hard done by, but I should have worked harder at making her feel special instead of wallowing in the juices of my extraordinary circumstances – my desperation in wanting to get back to Yasmin and Evie! My first concern should have been to grasp *truly* what I was here to do – to service my second chance at life far more graciously. I hadn't given one hundred per cent and she had been right to feel short-changed. And so her being angry with me sort of took the responsibility away from me, and her decision to make me go, well, in the eyes of a coward I couldn't do anything about that, *could I?*

Was a lesson being harshly dealt? Perhaps some of it was actually getting through to me. I couldn't help but chastise myself for being so slow on the uptake, and for the fact that I was still travelling with the same self-absorbed values. And so now, knowing how much Julie had been hurting deep down inside and not being able to hold her, to have one last chance to make amends, I accepted that my love for her came with a health warning for us both. I was in no doubt that an attempt to tell her the truth, explain about Yasmin and Evie, should perhaps have been considered. I shook my head, aware that the consequences would have been fatal for me, but then maybe that was expected of me. Had I failed the test? I scratched my head furiously. How could I have told her my story? How on earth was I supposed to have told her that I had died and come back for another go? There was a first-rate chance that she would have viewed me as a madman, ruing our fateful night and her inability to break her tie with me due to the mere existence of Lillie. But perhaps I could have said I had a wife and daughter living abroad, or something… All I knew was that I could have given a reason for my mind being elsewhere, and it didn't take a genius to work out that I could have done *so* much better.

Between heavy bouts of sleep, I would simply stare at the ceiling from the safety of my bed, and on a good day would look blankly out of the bedroom window. Going through my memories of Julie and Lillie, a thousand different scenarios, but always the same inevitable failure of an ending. But the long, heavy, self-indulgent days proved to be as pointless as the last, not a step forward being realised, and then something inside of me clicked. The sheer fact that we had spent time together, time that I had no right to experience, I would be wise to settle for that, and it proved to be vital. I painfully and unexpectedly broke into a smile at the memories, good and bad. The shouting, the accusations 'true or false', the hugs, the glares of disapproval, the tender kisses, the hurt and disappointment in Julie's eyes, the intense love-making, our time and life together, and the glue that bound us, Lillie's every playful joyous step and adventure intensified due to her incredible spirit – for Julie and I, her creation our greatest moment. I was eternally grateful for having the chance to get to know them both. And though my recovery from regression wasn't immediate, and with nightfall showing itself far too soon, guilt and regrets magnifying under the cover of darkness, the letting in of friends undoubtedly massaged progress. Alternate nights, Leoni and Tia would take turns in sleeping with me, platonic and beyond reproach, just being there for me in the early hours, and I was very grateful to them both.

But as this habit of self-indulgence was becoming tiresome for all concerned, many sorry days later – my birthday having passed without recognition – I woke with a start, and enough was enough. A far too realistic dream, Scottie exchanging places with me, his words biting deep: 'There you go, Ritchie lad, in you get. If you're not going to use your life to full effect, get yourself comfortable in my coffin and I'll make use of your wasted days. Oh, and I may be gone for some time!' He was suddenly up and out, and I was on my back, unable to move, the coffin lid firmly installed above me. I'd slipped into this same destructive routine after Scottie's death, and I was ashamed that I had let it happen again.

I stumbled out of bed, my muscles under-used and reluctant on sudden demand. I opened my bedroom door and could hear Tia and Leoni having a slightly heated discussion. I pushed my head out onto the landing. They were talking about going back to America for a few weeks, or perhaps longer, and Leoni was saying that she couldn't just leave me. I shook my head, horrified, and made my way downstairs with the agility of a century-year-old man. But with every painful step, I was extremely keen to give my friends their freedom. I pushed open the kitchen door.

'Girls! *Look,* I appreciate your concern, but you must go off and *do* whatever it is you need to do. In fact, I *insist* you do. I've been pathetic for far too long as it is, and I may be going away myself!'

The girls looked back at me wide-eyed and hanging on my every word.

'So please, both of you, you've helped me, I'm healed and I've got some serious business to sort out. I've left it a while, *far* too long in fact, but I think I'm ready to face something that shouldn't be put off a moment longer!'

CHAPTER TWENTY-THREE

On Your Marks, Get Set, Go!

After Death, 1997 – Lilac Sky
Midnight struck and I was in bed, alone, but I was finding it impossible to fall asleep. My body and mind were rejecting the usual routine of rest and recuperation, both prematurely ready for what lay ahead, and it was decidedly detrimental to the recipe for a good night's sleep. But in the depths of darkness and a well-known fact that some of the best-laid plans can be hatched via a bout of insomnia, I had my first port of call worked out – my first intrepid step towards being reunited with my beautiful wife.

And so, I finally stepped out of Sky Cottage, the cold

morning and the bright sunlight unsettling me – like the feeling you get when you've been unwell, tucked away in your house for a few days, and then you take those first few unsteady steps back into the *cold* outside world. I'd packed a rucksack with a few essential things: a change of clothes, cheque book, credit cards. After all, I didn't know how long I was likely to be away. Suddenly, just when I had convinced myself I had sneaked out of the house without the girls knowing, Tia came running out of the cottage, her short lilac satin nightie struggling to contain her.

'*Ritchie, Ritchie, you bastard!* What's this?'

I smiled defensively at Tia as she threw the leaving note I had left for her and Leoni firmly at me. She stood in front of me with her arms folded, before finally relenting and throwing them around my neck.

'Oh, Ritchie! Can't you come to America with us? I'd love to show you off to all our friends, our bit of *sexy* rough!'

I didn't know whether to react playfully hurt by her comment, but was laughing too much to scold her. And as she nuzzled into my neck, she smelt *so* good! But as she came up for air, her eyes met mine and I have to say, she was not easy to turn down. But as I hugged her again, I thanked her for her generous offer and said that perhaps in another lifetime I would have jumped at the invitation.

As I climbed into the pickup truck, I couldn't believe just how gorgeous Tia was. The look in her eyes told me that she felt a lot for me, but within a jet hop across the ocean there would be another guy to take my place. As their plaything, I had no doubt in my mind that I would be a fond and humorous memory for the girls.

'But no future in that!' I muttered as I turned the key in the ignition.

I had no qualms about leaving, my true happiness only possible with one lady. And so, as I waved goodbye I took in the richness of the lilac sky, and felt the strongest desire yet to change that painful reminder into a perfect blue. I suddenly pushed my foot onto the brake.

'Tia! Your nightie ... a perfect match!'

Tia followed my eyes skyward and pondered for a moment,

then tilted her head to one side.

'Mmm, maybe if you're colour blind. Then yeah, *a perfect match!*'

I laughed at my own madness and we were both now beaming at the other.

'Good luck, Ritchie Angel!'

As I finally pushed my foot onto the accelerator, I had to smile at the twitching curtains around the main green.

But as my thoughts focused onto the serious matter in hand, my head didn't seem to be attached to my body, such was my anxiety as I made my way towards Janey's. Surely she must have an idea where Yasmin was. After all, they had been friends since infant school. But of course the love triangle involving Scottie, well, it had taken its toll.

'Ritchie, she's not contacted me at all. I've sent *so* many letters and pictures of little Scottie to her mum's old address, hoping they would all be forwarded. But I simply don't have a clue as to whether she's received them…Well, I suppose I can't blame her in the circumstances, but I'm sure her old neighbour had said that Yazzy's mum had gone down south, to London? Perhaps she's in contact with her, I don't know, she didn't seem that keen to share much with me. Worth a shot for you though, I would have thought…'

As I drove away, I could see that Janey was intrigued by my sudden interest in getting in touch with Yasmin. I made my way to the top of Willow High Street and pulled up alongside the kerb, drumming my fingers anxiously on the steering wheel. After a few moments, I stepped out of the vehicle, dropping several letters into the mail box – all my loose ends were sewn up in those letters. I wasn't up to facing anybody, just finally ready to challenge my future. I'd not telephoned Mr Skirdle, I'd not contacted my solicitor or my accountant, I simply hadn't wanted to be asked any awkward questions – the letters would save me from *all* that.

I smiled to myself, muttering under my breath, 'Who knows, I could be back within a week!'

But the truth was, I simply didn't know. Whatever I had to do, whether it took hours, days, years, it simply didn't matter. I was now ready to reclaim my life – it may even result in me feeling human again, and if I could do that, then I would travel to the edge of the universe. But at least now, on a practical front, while I was away I could take every step necessary, not having to worry about my business matters, tenants' rent, etc. – all so crucial to the recreation of my original life. Though I had had plenty of time to get used to it, it still seemed strange being back in such an archaic time – mobile phones were fairly commonplace, but as for email, well, that was only for the very high-tech minded!

As I turned and jumped back into the truck, I felt that now was perhaps the most frightening bit of all. Would I be able to find her? And once found, *would* she be interested in me?

But there was one face-to-face meeting that was crucial, and to achieve it, my best chance was to stop off at the Water's Edge. When I had needed Rose the most she would come to my special place. My fear was that down in London, apart from dropping onto my knees and begging her to come to me, I was at a loss as to how to reach her. And there were certainly some important questions I prayed she had answers for.

The sky was beginning to cloud over, and a light lilac rain was starting to fall. I parked the pickup tightly against the Water's Edge hedgerow, the sharp brambles screeching tunelessly against the paintwork. I climbed out of the truck and quickly made my way to the five-bar gate. As I climbed over, I expected to see the surroundings take on its usual form – no lilac – but I screwed up my face as I realised that the Water's Edge wasn't going to give me that pleasure today, and it concerned me. I could feel the rain hitting my back a little heavier now. I knew I should have grabbed a coat, but the battered jeans and thin white T-shirt were all I'd chosen to wear to protect me from the day ahead. I ran my hands through my tousled mane, brushing it from my eyes. I started to run down the grassy overgrown embankment towards the main weeping willow, my favourite spot – a place that Rose had appeared many times. Just metres away from the cover of the willow tree, I stopped, almost slipping over but just managing to steady myself. I raised my eyes skyward, the force of the rain almost hail-like now. I screamed out, challenging the skies above, defying the ferocity of all that they were hurtling my way. Each kamikaze droplet blurred my vision with lilac explosions! I looked down at my chest, my T-shirt splattered as though victim to an ambush of blackberries but then fading almost instantly. My eyes welled up, my defiance not quite so resolute now as my mind was suddenly filled with images of Yasmin and Evie. I knew that I needed all the help the powers that be were prepared to give. I dropped my head, temporarily humbled in defeat, and stepped obediently into the thick undergrowth.

Drenched, I pushed through the heavy straggly branches of the willow and found a dry spot, right up against the trunk of the tree. My eyes were drawn to the rain hitting the surface of the canal, and it gave me hope. The water had never failed to calm me; it just made everything right somehow. And especially here, the same stretch of water that Yasmin and I had spent many a long hot summer's afternoon lying beside, daydreaming and making our many plans together, buying the land, our marriage, the building of our home and the true blessing that *is* Evie. I pushed my back hard into the willow's trunk, now biting the inside of my mouth as the memories became painfully real: Evie at my side, just two or three years of age, pushing her delicate little hands into mine. We would stand and watch for the ripples, for the tadpoles, the baby frogs – smiles and childish laughter from us both, not a care in the world. Little did I know that soon we would be parted, perhaps forever! I urgently doused the thought, quickly building the image of Evie, her proud and brave pose as the ducks came and fed from her impossibly petite fingers. And the soothing soundtrack of the narrowboats, the steady chug, and how the people would always wave at us without exception.

Suddenly unable to sustain the memories, to combat the increasingly sore, dry throat and the bitter sting of ready-to-roll tears, I started to shuffle around, desperate for Rose to show her face. I pushed back through the willow tree's rain-sodden branches and stared across the long green grass, tangled with blackberry bushes, wild flowers and assertive weeds that would in time have to step aside for the bricks and mortar that would become the Angel family home.

I was now standing in a clearing, just a dozen steps or so

away from the safety of the willow tree, and all I could feel and hear as I stood, *was* nothing. I couldn't move my feet or lift my head; the rain was still falling, but I couldn't feel or hear it – I knew I was soaked through to the skin, because I could remember from just a few moments ago, but I wasn't cold, wet or warm. I finally managed to blink my eyes and then an awareness that I was gradually able to hear again, as though a conductor had raised his baton very slowly. I felt a raw energy pass through me; nothing significant, just a stirring that seemed to rotate deep in my gut, and then within a few short breaths, pushing around my heart and into my chest a rising of an inner belief, pushing itself into my face, and finally, tingling my senses, my brain. My toes started to rotate, stretching in my boots, and I felt a smile spread across my face and a belief filling me up. And then I screamed out.

'ROSE!' I waited, my heart pounding, and then spoke a little softer. 'Please, Rose…'

As desperation sank through me, suddenly it dissolved, a smile beaming out, relief as I felt a small hand push into mine, leading me towards the willow tree. I wanted to pick my little friend up and crush her with the overwhelming emotion I was feeling, but denied myself – the same way that you have to with a small fluffy kitten or puppy.

'Thank God, Rose! I really thought you *weren't* coming.'

Rose ducked down, pushing the willow's branches to one side. A sharp pain shot through my face, like the sword of *Zorro* across my cheek, as the perturbed branch looked for its original favoured position. Rose offered a small nervous laugh.

'Ohhh! Sorry, Ritchie, that sounded painful.'

I shook my head, muttering sarcastically, 'You think?'

Once inside the safety of the willow's branches, I slumped down against the trunk, my hand checking for blood from my stinging cheek.

'You're fine, Ritchie, don't fuss!' Rose stood before me. 'Okay…you need some answers?'

'Rose, am I ready for this?'

My little friend nodded, folding her arms and then asking me whether I thought I was ready.

'Ummm, I *think* so… Yes, course I'm ready!'

Rose smiled, as though wanting far more from me.

'Okay, Rose, ummm, let me get this straight. You have wanted me to make sure that I achieve materially, you know, the houses, my business, just as I did before? To recreate my original life as closely as I can?'

Rose beamed back at me, her arms unfolding.

'Yes, Ritchie, exactly right! The powers that be have used the word seamless to enable a healthy, physically possible crossover. They're looking for seamless, because only seamless can work, ideally with all the bad from your old life cut out, replaced with good intentions and, *hopefully,* impressive results.'

I thought about what I had achieved, but saw images of Lillie, Jack, Ian, Sally, Harry and how I'd driven Julie to take her own ... well, you know. I wasn't convinced that I was remotely close to getting things right. Rose stood beside me, resting her hand on my arm.

'Ritchie, Jack, Ian, Sally, Harry, Julie ... you'll have to wait and see. But, you have got to know Lillie this time around, that's got to be a big plus?'

'Yeah, but I didn't take good enough care of her...' I stopped, swallowing hard. Rose pushed out a warm smile and gesticulated for me to carry on.

'Umm, okay Rose, but if we're looking for seamless from my side, what about Yasmin's life? What if her journey has taken a totally *non*-seamless route? What if Yasmin's circumstances are *so* different? Children of her own ... maybe she's been sterilised and so cannot have a child with me...'

Rose stood before me, placing a fingertip on my brow, dabbing a worry bead of sweat before gently wiping it away. She then took both my hands in hers and crouched down.

'Ritchie, you must relax. I don't know what you're going to find when you eventually meet up with Yasmin. Whatever she's achieved here, if for example she does have a child, or two, then you have to decide for yourself whether she is still the one for you. But, and I have to warn you of this, it may *not* be down to what you choose. Yasmin may be very happy with her new life! The kind of person she is, she may well not give you a second look! The Yasmin that was married to you was totally devoted, and I can tell you this much, she never, ever strayed, or even, as far as we could tell, was outwardly tempted. She may carry the same principals now, and her loyalty to you then could well be exactly the same for her new man, or woman, in her life. And when it comes to Judgement Day, one of three things will happen: if successful, you will be reunited with Yasmin and Evie – aged thirty-five – and hopefully left alone to live happily ever after! However, if there are major complications, but your efforts are deemed worthy, then Yasmin and Evie could be brought into your new created world. But thirdly, and I feel sad just saying this, *if* you fail your mission, then you will end up back on the decking, *dead*, your wife and daughter finding you there at sunrise.'

Rose squeezed my hands and stepped away from me, almost as though she was anticipating my next impertinent, albeit logical question.

'Rose, please excuse me, but surely you know how Yasmin's life is panning out? You can choose who you watch when you're up there, can't you?'

Rose turned and smiled, shaking her head, and I was convinced she was blushing a little.

'Ritchie, I don't get to watch *all* the soap moments. I still have my chores and a life, you know!' Rose looked uneasy and backtracked a little. 'Well, not a life as such, but, well, yes! A life! What I do from day to day, it *is* my life, yes!' Rose smiled smugly, and then quickly blurted out, 'Ritchie, there is no running total that I am being kept up to date with, the powers that be *don't* share everything with me, I am beginning to realise…But that said, yes, you can now go and track Yasmin down, but just as before, your time could skip ahead without warning. So please, Ritchie, make the best of the home stretch. The time will fly by, and only you can change history here!'

I tapped my taut, tightly clenched knuckles on my thighs, frustration rolling uneasily through me.

'Rose, I know you're not telling me all you know…' I looked for a reaction, but she wasn't being drawn at all. 'Okay Rose, I suppose I have to accept you have your reasons for that, and, well, I know that I cannot expect black-and-white answers… Rose, are you listening to me?'

Rose was here with me, but not saying a word, deep in thought, as though carrying the weight of the world on her young shoulders. I stepped back, churning over and over what she might be thinking, and then focused desperately, attempting to sum up exactly what I felt I had achieved. But the reality of concluding any individual's existence in simple terms suddenly felt naive. Surely a life lived well is a life lived with vibrancy and as many colours as there are available to us – not some black-and-white, uninspired two-colour existence? But then for depth, sinking deep within the soul, many layers: coarse, smooth, magnetic, repellent and even indifferent facets of my life cannot be summed up by colour. *Mmmm, so a good life?* An optimistic lived-to-the-full life? Surely, a life lived like that will be full of vibrant, startling contradictions, thunderous and inspired moments, depicted in combinations that stain the mind and graze the soul and eyes of the voyeur! That, surely, is a life used, abused and leaving you rightly breathless? *'Amen!'*

I glance up, taking in the thoughtful concern stretched across my young friend's face, her appearance as an eight year old being so misleading, as of course she has been around for the same number of years as me. So, a deceivingly wise head on extremely young shoulders. I look away from Rose, dropping my eyes and focusing on my muddy boots. And though my shoulders are slouched and feeling a little battle-weary, I try to recapture my optimism from just a few short moments ago, desperate to stir up enough energy in getting myself ready for the next stage. Rose wraps her arms around my head – the warmth of her gesture, though overpowered by her ice-cold touch, still reminds me so much of Lillie and Evie. I feel a gentle glow from within, pushing out the slightest of sighs. I lift my arms up and rest my fingers on Rose's hands, and realise that I see Lillie and Evie in the same way now. Evie was always going to be *so* special to me, as she was a product of my love with Yasmin, a beautiful baby born out of an incredibly spiritual union. But now, having got to know Lillie, my love for both my children is as it should be – equal and unquestionable. Yasmin? The way true love is supposed to be, or at least as I thought it should be. But recent experiences have taught me that love cannot be pigeonholed. So yes, I undoubtedly love Julie, but it is not a long-term workable love. Outside influences? Not really meant to be together? Lust perhaps? But what I did know for sure was that Lillie should never be touched by any uncertainty between her mum and dad – she just needed to feel loved and cherished, and I hope and pray that she did for the majority of her young life. And as I reflected on the little friend I had made in Lillie – her eyes, the way the trust would beam out of them, the little kisses and the warm, passionate hugs – I was so incredibly proud of her, and though Evie and Lillie would never meet, I loved them both more than life itself, and in realising this, it meant that so far my new life had some genuine worth.

The touch of Rose leaves me briefly, but her hands are now under my chin. I reluctantly lift my head, our eyes now locked together. No words are spoken – solemn questioning creases form across my little friend's brow. Suddenly, the seriousness of the moment is lost, a smile spreading across both our faces.

'Get out there, Ritchie, be strong! Know that I am with you!'

I started to nod my head, and though I had real fear as to where my adventure was going to take me, I felt okay. But then, without warning, tears started to stream from my eyes, rampant and heavy, drenching my face – I couldn't explain why. But as Rose placed a small gentle kiss onto each sodden cheek, I rationalised that it was just a build-up of emotion. And though my soaked clothes should be making me cold and shiver, I actually felt warm and my optimism was back. Rose seemed to read my every thought, squeezing my shoulders and nodding in approval. I was now beaming back at her, suddenly taking her arms and lifting her up, the vibrant orange of the sun fighting valiantly to overcome the monopoly of the lilac in its midst, framing us both, pushing impressively through the willow's branches. We spun around, my arms outstretched, Rose giggling infectiously. Just as I thought I was about to lose my footing, I pulled her to me, hugging gratefully for all I was worth, but then something made me put her down. We exchanged an embarrassed smile, and then, for what seemed like an eternity, silence. Several breaths in, I started to shake my head, and gratefully an order of words left my mouth that summed up exactly what I was thinking.

'Rose, if I hold you for more than a couple of seconds, well, you feel *so* cold.'

She dropped her arms and shrugged her small young shoulders – once again, silence. Her eyes crinkled, but then lit up.

'What do you *bloody* well expect?' she said, a welcome blush colouring her cheeks.

I couldn't help but beam back at her, but then, incredibly, she was gone.

I blinked my eyes, giving out a frustrated and exasperated sigh, and then yelled, 'I *HATE* IT WHEN YOU *DO* THAT' But as I pushed the branches back and stepped out of the willow tree, I looked up at the sky. 'Thank you, Rose!'

Despite the vibrancy of the sun from just a few moments ago, I was now left with a heavy grey canvas, little sharp droplets of rain making me blink uncomfortably. I continued to stare, and decided that I actually liked the grey – almost no lilac – and it made me smile, strangely reassured and ready for the day that I would only see normal sky 'no lilac'. I was ready for that.

I steered the pickup nervously, making my way across the swollen ford to Yasmin's old home. As I turned off the engine, I simply couldn't believe the increasing strength of the rain, each drop creating a small lilac explosion as they bounced off the windscreen. I stepped out of the pickup, taking in the cottage and the many memories I had – I knocked nervously and waited, but there was no sign of life at all. I then looked to the right – the end cottage. Perhaps it was the warm glow from the lounge window that lit up the black morning that drew me there. I clenched my fingers tightly, praying that she would know where Yasmin was.

As I rapped my knuckles against the rain-sodden door, I listened for any sign of life. Instantly, a dog started barking. I waited. There was a steady trickle of water running off the decaying porch roof, and it had just scored a direct hit, right down the back of my neck.

'You bastard!' I muttered under my breath.

As I stepped back, I frowned and shook my head, frustrated that even putting on my coat had failed to totally protect me. I quickly reorganised the collar and edged closer to the front door, avoiding the increasing trickle. I placed the side of my head against the fading blue timber, almost touching it, the curling paint brushing my cold ear. I could hear a shuffle of feet, and then silence. I held my breath as I tried to work out where my possible informer had gone. I suddenly gave a little jump as a frail voice spoke.

'Who is it? Who's there? Is that you, Billy?'

I answered the lady eagerly, explaining that I wasn't Billy, but in fact a long-lost friend of her old neighbour, and did she know where I could find her. I could hear the rattle of bolts and latches, until finally, the door was open. I expected to see the face of the old lady, but instead, all I saw was her back as she made her way down the hall towards her lounge at the back of the cottage.

'You'd best come in! Close the door, please! I don't want next-door's cat in. I thought *you* were Billy! Next-door's cat is always bullying Billy!'

I closed the old lady's door and quickly joined her in the small, cluttered lounge. There was a strange smell. I wasn't sure whether it was a whiff of cats or perhaps the old lady herself. I scolded myself for being so disrespectful, an embarrassed smile underlining the reddening of my blushing cheeks. But then I screwed my face up, seriously overwhelmed by the number of boxes, piled high and full of food tins, and bags straining under the weight of sepia-coloured newspapers, until finally, my gaze fell upon an old, wrinkled questioning face. She looked up at me, almost frozen to the spot, before finally shuffling herself backwards and into her chair.

'So what do you want with Lillie?'

The name shook me. Though of course I *had* known, I had never linked Yasmin's mum as being a Lillie! I had always – at her insistence – called her Mrs Holland. And finally, once Yasmin and I were married, she simply became mum, until she died suddenly, when Evie had just turned two.

'Umm, yes, Lillie! Well, it was Yasmin I was after really. It's just that I was desperate to catch up with her, but sadly, no one seems to know where she's moved to.'

The old lady looked intently at me, desperately trying to weigh me up.

'S'pose I could help you, good-looking lad like you! But tell me, you're not trouble, are you?'

I couldn't help but give a small chuckle, and then waited hesitantly as I gave a risky reply.

'Trouble, me? Yes, every time!'

The little old lady almost closed her one eye, and then a little cheeky smile curled her thin, colourless lips.

'Mmm, so what's your name then? You're not that Scottie, are you?'

I was quite taken back; I hadn't expected the question. I quickly tried to reassure my Judge and Jury.

I stepped forward, offering my hand.

'No, I'm Ritchie, Ritchie Angel.'

The old lady took the ends of my fingers, her cold, clammy grip tightening around the tips.

'Okay then, Ritchie Angel, what do you want with her?'

The old dear was still in possession of all her faculties, and rather keen to do the same with my fingers – her grip tightening, a little uncomfortably now. She huffed heavily, impatient for an answer.

'Umm yes, sorry, well, just an address! So that I could *perhaps* send a letter. If she's interested in replying, then great! It's just that I always got on with Yasmin, and ummm, when my mother died...'

The old lady's grip seemed to soften. Encouraged, I mumbled on.

'...Yasmin was so, well, she was wonderfully kind, and I, I felt it the right thing to do to see how she's doing. In fact, ummm, what *is* she doing? I would have thought married ... a baby ... or...?'

The little old lady suddenly let go of my hand.

'Did I know your mother?'

I shook my head.

'I wouldn't have thought so. I don't know really... She was a quiet, sweet thing, you know? Kept herself to herself.'

The old lady looked at me, and I could almost see the cogs

revolving through her thinning mane. She finally dropped her head and I let out a *rogue* breath, feeling a surge of hope that it might just mean a decision had been made. But as I waited anxiously, her eyes focused firmly on her well worn claret slippers for what seemed like an age.

'Okay, Ritchie, here's the deal! I cannot tell you *where* she is. Her mother's not very well; in fact, I'm not sure how long she's got left. But I do write to Lillie, and if she wants to get in touch with you, then she can!'

My heart sank.

'Please, ummm, just tell me that Yasmin is okay... *Please,* is she married?'

But the old lady didn't answer, and just pushed a piece of lilac parchment paper towards me. My eyes were drawn to the matching envelopes on her sideboard. She handed me a chewed blue pen.

'Put your name and address on there, Ritchie...'

I felt deflated, my head reeling with a number of ways that I could force the issue here, but there was a look in the lady's eyes that told me firmly to do as I was told. I scribbled my details on the paper, but in doing so, I knew that it wasn't enough. I suddenly wanted to grab the address book and run, never looking back, but a sudden inner chuckle and grateful clarity brought me back to my senses. Still churning over and over again in my head whether I wanted Yasmin to know that I was looking for her, I genuinely wasn't sure. Did we have a connection? And what if it was purely one-sided, wishful thinking on my part? Would she want to hear from me? With a view to actually agreeing to meet up? But as I made my way to the front door, the old lady rested her hand on my arm.

'I'll write to her tonight. My milkman will take it around 5 a.m., so you can be assured it will be in the first post, I promise you, Ritchie. If she wants to talk to you, wants to divulge her status, then that's up to her. Sorry, Ritchie, but I promised Lillie, so I have no choice!'

I seemed to accept what felt like defeat graciously, smiling and thanking the old lady before trudging away dejectedly. Three or four heavy-hearted steps down the pathway and I turned with just one last question.

'Ummm, Billy… Is he your son, grandson? It's just that you said the cat next door bullies him!'

The thought had lifted my mood, and I couldn't help but laugh as I spoke.

'Oh no, Ritchie, Billy's my ginger cat. It's just that he jumps up against the door, banging it; sounds identical to your knock!'

The old lady winked at me and nodded her goodbye. The fading blue door was finally closed. I smiled outwardly, having to accept that my knocking technique was the same as an old ginger cat.

'Well done to you, Ritchie, with your little fluffy cat knock!' I blurted out sarcastically.

As I took the few steps to my pickup, the rain was relentless, the sheer chill of the early afternoon seemed to fill me up, and then, as with an eclipse, the daylight was gone and the blackness shrouding me, physically and mentally. No street lights or glow from behind the cottage curtains – and that's how I was feeling inside. I climbed quickly into my dry pickup. My head was racing with so many thoughts, but so few viable options. As I turned the key, the roar of the engine seemed to take my mind elsewhere. I reversed back up the lane, splashing recklessly through the swelling ford, the truck rocking from side to side and then being violently handbrake-turned, and I winced as I caught sharply the edge of an ivy-covered stone wall, a small wooden house sign clattering against my bumper. Everything seemed to stop. I looked around me, but nothing. I shuddered, as though something or someone had passed through me, and then, impossibly, daylight started to build from the ground up, the rain vanishing with the climb of the darkness. A glimmer of light, shimmering behind the grey that is left. I pushed my foot gently onto the accelerator, almost urging the truck to tiptoe, discreetly out of the lane. As I pulled up against a timber bus shelter, my eyes took in the telephone and bright red letter box. I turned off the engine. The shoot of an idea came to me from deep within, but suddenly deserting me, I shook my head, determined not to accept my lack of power here.

'For God's sake, what on earth am I supposed to do now?'

I knew I couldn't simply sit around and wait for a reply that may never come. There had to be another way. I closed my eyes tight shut – my best ideas always came to me at 4 o'clock in the morning when sleep was resisting me, so I needed a little divine intervention to help me out here. And then just like that.

'Ha, got it!'

I turned the key in the ignition and pushed my foot excitedly to the floor. My shoot of an idea had just blossomed; *I had my plan!*

I headed back onto Willow High Street and drove down the side of Skirdle's, parking selfishly in front of the other cars. I ran towards the shop, going over and over what I needed to say.

As I walked in, Mr Skirdle was just on his way out.

'Ritchie my lad! Ummm, wasn't sure whether or not we'd see you. How are you coping?'

I nodded, and told him that I was okay. Mr Skirdle looked down at my wet clothes.

'Look, Ritchie, don't take this the wrong way, lad, but you look…*well,* rather dishevelled! I think you need to get yourself home, you know, have a hot bath, *shower…*'

I shook Mr Skirdle's hand, reassuring him that that was my plan just as soon as I'd had a chat with Mr Ball.

To pacify him further, I added, 'Oh, and the wet clothes … I was just wandering around trying to clear my head and got caught out by the heavy downpour, but once you're wet…you know, after a while you *don't* really notice the rain anymore!'

Mr Skirdle winked at me and placed his large hands onto my shoulders.

'Jolly good, as long as you're all super duper and on the mend. Well done, good for you! And I'm sure Mr Ball will accommodate, ummm, with whatever it is you need him to do, but Ritchie, I appreciate that Julie and you haven't seen eye to eye over the last couple of years or so, but, *well,* your lovely daughter, *ummm…*Well, these situations can build-up and create mayhem with *one's* sanity, so take your time! Don't give work a thought, okay? When you're fit and ready is good enough for me!'

I felt genuinely touched by Mr Skirdle's attitude, and as he closed the door behind him, the shop bell ringing in his wake, I took a moment to gather my thoughts. Finally, Mr Ball replaced the receiver.

'Ritchie, nice to see you, old chum. How are you feeling?'

I quickly tried to regain my composure, keen to get my thoughts back on track, and sat on the edge of his desk.

'Umm, okay, Mr Ball, umm, but it's like this. You know that young Dave Skirdle? Well, of course you know; he's got the postal collection round in Willow. Well, I need an *itsy-bitsy* favour!' I explained my predicament.

Mr Ball's eyes widened and then his brow creased into an almighty frown.

Then, shaking his head dramatically, he said, 'Not being funny, Ritchie, but that's not actually *itsy-bitsy*, as you put it. In fact, it's *totally bloody illegal!* You're asking Dave to take a letter and give it to you! He would lose his job, simple as that! I'm sorry, old chum, I can't, and won't ask him to do that, *no way!*'

The silence in the shop was deafening – my ears ringing, my heart thumping furiously. I felt as though I was being pushed into a corner, and was suddenly surrounded by a red mist.

'Mr Ball, if you *don't* ask David to do this simple thing for me... I mean it, I cannot begin to tell you how important this is to me! But if you cannot ask him to do this *one* special favour, then I will...' I could barely bring myself to say the words.

Mr Ball stood up, puffing his chest right out. I jumped to my feet, trying to intimidate him with my two-inch height difference, my voice exceeding stern.

'I mean it, Mr Ball, I'll have to tell Mr Skirdle that you've been *shagging* his son!'

Mr Ball slumped down in his chair, the wind totally knocked out of his sails, his face as red as a cherry-infused beetroot. He looked devastated, and I felt evil.

'So, Angel, you're, you're blackmailing me?'

I couldn't say a word. He was right, that was exactly what I was doing. A few moments passed and I wanted the ground to swallow me up, for me to simply burst out laughing and pretend that I was joking, testing and teasing, nothing more. But thoughts of Yasmin and Evie, firmly entrenched at the forefront of my mind, kept me going, justifying the means.

'Look, Mr Ball, I've known about you and Skirdle junior for years, you know that, and I genuinely hate doing this, but I *need* this letter! This may sound terribly dramatic, but it really is a matter of life and death!'

Mr Ball twiddled his thumbs, his puce skin matching the dowdy grey of his tie, and I was convinced there was steam coming out of his ears. My heartbeat seemed to quicken as I waited, searching desperately for the next threat should my work colleague deny me.

'Ritchie, I'll ask him, but it's *his* decision, and don't doubt, old chum, that I *will* be enlightening David with *all* the morbid details of *this* conversation!'

I went to offer my hand, but he looked as though he was prepared to die rather than accept the gesture.

He then spat out through gritted teeth, 'You are an *utter* shit for doing this to me!'

I stood motionless. Once again he was right, but finally, a dressed-up apology started to spill from my mouth.

'Look, Mr Ball...I *love* this girl! Our relationship has been disrupted in the strangest of ways, and, well, ummm, *well*, you'll have to trust me on this one! When I found out about you and David Skirdle, I was a little shocked, but it was obvious that it was extremely important to you both! I've never given you a hard time about it; it's your life, nothing to do with me! And if I wasn't so *fucking* desperate for that letter and the address on it, and if there was any other way, then please don't doubt that I would *never* have asked you or threatened you so, well, *so* appallingly! It's just that, well, look, please, just do this for me! It's nothing sinister, it won't harm anyone and certainly won't come back and bite David or you on the, ummm, on the bum, *umm*, so to speak!'

Mr Ball couldn't look me in the eyes, but muttered that if there was a problem, he would ring me at Sky Cottage later. I nodded, embarrassed, but then deep down in the pit of my conscience, realising what a crucial part of the jigsaw this was, I was ever so slightly pleased with myself.

As I left the shop, I accepted that I had no choice but to go back to Sky Cottage and wait. I wasn't looking forward to explaining my return, or having to say my goodbyes all over again.

As I pulled up, Tia was in the kitchen, almost doing a double take when she spotted me.

I was barely out of the truck as she raced across the lawn, finally jumping all over me, yelling at the top of her voice, 'WELCOME BACK, RITCHIE! AMERICA, *HERE WE COME!*'

I didn't have chance to explain a thing as I was manhandled and hurried into the cottage. As Tia finally slid off me, my body suddenly feeling weightless, a can of cold beer was thrust into my hands. Tia continued to chatter on, while pushing me backwards into the lounge until I fell helplessly onto the settee. I could only smile and shake my head, my eyes suggesting that they seriously broke the mould when they made Tia, and what a sad and inadvisable day that was! And as wrong, basic and inappropriate as it was, I just watched in awe. Tia was dressed in her tight faded jeans and white cropped top, showing off her glorious Californian tan to perfection, though realistically it was now about ten per cent Californian, ninety per cent Willow sunbed. Tia threw herself on me again, nonchalantly straddling my lap.

'Oh my God, Ritchie, your clothes *are* soaking! Oh, my poor baby, you look like shit!'

I laughed, nodding in agreement, as of course it wasn't the first time that had been said to me today, though not in such basic terms! Without a moment's hesitation, Tia pulled my damp T-shirt over my head before sliding off the settee.

'Come on, Ritchie, let's have those wet jeans off you, you'll catch your death!'

I looked at my gorgeous friend and obediently eased my jeans down. Tia smiled, her face beaming at me as she took hold of my sodden jeans with her finger and thumb, almost as though they had suddenly become radioactive.

'Tia, I need the biggest towel that our airing cupboard has to offer. I'm feeling *really* cold! Oh, and chuck that freezing cold beer back into the fridge, I think I need a brandy!'

Tia threw her hair back and ran upstairs, her voice just about audible.

'So, Ritchie, we're on, yeah? You'll come to America?'

Before I had time to answer, Tia bounced gazelle-like back into the lounge, my eyes ashamed to notice how aroused she was through her thin top. I took the towel off her, sighing gratefully at the sheer warmth of it.

'So where's Leoni?'

Tia resumed her straddle position on my lap, taking control of the towel and wrapping it around my head, then rubbing vigorously.

'Leoni won't be here tonight, should be back late tomorrow afternoon. She's gone to see her brother at university, as we may be gone a while!'

Tia lifted my arms, my hands replacing hers on hair-drying duty. Without batting an eyelid and her conversation not missing a beat, she attempted to slide my boxer shorts down my legs. I quickly stopped her.

'Hey, Tia! You'll leave me with absolutely no protection if you take those off!'

Tia's chatter was now replaced with a stern, playful look, her lips pouting as she explained why she felt it necessary to remove my last item of clothing.

'Ritchie Angel, you big baby, they're damp, they have to come off, you'll catch your death!'

Her face was a picture, dangerously sexy. I shook my head from side to side, a huge guilty smile spreading across my face, my thoughts I was sure almost audible. *Mmm, perfection, and then some!* I felt it time to ask exactly how the land lay between the incorrigible lady before me and my friend Leoni. Motive being, in asking the question I hoped that maybe Tia could lead the way in what was right and respectable, removing the need for inner strength from me. Tia's smile subsided a little, an air of seriousness diluting the mood as she slid off my lap and sat before me, crossing her legs.

'Oh, Ritchie, you know I wouldn't give my little ass to anyone else but you and Leoni. She's my soul mate, we're long term *for* sure! But you are my gift from Leoni. With you ... I don't know! You're, well, a little bonus! A well-judged need between two girls who would normally deny themselves someone like you! Am I making any sense?'

I smiled, now very clear as to my standing in their *cosy* relationship. Determined not to weaken now I had found the moral ground, I stood up, wrapping the towel around my waist before easing my boxers down and throwing them on top of my other damp, dirty clothes. I stood still for just a moment, contemplating so many things, but well aware that there was only one point to make clear – a conversation that was long overdue. Tia went to stand up.

'Sit back down, Tia, please.'

Tia resumed her cross-legged position on the floor. Though I had a need for seriousness, I once again smiled, almost chuckling to myself as she pushed her finger into her dark brown hair and started curling it around provocatively. I now laughed at her, shaking my head determinedly.

'It won't wash with me, Tia. You *are* gorgeous! Dangerous! Very nearly irresistible! And of course you've had me wrapped around your little finger from day one, you and Leoni! But now, and from this moment forward, physically you and I … forget it!'

Tia looked suddenly concerned, and a little shocked by what I had to say.

'Ritchie, please say I haven't offended you, I couldn't bear it…'

I smiled and shook my head, my eyes not leaving hers.

'You've not offended me, you could never do that! I know this sounds a bit cliché, but I'm saving myself!'

Tia's eyes widened, and she pretended to sulk. But then she jumped up.

'Oh, Ritchie! You're no fun; tell me, *who*…?'

As we both stood, an acceptable distance now between us, our fingertips entwined, I told Tia as close to the truth as I was able. That I was off to London to hopefully find the girl that I had fancied from afar, but not had the confidence to tell her when she was living in Willow – and now she was gone. My hands were now totally encased in Tia's enthralled grip. I even told her that she had boosted my confidence *so* much, that if someone as stunning and successful as her could find me attractive, then I couldn't be all that bad. Tia let go of my hands and threw her arms around me.

'Ahhh, *my* baby boy, go for it!'

Her grip loosened suddenly and she stepped back, her head tilted to one side.

'I have, well, been worried. It's just that it's been quite some time, you know? After Julie…'

I was well aware of just how short an amount of time had actually passed, but of course I couldn't enlighten my concerned friend. My uncomfortable, lost-for-words look provoked an almost immediate response from Tia.

'Oh, but I am not judging you, Ritchie. You should focus on this, it will help. Just tread carefully, make sure that this girl is worthy of you. If you've lusted after her from afar, then you don't *really* know her, do you?'

I shook my head. 'Mmm, I think I've got the measure of her, Tia! But I will be careful.'

And of course, with the facts as they presented themselves, she was quite right to be concerned. Chasing some fantasy girl. But as I pondered all the negatives, I simply had to focus on the facts that had brought me here. To argue my position, or to try to justify my actions, I would have to tell the truth, and of course the truth wasn't an option.

'Tia, it's a tricky road I'm going down with this girl, but I have to see where it might lead. She's simply somebody that I believe I might click with, that's all! Could be back with my tail between my legs within a week!'

Tia just squeezed and hugged me like the true friend she'd now become.

We both sat and chatted – from Tia, true and colourful life stories, from me, carefully chosen, gilded words – but at least it enabled the night to tick away without me climbing the walls. I suddenly jumped out of my skin and was instinctively on my feet, my half-filled brandy glass sent bowling across the heavy wool carpet. I ran to the phone and picked up the receiver. Mr Ball was on the other end. As he spoke, I glanced at the clock on the wall; it was several minutes after 8 p.m.

'Ritchie, David will get the address for you, but he won't stop the letter from going!'

I thought for a second, almost prepared to accept the offer, the brandy having softened my resolve.

'Mmmm, Mr Ball, please, I need that letter! I don't want her to know that I'm looking for her! It's delicate…'

Mr Ball put his hand over the receiver and then spoke again in a reluctant, lethargic tone, but to the point.

'Okay, Ritchie, lilac parchment you say? Old lady's handwriting? First post tomorrow?'

As I replaced the receiver, any guilt was overwhelmingly quashed by sheer elation and I felt strangely reborn. I stood for a moment, unable to move, think or otherwise, but then, painfully distracted, I was aware of tearing a huge chunk from the inside of my cheek, chewing unwittingly, before scolding myself.

'Bloody hell, Ritchie, that's really going to help, and will hurt like crap in the morning, and be a lump the size of Mike Tyson's knuckle!'

Tia suddenly boomed down the stairs, '*Ha!* Caught you talking to yourself! This love thing has really gotten to you, hasn't it, baby?'

I looked up at the surreal image of the movie goddess in my home and simply shook my head.

Tia squinted her eyes back at me and then impatiently yelled, '*What?*'

I laughed out loud and ran up the stairs, taking Tia's hand and dragging her back down into the lounge.

'Bloody hell, Ritchie, slow down! I was getting stuff to clean up your *clumsy* brandy carnage!'

I shook my head, kicking her glass over as well, the excitement bubbling out of me. To finally be allowed to go after Yasmin was hyping me up, making me act like a seven-year-old kid on Christmas Eve. As I danced up and down on the sodden carpet, I beamed manically at the highly amused, *bemused* Tia.

'My beautiful American friend, it doesn't matter! Let's just say, something to remember your bit of rough by! Let's open the red!'

And so the countdown to daybreak began, my platonic friend and I putting the world to rights, and within an hour or so, opening up our second bottle of red wine, followed by many hours of deep, slurred and idle chat, before finally drifting off into a drunken slumber.

My deepest sleep for as long as I could remember meant that my mind was dreaming more lucidly than ever. My now platonic friend was lying across me, her restless body every few minutes looking for a more comfortable position, sending my dreams off in a different direction. I was standing on the top of a gigantic skyscraper, the sky an electric blue. The clouds were child book – little fluffy sheep without legs, all the same size, equal distance apart. As I looked up, I felt a slightly out-of-control feeling ease through my body. I looked out straight in front of me, my arms raised, stretched out, like Jesus on his cross. I couldn't look down. I knew I was high up, and I knew I was right on the edge of the building. I wriggled my toes in my heavy, insensitive boots, but suddenly my feet were bare – the hard, rough asphalt sharp against the soles of my feet. I edged forward until my toes were feeling only fresh cold air! I now wanted to look down, but my neck became stiff, as though held in a vice. I strained hard and eventually managed to push my head forward a little – in doing so, I had the ability to move my head freely. I looked down, expecting to see the city below me, the city I envisaged in my mind of tooting car horns and the general buzz of a rush-hour symphony. But as I took in the world below, my eyes widened – everything seemed so far away. Then, as though almost touching distance, were fields of green. As I took in my panoramic view, there were no other skyscrapers, no other buildings, just lush green grass, every blade blowing in one direction. Out of the corner of my eye I spotted a mole hole appear, but it seemed to be miles away, barely a pinprick in the distance. Suddenly, my eyes seemed to become telescopic, beaming in on the freshly unearthed soil, and everything stopped for a few seconds. Then the earth fell back into the hole as a small face appeared. Instinctively I smiled and started waving. It was Yasmin! My heartbeat started to quicken and I desperately tried to shout out, but then she disappeared beneath the ground again. I was drawn in another direction, another hole, and after a few seconds had passed by there she was again – Yasmin's beautiful face. I waved furiously this time, trying so hard to shout out, praying that she would see me, but then she dropped

537

below the ground again. The scene just kept repeating itself. No Evie, just Yasmin, popping up and then disappearing, until the whole field became a dot-to-dot of brown on green.

Suddenly, I woke, beads of sweat running down my face, Tia's now naked body entwined with mine. We had crashed out innocently enough in the lounge, the scattered settee cushions having been our bed for the night. But my platonic friend's breasts were firmly pushed into my stomach, her silky long hair splayed across my chest and a little on my face. I pulled my head back jerkily as one of her stray hairs tickled my nose, and a shiver ran the length of my spine. I tried to sit up, desperate not to wake her. I just about managed to wipe the sleep from my eyes, focusing fully now on the misleading scene. Unable to sit up properly, I gently slid from under Tia, arranging her arms and legs neatly, and pulling the white cotton sheet over her vulnerable body. She suddenly wriggled as though nestling into position, moving her head from side to side, a barely audible whisper coming from her lips – 'Night, night, Leoni, love you,' before becoming quiet again and drifting back into a deep sleep.

I pushed the curtains apart and saw a rich marbled purple sky forming, splatterings of darkness, lifting and disintegrating slowly. I was relieved that the rain had cleared; I didn't want anything to stop Skirdle junior from getting that letter. I just prayed that my one link to Yasmin had indeed posted her letter as promised. I told myself to calm down. Of course she'd do it, why the hell wouldn't she? And so I told myself to be patient and to just wait. I pulled some fresh clean jeans on and was pleased that the heating had been churning for at least an hour. In search of a top, I made my way upstairs to the airing cupboard. To the left, there was a huge pile of white fluffy towels. I smiled childishly at Leoni's and Tia's silky bits of nothing lying in an assortment of vibrant colours to the right. I lifted a couple of bras off my navy blue T-shirt and dragged the warm garment out, pulling it roughly over my head. I made my way downstairs and into the kitchen. I sighed, disappointed that it was so early – 6.50 a.m. I prowled around the tiled floor like a caged tiger, wondering what time Skirdle would finish his round. And as I contemplated a thousand scenarios, I felt that in such a time of crisis I would fall back on a great English tradition and make a nice cup of tea!

Three cups of tea later and two hours having passed, I was starting to prowl anxiously again. Such was my desperation I even considered the unforgivable – aware of Tia's warm inviting body in our makeshift bed in the lounge, I had to fight the urge of killing some time in the weakest of fashions. But all thoughts of Yasmin put an instant stop to that, and so the momentary lapse passed. And as I reflected on all that my journey was teaching me, it was then, like a bolt of lightning, that my relationship with Leoni and Tia dropped into place. I shook my head, my naivety taking me by surprise. I hadn't seen the wood for the greenery and immature shoots on the trees. It had been the greatest of tests – did I believe enough in the true love story that Yasmin, Evie and I stood for? Presented with the ultimate fantasy, would my head be turned sufficiently? Would I be weak and succumb, momentarily or otherwise, and having fallen initially, would I have the strength to walk away forever? I reflected on my not so innocent night with the girls. Had I already failed the test? But then – and I wasn't trying to justify what had gone on – it was Julie I was cheating on. Totally wrong, but now it would be Yasmin. Would I have risked a night of passion with Tia and Leoni if it had meant the possibility of losing Yasmin? I truly believed that I wouldn't physically be able to. My mind started to drift into memories of how I had done the unforgivable with Julie just a day after returning from honeymoon with Yasmin. I tried desperately to shake the thought out of my head. I had blamed grief and… I shook my head from side to side, truly desperate to erase the memory and all the destruction it had caused. I started to jog on the spot, just willing young Skirdle to bring me what I so desperately needed.

I tried so very hard to relax, and pushed my back against the kitchen wall and closed my eyes. I conjured up the image of Yasmin and Evie, and there we were, just feet apart, before finally throwing our arms around each other. But as my mind started to feel the warmth and reassurance of being where I belonged, the sheer dread of maybe never going home created a surge from within. I don't know where I was heading, but then

I was aware that my eyes were in line with the letter box, my knees bedded firmly into the rush matting. I was unable to move. The ticking of a clock started to pound in my head, the now ear-splitting sound of the hands moving around the clock face, pounding, resounding, slicing open wounds in my throbbing brain. Still I couldn't move, and I blacked out. Then, as though a switch had been flicked on, I was conscious again, though my nose and face were now a foot or so below the letter box. I was aware of a hot burning sensation as my lips slid fractions of a millimetre every few seconds down the paintwork of the wooden front door. I don't know how much time had passed, but I felt my body jolt in response to a tear in my lip that I imagined would result in blood seeping out and running down the eggshell blue paint. The clock was now ticking in exaggerated slow motion, my heart beating in perfect echo, the pain to my lips intensifying. But then, without warning, I was able to lift my hands and pushed myself slowly away from the door. I looked down at the trail of blood, just an inch or so from running onto the matting. I stood, disturbed and spooked, staring at the rich-red blood merging with the eggshell blue and how it was turning a vibrant and disturbing lilac colour. My breath was short and sharp, and I wanted to run into the kitchen. But though I could move, it was as though rigor mortis was trying to take control of my body. I was in pain mentally and physically, and it took all my strength to break the constraints of whatever it was that had its hold over me. I ran the back of my hand slowly across my mouth as I stepped into the kitchen and grabbed a tea towel, before returning to the hall and dropping back onto my knees, desperate to wipe the now completely lilac blood off the front door. I rubbed furiously. Then I was aware of a *slam* and a letter bouncing off my head, before dropping to the left of me, and there it was, the lilac parchment envelope.

As I picked up the letter, I couldn't feel my fingers or my legs, such was the anticipation. My heartbeat quickened, and a huge smile spread across my face as I read the name and *oh so* crucially, the address:

Mrs L Holland
Old School House

150 Victoria Road
Dartmouth
Devon
I couldn't take my eyes off it. *The Old School House?* And
I'd presumed London, *but Devon?* I quickly tore open the lilac
envelope.

Dear Lillie,
I know I'm writing a little earlier than usual, but I've had
a handsome visitor. Seems a nice young man, but anxious
to find out where your Yasmin is living these days. I made
it clear that I wouldn't give out your address to anyone,
but felt that no harm could be done if I was to write to you,
providing you with his name and address...

Lots of gossip and idle chit-chat later, I lifted my head up as
though suddenly feeling the guilt of an unwitting voyeur.
Should I send the letter on? I knew at least where to find
Yasmin's mum now, but suddenly, without consciously having
reached a decision, I found myself tearing the letter and
envelope up into the tiniest pieces possible. I buried the letter
deep into the bin, submerging it beneath potato peelings and
old decaying tomatoes. I quickly pulled my hand out of the
carnage, rinsing the indescribable slime away under the tap. I
was then racing around pointlessly. I hadn't taken any of my
stuff out of the pickup, so I was ready to roll. But then, almost
jumping out of my already paranoid skin, a sleepy Tia stood
before me, white cotton sheet wrapped around her waist.
'Tia, you startled me!'
But then as the nerves settled, just seeing her seemed to
calm me, and I pushed my arms forward.
'Look, gorgeous, I'm off, for *real* this time. I don't know
how long I'll be gone.'
As she stepped towards me I took her face in my hands and
pushed my lips firmly onto her forehead. I smiled at her dazed,
barely conscious face, and then hugged her. Finally, I managed
to let go.
'Ritchie, it's not too late! California? We could all have a
great life over there, you would want for nothing! They pay me

millions of dollars for a few months' work!'

I pushed my finger onto Tia's lips. I didn't need to hear another word – not because I would weaken and let go of my future with Yasmin and Evie, but because my mind was made up. No doubts, no regrets, I knew what I had to do.

'Tia, you are offering me every guy's dream! Glorious sunshine, being spoilt by two incredible girls, one big party 24/7! But don't you see? I know why you've been sent to me, *you,* Leoni – you're both the ultimate test! I am in the middle of an incredible love story, and you've been sent by the *devil...*'

I stopped there, aware that I was *even* scaring myself. Tia looked uncomfortable, suddenly a little more awake than she had been the sheet now pulled up to her neck. Due to the fact that I had no other response to what I had just said, I burst out laughing.

'I'm *only* teasing, Tia. Come here and give me the biggest goodbye hug you've got!'

She started to giggle, a look of relief spreading across her perfect face, before finally stepping forward and throwing her arms around my neck and pushing her lips onto mine.

'Bye, baby! Go and get the girl! Good luck, Ritchie Angel!'

And as I stepped out of the front door, her final words rattled around my head. I prayed that luck, and all of it good, was on my side.

Tia had offered me so much, and as I pulled away, waving furiously, just for the most fleeting of moments it was Yasmin standing there, just how she used to be as I left for work in the mornings. I pushed my foot hard on the brake and she was gone. There was Tia, and suddenly she paled by comparison.

As I turned away from the main green – Sky Cottage now out of sight – I simply couldn't get Yasmin out of my mind. I loved her so much that it was haunting me. Not being able to be with her just hurt unbearably. And as I attempted to wallow in the warmth her vision would bring, I was suddenly struggling to get her image clear in my head – variations of a dazzling face, but an inability to build up a totally true picture of her. I tried to fill my mind with the journey that lay ahead. I had never been to Dartmouth in my life, but having checked it out on the map, I felt confident that I would be there within just a few short hours, though I felt slightly concerned by the strip of water that seemed to separate me and Dartmouth itself. But I shook my head and felt convinced that there must be some kind of ferry, or something.

I yelled out defiantly, 'NOTHING IS GOING TO STOP ME, YASMIN! EVEN IF I HAVE TO *BLOODY* SWIM ACROSS...YOU SHOULD SEE HOW INCREDIBLE I AM IN THE WATER NOW! *I'M ON MY WAY!*'

My trusty old pickup truck made its way steadily down the motorway. And beneath the monotonous drone of the engine – a little noisier than usual – I struggled to settle the nerves that were unavoidably fraying me around the edges. In an attempt to look on the bright side of optimism, several scenarios ran through my mind, but then a cloud of uncertainty and understandable pessimism would spoil the ending of each. So to take my mind off any negative thoughts, I simply turned the radio up. The song from Dirty Dancing came on – *I've had the time of my life,* Bill Medley and Jennifer Warnes. As the song filled my mind, I was taken back to when Yasmin would force me to watch the film with her – under duress at first, but in time, the music and the film became an important part of us both. We'd both loved this song in particular and even chosen it for our first dance as man and wife. I sighed heavily at the memory and wondered whether Yasmin – wherever she may be – was listening too. But of course, as the song played now, in *this* lifetime, Yasmin and I had *never* seen the film together and so of course all memories were purely mine. And as the fact sunk in, I realised that there were so many precious moments that were natural souvenirs of our falling in love – songs, places, everyday scenarios – that from day one of our setting eyes on each other were nestled in the soul. Nobody could take the memories away, but now, in this world? And though I dreamed that I would find Yasmin, and that she would be simply waiting for me to come and rescue her, take her away from her dull, mundane life, I calculatedly feared that the reality could be very different. Yasmin had a lust for life! A passion that I was fortunate enough to have shared. For her to be on her own now, living a half life – not a chance! Who has taken my place, and was I man enough for whatever lay ahead?

As I approached Bristol I noticed my temperature gauge starting to climb worryingly. I eased off the accelerator a little, but the gauge kept climbing. I moved into the inside lane and looked for the next exit. The temperature needle sailed into the red and the steam, right on cue, oozed out and covered the windscreen, making me jump.

'*Shit!* Come on, old girl! *Please,* don't let me down now! *Come on!*'

The knocking of the engine was now so loud it was making my teeth hurt, but I continued to coax the pickup on. I kept it quiet and gentle, reverse psychology, perhaps encouraging the engine noise to pipe down a little so that it could hear me.

'Come on, you beautiful little thing, come on, my best little Japanese buddy!'

As the steam billowed and dived, I could only make out the faintest glimmer of the road ahead.

'Come on, my little baby girl, keep going, you clever little thing, don't stop here, not now! Please, not today of all bloody days! Sorry, sorry, didn't mean to swear at you!'

A glimmer of hope was at least showing itself as a three-pronged sign began its countdown, just a few hundred metres away from an exit.

'Thank you! Oh, thank you!'

As I cut directly into the breeze, the steam was billowing in a V-shape, resembling a wake, enabling me to see a little more. I limped up to the island, but just as I prayed that I could get to the top of the incline and perhaps freewheel down the other side, the engine started to make the most horrendous noises, that could only be described as cries of death! With one last muster, my foot pushed firmly to the floor, I just about climbed up onto the verge. The engine simply spluttered, and shook, rattled and stopped rolling! *Bang!* Steam and then silence everywhere. I slammed my hands against the steering wheel.

'YOU *BASTARD!* YOU *ABSOLUTE FUCKING* BASTARD!'

I threw the driver's door open, grabbed my rucksack, which contained all my belongings for the trip, and jumped out, slamming the door shut as hard as I could. I didn't even bother to open the bonnet up, but just walked off in total disgust, my ankles trying to twist and dislocate on the uneven tufts of mud disguised as grass. As I looked up at the huge highway sign, I frowned as I looked down the long road that led into Bristol. Cursing under my breath, I walked a few metres, then stopped. I mulled over my immediate options, time and speed being the key factors. Maybe I should hitch, but it was something I had never done in my life. There were cars out there with empty seats; on the law of averages, someone was bound to take pity on me.

So there I was, just thirty metres or so from my steaming pickup, thumb faced skywards. After a dozen or so cars simply screamed past me, I almost doubted my decision to simply stand and wait. As my frustration rose, almost as quickly as my temperature gauge on my rusty *bloody* let-down pickup, a blue Ford Escort screeched to a halt, tyres rubbing unwisely against the high kerb stones. I ran as quickly as I was able along the minefield of a verge, the view of my saviour through her rear windscreen. A chunky arm attached to an impressively built lady now stretched across her passenger seat and wound down the window.

'Car trouble, my lovely?'

As I placed my hand on the top of her roof and bowed my head, I nodded, and the door was immediately pushed uncomfortably into my midriff. I struggled clumsily, trying to get my rucksack off my back and placed without damage to anyone or anything into the back seat of the car. As a bead of sweat ran from my brow, I slumped down onto the passenger seat, slamming the door shut firmly beside me. As our eyes met, the Cheshire cat-like smile suggested that she may be just a little amused by my less than coordinated entering of the car. She pushed out her generously sized hand and I shook it firmly. Finally, words of my own broke the surreal feel of all that was happening to me.

'Ummm, thank you for stopping. I'm Ritchie, Ritchie Angel, and you are a lifesaver!'

Her smile peaked and then dropped away ever so slightly.

Then, bordering on the threatening, she stated clearly, 'Well! This lifesaver's called Corinne! And I'm a policewoman, so be warned! No funny business, *my* lovely!'

I smiled inanely now, feeling suitably and proficiently warned. As we drove, Corinne quizzed me about where I lived, where I was going, and informed me that she had just finished her night shift and an early stint in the gym. Oh, and that she had lived in Bristol forever!

I was feeling far more at ease now, our chat effortless and fun. There was an incredible energy about Corinne that oozed life. Every line she uttered was framed in laughter, and a real twinkle of the unknown in her eyes totally belied any preconceptions I would have instantly come to in other circumstances. She was larger than life, and I liked it.

'So come on, Ritchie Angel, what are you going to do, call a tow truck?'

I raised my palms to the sky and Corinne just giggled filthily, seeming to have her own plan as to how I should proceed. She turned the steering wheel suddenly as we headed off onto an industrial estate, racing at speed towards some railway arches. Just as I was starting to fear for my life, she pulled down hard on the steering wheel and jammed the brakes on. Corinne stepped out of the car and gave a high five to a large black guy, who seemed to appear from nowhere. He beamed in my direction, while wiping a spanner with an oily rag. Against my better judgment, I stepped out of the car. The huge guy took a step towards me. I nodded, and then shook my head in admiration for my saviour, who was comfortably shoulder-to-shoulder with this black *Robbie Coltrane* lookalike. I decided my money was on Corinne should these two decide to fight *or* simply arm wrestle, and felt I had picked my winner wisely as the softness of his voice defied the menacing image.

'Sorry, my lovely!' he said, his huge white grin appearing to mock my predicament. 'It's just that there's been a huge pile-up ten miles down the motorway! All the tow trucks for miles around have got their hands full. You're out of luck, my lovely.'

I sighed and nodded. 'Okay, well, thanks anyway!'

Corinne hugged the mechanic, who screeched ear-shatteringly as she made her way back to the car, *'TELL*

BOBBY I'LL SEE HIM THURSDAY AT BOXING TRAINING!'
I slumped back into the car, soon joined by Corinne. Suddenly, painfully, I felt the full force of her hand slap my chest.

'Cheer up, Ritchie! Always more than one way of skinning that lovely little fluffy puss cat!'

Corinne turned the ignition key and slammed the gearstick into reverse, pushing hard on the accelerator. My head slammed against the headrest as she amazingly handbrake-turned the car around, dust and exhaust smoke engulfing all visibility. She thrust the gearstick into first and we raced off back down the road we'd come in on. Once the image of her skinning a poor innocent animal had just about left me, my nerves having been tested to the maximum with my friend's driving skills, I was becoming increasingly impatient and so made a decision.

'What car garages have you got around here, Corinne?'

She ran a few off. 'Mmmmm, you've got Ford, Vauxhall, Fiat, Alfa, Mercedes, Porsche ... oh, and there's a new Jeep dealership.'

I nodded my head immediately. 'That's the one, girl, Jeep! If you don't mind, could you take me there?'

Corinne smiled, her head nodding in approval. She raced through the streets expertly, as though knowing every lump, bump and curve, until finally, she screeched up outside a smart glass-fronted showroom. An impressive line of bright chunky four-wheel drive vehicles stood defiant and ready for battle, defending the building behind them. Almost in awe, Corinne and I stepped out of the car, both nodding in approval. Corinne seemed to hold back a little, checking her watch.

'Corinne, I cannot take up any more of your time, you're probably ready for your bed. You've been brilliant, but I should be able to sort something out here and get myself back on the road!'

Corinne pushed her hand forward again, but I felt her more than generous help required more than this formal goodbye gesture. I threw my arms around her, and pushed my lips firmly onto her soft rosy red cheek. For just a split second, my slightly overzealous gratitude seemed rather one-sided, and I was just about to step back and make my embarrassed apologies. But as I loosened my grip, Corinne responded by wrapping her huge arms around me, squeezing all the air out of my body, almost lifting me off my feet as she pursed her lips and pushed them firmly onto mine. When she finally let go of me, I stood, lost for words, and then shook my head from side to side. Corinne tilted her head, judging my reaction, slight puzzlement in her large brown eyes.

'What, Ritchie? What are you shaking your head at?'

I shook my head again, a ripple of giggles burbling in the pit of my stomach.

'*You* Corinne! *You*! I think you're amazing!'

Corinne blushed, and for the first time she was not quite so forthright and confident, her size twenty-plus skirt and jacket barely containing her generous figure. She jumped back into her car, her hand grappling around inside her glove compartment.

'Here, Ritchie, put a few pounds on, and if things don't work out, look me up!'

Corinne handed me her address, torn off an old envelope.

'But listen! If my boyfriend answers the door, make sure you run. He eats pretty boys like you for breakfast! He usually does nights alternately to me, week on, week off!'

The mischievous grin on Corinne's face simply dazzled me, but then, with a screech of burning rubber, she was gone.

I made my way along the line of Cherokee and Grand Cherokee Jeeps, but my eye was taken with an open-top one at the end of the row, raised up on a mound of earth and rocks – all black, inside and out. I instinctively shook my head in total approval.

'That could be fun! I like it!'

There was an air of romance about the vehicle, though the flimsy soft-top was going to be a challenge with the British weather. I walked around it like an excited kid, taking it in from every angle. I looked back down the line, the more practical Cherokee Jeeps – with their thick leather seats and all the extras that meant you could almost live quite happily in one if needs required – pulling at my more sensible side.

My busy mind was suddenly interrupted.

'Can I help you, sir?'

I turned and came face-to-face with a middle-aged gentleman in a pinstripe suit.

'Um, yes!'

I looked back longingly at the open-top Wrangler Jeep and then once again at the five-door Cherokee in front of me. The salesman looked at me a little doubtingly, the look in his eyes questioning my ability to actually afford one of these shiny petrol guzzlers.

I turned to him, my rucksack slung over my left shoulder.

'I'm not so sure the pinstripe suit's quite the right image for promoting these rough-terrain all-American mudslingers...'

The salesman's eyes creased slightly, as though preparing a suitable response.

'Quite, sir! What would you suggest, cowboy boots and a Stetson?'

I nodded, impressed by his reply, and pushed my hand forward.

'Ritchie, Ritchie Angel. I think I would like to buy the Wrangler open-top, but there's one condition!'

My pinstripe friend's jaw dropped.

'Um, yes, sir! And what would that *condition* be?'

'I need to be able to drive it away within the hour!'

The salesman shuffled from foot to foot.

'Well, sir, I'm not sure... It's just that these things take time! I mean, would you be requiring finance? Or is that backpack of yours filled with the folding stuff?'

I slid my rucksack off my shoulder and took out my wallet.

'As good as...'

I grabbed my Platinum American Express card and driving licence, and then delved into the bottom of my rucksack and pulled out my passport. I handed over the route of payment and proof of who I was.

'Hopefully all these bits will suffice?'

I followed the now quiet, not quite so sarcastic salesman back into the impressive showroom, where he sat me down and asked the young girl from behind the reception desk to get me a coffee.

'I'll be back in a moment, sir!'

As the salesman scurried off, I shouted after him, 'SORRY TO BE A PAIN, BUT I'LL BE LOOKING FOR AT *LEAST* A *COUPLE* OF GRAND OFF THE SCREEN PRICE!'

Within fifteen minutes the man was back, sliding into the chair opposite me.

'Right, sir! I've spoken to my boss, and he's said that the best we can do is twelve hundred off the screen price! *So*...subject to your acceptance, and of course payment being granted by your credit card!'

The salesman didn't look up, his eyes avoiding mine totally.

He continued his monotone methodical patter. 'The Jeep was in fact registered three days ago, and subject to half an hour or so of tests in our workshop, and our little 'Joey Gopher' nipping off to the post office to grab your tax disc, you could indeed drive her away this *very* morning! Do you have insurance, sir?'

I thought for a second, ready to insist on the full two thousand pounds off, but all I could see was the vehicle enabling me to get to Yasmin, and what price would I put on that? And so I said that I would call my insurance broker and get them to fax the appropriate details through. My salesman friend turned his phone around and pushed it my way. The next one hour and twenty-six minutes dragged like a rain-filled weekend, but none of it mattered when the nice salesman finally handed me a full receipt, all the necessary paperwork and, most importantly, a spare set of shiny Jeep keys. As I walked out of the showroom, the Jeep was driven round to the front of the building, the mechanic nodding in approval.

'Be good fun that, sir, it's a beauty, four litres! Drive carefully, my lovely!'

I nodded and thanked the mechanic, an unavoidable chuckle still stirring every time I heard that wonderful 'my lovely' localism, seeming to me to promote the world as a far less serious proposition, and I liked that. I dropped down into the heavy cloth seat and felt instantly ready for the road ahead. After a quick run-through of the basic controls that made my pickup truck look as though it was decidedly advanced, I was free to go. I pushed my hand forward, shaking the salesman's hand firmly, thanking him for all his help. He smiled warmly. I leant forward, offering a little encouragement in regards to one of his earlier suggestions.

'Umm, while it's fresh in my mind, the Stetson, the cowboy boots... I think you're onto something there!'

I turned the key, the engine roaring reassuringly into life. Thinking I had had the last word, the salesman wasn't done just yet.

'Sir...?'

I craned my ear towards him.

'Sir, perhaps *us* sales guys could have cowboy names to go with the cowboy outfits. For me, perhaps Three Tits Pete!' He laughed and stepped away from the vehicle, looking extremely proud of himself.

I also found myself laughing, but wasn't quite sure why. I was just about to pull away, bemused and searching desperately for a link to local historical legends or something, when I remembered there was just one little bit of business that I hadn't yet taken care of.

'Ummm, sir, Old Three Tits Pete! Could you take care of something for me?' I handed over the paperwork and keys for the pickup truck and told him where it was. 'If you don't mind, you'd be a lifesaver. Can you get it picked up and sell it? Scrap it? If you make any kind of profit, just give it to charity! If I end up owing you, then just contact me at the logbook address!'

We shook hands again.

'Thanks, Pete!'

'No, Mr Angel, the name's Michael, Michael Threebird!'

I was now more confused than ever. I grinned sheepishly and sped away as quickly as I could. Without warning, I was laughing uncontrollably, the penny having dropped, though still unsure where the Pete bit came from. However, I decided that today was going to be a good day, and as I pushed down a little harder on the accelerator, making my way towards the motorway, I prayed that it would be a *great day!*

As I pulled onto the motorway island, the traffic south was moving at a snail's pace, and though normally I would head off in search of a quicker route, I simply shrugged my shoulders. *No rush*, I thought. *But a bit of fresh air wouldn't go amiss!* I pulled onto the verge, the cars from behind me tooting and flashing signs of single-finger denomination.

'And to you! Yeah, yeah, have a nice day!'

I unhooked the Jeep soft-top and rolled it back. I sat for a moment, not quite sure whether I would be warm enough once the motorway traffic built up a little speed, should we actually start to move at all. But being the eternal optimist, I felt that I had better wrap up as best as I could. I jumped into the back of the Jeep and grabbed my rucksack, having to delve deep to find my battered leather jacket. I pulled it on and zipped it up to the neck, before jumping back into the driver's seat. I knew I was stalling for time, and accepted that I was messing around and being indecisive, the fear of what lay ahead undoubtedly getting to me. I sat, desperate to psyche myself up, only too aware of how deeply I was breathing, the very real possibility of disappointment almost paralysing me. I placed my hands firmly onto the steering wheel and let my head fall back, my gaze fixed on the cold, crisp, clear lilac sky.

'Bloody lilac sky... If I want to be rid of *that,* then we've got to do *this,* Ritchie!'

Everything felt *so* surreal, a simple date in time, but a day I'd lived before. I tried to recall what I had done on this very ordinary Monday morning originally, but of course I had no idea. All I did know was that I was happily together with Yasmin. I tried to recreate some details. Together? In our hearts, definitely! Together physically? Unlikely; realistically kept apart by work. But as I sat there, wondering whether or not I would ever get to hold Yasmin again, I realised how I'd taken for granted just how accessible and simple the rules of our relationship were. To have borne no major significance to the habitual gesture of picking up the phone and chatting about how our days were going in the absence of the other. And for it not to have been unlawful to have been able to recklessly forget work, and to simply march into Yasmin's busy day and carry her off to wherever our hearts desired – the countryside, the beach, or better still, home and our bed, just to hold each other, to kiss, to simply *be* with her! I took a very large breath and let my head fall forward.

I smiled to myself. From nowhere came the words of my

great-grandfather: 'Victory favours the brave, Ritchie boy!' I nodded instinctively. *Now is the time to see where Yasmin's life has taken her.* I turned the key and the engine roared into life.

'Okay, Jeep my new friend, we've got a job to do!'

CHAPTER TWENTY-FOUR

Angel's Wings Unclipped And Ready To Fly!

After Death, 1997 – Lilac Sky
Seven miles in two hours was starting to test my patience. But the open-top motoring was certainly keeping me sane, and the fact that the full glare of the sun and the warm breeze was fully on me and not simply bouncing off a metal barrier seemed to keep me smiling, despite my lack of progress. I also kept myself fairly amused by taking in the irate, ready-to-boil drivers that sat to the left and right of me, line after line of them, locked together on this endless stretch of tarmac. I stared up at my lilac sky, wondering how we looked from up there – a thin black line, assumingly insignificant, but such incredible stories of everyday life in each and every vehicle. I let my head slump sideways, taking in the acres of rolling fields, and imagined what lay beyond the horizon, first to the left of me, and then to my right. I wondered about the cars in front, to the side and behind me; what were their stories? Was I alone and unique in my adventure? Rose had made the comment that I was an experiment, pretty much a one-off! I wondered whether that was true. Would they share the details of other experiments with her? As I sat in my totally impractical Jeep, my music blaring selfishly, I decided that I wasn't going to worry about the answer; for me, my adventure in the here and now was all-consuming. Yasmin, Evie and me together, that's all that mattered.

I suddenly had the most incredible urge to slip my heavy boots off and let my bare feet feel the cold damp grass that surrounded me. But just as I was about to give in to temptation, the traffic started to move again, and then, slowly but surely, we started to gain a little momentum. Then I was back in neutral again and almost easing to a stop, then back into first gear and then a little faster … thirty … forty … fifty … sixty miles an hour, and then as the gaps between the vehicles got greater, seventy …eighty, and away. I pushed the heater up to maximum, and the combination of cool and hot air was battering my face beautifully. I could barely make out the music above the roar of the V6 engine, but it was an adrenalin-filled symphony that was taking me ever closer to my dream. However, there were black clouds building – not a metaphor, but real storm-threatening clouds.

My mind was being kept busy by the 'grimace and gamble' game that I was playing. As I passed unprotected under the black angry clouds, I had to smile as the short, sharp droplets of rain hit my windscreen, but then missed my head and landed miserably onto the tarmac that I was now safely leaving behind. I was dry and untouchable at this speed. But I laughed nervously, deep from the pit of my stomach, as the odds were about to be shortened. A band of vengeful wrath-ridden blackness filled the sky – the width of the horizon, and with a depth that promised me a serious beating – and almost made me stop the Jeep and pull the roof back on. But as the speedometer was reading just over eighty miles per hour and the rain was getting heavier, I had my audience to consider. The finger-pointing, the tooting of horns and the excited smiling faces in the cars that I was overtaking meant that the show had to go on. The rain became stronger, harder and was seemingly taking my resistance personally. I glanced back at my rear seat; the rain was leaving its mark. Suddenly, my head shaking in defiance, I could hear water on leather drumming furiously onto my back, a drop or two kissing my neck.

I pushed my foot even harder to the floor … eighty-five … ninety. I screamed out, *'YES!!'* as my back was now out of reach to the torrent of rain being released by the playful gods. Ninety-five… A quick glance; my rear seat was still taking a bashing. Ninety-seven … my wiper blades couldn't move the water any faster and my vision was minimal, but nothing was going to stop me now. *One hundred miles an hour!* Another look back and a victorious shake of the head; my Jeep and all that was in it were now out of reach to the rain. My Jeep and I were thundering our way down to Dartmouth, dangerous and out of control. I could no longer take in the amusement of my audience, I just kept going flat-out. And then I felt an overwhelming warming of the soul, as there it was, lilac clear sky edging ever closer, in the wake of the clouds; or for the more optimistic of you, chasing, triumphant, all-intrusive blackness away.

I had eased to a more acceptable *legal* seventy miles an hour now, and getting drenched was no longer an issue since the sky was good. The traffic was starting to thin out a little, twenty miles north of Dartmouth. Thick clusters of evergreens lined the hilly dual carriageway as we finally dropped from three lanes to two. My nose twitched, and I felt convinced I could actually smell salt, excitedly anticipating that the change in the air would mean a glimpse of the sea as I reached the top of each steep climb. I would shake my head; *maybe the next one…* But as the miles were eaten up, wanting a view of the sea was pushed aggressively into the background, and my heartbeat seemed to quicken with every sign that informed me I was getting closer to my chosen destination. My nerves were fluttering wildly, and the extent of my anxiety was uncomfortable, but I defiantly shook my head and knew this was to be expected. And so I would push the nerves and reoccurring doubts to the back of my mind.

As the roads started to twist and turn, I passed the many B&B boards that lined my route to the moment of truth. I finally saw the signpost taking me off the main road: *Dartmouth – 4 miles.* As I knocked down the right-hand indicator, my heart was in my mouth. I tried to steady my erratic breathing, the persistent anxiety seemingly determined to take over my entire being, but I wasn't going to let it. As I made my way down the twisting narrow lanes, the approach through vast greenery, vibrant and rich, pulled me further into my adventure. I slowed down and turned left by a peaceful centuries-old cemetery. My eyes were everywhere, trees to the left and right of the road joining their branches and cutting out the now forceful strands of lilac sun. The one-way lane climbed into the side of the hill, water tumbling down the moist craggy rock face, the lane twisting and turning as though determined to shake your sense of direction. Suddenly, my eyes were blinking back the sheer strength of dazzling sunlight as the trees broke hands and left me unprotected, but then my jaw dropped as a true vision of beauty filled my eyes. I instinctively pushed my foot hard onto the brake pedal and was immediately scolded by a blast from a car horn right behind me. I had not even been aware of anyone else being within a thousand miles of me. My eyes were wide and I was undoubtedly in awe, I simply couldn't take my eyes off all that stood across the water. 'Wow…that *must* be Dartmouth!'

The winding, almost single-file road ahead of me was lined with many pastel-painted houses, until the road almost appeared to reach a dead end strewn with cobblestones. I glanced a little more questioningly this time as I took in the strip of sea that stood between Yasmin and me. The guy behind me, quite rightly, blasted his horn for the second time and raced passed me, his fist and expletives ripe and warranted. But at this moment in time *he* simply didn't exist. I felt as though I was dreaming every moment of my journey. I lifted my hand and slapped it hard against my face, the sting making my eyes water. I chuckled at my increasing insanity. But it was getting genuinely more difficult to separate real life and a deep, dreamy stupor these days.

A dark cloud took away the feeling of warmth that had been disguising the cool sea breeze that was now tickling my travel-weary bones, and a small shiver passed sharply through me. I looked around for a friendly face, suddenly needing an answer.

'Excuse me! Do you know the time?'

The old gentleman stepped towards the Jeep, glancing down at his watch.

'Ah yes, certainly, it's just gone four!'

He smiled and tipped his cap; despite his thick, neatly pressed sailing jumper, it seemed very unlikely that he had ever actually been out to sea. And as he made his way back up the hill, I caught a reflection of his bright white trousers and stiff leather deck shoes that convinced me I was right.

I quickly jumped out of the Jeep.

'Excuse me, sir ... *sir!* Um, sorry to bother you again! But how do you get *over* to Dartmouth?'

The old guy turned around and pointed over my shoulder.

'The ferry, young man! Keep going to the bottom of the hill, and just join the queue!'

I waved my thank you and turned quickly, suddenly feeling a little foolish as I looked at the signs everywhere, giving perfectly simple instructions on how to get on the ferry! I jumped back into the Jeep, my face screwed up, as I felt that my inability to spot several well-placed signposts did not bode well for my new role as detective. But as another couple of cars passed me, I decided that I had best join that queue rather quickly.

Within minutes, as the steep hill dropped low and narrow, I pulled up behind a row of several cars. I glanced up at a sign asking for all engines to be switched off, nodded in humble acknowledgement and turned the ignition key. I smiled at my reflection in the rear-view mirror, sarcastically congratulating myself for actually noticing the sign. I sighed at the sudden peace and calmness that seemed to have dropped around me – it felt good. But any well-being suddenly drained away as I watched a young couple pass by, laughing and joking, their bodies virtually welded together, their arms and legs getting lost in the tangle – all I saw was Yasmin and me, a lifetime ago, in love and inseparable! Unable to take the torture for a split second longer, my instincts took pity and drew my eyes to the view. *Mmm, beautiful... this place would suit Yasmin... almost perfect!*

My mind raced as I stepped out of the Jeep. I pulled myself up onto the high wall, keen to get a better view of what I was dealing with. *Almost perfect!* kept repeating itself over and over again in my head. *Because surely, Yasmin anywhere without me, well, how could that be perfect?* I pulled my knees up to my chest, dropping my chin onto my hands as I wrapped my arms firmly around my legs. I was surprised how the lilac haze appeared to be very faint – it was still there, but it hung several shades lighter than usual as I looked out across the river. As the light bounced off the water, it was almost

557

hypnotic, crystals rolling hedonistically together, pulling me in. I had to blink hard to break the spell, and gave an almost defeatist sigh and the thought that was not going to help my cause: *Well, Yasmin, any comparison between here and the Water's Edge*...Well, I was lost for a positive response! The energy and brightness of what stood before me on the surface seemed to leave my world back home in the shade.

I had always believed that our little piece of nirvana was unquestionably perfect, beautiful, and that all I had to do was get Yasmin back home to the Water's Edge, and though of course it was still in its raw, natural state, I hadn't doubted that she would fall in love with it, that the magic it had raised in us both would be unearthed again. But I now realised that she had her own beautiful backdrop and all the spells that could well have captivated her in her new world. That was my challenge! All that Yasmin is *now* against all that she was *then,* with me. Was there a lost soul deep within her, simply needing to be reminded of a wonderful past life? I had no way of knowing, and it scared me.

Across the water, I could see a car ferry making its way towards Kingswear, the small place that I was waiting so patiently to leave. I was now reading every sign available to me. A cool breeze seemed to wake me from my trance. I looked to my right, where a trail of thirty or so cars were falling in line, snake-like, behind the Jeep. I let go of my legs, letting them dangle, and suddenly pursed my lips. Then I nodded my head, progressively faster, in a gallant effort to psyche myself up. *Come on, Ritchie, Yasmin loves you... she just doesn't know it yet!* And though I had to accept that my battle with devil's advocate would be ongoing, I had to be ready. Any chance of him slipping beneath my inept defences and I would have to swing the *willow*, batting him firmly away – stand strong! I started to make a mental list of the positives: Yasmin's likes and dislikes, and who would know better than me? And there was no escaping the simple fact that I did have an albeit unaccounted-for history with the beautiful lady, and it should not merely be dismissed, just as a marriage witnessed in the eyes of our good Lord should certainly count in the great scheme of the universe. Would we change so dramatically from one life to the next? Only a reshuffle of time was going to tell. So I had an upper hand against any potential rival, and if not an *upper* hand then certainly a *wild card!* Despite my pessimisms pressing relentlessly to unsettle my optimisms, my blood was up. I had to find the strength of character that had been the hallmark of all that Ritchie Angel stood for. I had to brush off the ego and confidence battering that had been a baying parasite throughout my nightmare adventure. My legs were swinging like those of a small, hyperactive child now. My steadily increasing buoyant mood would have undoubtedly raised a few concerned eyebrows for the majority of the waiting car passengers that I had my back to. But I let out a small chuckle; why would I care about that? In some sort of surreal way I had to ask the question, do any of them really exist?

But suddenly, interrupted by the very real sound of people starting their engines, I turned and jumped off the wall, walking self-consciously back towards my Jeep. My mind started to picture how the arrogance of Ritchie Angel would play this scene to his audience, should he be the leading man, and doesn't the leading man always get the girl? And so I jogged the last few steps and attempted to leap into the Jeep via the rear seats and swinging through the rollover bar, but unfortunately catching every protruding part of my anatomy on the descent. I winced as I landed harshly, but tried to maintain the pretence of having executed the move perfectly as I caught the eye of a young woman, her arm linked with her gentleman friend, her discreet smile suggesting that she was ever so slightly impressed by my agility; or perhaps embarrassed for me, I couldn't decide which. I nodded coolly in her direction, desperate to hide the pain that was presently shooting from buttock to buttock and up the length of my spine.

The cars in front of me started to roll down the hill a little and then stop. I could hear the heavy bass of a tugboat and then the loud slam of metal onto concrete. One by one, half a dozen or so cars came from around the corner and made their way up the steep hill. I waited, then finally, as we all started to roll forward again, I turned the elusive corner, and there it was, the ferry bobbing up and down on the slightly choppy sea, the front sitting on the greasy concrete slipway. As I drove the Jeep carefully onto the vessel, we were all packed tightly together, bumper to bumper. I felt a little conspicuous as people filed onto the boat by foot and squeezed in at the sides, arms and bottoms resting against the Jeep. Once we were full, the small tugboat that ran parallel to us manoeuvred aggressively, turning full circle, now pointing towards Dartmouth. We started to move effortlessly through the water. Suddenly, the full force of the spring sun slipped from behind the imposing hotel that ran alongside the ferry slipway and fell protectively upon us, the full glory of the day making the most of its last few hours. And though I accepted that I had to take full responsibility for what lay ahead, the sheer anticipation was incredible. So many thoughts over the last few years were now condensed into just a handful of possible scenarios, and in this instance – despite all I had kept telling myself – the pessimist in me was lurking unhelpfully in the background, pushing himself forward, determined to steal the lead.

It didn't take long, maybe seven or eight minutes, to finally reach Dartmouth. Once again the engines kicked into life and the foot passengers rushed forward, making their escape first. One by one, the cars were signalled off the ferry. I followed the line of traffic up the sharp slip road and along the small, narrow streets, my eyes everywhere. I was almost convinced that I would see Yasmin, just walking along with her throng of small children in tow, her six-foot-six husband lovingly at her side. But of course, and gratefully, it wasn't to be. I drove around the small town twice within twenty minutes, the steadily growing rumble in my stomach telling me that maybe I should park up and get something to eat.

Dartmouth was beautiful. There was an array of classy-looking restaurants, expensive art and clothes shops, but the place had an untypical seaside feel. The yachts in the estuary ranged from the magnificent to the traditional 'old money' antique vessels, moored, patiently waiting for their captains. There was a huge, intimidating battleship easing itself with dignity through the seemingly shallow waters, its crew of naval men waving at the intermittent gathering of well-wishers scattered along the promenade.

I finally found a parking space, undoubtedly a major triumph in itself. As I turned off the engine, I couldn't quite believe I was here. And though I was trying desperately hard to be relaxed, I felt that I was being watched. As I said the words, I smiled and looked up towards the skies, nodding and whispering a *hello* to Rose, and to whomever she might mingle with up there. But as I dropped my gaze, taking in my more immediate surroundings, it was still the chance of bumping into Yasmin that unnerved me. I was on my guard. After all, I wanted our first meeting to be impressive, our eyes to meet and for it to have a lasting impression. As I sat in my Jeep, I drummed my fingers against the steering wheel, and the thought hit me: *what if Yasmin wasn't here in Dartmouth?* I had presumed, from what people had said, that she and her mum were living either together, or at least close by. My mind started to race. *What if Lillie won't give me Yasmin's address?* And before the problem had even arisen, I was thinking of ways to get around such hurdles.

I needed to stretch my legs! As I stepped out onto the fancy cobbles that lined the length of the promenade, I took in the many, many people that were sauntering along, as though they didn't have a care in the world. Keen to do something other than spin aimlessly, I walked ten paces to the left, and then, devoid of direction, turned and walked twenty paces the other way. Then I stopped and took a deep breath, soaking up the stunning surroundings. I focused on a castle at the jaws of the estuary, the sun blazing across all it surveyed. The sheer strength of light that filled the opening to Dartmouth was the most powerful I had ever witnessed – an almost spiritual display. As I squinted my eyes, there was no mistaking the thread of lilac amongst the glow, but undoubtedly diluted compared to the strong shade I had been seeing back in Willow.

I suddenly turned and ran back to the Jeep, having forgotten to put the soft top back up, but as I stood looking at my new mode of transport, I simply shook my head. *Who cares?* I squashed my rucksack down beneath the soft top, having first removed my wallet.

Though I was hungry, I felt unable to settle. I knew I needed to relax, but I had so much to do. I had walked without direction for three or four streets, finally deciding that food was crucial to regain some kind of focus. My surroundings were a little quieter, I was aware of being amongst the backstreets slightly higher into the hillside. Common sense finally forced me into the doorway of an impressive seafood restaurant. The waiter setting the tables looked alarmed by my sudden appearance, his broad Scottish accent leaving me in no doubt that I was an unwelcome intrusion.

'Sorry, big man, but we're not open! Not until seven!'

I nodded my head apologetically, pleased that I hadn't bitten the man's head off, as my increased need for food was diminishing my patience; *So why not lock your fucking door then?!* so very nearly put out there. I walked backwards, a false smile spread across my face, and out of the doorway. I stood for a moment. Then I turned and looked along the small cobbled street, presuming that all the restaurants were likely to open at a similar time.

I hovered for a few indecisive seconds more, muttering under my breath, 'A fast-food place? I'm sure they'll sell me a pastie. Mmm, a Cornish pastie would be nice, yesss, a lovely Cornish Devon pas… Oh *do* shut up, Ritchie!' I scolded myself at the unnecessary inner chats I was having within my increasingly insane head.

I moved, suddenly aware of the restaurant door being opened.

'Oh good, big man, ye still here! If ye hungry, ye could perhaps do me a favour?'

Our eyes met, my hopes rising.

The waiter, briefly straight-faced, his laughter out almost before the words, bellowed, 'If you can grab *me* a bag of chips whilst getting ye wee self something… It's just that the food in *here* is *shite!*' I felt the red mist descend and my eyes bulge, and then within the flicker of my tormentor's eyes, my sense of humour took control as the waiter boomed, '*ONLY KIDDING BIG UN!*...If you're up for being a guinea pig? And I don't mean a wee bit of lettuce and half a carrot, but ye could try a couple of my new recipes if ye're up for it?!'

The same wonderful man that had *so* painfully turned me

away just a minute or so ago was now welcoming me with open arms. *What was the catch? Who cares?* I thought as I readily accepted his offer and stepped inside.

The restaurant door suddenly banged sharply against my back nudging me forward clumsily.

'Aye, that's it, och, just slide the wee bolt across!'

I did as he asked, nodding my head as he pointed to a table in the centre of the room. The man disappeared into the steam-filled kitchen, the stench of garlic and a subtle smell of fish tickling my nostrils and teasing my taste buds. I slipped off my jacket, placed it on the back of my chair and waited. The restaurant was only small, but in my present state of mind just perfect. I took in the tasteful decor, with the large chrome mirrors and solid sheets of glass across rough stone pedestals – incredibly similar to the design of my Italian tenants who ran their restaurant overlooking the canal on Willow High Street.

My waiter now being promoted to chef finally rejoined me.

'Okay, sir?' He shook my hand limply, his mind certainly elsewhere. 'Right, my friend! Sit, sit! If you are ready? I've experimented on three new dishes, I think they're good. I *pray* they're magnifico!' My friend's accent was now impressively Italian. 'But you, I want you to try each one and then you tell me, ahhh yes, or ahhh no! I hope *not* no, but be honest and I promise I *will* cope, okay?'

I sat down quickly, my schizophrenic friend keen to get this experiment started. My taste buds were being pulled this way and that. Each time my personal *waiter* swung in and out through his timber doors, an escape from inquisitive customers' eyes, an explosion of aromas would fill the air. I was increasingly confident that I was in for a major treat. The Scottish-Italian ran back into the kitchen and then returned, an impressive waft of steam starting to subside in his wake.

'Okay, sir…' He slid a large warm plate in front of me, strips of smoked salmon across a glistening sorbet. 'Sir, our own, indulgent Louis Roederer Cristal sorbet, and the finest strips of smoked salmon!'

The poor guy waited with bated breath. I wasn't sure that the delicate work of art before me was the choice of a hungry man, who only moments ago was craving a family size Cornish pastie, but as I dropped a sliver of smoked salmon into my mouth, the sacrifice of oak embers was certainly not in vain.

'Oh, that *is* very good,' was the result.

I then took a small spoonful of champagne sorbet.

'Oh my God! Wow, that is ... oh my, that *is* wonderful!'

The bubbles instantly burst into life, the alcohol bouncing on the palate. And as the remaining strip of smoked salmon and champagne accompaniment was gratefully devoured – before the warm plate denied me – I instinctively raised my hand.

'Bravo, sir, bravo!'

I was full of praise for my newfound friend. I asked the waiter – or should I say chef – his name.

'Cass!' he replied.

I smiled, shaking my head in worthy acknowledgment of a true genius.

'Well, Cass, umm, my name is Ritchie, and that, well, it was excellent, absolute top drawer! But please enlighten me, why do you serve the salmon and sorbet on a warm plate?'

Cass kissed the tips of his fingers, his explanation as potent as his glorious food.

'Good smoked salmon is like a red wine! As rampant as a living brie! It needs to breathe at body temperature, as though just plucked out of the sea, which is where the chilled champagne sorbet comes in. The warm flesh is then at its freshest, and its tastiest! I smoke my own salmon, and then, just like the bubbling ocean, my sorbet and the Cristal, ooohhh yes! Eh, eh, you approve? You liked it?'

I nodded my head with undoubted conviction.

'Oh yes, Cass, I *loved* it!'

I waited eagerly for my next course. There was a loud clatter, and the odd swear word coming from the steam-filled kitchen next to me. But then – an arrival worthy of *Merlin* himself – Cass was at my side, and an even larger warm plate was slid before me. I was convinced that he had just hopped on the spot, his hands pushed excitedly together. The look of anticipation on his small tanned face was like that of an expectant father. Finally, he took a breath and introduced his next creation.

'This, my friend, was caught just two hours ago; the

freshest, not a whiff, no aroma, just pure, fluffy, melt-in-the-mouth cod!'

My attentive chef gesticulated with his hands and continued.

'You can see that I have placed diagonally, equally fresh, torn-off strips of lobster. Cass only accepts those that are in their prime, at their tastiest best, yeah? My use once again of champagne in my sauce, with a subtle mix of wholegrain mustard! Oh, and the asparagus, young and perfect, kissed by the dew of this morning's dawn. Over the season I have personally visited and watched this very offering prosper, and as the sun rose today, I just knew, and so finally, I gave the thumbs-up, the time had come! Tomorrow would have been too late! Please taste! And tell me the truth?'

I hesitated for just a moment and then picked up the end of the asparagus, the hot butter glistening and running into the perfectly formed shoots. I bent my head down, meeting the delicacy halfway.

'Oh, Cass, mmmm! Oh! You were *so* right! If there was a better day than today to taste this fruit of the soil, I would call the man that challenges you on that a misguided fool! Ohh, wonderful!'

As I eagerly pushed the full length of the asparagus into my mouth, I nodded my head in full and total approval. I took my time, devouring and acknowledging the young life that was now taken away so barbarically, but then noticed Cass's short attention span urging me onto the rest of his creation. I dropped my fork into the natural fold of the white meat before me and lifted the morsel to my lips, well aware that every inch of my performance was being anxiously monitored. The cod simply melted in the mouth.

'Oh, Cass, this is good!' The necessary sharpness of the creator's sauce hit the spot to perfection. 'Yes, yesss, heavenly!'

I eagerly speared the sunburst orange over white lobster, turning it full circle in the sea of beige that once on the palate certainly didn't disappoint.

'Mmm, oh, that's *very* good!'

And it was wonderful, his work a masterpiece. The only exception was a rather salty miniature sandcastle *thing* that, as

I pulled the napkin away from my lips, remained only lightly dented on my plate. Cass's face and body language were that of a broken man. I explained to him that apart from the sandcastle, the rest was the creation of a sheer genius.

'That sandcastle...That *sandcastle* is an anchovy mousse!' Cass gestured towards it. 'You try again! You must! Hang on, *one* moment please!'

I sat and waited, my mind racing with many options as to what my new friend may be preparing for me. *More food, or the sharpening of his cleaver?* Without warning, he was back, and a small side dish with some torn lobster placed before me. He was pushing my fork into the plumpest piece, before dipping the end of the flesh into the sandcastle, and there it was, placed before me at mouth level.

'Try it now, sir!'

I took the fork and nervously placed the bespoke offering into my reluctant mouth.

'...Oh my God, Cass! That is heavenly!' And it *truly* was.

Within the hour, several inspired courses more, along with detailed techniques and over-my-head tips of how to recreate all I had tasted, I was totally and rather uncomfortably refuelled. Food and all thought of it were now firmly placed at the bottom of any imminent to do list! My pasty complexion seemed to bring out the elated in Cass, and he knew his work was done – well, almost! For his final trick, he pulled a gold bottle from behind his back.

'Shame not to finish the experience off with a glass of the very best, eh, Ritchie?'

Cass removed the silver spoon from the neck of the Cristal champagne.

'This clever little trick ensures that the fizz remains once opened, Ritchie. Trust me, it works!'

And not wanting to offend my new best friend, I took a deep breath and nodded my approval. Failing miserably in an attempt to buy some time for my digestive system to make some room for what it was about to receive, I watched contentedly as the bubbles danced.

'To you, Cass! You are a true genius!'

Cass beamed, proud and emotional, and I was convinced I

could see tears welling up in his eyes.

'And to you, Ritchie my friend. You are a man with a fine palate. I thank you, sir, I *thank* you!'

As the clock approached opening time, I was aware of staff milling about and energetically working around us. But Cass seemed more interested in my reason for being in Dartmouth than the preparation for the night ahead.

'So you see, Cass, I need to find Yasmin, she's the one!'

Cass raised his glass.

'To Yasmin! And don't you worry, laddee,' his broad Celtic accent reassuringly back with us. 'Ochh! I will make my enquiries. I am almost certain Victoria Road is only a wee few streets away, and the beauty you describe, mmmm, I am sure she has been in here. Och though, we have many beautiful ladies keen to try Cass's delights, *hey,* Ritchie!'

I laughed out loud as Cass rubbed his hands aggressively on his thighs, his cheeks reddened by our third glass of Cristal.

'Och, Ritchie! But there is one bonnie lass that certainly sounds like your Yasmin. Leave it with me, laddee, I will make some discreet enquiries for ye!'

The restaurant was full of noise and chatter now, and I was aware of a young waitress looking nervously towards where I was sitting.

'Cass, I think it's time I left, you'll be needing this table.' I nodded towards the girl, who seemed to relax a little. I bade Cass goodnight and wished him luck. 'How much do I owe you? Please let me pay for what I've had.'

But my friend convinced me otherwise. 'No, laddee! You have been a great help! It is I that should be thanking you!'

And with that, our internal organs rampant with champagne, we embraced firmly, and I made my way into the night.

Within minutes of being back on the street, I realised how cold the nights still were. I bounced up and down, trying to jump-start my circulation. I physically shook as the full extent of potent alcohol became apparent through the thinning of my usually warm bloodstream. The sky was filled with cloud, entwined with a rainbow of differing depths of lilac. I pulled up my jacket collar and retraced my steps back to the Jeep. I cursed myself for not putting the soft top back up; now I was even less keen than before! Good food and alcohol had left me longing for a warm and comfortable bed for the night.

I fumbled and cursed as I tried to pull the canvas roof back onto the Jeep – it seemed to take forever. But once my new friend was watertight and locked up safely for the night, I felt a little more relaxed. I smiled at my earlier craving for fresh air and sheer disdain at the thought of being cooped up inside a sensible, practical vehicle. Whereas now, the simple appeal of a warm confined space was all I wanted, my increasingly weary body desperate for rest. But as I turned yet another corner, convinced that I would soon have my wish, I reassured myself that come sunrise, and with a refreshed mind and spirit, I was going to let nothing stop me from finding Yasmin and making her mine!

But for now I was beginning to doubt my sense of direction, my head hazy from the generous amount of champagne that had been forced upon me. And just as I was smiling at the surreal pleasure of it all, I was swallowed up by a crowd of people, taking up the whole corner of the street. There was a carnival atmosphere and a hypnotic backdrop of a bass guitar and rattling of drums, and like a parting of the Red Sea, my eyes were drawn towards a hotel that stood at the foot of the small harbour. I was pulled towards the bright lights, and now the unmistakable sound of jazz music spilled out into the night air, seagulls and the lapping of the high tide joining in with the reassuring symphony. I looked up at the large gilt letters that ran along the full width of the white and blue building: Royal Castle Hotel. I paused for a moment, questioning whether I was actually going to manage to get a quiet night's sleep here. But then I shook my head as I realised that I could quite happily lie down in one of the adjoining shop doorways and probably sleep like a baby.

I turned and glanced at the modest harbour that was crammed full of small boats, and then took in the people who were now stood all around me, puffing on large cigars, wine, whisky and beer glasses in hand. They each nodded as I eased past them, finally stepping into the quaint hallway. The highly polished, but slightly worse-for-wear oak floor led me past the main bar on my left and the lounge-bar set to the right. I was suddenly aware of applause and cheering as the band introduced their next number. The place had a good feel about it – it was centuries-old, and oozed character from every beam and leaded window. At the end of the long entrance hall, a young lady sat behind reception, with a warm welcoming smile that was graciously maintained for every one of the twenty or so steps that it took to reach her.

'Good evening, sir, how can I help you?'

I placed my rucksack down on the floor, repeating in my head, *please have a room for me, please have a room for me!*

Finally, as I rested my hands on the counter, 'Umm, have you a room, preferably one that takes in that wonderful sea view?'

The girl glanced down at her list.

'Umm...Yes we do sir, just one sea view room left...'

I nodded gratefully.

'Okay then, sir, for that room, including your evening meal in our main restaurant, and of course a full English breakfast, one hundred and forty pounds per night.'

I gulped, and a little laugh eased out of me at the mere thought of ever wanting to eat again after all I had consumed this evening. The girl smiled and laughed with me.

As I passed her my credit card, I said, 'Can I reserve the room for a couple of nights? I really don't know how long my business will take here.' I glanced down at the gold name badge. 'Ummm, Kelly, if that's at all possible?'

Kelly beamed warmly. 'Of course, sir!' whilst running my card through her machine.

I had a collection of cards that I very rarely ever used, but today, well, I had certainly changed all that. And depending on how long it took to find Yasmin, and perhaps more importantly to convince her to come home with me, would determine just how much of a serious bashing these little bits of plastic would take.

Kelly showed me to my room. She apologised for the fact that the porter wasn't available, but despite her willingness to carry my rucksack up the many stairs for me, I assured her that I was quite capable, and that she had been helpful enough. But as she pushed the key into the door and let me into my room, I nodded approvingly. Kelly pulled the curtains across, straightening their fall. She turned and smiled, standing momentarily, before nodding and then making a hasty exit, closing the large heavy oak door behind her.

The room was perfect, steeped in tradition, elegant and stylish. But for me, the power shower and then the large four-poster bed had for now become my lifesaver. The hot water cleansed and relaxed my body, but as I wrapped the large white fluffy bath sheet around me, my heart felt heavy. I was very pleased to be here; after all, I'd waited twelve long years to get to this point. And despite a little fast-forwarding here and there, it had felt like several hectic lifetimes. But here I was, at the moment of truth. Nothing was assured, everything to gain... but then *so much* to lose. All my doubts had been based on the fact that I didn't really know *this* Yasmin at all; we didn't have an ounce of worthy history between us. But my hopes were hanging on one single moment, our kiss, in this life, very real, and the spark that was undoubtedly there. And though the powers that be made me erase the scene between us, was the moment really gone forever? Was that possible? But here and now, I had everything to play for, and what a prize. I knew I was beaming like a Cheshire cat at the mere thought of it. A good night's sleep and then, in the cold light of day, I would be back to my optimistic 'make anything happen' self. I smiled at my description, but that's what I needed to be. But as I rubbed my hair and body dry, for now I was happy to settle for sleep. After all, the morning would be here soon enough.

A pounding in my head brought the morning to me before I was ready for it. I jumped out of bed quickly, feeling a little nauseous as I opened the bedroom door.

'Sorry, sir! We knocked earlier, but wondered whether it was convenient to clean your room?'

I shook my head from side to side. 'Um, sorry, no, I'm a bit behind this morning. In fact, what *is* the time?'

I closed the door, a little perturbed that is was almost midday. The buzzing in my ears was uncomfortable, the side effect of being woken suddenly, and I was in no doubt that the fabulous champagne had played a significant part. I grabbed the water decanter and filled the glass tumbler. I felt really dehydrated, but as the cool clear liquid started to work on my body, I could feel all my internal organs falling back into line, back into their rightful, most productive positions. I walked towards the heavily patterned curtains and tried to pull them open. After a determined moment or two, it dawned on me that I might find it easier in pulling the cord which wasn't that invisible at the side of the window. I blinked my eyes furiously as the stark lilac sunlight filled the room. But as I regained focus on the glorious day outside, I was in awe. *Wow, what a view!* Dartmouth was indeed a beautiful place, the yachts, the people, the water … it was all so very inspiring. My heart was racing, my blood up.

I grabbed my clothes, feeling an overwhelming desire to find my beautiful wife. But though I was pushing myself forward, I couldn't deny the pounding in my heart, a burning sensation, a heady cocktail of fear, anticipation and excitement, but I was ready! I longed to see her, and I prayed deep down inside that today would bring us face-to-face.

As I stepped out of my room, the young girl that was on reception when I arrived last night was stood before me.

'Good morning, Mr Angel. We didn't see you at breakfast this morning.' Kelly's smile was warm and lifting.

'Ummm, no. I must have passed out when my head hit the pillow, hmmm, not really my way. Things to do, people to see!'

Kelly beamed again, her forehead creasing a little, undoubtedly at my rather un-cool response. I smiled apologetically. My nerves mixed with neat adrenalin were proving to be an interesting cocktail. I headed for the stairs, Kelly wishing me luck. I turned and waved, her encouraging eyes sparkling back at me, as though willing me on somehow. But then I was gone, down into the main hallway and out of the hotel.

A flood of lilac light stopped me in my tracks. I unwittingly rotated three hundred and sixty degrees, people tutting and stepping around me. Finally, I stood totally still, the sun warming me from head to toe. I took a deep breath and told myself to calm down as I felt that I was going ever so slightly mad. I let out a balancing sigh, and seemed to gradually take stock. I focused on the newsagents just over the road. I felt that they might be able to tell me the whereabouts of Victoria Road.

The old guy behind the counter didn't look up from his *Daily Telegraph*, his gold-rimmed glasses perched on the end of his crooked nose.

'Number?'

I informed him quickly.

'Yep! Turn left out of the shop, past the hotel, left again, a mile, mile and a half, almost to the top of the hill, wrought iron gates, the Old School House, just about still standing, but you can't miss it!'

I thanked the man, but he still didn't look up, and just lifted his hand in recognition of my gratitude.

Though the Jeep was only a couple of roads away, I simply couldn't stop myself from turning left, walking with purpose past the hotel, left again, and I just kept walking. I caught my reflection in a shop window, an inane smile fixed firmly across my face. I started to chuckle, my mind tripping up with all that could be waiting for me at the end of this road. Fearful, yet undeterred, my feet just kept walking, wobbly and strangely uncoordinated, but as long as they kept moving forwards I simply didn't care. *Oh God, Yasmin! Please be there! Please be in! Be single! Be...* I started to shake my head from side to side, and then very steadily started to run.

As I made my way up the hill, the noise of Dartmouth was being left behind, the many people that had been around me having vanished. My eyes focused on the long twisting road before me, lined with shrubbery and gate after gate, but I was alone, and not another living soul blocked my way forward. As I pushed my legs a little harder, my lungs burning under the forced pressure, I was aware of beads of perspiration forming on my brow. And then, just a hundred yards or so more, they dropped kamikaze-like into my eyes, forcing me to bring up my forearm, a broad sweep enabling me to simply keep running. My vision, albeit blurred, gratefully returned and I ran harder, my legs still shaking, but carrying me on heroically. As I turned another corner, I had the image of Yasmin opening her front door to me with a warm welcoming smile, and me all sweaty, looking a right state! But still I kept running.

As the hill became steeper and steeper, I knew I was slowing. I tried desperately to gain some speed, but my legs felt like lead. I pushed for a few minutes more, until finally I gave in and resorted to walking, just grateful that I was able to keep moving – I was prepared to crawl on my hands and knees if I had to. I noticed the number 132 on a high-gloss royal-blue door, then 134. The pounding in my heart took centre stage again, my mouth dry and throat aching. My hand brushed against the tops of the gates, somehow making my countdown to destiny official. Another house, then another, and the distance between each home started to increase. The road swept to the right, and with each step my heart was doing somersaults. I ran my hand along the top of a white freshly painted picket fence, well aware that once this fence ended, it would be just me and the Old School House.

I was desperate to keep walking, but my legs stopped. My full body weight was now in the palm of my hand, the timber point of the fence close to piercing my flesh. But I couldn't move, and the sharp pain reminded me that I was alive and I was grateful for that. I thought about my first year or two when I had been sent back, and how I hadn't always had control over my actions. And though I had been told all that had been in my mind, I was struggling to battle its incredible strength, painfully convinced that it was happening to me now. I took a moment, trying to breathe and calm myself. I accepted my fear, and that I was being paralysed by the enormity of what lay ahead. I let out a nervous laugh, relieved that my legs had stopped working for this reason and for *this* reason only. I slid down and onto the pavement, pleased to take a moment. The pounding in my heart and lungs dropped to an acceptable level. I bit at my nail and then attempted to psyche myself up for the final few steps that would lead me to Yasmin's front door.

A drop of blood bounced onto the concrete slab that was just visible between my legs. I turned my throbbing palm and watched as the blood ran freely between my fingers. For a moment I did nothing, just accepted the trail of life's fuel seeping out of me, happy to let it escape. But something made me place my finger onto the cut, and the flow stopped. I stood up, wiping my hand on the lush green tufts of grass that pushed for a better view from between the fence posts. I craned my head towards the Old School House, memories flooding through me of how my desperation for purchasing the Old School back in Willow in my original life had ended *so* badly. I prayed that this building would deal me a more prosperous hand.

I turned to face the way I had come. Dartmouth town just roof-tops in the distance now. A green bus passed me suddenly, and I nodded at the people that smiled my way, confirming my questionable existence. I ran my hands through my hair and pulled my T-shirt up to my face, wiping the sweat away. Despite my hand mildly throbbing, I nodded approvingly, as the cut was clean and strangely as though days old. I shook my questions away; I didn't want to know why. I pushed my feet forward, my eyes unable to look up, happy to focus on the picket fence. But I physically jolted as I became aware of a red brick wall and its crown of black ornate iron railings. I kept walking, my fingers trailing along each cold erect section, my eyes lifting gradually until I stood square-on, the Old School House directly before me.

Ten-foot-high black-iron gates stopped me in my tracks, and I was grateful for that. My eyes focused on the black-gloss front door twenty or more feet away, large and sturdy before me, an ornate timber and brick open porch framing the entrance, but then something broke me and my eyes were suddenly focusing on my boots. I hadn't wanted to step in front of the house, I hadn't felt quite ready for that, but here I was. I swallowed hard, almost convinced that the whole of the household would be staring out of the windows, each looking down at me, the mad stranger, his head bowed low, his shoulders drooped. I tried to laugh away my paranoia, and gradually took a much-needed deep breath.

Finally, my chest and shoulders regained some low level of pride and diluted composure, but however diminished it was, I gratefully believed it was enough. Gradually, warily, I lifted my head and stared number 150 right in the eyes. The once grand building was imposing, an acre of land at least wrapped around it. My eyes were drawn to a huge brass bell, centre to the tiled roof ridge-line, housed in a slightly decaying timber structure, the decorative but tired lead roof almost entirely lost under many layers of crusty seagull excrement. My eyes fell onto an overgrown field to the left of the Old School, and the estate agent in me shook his head in appreciation as I reflected on how out of place this home was amongst the tightly packed properties that lined both sides of the road, a postage stamp front garden for each if lucky, separating the front doors from the passing traffic. I felt an internal scream well up from within, an almost schizophrenic voice scolding me for my insignificant ramblings. I was suddenly overcome, a smile spreading across my face as I spotted a white soft-top Wrangler Jeep tucked up, almost touching the double-width garage door.

'Well, surely that has to be a good sign,' I whispered to myself.

My hands were lifting the latch, and an almost perfect-pitch chime resonated, backed up by a well-held lower note, as I pushed the heavy gate forward. My heart was pounding out of every part of me, and it seemed to raise a decibel with every step. I lifted my eyes, flitting from window to window, but I couldn't see anyone. Finally, I was standing in front of the black timber front door, having stepped within the safety of the porch. There were slightly overgrown Buxus to the left and right of me, and I gave a nervous chuckle as I reflected on how the Major, just along from Sky Cottage, would be unimpressed with their lack of pruning. A shiver ran up my spine with the realisation that I hadn't taken a breath for a few moments. I took a much-needed deep one, my lungs grateful, colour seeming to fill my ashen face in appreciation. I wanted to thump impressively on the front door, but could barely stop my hands from shaking. I pushed my finger against the brass-framed doorbell and almost wanted to run away, but of course, being frozen to the spot meant that I was bravely left to face whatever may be.

As the chime echoed inside the house, I wondered how on earth I had got here, as I certainly wasn't in charge of my actions. But this was heavy stuff, the sheer fear of losing Yasmin sapping all my courage, though I wasn't proud of the fact. So any help, and from wherever it was being sent, I was so very grateful for. I pathetically realised that if it were purely down to me, I would have still been impaled on the white picket fencing, possibly bleeding to death, perhaps meeting my demise at number 148. But instead, thanks to divine and necessary intervention, I was where I needed to be.

I could hear footsteps coming from inside the house and suddenly, a key turned in the lock. My heart was firmly in my mouth. And as the door opened, I found it hard to focus. I hadn't known what to expect – maybe a young child, perhaps Yasmin's mum, or my very worst nightmare, a husband or a fiancé. But as my eyes blinked repeatedly, cross-examining and double-checking all that stood before them, they concluded as a soft voice spoke.

'Oh my God! Ritchie Angel! How *on* earth did you find me here?'

I had no answer to the question, and my eyes instinctively filled, ready to burst. But somehow, pride – and the sheer unadulterated fact that anything other than cool would have had me down as a complete nutcase – seemed to gratefully step in and take control. I simply looked into the most beautiful blue eyes and gave my best smile. How words managed to then come out of my mouth, I was at a loss to fathom.

'Hello, Yasmin!'

The world for me had stopped. We just stood and looked at each other. For me, the entire human race could begin and end right here. For Yasmin, there could only be confusion. After all, why *would* I be here? But if she was perturbed by my surprise visit, then she hid it well.

'Ummm, would you like to come in, Ritchie?'

Just to hear her voice made me feel human again. I couldn't take my eyes off her – every gesture, her face, the curve of her lips. And as I studied and mentally questioned her possible circumstances, I focused on her figure, but for the first time in my life for very different reasons – it was perfect. A child...*or* two? Not possible! But then I reflected on how within a week of giving birth to Evie, Yasmin had gone back to her perfect curvaceous original shape, to the detriment of, through gritted teeth, and playfully acknowledged by all our female friends and new mums. A black shroud blurred my happy memories, a guilt for our parting filling my every pore. I reflected on Rose's reasons for my premature death; nothing had been set in stone by her. Just that I had done three unforgivable things. I had presumed: Jack De'Vil. Surely: Harry and Alice Christian. Ian: me, playing God, despite his despicable behaviour, the arrogance in being his Judge and Jury. Inhumane treatment of Julie and Lillie: denying my own daughter's existence, in every sense unforgivable. But my betrayal to Yasmin: how could I do that?

I was becoming increasingly hot. I had undoubtedly been a wiser man in my new life, but certain facts remained. How had I allowed myself in my second attempt in life, though an existence devoid of Yasmin, to walk the path with Tia and Leoni? Wasn't all that an equal measure of disloyalty? Yasmin should still have been my number one priority. I blinked my eyes firmly, desperate to erase all the thoughts that were going to be of no use to me in ensuring I move forward, so I was grateful for being reminded exactly where I was. And as Yasmin repeated her question, I couldn't help but ask myself a very important one first: When I had the love of the woman that stood before me now, how could I have gambled so foolishly?

I stepped inside, and a voice that I had missed *so* much cut into my engulfing thoughts.

'Ritchie, I'm not being funny, but please tell me, how on earth *did* you find me here?'

I found the strength to look in her eyes, afraid to talk, but felt it wise to.

'I …well, I saw you, down in Dartmouth! I wanted to come over and say hello, but, I don't know, I was enjoying a bit of time on my own, but it was the Jeep that did it! I have the same vehicle, except mine's black!' I was floundering with weak babble, and ashamedly continued in the same vein. 'Umm, and then before I got the chance, you were gone.'

Yasmin looked behind me, but I didn't turn around. I was searching desperately for something a little more dynamic to say.

'Ummm, your Jeep, outside your house. Having taken a stroll, I just saw it and put two and two together!'

Yasmin let out a small giggle, a warm smile easing the tension. I smiled back gratefully.

'I hope you don't mind me being here?'

Yasmin shook her head with a thoughtful smile, and said, 'No, of course not.'

The moment seemed to hypnotise me, but then I almost jumped out of my already over-sensitive skin as Yasmin yelled up the sweeping staircase, 'I'M MAKING SOME TEA, MUM, DO YOU FANCY ONE?'

A frail voice answered that she was okay for now.

'Um, and for you, Ritchie, or do you fancy something stronger? You look as though you need it!'

Yasmin glanced past me again, but I couldn't look. I was paranoid that perhaps her husband was pulling onto the drive, or something just as heartbreaking. She suddenly stepped towards me and I stood my ground, not quite sure what she was trying to do. She smiled, and then went to step to my left just as I moved and bumped into her. An awkward moment, and then she muttered something about closing the front door. I went red from the neck up.

'*Sooo* sorry, ummm, let me. Sorry, I must have been born in a barn!'

I pushed the door gently shut, and it was a joyous moment. Just knowing that I was in the same house as Yasmin, well, it felt incredible. I turned and leant back against the white paintwork, the palms of my hands strangely groping and absorbing this wonderful place. I stood and took in every millimetre of the grandness around me. The outside of the Old School House did not prepare you for just how beautiful the inside would be. I had adored the Water's Edge house – Yasmin and me together, having realised our dream. But here, in Yasmin's parallel world, I was totally shocked to see such similar ideas so clearly present in this house. I stepped away from the door, and took several small steps across the stone floor. I stooped and took in the aroma of the fresh white lilies standing on a round antique maple table.

'Yasmin's favourite,' I whispered gently under my breath.

I had always bought them for her. I was suddenly weightless, lost in the moment. The large goldfish-bowl vase was reflecting the lilac sunlight that streamed through the double glass doors, which I presumed led into her lounge. I could have been back at the Water's Edge. Yasmin's voice seemed to click me out of my trance, managing to grab my attention. I was undoubtedly on a high and almost in a world of my own, but I knew I needed to act a little less strangely.

'Mmm, sorry, Yasmin, coming through! I was just admiring your beautiful home!'

As I stepped into the kitchen, my heart leapt and landed uncomfortably, for on the fridge door were several children's paintings. I frantically scanned the rest of the room, and sure enough, standing at the back door, were a tiny pair of bright red Wellington boots. I felt myself go weak. I should have known, but the confirmation was a depth of pain that I had certainly underestimated. But through the barrage of *ifs* and *buts* flying around my head, I could just about make out that Yasmin was asking questions about certain people back home, and yet I hadn't answered once. To appear lethargic, devoid of conversation and to be concluded as perhaps high on drugs, or controversially worse *rude,* would have been way down on my wish list when I had been planning to greet her with such a wonderful impression after all these years.

'Ritchie, Ritchie, are *you* okay?'

I lifted my head, my eyes now locked onto hers, my mind reeling, as though waiting for the three angels to drop on a one-armed bandit.

'Mmmm, you *must* forgive me!' I coughed to clear my throat, but a far greater need was to actually assemble some sort of order in my brain. 'Yasmin, ummm, I was simply miles away. What *were* you saying?'

Her eyes squinted a little, followed by a small, intrigued frown. I had definitely unsettled her. This had to stop.

'Your home is *so* beautiful! I was somewhere else for a moment there. It was the lilies in the hallway, their smell reminds me of someone *very* special. I was being extremely rude...*please* forgive me!'

She smiled, all thoughts of perhaps having a madman in her home seeming to fade away almost instantly – at least I hoped so. As the kettle boiled, her back now towards me, I searched desperately for photographs – Yasmin and her partner, the children – but I couldn't see any.

'Sugar, Ritchie?'

I shook my head. 'Er, no, no thank you, Yasmin.'

It felt so strange to say her name, and especially *to* her, and to actually be standing in the same room; after all, it was twelve painful years, and I had felt bereft for every damn second of that time. But here, now, I was able to talk to her, able to pursue her, but my bumbling vacant act up to now was not perhaps the most fruitful way of igniting any romantic spark that I was so desperate to run with.

Yasmin placed my cup of tea in front of me and still I couldn't take my eyes off her. I gave a small sigh, though a little louder than I had intended. But as her eyes caught mine, her beauty certainly wasn't a memory through rose-tinted glasses. She was everything and more than I had remembered, and how my heart ached for her. But keen to prove not only to her but actually to myself that sanity was still with me, I felt that acting as normal as possible would be a very positive step forward.

'So, Yasmin, how long have you lived here?'

She tilted her head slightly. 'Oh, mmmm, quite a while now!' But she had questions of her own. 'So, Ritchie, how are the gang back home? How are Jimmy and Sally getting on, and the twins?'

I answered as quickly as I could, but every time I tried to find out a bit about her life, she expertly steered me away.

'I hesitate to say this, Ritchie, but I *do* miss my friendship with Janey. How is she?'

I told her what she wanted to know. I took my time, elaborated, joked, all in the vain hope of gaining her trust. But the more I tried to ask her personal questions, the more convinced I became that there was something not quite right. My mind started to run riot: bad relationship, unhappy with her life... But I wasn't convinced that it was her new life that was the problem at all. I recalled her contented look as she opened the front door, the untroubled spring in her step. The impressive home and all the beautiful and personal things in it all combined to convince me that I was simply looking for trouble where there wasn't any. And as my desperate prying seemed to have become a little obvious to us both, it wasn't long before the silences started to build. So in an attempt to try to steer away from all that was personal and private to Yasmin, my mouth and mind became dry and unable to act as I would have liked. Until finally, I simply ran out of relevant things to say, and so I was counting down the seconds to when the late, great Mrs Angel would simply stand up and ask me to leave.

Then the phone rang, causing an exhaling of air and relief for us both. Yasmin pressed the phone to her ear and I tried to look away, desperate to appear uninterested in her conversation, but of course I couldn't take my eyes off her. And any pleasure I may have got from her physical presence soon started to melt away in the heat of what followed.

'Hello, you! Yes, *no*, I'm fine! Missing you, though. Will you manage to get back tonight? You'd better! God, we've *both* missed you terribly! Look, I don't mean to rush you, but I have a visitor, so yes, yes, hurry home! Yes, love you too. See you tonight!'

And as Yasmin replaced the receiver, my head was swirling in a vacuum, giddy and nauseous. I felt destroyed, totally insignificant. All my hopes, all my foolish dreams, were being smashed to nothing. And in the blur of it all I was aware of Yasmin's eyes on me. I tried desperately to focus. My eyes widened as a man's voice breaks the silence, and I almost looked around to see who was talking, but realised just in time that it was me. I tried to smile through an instinctive need to grimace.

'Was ... was that your boyfriend, Yasmin?'

And the same dazzling eyes that once would sparkle with only love suddenly appeared not quite so reassuring, as for me, now, here, the eyes that I thought would only ever fill me with warmth suddenly offered me only pity.

'My husband, you mean!'

My heart seemed to shrivel up, my body weight suddenly a fraction lighter, deflated by a full twenty-one grams, the weight of my soul drifting off away from me. I gripped tightly onto the arms of the kitchen chair. Yasmin was now quiet and noticeably uncomfortable. I felt as though I was nothing more than an irritation and an intrusion into her world, and it hurt like hell.

The silence was hurting my ears. I had dreamt of this moment over and over again. I had so wanted to just be myself, to talk with confidence, to dazzle and impress her, but I was drowning fast, and then I heard the anticipated but nonetheless shocking words.

'Ritchie, I'm *so* sorry to rush you, it's just that I need to get on. In fact, I should have been out by now!'

. As I stood up, I couldn't feel my legs and I'll never know how I made it to the front door. I turned and looked at Yasmin, unsure of what to say. I went to shake her hand, and she smiled and leant into me, kissing me softly on the cheek. The optimist in me took the gesture and allowed it to lift my spirit a modicum above freezing. Though I knew that it probably meant nothing to her, the warmth of it and the sheer fact that her lips had touched my face, well, it gave me the slightest glimmer of something. And with the way things had gone, I was grateful for that.

The pain was soon back as I stepped outside. Yasmin waved and then simply closed the door ... heartbreaking. I dug deep to maintain some kind of control, to stop myself from running back to her front door, banging and screaming, telling her how much I loved her, but of course I couldn't do that, although the temptation was huge. And so I had to settle for the only other reaction I felt physically capable of: falling to the ground, crying uncontrollably until the men in white coats carried me away to spend my remaining days in the foetus position in the corner of a padded cell. The mere thought of it really did appeal to me, but it also made me laugh. For now I was still standing, albeit on the outside of Yasmin's world.

I finally managed to squeeze a breath, the full horror of our latest separation removing my instinct to do so. And though I was searching for the positives, all I got from deep within, rising through my numb body, was a surge of bewilderment, panic entwined with fact after fact, firing all at once: Yasmin's world, a husband, a child; confirmed! And all I could see, in every pore of her face and body, in every material thing that was now surrounding her, was a love, but a love that wasn't being allowed to flow from or to me, or that was even wanted and needed from me.

I stopped for a moment, counting to ten and taking small, shallow breaths. I turned and stood before the great house, and there was one fact that stood larger than all the rest – I wanted Yasmin; without her, I was nothing. So with every last breath in my body, I was going to do whatever it took. And should I fail, then I would give myself to death, and pray that it would take away the pain.

As I made my way back down the hill, despite my resolve to battle all, the tears were streaming down my face, the stinging in my throat unbearable, the facts as they were running rampant through my mind: *Yasmin's in love with another man, they have a child, a life, a history; she'll tell him every day that she loves him.* I just let the tears come; I wasn't going to stop them, I wanted them out! A couple of teenage girls walked past me, unable to contain their sniggers, understandably amused by my blatant show of emotion.

So what was I supposed to do now? The answer? I really didn't know! But as I made my way back into Dartmouth, I had the most incredible, suddenly impatient urge to reach the river. Any thoughts of how I was going to get Yasmin back were strangely overtaken by the desire to sink beneath the water. I started to run, getting faster. I made my way through the small park, the crowds of people forcing me to divert sharply, I was suddenly bounding up the steps of the bandstand, leaping from the side railings, landing sharply, but I just kept running. Within a zig-zag of moves I was across the main road; a car blasted its horn, missing me by millimetres. But within seconds, I was gone. My back arched, my arms outstretched, until the twenty-foot drop was eliminated and my body disappeared beneath the surface. The surge of ice-cold water shot through my body like a bolt of lightning. But a charge of energy that burst out of my outstretched fingers and toes instantly cleared my mind, leaving me cleansed and reborn, all my anger and hurt being blitzed and washed away. Being surrounded by nothing but deep black water seemed to baptise me and give me a fresh inner strength.

Anyone that had seen me disappear into the river would

have questioned their sanity, because I didn't come up for breath until about half a mile out. As my head lifted above the muting force of the water, I turned, suddenly focusing on the small crowd that had gathered at the water's edge. I smiled and felt like waving at them, but I doubted they would be able to see me. A small yacht passed by within feet of me. The tanned young woman on the boat, her feet dangling elegantly over the edge, raised her eyebrows and smiled, almost in disbelief at what she was seeing. I eased onto my back, the soothing water lapping in and out of my ears. I flipped back onto my front, and then proceeded to side crawl for a few metres. I felt so totally exhilarated. An image of an electric eel came to mind, and that's how I felt, a line of potent electricity running right through me. I dived down into the water, my arms at my side, just flipping my feet up and down, heading a little closer to the crowd that were still looking puzzled on the Dartmouth embankment. I slipped behind a small fishing boat and took in the animated chatter.

'Did you see that? My God! Did you see the madman? He just ran and dived in! But he's gone, as though I dreamt it, nowhere to be seen. Maybe I'm going mad myself!'

And as the crowd slowly dispersed with a shaking and scratching of heads, bemused laughter seemed to replace their concern, and shrugs of shoulders seemed to cast doubt on the sanity of the few that had witnessed my entry into the River Dart. But then the calling of my new playground and my ability to cut through the water at breathtaking speeds took me away from all that was a concern on dry land. And for me, I was just happy to be as free as a bird, or should I say as free as a fish.

I sank beneath the water again, darting this way and that. And as before, I was simply astounded by my new talent; I had such power. As my confidence and enthusiasm grew, I would drop a little deeper each time, before charging back to the surface. And with each fresh attempt, my belief pumped up another notch. I let my feet touch the bottom of the river, and as my imagination ran riot, I pushed myself at lightning speed, suddenly fresh air all around me, a metre or so above the surface, before executing a perfect dive back into the cool calm water. As I sank deeper and deeper, I was aware of the constant smile on my face; the speed I could move, and the length of time I was able to survive under the water, seemed to increase. In fact, it simply wasn't a problem any more, and I seemed to either be able to breathe or simply not need to.

As I moved steadily amongst shoals of fish, my toes brushing the outstretched pincers of defensive crabs and slightly more menacing lobsters, all I could think about was when my mum had taken me to see: *Bedknobs and Broomsticks*. And that's how this all felt, comical and utterly surreal. But then in a total reversal of mood, all around me became dark, far less comfortable, and suddenly I felt a need to move a little faster. I turned sharply, drawing my knees up to my chest, as though aware of something trying to grab me, but I couldn't see anything, and so desperately made my way towards the surface. I took a deep breath, as though kick-starting my lungs. I bobbed with the wake of the water for a few moments and finally felt a little calmer. I turned my body three hundred and sixty degrees and was astounded how far I had travelled. My eyes were drawn to a small sandy beach, secluded just below the castle that stood protectively at the mouth of the estuary. I dropped back beneath the water, my confidence seeming to return, with a keenness to reach that beach.

I kicked my legs harder than before, my arms at my side, a murky blackness surrounding me. I dropped a little deeper, and found the water to be clearer and bathed in the sunlight from above. I felt the hairs stand up on the back of my neck as a large octopus brushed against my face. We seemed to look at each other, and I felt a shiver pass through me. I instinctively nodded politely before we went our separate ways. I started to laugh, bubbles rising from my nostrils. I pushed forward, harder and faster now, but suddenly I felt a small hand slip into mine and an explosion of air left my mouth.

'Rose?!'

But as I looked to my side, there was Lillie, her dark hair streaming behind her, her beautiful little face beaming at me. I didn't stop, I just kept moving through the water, flipping my legs gently. I dared not stop, since I feared that I was dreaming and that Lillie would simply disappear, but she didn't. She clasped my hand even tighter and swam with me, as though it was the most natural thing in the world.

After about five minutes I came up for air, the light buzz of day-to-day life ringing in the distance. Suddenly, Lillie's head was bobbing up and down in the water too.

'Hello, Daddy!'

Not for the first time today, the tears were rolling down my face. I pulled Lillie to me; to hold her again was just wonderful, surreal. I pushed her out at arm's length, desperate to make sure it was *really* her. I was laughing and crying all at once, my legs kicking for all they were worth to keep us both afloat. She pulled closer, her tiny fingers wiping the salty seawater from around my eyes, her little smiling face bemused by my emotion.

'Daddy, I haven't upset you, have I?'

I shook my head from side to side.

'Oh, baby, no! I'm just *so* happy to see you. I can't believe you're here with me. I love you *so* much, Lillie!'

And though I expected her to just disappear at any given moment, she didn't. Then her small, perfect arms were around my neck, hugging me with all her strength, my legs kicking furiously now, enabling us both to keep our heads above the lapping waves. My mind was reeling, and I was just about managing to hold it together. But as crazy and beautiful as all this was, I knew I wasn't dreaming – Lillie was with me, and totally unfazed by our reunion. I couldn't take my eyes off her. She didn't appear to be any older than the last time I was with her. And though this time together was such a priceless moment, I just couldn't stop the hot stinging tears pouring down my sea-drenched face – for the sheer joy of seeing her, but then also the absolute fear of her vanishing before my very eyes.

Little by little, my composure returned. I pointed to the beach not so very far away now, and Lillie nodded in approval. We beamed at each other, before dropping beneath the sea. Lillie let go of me and I almost panicked, wanting to grab hold of her, but as my clever little girl swam in and around my body, I felt it wise to relax and trust whatever was happening. As we pushed even deeper into the water, Lillie climbed onto my back and held on for all she was worth as I darted off. I was beaming uncontrollably, loving every second of our high-speed adventure.

I clumsily slowed down, my chest skimming the bottom of the sea, but as I lifted myself a little higher, I could feel a mixture of froth and sunshine on my back. I was then on my knees, the water lapping around my shoulders. Lillie slipped off me, steadying herself before pushing her hand reassuringly back into mine.

'Daddy, we're here!'

We waded through the shallow waves. I turned my face towards the sun; a haze of lilac, but only a touch. I felt as though Lillie and I were basking in a spiritual glow, a warmth that seemed to have been turned up a notch or two, as our cold, wet bodies were drying nicely. We both slumped down onto the sandy beach, our eyes looking back out to sea, but as breathtaking as the view was, it was nothing compared to my beautiful little daughter. I brushed the tangled hair from her eyes and then pulled her towards me, her head now resting on my chest – she was ice-cold.

'Mummy and I have missed you *so* much!'

I didn't cry this time. I so wanted to, but I didn't want Lillie to see any more tears. I couldn't speak, though, and just held onto her.

'Mummy said to say hello! She may come and swim with us one day, but she said that I should come on my own and see you this time!'

As I lay back on the sand, getting comfortable and relishing this most privileged of moments, I just listened to my beautiful little girl's voice, her body pressed firmly against mine. I could feel her heart beating in unison with mine and I blinked my eyes as a thank you, directly into the powerful skies above. I couldn't help but question what on earth was going on, but then I wasn't sure that I wanted an explanation or an answer. Perhaps the here and now was enough. And as I held Lillie in the warmth of the afternoon sun, I drifted into a deep, contented sleep.

CHAPTER TWENTY-FIVE

Time Flies As You Get Older

After Death – Lilac Sky
It must have been a good three or four hours later when I could hear the ringing of the church bells cutting into my sleep. Strike one to six, seeing me gradually open my eyes. I felt cold as I stretched out. I sat up quickly, painfully aware that Lillie was gone. I jumped up, looking all around the small beach, hoping that she was simply playing close by. But then just as I was beginning to question our meeting, I noticed a large heart scrawled in the sand, in which was written *I love you, Daddy. See you soon. Lillie XXX.* A shiver ran the length of my spine, but then came a huge sigh of relief. I hadn't dreamt it!

I decided that I didn't want to swim back into Dartmouth, since the sea looked rough, cold and suddenly uninviting. My clothes had dried nicely, but as I wiggled my toes, my boots and socks were anything but. And so I was convinced that up to the castle and along the coastal road should lead me back towards the hotel.

I found the narrowest little pathway, and finally managed to get myself out of the castle grounds. I looked around at the fortress and reflected on the bloody battles that would have been won and lost here; the many intruders that had tried and failed to bring harm to Dartmouth. I shook my head as I questioned the very depths of my love for Yasmin, and how I should be prepared to fight for her, no matter the odds.

I turned and started to make my way back to the hotel, pondering how I could get her away from her new world, her beautiful world, but a world without Evie and me. My sodden boots pushed forward, squelching with every step, but my mind was filled with something so much more uncomfortable. I should have realised from the very beginning that Yasmin was always going to have been snapped up. She was an exceptional creature, she could have anybody. I was suddenly aware of people edging past me on the narrow pathway, a look of pity and disdain clearly and surprisingly evident. I looked inquisitively back at one of the ladies, who immediately dropped her gaze and concentrated on her feet. I shook my head. My eyes suddenly lifted and my ears pricked up as a car passed by, a song I had fond memories of filling the air: 'If you love somebody, set them free!' I questioned the sentiment, the melody pushing itself to the forefront of my mind, but I had my own questions: Who was I to disrupt Yasmin's life, with her 'on the surface' perfect existence? Maybe it was a test. If I really loved her, and as the song says, maybe I should set her free. But as I walked, my ranting seeming to amuse and concern the passers-by in equal measure, I decided to think rather than waste my energy speaking out loud unnecessarily. And so I pondered further the aphorism by Richard Bach who had written Jonathan Livingstone Seagull, a wonderful book that Yasmin herself had given to me: 'if they come back they're yours, if they don't they never were...' But then I shook my head in sheer defiance, this time raising my voice assertively in my conclusion to this flawed and unfortunately inappropriate advice, and my eyes turned to the powers that be.

'Set her *free? I* wasn't the one that set her free, *was I?* And if she loves me, she'll come back to me? *Wrong!* Thanks to *you*, I'm just some *'bit part'* player from her past! And so *how* can she love me based on *that?'*

But as I walked, desperate to calm myself, I finally reached the busy streets of Dartmouth. I caught my beach-bum reflection in a shop window, and was shocked at just how bad I actually looked. My hair was impressively matted from the sea and the sand, but for now I didn't care – a hot shower would come soon enough. My immediate concern for my personal hygiene was a little down my list – I just didn't want to bump into Yasmin. But then due to the increasing number of funny looks and an undeniable whiff coming from my seabed-infested body, I felt that perhaps a shower should be the very next thing I did. Once I had checked on my Jeep, though, as the chance of a parking ticket or, even worse, being clamped was a very real possibility.

I looked along the road, where I was convinced I had parked the Jeep, but it was gone. I walked up the street a little further, but it was nowhere to be seen.

'Shit! It's been bloody stolen!'

I scratched my head for a moment before finally running over and into the hotel, and there I stood face-to-face with the receptionist.

'Kelly! Look, who do I call? My car's either been towed away or stolen!'

The receptionist looked back at me, wide-eyed and distinctly puzzled, almost as if she didn't recognise me.

'Are you okay, Kelly? You do remember me from last night? Oh, and this lunchtime, coming out of my room? Ritchie Angel, ummmm, room twenty-seven?'

Kelly suddenly giggled nervously. I joined her and felt relieved at finally being recognised.

The girl scrunched her face up a little and seemed to almost whisper, 'Umm, sir, I *do* remember you, but that was probably over a year ago!'

I looked at her face, ready for her to smile, tell me that she was joking, but as I waited, frozen in the moment, her eyes convinced me that she was deadly serious. I was lost and spinning, and I dropped my hands down firmly onto the counter, steadying myself. I took a breath, my eyes suddenly looking for something. I turned and scoured the corridor, spun around and stooped, grabbing a copy of Devon Life off the coffee table. I turned back towards the receptionist.

'How old is this magazine?'

Kelly shook her head from side to side.

'It's about a month, maybe two months old. Sir, are you alright?'

My eyes finally gained focus as I took in the date on the front cover – the magazine was eleven months on from where I had started my day. I felt my entire body break into a hot sweat.

'Sir, can you *just* hang on a moment? I think the manager would like a word with you.'

I slumped into the nearest chair, running my fingers from the thick stubble on my chin up onto my face and through my matted hair. I felt as though I was a thousand years old.

After Death, 1998 – Lilac Sky
The manager stood before me, his hand pushed forward.

'Mr Angel, are you alright, sir?'

I took a deep breath and stood up, trying to appear as normal and sane as possible. I shook his hand firmly.

'Mr Angel, if you would like to come into my office, I hope I can clear a few things up for you.'

I walked as steadily as my shaking legs would allow, the squelch of my boots impressing all that took the time to drop their eyes and identify the comical noise. Finally, I was tucked away in a small office. Kelly stood at the door, with a look of genuine concern.

'Can I get you a cup of tea, Mr Angel?'

I nodded. The door was pushed to, and the manager beckoned for me to sit down.

'Mr Angel, hmmm, we felt it strange at the time! But it was, let me just check … ah yes, a year ago tonight, amazingly! You were seen leaving just after lunch and that was it, we never saw you again. You left your rucksack, your credit cards, the lot! Your vehicle was finally towed away by the police, but everything is safe.' The softly spoken manager turned to me, a concerned smile spreading diplomatically across his freshly shaved face. 'Are you okay, sir?'

I felt like a freak, and was particularly concerned about how much fuss had probably been made over the last twelve months. It crossed my mind that perhaps the papers had been involved. Questions and enquiries back home? The hotel manager seemed to read my mind.

'This happens all the time in the South West, though rarely do we get people turning up again the way you have! But no, the police are used to people coming down to this part of the world and disappearing for one reason or another, but we're not one for selling stories to the press!'

It wasn't long before I got the hot shower I so desperately needed. And as the powerful jets hit my numb and confused body, I juggled with the trivial practicalities that a disappearance of twelve months would rattle. Even though my credit card had been stopped, I was grateful that the hotel believed me when I said that I did have money. I assured them that first thing in the morning I would contact my bank and notify the police that I was indeed alive and well, and then get my Jeep back.

Once showered and shaved, I questioned what I wanted to do next. I closed the curtains, shutting out the madness. With the room reassuringly dark, I was drawn to the safety of the huge comfy-looking bed. I slid beneath the heavy duvet, convinced that a good night's sleep would help clear my mind ready for a new day. But despite passing out almost as my head hit the pillow, within ten minutes or so something startled me, mentally and physically forcing me to sit up sharply. I looked around the unfamiliar surroundings, searching for whatever had woken me.

'You idiot, Ritchie, there's no one here...'

I slumped back down onto my pillow. But as my mind raced and my heart pounded, many hours passed before I finally fell into a deep but disturbed sleep. And as I dreamt that the sun was rising and I kept telling myself I needed to be up, enabling me to see exactly how the pieces of my continually disrupted life had now scattered themselves, I was actually knocking on the manager's door. I pinched myself hard, convinced that I was still dreaming, but as I winced at the pain, I knew that I was very much awake.

The manager greeted me with a familiar look of sympathy.

'You must have needed that long lie-in, Mr Angel.'

I looked out of the window, disappointed to see the sun so high in the sky and that the day was ticking along far too quickly for my liking. The manager nodded his head, having offered me a free rein of his office.

'Phone, fax, computer, Mr Angel. Take your time. I'll be helping out on reception.'

I explained clumsily to my bank a naively thought-out excuse for my extended absence, but after being left on hold for about ten minutes, having first been asked for more personal details, passwords, date of birth, etc., I was finally, gratefully saved from yet another run-through of a distorted rendition of *Greensleeves*.

'Sorry to keep you, Mr Angel, sir. No, your accounts are looking very healthy indeed. Your tenants have obviously paid directly into your business account, yes, each month, and your accountant, Mr ... oh yes, Peter Crabtree, has been making sure that things tick over while... It says here on your file, *away until further notice!* Umm, but looking at your account, *no*, nothing particularly unusual. Money in, with a few monthly direct debits, etc. going *out!* One second! Ummmm, and yes, a payment nearly a year ago. Mr Crabtree had a cheque drawn up for your credit card company. Umm, American Express ... a hefty cheque?'

The Jeep, I thought, nodding to myself, relieved that everything seemed to have been taken care of in my absence. There was, however, one more crucial phone call to make, and one very serious question that I needed answering. I took a deep breath as I waited for my accountant to pick up his phone.

'Ritchie? My God, old son! Where the *hell* have you been?'

I brushed aside as quickly as I could his concerns and impossible-to-answer questions.

'Peter, the Water's Edge, how's that gone?'

Peter paused for a moment and then laughed out loud.

'It's done, it's done, as you clearly requested in your letter! Signed and sealed eight months ago! With respect, probably the *worst* bit of business I've *ever* had the misfortune to be involved with, but as you have reminded me on several occasions, the customer, the client, is *always* right.' Peter grunted, waiting for me to comment, but I didn't, and just sighed emotionally with pure unadulterated relief that the Water's Edge was mine.

I shook the hotel manager's hand, reminding him for the third or fourth time that a fax should arrive within the hour confirming that a new credit card was being sent directly to me here at the Royal Castle, and that as soon as it arrived, could he please let me know.

I made my way back up to my room, a thousand thoughts running through my mind, and I shook my head. I hated the way that I could just lose so much time like that. I felt sad that I had spent that afternoon with Lillie, and then bang, gone! I felt a sense of panic well up from deep within, concern that Lillie may feel that I had simply gone off and abandoned her. But in a moment of clarity, I remembered Rose telling me how she would watch my every move, so Lillie would know what I had been up to. *God, I hope so!* But then I questioned the fact that I couldn't have simply been left lying on the beach for a whole year, so what the hell had I been up to? And of course, an even bigger problem was screaming at me: Where would Yasmin be now? Still at Victoria Road? And I prayed until it hurt that I hadn't been allowed to do anything in my apparent physical absence that would jeopardise my increasingly meagre hopes of a reunion.

My thoughts were suddenly interrupted by a call from reception.

'Mr Angel, your Jeep is outside!'

I glanced at the bedside clock, not pleased that it was after four. I quickly made my way downstairs, where Jim the porter handed me the keys. He explained briefly about how things worked at the police car pound, etc. – his brother being a detective sergeant or a position similar – and though my mind was elsewhere, I thanked him, shaking his hand just a little too aggressively.

'No problem, Mr Angel. They seemed keen to get back a much-needed parking space! And as I had mentioned, you know, my brother being who he is enables us to do away with all the usual red tape!'

He winked and strode off towards the kitchens. Suddenly, he turned back round.

'Oh, Mr Angel! He told me to tell you that they have used the Jeep on several occasions, hence no charge for the excessive parking!'

The hotel receptionist, Kelly, smiled and enquired yet again, 'You okay, Mr Angel?'

I nodded, a slightly embarrassed laugh creeping out. *Nerves*, I told myself, *or cracking up?* I questioned.

'Yes, Kelly, today I'm fine. Look, I'm going out for a while, but I promise I'll be back tonight!'

Kelly laughed. 'I'll hold you to that, Mr Angel, but if not, same time next year, eh?!'

I shook my head, a smile beaming her way, well aware that many a true word is spoken in jest, and under my breath I couldn't help but mutter, 'I'd better be back tonight, *today*'s night … *please!*'

I turned and made my way out of the hotel. The Jeep looked

a little dusty and unloved, but it was almost like being reunited with an old friend. I placed the palms of my hands onto the bonnet, sweaty fingerprints proving my existence. I lifted my head and looked at the sky above. I squinted into a lilac haze, but as my eyes became accustomed, I thought the weather was good, so the roof had to come off.

As I turned the key, the powerful engine sprang into life. I noticed Kelly standing in the doorway of the hotel. She smiled warmly, and I reciprocated – I wasn't surprised to see a concerned, distant look in her dark eyes. But I shook my head and shrugged my shoulders, as though answering her very obvious thoughts, and she encouragingly stuck her thumb up. I winked and turned away, glancing and blowing a kiss before speeding off, narrowly missing three jaywalking teenagers. I took the next left and within minutes was outside number 150 Victoria Road. The Jeep ticked over gruffly. I struggled to turn my head and look at Yasmin's home. I wanted to turn the engine off, to simply climb out of the Jeep and go and knock the door. It seemed so easy, so very simple, but right now it was proving to be just beyond my capabilities. Suddenly, a toot of a car horn made me look back over my shoulder.

'Oh my God! Yasmin!'

Despite the intensity of the moment for me, for Yasmin I was simply blocking her driveway. I pushed my foot down on the accelerator, and the Jeep roared forward. Yasmin swung her white Jeep onto her driveway; she too had her roof down. Her hair was a little longer than last time, sun-kissed and wavy. She was hauntingly beautiful. As she jumped out of the Jeep, she made her way round to her passenger door, and there she was, the most exquisite little girl you have ever seen. My heart stalled, my breath just evaporated. The little girl was the spitting image of Evie; in fact, she was the absolute double. As Yasmin undid her daughter's seatbelt, I saw the little girl was wrapped up snugly in a white ski jacket, the collar touching her ears, wearing a baseball cap that was far too large for her, almost covering her whole head. But there was no mistaking the look. I felt my eyes go painfully hot at the memory of my own little girls. I took a deep breath, desperate to keep some sort of control. As I continued to watch, I presumed that

Yasmin's daughter was probably three or four years of age.

Suddenly free from the confines of her seatbelt, the little girl jumped bravely from the Jeep, her cap falling onto the driveway. My eyes widened, the hairs on the back of my neck stood rigid, my body went cold, a knife turning sadistically in the pit of my stomach. Dazzling blue eyes sparkled at me, but a tumble of jet-black hair framed the face of *Evie*, and I felt myself flinch uncontrollably at the image. I went to jump out of the Jeep, but Yasmin's narrowing eyes fell onto mine, the palm of her hand disrespectfully turned towards me. I waited for a moment, unsure of what I was supposed to do. I pulled the Jeep door shut and wound down the window and waited. Little black-haired Evie ran inside of the now open front door. As my breath returned gradually, I started to shiver uncontrollably. I dug my nails into my forearms, trying to break through the numb, deathly feel of my flesh. I could do nothing other than watch this hateful, stomach-churning nightmare unfold. I had genuinely believed that I had prepared myself for this, blindly convinced that I knew how I would feel seeing my wife with another man's child - *but shit, **this** hurt!* Yasmin finally pushed her Jeep door shut and seemed to hover for a second, but then dropped her head and walked over to me.

'Umm, hi, Ritchie...it's nice to see you.'

But I wasn't convinced. Yasmin seemed agitated and nervous about something, and whatever it was, I didn't feel welcome.

'You just down for a holiday, Ritchie?'

I nodded, wanting something bright and witty to come out of my mouth.

'Yeah, just a couple of days or so. Ummm, thought I would drop in to say hello!'

She stared at me, but almost through me.

'Look, Ritchie, I have a problem. You see, my husband is a very private man, he doesn't really like people just dropping in!'

She finally looked at me properly, and as our eyes met I felt the pain drain from me. My spirits were instantly lifted; there was something between us, and I prayed I wasn't kidding myself. But there was an intensity that was overpowering –

well, for me at least. It was like the kiss that cost me the extra two years. Whether the moment was erased for her, it was certainly set in stone for me. And though the powers that be may well have erased the kiss, surely they have no power over the spark that would have been building prior to such a passionate moment? Yasmin let out an impatient sigh, I felt it wise to say something, anything.

'Look, Yasmin, I understand, but I just felt this urge to see you, um, you know? Just to see how you're doing...'

Her faced softened, her guard seeming to drop ever so slightly.

'Yasmin, I'm sorry to hear that your husband's not particularly sociable, it's just that, well, I didn't come to see him, I came to see you!'

Her eyes gave an almost embarrassed glint, a diluted reminder of what used to be – a glimmer of what I would ashamedly take for granted on a daily basis. But then suddenly, her eyes broke away from mine as she looked down at the floor, her feet shuffling from side to side.

'Ritchie, I've got to go...'

She turned and made her way towards the house, taking what was left of me with her. I sat ice-cold and broken. But just before she stepped inside, it was as though she had a change of heart. She turned and smiled right at me, and in doing so I physically flickered back into life, as though her smile had ignited the dregs of my spirit. And for me, for now, it was my lifeline.

As I sat and simply stared at the closed front door, I just relived the few short moments that I had just spent with Yasmin, raking through the brief words we spoke over and over again. I could and would have stayed right there forever and just watched her world, but for now I would do as my wife had asked, and leave.

As I turned the key in the ignition, I mumbled under my breath, 'Anti-social git, I *hate* you already!'

But I pacified myself in the knowledge that I would be back; subtly, gently, but I was definitely going to be back. I pushed my foot down on the accelerator and sped off up the remainder of the hill. But there was something undeniably alien about driving away from Yasmin, which resulted in my pulling the Jeep to a halt, my wheels smashing aggressively up and onto the narrow pavement. Line after line of substandard ideas about how I was going to tackle this immense problem filled my head. Finally, gratefully, my mind emptied itself, and so I just sat and enjoyed the release. But though I closed my eyes, desperate to deny the building questions, it crossed my mind that maybe it was Yasmin who didn't want the link with her past; maybe it was her, not him, that was the anti-social one. And so my fighting spirit decided that I would call back later this evening; after all, the husband had to come home sooner or later. And when he did, I wanted to make sure I got to meet him. Gently thrust myself into their lives. *Surely a man that is confident and in love wouldn't feel threatened by an old friend of his dear beloved wife?* I took comfort in the belief that, given time, their feelings for me, good or bad, would leave an indelible impression.

I turned the radio on; the news at four-thirty was just ending.

'Right!' I offered the skies above, twiddling my thumbs, before wisely deciding that the quickest way to kill time was to perhaps do something; perhaps a little exploring would be fun, and what's more, take my one-track mind off my wife for a few hours at least.

I bounced off the high kerb and roared to the top of the hill. *Left or right, Ritchie boy?* I took in the many classy-sounding village names, but became fascinated by the presumably unflattering, I was sure, Blackpool Sands. *Just what I need, I thought; should be fun!* So I turned left and followed the winding coastal road.

It was a bright and clear late afternoon, the sun was warm, and I felt increasingly comfortable and calm. And as the lilac sunlight bounced around me, the day became beautiful. As I made my way, twisting and turning along the coastal road, I became mesmerised by the breathtaking scenery, the ocean hogging every shot. And as is inevitable with every climb, the Jeep started to drop its nose downwards, the trees shielding my descent, and suddenly I was aware of arrows pointing towards an opening to my left: Blackpool Sands. I smiled, suitably impressed. A little more crowded than I would have liked, but then something suggested that perhaps I could find peace amongst the madness here.

'Yep, that's what I need!' I spoke out loud, as was becoming a habit of late, but also nodding in approval at the new buoyant me.

I paid the car park attendant and drove off into the field, looking for a remote, peaceful parking space.

'Bloody hell, haven't you people got homes to go to?'

As I drove around for the second time I spotted a flock of sheep, tucked at the foot of the steep cliff face, and looked over my shoulder to see who might be watching. I reversed slowly amongst them, noticing their look of disgust and shaking of their heads at my sheer bad manners, but I had my private parking space. I turned the engine off. I was now aware of the bleating of a couple of sheep that had defiantly stood brave, as though keen to break the stereotypical image that these creatures have, as the other dozen or so huddled together and moved further away, these two made a stand – I was proud of them. But as I started to laugh nervously at my increasing madness, my mind turned very quickly to Rose. I smiled as I thought about my little friend, and as I relived some of our conversations, I realised that she was needed now more than ever.

I sat and willed her to come to me, but she didn't. I wondered if I should climb up the rocks a little, maybe finding a quiet spot. *Maybe then you'll come and see me!* So that's what I did. I found a less obvious pathway that appeared as though it hadn't been used in years; in fact, as I started to climb, it was bordering on the impassable, but the more determined I got, the higher I got.

Though my initial focus had been on getting to the top, I found I was being drawn to a small rock jutting out from the side of the cliff face. I scrambled dangerously – almost crab-like – grabbing brambles and gorse, anything to get me there. A deep breath, and a huge smile spread across my face as I finally slumped onto the dry moss, which cushioned gratefully my place of calling. As my heartbeat slowed, I was quite shocked at how sheer the cliff was. There was almost nothing below me, just the waves crashing against the sharp glistening rocks that did nothing to calm my fear of heights. But as though this moment was meant to be, a warm breeze brushed against my face. And as the distant voices from the crowds on the now out of sight beach seemed to fade to nothing, I felt an inner strength pass through me, as though someone or something was close by. I waited, not saying a word. All I could hear was the sound of the ocean, my eyes continuing to be dazzled by the strength of the early evening sun.

An hour or so passed by. 'Come on, Rose, *please!*' I continued to sit, not moving from my original position, as though movement would kill the moment. Gradually the sun was dropping, spreading itself like the red-hot embers of a dying phoenix, and so I remained rooted to the spot. But as another hour, maybe two, passed by, an icy chill brushed over me, and in response I stretched my arms and legs, but only as much as the confines of my new resting place would allow. I started to fidget, disappointed and desperate, painfully convinced that Rose was going to deny me on this occasion.

Out of sheer frustration I started to yell, *'ROSE...!'*

My body seemed to rock, the momentum of frustration making every muscle and vein in my body, my neck and my face stand proud and ugly, I then froze, waiting for a response – but nothing. Finally, I took a deep breath and let out a smile, as though accepting rejection. I slumped back against the cliff face and as a consolation prize took in the indescribable sunset, and as I watched intently the retirement of something so wondrous, I must have drifted off.

'What the...!'

I sat up quickly, aware of something falling around me, then aware of stones hitting me, prodding me sharply. My eyes struggled to focus, sleep and spears of fading light leaving me at a disadvantage. I turned and craned my neck looking back up the cliff face, and there forty or fifty feet up was a thick coated golden Labrador looking back at me, tail wagging furiously, waiting for a reaction from me. Instinctively I was ready to call out Fluffers, but the dog was then gone. My mind is then filled with pictures of Fluffers, Evie, Yasmin and me; the Angel family, together.

I laughed at my reaction to the dog, and scolded myself.

'You're losing it, Ritchie!'

I eased my head back and watched the tip of the sun, now just a moment away from disappearing, leaving its vapour trail of fire. My eyes became heavy, and without too much of a fight, they were closed. I just wanted to dream, to conjure up Evie's face, her mother's face, the three of us holding each other.

I must have drifted off again...

All beautiful thoughts were eaten up by black and the stench of hate, but then a calmness returned. I was then searching for why I had felt uneasy, and though diluted, I felt a modicum of calmness filter through me, an icy breeze whispered across my face, and then the feeling of someone walking over my *grave,* followed by the sound of falling rock. I tried to move quickly. I felt heart-wrenchingly uncomfortable, and a sense of danger urged me onto my feet. But as I tried to steady myself, I felt as though I had been hit by a steam train, and I was thrust face first onto the sharp unforgiving ground, the taste of dirt thickening my saliva. I tried to roll over quickly, desperate to face my attacker. But suddenly, my head was spinning as a kick, or a length of timber, was smashed against the side of my head; whatever it was, it had me reeling, and I was drifting in and out of consciousness. I couldn't see a thing; all I could feel was pain, and I didn't know when the next blow was coming.

I rolled into the foetal position, almost accepting defeat, but then a glimmer of clarity seemed to pass through me, a sudden surge of energy racing through my body. I scrambled, desperate to get to my feet, enabling me to put up some kind of fight. As I finally stood and turned, my back to the sea, I was once again caught full force, this time across the front of my face. Whatever I was being hit with seemed to rip into the side of my nose, the pain suggesting it was being torn off. Then, a killer blow was struck full force into my stomach, and I was falling. As my hands instinctively grabbed for something to hold onto, I felt the backs of my legs hitting the side of the unforgiving cliff face, and my body started to twist and turn as I bounced from rock to rock, my hands still grappling for something to break my fall. Just as I thought that every blackout was going to be my last, I seemed to be given a chance, and I was now falling feet first, my body sliding down the sharp, jagged rock face. The pain as I was flipped from my back onto my front, my legs, stomach and face, and then my back again, felt as though I was being cut to pieces. But just when I believed that this was it, that this was the end for me, something pushed into me, forcing me sideways, lifting me totally against the laws of gravity, until I slammed down onto a large piece of rock jutting out from the cliff, the wind being totally knocked out of me; but finally, gratefully, I had stopped falling.

I tried to open my eyes, my heart pounding with a crushing force, but slowly the breath was returning to my lungs. As I lay face down on the cold slab of rock, I managed to turn my head onto its side. This time I forced my eyes open, the harsh light drifting in and out. But just as my vision returned, I could see above the ledge, from where I had just been so ruthlessly evicted, a smiling face, peering over, hands on hips. I could see it was a man, but then my eyes widened as I took in the claret rugby shirt, and as though reading my thoughts, my attacker turned around, a white number seven proud on the back! He then turned to face me again and the smile started to slip away, a grimace of frustration taking its place. My attacker began to climb down towards me and my heart started to pound louder. I needed to get up, though my entire body was broken with pain.

I clasped my fingers tightly around the unforgiving gorse, hundreds of needles burning relentlessly, but that was the least of my worries and I knew it.

I tried desperately to pull myself up as my enemy got closer, my eyes widened, and through broken, blood-splattered teeth I just about pushed out with what little breath I had, 'Harry … Harry Christian!'

I forced my way onto my knees, blood filling my eyes. I wiped my face with my T-shirt, the dirt adding a fresh dimension to the pain. Though my arms and legs were badly cut, I was so grateful that the sound of rock on bone hadn't resulted in any obvious breakages. I stood, stooped and twisted. Harry was just fifty or so feet away, and gaining with every passing second. He suddenly stopped and looked straight at me, his eyes narrowing into black icy slits.

'YOU CHEATING, *SLIMY* LITTLE SHIT, ANGEL! I WON'T REST IN MY GRAVE UNTIL I'VE *GOT MY REVENGE!*'

My blood ran cold. I had been unnerved by Harry in this second life; there had been an undercurrent of something...*something* that I just couldn't put my finger on. As Harry continued his descent towards me, the stench of hatred filled the air. I scrambled nervously, desperately wanting to prepare myself for the next onslaught. I was totally trapped, unable to go up, and only the rocks of death a hundred or so feet below me. As Harry's excited eyes focused on mine, his taut pumped-up body getting ever closer, my thoughts pushed out under my strained breath. '*My God, that's a serious hate you've got there, Harry!*' And as I waited, I reflected on when he had attacked me at his bungalow. I had presumed, foolishly, that whatever had been going on had at least been settled when he died. After all, why wouldn't it be? How on earth can a dead man hurt me? Perhaps with words left behind, or an accomplice picking up the chalice, but personally, physically? But as I recalled my first attack from Harry at my school, and then the second at his bungalow, I now knew that he wasn't going to rest, not until he'd put me in my grave. I grabbed hold of a loose rock, lifting it above my right shoulder. I was tempted to throw it at Harry, but as I looked around, it was my only weapon, so I kept a firm hold of it. As my enemy scrambled against the laws of gravity, I could hear his hysterical giggles, mixed in with undecipherable words. He was now only forty or so feet away from me, and suddenly he looked *so* young, with the fitness and physique of a man a fraction of his age. I wasn't afraid to admit it, I was scared, and I had good reason to be.

My life of wrongdoing passed before me, overpowering the positive. The happy times with Yasmin and Evie were overawed with rampant ugly images. All I could see in my mind was the frail frame of Harry Christian leaving the Skirdle's shop, his finger tapping the side of his wine taster's nose. And as I recalled my last visit to Harry, such was his anger that had it not been for Alice, I believe wholeheartedly that he would have strangled the life out of me. He was a man possessed, and had certainly stepped it up a level in the here and now.

Harry was almost upon me, and he looked huge, now just thirty or so feet away, ready to pounce. I searched desperately for anything that could help me, but my rock was all that I had. My six or seven-foot-square ledge seemed to be shrinking by the second. I shook my head, feeling a certain inevitability about how this was going to end. Defiantly I met Harry's deathly stare, his hate boring into me. Despite the evil that he had become, it was as a result of *my* wrongdoing, and I had to accept that I was responsible for him being this way.

'HARRY, FOR GOD'S SAKE, WOULD ALICE WANT TO SEE YOU LIKE THIS, AN *EVIL DEMENTED ANIMAL?*'

But my tormentor was not for turning, and no words were going to pacify his conviction. I knew I would be wasting the little time I had left. I had to be prepared to fight to the death. But as Harry seemed to increase in stature with every painful breath, I was struggling to accept that my life had come down to this moment. The odds were not in my favour, with the amount of blood that I was losing, combined with the increasing strain to just keep breathing. And then I felt myself laugh, my shaking amused head now staring once again right into Harry's eyes. I started to bait him.

'You're one of my *lesser* evils, Harry, and yet it's only *you* who's taken the time and trouble to come back to *haunt* me!'

Harry was now purple with fury. I tried desperately to create a picture of Yasmin in my head, but I could only see her name in letters; no image, just a black mist and letters that seemed to fade with every tear-driven blink. I desperately searched for a memory of Evie and Lillie, and this time I saw faces, but not of anyone I knew. I looked down at the killer rocks below and then up at Harry Christian, and suddenly, as his evil grin surpassed itself, he lifted his arms, ready to pounce on me from the twenty feet or so that had suddenly become tiresome to him. And just as I felt that this was it and braced myself for a fight to the end, Harry seemed aware of something just above him. He turned quickly, and a small, dainty foot kicked out sharply, catching him perfectly on the temple, his balance being lost. Harry's legs and arms were flailing, trying desperately to grab hold of the rocks and gorse, but he dropped clumsily, vitriol and venom spewing from every pore.

I dropped back into the cliff as quickly as my twisted broken body would allow, Harry's breath burning within inches of me, his arms swiping desperately, a determination to take me with him. But as his body took blow after blow from the jagged unforgiving cliff face, within seconds his screams stopped and he was now silent and still on the rocks below, basked in fresh moonlight.

I started to shake; I couldn't believe what had just happened. But as I stood and stared, the waves were crashing around the twisted, bloodied body of Harry Christian – he had to be dead! Surely it would be impossible for him to have survived such a fall? But with all the madness that was surrounding me, how could I be sure? And so I just watched him, increasingly desperate to see that finally, his life here on earth was over. I crouched down, my arms wrapped around my blood-soaked knees. I was totally fixated on what lay below me, the waves crashing in and out, his body face down in the water for what seemed like an eternity. Gradually, as Harry's broken body was increasingly shaken and jolted by the renewed vigour of the frothing, crashing waves, I knew it was over for him, and a sense of calmness filled me up.

'Sit back, Ritchie, come on...'

A small hand was on my shoulder and then easing me back, forcing me to sit down on the small ledge. There was no mistaking the touch. And as I dared to look, Rose's hopeful eyes just melted me. She pulled my battered head onto her shoulder, her small hands cradling me.

'It's okay, Ritchie, he's gone, he *won't* be bothering you again.'

Welcome words, welcome words indeed.

And as we lay, two friends there for one another, we could have been seven years of age again. As we talked openly, innocently, the blackened embers of the night sky watched over us, until finally, after many hours, the sun began to rise on a new day.

The lilac sun was as bold and breathtaking as I had ever seen it, the spiritual glare almost blinding me. And with a fresh dawn rising, one question left and sidestepped in the vulnerability of the night quite rightly pushed itself forward. I sat up, my friend and I now cross-legged and facing each other. Rose stuttered, and ummed and ahhed, but then seemed to settle on a way in which to explain what I was so desperate to know.

'Ritchie, Harry had lived his life. He knew the rules, that once he was dead, that was it! But he was a man with a score to settle. He had been able to study the archives the same as anybody else. And whereas everybody else had to settle for forgiveness, wait patiently for the day that their former enemy would join them in the skies above to discuss further their gripes, etc., well, Harry wasn't quite so forgiving or indeed stereotypically patient as the majority of our residents.' Rose rolled her eyes. 'He just kept repeating the same question: if Ritchie Angel can go back, then what's stopping me? Well, we thought we'd convinced him. But remember when you kissed Yasmin?'

My eyes lit up. 'How could I ever forget a moment like that?'

Rose smiled and chuckled. 'Ritchie, you knew that by rights that was it! Well, Harry had been rubbing his hands together, counting the seconds to your arrival, finally his chance to confront you. But, as you well know, after shameful begging from me, the powers that be finally relented and gave you an undeserved pardon.'

I stopped smiling, realising just how much Rose had done for me.

'I can tell you, Ritchie, he was fuming! More anger than…well, I think you've just experienced for yourself!'

I rotated my neck and took a sideways glance at the lilac sun, Rose's fingers squeezing mine.

'Ritchie, he was unable to rest, and spent his entire time finding out exactly how you had been sent back, studying again and again the footage of our meeting on *the* fateful night at the Water's Edge. And having befriended certain old school influential members up there, he was gone!'

I went to stand up, but Rose placed her hand on my shoulder and firmly pulled me back.

'In order for your second chance at life to operate as before, time is simply turned back. You, and only you, were living it with a state of mind that gave you control and thoughts that would and could differ from your original life, enabling, hopefully, a positive and happier outcome for you and those that lived their lives entwined with yours. But when Harry escaped with the same ability as you, it was of course a problem. I'm sure you don't need reminding of the beating he gave you at your school. Well, at first Harry was happy enough with that, and he was brought back without too much fuss. And having given it much thought, the powers that be felt that as long as he stayed with us from now on, they didn't need to punish him for his blatant breach of the rules. But within a short time he became obsessed with watching you, and every scene just wound him up even more. What happened next became almost too delicate to stop. Harry was now sneaking away virtually unnoticed, timing to perfection his interjection, and doing gradually and with subtlety his own thing. And though it was imperative for your experiment that you continued unhindered by an anger-fuelled, unstable character, you had to be left to deal with it. And though I begged for help, as I was so worried about you, Ritchie, on one recapture of Harry he offered a deal. He promised that he would leave you alone, if the powers that be would kill off his wife, Alice, and have her join him; only then would he behave! He hated your visits to Alice, and he hated even more the fact that Alice had struck him with the poker when he had been so close to throttling you to death. Though he knew full well that Alice would never have wanted to kill him! But as for appeasing Harry and ending sweet innocent Alice's life prematurely, well, they could not and would not agree to it, as of course if it was done for one, well, you can imagine the knock-on effect. Harry prowled the corridors like a man possessed. I begged the powers that be to be strong and deal firmly with him. But then Harry befriended your mother, and we were convinced he'd tell her all about you, despite everybody warning him that she was totally out of bounds, that she deserved to keep her memories in tact, after all, she had made a *very* personal decision *not* to scan the archives, relating to you or your father's life! *So,*

Harry used your mother as a bargaining chip, and though outwardly the powers that be wouldn't condone being blackmailed, there were undoubtedly moments when Harry's ways became tiresome, and *so, inadvertently* they would turn a blind eye to his misdemeanours...'

I listened intently. Thoughts of my mother with Harry, well, it had never crossed my mind. To have imagined that my darker side could come into contact with all that was good in my life, and the good being made aware of any sinister side to my personality, was, in time, an inevitable scenario, meaning that no secret was safe. Rose gestured with her hands, almost as though she was apologising to me.

'And, Ritchie, I would watch him, preparing and plotting your downfall, and so I would beg them to try to help you. So they would grab him between scenes with you, try desperately to erase his bitterness; after all, it was putting everything at risk. But no matter what was done, Harry seemed to be immune to the usual tried and tested procedures.'

Rose took both her hands and ran them down the sides of my face, and then very slowly across my nose.

'In the end, I had no choice but to leave Harry to do what *he* felt he had to do, as he'd started to get close to Lillie and was threatening to tell her all sorts about you if I didn't butt out! It was then that I reluctantly agreed that you were on your own with him.'

She brushed the back of her hand across my lips, a small motherly smile pushed my way.

'I'm sorry, Ritchie, we had no choice!'

She ran her fingers ever so softly across my chest, lingering for just a few seconds around my heart.

'But, Ritchie, today, I knew he had to be stopped; it was him or you.'

She let her arms fall to her side and took in the scene amongst the rocks below.

'And now look at him, Ritchie. Though his body will be cleared away, as a penance for his total disregard for the rules his spirit will remain there on those rocks, and once Alice does die, they will not be reunited. We all warned him, and so his bitterness and inability to forgive has brought him here. He has only himself to blame.'

I held onto Rose's hands, an almost hysterical laughter building up from inside me, the depths of just how surreal and yet so life-threateningly serious this all was seeming to activate an equilibrium.

'You saved me, Rose.' I tightened my grip. 'It was you who pushed me onto this ledge as I was heading for the rocks and ultimately to my death.'

She just smiled, nodding calmly.

'And Harry, you killed him!'

Rose suddenly looked uncomfortable, her hands slipping from mine.

'I ... I ... yes, Ritchie, I did, but I had no choice. He would have just kept coming after you! I had been given the nod from the powers that be, and so I did what was necessary.'

I was battle-weary, but with every ache and pain I felt as though I had been taken to another level, physically and mentally, and I felt strangely incredible. I took Rose's face in my hands and simply looked at her. Her eyes stayed with me for a split second or two, but then she seemed to blush and looked away.

I gave her a moment, and then said, 'Rose, what kind of life have you had? I mean, you were eight. What happens to you when you die? What is there for you, ummm, for all of us?'

Rose scrunched her face up, and then looked out to sea. I watched her hair flickering very gently in the early morning breeze. She turned towards me, her head tilted and signs that she was chewing the inside of her cheek.

'Ritchie, life, or should I say death, isn't all that different really, it's just that the people tend to be a lot older, but of course there are still more young people than there should be.'

We both smiled together, Rose more out of fun, but me with a sense of loss and pity.

'I made a few friends, Ritchie, but not easily; as you well know, I wasn't exactly the most sociable in the class.'

I chuckled, this time due to amusement and the memory of how stubborn Rose had been as a child. But as I took in how my friend hadn't changed in all these years, I shook my head and blinked away the madness, and gave her another hug.

'You see, Ritchie, there is no television; in life I suppose you have your soap operas, but in death, well, you get to see the real thing! You tend to look down on what your family are doing, your friends, anyone really that you care about, or at least find interesting!' Rose gave a little blush again, but continued. 'And so for me, I followed *your* life, and I have to say, Ritchie, it's made pretty good viewing! In fact, you had quite a crowd of us watching your life in the end!' She chuckled, suddenly covering her face with her hands. 'And now, Ritchie, with your adventures in your second go at life, you have matched the viewing figures of some of the biggest stars on the planet!'

Suddenly, I was covering my face with my hands, an embarrassed laughter spilling out of me. I couldn't help it. My life in all its gory detail, there for public consumption? I recalled some of my more recent colourful moments, and Tia and Leoni filled my mind.

'Bloody hell, Rose! You've seen all of that?'

Rose was now covering her face again, the brightest blush yet colouring her cheeks.

'No Ritchie, but I did get to hear certain things about it…There is an age rating in place with certain chapters within the archives. If you happen to be watching as certain acts unfold naturally, then the powers that be can't do an awful lot to stop that being viewed, but there has been a time or two when I've been told sharply to go to my room! As events started to unravel…hot up with Tia and Leoni, well, lets say I was *relieved* to be sent to my room!'

Rose beamed at me, shaking her head from side to side in mock disgust.

'But seriously Ritchie, there are many unsuitable things that you have done that Lillie won't get to see, not until she's *much* older, and only then, if she takes the time to seek it out.'

Rose's eyes sparkled brightly, and suddenly, we were both blushing. We huddled and laughed together, the sun just lifting above the horizon.

'Rose, how do you think things are going for me? Do you believe that I will get my original life back?'

Rose turned her head and looked right at me, her eyes still

for a moment. They then started to dance again.

'Ritchie, I really don't know. The general consensus is that you're doing your best! I think really only you can say whether or not that's enough. It's what's in your heart... You might not always get the right result, but when solving a problem, there is a lot to be learnt from seeing how the person involved got to the answer, their approach, planning! The answer, the result, can often be secondary!'

I gave Rose a slightly puzzled smile. I understood what she was saying about effort and intent, but how I prayed it would be enough.

We just sat looking out to sea, our arms wrapped tightly around each other. The horizon was now reflecting a little of how I felt, the sun clean and tight as it rose into the clear blue of the sky, just faint tinges of lilac rippling neatly across its face. My mind was like that, clear and focused, just faint tinges of fear and the unknown rippling neatly across my future. I laughed at my analogy, but was prepared to stand by it. A sharp crash of waves drew my eyes down to the rocks below, but there was only sea and no Harry Christian. I swallowed hard and uttered my last respects for the man. I pondered thoughtfully for a few moments, reliving my history with Harry. I felt my shoulders drop with the sheer relief that he was gone, and then my newfound energy surfaced triumphantly. I wanted to stand up and then dive the hundred feet or so into the baptising cool waters of the ocean.

As I attempted to rise, Rose increased her grip and shook her head.

'Not now, Ritchie, you have much work to do!'

I didn't hesitate, the urge suddenly subsiding.

'Okay, but tell me, Rose, what's that about, my craving for the water? My wonderful reunion with Lillie?'

Rose took her arm from around my shoulders and didn't speak for what seemed like an eternity.

'It's ... well, it's a difficult one, Ritchie. But we, as humans, have a natural affinity with the elements, the basics of nature. For some people it's the sky, planes, air balloons, parachuting! It's just something that an individual is drawn to. For you, it's the water. I presume that you find it soothing and calming?'

I nodded, but questioning my answer before I'd even spoken.

'You're right, Rose, but before death…although I loved the water – after all, that's why I built my family home right next to it – it had been the sky for me, my plane, and despite my fear of heights it was something that I felt I had to do. And when I was up there, especially that day with Yasmin and Evie, the adrenalin was flowing and I was in heaven, in a literal sense of course!'

Rose smiled, but quickly jumped to her feet. She took a moment, running her small beautiful fingers through her glossy mane.

'I know, Ritchie, but I think that was down to thrill seeking! Wouldn't you agree that the water offers a kind of serenity unsurpassed, with no fear of falling to the ground?'

I laughed, and then, keen to explain myself, 'But, Rose, as I look out to sea, here and now with you, I ache for it, absolutely yearn for the freshness of it, the freedom, just to sink beneath its surface. The thought of it seems to soothe the terrible heartache that I feel, this continuing grief that I carry constantly for all that I've lost, all that I miss so terribly.'

Rose shook her head, discouraging my self-pity.

I let out a tired sigh and uttered, 'I know, Rose, but I do miss my wife and daughter *so* much.' I dropped my hands to my side, my face skyward.

'Ritchie, *stop* it!'

Relenting, I let my eyes fall onto hers and I accepted the scolding, and so continued.

'In my original life I would love to look at the water, but I would also feel a sense of fear. I think it's the enormity of it, not knowing what lurks beneath. But here, now, I think the sea offers me an escape from the unknown, from the skies above, the powers that be!' I realised I had answered my own question. 'Wow, *that's* it! Deep beneath the surface of the water I feel that I can escape all the prying eyes. No disrespect! More to do with my loyal audience you've been so kind to tell me about!'

Rose broke into soft giggles, her accepting smile acknowledging wholeheartedly what I was saying.

'The water it is then, Ritchie, in *this* life. But then in your previous life the skies offered you no fear, just a freedom to explore, totally unaware of just how close you were getting to us. The water, the skies, which one you desire all depending on your state of mind.'

She was laughing now, and yet I believed we really had solved our mystery.

Without warning, Rose's warm hand slipped away and she was gone. I looked around desperately, my eyes scanning furiously up the cliff face, but there was no doubt that I was on my own again. I suddenly felt as though a cloak had been thrown over my head; the sky was black, the early morning light instantly replaced by an unfriendly, cold backdrop. I turned and faced the sea, and as my eyes became accustomed to the sudden darkness, I took something positive from the silver glisten from the ripple of the calm seas. I took a deep and heavy breath, and gave an unexpected sorry sigh – perhaps the disappointment that my little wise friend was gone again. And then, as though being spoken to, day burst into light, the full glow and heady metallic plumage brighter and shinier than I had ever witnessed.

Though my body felt weightless and inspired, I was filled with an overwhelming desire to get back up the cliff and away from this place. But as I stood up, I seemed to be pulled backwards at speed, my arms and legs out in front of me, my hair forced forward; no control, just the inevitability of waiting to hit the bottom, *or* top, of wherever I was heading. And then everything stopped. My feet on the ground, my arms at my side, my hair now resting warmly over my ears and neck. My eyes focused on the sea in the distance, the sound of the waves rolling onto the beach a very different soundtrack to just a moment ago. I moved my head slowly and then gulped painfully, my throat dry and in shock. I was standing back on the beach car park, next to my Jeep. I raised my palms towards my face; all pain was gone, and they were clean; no cuts, blood and embedded gorse bush needles. I ran my healthy hands down my twisted and battered body, but my white T-shirt was white. Blood, sweat and tears, broken bones, torn muscles, all repaired, fit and healthy!

The door of my Jeep was unlocked, so I opened it and climbed inside. I tried to make sense of all that was happening, but how could I? And so I felt it wise not to dwell. My mind was suddenly clicking back, as though the scenes were rewinding and then falling and settling on the image of Yasmin, and then the practicality of one question in particular: would her husband be home? I nodded my head. I needed to see what I was up against.

As I pushed the key into the ignition I started to feel nauseous, and my head began to spin. I clamped onto the steering wheel, and in an attempt to shut out the flashing lights that were bouncing around the Jeep I just held on for dear life. Darkness and light beaconed before me, but I didn't move a muscle – I couldn't! I was simply stuck in the movement of time. The full glare of black and white flashed on and off, and then snow fell around me. Within seconds it was replaced by fresh green grass and the buds on the trees popped out, leaves within milliseconds darkening and falling to the ground, ice and then snow, buds, bright sunlight, wind, rain, ice, snow, buds, leaves. I was hyperventilating, but unable to move. I felt fear, as though the life was draining out of me, but I couldn't do anything to stop it. I was desperate to get the Jeep door open, to try to slide out, hoping that that would force my life to stop wherever it had landed. But then, as the seasons continued to roll forward before my very eyes, everything around me started to slow down, and within seconds I was surrounded by snow, with darkness deep-set around me.

After Death, ?

Finally, I was able to move my head. A sudden blast of light forced my eyes closed.

'Excuse me, sir! You shouldn't still be in here! Oh, it's *you*. So this is *your* vehicle then, sir?'

I pushed my door open and slid out, my feet sinking into about a foot of snow. A light flurry of flakes danced across my face. The torch man started to talk again.

'Sir, I'm sorry to be so direct, but you must understand, you can't just abandon your vehicle here. In fact, I need to ring the police, so if you could hang on a minute, sir!' The old man turned away from me.

'Umm, *no* police! I understand I've caused a problem here, but no need for the police!'

The torch was back on my face, a crease forming across the old man's brow, but then a glint in his eye suggested he was keen to see me on my way.

'Hmmm, I doubt it will start though; in fact, I'm *sure* it won't!'

I shook my head, batting away his negativity.

'I ... I ... don't see why not. Can I still get out?'

The old guy nodded.

'Hmm, yep! It won't be *me* stopping you from leaving. I'll help you get the snow off your windscreen!'

The full force of the bitter night hit me suddenly, and instinctively I wrapped my arms around my body, my totally inadequate T-shirt cold and damp. As the old guy brushed the thick slabs of snow off my Jeep, he looked star-struck and bewildered.

'We've had the police sniffing around this vehicle you know, but they simply told us to leave it. They'd had word that you'd be back, *someday!* Even 'ad a few *nosey* journalists asking questions about you! Personally, I thought we'd never see you again. But good God, what can I say? 'Ere you are, as I live and breathe!'

My hairs stood on end. I presumed the worst; I knew what had happened to me. I wanted to ask the old guy what the date was, but I wasn't so sure I wanted to know the answer. All I kept thinking about was Yasmin. Was she still at the same house? More children? I started to shake. I placed my hand beneath my jacket; I was a little thicker around the waist. I then lifted my hand to my face and there it was, a small mole that had appeared on my right cheek in my early thirties. A tear rolled from my eye. I felt stupid getting so emotional, but I was just *so* scared. Had I missed my chance to put everything right? I just felt it was all slipping away from me.

The old guy suddenly piped up, 'Bloody hell, sir! I knew it had been a while, but your tax disc is nearly six years out of date! No, hang on a minute, it's *nearly* seven years!'

I turned away quickly, slumping to my knees.

'PLEASE, ROSE, SHOW YOURSELF, I *BEG* YOU, ROSE, *HELP ME!!*'

She didn't come, and I suppose I didn't really expect her to. There was something about this that made me believe I was very much on my own. The old man stood back, his torch pointing at his boots, his sheepish expression seemingly as a result of my outburst to the skies above. He seemed to hesitate, but then lifted his torch, now full force into my face.

'Sir, are you okay?'

I nodded slowly. 'I'm sorry, it's just that...'

I was lost for words; after all, what could I say? I forced a smile for the old guy, which seemed to settle him a little, and then suddenly he was all arms, keen to get me onto my feet.

'Come on, sir, you'll catch your death down in the snow like that. Come on, you'll have to come and get warm in me hut, I'll get the police or summat.'

I stood up, thanking the man, but explained that I would soon be on my way. The old guy raised his eyebrows, not looking too convinced.

'Are you sure, sir? I'm pretty sure you'll be wasting your time!'

But a stern determined look from me seemed to kick-start a little optimism from my old friend.

'Oh well! Right you are, sir. Ummm, go on then, turn her over!'

I rubbed the key roughly between my hands and then lifted it skyward. The old man was shaking his head enthusiastically all of a sudden.

'That's it, sir, let's see just how good these Americans are at building their answer to our Austin Champ, eh!'

I shook my head, not following him at all.

'Come on then, sir, turn 'er over. If she don't start, I can always get the tractor; I've got some jump leads!'

I took a deep breath and watched intently as the snowflakes floated down and settled layer after layer onto the windscreen. Under torchlight, their deeply ingrained lilac tinge was worryingly rich and vibrant, far more so than ever before. I turned the key and the engine churned very slowly, as if the battery was close to death. My head was leaning against the steering wheel, my plea soft and whispered into the dimly lit dashboard.

'Please, my dear friend, you've waited for me *all* this time, come on, I need you now!'

But gradually, all life in the battery slipped away; a clicking of electronics, but nothing else. I took a deep breath, slowly raising my head and taking in my sorry reflection in the windscreen. I shook my head, my eyes suddenly wide and transfixed, as there were two little girls. I blinked furiously. It was Evie and Lillie kneeling on the Jeep bonnet, faces peering through the windscreen, willing me on. My face beamed back at them, emotionally confused tears rolling down my cheeks. I turned the key again, and *this* time, very slowly, the battery gave me a whisper of hope. Evie and Lillie were banging their little fists against the windscreen.

'Come on, Daddy! Come on! Daddy, *you can do it!'*

And then the engine fired up, grumbling, gurgling, misfiring for all it was worth. I pushed my foot down lightly, coaxing the accelerator, but the engine nearly died on me. I eased off quickly, wisely letting it burble at its own pace. I left it a few moments before looking up. My eyes were then searching desperately for my little girls, but they had gone. I swallowed hard, an intense disappointment filtering through me, and though my throat was dry and devoid of volume, I gave thanks to them both for their help.

Suddenly, the old man was at my door window, his eyes wide and highly bemused at what he was witnessing. I pushed my foot onto the accelerator again, just a light squeeze, the old man's fists tight and his head nodding in approval. Driven on, I pushed my foot down a little harder, and the engine responded with a far healthier growl. Just as my confidence was building, the Jeep gave a startling gunshot backfire and I eased off quickly. Gradually, the engine seemed to settle into an acceptable rhythm, and within a few heart-thumping moments, it actually seemed to dance to a far healthier beat, almost inviting my foot to try its luck, and so I did. This time, the engine totally cleared its throat and then roared, the full four litres blasting the cold and damp away.

The old guy was now jumping up and down at my window,

his torch pointed out to sea so as not to blind me as he had before.

As I wound my window fully down, he scratched his head and muttered, 'Well, sir, I never. I'd 'ave put my 'ouse on that not starting. Well, bugger me!'

I pushed my hand forward. 'Thank you. I suppose I'd better be off.'

The old man dropped his torch and gripped both his hands around mine, his head nodding in serious humble approval. We beamed at each other, his hands finally opening up and letting me go. I pushed the clutch down as hard as I could and battled gently with the gearstick, eventually, noisily, engaging first. I pushed onto the accelerator, my face screwing up with every painful grind of seized cogs, battling against more dry and corroded metal. But gradually, the Jeep started to shudder and creak reluctantly, an inch or two at a time, the resistance weakening, and then finally... it lurched forward. I was now grinning away like a Cheshire cat, my eyes scanning desperately for any sign of my beautiful daughters. I sighed; for now, they were gone. But then I smiled at the memory of their perfect little faces, and thanked them again for their love and support.

The Jeep creaked and cracked across the compacted snow, my old friend running alongside me, us both nodding our heads in triumphant unison, his torchlight bouncing furiously with every step. And as I gathered pace, we excitedly bade our farewells, his hands on hips and huge beaming smile now fading fast in my side mirror.

Six years or so later, and I was finally leaving Blackpool Sands. Despite a wealth of questions that were simply too mind-blowing to try to make sense of, I settled for perhaps the least appropriate and minor details. I was eternally grateful that the police hadn't compounded my Jeep as they had with my last disappearing act. And though this was a hard one to decipher, and not an easy detail to see the good and the positive in, the fact that the powers that be had deemed me worthy of being released back into the here and now, enabling me the chance to see this nightmare through, and be free to go and find Yasmin, meant the world to me!

I made my way up the twisting, winding coast road, the snow and ice evil beneath my tyres. But despite my spirits being high, it was a treacherous night, and my concentration was being dented by the images of Scottie and me on our fateful journey together. I could hardly see the road ahead, and as I focused heavily on the nose of the Jeep, I kept reliving the horrendous moment when all control was lost, and the horrific fatal scenes that followed. I swallowed hard, desperate to put all that behind me. But as the snow became thicker and faster, Scottie's battered face was now right in front of me. I struggled to catch my breath, but then anger, frustration and hell-bent determination erupted from within me, and I screamed viciously back at him.

'YOU'VE *NO* RIGHT TO TAUNT ME SCOTTIE…THAT WAS BEFORE, YOU'RE ALIVE AND WELL NOW!'

Then I was alone, the wipers going ten to the dozen, and as I swallowed hard and my composure returned I leant towards the windscreen, apologising to my friend, accepting that he may have been warning me to be careful? I prayed that that was all it was! As my attention on the road ahead increased, I noticed as the engine had warmed up that huge slabs of snow were sliding off the bonnet, and I could see how the once shiny black paintwork was now a patchy faded grey. And as more snow slid away, there were painful-looking rust holes everywhere. But the Jeep just kept plodding forwards, and with every grateful rotation of the wheels I kept my focus on the prize that hopefully lay ahead.

After Death, 2004 – Lilac Sky

So, as my life-threatening journey continued, physically and spiritually my head was spinning. But as for the Jeep, despite one or two close shaves with the sheer drop of the coast road, my man-made friend was doing me proud. Defiantly I just kept pushing my foot onto the accelerator. And as I passed yet another abandoned vehicle, my confidence steadily grew. Little by little, I started to get closer to civilisation, the bright lights seeming to warm up the icy-cold night. I even started to see people walking gingerly, holding onto each other. But as I passed them all by, my thoughts were well and truly on the fact that within minutes, I would be at Victoria Road.

I pulled the Jeep to a halt at the top of Dartmouth hill. As I looked down into the valley, the snow-covered yachts and row upon row of tightly linked houses convinced me that should I be successful in winning my wife and daughter back – then I would make sure that we made this our second home. The three of us together as a family! The image of us all together, I could almost touch it. I clicked down the right–hand indicator and turned the wheel, pushing my foot firmly on the accelerator, covering the final short distance to number 150.

As I took in the rambling house, the Christmas decorations sparkling with all the festive cheer they could muster, I turned off the engine. There was a small Mercedes sports car on the driveway, covered in snow; an impressive wreath of holly on the front door that framed – for me at least – the potentially life-destroying brass doorbell.

I pushed the Jeep door open, stepping onto the crisp white snow. I eased the car door gently back into place, desperate to keep my arrival quiet, my heart beating painfully as I lifted the latch on the iron gates. The pounding in my head, the increasingly building heart rate, and now the crunch of snowflakes with every step. I stopped just a metre or so from the house, taking in a merge of sounds that were coming from inside. Distant music, perhaps the television, radio? I shook my head from side to side, almost despairing at the strength of fear that was making me dizzy. I took a deep breath.

'Just ring the bloody bell, Ritchie!' I muttered aggressively.

Finally, I pushed my shaking hand through the holly and left it suspended just a hairs width away from the bell, for what seemed a lifetime…I then pushed it. I instinctively hunched my shoulders up towards my ears, scolding myself. *What was that? It will sound like Big Ben inside the house!* I was a bag of nerves, and I had stopped breathing as I listened intently. I could now hear a distant dog bark, getting much louder by the second. My breath forced itself out, and I could hear sniffing and gentle scratching against the door, and a young female voice in the distance.

'Good girl, Fluffers! *Good girl!'*

I smiled inanely, I couldn't help it. *Fluffers, Oh Wow!*

Yasmin must still live here! was all that I could say inside my head. But something made me want to run, such was the fear of what I was about to be faced with. I felt it safer to simply dwell on Fluffers. I was convinced it was me who had suggested the name, but I didn't care about any of that, I just felt such a warm glow at the mention of the name.

The door was suddenly opened, and a large black-haired man – early forties I presumed – stood before me.

'Yes?' he said.

I shuffled, desperate for words to come out of my mouth.

'Um, hi! My name's Angel...*Ritchie Angel!*'

I almost winced as I spoke, anticipating a negative response, unwelcome recognition of a name representing a past his good lady had chosen to leave behind. But a sudden scream from upstairs simply had the man apologising and running off in the direction of more shriek-like tones. I stood there, the door open wide. I felt it polite to pull the door to, keen not to let all the wonderful heat out, but instead I just stood there, once again on the outside of Yasmin's world. But whilst the door was open, I felt I was part of whatever was going on.

Suddenly, a door off the hallway opened and out toddled a young girl, perhaps about three, maybe four years old. Blonde, shoulder-length curly hair entwined with coloured ribbons.

'Where's my Daddy gone?'

'Oh, he's gone upstairs, someone called him! What's your name?'

The little girl smiled and popped her thumb into her mouth, not answering my question but seemingly prepared to wait with me. After a minute or two – but seeming like an eternity – I felt that polite conversation would help pass the time a little faster.

'Is your Mummy in?'

The little girl nodded.

'So what's *your* Mummy and Daddy's names?'

The little girl turned her head slightly to one side.

'Father Christmas is coming tonight!'

I smiled warmly and crouched down, total surprise that it was *actually* Christmas Eve, and feeling even more guilty about disturbing Yasmin and her family on such a night – though I batted the guilt away.

'So what's Santa bringing you?'

The little girl didn't say anything, and just started to giggle to herself. She then turned to go. I could hear the desperation in my voice as I asked her another question.

'You didn't tell me your name…'

The little girl stopped and turned to face me.

'My Mummy and Daddy are called *Mummy and Daddy*, silly!'

But then her father ran back down the stairs and into the hall.

'Go in the lounge please, Millie! I'm *so* sorry to have gone off like that, it's just that my wife is expecting our fourth child any day, and she's feeling a little uncomfortable, you know how these things can be.'

The man was talking, but I was almost out for the count. *Four children!* It was a worthy knockout blow. But somehow, as he spoke, I was just about hanging in there, floundering on the ropes, simply buying some time. My rival was running his fingers through his hair furiously, and finally, I was starting to take in some of what he was saying.

'I'm *so* sorry, I didn't catch your name. There's me boring you with my problems. How can I help you?'

The shock of everything had simply dried my throat up, but I just about managed to croak, 'I was simply looking for my cat. I've just moved in around the corner… *Very* sorry to have bothered you!'

I made my way back down the driveway.

'She'll turn up!' I assured him. The man called after me. 'What colour is she?'

I turned to face him, my arms gesticulating all over the place.

'Oh, um, white. A small white fluffy thing! Not the easiest thing to see with all this snow around!' I waved and turned away.

'Good luck! We'll keep our eyes open!' rang relentlessly in my ears.

I finally heard his front door close, and as simple as that, I was shut out of their lives. I clanked the iron latch back into place the gates shut securely. Despondently I climbed back into the Jeep and slammed my hands down hard onto the steering wheel.

'FUCK! FUCK! FUCK!' The frustration was just too much. *How on earth could I disrupt a family like that, how could I possibly get between a husband and wife...AN IMMINENT BIRTH, THREE OTHER CHILDREN?* And as I took in the beautiful home and everything it stood for, I was left questioning my right to mess things up for Yasmin.

Through tear-stained eyes I made my way back down into Dartmouth, the crackle of ice beneath my tyres a perfect backdrop for my breaking heart. I shook my head from side to side, desperate for some kind of inspiration. But as my tired soul craved a warm dark place to hide in, I accepted that I needed a bed for the night. The Jeep limped past the Royal Castle Hotel, but I knew I couldn't go in. As a desperate man, I questioned myself and tried to picture the scenario, but it was simply too much. I'd gone back before, but then hadn't an inkling that I'd been away a whole year, but now, nearly seven years later, well, they would be right in thinking I was a deeply troubled individual. And as I gave out a pitiful, almost defeated chuckle, I pushed my foot down on the accelerator and decided that for embarrassment's sake I would try my luck a little further along the Dartmouth front.

There was a broken line of public houses and restaurants open, with steamed-up windows, a vague scene of Christmas Eve cheer just about visible. I could see a more consistent light in the distance, and I suddenly longed for it. After about a third of a mile, I craned my neck to see what I had been drawn to.

'*Dart Marina Hotel*, that'll do!'

I excitedly scoured a parking space, finally having to pull up alongside a small covered yacht lying on an insufficient-looking trailer. As I stepped out of the Jeep, I was now aware why I had been left with perhaps the only available parking space. As the vicious whipping edges of a navy-blue tarpaulin complete with metal clips were twisting and bucking themselves ever so gradually free, despite the weight of a foot or so of a rust-stained slab of ice, a horrible thought crossed my mind. I suddenly panicked and ran to the back of the Jeep. I hurriedly grabbed the tailgate, which was heavy and creaking defiantly, and had to use all my strength to get it open just a foot or so. I squeezed in through the tiniest of gaps, the hinges not prepared to give me an inch more. My hands, shrouded in darkness, searched frantically for my rucksack, but nothing. I pushed my body back out, pleased to be able to breathe again. I frantically felt inside my pockets – a bit of change, and then I felt relief as I placed my hand on a credit card.

'Thank God!' left me through a cloud of solidifying breath.

As I stood at reception, grateful for the warmth around me, I was starting to hallucinate about the hot shower and thick heavy duvet that were waiting upstairs. The girl smiled as she checked her computer, a band of red tinsel wrapped around her wrist.

'You're in luck, sir, we have one room available. How many nights would you like?'

I uttered weakly, my throat increasingly dry, that I would be staying just for the one night, and would be heading back up north tomorrow.

'Well, at least the roads will be nice and empty, sir, though I don't envy you travelling on Christmas Day!'

As the girl processed my details, my hand was tightly clasped around my credit card. Finally, when asked how I would like to pay, I slid the card across the marble surface. But as the smile left her face, the obvious dawned on me as the card came back across the counter.

'I'm *so* sorry, sir, this card's out of date! By about four years, in fact. Do you have another form of payment?'

I shook my head despondently, embarrassment mixed with sheer exhaustion travelling the length of my body. Muttering my apologies, I grabbed the card and made a hasty exit.

As I stepped out into the treacherous night, I stood short of the Jeep. I looked up into the icy clear night sky, and for just a split second I saw crystal white stars, but then each one randomly became a deep lilac. I looked over my shoulder, the moon white and bright, but within seconds a wisp of unwanted familiar colour seemed to pass before it and then the moon looked to be sucking the blood out of the passing haze. I rubbed my eyes furiously – I felt desperate. Only now did I have a sense of what a tramp must feel like. I had my Jeep, but the temperature was several degrees below zero. I didn't have a penny to my name, I had no friends around me, and my fuel tank was running on empty. I stepped towards the Jeep and rested my hands on the bonnet, feeling grateful for the warmth that was rising from the engine. As the heat passed through me, I had an urge to ring my accountant.

'Peter would sort something out for me!' My breath almost froze as I said the words.

But as I stood with my head dropped, the negatives presented themselves. *It's Christmas Eve, Ritchie, and you have no money, not even for a phone call!* I turned full circle and slumped with my back onto the Jeep bonnet, attempting to remember Peter's telephone number, but I simply didn't have a clue. I pulled away from the Jeep, trying desperately to churn up his number from my disintegrating brain. But the truth was, I couldn't, not a digit of it. I stamped around the car park like a spoilt child, and as I let the search for Peter's number go, I simply kicked my boot into the snow, trying to dislodge a lump of grey ice welded to the tarmac, as though trying to kick some life into my battle-weary brain. Jimmy's number? Leoni's? Anybody's? But it was frighteningly hopeless. Without any thought or major direction, I simply turned around, and after a dozen or so heavy steps realised I was heading back into the part of Dartmouth that I knew. The bitterly cold wind was scarring my face with every slap. I tried to pull my head down into my jacket, desperate to cover the bottom of my ears. As I trudged, wearily making my way along the now uninviting water, the brittle wake slapping sharply against the moored yachts and boats, I wondered scathingly about my future – and if I had one? But the more I walked, the buoyant mood of Christmas Eve was grudgingly infectious, reminding me perhaps that I should be grateful to be alive at all. And so, as I passed by the many eateries, the fogged-up windows doing little to hide the merriment inside, and as the smell of indulgence filtered into the street, the hunger in my stomach was starting to growl, and it was that, that reminded me of my good friend the seafood chef.

'Oh my God, Ritchie, you *are* a genius!' And as a poor substitute for a spring in my step moved me on a little quicker,

I couldn't help but yell into the night sky, *'PLEASE BE THERE!'*

Cutting through the narrow sidestreets, finally, there it was – the large silver fish hanging over the glass front door, the subtle white Christmas lights twinkling invitingly. I almost ran the last few steps, until excitedly I was pushing the heavy door open. The sudden waft of garlic and general headiness of nirvana smacked me hard in the nose. I scanned the faces of the waiters, who looked indignantly back at me, before one of them stepped forward.

'Can we help you, sir? We *are* fully booked!'

I gesticulated, until finally, the right words came out of my mouth; and then a disappointment reminiscent of my absent father on each and every birthday.

'No, sir, he is gone. Two years now.'

And with that, I was subtly ushered back onto the cold street.

I stepped away from the restaurant and just stood, my brain as though closed down and unable to instruct any part of me to move, unable to accept that my last chance of help from my dear friend Cass had been cruelly snatched away from me. I simply didn't know what to do next. As maybe five, ten minutes passed by, my fingers and toes were now aching with the cold. And so, with no other choice open to me, my Jeep was my only option, and as the snowflakes started to flurry I was grateful for it. I walked as fast as was safe to do so, taking a more sheltered, hopefully shorter route through the almost deserted streets. Within ten minutes or so, a smile of relief spreading across my numb face, I pulled the Jeep door closed behind me. With fingers that seemed twice the size, I pushed the key into the ignition, my smile even bigger as the engine kicked into life. Though I knew it was unwise, I turned the heater on full blast. The ice-cold air hit my hands and face, but within minutes a lukewarm response started to offer some hope of future warmth.

I must have been in my Jeep for about thirty minutes, the heater now red hot, and my brain seemingly keen to come out of retirement, when I made a decision that I knew was mad, but I made it anyway. I accepted fully that I wasn't thinking straight, so before I changed my mind, I drove the short distance to where I wanted to be most of all. I pulled up outside the Old School House. I felt that Yasmin couldn't turn me away, not on a night like this, even though it was Christmas Eve. But surely our brief friendship counted for something. And her husband seemed quite normal, rather friendly in fact.

Before I knew it, I'd pushed the bell – there was no going back now. It must have taken a minute or so, but finally, the door was open. I grimaced towards Yasmin's husband, moving my head from side to side in tune with my feet. But before I could utter a word, I was extremely grateful, as he spoke first.

'Oh hi! Ummm, have you had any luck in finding your cat?'

Still grimacing out of pure embarrassment, I nervously explained that I wasn't in fact a neighbour, but an old friend of his wife, and that I desperately needed a bed for the night. The poor guy looked puzzled, his questioning eyes trying to weigh me up.

But then a glimmer of amusement shone towards me as he said, 'Look, umm, you'd better come in!'

I stepped into the large, but *oh so* warm hallway, and once the door was firmly shut behind me, I felt wholeheartedly that I was doing exactly the right thing. The two of us seemed a little unsure as to how we should proceed, but going along with the relaxed nature of my host, I found myself following him into the kitchen. He was uttering this and that, but nothing that was sinking in. He picked up an already opened bottle of brandy and raised it up. I nodded. I usually hated spirits, but unquestionably it seemed like the best idea in the world. We both stood in silence, clinking our glasses together. Suddenly, a scream tore the calm of the festive evening into shreds, my rival knocking over a kitchen stool and running up the stairs. I placed my glass down, ready to do something, desperate to help, but I just stood there, hands on hips. I could hear all sorts of commotion going on – heavy footsteps, raised voices. Yasmin sounded extremely distressed, and how I stopped myself running to her I'll never know. Within a few minutes the little daughter Millie came into the kitchen, tears in her eyes.

'What's wrong with my Mummy? Daddy told me to get out

of the way!'

I instinctively picked the little girl up, and it felt surreal. I touched the tips of her fingers, and her trusting eyes sparkled back at me. I felt the strangest of feelings, not quite able to get my head around *who* this small child's mother was. Suddenly, Yasmin's husband was at the kitchen door, out of breath and panicking.

'I'm *so* sorry!'

We were interrupted by a loud knock on the front door, and two paramedics were suddenly inside the house and running up the stairs. Within what seemed like only a handful of minutes, Yasmin was in a carry chair-type structure, wrapped from head to toe in a thermal foil blanket. I froze to the spot, but then, keen to avert the little girl's attention, I turned away. But then I couldn't help but look back over my shoulder as the two burly men carried her out through the front door, I winced as I noticed Yasmin's husband carrying a small bottle of gas, running clumsily in an attempt to keep up with proceedings. The front door was wide open, the rotation of a blue light circulating around the hallway. And so I just stood, the air filled with an almost eerie silence – all background noise rejected by me. My eyes widened suddenly as Yasmin's husband was back in the house, his arms flailing dramatically.

'Umm, oh God! I'm *so* sorry, would you mind? Could you please take care of the kids for us? I'll be back as soon as I can.'

I didn't have chance to say much, and just nodded my head as reassuringly as I could. I was in a major scene that just seemed to be unfolding around me, and I was seemingly helpless, but undoubtedly crucial to the plot. And though I just wanted to run out into the snow to be with *my* Yasmin, I knew that I shouldn't. I tried in earnest to pacify myself that I was being sympathetic to the needs of Yasmin's children, and for now I accepted that. But then in total defiance, I still wanted to run to my wife –yet I couldn't move. And as the front door slammed shut, the sirens screamed out. All I could do was stand holding Yasmin's little girl, as the woman I loved was carried off into the cold Christmas Eve night ready to give birth to another man's child.

A small warm cheek was suddenly on mine, Millie's arms holding on tightly around my neck. I felt one of her tears fall onto my face, and gratefully my concerns were now for my new little friend. I turned her face towards me, before wiping all tears away.

'Don't worry, your Mummy will be fine. She's just going off to the hospital, and soon they'll bring you back a new baby brother or sister!'

Millie beamed, suitably reassured, her little fingers wiping away a small tear that I hadn't realised *I'd* cried. We both walked into the lounge. The entire scene was the traditional Christmas card – the tree, the burning logs...Fluffers lying across the rug in front of the open fire. She lifted her head, acknowledging the stranger in her home, but then dropped her head again, her eyes closing effortlessly. I placed Millie very carefully onto the settee, and then crouched down and gently stroked her brow. My little friend smiled, but gradually her eyes started to flicker, and within a few short seconds her head dropped. Yasmin's little baby was asleep! I cooed as I took in the innocence of what lay before me, then stood up and took a deep breath.

As my composure returned, I embraced the incredible feeling of finally being close to Yasmin, and it overwhelmed me. Okay, I didn't have a clue as to what my next step was, and I was increasingly aware that I had little or no chance of sorting this mess out, but at least I was part of her life! I smiled smugly as I congratulated myself on being brave enough to come back here, and especially tonight. And to actually be so crucially needed! I felt that my being here would perhaps suggest to Yasmin that fate had brought us together, and all that considered, then maybe, just maybe, she wouldn't be too averse to accepting me as a family friend. Suddenly, my head was in my hands and I was laughing at my increasing insanity. But for now, compared to how I'd been alone in my Jeep, this was almost at the other end of the spectrum – a vast improvement on proceedings.

I took a long, deep breath and lifted my arms fully above my head, just happy to be taking in the smell of Yasmin's world. I turned full circle, my eyes suddenly drawn to a lady's cream cardigan lying on the back of a maple Regency chair. I winced as I stepped guiltily towards it. I let my fingers run around the cashmere collar, and then lifted it to my face – an unfamiliar perfume filled my head. But as I absorbed the full force of the new Yasmin, I couldn't help but wonder about all the changes that may have taken place without my influence. I looked up towards the ceiling, suddenly desperate to see her bedroom. How could I resist? Though I had imagined the moment a thousand times, I had presumed she would be in it.

As I climbed the wide staircase, I felt a little surprised by the heavy antique bits and pieces that decorated the house. Yasmin had always shown a preference for light and airy, nothing heavy, nothing too traditional. We both shared a passion for the creams and the warmer natural woods that gave us both a sense of space and minimalism, but then that was our taste together. Now, with her new husband, I had to accept that the ingredients had changed, and so Yasmin, her children, her house, her choices would all reflect that.

As I finally stepped onto the landing, I was drawn instantly to the large open doorway at the end of the imposing corridor. I knew that it was wrong to be snooping like this, and what if one of the children saw me? I felt my conscience disapproving on every level, but a totally understandable need pushed me forward, tiptoeing towards the impossible to resist open door. I tensed nervously as yet another floorboard decided to creak noisily back at me, and with each step I expected one of the less impressive doors to my left and right to open, a disapproving face questioning my actions. I wondered what the ages of Yasmin's other children were, but as I continued towards the Holy Grail, I prayed that I wasn't going to find out *just* yet.

As I approached the bedroom door, I shook my head as the facts actually sank in. Yasmin would be thirty-four, and though I knew and accepted that, there was no doubting how daunting it was, trying to imagine just how different she would be compared to the woman I fell so hopelessly in love with. My mind started to run riot with how my original deal with Rose was to get to see Yasmin at twenty-five, and yet for whatever reasons, here I was, nearly ten years late. But as I became increasingly hot at the uncertainty, I felt it wise not to dwell on it. I stepped into the large bedroom. I shook my head and smiled at the blankets just thrown all over the floor, drawers spilling, as though ransacked by a drug-hungry burglar. The rich mahogany wardrobe door was wide open and I could see Yasmin's clothes; just the thought of touching the fabrics that clothed her took my breath away. I ran my hand across the many different materials, and it was unnerving having it confirmed that there was nothing familiar here. My fingers ran across the hem of a heavy tweed skirt, my eyes now upon an open drawer, but gone were the expected silks and satins, sheer stockings and suspender belts. But here and now, in Yasmin's *new* world, was complacently strewn faded cotton underwear.

As my fingers picked through the uninspiring choice of a middle-aged prim and proper madam, I was left scratching my head, not sure whether to feel grateful at the obvious lack of desire this relationship inspired, or to feel frustration that the Yasmin I knew and so passionately loved seemingly didn't exist any more. I turned away from the wardrobe, covering my face with my hands. I stepped towards the bed, reluctant to carry on my snooping. But suddenly, I was picking up an open book off the bedside table: *How to Have it All*. I quickly picked up the book beneath it: *How to Become Friends with Your Husband and Children*.

'Shit, Yasmin! You don't need books for all that! God, woman, you're a superstar wife and mother!'

Suddenly, I was aware of somebody at the bedroom door.

'What are you doing? Who are you?'

I turned around quickly. A girl about nine years of age stood with her hands on her hips. I felt so guilty, but tried to appear as unfazed as possible, smiling as innocently as I could. The girl, her dark brown hair stuck to the side of her face as though she'd been in a really deep sleep, stood accusingly.

'Where's my Mum and Dad?'

I tried quickly to reassure her, explaining her parents' unexpected trip to the hospital, but she had other questions for me.

'What are *you* doing in *their* bedroom?'

I quickly grabbed a discarded blanket off the floor.

'Umm, I thought Millie might get cold, she's fallen asleep downstairs.'

The girl simply turned away. I hugged the blanket to my chest, shocked at the fact that I had just met one of Yasmin's other children. My mind raced. The little girl that had looked so much like Evie on the drive all those years ago was now, well, not how I had imagined her to look. I moved forward quickly and then stopped. I spotted a wedding photo on the dressing table, the first I had seen in the house. I picked up the heavy gold frame. *That's him, but that's not Yasmin...* I stared at the couple on their wedding day, and this fair-haired, quite plump lady looked back at me. I quickly ran out onto the landing, my inquisitor now presumably downstairs.

'Excuse me, *please...*' I whispered assertively, devouring the landing in four strides, and then descended two treads at a time, just as the older daughter marched into the hallway, once again hands on hips.

'*What?* You'll wake everyone *up!* James is a *light* sleeper!'

This girl was seriously intimidating and so I made my apologies.

'I'm *so* sorry, but have you got a recent photo of your mum? It's just that we're old friends and I haven't seen her for a good few years!'

The girl beckoned for me to follow her, index finger placed firmly on her lips, before disappearing into another room. I quickly joined her, waiting as patiently as I could.

'Here's one of Mum on her last birthday.'

I looked at the picture; it certainly wasn't my Yasmin.

'But your Mum *is* Yasmin? And your dog, Fluffers?'

The young girl laughed, highly amused, rolling her eyes, quite unfazed by the madman that she had been woken by.

'*No*, my Mum's name is Sue! Our dog is Fluffers, yeah, but Mum liked the name of the dog that used to live here; they had a puppy called Fluffers, she was *so* cute!'

I looked at the girl, my head spinning, many questions jockeying for position.

'When did the last lady move out?'

The girl ran her fingers through her deep-sleep bed hair.

'Mmm, just as Millie was born. So nearly...four years ago,

or so!'

The girl pushed past me and headed off into the kitchen. I watched, open-mouthed, but then ran after her.

'Where did they go? I mean, what was the lady's name?'

As I entered the kitchen, the girl put her finger on her lips.

'Ssshhh! If she wakes I'll never get her back to sleep.'

The girl grabbed a bottle of milk out of the fridge and poured herself a glassful. A little quieter this time, I attempted to repeat my question, but the girl beat me to it.

'Yeah, her name was Yazzy, well, that was what her husband called her. Pretty lady, I would *die* for hair like hers!'

I was about to explain that dying was overrated, but felt it wise to let the inclination pass. Instead, I just sat there wide-eyed, desperate for more information. The questions kept coming.

'How many kids did she have?'

The girl took a large quenching mouthful of her milk, leaving her with a white moustache.

'Ummmm, one, I *think*...I can't really remember! I *was* only five! But they were going somewhere abroad. Look, I'm sorry, but I'm going to need your help. If, as you say, Daddy isn't coming back for some time, then I've got to get all the presents from upstairs. Millie and James would be heartbroken if they thought Santa had let them down!'

She was right of course. And despite my mind reeling, but rallying with renewed hope after the full horror of genuinely believing that my wife had changed beyond all recognition due to mistaken identity, for now, the saving of Christmas was paramount, and I was more than happy to offer my services. Therefore, I awaited my orders from my new friend, nine-year-old Tilly, *not* one of *Yasmin's* four children!

With extreme care, we managed to get Millie into her bed. Though I did have a slight scare, attempting to hang a Christmas stocking at the end of her little brother's bed. James sat bolt upright, muttering a few tired words, his eyes looking directly at us, but something told me that he was of no harm to our plans, as he called Tilly and me *Jake* and *Milo*. I sighed at the instant memory. Evie loved the *Tweenies*. I shook my head in awe. Tilly was my hero as she expertly convinced him that everything was just fine. Her baby brother's head slumped reassuringly back onto his pillow and his eyes fluttered to a close. My heart sighed with relief. As we stepped out onto the landing, Tilly gave me a gentle high five, followed by a whisper.

'Thanks, Ritchie. That's the stockings done, now for the rest of it!'

I frowned a little as I followed Tilly into her mum and dad's bedroom.

'Do you not believe in Santa, Tilly?'

My friend stopped what she was doing and sat on the edge of the huge bed.

'I do, but you can't expect him to bring everything, *can* you?'

She seemed very interested in my response. I shook my head without a flicker of hesitation.

'Ritchie, I found some things this year, all wrapped up in Mum's wardrobe! I, well, I couldn't believe it! I knew that Mum and Dad would never lie to me, but I didn't say anything for days. I felt really sad. But then I knew I had to ask them both. I suppose I was scared that they would be cross with me. Do *you* believe in Santa, Ritchie?'

I didn't need to give the question a thought.

'Absolutely! I get things every Christmas! I send my letter off, thinking that maybe I'm too old and that this might be my unlucky year, but no, because I believe, he keeps coming back!'

Tilly beamed, her head nodding approvingly.

'That's what Dad said! As long as I believe! But because there's three children here, and of course another one on the way, they do like to buy a few of the presents, just to help Santa out! So come on, Ritchie, lets get them downstairs quick!'

I did as I was told. Once our mission was complete, Tilly pushed her hand forward, and I squeezed it and offered her a nod of approval. Though I was reluctant to break the mood, I simply heard the words come out of my mouth.

'You said...*that* Yasmin and her family had gone abroad, do you know where?'

Tilly slumped down onto the settee, pulling Millie's cast-off blanket around her. She didn't look at me, but between tired words she let out an almighty yawn.

'I don't know, you'll have to ask Daddy when he comes back...'

I smiled, frustrated and anxious, but Tilly looked so beautiful as she fell into a well-deserved sleep. But I really didn't want to be here when her father got back, though of course I couldn't leave the children on their own, so I settled myself down into the large comfy armchair, ready for the long night that lay ahead of me. I hadn't planned to close my eyes, and despite trying repeatedly to force them open, I finally accepted that half an hour or so wouldn't do me any harm.

But my sleep was soon filled with disturbed images. I was running from country to country, searching, looking anywhere and everywhere, silly and surreal places! But I simply couldn't find Yasmin and her family. I tossed and turned, Tilly's words just repeating themselves over and over again. And as my nightmare became gradually worse, I was in a hot sweat, convinced I was never going to find my wife again.

My eyes were suddenly wide open after hearing the sound of a front door opening and the excited barking of an overzealous dog. My head was pounding from being woken so suddenly. I tried to clumsily grab my discarded shoes, keen to look awake and responsible, but was beaten to it.

'Good morning! Oh, you look as though you've had a restless night.'

The guy whose name I still didn't know went to step towards me, his hand outstretched. But he was suddenly pulled back and shackled by his youngest children, each grabbing a leg, whilst their father tried to keep his balance. He threw me a beaming smile.

'Well, I have a very important announcement, a few days early I know, but...' The man rested his large hands on the head of each child. 'You two have a little baby brother!'

The now delirious siblings were leaping up and down, shrieking at the top of their voices. Their father's legs finally buckled under the onslaught as Tilly woke, and as though a switch was clicked on and a thousand volts released, she was now throwing herself at her proud father, who was now falling back onto the settee, laughing uncontrollably at the joyous response.

We all listened intently as a blow-by-blow account was relayed, which culminated in the triumphant arrival of baby Tim. The father finally wriggled free from his offspring and managed to stand up. I quickly joined him, pushing my hand out. We shook firmly.

A hesitant pause for breath, and then he said, 'Thank you for your impeccable timing, you really have been an absolute lifesaver! Sue seemed a little surprised when I mentioned you, but then she was a bit out of it, so maybe I can take an address and a number? I'm sure she'll be keen to contact you as soon as she's fit and able!'

I looked down at my feet, hoping that the following words were going to come out right. As I started to speak, I almost felt like I was pulling a *Prince Charles* or *Hugh Grant* face, and I was uncomfortably convinced that I had created an amalgamation of the two!

'I, I think we've got, well, a bit of a funny incident really! It's not actually *your* Yasmin, or should I say Sue, that I know, but the Yasmin that lived here before!'

The man's dark eyebrows raised themselves incredibly high, and then as I continued my explanation, they dropped low and an uncomfortable grimace seemed to spread across his now deeply furrowed brow. I felt it best to simply keep talking.

'Mmmmm, and the chances of your wife being Yasmin, and how at first I simply presumed it *was* her! So, well, you presumed ... I presumed! And here I am, a good few hours later!'

The guy had looked noticeably concerned for a sentence or two more than I would have liked, but finally, the furrows retracting, his face creased completely, and then laughter spilt out and filled the entire room. Fluffers ran for cover into the kitchen.

'Oh my God, I'm *so* sorry! And to have put on you like this!' His hands now pushed into his sides, another laugh pushed forward. 'Bloody hell, you're right, when we first met I don't think we even discussed a name, just that my wife was *your* friend. Oh my God! So you're after Yasmin! Wow! All night I've, I've just kept thinking about the man who arrived in the snowstorm, totally surreal! But you're after the lovely Yasmin. Well, I can't say I blame you for wanting to catch up with her! But, but, oh! I hope I'm not speaking out of turn.'

It was now my turn to laugh and offer my opinion of the beautiful Yasmin.

'No, not easily forgotten. You would be truly amazed if you knew the trouble I was having to go through to catch up with the lady!'

My mind started to wander at the sheer mention of her name, but was suddenly back with the crazy situation in which I found myself.

'My name's Hank by the way. And though I'm sure you've already been introduced, this is Tilly, and Millie, and my youngest, James, though that's not actually the case any more!' Hank ran off towards the kitchen. 'You'll stay for breakfast, Ritchie, tea or coffee?'

How could I refuse? And after a discreet word in Hank's ear, the rest of the Christmas presents miraculously appeared and Tilly looked delighted, her eyes raised to the ceiling, mouthing, 'Thank you, Santa!'

Finally, I left Hank and his beautiful children, I was now armed with valuable information about Yasmin. I couldn't help but shake my head. She wasn't abroad at all, she was actually back up north, as Hank had put it.

'A little town, Ritchie, umm, Willow? Yes, Willow!'

As he said the words, I simply had to catch my breath. But as a smile as full and as vibrant as life itself spread from deep within, I just repeated over and over again in my head, *Yasmin and Willow*, and thought how it sounded just right. And then, light ironic chuckles trickled out of me, as incredibly here was I, two hundred *bloody* miles away, and there was Yasmin, who nearly four years or so ago had taken herself home.

Hank's front door finally closed. As the Jeep roared into life, I waved back at the happy smiling faces in the lounge window, their extra special Christmas ready to begin. But I had one last question and the urge to run and knock on Hank's door just one more time, but instead, I just dropped my fist down onto the steering wheel.

'I don't know her married name!' But then common sense prevailed. 'If Yasmin is in Willow, then I'll find her!'

As the Jeep chugged slowly onto the main street of Dartmouth, I felt a little panicky, as the needle on the fuel gauge was dangerously low. I eased almost completely off the accelerator as I pulled level with the Royal Castle Hotel, but despite wanting to stop, I pushed my foot down a little harder, the prospect of major embarrassment just too daunting. But as I took in the reflection of the hotel in my rear-view mirror, I made a decision that was a little easier in the cold light of day. With a broad nervous smile I pulled the Jeep into a vacant parking space that was one of many – on my previous visits into Dartmouth, when actually finding a vacant parking space it had *felt* like Christmas! So for it to *be* Christmas and finding a parking space...I shook my head at my mindless rantings, and smiled inanely, apologising to my audience above who may or may not be monitoring me. I pushed the Jeep door open. I started to question what I was going to say, but felt it wise to proceed without thinking my actions through. It was a new system for me, and had worked last night in giving me the courage to go up to the Old School House. So now I had to face the hotel in the same way.

Once inside, the place was far quieter than usual, but then it was barely 11 a.m., and it was Christmas morning. As I approached the reception desk, my heart started to pound, many good reasons for not being here now at the very fore of my mind. My heartbeat was all I could hear as I pressed the bell, but was then joined with an internal chanting, over and over: *please let it be Kelly, please let it be Kelly*. I changed my stance a dozen times, ready to face a conversation that would offer only confusion for the poor individual that had drawn the short straw – not only to be working on Christmas Day, but to have to face me and my madness. I stood barely breathing and then pushed the bell again, my patience threadbare and desperate to get this over with. As a few more moments passed by, gratefully my thumping heartbeat softened. I placed my hands down on the counter, my confidence building a little. I craned my ears, as I was convinced I could hear a gentle sobbing and not too far away from me. I stood back, keen not to pry, but then felt concerned. I leant further over the counter and could now hear words mixed in with heavy sobs.

'You have left me with *nothing*, you're a *total* bastard! You ... you must have been planning this for months, Dave!'

I leant forward a little more, and then without warning the reception bell was ringing out. I quickly looked down and saw that my elbow had hit a bull's eye right in the dead centre of the hotel buzzer.

'Shit!'

Everything went quiet, the sobbing stopped and then came a hurried, 'Well, I hope you can sleep at night!' followed by a loud replacing of the receiver.

The sudden silence was quickly followed by a good blow of the nose and then a little gallop of footsteps, finally producing a defiant smiling face.

'Sorry to keep you, sir! *Oh my God, it's you!*'

And there she was, my prayers answered. As she travelled quickly around the side of the counter, she threw her arms around me, kissing me warmly on the cheek. I held on to her warmth and friendliness, recharging me physically and mentally, and so very welcome. But then naturally the questions started.

'Where on earth have you been?' She stepped back, taking my hands. 'Mr Angel, you look *bloody* awful!'

I shook my head. I had no opinion – I didn't know what I looked like any more. Kelly dropped my hands and stepped back behind reception, shaking her head and talking openly.

'Jim, remember Jim, the porter? He's still here, and he said that your Jeep was still standing on Blackpool Sands. But, oh my God, Mr Angel, you've become quite a myth, err, legend? I always get those two mixed up! But whichever, you're certainly a regular topic of conversation in Dartmouth!'

As I beamed back at the warm smiling face before me, I wasn't quite sure what to say.

'Mmmm, Kelly, you're lovely to have remembered me! I know you would like me to give you some sort of explanation, but the truth is, well, I don't really know what happens to me!'

Kelly took my hand then guided me around the counter, then led me through a small door at the side of reception. She pointed to a comfy-looking chair in the corner of the room and grabbed the kettle from off the top of the filing cabinet.

'Tea or coffee?'

I wanted to say that I simply didn't have the time, that I needed desperately to get back home, but somehow the words, 'Coffee, black,' came out of my mouth.

As I sank back into the ridiculously comfy chair, I tried to think of a plausible, but not too alarming explanation for my incredibly long disappearance. But I couldn't think of anything. After each question, I would react by simply pulling a silly face and just shrug my shoulders.

'Kelly, I know you must think that I am *totally* mad, but I have *no* explanation! I simply *don't* know what happens to me!'

We looked at each other, not a word spoken. As the kettle started to boil, I tried to inject some humour.

'Maybe I've been kidnapped by aliens, been used for experiments. All I know is that, well, the only thing I am sure of is that it really pisses me off!'

Kelly laughed out loud, shaking her head and repeating, 'Poor Mr Angel, poor, poor Mr Angel!'

But then I felt it was my turn to ask the questions.

'Enough about me and my problems, what about you? Are *you* alright? It's just that, well, was it you crying when I got here, on the phone?'

Kelly forced a smile, her cheeks blushing a little.

'Oh, I'm sorry about that, not very professional!'

I smiled, shaking my head.

'Look, Kelly, you've always been *so* lovely with me, it's just that you didn't sound too happy on the phone. I know it's none of my business, and I may be a mad stranger that keeps disappearing at the drop of a hat, but I have been told that I am an excellent listener!'

Kelly didn't say anything for a minute or two, but as she handed me my black coffee, she perched herself on the edge of the chair opposite me.

'Mr Angel, I've been so stupid! Everyone warned me, but I

love, well, *loved* Dave *so* much… *Oh God!'* The tears started to well up in my friend's heavily made-up eyes, but then an admirable resolve took over. 'You see, Mr Angel, I lost both my parents about a year ago in a horrific car accident. Well, I am an only child, and, well, I was left everything my parents had, and that's when Dave took a shine to me. I couldn't believe he would be interested in me. He was the handsome restaurant manager! Oh no, look at me going on!'

She dabbed her eyes, a wave of embarrassment creeping over her.

'Please, Kelly, what's he done? Got another girlfriend?'

Kelly stood up as though she was about to leave the room, but then closed the glass door and sat back down.

'I've lost everything. He's been incredibly cunning. Everything to do with paperwork, contracts for buying our new home, I just totally trusted him!'

She started to sob again. I heaved myself up out of the heavenly chair and stepped towards her, falling to my knees and wrapping my arms around her.

'Mr Angel, he … he…'

'Please, Kelly, call me Ritchie!'

And through her tears, I could just make out how my lovely friend had been so badly treated.

'He's taken the lot Ritchie, moved some other girl in. I thought we were *so* happy, but last night I went home, ready for our *first* Christmas together, and the locks have been changed! The house that I totally paid for, all my savings, *all* gone! My parents didn't have much, but I've let them down, and lost it all!' Kelly let all her tears out. 'And he told me to keep away, to take a room here at the hotel…'

After an hour or so, and a few well-chosen words, Kelly forced a smile, followed by a small giggle.

'Thank you, Ritchie, you're very kind.'

I assured her it was she that was the lifesaver, and though I hated to bring the subject up, I had a major favour to ask her. I cringed as the words came out, especially in light of her financial misfortune with the last man she had trusted with her money, but I was desperate.

'Kelly, um, my immediate problem *is*, I need to get back

home, back up to Willow! My credit card is years out of date, and I just wonder whether you would trust me and lend me fifty pounds?'

My face must have been an absolute picture as I asked for the money; I was certainly cringing inside.

'If it's any kind of problem I can ring my accountant friend, and he would be more than happy to give you his credit card details over the phone so that you can advance me some money from the hotel perhaps? But, well, it's just that I may give him a heart attack just ringing out of the blue, especially after nearly seven years!'

Kelly didn't bat an eyelid and just rummaged in her handbag.

'Here, Ritchie. But on one condition...you let me have a photo of us both together. The chef will take it, he's got one of those *Polaroid* cameras, you know? Just in case we get someone famous in here, *like* yourself! And I want you to sign and *date* it...because nobody will believe I've seen you otherwise!'

What could I say? I was certainly more than happy with the terms. Kelly handed me the fifty pounds, her mascara reminiscent of *Alice Cooper* after a heavy night out, but of course her kindness and natural beauty shone through.

'It's only my bonus, tight gits! The hours I put in here, even though it was my choice to do the dreaded Christmas Day... Well, without Mum and Dad ... and Dave *had* agreed to join me here for lunch.' Kelly paused for a brief moment, and then forced a smile. 'So I was happy to take the shift that nobody wanted. But the money's yours and it's up to you whether you send it back to me.'

I assured her that she certainly would get the money back. The chef soon took the picture Kelly had asked for, and once I had given her a big hug and an even bigger thank you, I left.

CHAPTER TWENTY-SIX

My Date With Destiny

After Death, 2004 – Lilac Sky

Christmas Day and it wasn't easy getting a ferry. The grumpy guy wanted to wait another hour at least, he said, as he'd planned to do a 2 p.m. and a teatime crossing only. But finally, with a begrudging smile, he took pity on me. And so, with me as the sole passenger, Bill the ferryman made the journey across the water. With the chugging of the tugboat, mixed in with the sound of the hungry seagulls, I couldn't help but look back at Dartmouth and the harsh memories that would stay with me forever. I searched desperately for answers as to how the horrific surge in time could possibly damage any possible reunion with Yasmin. But as my mind rambled, I felt it possible that sense and logic would only be obvious once this adventure came to its natural conclusion. To lift my spirits, I imagined the scene. My warm and rested body lying without a care in the world in the master bedroom at the Water's Edge, my wife sleeping and content at my side, our beautiful daughter lying across us both, dreaming soundly.

I jumped as the front of the ferry was slammed down onto the black oily concrete, and felt excitement as the ferry gates opened. I wound down my driver's window and shook the heavily bearded man's hand.

'There you go, Bill, you grumpy old bastard, have a Christmas drink on me!'

He didn't bat an eyelid. As the Jeep drove steadily onto dry land, I prayed that within hours I would have my answer to this madness. And as I pushed down onto the accelerator, I caught a glimpse of Bill holding up the ten-pound note I'd given him, checking to see it if was real, and I had to smile!

As I took the winding roads away from Dartmouth, so many thoughts ran through my confused mind, *so* many questions! I shook my head, bewildered, and pushed out with a large huff the mounting stress. As a chance distraction, I turned on the radio.

I pushed back into my seat, my arms outstretched on the

steering wheel, and just repeated over and over again under my breath, 'Almost eight years, gone just like that! What the hell am I going home to?'

When my life had suddenly fast-forwarded before, it was always with me playing my part, or at least I thought I had. Nobody questioned where I had been, because I'd never left! And each time varied; sometimes I would fast-forward just a few days, sometimes months and even a couple of years. But for some reason, this time things felt *so* different.

Once I'd put sufficient fuel into the Jeep, I jangled the loose change in my hand. I spotted a phone box by a bus shelter on the other side of the road.

'Hello, yes, Willow! Ummm, a Peter Crabtree, yes, it may be a residential number ... possibly, perhaps under Chartered Accountant?'

I waited; a calm exterior, but butterflies rampant inside of my stomach. *Think of nice relaxing things, Ritchie boy.* I pressed my face up against the telephone box window, forcing myself to take in this very special Christmas Day and all that it meant, but then found myself reading all and sundry emblazoned on the scratched and graffiti-riddled glass.

'Here's your number, sir.'

We exchanged our Christmas greetings, and the operator was gone. I punched in the now vaguely familiar digits, and then as I heard a voice I quickly pushed several coins into the slot. A huge smile spread across my face as Peter's voice boomed out, but then my heart sank.

'We're sorry that we are not here to take your call...'

I waited for the tone.

'Peter, God, I hope you're sitting down. It's Ritchie, umm, Ritchie Angel. Remember me? Well, as you can hear, I'm alive and well! Please forgive me, I am so sorry not to have been in touch before now, but as always, I have an important request. Oh, and I will be back in Willow very soon, or at least I hope so. Do you remember, my old friend, that I wanted to make good use of that fifteen thousand pounds that we'd simply put aside, ill-gotten gains and all that? Well, I've now got the deserving party! A Miss Kelly Harris, the Royal Castle Hotel, Dartmouth, the full fifteen thousand, Peter! Just sign a note for me, ummm, *lots of love, Ritchie Angel, aka The Disappearing Madman, kisses,* that sort of thing! All things being equal and such like, I'll speak to you or see you in the New Year. Take care, and *thank you!'*

I replaced the receiver and stood for a moment, hoping that I would be around to see Peter, and tried to shake away the doubts in my mind.

I finally climbed back into my Jeep, throwing my jacket onto the back seat and turning up the radio full blast, and it wasn't long before I was eating up the miles on the motorway heading north. Despite the volume, the questions kept banging around my head, nostalgic song after song being played but failing to avert a single probing concern at what lay ahead for me. As I drove, familiar signposts counted me down to my date with destiny, and I couldn't help but feel that my nerves were unravelling with every mile. My thoughts were distracted as a tune that meant so much to me filled the airwaves, every word familiar and painfully poignant: *Somewhere Over The Rainbow.* I felt my heart strings tighten with the memory of Yasmin, Evie and me, all together on the journey home from our first flight in *The Angel.* I recalled our close shave at the traffic lights, my fear that we could all have been so easily killed. But the song had meant so much to my wife and me. And as I relived the significance of it, I simply couldn't stop the sudden sting in my eyes. Evie singing her little heart out at her first nativity play; Yasmin in tears as she watched our little girl, fearless and triumphant! I had to shake away the images as they came thick and fast; it was just too much. I shuffled about in my seat, my bottom having gone numb. I ran my hand across my stomach, surprised at how much heavier I had become since my full-throttle projection in time. I couldn't believe how ageing eight years so quickly made me feel so aware of a few extra pounds on my body. Ageing on a day-to-day basis could be bad enough, *but eight years?* Click of the fingers, *gone!*

As the afternoon sunshine welcomed me into the Midlands, I was grateful that we were free of snow and the day was bright; it bolstered the spirits. Though the Jeep wasn't faring quite so well, coughing and spluttering a little worryingly, I just kept the prayers coming and the fingers tightly crossed, repeating over and over that as long as it got me back to Willow, then its job would be done – it was then free to rest in peace for the remainder of its days. But as the engine seemed to be progressively weakening, I went as far as to promise it that I would display the heroic vehicle in a glass cage at the Water's Edge as a symbol of my gratitude. I started to bite the inside of my mouth, deeply hopeful that the Jeep was listening.

The next motorway exit was mine, but the fear of what lay ahead made me ease off the accelerator, almost freewheeling up towards the island. In an attempt to come up with some sort of strategy, I tried to decide who I needed to see first. Jimmy? Scottie? Perhaps Leoni? Who would be able to give me the answers I so desperately needed? And as the roads became increasingly familiar, the same old scenarios just kept replaying over and over again in my battle-weary mind. Yasmin, she'd be thirty-four! Evie, she would be four and a half by now! God help me, how was everything going to work out for Evie? If I failed to get my old life back, if I was destined to stay in this world, where on earth would there be a place for Evie? The perspiration drenched me, and I was burning up at the mere thought of *no* Evie. But should it be so? Then like the acid that was filling my stomach at the very thought of such an evil atrocity, I would choose to let it dissolve me here and now – I would take my chances as a dead man, because this was an eternal hell. Suddenly, the tears were running from my eyes, my frustration and fears spilling out of me. *For fuck's sake, Ritchie, be a man! Take back what is yours!* I shook my head with such vigour that I was convinced I had dislocated my neck. But as I rotated my head from left to right, I felt my joints and muscles click back into position. I brushed my fingers across my eyes, determined that from this moment on, the bullshit negativity, tears and self-pity were going to have to stop. To see this through, to have any chance of success, I had to keep control and focus on the next few crucial hours.

I clicked down on the indicator: *Willow, one mile!* I grinned and started to nod my head. 'This is it, Ritchie boy, *this is it!*' My foot was now pushed to the floor, the reluctance and obvious pain of the Jeep engine not worthy of a second thought. The sky was blue and vibrant, but then as though it knew I was looking at it, clouds of dark and angry purple started to roll in like black sheep surrounding a cowering sheep dog.

As I turned into Willow High Street, the tyres squealing their disapproval, I finally pushed my foot hard onto the brake, disengaging the gears, freewheeling slowly, taking in the changes. *God, it's weird to be home!* I looked at the different buildings that I owned, and all appeared as it should. As I approached Skirdle's, I nodded my head in acknowledgment, and then across the street, the large McDonald's stood loud and proud on the Old Bakery site. I was convinced I saw a face at the upstairs window – not just any face, but evil and haunting. I blinked my eyes furiously, convinced I had just seen Harry Christian...I *slammed* my foot onto the brake, bringing the Jeep to a standstill. I left the engine running, just desperate to get out. But as the image of the Old Bakery seemed to spin around my head, the face was gone. I stood with my back to the Jeep, my feet either side of the white painted line in the middle of the road, a cold wind battering my body. Though all around me was calm, it was as though I was in my own personal bubble, caught-up in a destructive windstorm and a stench that made my hair stand on end, but I was ready to fight – to the death if I had to. The time had come. I struggled to move, to turn, but battled the intensity of a deathly pain, and finally managed to face back up the high street, the icy wind battering, pushing and pulling me, its strength and determination increasing, now riveting me to the spot. I wanted to force myself forward, but voices started to bounce off me, spitting and lashing around my head, getting louder by the second. Spikes of sound were drilling into me, deep and penetrating. I wanted to run, but my body started to shake, my ears at bursting point, and then it all stopped. I dropped to my knees.

I was now aware of ice and snow all around me. I could move my eyes to the left and right of me, but my body was not functioning. I started to panic, but I was totally devoid of doing anything physically, and *then* my body started to respond, my breathing heavy and my head spinning, my hands pushed instinctively forward, stopping me from falling face first into the thick snow before me.

And then nothing; peace and quiet surrounded me. *I think I have died.* And how I would imagine death to be, for what seemed like an eternity my mind totally closed down, pure blackness. No thoughts, just an emptiness devoid of any view, to the past, present or future.

And then a click, a shard of light in the distance, and with it a view, suddenly, to the past, present and future. And then, without warning, my head jolted sharply, my eyes stretched fully open. But then gradually, I was able to rotate my head and deep grateful breaths were drawn.

I slowly lifted my head up, my eyes blinking furiously, my nostrils filled with clean fresh air. My snowstorm madness was now extended to all and everything around me. But then I focused on a young couple, pulling their two small children on a home-made sledge. They could see me, but seemed keen to trudge past me. They tried not to look directly at me, but their children couldn't hide their amusement at the madman kneeling in the middle of the road, as though praying before his Jeep, deep snow and ice putting a virginal glaze on all it kissed. As they passed by, inhibitions seemed to kick in and I stood up quickly, over-exaggerating a smile and the manner in which I brushed myself down. I laughed in the family's direction; they were laughing, as if all they had seen was some huge joke.

As they turned the corner, I ran around the Jeep, desperate to get the driver's door open, but I was unable to. I pulled hard, but I must have locked it. I raced to the other side, but that door was locked too. I ran to the back of the Jeep, trying to lift up the tailgate and then the soft top, but all I found was a deep-rooted resistance. Suddenly, the town hall clock boomed out, startling me, making me turn; it chimed four times. I turned back around sharply as though someone was calling me, but there was nothing and no one, and then I blinked my eyes furiously, as the Jeep was *gone!* I couldn't move, my heart visibly pounding through my white cotton T-shirt. I ran my hands up my body and onto my heavily unshaven jaw, my head shaking from side to side, my fingers now firmly entangled in my hair. And then curt, demanding whispers made me turn around quickly. I froze to the spot. Then the voices got louder, and the bitter wind was slapping me sharply. As it got colder, it grew in its rage, like little razor blades swooping and slashing at my vulnerability. To save myself I knew I had to run, to get away, but as I was heading away from the wind, the voices were laughing and telling me to run faster! And then the voices seemed to be in front of me, calling me, drawing me purposely forward, and I realised that I was being summoned ... and then an image of the Water's Edge.

I just ran, and kept running as fast as I could. Nothing else mattered, I just had to get *home*. But who was calling me? What would I find when I got there? But then logic told me that perhaps it was only Rose; not Yasmin, not Evie. But still I pushed my heavy body, my heaving ice-filled lungs ready to burst, but nothing was going to stop me, though the now Ice Age surroundings were making it increasingly treacherous underfoot. I ran past the small row of bungalows. I glanced up, wondering how Mrs Heart was doing, and felt concerned as I noticed a Skirdle's 'For Sale' sign at the foot of her front garden. But I just kept running. And as the heavy drifts of snow crowned the wild and unkempt hedgerow, it wasn't long before I noticed a heart-sinking monstrosity just a hundred or so metres away. *Bloody hell! What on God's earth is that?* Though I had been looking for the tatty five-bar gate, with the 'Keep Out' sign reassuringly guarding my beautiful spinney, instead I found two great big red brick pillars. I stooped before them, my hands on my hips, desperately trying to recapture my breath that this unfit body so urgently needed. My sweaty hands were now wrapped around thick iron that formed a pair of black gloss gates, which stood guarding my dream home. I tried desperately to see what had been built here in my absence, but all that greeted me was a neat line of snow covered conifers twisting strategically down towards the Water's Edge. I stood back, my eyes were suddenly drawn to a plaque set into one of the pillars, frozen snow partly covering the enscribed brass. I rubbed furiously, my nails scraping urgently into the snow, my heart thumping painfully, and then, 'RED HOUSE.' I stepped back, my hands placed onto the top of my head, almost ready to tear my hair out. My breath was wheezing, tinged with heart splitting emotion, molten tears ready to burst out - but I refused to let them. I placed my hands over my eyes, comfortable within the dark. I then lowered them slowly, and yet nothing had changed.

'But Peter had assured me that I had bought this land, so *who* the hell is responsible for *this?*'

My mind was scrolling desperate for answers, both my hands back on top of my head, my breath being released in short, sharp bursts. I continued to stand, unable to do anything other than shake my head at this intrusion, wondering what on earth I should, or could do. But there was only ever going to be one answer: I was going in! I walked for several metres left and right of the gates, but felt a little unnerved by the buzzing noise coming from the layers of wire thread through the thickly formed conifers. So as I stood before the high imposing gates, I wedged my feet between the intricate wrought iron – minus fifteen-degree icicles – determined to resist my intrusion. But I wasn't for stopping. My fingers seemed to weld tight as I pulled my body up towards the next foothold. But the higher I got, the sharp arrow spikes felt as though they were going to puncture the soles of my boots – but I didn't care, I just kept climbing. Once at the top, I had run out of ideas as to my next move, though it soon dawned on me that the only way to get over the top of the gates was to literally throw myself over. I paused, and then having confirmed there was no other way I took a deep breath and hurled myself over the top spikes. I felt a sharp gouge as a lump of flesh was torn out of my thigh, but the stinging pain was soon replaced as I slammed hard onto the sheet of ice that encased the cobbled driveway below. The full force of my thirty-four-year-old bones slammed unforgivingly onto immovable ground, the shock of the impact leaving my entire body breathless and interestingly twisted. Despite the feeling that I was never going to be able to move again, I instinctively dragged myself into the welcome cover of the conifers. As I slumped amongst the undergrowth, I inspected the blood now seeping from beneath my torn jeans.

I shook my head from side to side, wincing and laughing sympathetically under my breath, grabbing a handful of snow and clamping it firmly against my wound. But then the desire to see the impostor that had destroyed my dream home forced me to my feet. I moved as quickly as I could, following more spaced-out conifers that lined the long twisting driveway.

Finally, I stood, my mouth open and my eyes wide, at the top of a sweeping lawn. I couldn't quite believe the palatial monstrosity that stood before me – expensive and grand. But lacking the subtlety, the timeless natural beauty that I felt Yasmin and I had succeeded in creating. But here, now, was something that looked as though... An angst-raised smile filled my mind, and then I laughed nervously at my ridiculous and totally irrelevant concern. This wasn't about *the* house, I simply wasn't interested in *this* bloody house! Something or someone had brought me here, and I was going to find out why.

I made my way along the edge of the lawn, and looked back at my footprints clearly obvious in the otherwise untouched snow. As I took in the jarring surroundings, I could see cameras and security lights, and was beginning to believe that I would be spotted at any second if I hadn't been already. I hesitantly made my way towards the edge of a paved patio, lined with even more conifers in huge beige urns. I crouched down, wondering whether or not the householder knew they had a trespasser. I kept totally still, and watched for some sort of activity. But all was quiet and still. My confidence building, I crawled a little closer to the house, my T-shirt and jeans soaked through to the skin, my fingers almost totally numb. I could just make out through large Georgian patio doors, the lights of a Christmas tree. There were a couple of lamps on in the lounge, but no sign of life. I urgently threw myself and rolled towards a huge brick-built barbecue area, as I could hear voices coming from the woods that ran alongside the canal. My heart was racing as I scrambled forward on my stomach to see *who* was coming. I peered through the icicle-laden branches of yet another conifer and sighed nervously, but was grateful for a better view of the approaching voices.

As I looked across the perfectly flat snow topped lawn, I could just make out a man and a woman, all wrapped up warmly. The woman had a red wool hat pulled down around her face; the man was wearing a similar hat, but his was black, with a matching thick wool scarf wrapped around his neck and mouth. I could feel the venom of the ice that was making itself known through my jeans, and my knees and shins were aching with cold. I was desperate to stand, so I eased myself up, now adopting a stooped standing position. The man pulled away from the woman as the bark of a dog tried to tease him into giving chase. My eyes were then drawn to a young girl, nine or ten years of age, running, smiling and laughing as she too made her way out of the woods. She was wrapped up festively in a thick red fur coat, with a matching fur hat and a white wool scarf tied loosely around her neck. Suddenly, the Labrador was spinning around, chasing its own tail, and as it got nearer, my heart seemed to stall. *Fluffers ... surely it can't be?* And then as my eyes were drawn to the woman, who was now well ahead of the man and girl, my breathing became intermittent, my throat starting to burn. It was Yasmin!

Her posture, her aura, just spiralled hypnotically around her. *Oh my God! Yasmin, I've found you...* I simply froze, physically, mentally; I really couldn't believe that she was *here* at the Water's Edge. I pressed my fingers to my lips, stinging tears now icy-cold running onto my nails. I could not move. But then I was eternally grateful as a surge of adrenalin kick-started my senses, and my hand dropped from my lips onto my heart, almost massaging a reassurance, faint but determined words: *Come on, Ritchie, you can do this!* My heartbeat was in my ears, my breath like a steam train in the zero temperatures.

I simply wanted to run out and hug my very existence into Yasmin, but just as I ill-advisedly stepped forward, the man and the young girl were running into the picture, their hands tightly together, being pursued by their clown of a dog. But then almost instantly the snow-covered beast stopped, dropped its head and turned its eyes towards me. I instinctively craned my head back, receding carefully, quietly, but then froze, and just as I was about to panic and give myself up, the dog appeared to blink at me, bark, and then turned and bound towards the canal. The man suddenly let go of the girl, beckoning for her to join her mum. As the girl spun around, singing her heart out, skipping and jumping, the tears started to run down my face, free now to drop off my chapped lips – just the memory of Evie, but having to accept that *this* was *not* Evie.

But as I revelled briefly, indulgently, in the fantasy that I was seeing my wonderful daughter, I had to accept that as amazing as it was to see Yasmin, there was no changing the fact that she was now mother to a beautiful young girl who simply wasn't mine. I was having to digest the fact that Yasmin was here at the *supposed* Water's Edge, but with two imposters. I swallowed hard and focused on Yasmin and her daughter now inside the kitchen. I edged closer, but suddenly had to almost lie on the snow-covered patio, face down, as the man walked towards the house. I lay down as low as I could, convinced that the hound would sniff me out. I couldn't see anything, but then my ears were full of Yasmin calling their dog, and suddenly the chill up my spine became a spear of ice.

'*Fluffers!* Come on, girl, come on, you *clever* girl!'

Though I had presumed a name for the dog here at the Water's Edge, and with all that Tilly had told me perhaps I shouldn't have been surprised, but to actually hear her name called in this lifetime, well, it was too much. But as I shook my head from side to side and lifted my eyes a little, I took my chance and crept towards one of the large urns just outside the kitchen patio doors. I could see Yasmin and her daughter clearly now. The man had his back to me. Yasmin was hanging her coat and hat up, and then dropped onto her knees, helping the young girl take off her boots. As the *perfect* little family laughed and joked, I caught the daughter's eyes, and they simply sparkled; there was no mistaking the deep dazzling blue, undoubtedly her mother's eyes! My heart thumped, a deep rooted sorrow, bereft of hope. Unjust surrealism filtering through me, its jagged, razor blade punctures repugnant and very possibly fatal as I attempted to proceed in getting back all that was mine: *but how the hell was I going to do that?* My attention was quickly averted to the man as he lifted off his hat and unravelled his scarf, his jet-black greasy hair looking horrendously, painfully familiar. And then, as though something drew his attention, he turned and appeared to look directly at me, and I couldn't stop myself. I was heaving, pungent sick splattering against the side of the urn, bouncing up against the red brickwork. As I ran my hand across my mouth, I stood up, shaking from head to foot.

'Jack De'Vil ... please, *no!'*

I couldn't stop staring at the nightmare in front of me: Yasmin, her daughter, and the supposedly dead Jack De'Vil. As I stood, a frozen lost soul, I expected them all to spot me at any second, but they didn't. And suddenly, instinctively, I found myself retreating back under the cover of the shrubbery. The tears were rolling down my face, the words in my head just repeating over and over again: *was this some kind of sick joke?* I forced my thumb and finger together, pinching my numb flesh for all it was worth, but I felt the pain sharply enough. I certainly wasn't dreaming. And as I watched the three of them hugging and kissing, exactly the way that we had as the *Angel* family, I heaved again, and the wrench that I thought would kill me forced me to slump down onto the snow, hot stinging tears falling like molten lava.

I must have sat there for hours, just watching - hyperthermia losing out to a cast iron will, a full and resolute refusal to simply accept the loss of such an all consuming love. I tried to make sense of all that stood before. How could this have happened? Jack was supposedly dead. The explosion. The body. Everybody just presumed. I couldn't believe that he was now back to haunt me. I knew that I was wrong to have sent him to the bakery, I knew that him going there meant he would possibly be killed, and though I often felt guilty, it was exactly what I had wanted. He was ready to terrorise me, and he was good at it. So, when he was gone, it removed a huge black cloud. As I continued to sit, numbly watching the horrendous scenes unfold, I began to think that I had been set up. This was all so very, *very* wrong. I was beginning to believe justifiably that I was in *hell*. Surely death was easier than all that I had been through, and *continued* to go through? This was a truly convincing form of hell on earth. And as I watched the love of my life and her daughter, I knew that they were with the *devil* himself. He'd won, and I was the fool! This wasn't about me, this was all about Jack getting *his* revenge. After all, the more I thought about it, he was the injured party. He loved Julie, but he found out that I was the father of his beautiful little girl.

When he tried to live with it, for the sake of keeping everything that was important to him, I stepped in and destroyed *his* life! Sleeping with his wife, her final betrayal, simply pushed him over the edge. I relived the confrontation in the lounge at the Old Church, the look of total agony on Jack's face, how he wanted me to get Yasmin to come over so she could see what a lying, useless shit I was. Jack didn't seem to care whether he lived or died, his eyes told me he was dead already, and I had done that to him. And yet, rather than equal things up, let him destroy my life with Yasmin, to protect myself, to save what was important to me, I had one chance to finish him off, and whether that was right or wrong – I took it!

The darkness fell around me, the severe frost crystallising all it touched. And that's how my heart felt, numb and close to flatlining, unable to fight back from all that nature had thrown at it.

When the time came for their daughter to go to bed, the way she hugged and kissed her father goodnight was just another nail being thrust into my coffin. I should have gone there and then, but where on this godforsaken earth was I supposed to go? I could see so clearly through the large windows the warmth and brightness of what was going on inside, and I was like a moth to the flame, knowing full well that every loving scene was signing my death warrant, but I found myself simply unable to move. Instead, the torture continued, as each window lit up another example of happy families being played out. And how I managed to watch what happened next simply defied my character and supposed feelings for Yasmin.

The daughter of Jack and Yasmin was now fast asleep, tucked up in her bed. Yasmin was lying next to the open fire in the lounge, and Jack had taken himself off for a shower. The more time Jack and Yasmin spent apart, I felt a seed of hope growing that perhaps they weren't as close as they first appeared to be. But as the bedroom light was turned off, within a minute or so the lounge door was open, and in walked Jack, his tanned, muscular body bringing a smile from Yasmin as she peered over the top of her novel. Jack stood dressed only in a pair of white and navy striped boxer shorts. I *prayed* that Yasmin would lower her eyes and carry on reading, but as she placed her book down, Jack stooped, pulling my beautiful wife to him. Yasmin's thin wool jumper was being expertly lifted over her head and thrown to the floor. He started to nuzzle her neck, Yasmin's eyes closing in response, the look of ecstasy on her face pushing the stake further through my heart. I looked around frantically, desperate for something to throw through the patio doors, anything to make this nightmare stop. But then Jack's hands were cupping Yasmin's naked breasts, caressing, then gently kissing, arousing her. Her fingers were firm and longing on Jack's back, then easing his boxer shorts down, and within seconds she was being lifted up as though a rag doll, her jeans and white lacy thong off and joining the rest of her clothes on the floor. I wanted to run, throw up, scream, but I couldn't do anything. There was Yasmin, the love of my life, being taken willingly by another man, and not just any man, but a sworn and sadistic enemy, and so hated that I had killed him twice. The tears started to fall, something that I was actually capable of doing, my blurred vision not hiding the fact that here were two people very much in love.

I finally managed to stand up, my legs shaking, barely able to put one foot in front of the other, but I had to get away. I staggered towards the main gates, security lights being triggered from every angle. But each time I turned around, I could see Yasmin and Jack, but both totally oblivious to me and *any* possible threat that I held.

The jolt of the hard road shot through me as I jumped down from the top of the iron gates. I didn't *disembowel* myself this time, just rolled and thumped against the compacted ice. But as I sat and looked up at the lilac-filled night, I knew nothing could hurt me ever again. I was now a hollow, empty soul, so how could a dead empty shell ever feel pain again? Suddenly, snowflakes started to fall and my eyes blinked, each flake trying to remind me that I wasn't dead yet and seeming to light something deep from within. A voice of existence emerged, and I let out an almighty roar.

'*MERRY FUCKING CHRISTMAS, ROSE!*'

Without warning or any particular plan to do so, I was walking away from all that I wanted, like an injured animal taking itself away to lick its wounds, and for a rock-bottom moment I pondered perhaps taking myself off to die. But as the falling snow became thick and swirling around me, I felt the urge to find shelter, a survival instinct rising from deep down inside of me. I started to imagine a hot shower, and was grateful that I was not giving up. I wasn't ready to die, I was being driven on, and so I went with it. Sky Cottage filled my head; an open door, friendly faces. I actually let out a small wry chuckle, as I doubted whether Leoni and Tia would still be there. But it was probably the closest place to get to, and so I trudged on. Then as my mind raced, I stopped, panic sinking through me, a flurry of 'what to do's,' and then wanting to go back to the Water's Edge, make them both see me! But as I approached the gates, within seconds I would be walking away. And then I would be at the gates again, desperate not to leave Yasmin behind, but then I would be walking away, my head in my hands, and each time the security lights would flick on, and the painful memories of what I'd seen would see me heading off into the night, this time determined just to keep walking.

The crunch, slip and slide of every step produced quite a beat, and I didn't want it to stop. I tried to focus desperately on getting some rest, to wake in the morning, to then challenge for what was mine. But despite trying to think only of the positive, there, pushing itself to the front of my mind, was the feeling that Rose had set me up. I was never going to be allowed back into my original world, I was just a disillusioned fool. And as my feet pushed forward, I had to accept that this whole adventure was getting worse as time progressed. After all, what on earth had I achieved? I started with the positive: Lillie – my only success! At least I had got to know her, love her, and I prayed that she knew I loved her. The fact that she now came to me, through the medium of water, convinced me that she did know that I loved her very much. And as for Julie, I hated myself for not being able to stop her from taking her own life. I swallowed hard at the mere thought. But then on a positive day, I could be found to accept that it was down to the shear grief of losing Lillie that had shown her no mercy. It was enough for any mother to consider that the pain was just too unbearable, and Julie had never once blamed me, so I needed to accept that. And as I pondered the thought, I smiled, shaking my head positively, as I recalled Lillie relaying that in time, her mum would join us for one of our swims together. I tried to keep my thoughts as rational as possible, but I was beginning to wonder whether or not I was actually dead, simply drifting around in purgatory. But as the bitterly cold snowflakes fell onto my tear-stained face, something told me that I was very much alive.

As I walked, I thought about Harry Christian, a major failure. But then I hadn't counted on him slipping through the net, making it impossible to put things right there. I tried to give him and Alice the extra money, but he knew I was simply trying to save myself, but then wasn't that the whole idea of me being given the second chance? Poor old Harry had no forgiveness in him, and so he paid the ultimate price. And what about my best friend Jimmy? How could I be trying to make things right, and yet get my best friend's future wife pregnant? I knew they were destined to be together, but for some insane reason, though I was convinced it was Yasmin at the time, a disastrous mistake was made, and Sally was pregnant by the wrong man! And though they seemed happy, they both had to live with this terrible fact. And though far less important, I of course blamed myself, and as a consequence, felt bad in their company, therefore tarnishing a cherished friendship. How can that be remotely positive? I could only chalk this one up as a complete and utter disaster.

As for Jack De'Vil, circumstances gave us a fresh start. He seemed to have respect for me at first, and so we both tolerated each other happily. However, the truth about Lillie was already set in stone. Therefore, it was only a matter of time before he realised we were never to be friends. It was then that I saw the old Jack. I may well have panicked, but I was convinced we were back to square one – him or me. Surely under those circumstances I had a right to defend myself? But it didn't change the fact that I had felt incredibly guilty sending him off to his potential death. Though as time often reveals all, my regret was a misplaced one, as it did appear that Jack was *very much* alive and well, and in the worst possible way; him, Yasmin and their beautiful daughter, the perfect family, all living at the Water's Edge or should I say *Red House!* So if you looked at the evidence, had Rose set me up? Was I being ridiculous, paranoid? I raised my eyes skyward, begging for an answer.

'ROSE, PLEASE!' And then more humbly, 'If you're out there, *please* come and talk to me, just let me know. I'm sure I deserve *all* that has happened, but please, can we put a stop to this torture?'

But as I walked, I remained alone. And as the moon shone down on me, flickering lilac flurries of snow appeared like angry angels' wings soaked in their own tears, and it was all that I could see, my hands now covering my eyes, unable to take it any more. As I cowered down, all I was sure of was the fact that all I dared to touch inevitably became tainted and diseased beyond all recognition. But then, when all the madness seemed to be bubbling furiously in my head, I heard a loud screech of brakes, and my body suddenly crumpled beneath the impact, my lungs squeezed dry of air, and then all was black.

As my body slammed onto the snow-covered ground, all I could hear was, 'Yasmin, Evie, Lillie...Please forgive me!'

The pain drained from my body, but the sadness remained. The snow was sticking, incredibly thick now. And as I looked down at myself lying on the crisp white snow, the lilac tinge, fading fast. I smiled as I took in the scene – not a mark of happiness, but perhaps a show that accepted my defeat. I didn't feel comfortable though at the amount of blood that was flowing out of my head wound. As the snow tried to settle on the rich red sea, from above I tilted my head, bemused how the little indentations looked like rose petals scattered on the ground. I thought of Rose; was this her form of calling card? And though the evidence against her was proving more and more damning, my deep guttural instincts scolded me. But as I shook my head anxiously, I begged for help. Had she, in her naivety, set me an impossible task? Or did she have a motive for setting me up?

Suddenly, when I think I'm above the pain, I'm back in my twisted body. I'm aware of a woman hovering over me. Through half closed eyes, I am just able to see – hair, tears and mucus falling onto my face. The woman turns her head skywards, screaming for forgiveness. Her face is now on mine, and my mind is wrenching at the sheer realisation.

'Oh, my dear Lord, please *no*, *YASMIN*...' I hear myself screaming out, my spirit able, but my body ineffective and seemingly redundant in being able to reach out to the woman I love most in the entire universe.

I genuinely don't understand how she has to be given the guilt of having killed someone, and for it to have been me. From within my tears start to fall, and as the calmness of the Christmas night ascends into turmoil, I could hear the evil laughing of people around me. But then, for me...*life stopped.*

And so, I lost everything. They say that what *goes around, comes around,* and maybe to anyone that doubts the saying, we will only get to find out when it's far too late!

But just as I thought it was all over, I found myself sitting quietly at the Water's Edge, the morning after I had collapsed and died on the decking, the warmth of a late summer sun, my feet dangling soothingly in the cool water. I felt a little uncomfortable, my cold dead corpse lying right beside me, but I tried to ignore it, preferring to take in the beautiful clear blue sky. I hoped that I would never get to see the lilac tinge again. I believed that I had paid my price, and I hoped the powers that be would feel that my debt was fully discharged. But though I was past questioning anything that happened in my life, before or after death, it seemed that someone was finally ready to talk.

'Good morning, Ritchie!'

I turned quickly. My dead corpse was suddenly gone, and there, sitting cross-legged on the decking, was Rose. I didn't know whether to smile or scream at her, though there was something in her eyes that stopped me doing either.

'Ritchie, it's *not* quite how you think. Please, let me explain.'

I nodded my head.

'Ritchie, I know you must hate me, but really, you must give me a chance to tell you everything.'

I pulled my feet from out of the water and turned to face her. I placed my elbows on my knees and waited calmly.

'Ritchie, I should have stuck with my original feelings for you. I told you how I had appreciated your friendship when everyone else ignored me; well, there was a reason for their lack of interest in me. When I first arrived at the school I expected people to be a little cool with me, you know, being the new girl and all that. But the truth is, Ritchie, I wasn't well. But I had begged my mum, dad and the doctors to let me spend my last few days where I was happiest – at school. But I was there for less than a week, and then I died in my sleep...'

I stared open-mouthed at Rose, not quite able to take in what she was telling me.

'You see, Ritchie, I was what's known as a restless spirit. I wouldn't just leave quietly, and so I would still go to school, and you had the ability to see me. I think we must have made a connection somehow. Well, anyway, for the rest of the term it was you and me. I suppose to everyone else you must have seemed a bit reclusive, a *bit* strange, but we had each other, didn't we, Ritchie? I'm sorry, I just wasn't ready to go! Even at my party it would have only been you and me, and I was going to tell you then, but they finally put their foot down, and the man at the gate, on the day of my party, *well,* he had been sent to get me. He was my wonderful, but dearly departed grandfather. I begged for someone to be there to greet you, to explain, and though I felt you deserved the truth then, the powers that be, well, they forbade it. I'm *so* sorry, Ritchie!'

I was truly stunned, and felt a little sick. I couldn't help but question my entire history. Was I *mad*, befriending a *dead* child? I had delved into the depths of insanity without realising it. But then, how would you know how sane you actually are? We think and act as we feel, and to the individual, isn't that normal? I rubbed my eyes, not accepting that I was anything but stable.

'Please, Ritchie, there's more, much more! Remember when I told you before, how we would sit and watch our very own soap opera, and how I would tune in religiously to catch up with your day-to-day activities? Well, when Lillie was rejected by you I felt sorry for her, and though of course I understood your reasons, the pure hostility between you and Jack made it impossible for you to have any kind of relationship with her.' Rose was screwing her face up, suddenly unable to look me in the eyes. 'You see, Ritchie, I had always taken your side, it was natural for me. I never questioned your actions, I was your friend, and *I am* a loyal friend!'

I waited for the but…

'*But*, Ritchie, when Lillie came to us, she was totally in the dark about you being her father, and that's where I made a terrible mistake. She was missing her mum and generally a bit down, and I suppose having such an important piece of information, well, I suppose I used it to ingratiate myself, form a bond. And then I convinced myself that Lillie had a right to know who her real father was!'

I let out a deep breath, and Rose continued her confession.

'Oh, Ritchie, poor Lillie was mortified, she didn't speak to me for days. I knew I'd made a terrible mistake, but sort of, well, genuinely believed that I would have wanted to know if it was me.'

I shook my head in agreement, but was a little too numb to say anything, as I felt the really bad part of Rose's story was yet to come.

'Lillie pondered for a few days, kept herself to herself, but then I caught her looking back through the archives, trying to find out a bit more about your relationship with her mum, and when she saw how you didn't want to know her, well, it broke her heart. But then she became more animated, and then verbally hateful towards you!'

I dropped my head into my hands; any vision at all of one of my girls hating me, well, I just couldn't bear it.

Rose continued. 'She simply wouldn't accept you as her father, and when I tried to comfort her, she would scream at me that Jack was the one that took care of her, loved her, so *he* was her father! And as she watched your battle with Jack, her allegiance was totally with him!'

I lifted my head up, trying to catch some sympathy from Rose, but she just continued the horror story.

'Bloody hell, Ritchie, the day you and Julie were at the Old Church, the powers that be told her that it wasn't suitable for young eyes, but no sooner had they turned their backs and she was watching again. It was heavy and horrible, Ritchie. I couldn't leave her! So I stayed with her as that day unfolded.'

I lifted my face skyward, the sun suddenly disappearing

behind a large grey cloud.

'Ritchie, when Jack killed Julie, Lillie was hyperventilating, but through her fingers she watched the stand-off between you and Jack. Bloody hell, Ritchie, when you killed him, she was uncontrollable, screaming as she ran off down the corridors!'

I just sat there shaking my head in disbelief, totally amazed that whatever you do, however alone you think you are, however great, however minor your actions, someone, somewhere, is keeping score. Rose muttered an apology, her words barely audible.

'But, Ritchie, Lillie became obsessed, desperate for a way to make amends for Jack and Julie's death, and I suppose because I was her friend and yours, I felt that maybe there was a way of proving to her that you were a decent guy. So between us, we begged the powers that be for your second chance!'

I scratched my head furiously. 'So, Rose, why was Lillie okay with me when I had my second chance? She showed no signs of hatred.'

Rose smiled. 'You're missing the point, Ritchie. Only you knew that it was your second chance at life, except for Harry Christian of course. But for Lillie, *no*, she didn't get to relive *her* life again, she simply lived it second by second, day by day, just as before. Any changes would be down to you and your actions. The only time she would get to see any new direction in history was when she died, when she would have access to the archives, though there is good reason for the age rating on certain scenes, so your time with Tia and Leoni would not be shared with someone so young... *Thank goodness!*'

Rose smiled, her eyes rolling sky-ward. 'And Ritchie, I certainly wasn't going to make the same mistake and share *any* of your night with Tia and Leoni with her! Plus my knowledge of it was limited anyway, just bits that I had heard through the grapevine! So you see Ritchie, Lillie would only be aware of *all* she experienced with you!' Rose beamed at me. 'And the verdict, the proof was there for all to see! There was the full father and daughter love in your second life, whereas the first life, your actions, foolishly, despicably denying her mere existence...!'

I winced and scowled at Rose, but her look of, 'well, if you commit the crime' was not something I could fairly dispute.

'And, Ritchie, despite your far less ominous failings this time, she knew you loved her with all your heart, and it is totally natural that she would want to come and see you whenever possible!'

I nodded my head. 'So how could Lillie come and join me in the water? I loved it, but how was it possible?'

Rose stood up, her hands placed firmly on her hips, and then walked up and down the decking as she explained.

'I have certain privileges. It's an age thing... The powers that be, well, they feel that people like Lillie and me didn't get the life that we deserved, so a little treat that is granted is being able to come back in some shape or form.'

I stood up, placing my middle fingers on my temples, pushing firmly.

'Do you mean *like* a ghost? I mean, *are* there such things?'

Rose laughed, throwing her head back.

'No, stupid, Lillie and I are *not* ghosts! You can touch and hold Lillie, can't you? You and I...' Rose stretched out her small pale hands, our fingertips connecting gently. '...can touch. I feel *just* like you! I just have the ability to go back and forth, within reason, but each visit has to have total clearance. Lillie chose to come back and visit you.'

I had so many questions, and there was so much that I didn't quite understand.

'Okay, but why the water? How come Lillie could only come to me when I was in the water?'

Rose smiled. 'That's down to you. Do you remember how we discussed affinity? Some people feel it when amongst the clouds. Some people, like you, Ritchie, feel at their most relaxed in the water, deep beneath the surface, you expressed the need to escape the prying eyes of the powers that be! Your ability to swim at high speeds and stay under water for so long is simply *partly* because you believe that you can! But mainly, there are certain changes that take place when a body is sent back to earth. The soul will always remain constant, but the body, well, a crude way of putting it is that we almost have to jump-start your dead human shell, recharge it! And so there are certain areas that you will excel in, and for you, it was the water! There are just a handful of people walking the earth that do have incredible powers, all due to pioneers like me trying to be clever, messing about with nature, playing Russian roulette with life and death!'

I couldn't take my eyes off her; I was fascinated.

'You see, Ritchie, people who watch these special few will accept that they are witnessing greatness, a prolific sportsman, constantly breaking world records! Mmmmm, yes, there was much debate, idle gossip that Houdini had escaped the powers that be in his teenage years. In fact, he made quite a career out of doing just that. There are a least two great sportsmen over the last thirty years that are rumoured to have slipped from the net, and there is one particular illusionist, magician if you like, who still walks your world. He can be a little sullen, undoubtedly crazy, but he is nonetheless astounding, and excites and entertains people, can close down his body's natural functions to stand without movement for days, ummm, submerge his body in water for ridiculous lengths of time. At the moment he is not doing any major harm, but the powers that be are aware of one or two unacceptable things he is planning, so he could well be on borrowed time, and undoubtedly he will be grabbed back soon! But the facts are that for these privileged few, there is no magic, no illusion, just a unique ability, brought on by an overzealous jump-start!'

Rose stopped for a moment, nodding at me, placing the top of her hand beneath her chin, playfully advising me that my mouth was now wide open. I shook my head, urging her to continue.

'Okay, Ritchie, but there is one, maybe two high-profile names that use these powers to bring them fame and fortune. It's extremely frowned upon by the powers that be, but they're getting less stuffy these days, hence me being allowed my little game with you!'

I suddenly interrupted. 'Little *game*, Rose? Is that all I am to you?'

Rose shook her head, the palms of her hands turned skywards.

'Please, Ritchie, whatever I've set out to do here, well, I

prayed for only good to come of it, nothing sinister, you *must* believe that.'

Rose could see how scared I was, and surely couldn't help but notice that I was a lost soul.

'Come on, Ritchie, look at me!'

But the truth was, my world was destroyed. I was beginning to wonder whether I had died naturally. I was ready to believe that maybe Rose had instigated my death, so she could play her so-called game – something to amuse her, while away the long, tedious days. Rose suddenly cut in.

'Ritchie! You must *stop* that. I told you right at the beginning, this had never been done before, well, not quite these circumstances anyway. Many people dream that they could go back to when they were young, to do exactly what you have been allowed to do, make amends, make subtle changes!'

Rose was now right in front of me, her hands resting on my chest.

'Ritchie, certain people, given the chance, would want to change their lives completely, they would simply go off in a totally different direction! But this, with you, it was the power of your love story. I gambled on the genuine belief that your love for Yasmin and Evie was the real deal. In every scene that I watched of you, it was clear how much you loved your life! How you would, and indeed did, kill to preserve the sanctity of it at any cost! Okay, there was no escaping the fact that you destroyed a few people's lives in the process, but please accept that I didn't instigate *your* death. It was *your* stress, *your* sincere regrets, that set the clock ticking on *your* demise, and it was that, and *that* alone, Ritchie Angel!'

I let my eyes fall onto hers, and she then softened her tone.

'It was that, Ritchie. I swear I couldn't stop any of that, and all I could do was get you a second chance. I was warned that no good would come of it. I was told that they frowned upon second chances, and for the very reasons that you have unearthed. But, like I say, they're not quite as stuffy as they used to be, and so, finally, like most adults with nagging small children, they gave in to me!'

I pulled Rose to me. I knew that she was telling me the

truth, but it didn't change the fact that I hated what I had created with my new world. I didn't have to say a word; she pushed her arms around my waist and gently squeezed.

'I know, Ritchie, I know, and it's why I have brought you here to explain, and then to give you one last option.'

I gripped her shoulders and pushed her away from me, holding her at arm's length, my mouth looking for the right words. *Last option?* resonating large in my mind – after all, just moments ago I had settled on submission and defeat, resigned of hope of any kind.

Rose shook her head and placed her finger to her lips, then pulled away. She scratched her head, and took a deep breath.

'Ritchie, before I talk about any kind of choice you may have, I need to stress just how we view the new you.'

I placed my hands together and lifted them to my lips, as though praying for the best.

'Ritchie, originally, in your first life, it would have been easy for us to judge you harshly and cast you as a weak and evil individual, and simply walk away. But the bane of your life, Jack, was trouble for you the moment you stepped into Julie's life. Without any knowledge of Jack's place in her world, you had taken a very dark path, and there was always going to be an extortionate price to pay. He made your life hell! And though it appeared inevitable that he would use his vindictive and physical strength to destroy you, you showed an inner will of character that perhaps even surprised you. In the final scene, it really was kill or be killed. He destroyed the most important thing in his world, and so he would have taken immense pleasure in seeing you die! We also believe wholeheartedly that Jack would have taken his own life, so that would have been the end of you both, but you were quick, Ritchie. You had one chance and you took it … you survived!'

Rose went quiet for a moment and then wagged her finger in the air.

'What I expected of you second time around nearly worked. You were stronger, and Jack had respect for you. But the delicate detail that you and Julie had created was a complication that was never going to go away. Regardless of what you did, unavoidably history was playing its part. You and Jack would always come face-to-face, and within a certain space of time do battle. Just as your bond with Jimmy was never to be broken, set deep in the veins of the rich tapestry of fate. But if you compare your wrongdoing in Jack's world, and then consider that you did exactly the same in Jimmy's world, hatred in equal measure with both should have been the result. But such is the difference in personalities, you and Jimmy remain friends, whereas Jack and you become enemies of the highest order!'

My head was reeling. My thoughts turned to Scottie, his death and how I managed to avoid that. Rose as always seemed to pluck my thoughts from the air.

'Ritchie, there is no easy way of saying this, but Scottie will die within a handful of years. It's tragic, I know, but it will happen. You've simply bought him more time, so be grateful for that. The death of Ian was inevitable too; he was never going to make old bones. He died a few years earlier this time around, and Scottie will die a few years later; you traded one for the other, but without realising it. It's allowed by the powers that be, as Scottie's delayed demise means that Janey and little Scottie miss the hateful section of their life with Ian because he's no longer around, which is brilliant, right? Time and schedules are simply juggled up a bit, a phase-two principle, and all the better because of it! You have thrown fate a different course, an alternative route. Look at how a satellite navigation system works – you defy the nice lady's instructions and take a left turn rather than a right. She immediately tells you to turn around when possible, but you keep going. By design and with your compliance, she will ensure she comes up with an alternative route, and so, regardless of how many deviations you make, you will reach your journey's end! And though a fairly liberal estimated time of arrival is pushed to the limit, in the overall scheme of the universe, the end result, the final destination, will always be the same!'

I sat totally still, absorbing mechanically all that Rose was saying to me.

'Okay, if we're talking about fate here, what about love? What about Yasmin and me? If we're talking about things carved in stone, then what about Evie? Surely her existence and links to me are set in the veins of this *so-called* rich tapestry of fate? How has it been possible that we've averted that?'

Rose looked nervous, but beckoned me to the edge of the water.

'I'm going to show you something that may disturb you, but I feel that you have a right to see it.'

I stepped nervously over to Rose, and taking her outstretched hand, I crouched down and looked deep into the water. At first I could only see my reflection, but then a vision appeared. There was the lilac sky, and a cliff face at the edge of the ocean, and as I looked at the scene, it was almost as if I was watching video footage, with the date at the bottom right-hand corner of the frame – 23rd December, 2004. There was a man sitting on a rock, high up, almost at the top of the cliff. We seemed to zoom in suddenly, and it was me, the strong wind blowing my hair this way and that. And then something pulled me in. I wasn't watching any more, but living the scene and what was to follow, with no memory past this moment.

I had sat alone for hours and days at a time, just looking out to sea. All I could think about was Yasmin and Evie, but I had no power to move. I felt as though I would end my days here, finally dying and falling into the ocean. But there was something different about today. I felt deep within my soul that this fresh sunrise had more to offer, something life-changing.

In the distance I could hear a dog barking. I would often hear dogs barking, voices, see people peering down at the sea, but no one ever seemed to notice me. But today was to be different. The barking got closer, and instinctively, excitedly, I recognised the noise, a heavy breathing, and then instantly I was being licked, almost pushed over by this great big fluffy lump. How on earth the daft animal had got even remotely close to me defied logic. I couldn't talk, I was too emotional; it was Fluffers, and it could only mean one thing. I was unable to move momentarily, but a bubbling energy was ready to burst out of me, a feeling I hadn't had since I was a young child on Christmas Eve. Finally, all restraints lifted, I was able to move my head, and instinctively I looked up the cliff face. Peering down at me, like an angel sent from the heavens above, was Yasmin.

'Oh my God! Is that *you*, Ritchie Angel?'

I beamed, and stood up. I was about to apologise for my dishevelled state, my dirty grass-stained jeans, but suddenly I didn't feel as though I needed a good hot shower or a fresh set of clothes. My face felt smooth, my hair was light and clean, and as for my attire, I was dressed in a pair of old Levi's that had been my favourites when Yasmin and I were together. But more importantly, I was wearing a thick black cashmere jumper that Yasmin had bought for me just before Evie was born; she'd loved it, and her eyes would light up every time I pulled it on. She always said how she couldn't resist me in it, how she loved how soft and cuddly I was when wearing it.

I don't know how I stopped the strength of emotion spilling out of me, or how the nerves weren't making me a quivering wreck, but there was a calmness, and I was at ease. There I was, on my jagged rock ledge, just staring up at my wife as though it was the most natural situation in the world. Yasmin looked more stunning than I had ever seen her; the sea air always seemed to bring out the deepest blue in her sparkling eyes, but today, well, they'd never looked quite so incredible. I pulled myself up, almost cat-like, level with Yasmin at the top of the cliff. Confidently I pushed my arm around her, kissing her gently on her cold flushed cheek. She beamed at me, returning the gesture.

'I can't believe you're here, Ritchie. Is this little spot, ummm, a usual haunt for you?'

Not really knowing what to say, I was convinced that I blushed as I pictured how my perching on the edge of the rock face would be viewed as a *little* strange. But none of that seemed to matter. Yasmin simply took a huge breath of fresh sea air, her face skyward, her words wistful.

'Mmmmm, I love it here!' She closed her eyes for just a moment, soaking up the sun, but then turned to face me with an inquisitive look. 'Ritchie, you seemed to just disappear off the face of the planet. I've asked after you, but no one had heard from you. You have some very upset friends!'

I just shook my head; I didn't know what to say. We started

to walk together. Yasmin said nothing for a few steps, her silence reflecting that she was unsure of how to handle my lack of response, but then she spoke again.

'I don't actually live in Dartmouth any more, Ritchie, I've moved back up to Willow. Well, when I say I, I mean my daughter and ... my husband and I...'

I tried to keep my face the same, desperate to keep the disappointment tucked deep inside.

The three of us walked, Yasmin, Fluffers and I, just like our early years. But somehow, the intensity of how precious it was – being reunited with someone you've lost, and presumed that it was likely to be so forever – just created an indescribable feeling.

'So, Yasmin, where is your daughter now? Is she at home, in Willow?'

Yasmin nodded, and then explained how she hated leaving her, but how she'd needed a bit of time to simply blow a few cobwebs away, and so had rented a little cottage almost on the beach, just a few miles away. As we walked, there was a certain inevitability about our meeting; everything seemed so natural, as though this day together was always going to come. I took her hand as I guided her down a steep section of rock until we both stepped onto a firm well-trodden pathway leading down towards the car park. I shook my head and had to blink hard, as there was my Jeep.

Fluffers had run ahead and was now relieving herself up against the rear tyre. Yasmin covered her mouth in horror.

'Ritchie, I'm *so* sorry. I take it, seeing as we're the only two cars parked, that that's *your* Jeep?'

We both laughed, Yasmin bumping into me, my steadying arm resulting in another wistful sigh, but an end to the nervous laughter. My eyes were locked onto her face, unable and unwilling to look anywhere else, but then her head dropped, as though afraid to engage in what was happening here. I willed her to look back up. The sea breeze dived and buffeted around us, and then, gradually, Yasmin's eyes moved up my body until finally meeting my stare, and she didn't look away. Fluffers seemed to stop and watch us both, neither one of us daring to break the spell with anything as crude as actually talking. But inevitably words would have to be spoken eventually.

'So, Yasmin, does this cottage of yours have fresh coffee?'

She looked a little awkwardly at me, but such was my building confidence that I believed I had taken the words out of her mouth.

'Um, yes, but you'll have to excuse the mess of the place, I've just taken it very easy and haven't really unpacked properly!'

I smiled, mesmerised by her every word, every breath she took, the sparkle of her eyes, the agility of her perfect mouth. I then assured her that I wouldn't look below eye level, and as her smile disarmed me, as it always could, she suddenly lost her nerve and looked down at the cold damp sand. My thoughts started to race ahead. I was increasingly keen to ask her the name of her husband, but the fear of tainting this moment stopped me. Something moved us both on, and as she walked towards her silver four-wheel drive Mercedes, she turned a quick glance at me. She went to look away again, but I followed her eyes and ensured she stayed with me. I instinctively winked, and she seemed to blush ever so slightly. I was then aware of myself speaking again.

'Okay, Yasmin, don't drive too fast. Hot coffee at the ocean's edge!'

She beamed at me, a renewed confidence oozing out of her. Fluffers barked and then jumped up into the Mercedes, the tailgate barely open. Yasmin laughed at the animal's impatience, whilst Fluffers wagged her tail rapidly, as though she didn't want to hold anything up. I stood back, just taking in the moment. Yasmin climbed into the driver's seat, with little glances back at me, simply lifting me higher and higher. As her vehicle eased steadily across the sandy grass, I couldn't help but shake my head from side to side, euphoria passing through me, the memories of all that had happened since we parted now simply a blur. Yasmin was here with me, wanting me to spend some time with her! I was that teenager finally getting the date with the girl he had worshipped from afar, the beautiful fantasy girl that you felt would never give you a second glance.

Yasmin suddenly tooted her horn, and I waved, mouthing

'sorry' and hurriedly made my way to the Jeep. I was dumbfounded as to how good it looked, as though waiting for this moment, glistening in the morning sun – a few specks of sand, but as I jumped inside, it smelt fresh and almost factory new. I instinctively dropped my hand down to the ignition, and there was the key. I didn't say a word or dare question the madness of it all, and then with one simple turn, the engine roared into life.

As I followed Yasmin along the twisting, winding coast road, there was a fixed smile across my face – I couldn't help it. I simply adored everything about her. Just to be spending any time at all with her was erasing all the heartache, scene by dreadful scene! But many crazy thoughts ran through my mind. I mean, how incredible that Yasmin should have Fluffers! I simply couldn't take it in. And just the one child, and a daughter. As I continued to follow her, I was aware of how I even loved the way her brake lights would come on, the way she would twist and turn around every corner, her way, beautifully done.

As we finally pulled into a small, *blink and you would miss it* sandy driveway, the Jeep bobbled and bounced its way down the part sand and coarse grass access, which finally led us to Yasmin's romantic thatched cottage. I pulled the Jeep to a premature stop, making sure I could watch every move as she climbed out of her vehicle, each and every footstep as she lifted the tailgate and freed Fluffers, her poise and elegance as she made her way to the front door. She was wearing a long navy-blue skirt; her brown leather boots looked dusty, but perfect. She had on a thick cream highland wool jumper, a powder-blue scarf wrapped warmly around her neck. As I watched every detail, devouring her every movement, she threw her gloves and hat into the porch, then ran her hands through her tousled blonde mane. She turned to me, amused that I had not yet parked up, and a small teasing smile crept across her lips. In response I roared forward, turning the engine off and quickly stepping out of the Jeep. I dramatically slammed the door shut, and then ran after Fluffers. I was showing off like an idiotic teenager high on love and life, anything to impress the woman I would give my last breath for. All I could hear was Yasmin's

673

laughter as I jumped over the small sand dune that stood protectively in front of the cottage. But as Fluffers ran off towards the crashing waves, I didn't feel comfortable running away from the love of my life, so I stopped and turned around. And there she was, just standing, holding open the entrance to my reoccurring dream that I had woken with for every single day of my second life.

Every hope, dream and unrealistic expectation was wrapped up in this moment. I know it's a cliché, but I couldn't catch my breath; she was hypnotic. And as I walked through the open doorway, she just stood in front of me, her hands untying the loose knot on her scarf, and our eyes were locked onto each other – but this time, it was me that broke away, as across the room was the picture that I desperately needed to see. Yasmin stepped into the kitchen.

'Umm, Ritchie, do you take cream, or do you like it black?'

Suddenly, the picture was all I could focus on. My mind was racing, and as the word 'black' was harshly bellowed back towards the kitchen, my hands started to shake as I held the photograph. There was Yasmin and her daughter, a handful of years older than Evie, but the spitting image of my beautiful sorely missed daughter. Her eyes, her perfect nose, but every strand of her platinum mane besieged by black... And suddenly I couldn't stop rocking, my breath hot and painful. The man in the picture, the black eyes, the jet-black hair... And as I stared, almost boring a hole into the photograph, there in full blazing colour was my worst possible nightmare.

I tried to talk, searching desperately for something composed and cool to say, but instead, 'Oh my God, Yasmin! You're *married* to Jack De'Vil...'

She walked up behind me.

'You sound surprised, why?'

I couldn't say anything. Sure, I wanted to say *so* much, but there was nothing that I could say that would be suitable. I tried to calm my breathing down, to forget about what was in the picture, to simply look away, to concentrate on the here and now, because who knew when this moment was going to be snatched away from me? But my eyes and then words betrayed my wishes.

'Your daughter Yasmin, she reminds me so much…of someone very special to me…a little girl called Evie!'

I swallowed hard, praying for some kind of recognition to the name.

'That's a pretty name Ritchie, and that's my Holly!'

I leant forward, my arms outstretched onto the cabinet. I knew I was breaking the mood, and I was so desperate not to. I wanted to turn around and scream accusingly, demanding an explanation as to how she could have had a child with such a vicious bastard. But I knew it would be suicidal. I knew also that there was only one thing that could lift my mood. I turned around slowly, and in the split second it took me to do so, I was desperate to project calmness personified. Yasmin's eyes met mine. I gave a subtle sigh of relief; here, us both alone, nothing else mattered. She looked straight at me, and though this antidote was extremely powerful, the thought of losing her meant that my mind was spiralling with raw panic, my wife's new world getting the better of me! She suddenly turned away at exactly the right moment, retreating none the wiser into the kitchen as I simply stood and shook.

As Yasmin prepared the coffee, her raised voice explained Jack's reappearance.

'Ritchie, when I met up with Jack it was a total shock. I, like everyone else, had believed him to be dead. But when my mother was in and out of the city hospital I'd got friendly with one of the nurses, and she kept me up to date with the progress of one of her outpatients that had totally lost his memory! And by chance, I was introduced to the poor man – it was Jack! I simply couldn't believe it! But it wasn't the cocky Jack De'Vil that we all knew, but a gentle, soft, caring man. And in time, I suppose I fell for him. Little by little, with my help, he got the majority of his memory back, he was paranoid about going back to Willow, and so we put a pin in a map – and Dartmouth was to be our home for a few years. But as he regained his confidence he felt ready to go home, face the *music,* so to speak. He's still fairly vague about the explosion, but, oh, I don't know, just recently, I suppose back in his old environment, it saddens me to say it, but he's changed. He's more like the old Jack we were all so aware of. Perhaps you can remember the reputation he had?'

Yasmin finally re-entered the lounge, her eyes inquisitive, as though trying to judge my reaction. I smiled, calm and collected, as though I didn't have a care in the world. But simmering beneath the surface I was totally horrified! At ease, she went back into the kitchen to check on the coffee.

I lay the photograph face down. There were three smouldering lumps of charcoal on the fire.

'Yasmin! Do you want me to throw a couple of fresh logs on?'

She suddenly re-entered the room, a cafetière and two mugs on a tray. She smiled from beneath a large curl of hair.

'Yes please, Ritchie. I'd meant to do that as soon as I came in.'

In the midst of our domestic bliss, everything about her new world killed me, but as long as she stayed very close indeed, I was going to have to rely on possession being nine tenths of the law!

She placed the tray on the magazine-laden table and then slumped back into the deep cushioned settee.

'We'll give it a few minutes, Ritchie, and then I'll pour.'

Addictively, without saying a word, I couldn't take my eyes off her; she didn't seem to mind and just looked back at me. Five minutes must have passed, and then she slid forward, unzipping her boots, kicking them to the other side of the room. She then proceeded to pour the coffee, finally handing me mine, our fingertips touching and lingering, still without a word being spoken. She eased back into the thick cushions and her long skirt rode up, showing off her slender tanned legs. Several minutes must have passed, synchronised sips, our eyes taking in the other. And then words that diluted the moment, paling in comparison to the beauty of silence between two people that undoubtedly connected, lovingly, lustfully, and yet for me, a pain, an anxiety, that threatened to take my last breath away from me at any given moment.

'So, Yasmin, why do you need to blow the cobwebs away?'

So I had asked *the* question. I knew I should have waited for her to tell me when she was good and ready, but a raised eyebrow and breathy chuckle, just about audible, seemed to forgive my bold approach. After all, it was her who had told me that Jack had changed. I had my fingers so tightly crossed that I thought they would twist out of their sockets. Whilst she appeared to be mulling over whether to answer me or not, I sat down beside her, my face trained on her side profile. Sun-kissed curls and eyelashes that crowned pools of sparkling blue, and as she intermittently closed her eyes, their length would touch her perfect cheekbones. My fingers wanted to touch her...her face, her hair, her breasts, restrained under her tight jumper, but I decided it was probably better to look away. She may be married and have a beautiful daughter, and we may have been only passing acquaintances in this life, but I knew that there was something incredibly powerful between us, and there was of course that fateful kiss! First life, second life, I had to pray that lightning could strike twice.

Yasmin started to talk, her words sad, regretful; no bitterness, but wistful disappointment, heartbreak for Holly, falling in and then out of love, and blaming herself. I stopped her there. I stood up and took her coffee from her. I walked over to the fireplace, resting our mugs on the mantelpiece. I turned and looked at her and then spoke softly, asking her to trust me. She didn't question me, and just nodded her head. I threw her boots back at her, both landing entwined just inches from her feet. She beamed at me. I turned the key in the patio door and opened it, the power of the ocean, smell and volume suddenly filling the lounge. Yasmin had her boots back on within seconds and then stood up, her breathing starting to quicken. I stepped towards her, offering my hand; hers were now in mine, and that was it, as though we'd never been apart. I kissed the tips of her fingers, her warm, soft skin, but my lips recoiled slightly, as I became aware of a silver ring encasing a black jet stone. I froze. Thoughts of Jack. I looked into her eyes, and then boldly slid the ring off her finger. Her eyes widened, questioning the gesture, but within a breath any concern was washed away, her sparkling and smiling eyes offering only trust. I threw the ring onto the settee and pulled her to me.

Fluffers suddenly ran into the room, shaking the cold sea water from her thick fur, but as she took in the scene, she stopped what she was doing, her eyes fixed on us both. She then seemed to nod in approval, and quickly took herself out of the room. A pang of guilt spread across Yasmin's face, but a smile from me seemed to erase her doubts almost instantly. We were both now caught up in each other, my hands, unable to resist a second longer, now on her beautiful face. I took in the moment, my battle-weary body being recharged and wiped clean of pain. I kissed her nose, Yasmin's encouraging hands now on my back. My lips, soft and gentle, teasing the edges of her mouth. One of her hands was now gently massaging the back of my neck, and then a little more roughly her fingers pushing through my hair. My lips suddenly became hungry and impatient, but I pulled back my head just for a second and saw that her eyes were closed. I had believed that I would never live this day, that I would never, ever get to hold my wife again, and as my mouth fell onto hers, I felt the sting of tears welling up. I dared not open my eyes; I simply didn't want to frighten her.

As our lips parted, a red-hot beam of sunlight fell upon us. I took Yasmin's hand and led her down towards the ocean's edge. We started to run, her fingers entwined tightly with mine, heady and giggling laughter with each step, the sand light and unsure under our feet. As we both finally stop, trying to recapture our breath, we just stand, our arms suddenly at our sides, our faces just inches away from the other. Slowly our fingers touch, the sea lapping around our feet, and Yasmin squeals and jumps back, but then laughs and kicks the froth of the ocean all over me. She then quickly takes off her boots, throwing them back up the beach. And though it is just forty-eight hours or so until Christmas and the day should be bitterly cold, the exaggerated sun seems to be taking care of us both.

Yasmin pulls me further into the rolling waves, and then presses her body against mine, my jumper being lifted over my head, her soft lips exploring my bare chest, tender kisses on my stomach. All I keep thinking is how this feels as though it's our first time together, despite having made love to each other a thousand times. For the here and now, the excitement, all the wondering, every fantasy, each wish being granted a zillion times over. Suddenly, impatiently, I'm lifting Yasmin's jumper above her head, throwing it towards the sand. Her fingers are now undoing my jeans, the ocean now around our knees. With every roll of the waves, froth splashing onto our bare backs. She suddenly stops, her lips pulling away from mine, stepping back, our arms at full stretch. But the passion in her eyes is just taking me in fully, as though desperate to savour the intense, wonderful moment. She steps towards me, my arms placed at my side, her fingers now on my forehead, lowering them and taking in the contours of my eyes, then my nose, and then gently around my lips, and then her mouth is pressed firmly against mine, her tongue sending little darts of electricity as we totally connect. And as our clothes fall away, not a fumble or a clumsy moment between us, within priceless minutes there's not a strand of man-made fibre on either of us. The spine-tingling warmth of the crashing, rolling ocean is all around us, and as our knees start to weaken and our bodies lower into the lilac surf, even the odd splash of sea on our faces tastes like nectar. As the waves breathe in and out, Yasmin and I become one. My head is spinning, and nothing else matters; nothing but the here and now. My breath finds a rhythm that isn't threatening to see me leave this mortal coil. And then my eyes take in Yasmin's face, lost in the excess of the moment, and there is an honesty that defies legal paperwork. She is married to Jack; just bullshit and wrong, nothing cleverer than that to say. There was always going to be an inevitability about us finally finding each other, but despite Jack De'Vil, and despite my fucked-up second life, there is nothing but us. The connection for me is as it has always been.

But as all logic and thinking desert me, the intensity and science of our bodies moving in time with the crashing waves, my head is now well and truly lost in the moment. If it is possible to physically love somebody to death, then it could happen now, right here at the edge of the ocean. And as we cling onto each other, our bodies pushed and locked intensely together, finally a shard of lightning travels the length and breadth of our souls!

I ease onto my back, taking Yasmin with me, her head now resting on my heaving chest. As my breath little by little returns, I run my fingers through her damp tousled hair, and I am aware that the waves are receding, leaving us to recover on the soft lilac sand. And as a paranoia creeps over me, I keep repeating over and over in my head, *please don't let this end, please don't let this end!* As I look out to sea, the sparkling crystal water seems to give me hope, and as Yasmin lies with me now, I feel so tempted to tell her that, in another life, we have both created the perfect world. I so want to tell her about our daughter Evie, and how she has her mother's eyes, her hair and the same infectious laughter. But with every second that passes, I start to feel an intuitive sadness fill me from the bottom of my naked feet, and up through the spine of my entire being. A tear spills from my eye, but is quickly carried away by the lilac froth of the waves as they wash over us both, and then, as though the volume has been turned down, I'm drifting skyward. But my eyes are still firmly fixed on Yasmin and me, lying together, the lilac tinge fading as the golden beach and the perfect blue sea leave me with a memory of us both that I will never, ever forget.

There was something about that afternoon that, regardless of what happens, meant that Yasmin and I had connected one hundred per cent in both of my lives. I will never experience with anyone else the physical, mental and spiritual pleasure of being with the perfect woman. Julie was wonderful, but she wasn't Yasmin. Tia and Leoni, an incredible experience, physically very satisfying, but mentally, spiritually, I was unmoved. It had been a test. And so, if my life were to end now, today, tomorrow, I felt privileged to have known this. My heart was now truly full. My head, undoubting and wise. My spirit, restful and *home.*

I sat and looked into the misty water, the image of Yasmin and me fading away. Suddenly, all I could see was my reflection, tears rolling down my face.

'You see, Ritchie, fate didn't let you down, you got together. But inevitably Yasmin went back to Willow. And though she fell head over heels in love with you, Jack was Holly's father! She knows the power and intensity of the man and she is well aware that she would never be allowed to leave him! Yasmin is undoubtedly a bright woman, bar her one error of judgment in falling for Jack. But in her defence, she simply confused the kindness, the tenderness, for love. Now, her relationship with you has taught her just how deep real love can burn. But for Holly's sake, she will stay with Jack, and I have to say this, Ritchie, I think she doubted that you would challenge Jack's world; in fact, she was convinced that her love story with you had started and ended at the ocean's edge...'

My eyes stared into the water. Rose's words did not surprise me. I had felt that closure had been forced upon me. I wanted to fight it, to deny that I understood what was being done. I lifted my face up and looked out across the canal, taking in the sandstone bridge, desperate to run across it and see where it would take me, escape the clutches of whatever it was that was deciding my fate. But then I felt a smile spread full and warm across my face as the memories of Yasmin and me, from what seemed like only brief moments ago, filled my mind. I sighed, dropping my head; *it's too painful to let her go!* But as I sank my teeth into the side of my mouth, a welling of calmness seemed to lift me up. And suddenly, I felt so incredibly grateful. There was no price too high for the afternoon that I had *just* had with Yasmin.

I stood up, letting out a huge wistful breath, looking around at all I had created. I loved my home, and loved even more the two special people who were fast asleep inside of it.

'Rose, please can I go inside and take a look at Yasmin and Evie?'

Rose pondered for a moment, as though waiting for a word of guidance, but then shook her head from side to side.

'Sadly, Ritchie, I can't let you do that. If you go in, it would disturb our final time together, perhaps jeopardising the last option that I have for you.'

My eyebrows raised, I sat back down.

'Okay, Rose, I'm listening.'

We both sat, cross-legged in the centre of the decking, our knees touching.

'Well, Ritchie, though you haven't witnessed your departure from Yasmin's cottage on the beach, inevitably you did leave. And not long after, Yasmin left too. She was desperate to get home to Holly back at Red House. Where else would a mother be at Christmas time, but with her child?'

At the mere mention of *Red House* and my blood pressure was rising to surpass a level that would induce death within my next heartbeat. I swallowed *so* hard in response to Rose's nonchalant mentioning of the place, that I thought I had broken my Adam's apple in two. But the truth was…But the *truth*, the cold hard facts were simple: here I was at the Water's Edge, and so Red House was no more than a splash in the memory pool, I refused to believe for one moment that *that* monstrosity could root itself long-term into history – I was scolding my dear friend, and this time wanting her to read my mind!

'*So* touchy Ritchie…I wasn't looking to upset you! But Yasmin with Jack, *then* home is Red House! But I promise I won't mention the place again!'

Rose put her hands on top of her knees, and I gently, guiltily entwined my fingers with hers, she had my forgiveness. She giggled childishly, exactly how I remember her from our school days together. She beamed at me, and then continued.

'Ritchie, it turns out that Jack wouldn't let Yasmin take Holly with her on her trip. He was petrified that she would run away forever, and he was probably right. But without Holly at her side, Yasmin had only ever planned to have a couple of days away, with every intention of being back at home for Christmas Eve.'

I pursed my lips, feeling deep sadness at the mere thought of Yasmin being unhappy, but I was powerless, I couldn't change it, and so I had to wipe all thought of it from my mind. Rose's words were washing over me unheard, but I quickly rotated my neck, aware that I needed desperately to be concentrating.

'You see, Ritchie, it's been a life defining moment, you and Yasmin having some time alone, priceless to be with the love of your life, right? Or *lives,* as in your case!'

I scolded her with a withering look, and then smiled.

'I'm sorry, Ritchie, couldn't resist it. But anyway, you had your time together, and found yourself back at Blackpool Sands, and then your interesting night at the Old School, which eventually saw you return to Willow. It's what happened next that is the most disturbing!'

Rose pulled her fingers away from mine, suddenly pushing her hands together, as though praying for divine intervention.

'Ritchie, Yasmin had gone home, and you'll be pleased to know that she couldn't get you out of her mind. But as I said before, she was convinced that she'd never see you again. And so, for Holly's sake, she would give her marriage to Jack every possible chance.' Rose pushed her hands into mine this time, her eyes suddenly intense. 'But oh God, Ritchie, it was only when she saw you on the security camera, standing outside the iron gates, that she realised you were prepared to fight for her. But by the time she was dressed and had made her excuses to Jack, she thought you would be miles away. She was driving far too fast, and that's when, well, you know what happened...'

Rose and I sat quietly, our fingers locked together, my mind, body and soul in no man's land.

She loosened her grip and placed her hand under my chin, lifting my head to face her.

'Ritchie, my wonderful friend, I pray that you forgive me for all that I've put you through. All I would say in my defence is that you now have a wonderful relationship with Lillie, and I hope that you believe she deserves that?'

I took her hand and placed it on my cheek, nodding in agreement.

'She deserves nothing less than that, Rose!'

But as I questioned the sincerity of my answer, I felt that maybe the price had been a little *too* high. I struggled to get the words out, the subject was just too painful.

'Rose, what about Evie, please, what about my beautiful Evie?'

Our eyes locked together, and then, as though all the answers were unfolding with each crinkle of her face, the sudden upturn of her lips and the increased sparkle from her eyes, for once, I was reading her mind.

'Yasmin is carrying my baby, *my* little Evie?'

Rose started to cry, nodding her head, and mixed in with her emotional sobs,

'Yes, *yes, Ritchie!*'

I gripped her hands, pulling her to me, and we both held onto each other, the tears rolling down our faces.

The sun was now starting to rise at the Water's Edge. It was always a spectacular sight, spring, summer, autumn or winter.

But I felt the inner bitter chill of all that it meant. Rose was now up and on her bare little feet, pacing and visibly uncomfortable, but then seemed to compose herself.

'Ritchie, we don't have much time. I teased you with an option, but in fact I have *two* options, *a choice*! And though the powers that be have battled amongst themselves, this final offer is down to me, my judgment, based on the lessons I think you have learned from your adventure.'

I held my breath; the next few words from Rose's mouth were going to make or break me.

'Ritchie, you *do* have a choice. I can offer you life, but at a price. You can go back to the night that Yasmin ran you down and survive...'

My palms were suddenly hot and sweaty, my mouth dry, and I was unable to speak, my heart racing.

'Ritchie, you can take your chance with Yasmin, but these are the things that will happen. As we have discussed before, fate has control! You may well only have a handful of years at the very best.'

Handful of years! just kept repeating itself around my head.

'Minutes, hours, days, *handful of years with Yasmin and Evie!* I would take whatever you offered me, Rose, if it meant *just a day* with them!'

Rose brushed aside my desperation, shaking her head.

'Please, Ritchie, this is difficult enough, let me continue.' Rose didn't, couldn't, wouldn't look at me. 'Should you choose option one, then it will be war, Ritchie. The chances of Yasmin having the strength to leave Jack, to risk losing Holly...'

But my irrepressible emotions were bubbling over, and I was ready to fight. Evie was my child, but I knew I would love Holly; born from the loins of Yasmin, how could I not? I was up on my feet, my words falling over each other in their excitement and over-eagerness to be heard! Rose was suddenly right in front of me, her eyes now boring into me.

'Ritchie, as soon as Jack knows you're in Willow, he'll come after you, and this time his luck might just be in. He will bad-mouth you to hell, Ritchie, he'll tell Yasmin about Julie, how you were the father of Lillie! But what really scares me the most is that Jack made Yasmin have a DNA test done when she was pregnant with Holly, such is his paranoia! He'll do the same again, Ritchie, and how do you think he will react to the fact that Yasmin has *also* betrayed him, and with *you*? Her life, it will be over!'

I sat back down, my legs unable to support me. My fears were not now for me, but for Yasmin and my unborn child.

'Ritchie, I'm sorry, you may believe that you can take him on, get him before he gets you...' Rose was now at my side, her hands firmly wrapped around mine. 'But please accept, it really could be Jack's turn to kill you, and with the law of averages, you cannot count on surviving your third battle with him, and it's fate that is putting forward your *handful of years* scenario Ritchie...Fate's interpretation of your realistic lifeline! Though nothing would be set in stone...'

My mind was suddenly blank, devoid of an answer, and I was so desperate for one.

'Ritchie, Jack's destiny has a similar swing to yours, it's a gamble, but you are playing with the lives of loved ones here...You have to think of all that is involved.'

Rose's fingertips were cutting into my hands, and as I looked down, small drops of blood had spilt onto the decking, each droplet as though a symbol of my life ebbing away. I lifted my head and looked deep into my little friend's eyes.

'And my other option, Rose?'

Rose looked increasingly uncomfortable, her eyes suddenly dark and sad, and then she was unable to look at me. She fixed her eyes firmly on her bare feet, her words nothing more than a whisper.

'Well, Ritchie, I know it was what we set out to avoid, and I know you'll hate me for even suggesting this one, and I have thought of nothing else for days...' She lifted her head, a tear in her eye. 'But you could, perhaps should choose to be found here, dead on the decking at sunrise...'

There was a numbness that disabled all movement. The very moment that my little friend had made her absurd suggestion seemed to suspend any physical reaction. Whereas inside, I was screaming, questioning, laughing manically, hysterically, anything really to try to kill off this totally insane recommendation. But as Rose continued, a sliver of logic was wrapping itself effectively around all my hopes and dreams, anaesthetising, slowly murdering them, the life of each simply allowed to drain wastefully away.

'Ritchie, it would be Yasmin and Evie that find you!'

My head was shaking at the very thought, and internally I was telling her no! But every thought-out, soul-researched, justifiable word that she spoke forced me to absorb, and gradually painfully understand what she was *so* right to be saying to me.

'And, Ritchie, at least your memory will be intact, your wife free from any influence Jack De'Vil would have. He'll kill Yasmin and your unborn child, you do know that, don't you, Ritchie?'

I shut my eyes to it all.

'If you sacrifice yourself, Ritchie, then your daughter is able to grow up hearing only good things about you, from friends and all those that stood you in such high regard. Ritchie, when you leave, until you are able to defend yourself face-to-face, for now, and for many years to come for those that are left, all your secrets will die with you. Who knows what will happen to Yasmin, whom she may or may not marry? But now she has a wonderful example of what real love is all about, and so for her...why would she settle for anything less?'

I was set in stone, frozen to the spot, my eyes and crying heart burnt out and swollen. How could I let my wife and daughter find me here, dead? Surely it would haunt them forever. But as Rose's wise words and heartfelt logic continued to sink in, I knew that Yasmin left alone with Jack, carrying our baby, was not an option. As my mind started to clear, the depth of my love for Yasmin and Evie, and all that we stood for was a legacy that I was most proud of, above all and everything else. To have anything, or anyone, harm or taint that, no price would be too high. But as I absorbed the very thought of it, signing the death warrant on any possible reunion with my wife and daughter, it was an incredibly high price, and it was sticking hot and throttling in my throat. Was I strong enough to do this?

I just wanted to hold Evie for a final time, then I would go. I had my memories of Yasmin, our time together in both lives powerful and still so fresh in my mind. But a selfish man would forsake what was best for those he loved, if it meant forsaking himself.

I was now flat on my back, my arms stretched out in a cruciform position, the tears of an undeniably emotional man that is Ritchie Angel spilling uncontrollably at the very thought of doing what was so undeniably right, but the pain was excruciating.

'My God, Rose! *This* hurts like hell!'

My little friend lay beside me, her hands pushed into mine. As we lay there, and the self-pitying tears became tiresome and crass, a clear picture was forming in my head.

A strong man would rather die than have his wife and daughter walk through hell!

Rose was now sitting up, her hands resting on my face.

'You are a strong man, Ritchie. You're clouding the issue with a reluctance that is natural and totally understandable. We've talked about the working out, the rough scribblings when solving a problem, but for us now, we know that the tattered, dirty steps to how we get to the only result open to us is not important. For Yasmin and Evie, only the right answer matters! Ritchie, my dear friend, it's time to go!'

I shook as I got to my feet. I stood, looking out across the water, my arms wrapped around my body, and as the morning sun rolled warmly onto my face, I nodded in approval. At least I could watch over my family and friends, and with all that I had learnt from Rose, I now knew that death wasn't such a fearful prospect after all. And perhaps the powers that be would grant me time with Lillie, and a front row seat to watch my family soap. I could feel the tears welling up, fragmented thoughts dropping hazily onto what all this would mean to Jimmy. He was my best friend, and if I let life number two go, then his children were his, not mine, no longer a mistake and a dark secret that we all had to live with. And though the image of Yasmin and me together was all I was left with, it was simply a matter of time, lots of it, simply waiting, but I assure you, I will wait!

As I drifted off into the clouds, the sun was shining extremely brightly over the Water's Edge, the lilac tinge burnt away. As for Yasmin and Evie finding me there that morning, well, I couldn't watch, and it was that way for a while. But when I finally tuned in, they were bearing up, good friends surrounding them. Evie was playing in the garden, and every now and again she would run over to her mummy for a hug and reassurance, and would then rejoin her friends. And from then on, as I watched religiously, I would be *so* grateful, as Evie would be laughing and having fun, and though the day would roll on and nightfall would see her tire, it was then that I found it the hardest to watch. I would catch her secretly trying to wipe her tears away while Yasmin read her a bedtime story. But their little prayers together always ended with a word and a kiss for me. I knew that my little girl would survive. As for Yasmin, I simply couldn't take my eyes off her: nothing new there. But as resolute and as dignified as she would appear in public, behind closed doors it would all become a bit too much, and I would just stretch out my arms towards her, desperate to comfort her. And the pain that I felt with my sheer inability to help my wife, well, I felt as though my heart was breaking over and over again. But I had faith that she would get stronger with each passing day.

Forward planning had meant that I had left a videotape with Peter Crabtree, my accountant, and when the girls finally found the strength to watch it, I thought our tears would never stop. But I made it clear on the footage of my eternal love and commitment to them both. I regretfully left them lots of daft jokes that my special friend Peter had provided me with. But far better advised was a scene of Yasmin and me dancing at midnight. Playing in the bath with Evie. Even our taking off and landing, our first and last trip in *The Angel*. Many, many priceless moments. But I kept firmly to myself the regret and belief that I had nonchalantly carried prior to being told of my demise – the taking for granted of having a lifetime with Yasmin and Evie, and just how little we realise that none of us are guaranteed a full innings.

I prayed every morning, noon and night for them both.

It was only yesterday that I got to talk to Julie, a conversation that was poignant and momentous in equal measure, but at least *now* she finally understands why she couldn't quite reach me when we were together. And Lillie and I? Well, inevitably we're inseparable, and as a consequence, Julie and I have become the closest of friends. But of course, choosing the reality of my original life means that poor old Scottie has been a resident for quite some time, but he assures me with a wry wink and a strained smile that there are no hard feelings. He states that it was just as much his choice to go off to Scotland in such treacherous weather, and he says he forgives me for my poor, erratic driving, always following up with an overzealous punch on my upper arm, brutally managing to hit exactly the same spot. And as this routine has become our daily meet and greet, my arm is a constant array of colour, but this is perhaps a small price to pay for killing the poor boy.

Harry Christian has had all his memories of him and I scrubbed, and though his spirit was supposed to stay around the jagged rocks on which he died, when Alice suddenly joined us I begged for his release, and a sweeter old guy you couldn't wish to meet. And I get to see my mum far more than I ever did down on earth. And as for the evil Ian, I've not seen him. But I've heard there's a special place for people like him. And so to Jack De'Vil. Well, we pass each other in the corridors, but we've both been warned that any trouble, and the special place beckons! And of course our mutual love for Lillie and her love for each of us means that we have both had to adopt a maturity, befitting two alpha males that have *had* and *lost* so much!

But to a moment that made the hairs stand erect on the back of my neck. A reunion with a man that had lost his way down on earth, broken-hearted and unable to cope with the day-to-day requirements of a demanding world. As though I had met death himself on that foggy night, I recalled vividly the lost extinguished eyes, blackened burnt-out embers. But the man stood before me now, almost unrecognisable – my hitchhiker, his eyes dancing with sheer unadulterated joy as he hugged tightly, proudly, his beloved daughter.

'Ritchie, I think you know my little flower girl, Rose.'

My heart leapt for them both.

And for Rose, one question that had waited long enough finally had an answer – her little bare feet. Well, now I'm here,

I've found out first hand. When we die, we lose our shoes and have no socks, just warm bare feet, enabling us to have our connection with the planetary crust, the natural electricity that flows from the universal core. And so, to keep our souls housed in our weak, demised bodies, the powers that be inform me that we need the natural energy that *we* in the Western world choose to shun, albeit foolishly; those deemed less fortunate in the poverty-stricken Third World countries, suitably nourished via natural ingredients, can outrun us effortlessly.

So Rose, Lillie, Julie and of course yours truly, we all make our way in our new environment, with our bare feet.

But as for my new home ... there are subtleties and extremes in equal measure. There is an aroma of love, compassion, positivity and goodwill that fills the air, it simply flows from us all, a peace and serenity that is blissfully intoxicating. And it's this that gets me through. Amidst the reassurance of such well-being, for me there is one thing that tops all others, and though I've not been allowed any special privileges directly, I do get a pass out with Lillie, so we can go and swim wherever our hearts desire. And Rose, she joins us when she can, which is as wonderful as it is spellbinding. Our first and only choice, every time, just happens to be the river that runs beneath the old sandstone bridge just a stone's throw away from the Water's Edge.

On each occasion and regardless of how the weather starts off, by the time we are submerged beneath the cool, fresh water, a perfect sun-lit sky of blue protects us. Each time, as I wait patiently, my heart is in my mouth, my fingers and toes crossed, my prayers repeated a thousand times over. Until finally, the patio doors are thrown open and Yasmin and Evie are running at full speed towards the bridge, their faces beaming, mother and daughter joining hands, before jumping, a wake of infectious laughter as they drop beneath the water beside me. And as I swim amongst them, I am as happy as I dare to remember, their warm breath on my face reducing me to an overwhelmed wreck. As a consequence, Lillie and Rose mercifully tease and cajole me. But after our last visit, they too are convinced that Yasmin and Evie know I am there.

And that is where I am now. Lillie sat, happily threading daisies on the river bank; Rose doing handstands against the base of the bridge, before slumping to the ground and laughing in embarrassment at her clumsiness. They then both look my way, taking in the Angel family, smiling approvingly as I effortlessly tread water, hardly a ripple to be seen, but our hearts a little heavier as that inevitable moment seems to come around a little quicker with every visit.

As dusk descends, a sudden chill replacing the fading sun, Yasmin and Evie reluctantly, almost silently climb out of the river. They look back, and then at each other. Evie suddenly, anxiously, runs around gathering daisies. She hands several to her mummy, and they both start to smile, tears rolling down their perfect beautiful faces. With synchronised timing, the flowers are thrown towards me.

With every visit, they repeat their goodbye, throwing their daisies directly to where I am. Then comes the unrelenting pain as they take a step back, as I know that it's time for them to go. But with bated breath I wait as my wife and daughter shout out in perfect harmony, *'WE LOVE YOU! PLEASE COME BACK SOON!'*

And so, if I can ask you one question…

'If you have ever lost a friend through death to whom you were particularly close, and at the time of your death they show themselves to you, offering you a chance to live your life again, will you *stick*, or will you *twist?'*

THE END

Acknowledgements

First and foremost, to my wife Sarah, who has dedicated her heart and *sanity* into fact checking, proofreading and establishing a network of like-minded souls who have all played their intrinsic part in bringing this book into the public domain. A huge beaming smile for my ongoing inspiration, our daughter, Izzy! Heartfelt rapturous applause goes to our website, book cover and promotion designer, Andrew West, the creative genius that takes on board all your dreams and aspirations and delivers to the letter – courtesy of David Parr, *Rapid Web Ltd*. I would like to offer grateful thanks to Sarah Cheeseman, our editor, who became a crucial member of the team, and her official review filling me with pride. To Riccardo Scuotto our printer extraordinaire, for his attention to detail and in sharing our obsession for all things *beautiful*! To those that have read the first draft and expressed such unexpected enthusiasm that I had no choice but to complete and publish. To Jane Youde, my mother-in-law, for her detective eye in proofreading the final draft, magnifying glass in hand - you did a grand job.

Last but certainly not least, my full and final thanks goes to all of you that have taken the time in reading this book, dedicating *your* time on joining us on this roller-coaster of a journey, that is the life and death and *life* of Ritchie Angel. I hope that this is simply the beginning of a wonderful and inspired relationship between us. I am now working studiously on my next offering. Please accept my sincere gratitude: to each and every one of you!

Coming to you in the Summer of 2015

The Human Jigsaw

STEVENSON-OLDS

How far would you go for perfection… ethically, morally?
Would you strive with such a burning passion, that your
obsession becomes *all*-consuming… *murderous?*